◆ C O L L E C T I O N ◆

—— BOOKS 6~10 ——

CRAIG HALLORAN

CONTENTS

Dragon Wars Collection: Books 6 - 10

By Craig Halloran

★★★★★

Copyright © 2019 by Craig Halloran

Amazon Edition

TWO-TEN BOOK PRESS

PO Box 4215, Charleston, WV 25364

WWW.DRAGONWARSBOOKS.COM

ISBN PAPERBACK: 979-8-462940-03-3

Publisher's Note

This book is a work of fiction. Names, characters, places, and incidents either are the product of the author's imagination or are used fictitiously, and any resemblance to actual persons, living or dead, events, or locales is entirely coincidental.

 Created with Vellum

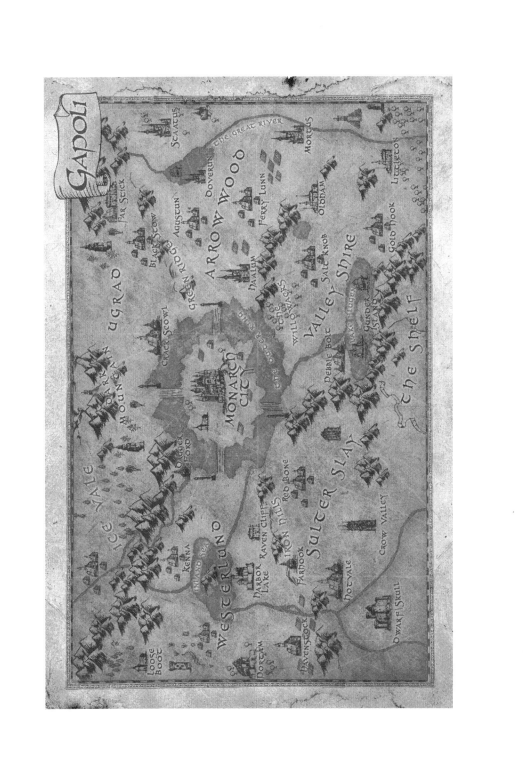

• MONARCH MADNESS •

—— B O O K 6 ——

CRAIG HALLORAN

1

MONARCH CITY

GREY CLOAK PACED THROUGH THE COZY APARTMENT THAT CRANE HAD SET UP FOR Zora, Dyphestive, and himself. Coffee was brewing on the stove, and Dyphestive sat half-filling the sofa, admiring his statue of Codd. Thanadiliditis, the hermit, sat on the other side of the sofa, stroking Streak's back, who was nestled in his lap. Leena, a monk from the Ministry of Hoods, was squeezed in between the two men, her typical intense look in her eyes.

Jakoby sat at a small table. The dark-skinned warrior wore an easygoing expression as he sipped a mug of coffee.

"Yonders. Of all things, they have yonders everywhere. It's going to be impossible to get Codd's shield out of Monarch Castle unseen," Grey Cloak said. He'd been muttering to himself ever since he departed the castle, trying to think of ideas for how he could rescue Zora from Irsk Monco, the leader of the Dark Addler. "It's no wonder *you* wanted me to see for myself." He looked dead at Jakoby.

Jakoby, the former Monarch Knight, set his mug aside. "It's one of those things that you need to see for yourself. You have to understand what you're up against. Yes, you have the yonders, not to mention the Honor Guard as well. That makes the very notion of stealing Codd's shield unthinkable."

Grey Cloak wrung his hands. "It would be doable if it weren't for the yonders. Flying eyeballs with wings? Who comes up with these things?"

"The castle's enchanters," Jakoby replied. "They're weird people. At least that's what people say. I only saw the yonders a few times when I was a knight. Spooky."

Grey Cloak stopped pacing and crossed his arms. "Well, that helps a lot. Thank you. Does anyone else have any useful information that they would like to share? How about you, hermit? You're awfully quiet. Any ideas?"

Than combed his scaly fingers through his stringy red-streaked white hair.

"If I did, I would have shared them. I do think you're on the right track to infiltrate the castle, but you'll be on your own once you're in there. We can't help, seeing as they're hunting for us as we speak."

Grey Cloak watched Dyphestive intently playing with his toy. Grey Cloak snatched it out of his hand and set it on the mantel above the small fireplace. "Will you pay attention?"

Dyphestive frowned. "I was."

"No, you weren't. You've been obsessed with that statue ever since you brought it home."

"But the detail."

"I don't want to hear about the details. I want to hear ideas about how to help Zora." Grey Cloak's nostrils flared. He was losing his composure, and he knew it. It wasn't like him, but he'd never felt pressure like this. He gathered his thoughts. "Let's hash this out again, shall we?"

Jakoby leaned over his coffee. "Hash it out as many times as you want. You never know what might come to mind. I'll tell you what. Let me hash it out, and you listen. It might spark an idea."

Grey Cloak nodded.

Jakoby pushed a chair out with his foot. "Have a seat and listen." Grey Cloak obeyed, and Jakoby continued. "We all know Irsk Mondo. Part elf, part goblin. The leader of the Dark Addler. He came after you"—he pointed to Grey Cloak and Dyphestive—"because you freed the Gunthy children and us in the process. Now he's taken Zora hostage, and he wants ten thousand gold chips and your dragon or the shield of Codd in exchange for her. Correct?"

"Correct. I don't see how this is helping," Grey Cloak added.

Jakoby drew himself up in a noble manner. "Keep listening. I'm not at the end yet."

Grey Cloak nodded.

"Codd's shield is guarded in the very heart of Monarch Castle. The two of you have seen it, and I've seen it. Twelve Honor Guards are stationed in Codd's crypt *and* who knows how many yonders? It sounds like the yonders focus more on the castle tours, but I could be wrong.

"We have two choices. First, we can steal Codd's shield and exchange it for Zora. That sounds impossible. Or we can shell out ten thousand chips and your dragon." Jakoby eyed Streak, who was still lounging comfortably on Than's lap. "But that is the same as exchanging one friend for another. You won't win anything by doing that." He eyed Grey Cloak. "Does that help?"

"No, that doesn't help. All you did was hash out what we've already been talking about for over an hour." Grey Cloak sighed, leaned his elbows on his knees, and rubbed his temples. "It's making my skull ache."

"Just because Irsk Monco gave you two options doesn't mean those are the only two options you have," Jakoby said.

Grey Cloak lifted his head. "What do you mean?"

"He gave you parameters. You need to think outside of those parameters. That's what they teach the Monarch Knights. Change the game. You've shown a knack for that by infiltrating the castle. Build on it. Use your creativity," Jakoby said. "There is more than one way to skin a dragon, we say." He glanced at Streak, who turned his head toward him and flicked out his tongue. "No offense."

"I'm trying, but I've hit a wall. I have a way into the castle, but I don't have a way out with the shield. Don't any of you have anything creative?"

"I'm fine with a sword, but I'm not the most creative thinker," Jakoby said as he patted his pommel. "I prefer to let my steel do the heavy thinking for me when I'm in a bind. Irsk Monco and his brood are evil. I prefer to kill the likes of him outright."

"I would like to do so myself." Grey Cloak envisioned the last time he saw Zora's pretty face. She was in the rough hands of the Iron Devils. The robed men's iron masks were fashioned with sinister expressions, and she was scared for her life. Her voice had cracked when she spoke. He'd never heard Zora like that before. "But we don't know where she is. Should we go after them? We could try to trail my contact, Orpah."

"I don't think you have enough swords to take on the Dark Addler," Than said. He leaned forward with Streak resting on his shoulder like a baby. "I'm all for looking evil dead in the eye and destroying it. People like that don't often change their ways. I believe in redemption, but I believe in killing, too, as a last resort, especially when it's them or you. Don't blink."

"Should we try to find Zora, then?" Grey Cloak asked.

"Let us handle that." Than scratched Streak between the small horns on his head. "I think your plan to infiltrate the castle is a sound one. You might find the crease you need."

Dyphestive stood up, walked over to the mantel, grabbed his figurine, and sat back down. His eyes were intent on every detail of Codd's suit of armor. He was fascinated with it.

Grey Cloak's jaw tightened. *I have one hundred ideas racing through my mind, and my brother wants to play with a toy.* He stood up and headed for the exit.

"Where are you going?" Jakoby asked.

He opened the door. "To take a walk and clear my mind." He slammed the door behind him.

2

GREY CLOAK SAUNTERED DOWN THE STONE-PAVED STREETS OF MONARCH CITY, deep in thought. On the one hand, Jakoby had opened a door for him. On the other hand, it didn't make his task any easier, and Zora's life was on the line.

Ten thousand chips and my dragon. Preposterous. Irsk knows I can't do that. Is he toying with me?

It might be a game to the leader of the Dark Addler, but Grey Cloak had cost the man a lot of money, and thieves didn't like that. He knew because he wouldn't like it either. Irsk wanted his money back or something of equal or greater value. So far, that was Zora.

I could steal the money from someone else. Perhaps I could pilfer a money lender's vault.

He passed by one such institution as he thought about it. The money lenders had vaults spread throughout the city. The stone buildings were under heavy guard. Two orc sentries stood at the entry to the vault he was passing. Their heavy stares locked right on him. He averted his eyes and moved on.

Grey Cloak's tummy rumbled. He hadn't eaten much, and it was catching up to him. Since he was near the Tavern Dwellers Inn, he decided to stop in, as an idea had crossed his mind. It was early evening, past sunset, and the tavern was at full capacity. He waved to Aham the Watchful, a slink with a gelatinous body and tentacles with many eyes.

Aham wobbled across the floor toward him, his tentacles waving. "Have you come to work? Busy night," he said in a bubbly voice. "We need all hands on deck."

"Sorry, I have other business, Aham. If you'll excuse me." He pushed by his employer and slid toward the back.

He nearly bumped into Teena, a cute waitress with bouncy curls, on his way through. She had a full serving tray on her shoulder.

"Glad you're here. I could use some help."

He patted her on the hip. "Sorry, not tonight."

"What?" she asked with disapproval. "Ah, I knew you wouldn't last."

He pushed to the back corner of the tavern and caught the eye of Irsk's envoy, Orpah.

The husky orcen woman, who packed on the makeup and squeezed into tight, gaudy clothing, waved him over with her flabby arms. Her valuable bracelets jingled along her meaty wrists. Orpah swept her hair from her eyes when he sat down. "Would you like something to eat, cute one? You look hungry."

The table was covered in what could have been every meal from the menu. Even though he was hungry, he didn't want to touch any of it. It was all half-eaten.

"No, thank you. I want you to tell Irsk that I need more time. Two days."

Orpah belched and tapped her chest. "Excuse me." She dabbed gravy from her chin and picked up a ham bone. "That's going to be as impossible as your mission."

"But I can't do this," he pleaded. "It's impossible. Please ask for more time. I need it. I'll come up with the money somehow."

She gave him a sympathetic look, bit into her ham bone, and with her mouth full, she said, "Oh, you poor dear. I really feel for you, but he won't change his mind. If you don't deliver, then your adorable little friend will be gone in one way or another." She lifted a greasy finger. "But you can learn from this, can't you?"

"Learn what?"

"To keep your nose out of other people's business." She snorted as she ate. "Now, run along. I'm expecting someone with a situation very similar to yours, but I don't think they'll make it either. See you in two and a half days." She winked. "I hope you have what we want."

He stormed away from the table and hurried outside. He knew asking for more time was a long shot, but it was worth a try. Besides, he had an ulterior motive.

Let them see my desperation. Perhaps they'll lower their guard.

He walked the streets for the longest time, trying to visualize how he could pull off the heist. He thought inside and outside the box.

I have to figure it out. It's like Jakoby said. There's more than one way to skin a dragon. And if it can be done, I can do it.

He felt a chill and looked sideways. He stopped. Crammed in what he knew used to be an alley between two stores was a tall, slender wooden building with a large red door. The sign over the door read: Batram's Bartery and Arcania.

Grey Cloak was pretty sure Batram was mad at him about the last time they met. He turned his foot toward the strange store. *I'll take my chances.*

3

"MAY I SEE THAT STATUE?" JAKOBY ASKED DYPHESTIVE.

Dyphestive leaned over Leena and slid the figurine of Codd to the end of the table. "Be careful with it."

"Oh, I will be," Jakoby said as he picked it up and gave it a close examination. "How much did you pay for this?"

"Five gold chips."

"Really? That's a lot of money, but I have to admit that the detail is remarkable." He slid the small sword out of the scabbard. "Hah!"

"Be careful with it, will you?" Dyphestive started to go for the figurine, but Leena pulled him back down onto the sofa. She had both of her small arms locked around his. "What are you doing? Let me up." He tried to stand.

Leena leaned back into the sofa cushions, crossed one leg over his, and held him fast.

"What's she doing? Leena, let go of me."

The monk with the long ponytail of cherry-red hair stared at him with intense dark eyes.

Jakoby and Than chuckled.

"She likes you." Jakoby set the figurine down on the table. "You shouldn't fight it."

"Yes, don't fight it. That will only make her mad," Than added.

"What do you mean she likes me? Why would she like me?"

"It doesn't matter why. It only matters that she does," Than said. "Remember that."

"But she tried to kill me with those little sticks," Dyphestive said with a glance at Leena's belt. "I have little lumps on my skull. What are those sticks?"

"They are called nunchakus," Jakoby answered. "They're one of the many unique weapons that members of the Ministry of Hoods specialize in. Your friendly companion is a weapons master of sorts. It's primarily a discipline of her body, which I see you are getting very familiar with."

"I am not." Dyphestive tried to pull away even though he didn't mind Leena wrapping him up. "Leena, will you let go of me?"

He gave Than a pleading look. The hermit managed a grin and shrugged.

"Leena, I need to go after Grey Cloak. I'm not going to sit here and wait any longer."

"He'll be back," Than assured him. "But he carries too much on his shoulders. He needs to learn to rely on his companions more. Especially you, his blood brother. If he tries to do it all, it will only get worse. Trust me."

"It sounds like you're speaking from experience," Jakoby said. "And I agree. You have to be a team and trust each other."

"We've been together a long time, and one thing I know about Grey Cloak is he won't let me or Zora down. He'll die first. I would too." Leena hugged his arm tight. It looked like she might be smiling at him. "Jakoby, I have to report to Cleotus in the morning. Can you tell me about that?"

"Ah, Cleotus is lining you up to be a squire to the Monarch Knights or possibly a novice to the Honor Guard." Jakoby gave an approving nod as he stroked his moustache. "Cleotus is a good man—most all of them are—but make no mention of me. They will test you right away."

"How?"

"Even though I am a banished knight, I'm still bound by my oath, so you'll have to learn for yourself what that's all about. But something tells me you might surprise them more than they surprise you, seeing as you've been trained as a Doom Rider. Maybe try to keep your skill demonstrations to a minimum since you don't want to call too much attention to yourself."

Dyphestive hung his head. "Don't remind me. I want to forget all about being Iron Bones."

Than reached over and put a hand on his shoulder. "That's in the past, and it will always be a part of you. But use the skills they taught you to serve a greater good. Let that light shine inside you."

Than's words lifted the dark cloud hanging over Dyphestive's spirit. He felt so ashamed of his time with the Doom Riders and having killed the people he had as a result. It was a dark blot on his heart that he couldn't wipe off. "I'll try."

Jakoby pointed a finger at him. "The Honor Guard and Monarch Knights can teach you something about turning the darkness into light. They are stalwart men and women. I don't know how these events are going to unfold. It's risky trying to fool them, but make the most of your time with them, and try to be sincere." He clenched his fist. "Nothing is stronger than the bond between soldiers."

"Funny, the Doom Riders used to talk like that too," Dyphestive said.

"A man's actions determine his heart," Than offered. "Remember that."

Dyphestive nodded. "I'll try."

Leena elbowed him in the gut.

"Ow, what did you do that for, knobby elbow?"

Jakoby chuckled. "Apparently, your reply didn't convince her."

Dyphestive put his mouth right next to her ear and raised his voice. "I'll remember."

Leena nodded, and her eyes smiled. She suddenly stood up and pointed toward the door.

"What's happening?" he asked.

"I think Leena's getting antsy." Jakoby drained his coffee and set his mug on the table. He stood up and buckled on the sword belt hanging from the back of his chair. "I am too."

"So am I." Than placed Streak in Dyphestive's arms. He patted the dragon's head. "This little dragon likes the blood brothers. That's a good sign of things ahead. Take care of him, and he'll take care of you. Tell Grey Cloak we'll track him down later. Have faith."

All three of them headed for the door.

"Where are you going?"

"We'll try to figure out where Zora is." Jakoby winked. "In the meantime, get some rest. You'll need it for tomorrow."

The door closed.

Dyphestive sat with Streak tucked in his arms and the dragon's claws digging into his chest. He didn't even notice. He stretched out his hands and grabbed Codd. "I am Codd."

4

"Welcome!" the boar's head rug said the moment Grey Cloak stepped on it as he entered Batram's Bartery and Arcania.

Paying the hoarse-voiced rug no mind, he sauntered toward the bartery's display counters. Batram was nowhere to be seen, but a tall older man with long gray hair, wearing ruffled and well-worn gray robes, peered down at him with all-knowing eyes.

They stared at each other in the awkward silence without introducing themselves. The venerable man seemed to look right into Grey Cloak's soul as he leaned on a gnarled wooden staff that was almost as tall as he was.

Grey Cloak's eyes started to water, and he glanced away. He noticed a finely crafted short sword lying across the glass display counter. Rocking back and forth on his heels, he said, "That's a nice sword." He looked the older man up and down. "Are you trading up from that ugly staff?"

With his intense eyes glued to Grey Cloak's, the older man said, "No, I'm keeping the staff, for it keeps me upright when I'm upside down. And I don't have a need for the sword anymore. Not my style."

"I see. May I?" He reached for it.

As quick as a cat, the older man smacked him on the hand. "Hands off. I'm negotiating with this rogue."

Grey Cloak rubbed his stinging hand. "Good luck with that."

From way back in the shop, Batram the halfling waddled down the aisle between the tall ancient blackwood shelves and brass-handled drawers. The shop had a musty smell to it, and cobwebs covered the ceiling, nooks, and crannies. Spiders of all sorts and sizes crawled over them.

Without giving Grey Cloak a glance, Batram hopped up on the counter and stood eye to eye with the older wizardly fellow. He wore a black-and-white-striped vest, a red long-sleeved shirt, and had a yellow daisy in his front pocket.

The cotton-headed halfling rubbed his fluffy goatee and eyed the short sword that shone in front of his bare feet. "I've thought about it and checked my inventory, and I've not seen the likes of that sword in this world. I'll give you five hundred gold chips for it."

"Five hundred! Outrageous! I didn't travel across the universe to be insulted!" the older man said. "Five thousand chips. Not one chip less!"

Batram wrung his hands. "One thousand. That's the best I can do." He shrugged his narrow shoulders. "The truth is, there isn't a very big market for an enchanted short sword. It would be a tough sell."

The older man got nose to nose with Batram. "Your offer stings, Batram. I'll do it for fifteen hundred. Not one chip less."

"Sold!"

Before Grey Cloak could blink, Batram's quick little hands whisked the sword underneath the counter and replaced it with a full leather bag of chips the size of his head. "Oof! It's all there. I promise."

The wizardly fellow snatched the bag of coins in his big hand. "It better be, or I'll be back, Batram." He gave Grey Cloak a hawkish look. "What are you gawking at? Let's see how you look after you've saved the world as many times as I have." He tapped the butt end of his staff on the ground, and with a puff of smoke, he vanished.

Batram coughed and fanned the smoke from his face. "I hate it when he does that." He instantly turned into a giant with eight spider arms and a tarantula head, wearing a striped vest. He turned his attention to Grey Cloak and drummed his tentacle-like fingers on the counter. "Now, what do you want, thief?"

5

"I hope you've come to return the Cloak of Legends to me." Batram wrung his eight spidery hands together. He stretched the bottom two out. "I'll take it now."

Grey Cloak pulled the cloak tighter around his body. "No, we're even. Besides, no one else can use it, so why do you want it? Can you use it?"

Batram pulled his hands back, but his hungry eyes were locked on the cloak. "No, but it has sentimental value to me."

"I don't think that's true." He hopped up on the counter and sat down. "I think you're tormented by the fact that you gave it to me in error only to find out later that it had power." He reached into one of the many pockets inside the cloak and pulled out a potion vial. One by one, he placed three glass cylinders with corks and wax-coated tops on the counter. One potion restored wounds, another was for shrinking, and the third he didn't know what its purpose was, but it had been given to him by the Gunthys. There was a fourth potion for flying. Dyphestive had that. "I want to sell these."

"Interesting." Batram reached for the potions.

Grey Cloak pulled them away. "I want ten thousand gold chips."

Batram laughed. He tossed his head back and belly laughed harder and louder. The boar's head rug on the floor started up in rollicking laughter as well.

Grey Cloak's cheeks flushed. "Fine, if you aren't interested, I'll take them somewhere else." He started to slide them off the counter, but Batram seized him.

"Don't be so hasty, young one. I didn't say I wasn't interested. I only laughed at your ludicrous price. I'll give you five hundred. A very fair price."

"No, ten thousand."

Batram rolled his eyes. "I've been in the business for a very long time. I see all sorts and kinds. I can judge people. You're desperate, Grey Cloak. Tell me, what do you need ten thousand pieces of gold for?" He leaned on two sets of his elbows and shrugged his weird eyebrows over his bug eyes. "Tell me, what do you need a king's ransom for? A kidnapping?"

Grey Cloak turned hot under the collar. "What do you know?"

"Ah, so it is a ransom." Batram sucked his teeth and took a seat. "Take no offense. I don't have knowledge outside these doors other than that which is brought in to me. You aren't the first one to cross my threshold to save a friend. I've seen that desperate look in all sorts." He transformed back into a halfling and sat on the counter. "Tell me more."

"I don't see the point in it."

"Come now, I might have valuable insight. Humor me."

Batram was right about one thing. Grey Cloak was desperate, and he needed all the help he could get. He spent the next several minutes telling the halfling everything about Irsk Monco and his plan to steal Codd's shield. He was exhausted by the time he finished, and with his shoulders dipping, he said, "My head hurts from thinking about it."

"Interesting." Batram smoked a pipe that a pair of huge tarantulas had brought over to him while Grey Cloak was talking. He blew out a stream of smoke. "Very interesting."

"Is that all you have to say? Any advice?"

"I have plenty of advice, but that isn't free either."

He had a sudden urge to swat Batram upside the head. But deep down, he respected the way the little man did business. "How much?"

"How much advice do you want?"

"Enough to tell me what to do. Zooks, you're greedy. I thought we were friends."

"No, this is business. Friends help one another for free."

"I don't have time for this." He slid off the counter and headed for the door.

"You don't have much time at all." Batram's voice lowered to a hungry whisper. "Tell me, do you still have the Figurine of Heroes?"

Grey Cloak turned on his heel. "Yes. How much will you loan me for it?"

"I'll loan you one thousand chips. I'll buy it for five."

"I see." He approached the counter. *Let's see how much he'll pay for everything.* "So, five hundred for the potions. Five thousand for the figurine." He eyeballed Batram. "In gold?"

"Yes, in gold."

He dusted off his cloak in showy fashion. "How much for the cloak?"

"The cloak is mine. I'm letting you borrow it. You won't get a chip from me for it," Batram answered bitterly.

"No, it's my cloak. You gave it to me. I thought we were even on this." He ground his teeth. He was getting used to Batram and learning from him too. He was getting a better idea of what his enchanted items were worth. And the truth was, he enjoyed the haggling. "Well, I'm certain what you would pay wouldn't be enough. Plus, I'm not going to give up my dragon to Irsk. Chances are, he won't honor the deal either way."

"Perhaps he will. Perhaps he won't," Batram responded through his cloud of smoke. "One never knows the heart of another man's intentions. That was free advice, my friend. Remember it." He scratched the sideburn on his cheek and stretched out his stumpy arms. "If you steal the shield, and he doesn't take it, I'd be very interested in acquiring it. I'd like the entire suit actually. I know someone in the market for it. If you snatch any interesting pieces, bring them to me."

"You sound confident that I can do this."

Batram dangled his short legs over the counter and offered the palm of his hand. "Let me have the vial, the black one that you can't identify."

Grey Cloak reached into his pocket and withdrew the vial filled with churning black liquid. He hesitated and said, "For advice."

Batram nodded and took the potion vial. "Open your hand. These are flash-ings." He sprinkled several acorn-sized pellets into Grey Cloak's hand. With a sparkle in his eyes, he said, "Now you have everything you need."

An unseen force whisked Grey Cloak off his feet and flung him through the wide-open front door and onto the street.

"Hurry back!" the boar's head rug said.

He caught one last look at Batram waving before the red door slammed shut, and the entire building vanished before his eyes.

"That dirty chipmunk got my potion for a handful of acorns!" He kicked the loose gravel on the street. "I have everything I need, my behind!" He stormed down the road.

6

THE SHELF

ANYA'S DRAGON BLADE SLICED DOWN IN AN ARC OF FLASHING LIGHT. THE SHARP metal sliced deep into the body of an enormous centipede with a lizard's head. The monster was as long as she was and as thick as her thigh, and its ugly plum-colored body had coiled around her leg. She sliced it again, splitting its shell in two. "Uck! Get off me!" She kicked the thick carcass away.

Three more lizarpedes scurried out of the dry hole in the dusty ground. They moved like snakes, with thousands of tiny legs rapidly propelling them forward from underneath. With flat heads like salamanders and sharp jackal teeth, they pursued her with their jaws opened wide.

Anya climbed higher onto the rocks of the barren landscape. "Come on, you dirty worms! Come!" She slashed the nearest lizarpede in twain and sent its gooey innards flying. She butchered the next one's face as it crawled up the rock. "Taste my thunder!"

The third, and last, lizarpede coiled at the bottom of the rock. Small spines popped out of its wriggling back and shot toward her. Tiny black spikes filled the air.

She crouched down and covered her face behind the metal of her armor's bracers. The spikes bounced off with a sound like the loud pitter-patter of rain. She dropped her guard and caught another barrage of needles in her face. "Ugh!" she cried out. "That's it!"

Her jaw tightened as she stared down the monster. She leapt off the rock and landed right on top of it. Her steel-shod boots crushed through the monster's ringed exoskeleton and smooshed into the gummy parts of its body. She sliced its head off with a backhand swing.

Tiny spikes, like a porcupine's, stuck out of her face. They burned like fire. She leaned back against the boulder and started pulling the thin spikes out, one by one. The needles had little barbs that clung to her skin. She ground her teeth.

Cinder popped up from behind a rise. The grand dragon had a lizarpede hanging from his jaws. He sucked it in like a wet noodle, and his big eyes brightened when he saw more of the monsters lying dead on the deck. "Ah, more sustenance. I thank you, Anya. Well done. This is much easier than digging them out of their holes."

"I'm so glad I could be bait for you," she said in a dry voice.

Cinder scooped the parts of two more lizarpedes from the dusty deck and guzzled them down. "Mmmm... not the same as meat but very satisfying. Shall I save you some?"

She made an icky face. "No, I want you to have it. After all, you worked so hard for it."

"You sound bitter. Perhaps you are hungry." He nudged a lizarpede toward her feet with the horn of his nose. "Eat. It's good."

"I've eaten enough things that creep and crawl in this water-forsaken land." She wiped the goo off her sword with a rag. "But it felt good killing something. I needed it."

Cinder slurped down another lizarpede.

Anya's stomach turned. "That's disgusting. I need to remind myself not to look." She sheathed her blade and slid down to her seat. Her long beautiful hair was matted and hanging over her shoulder, and her sunburnt skin peeled and cracked. She couldn't remember the last time she'd properly bathed. Eyeing the sky, she said, "What does one have to do to get a breeze in this suffocating land?"

Cinder blew at her. His breath was warm, like a fresh-baked biscuit's, but it smelled like rotten lizarpede guts.

She pinched her nose. "No thank you, no thank you. You're making it worse."

"Sorry," he said politely as he laid his huge body down on the ground at her feet like a loyal hound. "We could take a flight."

"Not now." She closed her eyes and rested her head against a rock. "Maybe tonight."

Anya and Cinder had been on the run and hiding for the better part of a year. Since the Sky Riders had been wiped out by Black Frost and his force, they'd been seeking refuge. They'd started with the Wizard Watch near Littleton, south of Gold Hook. They'd told the strange and aloof wizards what had happened. The brooding men and women in robes had received their message with looks as stony as the rocks that surrounded them and had coldly brushed them off.

The Wizard Watch infuriated Anya. She'd shaken her fist in their faces and left quickly, as she was completely uncertain of whose side they were on.

That left her and Cinder to care for the twelve fledgling dragons that had survived Black Frost's flame at Hidemark on Gunder Island. The fledglings were hidden in one of the plethora of caves that littered the Shelf. But the dragons grew fast, and hiding in the Shelf provided little to eat. It made their job all the more troublesome.

Anya plucked a spike out of her forehead that she'd missed. She eyed Cinder. The big dragon's stony lids were closed. If it hadn't been for his steadfast friendship, she didn't know what she would have done. He had been her rock. To make matters worse, he'd become the last one of his kind, a grand, unless one of the fledglings blossomed late. Otherwise, they were all middlings. But as the dragons grew bigger, it became harder to hide an entire thunder of them, which brought them to this desolate place.

"Cinder," she quietly said.

He opened one eye. "Yes, my dear?"

"Can you take care of the fledglings without me?"

He lifted his head. "You know I can. Anya, what are you planning to do?"

"You know I'd never leave you voluntarily, but traveling north is too risky for all of us. Black Frost will sniff us out for certain. Even if he thinks we're still alive, I don't think he's worried about us starving to death down here."

"What do you propose?"

She stood slowly. "I'm going north. I don't know why, but my gut is telling me I have to find Grey Cloak."

7

MONARCH CITY

Late that night, Grey Cloak entered Crane's apartment and found Dyphestive sleeping on the sofa, with his Codd figurine resting on his rising and falling chest. He snored softly. Streak was curled up underneath the big youth's feet, propping them up like a pillow.

Thank goodness everyone else is gone.

Several candles lining the walls of the room had melted down to nubs, but they provided a warm and welcoming illumination. He pulled off his leather boots. They were the same pair Zora had sold him the second time they officially met, when she helped dress him. He could still see her pretty face and big green eyes. It made him smile inside.

I'm going to save you, Zora. I promise.

The window overlooking the streets was open, and a gentle breeze stirred the cotton sheers. He sat down at the small kitchen table and started removing items from his enchanted pockets. The pockets were so deep that he could fit a sword inside one and not feel as if it were there at all.

The Cloak of Legends was interesting. If an item was too wide to fit in the pocket slit, the cloak would gobble it down—so to speak—like a great fish. All the while it kept him cozy, never too hot and never too cold, and as long as he wore it, his footfalls were as silent as if he were barefoot.

As he emptied his pockets, he reflected. He'd wandered the streets for hours trying to come up with a plan. According to Batram, he had everything he needed. He set the flashings on the table. They might have been the size of acorns, but they were as round as river stones and had tiny runes carved into them. He found it hard to believe that the stones were all he needed. He had five of them, but he'd tested them in an alley by tossing each on the ground. They made blinding flashes that dazzled him for moments.

I'm not so sure that's a big help. For a getaway perhaps.

He set a potion for wound restoration and a potion for shrinking on the table. He rolled the restoration potion between his fingers and watched the sparkling yellow fluid twist like a tiny tornado. He flipped it from one hand to the other.

I don't see how this will help.

During his long stroll, he caught on to what Batram meant when he said that Grey Cloak already had everything he needed. He realized that Batram wasn't talking about the flashings but everything else. The potions, his cloak, the figurine, his friends, that was all he needed, that and a good plan. He'd been bending his mind, trying to come up with something that might work before they reported to Captain Cleotus on the morrow.

He set the Figurine of Heroes between the two potion vials that he'd stood on their corks. He studied the faceless humanoid made out of black onyx. He recalled the words that ignited the enchantment in his mind—he always did once a day—and made sure that he never uttered it out loud. The powerful magic was both dangerous and exhilarating at the same time.

Perhaps this is all I need.

Of course, the Figurine of Heroes summoned powerful heroes from another world who quickly dished out punishment. He didn't think that would work in Monarch Castle. Jakoby said the guards were good people and that he shouldn't cross them. Grey Cloak had to come up with another plan, a plan that was subtle and nonviolent.

I think I can fool the guards, but how can I fool the yonders?

Dyphestive stirred. His Codd figurine rolled off his chest and plunked onto the floor. He sat up, bright-eyed and bushy-tailed, and eyed Grey Cloak. "You're back."

"I haven't been here long. Are you resting up for your day tomorrow?"

Dyphestive scooped his figurine off the floor. "I'm ashamed to admit it, but I'm excited."

"We're doing this for Zora, not ourselves."

"I know that. But I'm curious." Dyphestive eyeballed his figurine. "Ah, the shield fell off!" He bent over and jammed his fingers under the sofa. "There it is, I think."

"You better get it before Streak does. He'll squirrel it away with his hoard."

"I have it." Dyphestive held the tiny shield up proudly between his thumb and index finger. "Just like the real thing but smaller."

Grey Cloak's gray eyes widened like saucers. With a devilish smirk, he sat up. "That's it!"

8

MONARCH CASTLE

"Bloody Monarch Knights think they own this castle," Airius said as he led Grey Cloak through the castle's corridors. In a snobbish voice, the elven head servant continued. "I'm in charge of the servants, not them. They always see fit to make my choices for me." The short and rawboned elf turned his chin over his shoulder and looked back at Grey Cloak. "At least you're an elf."

Grey Cloak trailed behind the refined man's slow and unique gait. Airius's arms shoveled out in front of him as he walked, his torso leaning back in an odd balancing act. Airius was older, and he didn't move very fast, but his black clothing was neatly pressed, and his silver buttons and cuff links shone like the morning sun.

Beside Grey Cloak was another servant, Sayma. She was an attractive elf, young like him, with silvery-white hair tied back in a straight ponytail, with black ribbons woven into it. She wore black garb with a white apron and had a white servant's cap on her head. She maintained a serious expression.

Airius opened a door in the alcove underneath a stairwell near the bustling kitchens. It was morning, and Captain Cleotus had introduced Grey Cloak to Airius only minutes ago. It had been a quick introduction, and Captain Cleotus had whisked Dyphestive away to the Honor Guard's training grounds.

A set of stairs led down into a dormitory of small rooms. Each room held two small beds with wooden chests at their feet. Airius reached down and opened a chest. "You can store your belongings in this chest, and this will be your bed. It will always be made when you're not sleeping in it. I want the corners tight." A silver chip appeared in his hand. He bounced it off the bed's woolen blanket and snatched it away. Airius had a way of looking down at Grey Cloak even though he had to look up. "Very tight. You can make a bed, can't you?"

"Yes," Grey Cloak replied.

"And don't smirk. I don't like smirking. I don't like smiling either. We're here to serve, not be happy." Airius combed Grey Cloak's hair behind his ears. "Hmm... you're a bit shaggy but well-knit. Good cheekbones. Tell me, have you served before, as Captain Cleotus, the oaf, said?"

Grey Cloak nodded.

"We'll see. Sayma, find him a uniform, but take him to the barber first. I want him serving this morning. I want to know if he has the chops to do this or not." He slowly turned around and walked out of the room in his strange gait.

Grey Cloak did a quick imitation of Airius. He mimicked his walk. "I don't like smirking. And I don't like smiling either."

Sayma didn't crack a smile.

"Sorry," he said guiltily, recognizing Airius's no-nonsense expression in her features. "I didn't realize you two were related."

The soft-angled features of her straight face broke into a smile, and she burst into warm laughter. Holding her belly, she dropped down on the bed. "Oh my goodness, that's the best imitation of Airius I've ever seen. You did him perfect-ly." She popped up and peeked around the door. "Good, he's gone. You have to be careful with the old man. He likes to linger." She extended her hand. "Let me formally introduce myself. My name is Sayma."

He squeezed her warm hand with both of his. "I'm Grey Cloak."

"You were named after a garment?"

"Why does everyone say that?"

"Isn't it obvious?" She pulled on the shoulder of his cloak. "You weren't born in that thing, were you?"

"No."

"Here, let me help you out of that. As much as I'd like to chat, we need to get moving, or Airius will be on us like flies on dung."

"Good to know."

She tousled his hair with her slender fingers. She wore a faint but pleasant flowery fragrance. As she ran her hands over his shoulders and body, she said, "Don't get any ideas. I'm sizing you up for your uniform. But Airius is right. You are well-built."

"I know."

Sayma smiled. "Come on, let's trim those bangs and get you suited up. We can't keep the dubious Monarchs waiting." She led him from the room and down the long, narrow hall adorned with wooden doors to the servants' quar-ters. They squeezed by other servants coming and going and finally made it to a back room with a gnome standing on a high stool, who quickly trimmed his hair.

After the haircut, they made their way to the uniform closet, which had wooden shelves loaded with shirts, pants, dresses, aprons, and boots. Sayma pressed a set of clothing into his arms. "This will do." She led him back to his room. "Hurry up. Chop-chop. The Monarchs are waiting."

"A little privacy, please?"

She rolled her eyes. "And I thought you weren't shy."

"Not shy, only modest." He closed the door to change, and in seconds, he looked like he belonged, the same as the other servants. He folded up the Cloak of Legends and the clothing Zora had picked out for him. He focused on the mission. He had a plan. Now all he had to do was execute it.

Must save Zora. Only two days to go.

He couldn't find a way to lock his footlocker. *Zooks.* "Uh, Sayma, don't these boxes have locks?"

"No, none of us have anything to steal, and by the looks of it, you don't either."

I don't know about that.

He flattened his cloak and hid it underneath his mattress.

Sayma knocked on the door. "Are you taking a nap?"

He flung the door open with a smile. "I'm ready."

She chuckled. "We'll see about that."

9

DYPHESTIVE STOOD AT ATTENTION IN THE SMALL COURTYARD OF THE HONOR Guard's training grounds. Two elven men stood to his right, and a human man and woman stood to his left. He stood half a head taller than the tallest of the strapping people, all of whom were well put together. They'd been given padded-leather chest plates, and each held a jo stick. All eyes were on the soldier standing before them, a member of the Honor Guard, complete with scale mail armor and a golden sash. The man was broad faced, flat nosed, and clean-shaven, with thinning, wavy brown hair hanging past his ears and a stout but squatty build. The whites of his eyes shone like he was crazy.

"My name is Tinison! Sergeant Tinison!" He spit when he spoke. His harsh voice was loud. "I don't know what wormhole the likes of you were dragged out of, but I aim to stuff you back in!" He marched up to Dyphestive and stood nose to nose with him. "Do you find me amusing, boy!"

"No, Sergeant!"

"Then why are you smiling?"

"I'm not. I always look like this... I think."

"Listen here, Baby Face. I've seen big boys like you waltz in here like they're going to be king of the world only to run out of here crying like halflings." Sergeant Tinison bumped chests with Dyphestive. "I don't know what Captain Cleotus was thinking, dragging you to me. I'm going to turn your big bones into goo! Do you agree?"

"Er—"

"My name's not ER! It's SERGEANT TINISON! Answer me! Answer me!"

Dyphestive swallowed the lump building in his throat and shouted back in the sergeant's face. "No!"

Sergeant Tinison rose on tiptoe. "Are you yelling at me?"

"Yes!"

"Did I give you permission to yell at me?"

"No!"

"Stop yelling at me!" Sergeant Tinison fingered his ear, cocked his head to one side, and casually moved to the elf standing beside Dyphestive. "The big boy has some lungs on him, doesn't he?"

"Yes, Sergeant," the elf said in an agreeable tone.

Dyphestive could see the elf was gaining the sergeant's confidence out of the corner of his eye.

Sergeant Tinison nodded, his big chin bobbing. He put a hand on the elf's shoulder and gave him the once over. "Say, you're an elf, aren't you?"

The elf puffed out his chest and said in a more confident tone, "Yes, Sergeant."

Sergeant Tinison got in his face. "I hate elves! I hate your ears and your pretty little features. I hate your tiny little noses. Look at my nose, elf! Look at it! Do you like it? Tell me, do you like it?"

"Yes!" the elf said in a shaky voice.

"You're lying to me! I hate my nose! It's been broken eight times! Look at it! Look at it!" The sergeant moved over to the only female in the group. "What do we have here?" He touched her chestnut-brown hair. "A female." He crossed his arms. "How nice. Tell me, what are you?"

"Pardon, Sergeant?" she asked.

"I said, what... are... you?"

"I don't understand the question."

Sergeant Tinison's voice rose to new heights. "I'll tell you what you are. You're an overachiever. That's what you are! A woman in the Honor Guard? Is that a jest?" He got in her face. "Is it? Is it? Is it? Answer me! Say it! Say it! Say it! Auuuuuuugh! Say it!"

"It's not a jest, Sergeant. I've seen other women in the Honor Guard," she said.

Sergeant Tinison punched her in the belly and dropped her to her knees. He screamed in her ear, "They aren't women! They're Honor Guard!"

BY MIDAFTERNOON, the hot sun was beating down on the Honor Guard trainees like a dragon's breath. They'd soaked through their padded-leather armor, and they marched behind Sergeant Tinison with their heads low except for Dyphestive.

The strapping youth kept his chin up and a humble smile on his face. He'd been through worse, much worse with the Doom Riders, who made him push wheelbarrows full of rocks up a mountainside. The calisthenics and the hard running were routine to him. The weapons training was rudimentary as well. Sergeant Tinison hadn't shown him anything he hadn't seen before, and it was driving the sergeant crazy.

Dyphestive had finished his one hundredth push-up with Sergeant Tinison on the ground yelling in his ear. "Is that all you can do, Baby Face? Don't you have more in you?"

Dyphestive did ten more and kept going. Sweat dripped off his chin, but he could do one hundred more if he had to. He suddenly remembered what Jakoby had told him about blending in and not overly demonstrating his well-honed skills. He decided to take a break and collapsed on the ground.

"Look at this! A quitter! Same as that elf who tucked tail and scurried out of here!" Sergeant Tinison said. "Quit now. Run home, and you'll be back in time for Mother's dinner. I bet she'll have a big hug and kiss waiting for you."

"I don't have a mother," Dyphestive muttered.

"Oh, boo-hoo, orphan boy!" Sergeant Tinison smacked him on the back of the head. "How about this, loser? I'll be your mother! Loser! Loser! Loser! Auuu-ugh! Auuuugh! Loser! Get up, Baby Face. Get up! The orphan snatchers are coming!"

Dyphestive bounced to his feet and glared down at Sergeant Tinison. "You're not very nice."

Sergeant Tinison clapped his thick hands together. "That's the smartest thing you've said all day, Baby Face." He glanced sideways at the young woman in the group. She had a crooked nose. "Beak! Fetch the sticks. It's time to see which one of you has enough stones to be an Honor Guard."

10

Jakoby, Leena, and Than sat in the pews of Monarch City's main cathedral. The Cathedral of Saints was a massive structure, capable of hosting thousands, with tremendous stone archways holding up the hundred-foot-high ceilings. An occasional dove flew overhead and roosted in the nests of the archways. Stained glass windows decorated the walls, and bright sunlight shone fully through the purple and ruby-red glass with eerie effect. Monks in drab, loose-fitting clothing sauntered between the long swath of pews, offering to help the needy people who entered and sat down.

"I'm not so certain this is the best idea," Jakoby said to Than as he drew his hood higher over his face. His skin prickled at the thought of the dungeons below, where he'd been locked up. "Do you really think it's wise to go back?"

Than cleared his throat. "This is where Orpah came and went. It's the only advantage we have."

A big-eared monk teetered over and offered them a donation basket.

Than waved him off. "If we had money, we wouldn't be here. We're hungry."

Jakoby watched the monk move out of earshot. The large cathedral had many people scattered all over the parish, perhaps a hundred or more, but the place was so large, it appeared barren. "Do you really think they would keep Zora in the same place they kept us? That seems obvious."

Leena, who sat on the other side of Jakoby, leaned forward and glared at Than.

"True, it might be a trap, or it might be the last place they think we would look." Than winked at Leena.

She stuck her tongue out at him.

"I don't suppose we're going to sit here all day," Jakoby said as he rose. "Let's pay our jailers a visit."

He led the way to the front of the cathedral and moved up onto the stage.

Several candles burned on a tiered stand in front of an enormous statue of a man in flowing robes with a solid-gold sun for a face. He lit a dry candle wick with another candle while a nearby monk stood by, staring. He nodded at the long-faced man, who headed his way.

"Are you lost, young man?" the monk asked in a haunting voice.

"In a manner of speaking, you might say that." Jakoby put his arm over the fragile man's shoulders. He walked the man beyond the curtains toward the back. "You see, I've been wandering the streets a long time, trying to find a purpose. Could you give me guidance?"

"Of course. We're always looking for volunteers to serve the needy. Willing servants of the sun gods."

"This is a big place. If I volunteer, do you have somewhere for me and my friends to stay?"

The monk squeezed Jakoby's strong shoulders. "You are well-made. If you use that brawn, we will board you, but only long enough for you to get back on your feet. Come with me."

Jakoby nodded at Than and Leena. They quietly followed.

The monk led them to a storage room located down the stairs in the back of the cathedral. They passed a labyrinth of small rooms.

"There." The monk pointed from just inside the doorway. "Find a set of robes. Dress. I'll return, and we'll swear you in."

The moment they turned to look at the robes hanging on the walls, the monk slammed the door closed.

Jakoby rushed to the heavy wooden door and tugged on the handle. "That spooky snake handler locked us in!"

Than donned a set of monk's robes, and Leena did the same.

Jakoby stroked his moustache. "Do you really think we're going to fool them by playing dumb?"

"It got us this far, didn't it?" Than asked.

"Are you suggesting we get ourselves thrown in the dungeon? I'm not getting locked back up. No thank you," Jakoby said. "Leena, pick this lock, and get us out of here."

Leena hurried over to the door and pulled a hairpin from the neck of her ponytail. As Jakoby dressed, she picked the lock.

"I'm not putting the cuffs back on. I'll fight and die first."

"Great words to live by," Than said. "You're doing exactly what I thought you would."

Leena opened the door, and the trio entered the hall.

"It won't be long before they figure out we escaped, and this place is crawling with monks and whatever else."

Than closed the door, stuck a long yellow finger in the keyhole, and zapped it with a charge of light. A tiny plume of smoke drifted out of the hole. "That conundrum should keep them busy." He stepped aside. "After you."

"Are you a wizard?" Jakoby asked as he led them down into the bowels of the cathedral.

"No."

"A druid?"

"No."

"Then what are you?"

"On your side. That's all that matters."

After several twists, turns, and backtracks through the network of corridors and staircases, they came to the dank levels deep below the surface. They stepped into a corridor of stone, slick from the water dripping from the ceiling. At the end of the corridor, a pair of burly lizardmen stood guard in front of an entry made of iron bars.

Jakoby's fingertips tingled as they went deeper. Disguised as monks, they moved over the watery floor, and he quietly said, "I'll handle this."

The lizardmen stood upright and jabbed their spears at them. "Halt!"

Jakoby lifted his hands and smiled. "Brethren, I exalt you." He dropped his hood and smiled. "I have a prisoner with me." He grabbed Than's arm and pulled him forward. "This old crone was caught stealing from the coffers. I was told to bring him to you. Will you take him?"

"A petty thief," the tallest lizardman said. "Hah. He's not worthy of our dungeons. If he stole from the sun gods, then there is only one thing to do. Execute him." Without warning, the lizardman thrust his spear and stabbed Than in the chest.

Jakoby couldn't hide his shock as Than dropped to a knee. Jakoby fumbled for the sword underneath his robes and pulled it free just as the second lizardman attacked, shouting, "Intruder!"

11

"Try to keep up," Sayma said to Grey Cloak. "We can't keep the Monarchs waiting. And remember, don't look at them directly, ever. Think of yourself as a piece of furniture. We serve. We vanish."

Grey Cloak hurried behind her, a silver serving tray loaded with covered platters of food on his shoulder. They traversed the hidden corridors that led from the kitchen to the castle's main interior rooms. It was a veritable labyrinth when he didn't know where he was going. He quickly picked up on it, however. "Are you telling me that you've never looked a single Monarch in the eye? I find that hard to believe."

"No, I haven't."

"I bet you have."

"Are you calling me a liar?"

"Come now, how could you not look? The finest people in Monarch City are gathered there."

She stopped, turned, and faced him. "Listen to me. You aren't going to last very long as a servant if you can't control your curiosity. I've caught you staring at the castle's guests. You need to watch it because *they* are watching." She glanced up.

"Oh, you mean the enchanters and the yonders, don't you?" he asked, fishing for information. "Captain Cleotus told us about them. Creepy. Do they bother you?"

"Doesn't being watched all the time bother you? I can't go into a room without seeing one. The only time I have any privacy is when I'm in my quarters." She tipped her head. "Come on."

They'd been on the go for hours, hustling back and forth between the kitchens and the dining and living rooms. Monarch Castle wasn't so much of a residence as it was a government where the leaders of the city and the

Monarchs' guests gathered. The entire day was a well-planned and tireless event.

"So, you can see the yonders even when they're hidden?"

"In time, you get an eye for it. You can feel them. Creepy things. The only way to avoid them is outside in the daylight."

"They don't like the sun?"

"It's an aversion to bright light. We'd probably have the same problem, too, if we were a giant eyeball."

Grey Cloak grinned. *Perfect.*

He followed Sayma's lead into one of the extravagant dining chambers. Ten men and women were sitting at an ivory dinner table painted with golden trim. As the group of dignitaries talked amongst themselves, they set the covered plates before them.

Grey Cloak couldn't believe his eyes. *Look at the wealth.* In such close proximity, he gained a quick feel for the people at the table. They wore lavish and gaudy jewelry. Their clothing was cut from the finest cloth and silk, and their perfume reeked of shameless spending.

He got a feel for the Monarchs as well. They always sat at the head of the table, at one end or the other or both. When they spoke, their guests quieted. They had a domineering presence but were polite and well spoken, and the guests at the table were quick to suck up to them.

After he and Sayma served the food, they both stepped back and stood on the side of the bay window. They stood as still as cranes, only moving to refill the silver goblets with wine. After half an hour, the Monarch at the end of the table, a woman in a full satin dress with a pillowy bottom, rang a crystal bell. Sayma and Grey Cloak quickly dismissed themselves behind the curtains and hustled down the hidden corridor.

"I'm glad that's over with. Come on," Sayma said.

"Where to now?"

"It's time to give my aching feet a break. We'll swing by the kitchen and grab some scraps to eat. Monley always sets something aside for me. I'll share." She eyed him. "Hungry?"

He patted his belly. "Famished." He couldn't remember the last time he'd eaten because, when he had, it hadn't been much, and he hadn't cared for it. But his hunger had caught up to him. Anything would be nice.

Sayma whizzed through the kitchens and grabbed a napkin stuffed with food from the end of a butcher-block prep table. "Thank you, Monley!" she shouted to a sandy-haired dwarven man hammering bread dough with his fists.

He winked at Sayma and glared at Grey Cloak.

Sayma grabbed a burning candle from a tabletop on her way. She led them up a narrow staircase into a small tower that overlooked one of the many castle gardens. It was a crammed lookout post with two three-legged stools and some dried scraps of bread on the floor. Sayma scooped up the bread scraps and set them on the ledge of the portal window. A yellow bird with white wings landed on the windowsill and pecked at the bread. Sayma opened her hand and fed the crow-sized bird. "This is Lenny. A garden bird. My best friend." She touched the bird's beak with her nose.

"That's interesting."

"Go ahead and eat. You sound like you're getting cranky." She fished a small pipe out of her pocket and stuffed a pinch of tobacco into it. Using the candle, she lit the pipe and huffed out smoke. She offered it to Grey Cloak. "I love the sweet aroma of tobacco. Care to try?"

"No thanks." He opened the cloth napkin and grabbed a biscuit, a strip of bacon, and a hunk of cheese. He loaded the bacon and cheese inside the biscuit. "Are you allowed to smoke a pipe?"

She shrugged and blew smoke out the window. "It keeps the yonders away. But Airius would kill me. Of course, most of us pipe smoke, and he can't do away with all of us." She gave him the mature look of a much older woman. "So, how do you like your first day?"

"I've had worse days," he admitted around a mouthful of food.

"Huh, many can't do this job. They quit a day or two into it, but you're doing very well. I'm impressed."

"Thanks."

"Now tell me, why are you really here?"

He lifted his gaze and met hers. "What do you mean?"

"I've been doing this awhile, and I'm a good judge of people. You're here for something else. What is it? And be honest, or I'll turn Airius onto you." She gave him a deadpan stare. "I'm serious."

He swallowed. "Well, if you must know, I'm here to steal Codd's shield."

"GET AFTER IT, YOU TWO BAGS OF DONKEY DUNG!" SERGEANT TINISON HOLLERED. He crouched down with his hands on his knees, a menacing look on his face. "We're waiting. Somebody hit somebody! Do you want to be an Honor Guard or not?"

The four trainees stood amidst fifteen members of the Honor Guard, there to watch the new recruits, in what they called the Ring of Battle. Dyphestive stood among the stalwart men and women as well as a man he trained alongside named Hodges.

Inside the Ring of Battle, the woman Sergeant Tinison fondly called Beak squared off with the remaining elf trainee, named Fancy Feet. They both twirled their jo sticks and jabbed at each other.

"What's going on, Sergeant? Is this a dance or a fight?" a gusty orcen female member of the Honor Guard asked. "Pitiful!"

"Stuff a fist in it, Tulip, before I do," Sergeant Tinison said. "If you don't want to watch, go braid your beard or something."

The Honor Guard erupted in throaty laughter.

Tulip grabbed her chin and blanched.

"Let's go, Fancy Feet! Quit twirling that stick around! What are you trying to do, fly away?" Sergeant Tinison clapped his hands. "Somebody make somebody bleed!"

Beak was quick, but Fancy Feet was quicker. She jabbed, he juked. Off and on, their jo sticks would clack together, and they would break away again.

Dyphestive had seen his fair share of fights in his lifetime, and this show was boring. The two fighters used the long lengths of wood like swords, but a well-trained weapons master could use them for more than that.

I shouldn't have any trouble whipping either of them.

"Whoo boy! Somebody get me some coffee because it's going to be a long time before one of these toads hurts the other. Why don't you both lie down, and we'll wait and see who dies first?" Sergeant Tinison thumbed the sweat from his eyes. "Come on, sandbags! My eyes are falling asleep!"

Beak went on the aggressive. She swiped at Fancy Feet's legs. He jumped over the long stick with ease. She jabbed, stepped, and lunged. He evaded with feathery ease and countered with a sideswipe of his own. Beak ducked underneath it.

"Oh my! Listen, everyone!" Sergeant Tinison cupped his ear. "It's the sound of boredom! Aaauuuuuuugh! Somebody hit someone!"

"You want a show? You shall have it!" Beak went berserk. She attacked Fancy Feet with a brutal but precise fury. Her sudden lunge with her jo stick slipped past the elf's quick reflexes and knocked him hard on the shoulder. He let out a pained groan.

Beak's onslaught ramped up. She busted his shin, jabbed his belly, and cracked her jo stick against the side of his head.

Fancy Feet staggered away on noodling legs.

The Honor Guard exploded into thunderous cheers.

Beak whipped Fancy Feet like a borrowed mule.

Crack! Smack! Chuk! Thok!

Fancy Feet didn't know what hit him. He frantically flailed away, but a fast swipe by Beak swept his feet out from under him, knocking him flat on his back.

Beak pounced on Fancy Feet. She pinned him underneath her thighs and put her jo stick against his throat. Red-faced, he pushed back against her jo stick for a moment then quickly tapped out. She screamed gutturally in his face before releasing him and stood to the sound of thunderous applause from her superiors. Even Sergeant Tinison had an approving sneer on his face.

Dyphestive couldn't clap loud enough. He had clearly underestimated Beak. She was good.

Sergeant Tinison gave Fancy Feet a kick on the rear as a pair of Honor Guards carried the broken and bloodied man out. "Let him dance with the moat monsters. Get the elf out of here!" He eyeballed Dyphestive and Hodges. "Get in the circle, you two hootenannies! And I better get a stronger start than the last one."

Dyphestive and Hodges squared off with their jo sticks in hand. Hodges had a heavy build and tired eyes, which gave him a lazy look. He was older than Dyphestive, built like a dwarf, and had short, coarse black hair and a beard that looked like a fuzzy helmet keeping his face safe.

Dyphestive nodded at him. "Good luck."

Hodges sneered back.

Sergeant Tinison shouted, "What are you waiting for? A bell to ring? Get after it!"

Dyphestive glanced at Sergeant Tinison. Hodges smacked him right upside the temple with his jo stick with a resounding *whack*. The precise blow made his legs wobble and dropped him to one knee. All he could hear was a sea of the Honor Guards' cheers lifting into the sky. He was hit again. *Whack! Whack! Whack!*

13

LEENA FLICKED HER NUNCHAKUS IN THE WINK OF AN EYE AND SMOTE BOTH lizardmen across the jaw.

Chuk! Crack!

The iron-jawed lizardmen wobbled a moment before they straightened their backs. Leena rammed her knee into the shorter lizardman's groin, doubling him over, and cracked him in the earholes with her sticks. The lizardman dropped.

Jakoby sliced the tip off the taller lizardman's spear, which was still in Than's belly. As the lizardman went for his sword, Jakoby thrust his sword deep into the lizardman's chest. "Mercy on him."

With both lizardmen down, they went to Than's aid. Than was on the ground, clutching his gut. "I'm fine. I'm fine."

"You aren't fine. You were stabbed in the gut," Jakoby said as he searched for the wound.

Than slapped his hands away and said in a cranky voice, "I'm fine. The lizardman caught me off guard is all, leaving me wounded with shame. I should have seen that coming." He stood up. "Let's get going."

"Hold on a moment." Jakoby picked up the end of the spear he'd severed. The point was bent. "Care to explain this?"

"It explains itself. The lizardman forgot to sharpen his spear. How lucky for me," Than said.

Leena snuck up to Than and lifted his clothing. She gasped quietly.

Jakoby dropped his gaze to Than's belly. It was covered in thick gray-and-black scales, like the man's arms and hands. It looked like snakeskin. "You're like that all over. What is that?"

"My business." Than grabbed the key ring from one of the guards and unlocked the gate. "We have a mission. Stop with the questions."

"Are you a lizardman?" he asked.

Than stopped and gave Jakoby a serious look. "Call me a lizardman, or even suggest it, and I'll wrap that sword around your neck."

Jakoby smiled tentatively. "Don't take it personally, old man. You're the one with scales. What was I supposed to think?"

"Think smart. Lizards aren't the only creatures with scales." Than jogged down the long corridor on feet as light as a feather. The passageway opened into an inner sanctuary of a larger network of rooms. "We're close. I can hear people screaming."

Jakoby didn't hear a thing, and Leena shrugged her eyebrows at him. "Why don't you lead the way?"

"A good idea." Than took off like a ghost.

Jakoby had a hard time keeping up with the scruffy-looking man who moved like a will-o'-the-wisp. Than would rush to a spot and duck into an alcove or room while lizardman soldiers marched right by him. Than clearly had more to him than met the eye.

With the coast clear, Jakoby said, "What are we supposed to do, waltz down to the dungeons and do roll call?"

Than clawed at the ends of his hair. "I hadn't really thought this far into it. But your idea is sound. I like it."

"What idea, roll call?"

Than pointed inside a storage room. "Grab some buckets, shovels, and pans. We have some cleaning to do. Come on."

The trio ventured down a wide stone staircase that led to the very heart of the same dungeon that they had escaped from. At the very bottom of the stairs, the iron gate was closed. A lizardman guard sat snoring in a chair leaned back on two legs against the wall. He was stationed by the lever that opened the gate.

Beyond the gate, four lizardmen made their rounds. Six cages hung suspended over the floor, and at the far end on the left, a four-armed ogre sat on the ground, with his head between his knees.

Jakoby pressed his face to the bars. "I don't see her. Do you?"

Than's nostrils flared. "I don't see or smell her, but I can't be certain. My senses are not what they once were here. We need to get inside." He rapped his knuckles gently on the gate.

The lizardman leaning in the chair opened his eyelids. His yellow eyes slid over to the trio on the other side of the gate. He wiped drool from his mouth and dropped the two raised chair legs to the floor. Rubbing his eyes, he approached. "What do you want?" the husky-voiced lizardman asked.

Than nudged Jakoby. Jakoby cleared his throat and improvised. "We come to do our service to the sun gods. We come to clean. To serve. To ease the burden on your shoulders," he said in a soft, awkward voice. He raised a bucket and brush. "We clean."

"I've heard nothing about this." The lizardman eyed the trio warily. "Who sent you?"

"The sun gods," Jakoby innocently said.

"Bloody moons, I don't have time for this." He shouted down the stairs,

"Haavers! Do you know about a monk cleanup? Apparently, the sun gods sent them!"

The brood of lizardmen broke out in hissing laughter.

"Of course, send them in."

"Ah, stifle yourself! You just don't want to clean!"

"None of us want to clean! We say let them in, Adsel!" Haavers shouted back.

"Bloody moons!" Adsel grabbed the lever and pushed it up. He hollered back over his shoulder, "You better keep a close eye on them! This watch can't foul up like the last one."

The iron gate rattled upward.

The trio stepped past the threshold.

Adsel pulled the lever and closed them inside. "Get at it, and don't be down there trying to convert those people. You clean. I want none of the warm and friendly treatment, or I'll send you out of here with your heads tucked between your legs."

"Where should we start?" Jakoby asked.

Adsel the lizardman sat down, leaned his chair back against the wall, and smiled. "You want to clean? Then start in the ogre's grove." He closed his eyes and laughed. "Hah-hah."

As they walked down the stairs, Than said under his breath, "Try to split up and search the cages. By the way, that was some pretty good acting. Have you done it before?"

"Acted? No. Been a sun-god monk? Yes," Jakoby said, shamefaced. "Don't ask. You two take the front. I'll move back to the ogre's den." He eyeballed the suspended cages along the way. No one in the cages resembled Zora. He made a beeline for the ogre's lair, walking by the dungeon cells on the way down, and peered inside each one.

The prisoners were in awful shape. Their stomachs groaned as their sunken eyes locked on Jakoby. A feeling of dread came over him. It was the same feeling he'd had when he was a prisoner before Grey Cloak, Dyphestive, and Zora came. He owed them. He owed her. He didn't see any sign of her on his way to the ogre's lair.

The four-armed ogre didn't budge from his spot. Jakoby pinched his nose as he stood at the threshold of the big humanoid's den. *This is awful. Nothing could clean this.* He ventured a foot inside. The den was a deep cave, big enough for three ogres to huddle in. He dug his shovel into the grit and started scooping the waste. He loaded up a bucket and headed to the fire pit, with his nose tucked into his robes. *Ugh, this is awful.*

A deep stone fire pit where all of the waste could be burned sat at the back of the dungeon row. He met up with Than and Leena by the stones. "Did you find her?"

"No," Than said as he dumped his bucket into the fire. "I take it you came up empty-handed as well."

"I didn't see her. I say we move on before these green toads sniff us out," Jakoby responded.

"Agreed." Than headed toward the steps leading out. As soon as his foot stopped on the bottom step, the stone landing erupted in smoke.

The trio moved back and watched with big eyes as the smoke faded. Six warriors wearing iron masks and crimson robes stood tall on the platform. They were accompanied by a bald man with sunken eyes and vulturelike features. He wore black robes with a tight collar, and he stared the trio down with haunting eyes. "I am Finton Slay. These are the Iron Devils. I've been expecting you." He stepped away from the masked men. "Kill them."

14

Sayma belly laughed so hard she fell off her stool. "You really are a jester." The flummoxed young woman tilted her stool back onto its legs. "You really shouldn't joke about something like that though. If the wrong person hears it, you'll be fed to the moat monsters."

"Do they really feed people to the moat monsters? And I'm not joking."

"Hah. You don't know when to quit, do you, little Grey Cloak?" She pinched his cheek. "But I admire your ambition. Tell me, if you stole the shield, what would you do with it? Sell it for a fortune?"

"No, I thought it would look really good in my quarters." He smirked.

She giggled. "I don't think there's room for it." She tapped her pipe ashes out over the windowsill. The garden bird flew away. She crumbled up a biscuit and left it on the windowsill. "Come on."

"But you didn't eat anything."

"I save my tummy for dinner. I just wanted to feed you and the birds." She put her pipe away and dusted off her apron. "Did you get enough to eat?"

"Plenty."

"Good, you're going to need plenty of energy if you're going to steal Codd's shield. Tell me, how would you do it?"

"Ah, I can't tell you that," he said on his way down the stairs.

"Why, because you'll have to kill me?"

"No, because I don't know yet."

She nudged him with her shoulder. "You're funny. I hope you stick around."

He nodded and took a step back. "So long as they will have me." He almost bumped into Airius at the bottom of the stairs. He quickly hopped away. "Excuse me, sorry."

"I've been looking for you two," Arius said with disappointment. "Come with me, both of you." He led them through the busy kitchen to a small neatly organized office in the back. "Close the door and sit."

Sayma had a nervous look in her eye as she closed the door and sat down in a small wooden chair beside Grey Cloak.

Airius glanced down his nose at them but focused his attention on Sayma. "How is this newcomer handling his duties?"

She sat up and leaned forward. "Very well. He's proven to be an apt and quick learner."

"Very good." Airius scribbled notes on a parchment with a feather quill he dipped in an inkwell. "Is he capable of backing up your duties?"

"I'm confident he could master all of them over time." She rubbed her hands on her apron and chewed her lip. "He's very apt."

"Yes, you said that." Airius opened a wooden drawer and produced a small coin purse. He tossed it to the end of his desk in front of Sayma. "Take that."

She grabbed the coin purse and glanced at Grey Cloak. She seemed to shrink in her seat, and with a shaky voice she asked, "Headmaster, what is this for?"

"It's called severance pay. The monarchy is releasing you from your services."

She gasped and sobbed. "But why?"

"Why? You need to ask why, you little pipe smoker? I warned you about that." Airius shoved a parchment and quill over to Grey Cloak. "I need you to sign this. You're a witness."

"Uh, um, but—"

"Sign it, or I'll show you the door too."

Grey Cloak scratched his name down on the paper. He gave Sayma a sorrowful look. Her cheeks were wet with tears, and her shoulders heaved.

"Sayma, grab your belongings from your quarters, and see yourself out. You know where the exit is." Airius gave her a disappointed look. "I'd hate to have to notify the Honor Guard."

Sayma removed her apron and threw it at him. "I'll be gone before you know it!" She stormed out of the office. A clatter of broken glassware followed her departure.

Grey Cloak swallowed. *What was that all about? She didn't do anything. She was good.* He gave Airius a puzzled look.

"Don't look so long faced. We don't have a place for that here. Finish her assignments for the day, and tomorrow I want you to serve those on the castle tours."

Grey Cloak nodded. "Yes, Headmaster."

Airius grabbed the parchment, rolled it up, and stuck it in a drawer. "Off with you, then."

Grey Cloak hurried out of the office and after Sayma. He caught up with her down in the servants' quarters. She was coming down the hallway, with her things gathered in a leather satchel, her eyebrows knitted together and a stormy look in her eyes.

"Sayma, I'm sorry. I don't understand."

"Sure you don't. Get out of my way, job snatcher. This isn't the first time someone's tried to steal my position." She pushed past him. "Best of luck to you, Grey Cloak. I guess you got what you wanted."

"But I didn't want it. I just arrived." She moved up the stairs, and he hollered after her, "Go to the Tavern Dwellers Inn. Tell Aham I sent you. He'll take care of you."

Sayma was gone.

He kicked the wall. It had all happened so fast, and he was powerless to do anything about it. He might as well have been a fly on the wall. With his head down, he headed to his room and closed the door. His stomach felt like a giant pit.

This is awful. I like Sayma. She wasn't rigid like the others. Like Airius. Oh well, I'm not going to be here forever. I'll find her later, now I have to find Zora.

That was when Airius's orders hit him.

Did he say I'll be serving for the tours tomorrow? He stood up. *Zooks, yes!*

It was the break he needed. The tour ended at Codd's crypt.

Perfect! I'll be right where I need to be to steal Codd's shield.

He dropped to a knee and reached for his cloak where he'd placed it underneath his bed. His fingers came up empty. He flipped the bed over.

"Oh no, my cloak's gone!"

15

Dyphestive took two more hard licks from Hodges's jo stick to the side of the head.

Whack! Whack!

Hodges beat him like a drum for a few more seconds.

Dyphestive drew his legs up underneath himself and lunged at Hodges.

Hodges skipped away, but not before Dyphestive hammered the smaller man's shoulder. Hodges stumbled back and deftly caught his balance using his staff for support.

With a grunt, Dyphestive scrambled to his feet. He turned away from Hodges's next assault and blocked Hodges's jo stick with his own. The young fighters blasted away at each other, stick against stick.

The Honor Guards practically jumped out of their boots, hooting and hollering. One wide-eyed man held the surging crowd back with his arms.

"Stay out of it! Stay out of it!" Sergeant Tinison screamed. "Let the inbreeds fight their own fight!"

Seconds into the match, it became very clear that Hodges could handle a jo stick like a master. He aimed for knuckles and cracked it against bone. Dyphestive held on and loosed a savage assault of his own. Using powerful strikes propelled by raw brawny muscle, he beat Hodges's twirling attacks aside. He struck harder and faster.

Clak! Clak! Clak!

Hodges spun away from Dyphestive's attacks, slipped past the bruising stick, and jabbed his stick into Dyphestive's ribs. Dyphestive let out a grunt, twisted at the hips, and whipped his stick flat into Hodges's back.

Whack!

Hodges's arms spread out, and he arched backward as if struck by lightning. He dropped flat to the ground just as a second attack swished over him. He rolled to the side, evading Dyphestive's heavy-handed blows. He cocked his knee back and kicked Dyphestive square in the nanoos.

The entire Honor Guard, including Dyphestive, doubled over and groaned. "Ooooooooooh!"

Dyphestive limped away, using his stick to prop himself up. His nostrils flared, and his blood ran red down his face. He squared off with Hodges and glared at the man, with fire in his eyes. He waved Hodges on. "Come on! Come on!" He pointed to his skull and dropped his jo stick. "Take your best shot."

Many of the Honor Guards gasped.

One of them said, "He's crazy."

"I like crazy," said another.

"Bust the fool's melon open, Hodges! Teach him a lesson!"

Hodges jumped at the opportunity. Holding his jo stick high over his head, he brought it down with a wroth force on Dyphestive's skull.

Crack!

The jo stick broke on the brawny youth's head. It didn't leave a scratch.

The Honor Guard fell silent for a moment, then one of them said, "His skull is harder than Sarge's."

Hodges stepped backward, his face ashen.

Dyphestive snatched the other half of Hodges's staff from his hands and proceeded to beat him half to death until the Honor Guard finally pulled him off. His chest was heaving, and he lifted his eyes to the sky and let out a triumphant howl.

Sergeant Tinison wandered into the ring of stalwart men at a leisurely pace with his hands behind his back. "Well, well, well, look what we have left, a Beak and a Baby Face." He eyeballed Dyphestive and the woman nicknamed Beak facing off in the middle. "It's been exciting. It's been very exciting, but now you're the last two, and we're only going to take one." He stopped and faced them. "You both have shown grit. I like it. You can fight. But let's change it up. Corporal, bring the buckets."

A clean-shaven pie-faced Honor Guard with a scar on his cheek brought over two wooden buckets. He set them upside down at Dyphestive's and Beak's feet. He checked for an approving look from Sergeant Tinison.

Sergeant Tinison shooed him away. "Get over there." He paced around the two competitors. "Stand on the buckets, donkey skulls."

Dyphestive stepped up on the round platform. His big boots hung over the edges. He glanced over at Beak. Her feet were much smaller, and she stood within the circle of the bucket's rim perfectly.

"Come on, Sarge, not the bucket test. Let them fight," one of the Honor Guard said. He was a long-limbed orc who stood half a head above the rest. "This is boring."

"How about all of you do the bucket test?" Sergeant Tinison shouted. "Would you like that? Or would you rather watch?"

The orc shrank away from his comrades' hot stares. "Did I say it was boring? I meant captivating." He offered a humble smile and clapped gently. "Very captivating."

Sergeant Tinison rolled his eyes and muttered under his breath, "One orc spoils the whole bunch." He raised his jarring voice again. "Listen up, Beak and Baby Face. You're going to stand on those buckets in the hot sun all day or until one of you falls off. I bet you think that it sounds simple, but it's not. You're going to stand like a crane, one-legged. That's the rule. You stand on one leg, so pick your favorite." He glared at each of them. "Well, get a knee up, or I'll pick one for you!"

Dyphestive lifted his right knee. He spread out his hands and balanced himself.

Beak, who stood to his right, lifted her left knee.

"Outstanding!" Sergeant Tinison shouted at them. "Let's see which one of you tick turds wants this the most!" He turned on the Honor Guards. "What are you gawking at? We aren't going to watch them all day. We have work to do. Scatter, pigeons! Except you, Half-Wit. You stay with me." He pointed at the pie-faced soldier with a scar. "We'll keep an eye on them." He dabbed his sweaty forehead with a cloth. "Over there in the shade." He waddled off.

Dyphestive and Beak stood for hours without talking.

Beak broke the silence. "You might as well drop out," she said with the sun shining in her face. "I can do this all day."

"Huh," Dyphestive replied. "I can do this all day and all night."

She let out a pleasant but confident laugh. Aside from her crooked nose, Beak was an attractive young woman with refined features and long chestnut hair. "A big oaf like you might be able to beat a man with sticks, but I have the balance of a palace dancer. This challenge will be a breeze."

Dyphestive turned his head and started blowing at her.

"What are you doing?" she asked with an incredulous look.

"I'm trying to blow you over." He wobbled a bit, swung his arms, and regained his balance.

"You really aren't very good at this." She offered her hand. "My name isn't Beak, even though it's fitting. I'm Shannon."

He accepted her firm grip. "Nice to meet you, Shannon. I'm Dyphestive."

"Interesting name."

"How come you want to become an Honor Guard?" he asked.

"My father was a Monarch Knight. I'm going to be one too. This isn't my first crack at the Honor Guard either. It's the fifth and my last chance to make it." She stood as still and composed as a post. "I'm not going to lose."

"A shame because I don't intend to lose either." He decided to get into her head. "And I never lose, but it sounds to me like you've lost four times so far. That doesn't sound good for you. It sounds like you're better at that than winning."

"We'll see."

"You said your father was a Monarch Knight?" he asked. "What happened?"

"He died not so long ago."

"Oh, I'm sorry to hear that. My sorrows." He wobbled again and regained his balance.

"Don't fall off, Baby Face!" Sergeant Tinison hollered. "Or you'll crack the courtyard!"

"Did he die in combat? What was his name, if you don't mind me asking?"

"Yes." Her eyes narrowed and focused on the courtyard wall in front of them. "His name was Adanadel. The Doom Riders killed him."

Dyphestive's heart jumped. *Adanadel!*

Beak finished with a heated stare, "And I'm going to avenge him."

16

"SO MUCH FOR SLIPPING IN AND OUT," JAKOBY SAID AS HE DREW HIS SWORD.

The faceless warriors pulled curved blades from the folds of their crimson robes and slowly advanced down the steps. Behind them, at the top of the stairs, the wizard Finton Slay looked on with a crimson glow in his haunting eyes.

"I hope you're really good with that thing," Than said, nodding to Jakoby's longsword.

Jakoby's sword had been made in the Monarch Knights' forges and blessed by their enchanters. Its straight two-edged blade was razor-sharp, and the sword guard had crowns on the end. It was a work of beauty.

As the Iron Devils advanced, the lizardmen guards crept in from the other side with studded clubs in hand. Jakoby, Than, and Leena formed a circle back-to-back. Leena whipped out two pairs of nunchakus.

"She really likes those little sticks, doesn't she?" Than commented.

Jakoby held his sword in front of his chest and closed his eyes. "Yes," he said, "but not as much as I love my sword. Watch yourself, Than. I'm about to unleash steel wind on these vermin." He channeled the energy of a sword saint, turning his blood to fire. Energy spread from the pureness of his heart and pumped into the rest of his body. His longsword shimmered, and he opened his eyes and attacked.

WITH A DETERMINED LOOK in her eyes, long-haired Leena stepped toward the lizardmen, twirling both pairs of nunchakus.

The savage expressions of the lizardmen almost turned to laughter as they watched the spinning sticks. They were monsters compared to Leena, with bulging muscle underneath their scales. A lizardman with gummy eyes slapped another in the chest, hissing a chuckle.

Leena whipped the nunchakus faster. The spinning halves of the ebony sticks ignited with mystic cherry-red fire. The weapons spoke to the wind.

Whiiiiiirrrrr!

The lizardmen's slanted eyes widened, and their jaws dropped.

The nunchakus flicked out like lightning. In a split moment, the nunchakus in Leena's right hand clobbered a lizardman in the jaw so hard it spun him around.

Pow!

Her left set struck another lizardman in the shoulder with explosive force.

Kapow!

The cherry fire of the nunchakus formed shields of bright energy. They cracked knees and busted bones.

Pow! Kapow!

Leena attacked the brawny guards like a swarm of stinging hornets. The fire of her nunchakus sent them flying backward.

Kapow! Pow!

The gummy-eyed lizardman snuck in behind her. She back-kicked him in the groin, spun around, and clobbered him like a drummer doing a solo.

Nocka-nocka-nocka-nocka-pow!

Using her blazing speed and skills, she beat the scales off the inferior lizard-men. The brutes sprawled on the stone floor, knocked out or licking their wounds. That was when the four-armed ogre crept in behind her and scooped her up in his massive arms.

THE IRON DEVILS' body language told it all. They moved with the subtle ease of assassins and night prowlers. Silently, they descended the steps as one, their stares icy behind their iron masks.

Assassins! Jakoby lunged at the nearest assassin. He pierced the man's chest and killed him with a lethal strike. *I hate assassins.*

Two more assassins flanked him and struck. Jakoby anticipated the maneuver and dove to the ground to avoid their strike. The assassins gored one another and collapsed. Jakoby aided their descent, cutting one assassin's leg off at the knee. He spun on his back like a turtle and chopped through the other one's ankle.

Three down, three to go!

He had focus. Strength. Speed. He had it all.

An Iron Devil jumped from higher up the stairs, his robes billowing as he seemed to float through the air.

Jakoby deflected the strike and countered with his own. He split open the assassin's mask. Metal sank into solid bone. The mask fell away from the assas-sin's face, revealing a skull with decaying muscle and flesh hanging off it. Its burning blue eyes dimmed.

"Ghouls! I should have known, with a wizard involved. Don't let them touch you, Leena!"

The ghouls were men hovering between life and death. They were servants of the dark arts, who killed and fed off the living. Jakoby stepped up his game. A part of him held back when it came to killing men, but when it came to the arcane abominations of the world, he didn't hold back.

Four down, only two to go!

Two of the undead assassins came at him, their steel spinning. They struck with supernatural strength and speed.

He parried one blade and boot-kicked another assassin in the gut. He gored another assassin in the belly and let him slide off his blade. The faceless assassin that he cut through the knee grabbed his legs. Its ice-blue eyes were burning again. It opened its jaws and bit him. "Get off me, fiend!" Jakoby screamed as he hacked into it.

All the Iron Devils that had fallen by his blade were coming at him again. If they couldn't walk, they crawled. They would not die.

Finton Slay cackled with glee. "What's the matter? Can't you kill them? Hah-hah-hah-hah-hah!"

Jakoby's sword rose up and down. It ripped through robes and dry bones and flesh. Even the Iron Devils' severed appendages crawled at him. Fingers flexed and stretched and scurried across the floor. He stabbed a loose hand he'd severed and flung it away. The Iron Devils—hacked up with hunks and bits missing—clawed at him and kept coming. Their strong fingers and teeth locked onto his robes and started to drag him down. "Nooooo!" he shouted. He stabbed downward again and again. "Noooooo!" The swarm of darkness was taking him.

THE FOUR-ARMED OGRE squeezed Leena so hard that her shoulder popped. Her eyes bugged out, and she couldn't catch her breath. She threw her head back with all her might, busting the back of her head on the ogre's rock-hard chin.

The ogre moaned with triumph as the glow of her nunchakus faded. It squeezed harder.

Leena's eyes bugged out of her head. The nunchakus slipped from her fingers and clattered onto the stone floor. The ogre crushed her body like a vise. Her ribs cracked. She kicked and squirmed as her eyes rolled up into her head, and she let out a final painful breath.

17

"No-no-no-no," Grey Cloak cried under his breath as he turned his quarters upside down. The Cloak of Legends was nowhere to be found. He'd looked under his bed and mattress as well as the one beside it. He'd looked in the wooden footlocker too. It had vanished. He balled his fists and screamed inside himself.

EEEEEEYAAAARGH!

He made a quick trip to the other servants' quarters and searched them high and low. The only person he thought could have taken it was Sayma.

She must have done it to spite me, but why? I didn't wrong her. Airius did! He snapped his fingers. *Wait! I can catch her.*

Grey Cloak barreled down the servants' hall and headed up the stairs. Airius stood at the top of the steps and was on his way down. With his hands on his hips, he said, "Why aren't you upstairs working? Do I have to release you before you've even started?"

"No, I..."

Arius eyed him suspiciously. "I what? Let me guess. You're going after Sayma. Well, so you know, she's cleared the moat."

"But—"

Airius hooked his arm before he could pass. "What is this about, Grey Cloak? Hmmm?" he droned. "You are flummoxed. I can't have you flummoxed in front of the Monarchs. Tell me. A little honesty can go a long way with me."

Grey Cloak's fingers needled the palm of his hand. With his chin down, he admitted, "I lost something. I thought Sayma might have taken it."

"I see." Airius stepped aside, and with a snap of his hand, the Cloak of Legends hung suspended in front of him. "Is this the item you're looking for?"

"Yes," Grey Cloak said with a sigh of relief. He reached for it.

Airius pulled it away. "This garment belongs in your footlocker, not underneath your mattress. If I had a silver chip for every time I found a servant squirreling away something below their mattress, I'd be a Monarch." He rubbed the cloak between his thumb and fingers. "It's of a remarkable quality for an unremarkable cloak. Where did you come by it?"

Grey Cloak rubbed the back of his head. "Uh... Red Cliff. I bought it there some time ago."

Airius shoved it against Grey Cloak's chest. "There is a peg on the back of your quarters door. Use it. Put that rag away, and get to work."

"Right away," Grey Cloak said, as he took several steps at a time.

"Youths," Airius said smugly as he turned away. "They are so attached to the silliest things."

Grey Cloak paid him no mind.

Yes! Yes! Yes! I have it! Zora, I'm coming to get you!

"WHAT'S THE MATTER WITH YOU?" Beak tilted her head. "You look like you swallowed a bug."

"No, I-I lost my train of thought," Dyphestive replied. "What were we talking about?"

"My father. Thunderbolts, you're as bright as a bug bear, aren't you?"

"I wish," he said. He caught her smiling. "I didn't mean to pry about your father. I hope I didn't stir up too much."

"I'm always stirred up."

He didn't reply. *Bend my horseshoes! I can't believe Adanadel is her father.* The sinking feeling in his gut quickly became worse. He hadn't thought about Adanadel in a long time. The former Monarch Knight had recruited him and Grey Cloak into Talon. Their adventures had been short-lived. When the Doom Riders had arrived in Raven Cliff, Adanadel had died at their hands while trying to rescue Dyphestive.

This is awful. Should I tell her or not?

The wooden bucket groaned underneath him as if a heavy weight had landed on his shoulders. The shame of being a Doom Rider assailed him, and his guilt grew.

"Are you well? Now you look green, and you're sweating awfully bad," she said.

"It must be the sun, I guess. I can't take the heat."

"We haven't been out here that long. You aren't going to quit, are you?"

Flashes of all the horrible things he'd done as a Doom Rider filled his head as a flood of terrible memories came back.

Focus, I need to be here. I need to be here for Zora. He gave Beak a nervous glance. *I can't believe she's Adanadel's daughter. It's my fault her father died. I can't take this away from her too.*

Dyphestive wobbled. He was about to let himself slip off. The wooden bucket gave way under his great weight.

"Bloody biscuits, Baby Face! You owe me a bucket!" Sergeant Tinison said. He and Half-Wit hustled over to Dyphestive.

Half-Wit scratched his head. "If the bucket breaks, who wins?"

"Beak wins," Sergeant Tinison stated.

Dyphestive's competitive fire flared, and he shot back, "I'm still standing on one leg. It's not my fault the bucket broke."

"It is your fault anvi-arse," Sergeant Tinison retorted.

Honor Guards broke away from their duties and gathered around. "What's going on?"

"Baby Face broke his bucket, so Beak wins."

The Honor Guards murmured amongst themselves.

"That hardly seems fair."

"They should do it again."

"How is it his fault the bucket broke?"

"Gum up!" Sergeant Tinison said. "We can only take one!"

"Says who?" Half-Wit asked.

Sergeant Tinison got in Half-Wit's face. "Are you challenging my authority?"

Half-Wit stammered, "Y-yes, Sarge!"

"What about the rest of you?" Sergeant Tinison argued. "Are you challenging my decision too?"

"We're all Honor Guard," the long-limbed orc said. "I think we should put it to a vote."

"Well, I'm so glad that Long Neck has something to say. Say, Long Neck, after you finish voting, you can clean the squalor stalls for a month. How does that sound? Huh? Huh? Huh?" Sergeant Tinison asked.

Long Neck crossed his arms. "If it means righting a wrong, I'm behind it."

"Fine, you bunch of slack-jawed ninnies. We'll put it to a vote, then! It has to be unanimous too!" Sergeant Tinison glanced at Dyphestive and Beak. "Will you put your feet down? You look like you belong in a cornfield." He faced his men. "By a show of hands, who wants Beak?"

No one lifted their hand.

Beak's chin dropped.

"I see, I see," Sergeant Tinison muttered. He lifted his glass-breaking voice. "And who wants Dyphestive to stay?"

The soldiers' hands remained at their sides.

Sergeant Tinison grinned. "Who wants both?"

Every Honor Guard lifted their hands high.

Sergeant Tinison casually lifted his. He turned on his heel and addressed Dyphestive and Beak. "Welcome to the Honor Guard."

Beak jumped into Dyphestive's arms and wrapped her limbs around him. "Yes!" Noticing all eyes on her, she quickly jumped away and said to Sergeant Tinison, "Sorry, sir."

"Heh, don't do it again. Honor Guard, what do we say?" He cupped his hand to his ear.

"Long live the monarchy!"

"I can't heeeeaaaaar yoooouuuuuu!"

"LONG LIVE THE MONARCHY!"

Sergeant Tinison saluted his men. "See these donkey skulls to their quarters, and go to the galley and get some chow." He eyed them. "What are you waiting for? Move it! Move it! Move it!"

Dyphestive bounded after the others, with his heart racing. He was a novice in the Honor Guard. It meant something. Sergeant Tinison hooked his arm as he passed. "Sir?"

"I'm going to be watching you, Baby Face, because something tells me there's more to you than I see. I hope you don't disappoint me."

"I won't, sir. I won't."

Sergeant Tinison stuck out his chin and nodded. Under his breath, he said, "We'll see about that, won't we?"

18

THE FOUR-ARMED OGRE FINISHED SQUISHING LEENA AND DROPPED HER LIMP BODY to the floor. The hairy eight-footer with a bulging belly squatted over the monk. He nudged her with his fingers and tilted his head.

With the ogre's fetid breath in her face, she opened her eyes. The ogre let out a surprised grunt. Leena sprang up and heel-kicked the ogre in the beans five times in rapid succession. With a groan, the ogre dropped his hands over his crotch.

Leena snatched up one of her nunchakus with her good arm and clocked the ogre in the throat. Her small sticks spun with wildfire, and she battered his thick skull. He tried to cover up his head and took a shot to the knee.

Whackatahkrak!

The ogre flailed wildly, trying to smash the woman.

She busted his elbows and wrists. A quick and mighty strike cracked his nose. She spun around and roundhouse kicked him in the groin. The furious ogre beat his chest with four mighty fists, howled at the top of his lungs, and ran like a huge ape to cower inside his den.

Leena set her eyes on Jakoby just as the Iron Devils dragged him down. She dashed his way, her dislocated shoulder hanging limp. She hit the fiends with everything she had. Than stood in the knot of the unliving, pulling them away.

Finton Slay cackled with triumphant laughter. "Die, fools! Die!"

Than ripped a ghoul's skull from its narrow shoulders and hurled it at Finton Slay. The skull caught the bony man square in the chest and knocked him backward. Than ripped his legs away from an Iron Devil and charged the stairs. "Nogard! Nogard!"

Jakoby spun his sword in and out of the attackers' bodies. They started to pile up at his feet. He brought his sword down with two hands on a ghoul that lost its life. "The harvest is ripe!"

Right by his side, Leena blasted away with her nunchakus. The fiends would fall then climb up again with broken jaws, knees, and elbows, giving them a staggered gait.

With a twist of his hips, Jakoby cleared a ghoul's head from its shoulders. "There's no coming back from that!" Up and down his sword went, tearing one down then another.

Leena watched the last one fall with the final spin of her whirling stick. She hit the ghoul so hard, its face exploded. Bone chips and dead skin went flying.

"Up here!" Than hollered. He had Finton Slay in a headlock.

Leena's and Jakoby's clothing was torn to shreds. They had cuts, scrapes, and bite marks all over as they ambled up the stairs.

"You're looking for Zora, aren't you?" Finton Slay asked.

"No, we're looking for the nearest necromancer. Oh, it looks like we found one," Jakoby said. He suddenly grimaced, and his sword arm shook.

"What's the matter? Feeling rigid? Is your blood turning cold? Soon you will be one of those Devils—*urk!*"

Leena groin kicked Finton Slay.

"You little witch, I'll fry you after your bones turn brittle."

Than cranked up the pressure. "Where is Zora, you little worm?"

"You have more important matters to worry about, it seems. At least Zora is still among the living. They are not." Finton Slay's body collapsed into smoke, his head drifting away last, saying, "Goodbye, fools. Don't forget the shield." His body vaporized and was gone.

Than stood with his jaw hanging and his arms empty. "I hate it when that happens."

Jakoby and Leena collapsed on the floor, their faces turning ashen.

"So cold." Jakoby's teeth chattered. "My bones are freezing. My breath is frosty. I don't want to die like this."

Than kneeled between the two of them and locked his strong hands on their wrists. "You won't." His hands radiated with quavering golden light. His eyes shone like the sun.

Leena and Jakoby gasped as if taking a breath for the first time. Their wounds healed. Leena pushed herself to her feet, bowed to Than, walked to a wall, and shoved her shoulder against it. The shoulder popped into place. Her eyes didn't even water.

Jakoby offered his hand, and Than hauled him to his feet. "Thanks, my friend. I owe you my life."

"Save it for someone else." Than staggered. His jaws and cheeks looked more sunken than before. He swayed.

Jakoby caught him by the waist. "What's wrong?"

"Nothing," Than grunted as he straightened. "At least we know where Zora isn't, but they're onto us. We better go. It's up to Grey Cloak and Dyphestive now." He eyed the prisoners' arms stretching out past the bars. "But let's free more prisoners first."

19

After performing his daily duties, Grey Cloak tracked down Dyphestive at the Honor Guard barracks. It was there that he ran into Captain Cleotus, who was talking to Sergeant Tinison. They were smoking curled pipes made from elk horn.

"Ah, it's Grey Cloak. It looks like you survived your first day with Airius," Captain Cleotus said with amusement. "Let me guess. You want to see your blood brother."

"If possible, Captain."

"It's not my call. He's a novice with the Honor Guard now. Allow me to introduce you to Sergeant Tinison."

"Nice to meet you—"

"Stifle it. Can't you see I'm smoking?" Sergeant Tinison spewed a stream of yellow smoke. "He's in there somewhere." He hitched his thumb toward the open door.

"Thank you." Grey Cloak started to duck inside, when Captain Cleotus placed a hand on his shoulder. "I hear you'll be serving on the tours tomorrow."

"The tours." Sergeant Tinison rolled his eyes. "Waste of resources."

"Anyway, I look forward to seeing you in action. Not so much as your brother. It seems that his first day was quite impressive. *Quite* impressive."

"It does me good to hear it." Grey Cloak nodded and headed into the barracks. Inside were rows of single beds with footlockers in front of them. It was much like the servants' quarters but more military-like and filled with stout men and women, mostly men, wearing their evening shirts and britches. He caught a glimpse of Dyphestive lying down on a cot at the very end. Waving his hand, he caught his brother's eye.

Dyphestive sat up and smiled. He waved his brother to the back, but Grey

Cloak shook his head. He didn't feel comfortable wandering among all the soldiers who didn't know him. He preferred to use more discretion.

Dyphestive got up and met him at the barracks' entrance. "How did your day go?"

"It could have been better. Yours?"

"Great!"

"Is there somewhere we can talk in private?"

"There's a garden in the back that the Honor Guard keeps up. Follow me." Dyphestive led them to the backside of the barracks and through a door into a fairly large vegetable and floral garden. Stone benches lined a stone walkway that surrounded the separate gardens. They took a seat farthest from the barracks while still facing it.

Dyphestive quickly started talking about his day with the giddiness of a five-year-old, maintaining one long run-on sentence.

When Grey Cloak realized that his brother wasn't going to stop, he cut him off. "Enough, enough, I get it," Grey Cloak said, trying to be polite. "Honestly, I didn't think you would embrace it so much."

"I love it! I've been talking to the other guards, and they said if I complete the training and become Honor Guard, I can work as a knight's squire then become a Monarch Knight, like Codd."

Grey Cloak's head dropped. "What are you talking about? We're here to find a way to save Zora. I'm going to need your help."

Dyphestive frowned. "I know, but—"

"But nothing, we are here for one reason." He pulled Dyphestive's chin toward him and looked him in the eye. "We have to save Zora. Our friend."

"They're going to swear me in tomorrow. I can't break my word."

"Don't do it. Quit."

"I like it."

Grey Cloak tapped his heel. He had no idea what was happening to his brother, but it seemed that Grey Cloak was losing him. He didn't like it. "What about your oath to me? We're blood brothers."

Dyphestive's broad shoulders deflated. Sadly, he said, "I know." He sighed. "I really like this though."

In all their lives, Dyphestive had never asked for or wanted anything. Now it seemed he'd found something he wanted. He seemed determined to be a Monarch Knight for some crazy reason.

With the crickets chirping and a gentle wind rustling the fragrant flowered vines and bushes, Grey Cloak sat silently by his brother in what had suddenly become a glum evening. With sadness in his heart, he said, "The entire reason we left Dark Mountain was to be free to become whatever we wanted to be. I always thought whatever it was, we'd be together. If becoming a Monarch Knight is what you want, I want you to know that I support you." He patted his brother's back. "I'm sure Zora will understand too."

"I'm sorry. I didn't really think I'd like it that much. I don't know why, but I do. It feels right. And Sergeant Tinison, he's really funny. He doesn't mean to be, but he is. But I can't laugh out loud about it. Everyone else does behind his back." He squirmed in his seat. "There's another thing. I made a friend of sorts."

"I imagine you did."

"No, she's different. Her name's Beak, well, Shannon actually. Everyone has a nickname. I'm Baby Face."

Grey Cloak picked a flower from the garden and started plucking the petals off. "It sounds a lot more pleasant than Iron Bones. I was actually fond of that one."

"Funny that you mention it. Beak is Adanadel's daughter."

Grey Cloak sat up. "What?" A light went on in his head. "Ah, that's why you want to stay. You feel guilty, don't you?"

"No. Yes. Well, it's not why I want to stay, but I need to tell her what happened and why. She doesn't know, Grey. She deserves to know."

"Tell her after we save Zora."

Dyphestive shook his head. "I can't." He fished the flying potion out of his pocket. "Take this. I won't need it."

Grey Cloak stood up. "No, you keep it as something to remember me by. Goodbye, blood brother." He stormed away.

20

GREY CLOAK SAT INSIDE HIS QUARTERS, BROODING.

How could he do this to me? To me? I have one day left to save Zora, and he's going to abandon me? Ridiculous!

He lay flat on his back, tossing an acorn-sized flashing in the air and catching it. As aggravated as he was, he envisioned exactly what he was going to do.

You can do this, Grey Cloak. You can do it. All alone. I'll take my chances.

He'd been up all night. He tried to sleep, which he never did much of, and he tossed and turned when he succeeded. He was torn between being hurt and angry, wrestling with whether or not that was it for him and Dyphestive. They'd been through so much together. Dyphestive had been as loyal as a hound.

Did I do something wrong?

He blamed it on the Doom Riders. They'd changed Dyphestive when they'd manipulated his mind. He hadn't been the same since.

Outside the door of his quarters, he heard the soft footsteps of the servants shuffling by. It was the wee hours of the morning, before the monarchy woke, and the servants were preparing the morning meal.

He rolled off his bed and kneeled by his footlocker.

It's time.

He pulled out his servant's clothing, dressed, and loaded his pockets with the slender potion vials and flashings. He pressed his hands over his clothing to make sure they were well concealed.

Airius doesn't miss anything. I have to be careful.

He lifted the Cloak of Legends out of the footlocker by its shoulders. He felt naked when he didn't wear it, and it had been over a day. "I wish I could take you with me. Don't you go anywhere." He folded it neatly inside the footlocker, as opposed to hanging it on the door peg, and closed the lid. He patted himself down once more and exited his quarters.

I can do this. Even without help. I'll take my chances.

CODD'S domed crypt was half-full of excited observers. Captain Cleotus gallantly shared the heroic exploits of Codd, the father of the Monarch Knights. It was the first tour of the day, and Grey Cloak's palms hadn't stopped tingling. As he and his crew of servants served the tour, he made a mental note of every detail of the crypt.

Nothing had changed since he took the tour two days ago aside from the new tour guests. Surrounding the ominous and imposing figure of Codd were the twelve outer columns. In between those columns were twelve statues of knights, with Honor Guards in full armor beside them. The Honor Guard stood as still as fence posts, not blinking. They wore round open-faced helms, and one of them was Dyphestive.

Grey Cloak didn't make eye contact with his brother.

He'll probably turn me in.

Between serving the tour delicacies that the children couldn't keep their grubby fingers out of, Grey Cloak stole glances at the yonders lurking at the tops of the columns. He'd counted twelve of the winged eyeballs in all. They had fastened themselves to the marble pillars and blended in like fixtures, but he could still see the whites of their eyes.

He nonchalantly patted the flashings in his pocket.

This better work. It has to work.

He was putting his faith in Batram's words and hoping he got it right. He only had one shot, and if he failed, he would probably be locked in the Monarchs' dungeons for a lifetime or quickly fed to the moat monsters.

Focus. Focus. Focus.

Captain Cleotus was only a few minutes away from winding up his spiel about Codd.

Grey Cloak's heart started to race. He could try to steal the shield on the next tour and do more planning. He shook off the doubt.

I'll take my chances.

After one last look at Codd and the shield, he locked the image in his mind. The flashings were powerful enough to temporarily blind a person. He felt bad for the children. It might scare them, but at least no one would get hurt. As for Codd's shield, he didn't think of it as stealing so much as borrowing it. After he freed Zora, he planned to put it back or at least let the Monarchs know who really stole it. Perhaps they would understand.

Grey Cloak fished three flashings out of his pocket. With his back to the columns, he casually dropped one flashing to the floor and squeezed his eyes shut.

Booomph!

The blinding flash was so bright that he could see the veins on the insides of his eyelids. The tour erupted in screams.

Captain Cleotus barked orders. "Attack. We're under attack!"

Grey Cloak set down his tray and moved toward Codd's pedestal. Everyone fumbled and stumbled over the floor. The yonders dropped from their perches. As fast as a cat, Grey Cloak crawled up beside Codd's massive oval shield while everyone fought to regain their senses.

"I can't see!" members of the tour cried.

"I'm blind!" the children screamed.

As the sea of commotion built up in the crypt, Grey Cloak grabbed his shrinking potion. He knew it was meant for consumption, but he decided to take a risk and try something different. He tore off the cork and poured the swirling orange contents onto the shield. Nothing happened. *Zooks!*

"No one move!" Captain Cleotus shouted. "Be still! Don't panic! Can anyone see?"

The people replied with a bunch of mumbling and groaned nos. Many of the people sounded like they were about to die.

"Castle Monarch is under attack!" one woman screamed.

"Black Frost comes to put us to sleep!" said another.

Grey Cloak noticed some of the yonders rising up from the floor and flying erratically.

One of the soldiers said, "I think I can see, Captain."

Grey Cloak closed his eyes and kept his head down. He busted another flashing on the ground.

Booomph!

The crypt erupted in earsplitting screams.

Grey Cloak opened his eyes. The shield still hadn't shrunk.

Bloody horseshoes! What do I do?

21

GREY CLOAK DUMPED THE REST OF THE POTION ON THE SHIELD. THE ORANGE liquid dripped around the six-foot-tall oval shield's rim. In the meantime, he tried to pry the shield away from Codd's iron grasp. It didn't budge.

"Honor Guard! Man your positions!" Captain Cleotus stumbled through the crowd. "Everyone on the tour, breathe easy. There is no danger here. The Honor Guard will protect you!"

"We are doomed! Doomed!" a woman cried out as she huddled over her children. "The Monarchs have been slain!"

"No one has been slain!" Captain Cleotus rubbed his eyes. "I assure you. This is only a mishap—ulp!" He tripped over a member of the tour and fell to the ground.

"The captain's dead!" the same woman shouted.

"I'm fine! I only fell! Thunderbolts, quit your crowing, woman!"

The yonders started to rise again and fluttered like moths through the crypt. Grey Cloak used his last flashing.

Booomph!

When he opened his eyes, the yonders clinging to the walls and columns were dropping like flies. He reached for the shield. It wasn't there. It had shrunk to the size of a medallion he could fit between his thumb and finger. Its tiny straps were pinched between Codd's knuckles.

Sweet Gapoli!

He pried the shield away and stuffed it into his pocket. As the grumbling crowd came round, he made his way back to his serving tray. He took out the shield, wrapped it in a cloth napkin, and set it on the serving platter.

Now it's time to sell it.

Over the next several moments, the crowd and soldiers calmed down. They all rubbed their eyes and blinked. Grey Cloak helped many of them to their feet.

"Is everyone all right?" Captain Cleotus asked. His pupils were huge, the same as everyone else's. "What in the blazing furnaces happened? No one leaves the crypt until I get it sorted out. No one!"

Propelled by their creepy bat wings, the yonders rose into the air. Their staggered flight patterns steadied, and they whizzed around the people like a swarm of hornets. Grey Cloak found himself eyes to eyeball with a yonder that floated right in front of him. He feigned dizziness, and it flew away. The yonders combed the entire room, exhaustively searching every person, place, and thing. Suddenly they swirled around Codd like a hive of angry bees.

Captain Cleotus stood beside Grey Cloak, scratching his head. "I wonder what that's all about." His eyes widened. "Burning cornstalks! The shield is missing! Honor Guard! Nobody leaves this room. I mean no one! I want every person, every nook and cranny searched." He caught Dyphestive's eye as he was standing near the exit. "Close that door now! Half-Wit, make sure every tour member, servant, and soldier is accounted for."

In military fashion, the Honor Guard thoroughly patted every person down, including one another. Grey Cloak stood by his serving tray, not moving. He put his hands up while a comely woman Honor Guard searched him.

"I haven't seen you before," she said.

"I'm new. Airius brought me in yesterday."

She patted his backside and whispered in his ear, "I hope you stay around. Go stay over there with the others who have been searched."

"Can I grab my tray? Uh, I didn't catch your name."

"Olive." She squatted down and picked through the platter of desserts. She even lifted the cloth napkin with the shield inside it, tapped it in her palm, and set it down. "Take it away, handsome."

"Olive, cut the chitter-chatter," Captain Cleotus said. "Did anyone see anything?"

"All I saw was a bright flash, three times," a gusty half-orc woman said. She was as big as the captain and wore her hair in multiple black braids. She had two children with her. "I still have huge spots in my eyes. I say a wizard snatched it. Zapped in and zapped out. And I want a reimbursement for my tour. All of it!"

"Don't make me tell you to gum up again. Do you hear? No one goes anywhere until that shield is found."

The half-orc woman looked around the crypt. "That shield's bigger than me. It's impossible for anyone to hide it. Lords of thunder, let's go. I'm getting hungry."

There was a distinct knock on the door.

Captain Cleotus approached the door and said to Dyphestive, "Open it." When the door parted, he briefly stepped outside and had words with somebody. When he came back in, his face was ashen. He cleared his throat and spoke up. "If I can have your attention, everyone. All members of the tour will be seen out. The rest of us stay."

The tour was escorted through the doors, and Captain Cleotus closed the door behind them.

He stood before the men and women in the room while the yonders hovered over them. "Codd's shield is gone. I alone am to blame." He took off his sword belt and dropped it to the floor. "I've been stripped of my rank and have been asked to leave the premises immediately. I want to say that it's been a pleasure to serve the Honor Guard. Long live the monarchy."

The yonders surrounded Captain Cleotus and swirled around him like a tornado. They moved so quickly the captain was blurred from sight as they created an eerie whistle of wind.

Grey Cloak covered his ears. He wasn't the only one.

The yonders slowed, and Captain Cleotus had disappeared. Only his armor and gear remained.

With his arm hairs standing on end, Grey Cloak caught Dyphestive's shocked and disappointed look. He glanced away.

It's not my fault.

22

AFTER THE CRYPT INVESTIGATION WAS OVER, GREY CLOAK WAS SENT BACK TO HIS quarters and told to wait. He quickly closed the door and grabbed his cloak.

It's time to move on. I don't know how long this shrinking potion will last.

He'd been sweating sling bullets ever since the investigation began. According to the Honor Guard, the Monarchs wanted to interview everyone individually. *There's no way the potion will last so long.*

Grey Cloak's inner hourglass was draining. He moved with urgency, knowing that at any moment the shield could enlarge again. He had no idea how long it would last, but he'd made it this far. Now, he had to find a way to depart unnoticed.

He tucked the shrunken shield into the back of his pants. *I can't put it inside my cloak pocket, or it will get trapped.*

He opened the door to his quarters and looked down both sides of the hallway. The way was clear. He headed out. Up in the kitchens, the servants buzzed with gossip. Grey Cloak evaded their prying eyes and aimed for the back exit that led to the courtyard gardens. From there, he would blend in with the tour that might not have exited yet or possibly latch onto one of the dignitaries being herded out.

At the threshold of the back exit, Airius stepped in front of him. "Where do you think you're going? The Honor Guard hasn't released anyone as far as I'm aware." He fingered the Cloak of Legends. "And what are you doing with this?"

Thinking on his feet, Grey Cloak replied, "After today, I don't think that I want to be a servant. I'm shaken up. I'm not fit for this."

"Don't be silly." Airius nudged him back inside the kitchen. "From what I heard, you handled yourself quite well. Go back to your quarters, and we can talk about it later."

"I really don't want to. I'm sorry."

"No one is leaving without the Monarchs' express permission. Believe me when I say that you aren't going anywhere." Airius grabbed his shoulders and started to turn him. "Wait in your room."

The shield bulged in the back of Grey Cloak's pants. He could feel it suddenly growing. "Oh my!" He faced Airius as he pulled the shield from his backside. "I really have to go."

Airius raised an eyebrow. "What's wrong with you? You look sick. Are you unwell?"

Grey Cloak concealed the shield behind his back. It was growing in his hands. He smirked guiltily. "I'm feeling well enough, but I'm not so certain about you." The shield grew so big, his arms could no longer contain it. Its great size covered him like a shell.

Airius's eyes widened. "Th-th-the shield?"

"Sorry, Airius." Grey Cloak clobbered the elf in the jaw. "That's for Sayma." He glanced behind him. The kitchen was a commotion of jabbering servants not paying attention. He hauled Airius's limp body into a pantry and closed the elf inside. Just before he departed, he said, "Have shield, will travel."

The kitchen was located at the back end of the castle's front entrance. The castle wall was only thirty yards away, with a vegetable garden containing rows of cornstalks in between. Grey Cloak slipped into the corn rows and hunkered down. *So close, but how am I going to get beyond that wall?*

As far as he knew, the only way in or out was Monarch Castle's main drawbridge. He didn't have time to find another way. He eyed Cod's shield. It was a beautiful oval shield with an elegant sunburst pattern on the front and two leather straps behind it. It was easily big enough for him to hide completely behind.

Hmmm... it would make an excellent canoe. I wonder if it would float.

He ducked through the corn rows near the edge and looked skyward. Honor Guard manned the top of the castle wall and the towers sitting forty yards apart. Many of the guards leaned over the edge, looking down on the courtyards. They were spread out along the wall as far as the eye could see, and they weren't alone either. The Monarch Knights, in brilliant full plate armor, stood among them, shouting commands with authoritative voices.

I'm never going to make it out that way.

He noticed huge storm drains that sloped away from the castle and dipped out of sight underneath the wall. Leaving the shield behind, he stole over to a drain and crept close to the wall. A grid of metal bars blocked his passage, but they looked wide enough for him to squeeze through.

I might make it, but not with the shield.

With time running out, he moved back into the small cornfield to come up with another plan. He spied a small wagon at the end of the garden. He pulled the wagon to the edge of the corn rows, covered the shield with his cloak, and wary of the soldiers on the wall, he loaded it quickly into the wagon. From there, he nonchalantly rolled up his white sleeves and loaded the wagon with stalks of corn. Once the wagon was half-full, he pulled it by the handle toward the front gate.

A horrible plan, but I'll take my chances.

He kept his head down and whistled a cheerful tune, and no one paid him any mind. As he traveled closer to the drawbridge gate, he noticed that the portcullis was closed.

Now what? Shall I abandon the wagon and return later? I'm so close. All I need is a way past the gate.

The Honor Guards at the wall entrance waved him over. He lifted his head and eyed them. Dyphestive stood among them in a full scale-armor uniform with the yellow sash of a novice.

Zooks. There's no turning back now.

23

"WHAT IS ONE OF AIRIUS'S SERVANTS DOING ALL THE WAY OVER HERE?" A GUSTY Honor Guard asked. Grey Cloak recognized him as Sergeant Tinison, who Captain Cleotus had introduced to Grey Cloak the night before. "No one comes or goes. Weren't you supposed to be confined to your quarters?"

"I've been cleared," Grey Cloak said. Thinking on his feet, he added, "Airius told me to gather food to take to the cathedral to give to the needy. But I must admit, he seemed very distracted."

"You think, Big Ears?" Sergeant Tinison scoffed. "We've got a heap of woes on our shoulders, and Airius wants to feed the needy? If it were me, I'd toss all those vagrants in the moat." He grumbled curses under his breath. "Lazy alley trolls."

"I'll take the wagon back if you wish, Sergeant, or I can wait until the commotion is over," he offered.

Sergeant Tinison plucked an ear of corn out of the wagon. "I hate corn, but I wouldn't feed it to street dung either. Take it back to the garden until the smoke clears. If it ever does. Thunderbolts! Someone's probably going to get the guillotine if that shield isn't found." His eyes slid over to Dyphestive and the young woman with a crooked nose standing beside them. "Baby Face and Beak, first assignment, search that wagon and get it out of here."

"Aye, Sergeant!" Beak said as she snapped her heels together.

Dyphestive followed suit. "Aye, Sergeant."

Perfect, the fortune I needed.

Grey Cloak dared a look at his brother and shrugged his eyebrows. Dyphestive glared at him. He tilted his head toward the wagon to silently say, "Get on with it before she does."

Dyphestive moved to the back of the wagon and muscled his way in beside Beak. "I'll do this."

"What do you mean, you'll do this?" she exclaimed. "I don't need anyone else to do my work for me. How about I do this and you do something else?"

"Something else such as?" Dyphestive asked as he wrapped his fingers around stalks of corn and tossed them out.

"Look under the wagon," she said.

"You look under the wagon."

Grey Cloak stepped in. "If you'd like, I'll look under the wagon. I don't think I've ever looked under a wagon before."

"No!" Dyphestive and Beak said simultaneously.

Grey Cloak backed off. He noticed Beak's resemblance to Adanadel. She was attractive, with strong, refined features, but her crooked nose was puzzling. "It sounds to me like the two of you have some unresolved issues."

As Beak slung stalks of corn aside, she gave him a heated stare. "Stay put, elf."

"My name's Grey Cloak." He offered his hand. "Beak, is it?"

"Don't make me plant this cornstalk in you. Now get out of the way," she warned.

Grey Cloak lifted his palms and stepped back. "Testy. Sorry, I should have seen the signs of two young lovers quarreling."

Dyphestive gave him an embarrassed and dumbfounded look and said with incredulity, "What?"

Beak let out a dry laugh. "In his dreams."

She and Dyphestive started to quickly empty the wagon. Dyphestive gave him a subtle shrug. His blood brother could do nothing more. They would discover the shield in moments.

Somebody's about to have a really bad day.

He scanned his surroundings. The courtyards were clear of any guests, leaving only the Honor Guards, Monarch Knights, servants, and Monarchs on the grounds. The Monarchs stood in their lavish clothing, watching from the castle's tiers and windows, talking with one another and overlooking the grounds. The Monarch Knights gave the orders, and the Honor Guards executed the searches.

Grey Cloak searched for any avenue of escape. He didn't see one. *There has to be a way.*

A flock of yonders whizzed overhead. They spread over the courtyards, flying across the grounds. From one of the castle entrances came a group of men and women in purple-and-gold-checkered robes, escorted by a pair of Monarch Knights.

"Great, the enchanters are here," Sergeant Tinison said with disgust.

Dyphestive and Beak stopped to look.

Grey Cloak's blood froze. *From bad to worse.*

He caught Dyphestive's eye and fluttered his hands like a bird, then made a drinking motion by tipping his thumb to his lips like a jug. Dyphestive shook his head.

Eyeing the yonder scouring the area above, Grey Cloak said, "Sometimes I wish I could fly."

Beak scowled at him. "Stitch your lips." She resumed clearing out the wagon.

Grey Cloak gave Dyphestive a heated stare. "Don't you wish you could fly, Dyphestive?"

Dyphestive gave him a blank look.

"Wait, you two know each other?" Beak asked.

"Well, I thought so. We started on the same day," Grey Cloak said. "Captain Cleotus recruited us."

"Really?" She kept hauling cornstalks out of the wagon and eyeing him. "My father was great friends with him."

The wagon was almost empty. Grey Cloak could see his cloak showing underneath the cornstalks. "Can I head back now?"

Dyphestive's eyes grew the moment he saw the cloak. He started tossing cornstalks back in the wagon.

"What are you doing, buffoon?" Beak asked him.

"Loading the wagon," he admitted sheepishly. "I thought we were finished."

"I don't know about you, but the job isn't done until it's thoroughly done." Beak grabbed a handful of cornstalks and slung them out of the wagon. Her gaze caught the cloak. "What's this?"

Grey Cloak eased his hand into his pocket. "Oh, there it is. That's my cloak. I must have absentmindedly buried it. Thank you so very much for helping me find it. I would have hated to lose it."

Beak peeled the cloak back with her fingers. Her eyes widened. She jerked the cloak all the way back and gasped. Codd's shield shone against the sun. She lifted her eyes to Grey Cloak's and caught his guilty look.

"It's not what you think," he said.

She drew her sword. "Thief!"

24

GREY CLOAK EASED A FLASHING OUT OF HIS POCKET AND RAISED HIS HANDS. HONOR Guards came rushing over along with the yonders hovering above. "If you'll give me a moment, I can explain everything," he said.

"Seize him!" Sergeant Tinison hollered.

Dyphestive slipped behind Grey Cloak and pulled his hands behind his back. As he did so, he whispered in his blood brother's ear, "Should I close my eyes now?"

With yonders circling overhead, Grey Cloak replied, "Yes." He dropped the flashing.

Boooomph!

As Dyphestive's hands loosened, Grey Cloak jumped into the wagon, donned his cloak, and grabbed the shield. No one was looking his direction, and everyone was shielding their eyes. The yonders dropped from the sky like dead birds, and he jumped out of the wagon holding the massive shield overhead. He could only see one way out: up and over the castle wall.

This is madness.

At full speed, Grey Cloak ran toward the portcullis and headed up the stone staircase on the backside. Many of the soldiers on the wall had been caught looking toward the flashing and were still rubbing their eyes. He plowed them over.

At the top of the wall, he was confronted by two men in plate-mail armor and helms. They were Monarch Knights, the castle's elite. The formidable men drew their longswords and advanced as one.

Grey Cloak lowered the shield and charged them at full speed. "Yaaaaaaah!" Codd's shield slammed into the knights' longswords as they struck. A resounding *kraaaaang* followed. The shield absorbed the blows and knocked the knights backward. Grey Cloak plowed right over them.

Behind the battements, Grey Cloak stopped and took a quick look over the side. It was a straight thirty-foot fall into the moat and another thirty-plus feet across. The behemoth-sized moat monsters lurked just below the waters, waiting to strike.

Can I jump it? Can I swim it fast enough? Zooks, what have I gotten myself into?

All of a sudden, the shield swung him around with a life of its own. A ballista bolt fired from one of the high towers would have skewered his back. Instead, the oversized shaft of deadly metal ricocheted off the shield. Another bolt streaked through the sky with pinpoint precision. Grey Cloak watched it bounce off the shield like a dart falling from a board.

He eyed the shield.

This thing is fantastic.

The soldiers' eyes had cleared, and they advanced from both sides of the walls. Over two dozen Honor Guards and Monarch Knights closed in, escorted by giant winged eyeballs.

Grey Cloak crept between the castle's battlements and hid behind the shield. Ballista bolts whistled overhead and blasted off the shield, chipping rocks from the battlements.

A trio of yonders dropped in behind him, hovering in the air, keeping their distance.

"Oh, go away, ugly things!" he shouted.

The moat monsters gathered in the murky waters below.

He could hear the soldiers' heavy footsteps closing in.

Grey Cloak stuck his tongue out at the yonders and jumped. With his free hand, he grabbed one of the yonders by the wings and dragged it down with him. The gray folds of the Cloak of Legends billowed out. Grey Cloak floated down slowly to the astonishment of the soldiers leaning over the wall and shouting in dismay. Ballista bolts rocketed by.

Grey Cloak's feet dangled only twenty feet above the surging moat monsters, whose massive jaws snapped in anticipation. Aided by his cloak's magic, he sank to his doom. In a few moments, the moat monsters would chew him to bits.

"Well, if I'm going to die," he said to the eyeball that he cradled to his chest, "I'm not going to die alone. You're going first."

The yonder quivered like a frightened puppy.

"And just so you know, I only took the shield to save a friend. I plan to return it." With his fist locked around its wings, he hurled the yonder into the mouth of the largest moat monster, which swallowed it whole. "Ick."

No more ballista bolts whistled by him. He lowered the shield and looked at the crowd waiting for him to die. He strapped the shield across his arm, saluted them all, and said, "For Zora."

The moat monsters jumped from the waters, nipping at his toes. He lifted his knees to his chest. "I'm all out of tricks. Or am I?"

He fumbled to find the Figurine of Heroes in his pocket. It was his last hope. He started to say the words, but he caught something hurtling at him out of the corner of his eye. Dyphestive slammed into him while at the same time scooping Grey Cloak into his arms.

"Dyphestive, you're flying!"

"Forgive me for being so thick-skulled." Dyphestive flew straight toward the city and away from the castle. "You know me. Sometimes it takes a while for things to sink in."

"Your timing couldn't be better," Grey Cloak said as he waved goodbye to the red-faced soldiers shaking their fists from Monarch Castle. "But I think your new friends might be disappointed."

"Where to now?" Dyphestive asked, the wind rustling his hair.

Grey Cloak pointed behind them. At least a dozen yonders were in pursuit. "As far away from them as possible."

25

Dyphestive blasted by the pigeons roosting in the eaves of the cathedrals, scattering them like leaves.

Grey Cloak laughed. "I hate pigeons."

"I thought you hated flying."

"I do, but not when my life depends on it." He glanced down at the people pointing up at them from the streets. Women in bonnets screamed and hauled their astonished children into stores. "What's the matter with them? They have to have seen men fly before."

"Where should I go?" Dyphestive asked.

"I don't know. Keep flying in a circle. I'm thinking."

The yonders stayed on them without getting too close, like some sort of aerial escort.

Grey Cloak patted his pockets. He was all out of flashings. "You know, I was surprised that you came for me. I thought you were mad."

"I thought you were mad."

"I was mad."

"I was too," Dyphestive said as he swooped over the rooftops. "But I couldn't sleep, and you know me. I sleep like a baby. I couldn't let you down, Grey. You're my best friend. I'll never let you down."

Grey Cloak nodded. "Not even over a woman. Beak was fetching, well, aside from her nose. In a strange sort of way, it was charming."

"She's too much like Adanadel, but I feel guilty. You know he died because of us."

"He died because he was a good man, and that's what good men do. He wouldn't want us to feel guilty." He watched the buildings pass by beneath him. "Head toward the Outer Ring, away from the bridges. There won't be so many soldiers there."

Dyphestive grinned.

Grey Cloak caught his smile. "What are you thinking?"

"You did it. You actually stole Codd's shield."

Grey Cloak smirked. "I did, didn't I? Did you ever doubt me?"

"I wouldn't put anything past you, especially when you put your mind to it, but I'd be a liar if I said I thought you could pull it off." Dyphestive flew over acres of farmland surrounding Monarch City. "That was amazing."

"Thank you, but stealing it is one thing. Getting away with it is another. Every soldier and giant eyeball in the city will be looking for us." A yonder flew within striking distance. He lashed out at it, but it drifted away. "I'm sorry you couldn't stay with the Honor Guard, but if we get caught, you might stay with them the rest of your life as they guard your dungeon cell."

"With you around, I probably won't be that lucky." Dyphestive suddenly dipped in the air. "Uh, do you have any idea how long that potion will last?"

"No idea. Why?"

Dyphestive shrugged as they skimmed the ground, heading toward the Outer Ring. "Because I think it's coming to an end." Dyphestive crashed on top of Grey Cloak. They slid through a vegetable garden, riding the shield like a sled, and plowed over a scarecrow that looked like an orc as they entered a cornfield.

Grey Cloak squeezed out from under Dyphestive's body. "Zooks, you're heavy. More corn." He flung an ear at a yonder and knocked it out of the sky. "Bull's-eye."

The blood brothers hurled one ear of corn after the other at the flying eyeball vermin, but the enchanted creatures scattered like flies.

Nothing but wide-open countryside, cottages, and farm buildings stood between them and the Outer Ring Moat of the city. "Soldiers will be galloping our way soon enough." He slapped Dyphestive on the shoulder. "Come on."

They ran toward the Outer Ring and stopped on the ledge. Grey Cloak walked along the lip, staring downward.

"You don't want to climb down there, do you?" Dyphestive asked.

"If we have to, but that isn't what I had in mind." He pointed down. "There!" Several dozen yards ahead, he could see water draining from the side of the cliff. "Those are huge drainage tunnels coming from the city. I saw them on the way in. We should fit." He ran until he stood over one then strapped the shield on Dyphestive's back and lowered himself over the edge. "Are you coming?"

"You know I'm not a strong climber." Dyphestive wiggled his beefy fingers. "They have trouble grabbing some things."

"We don't have a choice. We have to try. And it's only a few dozen feet down." He began to lower himself. Glancing at the yonders hovering around, he added, "Get moving!"

Dyphestive lowered himself over the rim. He looked like a giant terrapin with the shield on his back. His fingers found solid purchase on the first several feet of descent.

"Good, good," Grey Cloak said. "Take your time. Not a lot of time, but well, you know…"

Dyphestive looked down. "I think I have it." He slipped and crashed straight down into Grey Cloak, knocking them both off the cliff face.

"Noooo!" Grey Cloak cried as they fell. Dyphestive latched onto him like a tick. The Cloak of Legends feathered out, and they floated downward. "Stop squirming!" He stretched for the rock, trying to grab the rim of the drainage tunnel as they passed. He gripped the edge, but he couldn't hold on. Though the cloak had slowed them, their weight was still the same. Dyphestive was dragging him down, and Grey Cloak's fingers were slipping. "You're too heavy!"

Dyphestive swung his arm over Grey Cloak's head and fastened his fingers on the tunnel's lip. "I can hold on. Go!"

Grey Cloak climbed inside the six-foot-high pipe. He reached down and grabbed his brother's arm. "Get in here!"

"I have it." Dyphestive crawled on his elbows through the sloppy, stinky, trickling water and into the dark hole. He looked down the pipe. "What now? It stinks."

"It's either this way or down." Grey Cloak led the way.

They made it forty feet in the pipe and ran into a grid of corroded steel that blocked their passage. Grey Cloak locked his fingers around the bars and knocked his forehead against the steel. "And I wanted to be an adventurer."

Dyphestive tapped his shoulder. He had to stoop down to avoid hitting his head. "We still have company."

The yonders had followed them into the tunnel. The white globular eyeballs cast a green hue around them.

Grey Cloak sighed. "Thanks for the light, rodents." He pulled a dagger from one of his pockets and chased them out of the tunnel. "Haven't you seen enough?" He beat his chest. "Come and get me now, why don't you?"

"Grey?"

He turned. He could see Dyphestive's white grin. "What?"

"I can handle this," Dyphestive replied. He grabbed the metal grid at its base with his bare fingers. His shoulders bunched and heaved as he pulled backward.

The metal groaned and separated from the stone wall. Thrusting with his mighty legs and pulling with all his might, the red-faced young warrior peeled the metal back like a banana. He let out a deep breath and stepped aside. "After you."

Grey Cloak slipped through the gap. "You're the best brother an elf could ever have."

"Thanks." Dyphestive followed him and caught Grey Cloak's disapproving eye. "What?"

"We can't have them following us."

"Oh." Dyphestive turned around and pulled the metal back into place as a wall of glowing eyeballs watched.

Grey Cloak took one last moment to face them. He put his thumbs to his temples, wiggled his fingers, and let out a funny *phylllt* sound. He pushed his brother along, and they vanished into the dark sewer tunnel.

26

Night had fallen over Monarch City. It was day three of Zora's abduction, and every soldier in Monarch City combed the streets, looking for Grey Cloak and Dyphestive.

After hiding in the sewer pipes the majority of the day, the blood brothers finally caught a break, hit the cobblestone streets, and in the dark of night, stole back to Crane's apartment, where a group of soldiers were departing. Jakoby, Leena, and Than were waiting for them there.

Grey Cloak sat on the sofa, petting Streak, who was lying on his lap. Dyphestive sat beside him, drinking a jug of water. Leena had squeezed in between them.

Jakoby stood by the small kitchen stove, holding Codd's shield. "I can't believe I'm holding it. It's even bigger up close." He polished the front with the palm of his hand and hugged it. "I don't think any man has laid a finger on it in centuries." He eyed the brothers. "You've earned my respect. Great respect, and that does not come lightly. Saving me was one thing, but this, well, this is astonishing. Hah."

"So you weren't able to locate Zora?" Grey Cloak asked.

Than stood by the small bay window with his shoulder leaning against the wall and his arms crossed. His eyes combed the streets. "We took a chance and tried the dungeons that you freed us from again. They were waiting."

"You went back?" Grey Cloak asked.

"It seemed logical that they might hide her there and hope we would attempt a rescue. We sprang the trap and eliminated the dungeon as a possibility. We exposed the enemy's resources too," Than calmly said.

Grey Cloak ground his teeth. Whatever they did would have agitated Irsk Mondo. If anything, the rogue leader would have buried Zora deeper if not quicker. "What happened?"

"We came across one of Irsk's minions, Finton Slay, and the Iron Devils. It turns out that the Devils aren't ordinary thieves and assassins but ghouls that almost killed us. Thanks to Than, we live," Jakoby said.

"Thanks to Than, all of you almost died," Grey Cloak said dryly.

"It wasn't all his idea," Jakoby admitted.

The door handle to the apartment rattled. Jakoby stole over to the door, pulled his dagger, and hid to the side. Everyone quieted. The door quietly swung open, and a paunchy man with wavy hair entered. Jakoby slipped in behind him and brought him to the floor.

"Crane!" Dyphestive said.

"He's one of us," Grey Cloak added.

"Sorry about that," Jakoby said politely as he effortlessly hauled Crane back to his feet.

"I had a key," Crane replied with a bewildered look. "And it's my apartment."

Jakoby closed the door. "Jumpy times."

"I can see that." Crane unrolled a piece of parchment and handed it to Grey Cloak. "Literally."

Grey Cloak looked at a perfect picture of his and Dyphestive's faces. It read: **Wanted: Dead or Alive. Reward. 1000 gold chips each.**

"That's a fortune!" Grey Cloak exclaimed. "Every man, woman, and child will be hunting us down."

"Well." Crane shrugged. "Not the rich ones. I just returned. What did you do?"

Grey Cloak pointed to the kitchen, where the shield leaned. "Stole Codd's shield."

Crane's mouth dropped into an *o*. He half-covered his mouth. "Why did you do that? *How* did you do that?"

"We crossed the Dark Addler. They kidnapped Zora and wanted the shield in exchange for her," Grey Cloak said.

Crane sniffed. "What stinks?"

"We escaped through the sewers."

"I see. Stink happens." Crane sauntered over to the blackwood wine cabinet. Using a small key, he opened the doors and removed a glass bottle with a round bottom. "It's called Brandy. She's a fine gal. Any partakers? I hate to drink alone."

"Knights don't drink," Jakoby said as he came forward, "but I'm not a knight anymore. Fill one up for me."

Crane filled up two pewter goblets and corked the bottle. "Now what?"

"With everyone in the city combing the streets for us, I can't even get to Irsk Mondo." Grey Cloak picked Streak up off his lap and set him on the table.

Crane sipped his brandy. "Who's your contact?"

"Orpah the orc. She'll be waiting at the Tavern Dwellers Inn. She's probably the one who drew those pictures," he said. "That place will be filled with people looking for us. They know we used to work there."

"All of us are wanted," Than added.

"Sounds like I'm in good company." Crane polished off his brandy. "Wait here. I'll set up a meeting." He refilled his goblet. "One for the road. Tell me, this Orpah, any distinguishing marks?" He shrugged his eyebrows. "Is she pretty?"

"Don't worry," Grey Cloak said as he showed Crane the door. "You can't miss her."

"Perfect," Crane said. "Sounds like the kind of woman I'm looking for."

27

CRANE RETURNED WITH A GUILTY EXPRESSION. "SORRY, BUT THERE WAS NOTHING I could do. Orpah's a tough negotiator. Cute but tough."

Grey Cloak's jaw tightened. Once again, Irsk Mondo was calling the shots, and once again, he had to cave to the fiendish goblin-elf's demands. "Didn't you explain that the entire city is looking for us?"

"Orpah said that's the reason for the additional discretion. It's Irsk's place or no place at all," Crane said.

Grey Cloak picked Streak up by the tail and let the dragon latch onto his back. He winced. "I don't guess those claws are going to get any softer." He swung his cloak over his shoulders. "And he insists that only I come?"

"Those are the terms."

"You can't do this alone. You know you can't trust him," Dyphestive said. "I'm coming too."

"I'll take my chances," Grey Cloak said.

"If you go, Dyphestive, they'll scatter like rats, and we'll never see Zora again," Crane warned. "Orpah promised me that. Again, I'm sorry."

Grey Cloak laid a hand on his brother's shoulder. "Don't worry. I'll figure something out. I always do."

"At least we know where you're going," Jakoby said as he opened the apartment door. "We'll be close by but not too close."

Grey Cloak nodded, lifted Codd's shield, which he'd wrapped in burlap, and eyed Crane. "Lead the way."

Crane headed down the stairs. "Orpah gave specific instructions and said she'd make sure the way was clear. I'll take you as far as the sun gods' cathedral. I'll stay close." He peered out into the street and led them through the dank back alleys and stopped for a peek around the corner. Across the road, a candle with a blue flame burned in a window. "There."

Grey Cloak and Crane jetted across the street into a general store's open front door. A man with long sleeves and a vest met them there. Hair hung over his eyes. He carried the blue candle. They followed him to the back of the store and crossed through an entrance that connected one store to another. They went down a set of steps into a musty stone corridor that ran beneath the road.

Whoa! No wonder I couldn't figure out where we were going before. It's an entire subterranean network.

A network of tunnels ran underneath the city, separate from the sewer lines that the soldiers had already been searching. The tunnels connected city block to city block and opened into the basements of many stores. They popped up inside a candle, tobacco, and incense shop on the same block as the cathedral.

The long-haired rogue said in a rusty voice, "Come on."

Grey Cloak gave Crane one last look.

"I'll wait right here," the older man assured him.

Grey Cloak and the rogue jetted into a side entrance underneath the cathedral's grand stair. Another rogue, a lean lizardman with a droopy head, opened the door for him. He was met by a host of Iron Devils, twelve in all. Each held a sword with hands wrapped in old cloth.

Ghouls. Sickening.

The Devils led him straight through the cathedral's basement, which was a network of ancient crypts of high-ranking priests, ornately decorated with stone sculptures of the sun gods, and sarcophagi plated in precious metals. They entered a stairwell and moved silently upward into a tunnel that backtracked to the cathedral's main foyer. One of the Devils pointed toward the apse. The pews in the nave ran nearly a hundred rows deep.

Grey Cloak entered, and the brass double doors closed behind him. The pews were modestly filled with people wearing iron masks and crimson robes. They turned their metal eye slits toward him.

What's going on? Is this my wedding day?

At the end of the aisles, sitting in the high priest's chair, was Irsk Mondo. The half goblin, half elf leaned back in his throne with a foot up on the chair and his arm dangling over the side. He still wore Zora's Scarf of Shadows around his neck. To his right was Finton Slay, the bald necromancer, dressed in all black. Kneeling between them was a disheveled Zora with a gag in her mouth.

Grey Cloak locked eyes with Zora and fast-walked down the long aisle, carrying the shield in both hands.

"That's close enough," Irsk said in his condescending tone, stopping Grey Cloak twenty feet from his grand chair. He leaned forward, eyeing the shield that was covered by a blanket. "You've created quite a stir. Quite a stir." He tapped his fingertips together. "Why, the Monarchs hold the Dark Addler responsible. Can you believe such a thing?" He combed his greasy hair behind his long ears. "Let me see it."

Grey Cloak dropped the blanket on the ground, fully revealing the shield in all its glory. "The shield is delivered, as you requested. Now release my friend."

Irsk showed off a mouthful of long, crooked teeth. "Not so fast. I have to test its authenticity."

28

"WHAT SORT OF GAME ARE YOU PLAYING, IRSK? MY PICTURE IS EVERYWHERE. THE entire city is tearing down the walls trying to find me. You know it's real. Stop fooling," Grey Cloak said. "Let Zora go!"

Irsk's hollow laughter echoed throughout the cathedral's chambers. "I've been doing this a long time. A very long time. Codd's armor is often replicated." He reached down and picked up a flail with a spiked metal ball attached to the end. He stood, stretching toward the rafters, over seven feet in height, with the crude weapon hanging by his side and walked down the steps.

"This is Bone Crusher. A personal weapon of mine." Irsk started to gently swing it. The spikes glowed. "A single strike can bust apart shields of the finest craft. Now we shall see whether this shield is real or a replica."

Grey Cloak braced himself behind the shield.

Irsk wound the flail up, creating a ring of energy with an angry golden glow. It sounded like a swarm of buzzing hornets. With a snap of his wrist, he struck the nearest pew. The ancient stone exploded, and a hunk of rock went flying toward an Iron Devil in the back.

With triumph in his dark eyes, Irsk wound the weapon up again. Using both hands, he swung the flail into the shield with all his might.

Grey Cloak waited to be knocked from his feet. Instead, Codd's shield hummed like a low-keyed tuning fork. He stole a glance at Irsk.

The leader of the Dark Addler grimaced and flicked his hands, one after the other, as if shaking away pain. Irsk pitched the flail aside. "It's authentic."

Finton Slay nodded.

"You have your shield. Now let Zora ago," Grey Cloak demanded. "And when I say go, I mean both of us walk out of here alive."

Irsk stroked the scraggly hairs on his chin. "You do realize that you're safer inside than outside. I can offer my protection."

Grey Cloak scoffed. "I want nothing to do with vermin like you."

"Oh, don't be so quick to judge. A man of your skill, and so young, would do well in the service of a man like me. I have to admit, you impressed me."

"I don't want any part of the Dark Addler."

"Don't be so hasty, because you might not have a choice." Irsk resumed his seat on the chair. "Think about it. You're a wanted man. The Monarchs won't stop until they have you. You need protection. All of you need protection. Besides, you owe me."

"Owe you for what? I brought the shield."

"There's the matter of the other prisoners your friends freed."

"The shield is worth one hundred times anything you might have lost. Quit playing games with me, and let Zora go." He eased forward. "I thought there was honor among thieves."

Irsk spread his hands. "I have to admit that I'm not very used to this. Typically, when I give men impossible tasks, they fall flat on their faces, but not in your case. No, you actually pulled it off. It makes me curious."

"I'm a determined elf. You underestimated me."

"I don't like being made a fool of. I have a reputation to protect," Irsk said.

"But you have the shield. What more could you ask for?"

Irsk tapped his fingernails on the arm of his chair and shifted back and forth in his seat. "This is very difficult because I like you. You carry yourself with the edge that I need. Let me offer one last time. Join the Dark Addler. You'll need my protection."

"No," Grey Cloak said firmly. "Let Zora go."

"The Monarchs will hunt you down and flay you alive," Irsk warned.

"I'll take my chances."

Irsk leaned back in his chair. "Speaking of chances, I can't take any and have you lead the Monarchs back to me. It seems that you leave me with little choice. Finton Slay?"

"Yes, Dark Addler," the hollow-eyed necromancer said in his cryptic voice.

"Slay them."

Surprise, surprise.

Grey Cloak's fingers fished coins from his pockets as he watched the Iron Devils rise from their seats. He summoned his wizardry and charged the coins with power. He gave Irsk Mondo a warning glance. "Are you sure you don't want to reconsider?"

"I stand by my decision."

As the Devils advanced, Grey Cloak said, "So be it. Zora, duck!"

Zora flattened on the floor as Grey Cloak hurled a handful of glowing coins at Irsk and Finton.

With catlike speed, Irsk dove out of his chair. Several coins hit the chair and blew the wood to pieces. The rest of the coins hit Finton Slay square in the chest and blasted the flat-footed wizard backward behind the altar.

Irsk pushed himself off the floor, snatched up his flail, and shouted with rage, "Kill them! Kill them! Kill them!"

Grey Cloak had counted at least fifty of the Iron Devils in the pews on his way in. It appeared that even more were popping up. Some moved with a jerkiness while others were more fluid, like normal men. He swung his shield around and knocked two close attackers over and hollered, "Zora, come on!"

Zora rolled away from Irsk just as he brought the flail down to smash her head open. She popped up and sped toward Grey Cloak. By the time she arrived, she'd wriggled out of her bindings and removed her gag. "Do you call this a rescue?"

"I missed you too." He plowed into two more sword-bearing attackers filling the aisle.

"Is that why you took so long?" She ducked under a sword swipe and kicked her attacker in the groin.

"Well, you were pretty steamed that last time we spoke. I thought you needed more time." Grey Cloak jumped from one pew to the next with Zora right behind him.

The masked Devils came at them from all directions, slicing and chopping at their knees, ankles, and toes. All of the exits were blocked by crimson-cloaked bodies, and every door was barred shut, sealing the desperate heroes in. There was nowhere to turn. Nowhere to run.

Irsk Mondo jumped the pews two at a time and closed the gap. He pinned Grey Cloak and Zora between two columns. "You fools can't last forever, shield or no shield." Using Bone Crusher, he whacked the shield with one hard, resounding blow after another.

Several of the Iron Devils climbed the columns like spiders and prepared to jump down on top of them with blades poised to kill.

Grey Cloak and Zora hunkered down underneath the shield. She kissed his cheek.

"What was that for?"

She gripped him tightly by the waist. "I wanted to thank you for trying."

Irsk pounded away. The Devils jumped.

29

"You can thank me later. I'm not finished yet," Grey Cloak said through clenched teeth. He snagged the Figurine of Heroes out of his pocket and started saying the enchanted words under his breath. The strange syllables twisted inside his mouth as he spewed them. He rolled the figurine under the shield to the pew rows below Irsk's legs.

"What's this trick?" Irsk demanded as he backed away from the shield.

An inky black smoke spilled over the floor and spread rapidly.

"We're going to die, aren't we?" Zora covered her nose. "Tatiana warned you about abusing that."

"We were about to die, one way or the other," he said.

"Who are you?" Irsk stammered.

The tip of a scaly black tail swiped underneath Codd's shield. A cold and husky-voiced woman answered, "I am Selene."

Streak popped his head out from under Grey Cloak's cloak. His pink tongue flickered out of his mouth.

Zora let out a squeal and clutched her chest. "You could have told me you had him packed in there."

"In all the excitement, I forgot. He's like a part of my body."

Streak scrambled down to the floor and squeezed underneath the shield.

"Get back here!"

"Whoever you are, you won't last long," Irsk Mondo warned. The flail, Bone Breaker, hummed by his side. "Iron Devils, kill her!"

"Her?" Grey Cloak and Zora shared a surprised look. They peeked over the rim of the shield.

A beautiful woman stood in the smoke, surrounded by Irsk's minions. Her long raven-colored hair had a white streak on one side. Her sublime body was covered in black scales, like a dragon, and a long tail flicked from side to side beside her. She had a dangerous look in her violet eyes, and she held a dagger burning with purple flame.

"Whoa," Grey Cloak said.

The dragon woman stared down at Irsk. "Whoever you are, I don't like you." She glanced at the Iron Devils like they were fleas. "You will all die today."

Irsk spun his flail in a bright blur between them. "We'll see about that, dragon wench! Slay her!"

The Devils converged on Selene as one. Irsk struck out with them.

In a blur of dazzling speed, Selene pumped her dagger into attacker after attacker. Their bodies burned from the inside out, catching their robes on fire. Her black tail cracked like a whip, and four of the Devils went flying head over heels. A bolt of fire blasted out of her hand, knocking one ghoul back into another.

Irsk Mondo saw a clean shot and brought the flail down on her head. She slipped under the attack in the blink of an eye and punched him hard in the chest, sending Irsk flying into a column. His back cracked against the stone, and the flail went flying from his fingers.

Streak jumped on a ghoul's face and coiled his tail around the man's neck. Grey Cloak handed Zora a dagger from his pocket and grabbed his sword. They sprang into action.

"Careful, they're ghouls," Grey Cloak said.

"Some are, some aren't. You can take the ones that are," Zora said as she jumped behind a man and stabbed him in the back.

Selene tore through the ranks of the dead and living like a saw blade in a windmill. The crimson assassins' blades shattered against her steely hide. She made them pay for it with dagger thrusts in the chest that exploded them from the inside. The dead fell. The living died in droves. Yet more came.

Grey Cloak flicked a handful of magic-fired coins, sending more men flying over the pews.

"Where'd you pick that up?" Zora exclaimed as she ducked a razor-sharp thrust and kicked a man's iron mask off his face.

"Gunder Island. I'll explain later."

Selene tore through the ranks of Iron Devils with ease. One ghoul exploded after another. From out of nowhere, a blast of hellish fire knocked her from her feet and sent her crashing through the backrests of the stone pews. She lay still in dusty gray debris, the colorful moonlight through the stained glass windows shining on her body.

Finton Slay stood on the stage, his hands smoking with radiant power. A victorious sneer stretched across his face as Irsk Mondo limped over.

"Well done." Irsk patted his top henchman on the back. "Well done indeed."

Selene rose from the smoke with fire in her eyes.

Finton's haunting eyes grew to the size of saucers. "Impossible, I hit her with everything I had!"

The dark-haired warrior advanced. "Then you're a dead man."

"Stop her!" Irsk commanded. "Stop her!"

The Iron Devils swarmed her in droves of ten and twenty. They piled on her arms and legs.

Grey Cloak and Zora fought with everything they had, but the numbers were too many. "Zora, stay close!"

The half elf had a weary look in her eyes. Her dagger hung at her side. "I don't have anything left. There are too many."

Selene killed the men two at a time. She was a juggernaut of power, but even she was overwhelmed.

"Streak, give us some cover," Grey Cloak commanded.

Smoke rose from the floor, obscuring the enemies' vision.

Grey Cloak shoved Zora to the floor. "Stay down for now." He sprang up behind two men and cut them down with a single swipe of his blade. One dropped dead. The other turned. It was a ghoul with glinting eyes behind its metal mask. Grey Cloak lopped its head off with a quick stroke of steel.

The Devils swarmed. He couldn't kill them all but tried, thrust after thrust, until a ghoul grabbed ahold of him. "Eeeargh!"

30

As Grey Cloak fought to stay alive and on his feet, he glimpsed movement on the other side of the surrounding violet-and-crimson stained glass windows above. In a violent explosion, the colorful shards of glass burst into the cathedral.

Four figures descended from separate windows and landed on their feet in the pews. Dyphestive, Than, Jakoby, and Leena arrived with fight in their eyes.

With Lythlenion's war mace in hand, Dyphestive shouted at the top of his lungs, "It's thunder time!"

Two of the Iron Devils converged on him with stunning speed. He cranked the war mace back and sent them flying.

Leena's nunchakus spun with fire. She knocked an iron mask off a man's face and clobbered him with lightning-quick strikes.

Blood surged through Grey Cloak's veins, and he shook off his attackers and punched holes in their bellies.

Jakoby let out his battle cry, "Long live the monarchy!"

Than furiously pulled crimson-robed men away from Selene and slung them over the pews. His wild hair flew all around him. His brown eyes burned with golden light.

The Devils lost the upper hand but fought on. Leena busted their bones with rapid strikes, cracking jaws and elbows. Dyphestive fought a ghoul on his back while he pounded another one to the ground. Jakoby batted swords aside and skewered men with his own. Everyone fought for their lives in a clamor of pain and battle cries. The cathedral of the sun gods turned into a bloody battlefield.

Grey Cloak chopped a Devil lizardman down. Out of the corner of his eye, he caught Irsk and Finton backing farther into the apse. Standing on a pile of the dead, he pointed his sword at them. "Don't let them get away!"

Dozens of the Iron Devils fell under the heroes' might, but still more came.

"Retreat!" Irsk ordered. He winked at Grey Cloak and grabbed Finton's shoulder. In a puff of smoke, they vanished.

The surviving Devils scurried out through the doors like drowning rats.

Than lifted a man over his shoulders, revealing the struggling dragon woman underneath. His golden eyes widened. "Selene!" He flung the man into a pillar and embraced her. "You're here, how?"

"I don't know," she said as her tail lashed out. She knocked a mask from an attacker's face and sent him spinning over the pews. "Where are we?"

"Gapoli. Another world. How did you get here?" Than asked again.

"I don't know."

He wrapped his arms around her. "I missed you. You look beautiful."

"And you look old." Selene broke their embrace. Her sublime body started to fade into smoke. "What's happening?"

Than's fingers passed through her. "Noooo! Noooo!"

"Keep fighting, Dragon. We'll find you!" Selene stated as she vanished.

"I love you!" he shouted.

Selene was gone.

Grey Cloak approached Than. "You knew her?"

Than had fire in his eyes. He grabbed Grey Cloak by the collar and lifted him off his feet. "She's my wife. Bring her back. Bring her back!"

"I don't have any control over who comes and who goes," he said.

Than shook him. "How did you do that?"

"You know, you're a lot stronger than you appear. Will you please put me down?"

Than lowered him to the ground with a hopeless look in his eyes. "Sorry." Than sat down on a pew and sighed.

Zora drew near Grey Cloak with the Figurine of Heroes in her hands.

He put his arm around her. "I'm glad you're all right."

With weary eyes she said, "I am, but I'm exhausted."

Grey Cloak sat down by Than as the others gathered around. All of them were scratched up and splattered with living and undead blood.

Grey Cloak fished the potion of restoration out of his pocket and handed it to Zora. "Pass it around." He showed Than the figurine. "I have no control over who or what it summons. All I know is that they come from other worlds."

"May I?" Than asked.

Grey Cloak held it to his chest. "No, it's mine."

Than frowned and said dejectedly, "At least we both know the other is alive."

"Did you say that she's your wife?"

Than nodded.

"I'm glad she was on our side. She came across as frosty." Grey Cloak patted Than on the back. "Everyone, the old hermit has a wife. How about that?"

Leena drank some of the potion and made a bitter face. She handed it to Jakoby. He passed it to Zora, whose arm was bloody. She drank the rest of it.

Dyphestive slapped Than on the back. "Congratulations. I only caught a glimpse of her, but she was very pretty. How long have you been married?"

"A thousand years or so," Than said.

"Oh." Dyphestive exchanged doubtful looks with the others.

Grey Cloak rose and looked about. "Codd's shield!"

The shield lay between two columns. Dyphestive fetched it.

Grey Cloak let out a sigh of relief. He wiped the sweat from his brow. "Whew! We did it." He tucked the figurine away, felt eyes on him, and looked up. "Zooks."

Over a dozen yonders entered through the broken stained glass windows. The flying eyeballs slowly floated above them.

Grey Cloak gave them a casual wave. "I guess they found us." He stood with Streak in his arms. "Now let's hope I can explain all of this."

The heroes pushed through the double doors of the cathedral. Their jaws dropped as they froze. It looked like the entire Monarch army had filled the streets. Monarch Knights, Honor Guards, and horse-drawn wagons and chariots stretched on as far as the eye could see.

Grey Cloak set Streak down. "Hide, little brother, hide."

Dyphestive set the shield before their outnumbered group, and they raised their hands in surrender.

31

"Dungeons aren't so bad once you get used to them," Grey Cloak said. His arms and legs were shackled to the wall. "It's the additional restraints that make it so unpleasant. Well, that and the smell."

He wasn't alone in his shackles. Dyphestive, Zora, Than, Jakoby, and Leena were in the same condition, stripped down to their undergarments with their backsides against the wet, moldy wall. At least all of them shared the same large cell.

"At least we have one another's company," Dyphestive said with a warm grin.

Jakoby sighed. "It will probably be the guillotine or hanging. It wouldn't surprise me one bit if it wasn't tomorrow at first light. I knew my past would catch up with me. My only hope was to have a few more years to live."

"Why do the Monarchs want to kill you?" Grey Cloak asked.

"Some Monarchs are good, and some are bad. I crossed the bad ones, and it was their word against mine," the dark-skinned knight said. "The same thing happened to my brother, Adanadel. That's why we left the Monarch Knights. They were being corrupted. I caught them slave trading with the Dark Addler. They were trying to make me a slave as well."

Dyphestive leaned forward in his chains. Grey Cloak was on the end to his right. Leena was on his left, followed by Zora, Jakoby, and Than. "Jakoby, I met your niece, Beak—I mean Shannon. She's training to be an Honor Guard and strives to be a knight. I never thought to warn her about what you said. I-I," he stammered, shamefaced. "I didn't want to tell her that I knew her father since he died because of me."

"Don't blame yourself," Jakoby assured him. "Revealing that information might have placed you and her in greater danger. When the time comes, if it comes"—he eyed his glum surroundings—"you'll know when to tell her."

Grey Cloak watched water drip from the ceiling. They were secured behind a row of solid steel bars two dozen feet away. The steel door was locked with a padlock, which he knew he could pick easily, but he didn't have his cloak anymore. The soldiers had taken it.

He looked down the row of heroes. "So this is Talon."

"What?" Jakoby asked.

"That's the name we chose for ourselves. Rather, Adanadel and Dalsay did when they recruited us." He smiled. "Now that I think about it, we've had many members, albeit briefly. Zora is the oldest member left."

"I'm not the oldest," she disagreed.

"That's not what I meant," he assured her as he looked her way. "It started with Adanadel, Dalsay, Browning, Tanlin, Tatiana, and Zora. We added Rhonna, Lythlenion, and Bowbreaker."

"I miss Bowbreaker," Zora said sadly. "He's so—"

"Reginald the Razor and Grunt came along. Now, the three of you," Grey Cloak said, speaking to Jakoby, Leena, and Than. "We are adventurers. This is what adventurers do. Did I miss anyone?"

"Does Cotton count?" Dyphestive asked of the old halfling that he almost killed when he was a Doom Rider.

"Ah, I suppose."

"Is there an oath we must swear to become a member of Talon?" Jakoby asked.

"No, we mainly do it for treasure and dragon charms, which we give to the Wizard Watch. Somewhere along the way, we should save the world, but I think Tatiana is working on that now."

"I see," Jakoby said. "This group has had many people. Perhaps the others will rescue us."

"I doubt it, but we'll find a way." Grey Cloak noticed Than's head hanging low over his chest, and Than hadn't said a word. "Is he well?"

Jakoby managed to kick Than.

Than lifted his head. "I am well, but my heart yearns to see my wife. You must tell me more about the Figurine of Heroes. Has it summoned others from my world?"

"I have no idea what world the others came from," Grey Cloak said.

Than stared at Grey Cloak with his hair hanging over his eyes. "Pry deeper into your gray matter, and pull out more details."

"Let's see. There was Selene, your wife, the dragon lady, an elf with a staff, very polite by the way," Grey Cloak added, "who called himself Bayzog?"

"Bayzog!" Than made and incredulous look. "I haven't seen him in hundreds of years. I thought he was dead. How is that possible?"

Grey Cloak shrugged. "Shall I continue? This seems to be helping. Uh, aside from Bayzog, there was a sorcerer who called himself Finster. Very cold and calculating. Merciless too. He turned my enemies' swords against them and turned them into meat on sticks." His chains rattled when he scratched his head. "Who else?"

"There was the muscle-bound warrior who rode a two-headed dog." Zora couldn't fight her big smile. "I wouldn't mind summoning him again."

Than's gold-flecked eyes widened. "Did he carry a double-bladed war axe and have a gusty voice filled with thunder?"

Grey Cloak and Dyphestive glanced at one another.

Zora said, "Oh yes."

"Is he from your world too?" Dyphestive asked.

"No, he's from another," Than answered.

"How many worlds have you been to?" Grey Cloak asked.

"Many, but believe me when I say no world is fouler than Bish," Than said.

"Well, this one is looking pretty bad," Grey Cloak commented as he tugged on his chains. "Jakoby, can you give us some idea of what to expect? Or are they going to make us rot here in these chains?"

"It's difficult to know what to expect when it comes to the Monarchs," Jakoby answered. "The worst thing you can do is make them look bad. Believe me when I say that they're trying to cover up the damage to their reputation that you caused." He cracked his neck from side to side. "Once they assess the damage, I imagine that we will get a chance to face our accusers. And believe me, there will be plenty of witnesses to our crimes. But at least we'll be given a chance to speak. Matters like this are entertainment to them. They thrive on drama. The truth is, some Monarchs might even support our efforts, but it will only be for show."

"You make it all sound pointless," Dyphestive said.

"Look at us." Jakoby eyeballed everyone in the row. "All of us have committed crimes against them. I attacked them, and Leena did too. You," he said to Grey Cloak, "stole the shield, and Dyphestive aided you. I'm not really sure what Than did."

"Or Zora," Grey Cloak added. "But we were blackmailed."

"We'll all be appointed an advocate. If you can convince them of your innocence, perhaps they can convince others." Jakoby grimaced. "Otherwise, I imagine we will all die or be buried in the dungeons until our flesh rots from our bones."

32

"This wouldn't be so bad if we could sit down," Zora said. Her hair was messed up, and her legs quivered. "How long do they expect us to remain like this?"

"I don't know." Grey Cloak's guilt grew with every passing hour. It seemed that his friends were suffering because of him, all because he wanted to be an adventurer and have a fortune to himself. "Be strong, Zora." Then he hollered, "Guards! Guards! Some of us could use a reprieve!"

"Don't waste your breath on my account," Zora said indignantly. "I can yell for myself."

"I was only trying to help," he said, trying to catch her eye.

She wouldn't look at him. "Do I look like I need your help? Worry about yourself," Zora fired back.

"Sorry," he snapped.

"Save your apologies!"

Grey Cloak blanched.

Dyphestive's eyebrows lifted, and he wasn't the only one. Jakoby and Than looked surprised too. Leena, however, looked perfectly comfortable with her eyes closed.

Guilty butterflies fluttered inside Grey Cloak's stomach as he second-guessed himself. *I never should have rescued the Gunthys. That's how all of this started. I never would have imagined saving someone could have such dire consequences. Now look at where I am. All of my friends are in the dungeon, and I've lost everything.*

"Everyone, keep your chins up," Jakoby said. "The Monarchs might be quirky, but they aren't trying to torture us. That will come later, maybe."

Zora let out a long sigh. "Grey Cloak, I'm not mad at you so much as I am at myself," she admitted. "I tried to escape on my own, and I failed. And I'm really mad that the scarf Tanlin gave me is gone. That fiend, Irsk, still has it. Back in the cathedral, I should have grabbed it."

"Yes, you should have," Grey Cloak replied. "I mean, what were you doing anyway, fighting for your life and trying to save others? You are so selfish, Zora. You should be ashamed."

"If you're trying to make me laugh, it's not working."

Jakoby chuckled.

"And what are you laughing at, Jakoby?" Grey Cloak asked. "You were swinging your sword like a blind man fighting with a broom."

The former Monarch Knight erupted in laughter.

"Did you even kill anybody, or were you too busy tucking them in for the night?" He saw Zora chuckle. "And, Dyphestive, what sort of battle cry was that? How did it go? 'It's thunder time!' Who are you trying to frighten? Children?"

By that time, everyone was laughing out loud except for Leena, who still had her eyes squeezed closed.

"And look at the man we follow, a hermit named Thanadiliditis. Not only is he older than all of us put together plus a thousand years, but he looks every bit one thousand years too. Tell us, Than, what is your secret to longevity? Do you bathe in dragon's milk, or is it because you married centuries younger?"

Than gave him a heated look. Everyone fell silent.

"Actually," Than offered, "she's much older than I am."

The dungeon erupted in laughter so loud that the metal bars hummed like tuning forks. Everyone's faces grew as red as beets. Their chains rattled when they clutched at their guts.

Jakoby was the loudest one of all. "Bwah-haaaa-haaaa-haah!"

Zora let out a couple of snorts that she tried to cover with her hands, but she couldn't stop laughing.

A blinding flash of light interrupted their laughter.

Someone with a booming voice said, "ENOUGH!"

33

THE IMPRISONED MEMBERS OF TALON WATCHED IN SILENCE AS A MAN materialized inside their cell in a puff of smoke. He was above average in height and broad shouldered with white woolen hair that fit his head like a helmet parted in the middle. Fine rings covered his fingers. He wore lime-green silk robes decorated with black geometric symbols. He had a warm countenance but was odd looking with his hard eyes, and he appeared to be aggravated.

The newcomer fanned the smoke away with his robes and said in a deep voice, "I don't think I've ever heard laughter in the Monarchs' dungeons." His voice carried well. "Wooza! I suppose there's a first time for everything."

"Who are you?" Grey Cloak asked. "Are you here to save us?"

"Did the Wizard Watch send you?" Zora asked.

"No, no, heavens no, I'm not part of that ramble," the wizardly man said.

"You're Lord Hyrum the Sol," Jakoby said. "We met before, long ago, in the ceremonial chambers."

"Yes, Jakoby, I never forget an introduction." Hyrum shook the knight's shackled hand with both of his. He walked by the prisoners, inspecting each of them with probing eyes. He didn't say a word as he checked them over, from the boots on their feet to their hands and fingers. He got nose to nose in their faces.

Grey Cloak exchanged looks with Dyphestive and Zora. They shrugged. "Excuse me, Hyrum, but who are you?"

"I'm a Monarch." Without looking, he showed Grey Cloak the rings on his fingers. "See my signet ring, the onyx with a platinum crown? I'm royalty and also an enchanter as well as a diplomat, guild guider, and high giver."

"Oh," he said, his eyes fastened on the rings. The golden gem-studded jewelry reflected in his eyes. "Those rings are very nice. Do they do anything special?"

"Of course they do. That's interesting." Hyrum lifted Than's hands and rubbed his fingers. "Are these scales? Like a lizardman?"

"No," Than said.

"I always wished I had scales." Hyrum searched Than's eyes. "Not from this world, are you? Wooza! There seems to be a lot of that going around. It makes me wonder." He moved in front of Leena and waved his hand in front of her closed eyes. "The Ministry of Hoods. I like them. Very quiet people. This one's much cuter than the rest I've seen."

"Are you here to help us?" Grey Cloak asked curiously.

The older mage rubbed his face like he hadn't slept in days. "I wish I weren't, but I am. I have enough to deal with as it is. But I've been watching you. You intrigue me." He waved his hand at the ceiling.

Two rocky bulbs in the corners of the dungeon detached from the walls and sprouted wings. The yonders floated down to Hyrum.

"You've been spying on us?" Grey Cloak asked.

"And you should be glad I was. No one else wants to defend you, but based on what I've seen, I will. You're not innocent, by any means, but given your circumstances, it's possible the courts could be persuaded."

"You'll be our advocate?" Jakoby asked.

"No, but I'll sponsor your advocate." Hyrum massaged his cheeks for a moment and poked Grey Cloak's chest. "You'll have to find your own advocate. Do you have one?"

Grey Cloak shrugged.

"That's not a good answer. If you don't have an advocate, the Monarchs will appoint you one, but I don't recommend that. It's a very delicate case, and the Monarchs are determined to make examples of you. After all, you embarrassed the manure out of them, and they can't stand the thought of anyone chuckling behind their backs." Hyrum grinned. "Oh, the look on their faces when they learned that they had been duped by a pair of youths. It was glorious."

"Hyrum, what happens if we don't win?" Zora asked.

"There will be a sentencing. Most likely death. More than likely, you'll be fed to the moat monsters. The citizens really enjoy that." Hyrum scanned their dreary settings. "Or you'll be left here to rot, the same as my good man, Jakoby, said. As for finding an advocate, if you can think of anyone, I suggest you do it. And it better be a good one. I shall return." Hyrum walked straight between the bars, like a ghost. The yonders squeezed their eyeball bodies between the bars as well, fluttering their wings until they popped out on the other side.

"Can you at least give us some relief?" Zora shouted.

Hyrum winked at her. "I will." He walked down the hall and vanished around a corner.

"Who are we going to use for our advocate?" Grey Cloak asked. "Jakoby, do you know anybody?"

"I did, but no advocate within these walls would help me. I'd need an outsider, but I don't know anybody."

"What about Crane?" Dyphestive suggested.

"Is he an advocate?" Grey Cloak asked.

"I don't know, but he should be able to find one, shouldn't he?" Dyphestive asked.

Hyrum slid back in front of the bars. "Did you say Crane?"

"Yes," Grey Cloak replied.

"Funny, I've heard that name before. Where shall I fetch him?"

Grey Cloak told him where to find Crane.

"Excellent. Your fate is looking up." Hyrum looked down the dungeon hall and hollered, "Guard! Guard!"

Two Honor Guards in full scale armor appeared. The taller one carried a ring of keys. "Yes, Lord Hyrum of Sol."

"Take those chains off, and get these people something to eat. They're under my protection now."

The Honor Guard unlocked the door, and just as he pulled it open, a dark womanly voice said, "Not so fast."

34

"ELISHA!" HYRUM SAID HER NAME MORE LIKE A DISAPPROVING GASP. "WHAT ARE you doing here?"

The woman stepped into full view. Elisha was the skinniest elf Grey Cloak had ever seen, with skin so pale it was almost translucent. She had delicate but haunting features, and her head was smooth and bald. The midnight-blue dress she wore hung loosely from her body like a dry sheet. As haunting as she was, she was pretty, very pretty. She was escorted by four Honor Guards.

Grey Cloak's heart started pounding at the sight of the odd but captivating woman. His throat turned dry.

Elisha looked down her nose at Hyrum. "There's no time for pleasantries. They will all be heading to trial now."

"Now?" Hyrum balled his fists at his sides. "What's the hurry, Elisha? Is this going to interfere with one of your hundred eighteen boorish dinner parties?"

"We're expecting company, and we don't want to be in the middle of these proceedings when they arrive," she said as she glanced at the prisoners from the corner of her eye. "They could arrive at any moment."

"The monarchy is always expecting company." He shook his fist at her. "That is all they do, entertain company. I'm sponsoring the accused, Elisha. And let me warn you that you are not to talk to them without me being present."

"No, I'm not to talk to them without their advocate being present." She stepped inside the cell. "You are not their advocate, but the court can certainly appoint one."

"No! I'll be back," Hyrum hollered at Grey Cloak. "Don't tell them anything!" He hurried down the hall.

Elisha stroked Grey Cloak's cheek with her slender fingers. "So, you're the mastermind behind the theft of Codd's shield. You're very... young. Impressive."

He felt her cool, minty breath on his face. Her dark, haunting eyes drew him in. He wanted to tell her everything about himself.

"Is there something that you wish to say?" Elisha turned her ear toward his lips. "I'm listening," she said seductively.

"Gum up, Grey Cloak," Zora said. Her eyes were boring a hole through Elisha. "Who are you?"

"The Monarchs' personal counsel. I've never lost a case for them. I don't plan to either." Elisha stepped back and scanned their faces as she slowly rubbed her hands together. "The question is, shall I try you individually or as one? You're a group, are you not?"

"We are called Talon," Dyphestive innocently offered.

"Stifle it," Zora said.

"Talon," Elisha said as she drummed her long black fingernails on her shoulder. "It sounds threatening. I like it. If anyone would like to say anything else, even though I am opposing counsel, I can still be very persuasive to the courts. For instance, if you were to confess, your sentence would be lighter and painless." Four yonders flew into the cell and hovered behind her. "You can trust me. Tell me everything."

Grey Cloak found himself wrapped up in her hypnotic eyes. Her voice was so soft and soothing, like a purring animal. "I..."

"Yes?" she asked as he came closer. "Talk to me, Grey Cloak. Make this easy."

"Grey Cloak!" Zora shouted. "Don't say a word! She's trying to trick you! Get away from him! Get away—*mmmph!*"

With her eyes fixed on Grey Cloak, Elisha stuck her hand out and made a fist.

Zora's mouth clamped shut.

"You were saying?" Elisha encouraged.

He could feel her words pulling the thoughts from his mind and down to his lips. Grey Cloak wanted to admit to everything. After all, his intentions were good, and the court would have to understand.

"Tell me what you're thinking, Grey Cloak," Elisha continued in her soothing voice. "Tell me, and everything will be fine. What happened? Did you steal the shield? Did you steal Codd's shield? Tell me, Grey Cloak. Tell me."

Grey Cloak's voice swam inside his mind, wanting to scream out everything inside. His lips parted. A guilty admission emerging.

A familiar voice cut him off. "Crane! Advocate Crane, that is!"

Crane eyed Elisha and looked her up and down approvingly. "And who might this enchantress be?"

Elisha's long neck slowly twisted. Her stare could have burned a hole straight through Crane and Hyrum. "How did you get him here so fast?"

"As it turns out, he was waiting by the drawbridge." Hyrum walked inside the cell and put his arm around her skinny waist. "We'll see you in the courtroom, Elisha."

Elisha stormed down the hall with her yonder and Honor Guard escorts hurrying along behind her.

"You didn't say anything, did you?" Hyrum asked as he motioned for the Honor Guard to give him the keys.

"No," Grey Cloak said, blinking heavily. His head swam. "She's very persuasive though. I wanted to tell her everything."

"Yes, Elisha is a veritable mistress of charisma. An enchanter, like me. It looks like we made it back in time," Hyrum said as the Honor Guard unchained the prisoners from the walls.

Zora was the first one to stretch out, groan, and take a seat on a damp bed of straw. She rubbed her ankles. "My legs were burning like fire. In a few more moments, I would have admitted to anything."

As the group wandered through the cell and stretched their aching limbs, Grey Cloak huddled with Crane and Hyrum. "Crane, I didn't know you were an advocate."

"I didn't either," Crane said with the same surprised expression. "But don't worry. I can handle this. I'm a good talker."

Grey Cloak rolled his eyes. "So, we don't have a true advocate, do we?"

"It seems so." Hyrum let out a raspy sigh. "Once we get into that courtroom, Elisha is going to eat us alive."

35

THE COURTROOM WAS A MAJESTICALLY BUILT ROTUNDA MADE FROM SMOOTH sections of pure marble. A dome of golden stained glass bathed the large chambers in warm light as the sun quavered high above.

At the front of the room, three judges wearing black robes sat behind a boxed-in dark-oak stand on a high stage. One woman sat between two men, an orc and an elf. All three had hard looks in their eyes, and their lips were drawn tight, like bowstrings.

To the left of the judges' stand was the witness stand, where Zora sat, wearing chains around her wrists and ankles. Her hair was messed up, her face still scratched and bruised.

Elisha asked questions, while Crane, Hyrum, Grey Cloak, Dyphestive, and the other members of Talon watched from their heavily guarded seats in front of the High Council.

Honor Guards in scale armor surrounded the room as well as many Monarch Knights in shiny platemail of the finest craft.

A circular balcony looked down on the main chamber floor. Every seat was filled with Monarchs, who wore the finest clothing, but their faces were covered with cowls or veils. The only other people in the room were the witnesses sitting behind Elisha, who she would call to the stand.

Elisha continued with her hard line of questioning. "Zora, when did Grey Cloak tell you that he wanted to steal Codd's shield?"

"Objection," Crane said. He sat with his hands on his belly, rolling his thumbs. "Counsel is insinuating that my clients had a plan, and they did not."

The woman judge frowned at Crane. "Overruled."

Crane winked at the judge. "Thank you, Mighty Councillor."

The judge turned her head away.

Zora continued, "Grey Cloak never mentioned anything to me about stealing the shield. I was being held for ransom by the Dark Addler. Stealing the shield was one of his terms for my release."

Elisha ran her fingers across the railing of the witness stand. "I see. So, it was either steal Codd's shield or assassinate members of the monarchy?"

"What?" Zora exclaimed.

Loud gasps filled the chamber.

Crane stood and put his knuckles on the table. "Objection. Counsel is putting words in my client's mouth. No one was attacked or killed. No one even mentioned anything about assassination."

"Overruled," the lady judge said.

Crane flopped down in his chair. "What sort of trial is this? They won't listen to common sense."

"Get used to it, but you're doing well for someone who hasn't been an advocate before," Hyrum assured him.

"My great-great-great-great-grandfather on my father's side was one. That's who I was named after," Crane proudly admitted. "I think I have a knack for this."

Grey Cloak leaned across Hyrum to Crane, who sat on the end. "We're getting slaughtered."

"Don't worry. I'll straighten this out when I cross-examine the witness," Crane said.

Grey Cloak leaned back in his seat and looked up at the dome. He imagined Cinder crashing through the glass, rescuing them, and setting all the fools of the monarchy on fire.

It's outrageous that I am sitting here, accused by these blind people. I'm a Sky Rider. A Sky Rider! One of the most powerful warriors in the world, and here I am, being judged by a bunch of wealthy fools. He scanned the crowd of hidden faces above him. *And for their amusement. What a shame!*

"High Councillors, my inquiry with this witness is concluded," Elisha said.

The judges on the High Council nodded.

Elisha took her seat at the table adjacent to the defendants and said, "Your witness," to Crane.

Crane stood and strutted across the courtroom with a warm smile on his face. He faced the judges. "May I please address the High Council?"

"No," a high councillor said. "Question your witness."

"But I believe we have a severe misunderstanding," Crane argued. "If I could only have a few moment—*ack!*"

A sliver of lightning shot out of a wand in one of the judges' hands.

Crane's back arched, and he rose on tiptoe, shaking uncontrollably.

"You will not speak freely to the High Council," the woman warned. She tapped the wand on the judges' stand.

Crane clung to the witness stand, gasping for breath. With his forehead beaded in sweat, he shuffled back to his seat. "No further questions."

THE NEXT HOUR WAS AGONY. Elisha carved up every witness she put on the stand and jabbed them with false allegations.

Crane objected to all of them but did so while ducking underneath the table. Every one of his objections was overruled. So far, the defense had nothing to support their case.

Hyrum brought them into a huddle. "Listen to me. We've made it this far, so they are listening. Don't give Elisha what she wants. She wants you to look guilty. Don't act guilty. You aren't guilty. You're heroes. Keep your chins up, and act like it."

After Talon and their advocates huddled, Elisha called her next witness. "The people of Monarch Castle call Grey Cloak to the stand."

Grey Cloak shuffled toward the witness stand with his chains dragging behind him. He winked at Elisha and sat.

Elisha didn't bat an eye as she ran her slender hand over the smooth skin of her bald head. "For the record, state your name for the court."

"Grey Cloak."

"Interesting, so your mother named you after a garment?"

The court rotunda filled with chuckles.

"Order, order," the leader of the High Council said.

The room fell silent.

"I never knew my mother. I was an orphan, so I named myself," he said.

Elisha rolled her eyes. "I see. An orphan with a habit of stealing. Grey Cloak, tell the court why you stole Codd's shield."

"I'd be glad too." He managed a smile. "You see, my friend Zora"—he pointed to her—"was taken hostage by Irsk Mondo, the leader of the Dark Addler. He wanted Codd's shield in exchange for her freedom. He said that he would kill her or sell her into slavery. I had to do something."

Elisha paced away with her hands behind her back. "That's interesting. Very interesting. Have you lived in Monarch City very long, Grey Cloak?"

He shrugged. "Only about a year."

"That's not very long. But you've lived here long enough to hear rumors of a secret society called the Dark Addler?"

"Secret society?" He raised his voice. "You must have seen the Iron Devils we fought in the sun gods' cathedral. What could explain their presence besides the Dark Addler?"

The head councillor tapped her wand on her stand and pointed it at him. "No more outbursts."

"Thank you, High Councillor." Elisha sauntered in front of the judges' stand. "If it pleases the court, I would like to bring in the man in question, Irsk Mondo."

"I'll allow it," the judge said.

Elisha pointed to the doors in the back of the room. An Honor Guard opened the large brass doors, and Irsk Mondo entered in a wheelchair pushed by Finton Slay.

Grey Cloak's stomach dropped to his feet.

Zooks!

36

F<small>INTON</small> S<small>LAY PUSHED</small> I<small>RSK</small> M<small>ONDO DOWN THE AISLE IN HIS RICKETY CHAIR WITH</small> squeaky wheels. Irsk crouched in the chair. His arm was in a sling, and he had a heavy blanket covering his knees. With his swollen face, he looked pitiful. His skinny fingers stroked the Scarf of Shadows.

"I object!" Crane said as he cowered behind his chair.

"What are you objecting to?" the councillor asked.

"I didn't know about this witness."

"You didn't know about any of them. You were poorly prepared," the high councillor said.

"But none of us—"

The high councillor waggled her wand.

Crane deflated as he sat down.

"High Councillor, the prosecution would like to call a new witness," Elisha said with a smug look.

"The witness is dismissed," the high councillor said to Grey Cloak.

Grey Cloak returned to his seat with his shoulders slumped. He glared at Irsk the entire way, but his stare wasn't half as hot as Zora's. She had murder in her eyes.

"I would like to call Irsk Mondo to the stand," Elisha said with a sympathetic look in her eyes.

"If only I were able," Irsk replied feebly.

The chamber was filled with a chorus of sympathetic "aws."

"You can provide witness for us from where you sit, Irsk Mondo," the high councillor said. "We thank you for your courage to even come here. Please, continue, prosecutor."

"Thank you, High Councillor." Elisha nodded at Finton Slay, and he took a seat at the prosecutor's table. "For the record, what is your name?"

"Irsk Mondo."

"Tell us a little bit about yourself, if you will."

"Objection," Crane said. He caught a frosty look and sat down. "Never mind."

"I've lived in Monarch City most of my life. I was an orphan, not that that was so bad, but what was bad was being an orphan who was part elf and part goblin." Irsk shivered in his chair. "The horrible things that the other children would say about me. And the adults too. Life was hard on me."

Grey Cloak looked up at the sobbing people. He couldn't believe his eyes and ears. He caught Dyphestive sniffling and elbowed him.

"What did you do that for?" Dyphestive whispered.

"You don't believe this, do you?"

"I don't know what to believe. It all sounds so good."

Grey Cloak slapped his face.

I'm starting to wonder what I believe. She's starting to confuse me.

"Well, I learned at a very young age to always treat others with kindness, no matter how poorly they treated me," Irsk said as he rocked back and forth and coughed from time to time. "You see, I was raised by some very kind women in the orphanage. They took care of me, and over time, I came to take care of them when they were in need. They were all so very sweet, and I felt that I owed it to them to carry on with their work and take care of the orphans in Monarch City and find them good homes." He coughed. "It is my passion."

"I think that most of us here are well aware of your contributions to the abandoned children in this city. I for one would like to thank you for your great efforts," Elisha said.

The chamber broke out in applause.

The high councillor tapped her wand on the stand. "Order. Order. As much as we'd like to commend Irsk Mondo's achievements, it's more important that we carry on with these proceedings without further distraction. Please continue, Advocate."

Elisha pointed at Grey Cloak's table. "Irsk, do you know these people?"

Irsk wheeled his chair around to face the table. It squeaked as he did so. He squinted his eyes. "I don't know all of them, but yes, I've seen them before."

"But do you *know* them? Like friends or in business?" she asked.

"No, the first time I ever saw them was yesterday when I was worshipping at the cathedral." He pointed at Grey Cloak. "He was in an awful rush, and I asked him if I could assist them. That was when I noticed Codd's shield. I've been to the crypt many times before. I take the orphans there, as they so enjoy it." His jaw tightened. "That's when I confronted these thieves! These cowards! They tried to kill me, a cripple, for it."

"Cripple my arse!" Zora jumped up and screamed. "He's a liar! He's a filthy rotten liar!"

"Remove her!" the high councillor ordered.

Honor Guards dragged Zora, kicking and screaming, from the court chamber. Zora cursed Irsk Mondo the entire way.

"If anyone else behaves like that, the punishment will be swift and painful."

The high councillor pointed her wand at Crane. "Very painful." She gave Irsk a sad look. "Please, continue."

"Well, there isn't much more to say. I did my best to fight them off, but there were so many, they simply overwhelmed me. Some brave parishioners, however, fought against them. I believe a few died in the process." Irsk let out a long, wheezing sigh. "All of this in the house of the sun gods. Such a blasphemous event to occur in a sanctuary well-known for spreading peace. I am so glad that the horrific event is behind us and that I can be a witness to justice and help see that these rogues are put in their place."

Silence fell over the rotunda.

Talon's members' shoulders slumped, and their faces were blank. They were all being cornered with lies and deceit, and the Monarchs were a party to it all.

Elisha broke the quiet. "I don't have any further questions, High Councillor."

Crane stood. "I do."

The high councillor narrowed her eyes. "Irsk Mondo has been through enough. Have a seat, Advocate. It's time for closing arguments." She tapped her wand on the stand. "We'll take a short recess."

There was no mistaking the subtle smile on Irsk Mondo's face as Finton Slay wheeled him out of the rotunda. He winked at Grey Cloak on the way out, blew a kiss at the others, and waved a final goodbye.

Crane brushed his hands over his brass-button coat. "Well, at least I get to have a closing argument."

"It better be a good one," Hyrum said.

37

ELISHA STOOD DIRECTLY IN FRONT OF THE THREE JUDGES, WHO LOOKED DOWN ON her from the stand with heavy eyes. She cleared her throat. "A great crime has been committed against the monarchy. Not just the Monarchs themselves, but the entire city that they protect. Why? Because of thieves—greedy, self-centered, cold, heartless, murdering thieves."

She spun on her heel, smoothed her hand over her bald head, and faced the accused.

"Look at them, High Councillors. Hard-faced, dirty, and with innocent blood on their hands. They taint this very courtroom with their vile presence." Elisha sneered at them. "Who do they think they are? They plan and scheme to take your, our, historical treasure. The very shield of Codd himself. A symbol of freedom, liberty, hard work, and sacrifice. What would compel them to do this?"

She faced the High Council.

"They will try to convince you of a wild tale about how they didn't have a choice. That they were blackmailed. By who? Irsk Mondo, one of the most, if not the most, benevolent citizens in this entire city. They accused him of being the mastermind behind the Dark Addler, a secret society that rules Monarch City's devious underbelly." She laughed. "It's outrageous."

She approached the bench and looked each of them directly in the eye. The high councillors leaned in, hanging on her every word.

"Monarch City cannot stand for this crime. It cannot show mercy to these thieves. We would be the laughingstock of all nine territories for letting a pack of mangy curs get away with a crime like this. And what about Codd? Yes, Codd himself, who fought so hard, so valiantly, to create a foundation of safety. What about his sacrifice? The sacrifice he and his brave knights made to boldly carve our future by shedding their blood. Is this what those men died for? They died so that the hard-working, benevolent, kind, generous, and loving Monarchs of this fair city could be robbed by the very face of evil?"

Elisha turned and pointed at Talon. "Those men and women are the face of evil. They are the face of everything Codd stood against, everything that he died to prevent. His bravery brought order to a wild territory and made it a haven for all who are good in this world, and these rodents came to steal that away."

She faced the High Council once more. "Talon. That is what they call themselves. A talon is a weapon." She made a claw with her hand and held it up. "It is a weapon used to tear flesh from the bone. To rip the heart out of its prey so the predator can feed on it." Elisha slashed her hand through the air twice.

The audience gasped.

"I warn you if you don't declaw or destroy this Talon, there will be more. There will be more." She nodded to the High Council, turned, and quietly walked back to her table, her heels echoing on the floor.

"Blood horseshoes," Dyphestive said under his breath. "Even I feel guilty."

Grey Cloak's throat tightened. They didn't stand a chance unless Crane pulled off some sort of miracle. He eyed the glass-domed ceiling, hoping the Sky Riders would drop in and save the day. It didn't happen. It was all up to a tubby, wizened fellow named Crane, who had his eyes closed and fingers locked over his belly. The man was snoring.

We're doomed.

38

THE LEADER OF THE HIGH COUNCIL RAPPED HER WAND ON THE BENCH. "ADVOCATE Crane," she said in an irritated voice. "Advocate Crane!"

Hyrum nudged Crane.

Crane's eyes popped open, and he wiped drool from the corner of his mouth onto his sleeve. "Is it my turn?"

"Yes," Hyrum said. "What were you doing?"

"Meditating." Crane rose. "She's really going to let me speak?"

"She always does. You have to persuade two councillors, Crane," Hyrum urged him. "I believe you can do it."

Crane lifted his brows. "I didn't think she would let me, or I would have prepared something." He saw everyone's heads drop. "Oh well, it's go time."

"Hurry up, Advocate Crane. The High Council has more than one case to review today."

"Of course." Crane walked right up to the bench and rested his arm on it. "This is a beautiful, just beautiful, rotunda. I've been all over the world, and I have never seen one so grand." He ran his hand over the lacquered finish of the dark wood and looked at the leader of the High Council. "I bet your skin is this smooth."

She pointed the wand at him. "Be careful what you say, Advocate Crane. This court does not cater to flattery."

"No, of course not. My apologies." He stepped away from the bench, spread his arms wide, and backed up. "Flattery. Monarch City is full of flattery. Everyone is always patting each other or themselves on the back, saying how perfect they are. How perfect Monarch City is. Why, it is perfect." He spun around in a full circle and pointed at Elisha. "Or is it?"

Crane walked as he talked, with his arms swinging at his sides, in a slow gait.

"Everything that Monarch City's advocate has said is pure bunk. A lie. Not true. All she has done is build a wall that is no thicker than the hairs on her head. That's right. She's lovely but bald, and so is her case against Talon. It's all a bald-faced lie."

The audience sat on the edge of their seats. Many leaned over the railing.

"Monarch City, its citizens, say that they want the truth. Well, if you want the truth, if you want justice, then you need to listen." He pointed to Talon. "These men and women are heroes, heroes fashioned from the same mold as Codd himself. That's right. Their friend was taken captive. She was starved, beaten, and tortured by the very same Dark Addler that you claim exists, but when it's right in front of your face, you deny it.

"I want you to ask yourself this. What would Codd do if an innocent woman, a friend, or a family member was taken against her will? Would Codd stand around and do nothing, or would he do everything in his power to save her? Would he give up his shield to save her, or his, life? You know the answer to that. You know he would." Crane's voice was strong and compelling.

"Codd saves lives. Plain and simple. Why, he is the very inspiration for heroic men and women such as the members of Talon. They do good because they feel compelled to. They risk their very lives to fight for what is right."

He faced Talon. "Look at them, battered and bruised. Those are the faces of people who fight the good fight. Those are the faces of people willing to make a sacrifice. If you are going to face evil, then you're going to get your hands dirty. Isn't that what Codd said? Fighting for good is a bloody business! That is what he said."

He ran his meaty hand over his jaw.

"My, what would Codd think if he were here? Don't you think that he would sniff out the truth? Don't you think he'd see right through the veil of lies and deceit?" He looked right at the High Council. "We all know he would.

"Yes, a crime was committed. It was committed right here in this courtroom, where a villain was glorified and these heroes were smeared." He shook his head. "I am hurt, wounded, saddened, and ashamed. How can the monarchy be so blind?

"Well, whether it comes today or tomorrow or years from now, we all know this: the truth will come out. And when the truth does come out, will this court be found on the side of truth, on the side of Codd, or will it be on the other side of the flaming fence?"

Crane patted the judges' stand. "The truth will come out." He returned to his seat.

Elisha sat quietly with her face drawn tight. The dark-eyed woman nodded at Crane. Grey Cloak reached behind Hyrum and patted Crane on the back. Dyphestive's face glowed.

The citizens in the balcony murmured, but the high councillor quieted them down with a tap of her wand. "Order. Order. The High Council will deliberate and return with a decision." She stood and stepped down from the bench, and the other two High Council members followed her out of the chamber.

Hyrum rubbed Crane's shoulders. "You did fantastic! Wooza! You definitely bent their ears and gave us a chance."

"Now what?" Grey Cloak asked. All the members of Talon crowded behind his back. "How long does it take them to deliberate?"

"Maybe an hour or so. Sometimes it can take days. If that's the case, you'll have to wait in the dungeon," Hyrum said. "Wooza, you really stuck it to Elisha. I could hear her rear end pucker when you called her out. I've never seen anyone get the best of her, but you did."

Crane gave a clever smile. "I did, didn't I?"

"What happens if we win?" Dyphestive asked.

"If the High Council rules in your favor, because they tried you all as one, you will be set free immediately."

"Even me?" Jakoby asked.

"Yes, you'll be cleared of all accusations."

Jakoby pumped his fist. "Yes."

The lizardman bailiff standing near the door to the High Council's private chambers said, "All arise!"

Everyone in the courtroom stood as the high councillors entered and took their seats behind the bench.

"That was fast," Grey Cloak said. "Wasn't it?"

"That was too fast," Hyrum replied.

Grey Cloak glanced at Elisha. She had a confident look in her eyes. She offered him a subtle nod that made his skin prickle.

"Sit," the leader of the High Council said. "During our deliberation, the High Council made a unanimous decision. The party that calls itself Talon has been found guilty of theft, treason, wanton endangerment, public menace, and lying under oath. Sentencing will follow immediately. Guard, see to it that this rabble is firmly secured."

39

IN STUNNED SILENCE, TALON REMAINED STANDING AS THEY LISTENED TO THE verdict.

"All members of Talon will be executed by hanging as soon as the gallows are erected." The leader of the High Council's eyes swept through the room and locked on Sergeant Tinison, who stood near the front. "Notify the high executioner immediately, Sergeant. In the meantime, remove the accused from this council room to the appropriate holding chambers."

Sergeant Tinison nodded. "Right away, High Councillor."

As the High Council departed for their chambers, Elisha passed by the company and offered her hand to Crane. "Well done, for a novice advocate. You actually gave me a shred of doubt, which I haven't felt in a long time."

Crane kissed her hand. "Perhaps we can talk more over dinner."

"Perhaps." Elisha waved goodbye and walked away.

"Well, don't let us get in the way of your dinner plans, Crane," Grey cloak said. "Be sure to dine on a balcony where you can get a full view of us hanging."

Crane's mouth opened in an *o*. "I'd never do something like that. It would make the lady uncomfortable."

Grey Cloak bull-rushed Crane. Several Honor Guards pulled him back. "Whose side are you on anyway?"

"I tried my best. I'm sure you'll think of something," Crane said. He grabbed his leather satchel and stuffed his notes inside. "If you'll excuse me, I have to make plans for dinner before she gets away."

Honor Guards escorted Talon to the holding cells in a lockup just outside the courtroom. Gray clouds rolled across a bleak skyline. Everyone slogged along, their chains dragging behind them.

Zora sat on a bench in the cell with her shoulders leaning against the wall. Her bottom lip stuck out, and her cheeks were red. "Let me guess. We lost."

Grey Cloak slumped beside her as an Honor Guard locked them all in the same cell. "You're a good guesser. Care to guess what our sentence is?"

"Does it matter?" she asked. "I knew I was dead the moment I came in here. Monarchs, dirty, rotten, filthy Monarchs. I thought they were supposed to be good."

"They're a mixed lot," Jakoby said as he stared out the barred prison window. "I really thought for a moment that Crane had pulled it off. He gave me hope, even after Elisha spewed her sea of lies. I don't know how people live with themselves."

Dyphestive was leaning against the steel bars sealing them in the cell when Hyrum approached.

"I'm sorry. Very sorry," Hyrum said as he wiped his sea-green sleeve over his eyes. "Even for my kind, this is extreme, and I'm not sure what's driving it. Of course, I've been on the outside a long time. The monarchy has become a hard nut to crack. Wooza. I bet Elisha knows something. Perhaps Crane can get something out of her before they get the gallows built."

"Well, he better talk fast because the gallows are halfway up," Jakoby said.

Grey Cloak approached the window. A group of Honor Guards were lifting posts, setting them in the ground, and hammering pegs into the long timbers. Every loud hit sent a tingle down his spine.

I'm going to have to figure out a way out of here.

Soldiers stood all over the castle's courtyards and paced the walls. Nothing but open ground stretched between the castle and the drawbridge. They would all be shot down by a thousand arrows before they made it halfway. Not to mention, he had no desire to hurt anybody.

He approached Hyrum. "If you know a way out of here, now is the time to spill it."

"Their eyes are everywhere," Hyrum said. "I have powers but not enough to overcome this. I'll do what I can to stall. I'm fairly good at talking." He left, and a pair of Honor Guards entered.

"Jakoby," Sergeant Tinison said. "Someone would like to speak to you before your time in Gapoli ends."

"Beak!" Dyphestive exclaimed as he pressed his face to the bars. "It's good to see you."

"Don't talk to me, you traitor. You are going to get what's coming to you," Beak said bitterly.

"But I had to, and you would have done the same thing," Dyphestive stated.

Beak turned away from Dyphestive and faced Jakoby. She stuck her hands through the bars and clasped his. "Uncle, I don't want to see you go. Not like this. Not without honor. Tell me why."

"You wouldn't understand. I was betrayed, the same as my brother, your father," Jakoby said with watery eyes.

"The Doom Riders killed my father, not the Monarch Knights. They would never do that. They would never betray their oaths," she said.

"A wise man told me that oaths are made to be broken," Jakoby said. "That was your father, Adanadel."

Her jaw dropped open. "Why would he say that?"

"He didn't say it because he didn't believe in the oath and what it stood for. He said it because men are not perfect. Your father understood that. We all strive for a higher standard, but we all make mistakes. Our words can be turned against us." He glanced back at the company. "These are good people. They risked everything to do the right thing. They sacrificed their lives for each other. That is the truth, Shannon." He stroked her cheek. "Remember that."

"I know what I saw," she said with a sideways glance at Dyphestive. "He helped steal Codd's shield."

"Your judgment cannot be so rigid. Tell her, Dyphestive," Jakoby said.

"Tell me what?" she asked.

Shamefaced and using a soft tone, Dyphestive said, "I'm the reason your father died."

40

"What is this?" Beak's face turned red. "I'm in no mood for games. My father was killed by the Doom Riders. I was told this. Is that a lie too?"

"No, Beak, I mean Shannon, it's true. I swear it," Dyphestive said. "And I'm not proud of it. It happened when your father was trying to save us."

"Why would he be trying to save you?" she asked.

"Because—"

Grey Cloak cut Dyphestive off. "Because the Doom Riders came after us. They had a bounty on our heads. It's a long story, and it doesn't look like we have time to get into the details. But the Doom Riders killed your father and many others that night in Raven Cliff. And we aren't finished with them yet."

"I don't believe you." Beak wiped a tear running down her cheek.

Zora came forward. "It's true. I was there, too, and witnessed three of my closest friends die. Dalsay, Browning, and Adanadel." She clutched the bars. "I know your pain, but you need to know the truth. Your father would only have given his life for a good cause."

Tears streamed down Shannon's cheeks. With a sob, she turned to Dyphestive. "Why didn't you tell me before?"

"I was going to when the right time came." He wrapped his big hand over her fist. "I'm sorry."

She sniffled. "If my father gave his life for you, then I know that there is good in you. But I want to know why. Why did the Doom Riders come for you?"

"I would like to know that myself," Sergeant Tinison asked. He narrowed his eyes at Grey Cloak and Dyphestive. "What is so special about you two?"

"It's a long story," Grey Cloak said as he grabbed Dyphestive by the wrist and squeezed. He could tell that his brother was about to blurt out everything, but he didn't want to reveal everything. Telling their enemy who they were could be used against them. He thought fast and said, "If you want to know the truth, you'll have to seek out the Wizard Watch after our deaths. Talon," he said as he looked at Beak, "worked with them. Ask for Tatiana."

"That's all? I must live with my father's demise shrouded in mystery?" Shannon wiped the last tear from her eye. "I'm disappointed. I'm disappointed with all of you!" She stormed away.

Sergeant Tinison remained. He said to Jakoby, "I'll look after her." His eyes scanned the bars. "Looks like you have enough to worry about as it is." He looked at Grey Cloak and Dyphestive. "I have to admit, I'm curious what all of this is really about. It's a shame I won't find out. After all, duty calls. I'm sorry it didn't work out for you, Baby Face. Hopefully it will in the next life."

The members of Talon took turns looking out the window to watch the gallows being erected. The soldiers were hammering down the floor of the platform. A bearish bare-chested orc wearing a loose black hood carried a coil of rope in his thick arms. He carried the armful to the top of the platform. Sweat glistened between the patches of hair on his shoulders and chest as he spooled the rope into the shape of a noose.

"They're going to need a lot of rope to hang all of us," Jakoby said dryly as sweat trickled down his temple. "It looks like they have plenty."

"We have to find a way out of this," Grey Cloak said.

Than sat silently on the end of the cell's bench.

"Well, hermit from another world, don't you have anything to offer? Certainly, a man who's lived a thousand years has gotten himself out of predicaments worse than this before."

"This old hermit isn't what he used to be. I don't see an easy way out of this without killing or harming a large group of people severely," Than said as he brushed his long strands of hair away from his eyes. "I'm thinking."

"Well, think faster!" Zora said. She paced the cell with her eyebrows knitted. "These Monarchs really are something. We're going to die, and we didn't even kill anyone aside from the Iron Devils. Why weren't they brought up in all of this? And Irsk Mondo, that vermin, flaunting my scarf right before my eyes. He comes out smelling like a rose while sitting on a stinking pile of lies. I don't care who gets hurt. These people deserve it. It's us against them, and we have to do whatever it takes to save ourselves."

Leena stood beside Zora, crossed her arms, and nodded.

"Fine, Zora, I'm convinced. We're going to have to make a run for it the first chance we get," Grey Cloak said. "The way I see it, if we're going to die anyway, we might as well die fighting. Hopefully, some of us will escape."

Jakoby lifted his chains. "We won't get far in these shackles."

"No, but they'll take them off before we hang, I would think," Grey Cloak said. "That should give me the freedom I need." He moved back to the cell window. Outside, the burly orc tossed the nooses over the support beam.

Jakoby stood beside Grey Cloak. "That's the high executioner. Though many have tried, no one has ever escaped the grip of the gallows." He put a hand on Grey Cloak's shoulder. "At least in my lifetime."

41

A CHILL CAME WITH THE DARKENING SKY AS TALON WAS LED TO THE GALLOWS. They snaked through the corridors and out to the courtyard, surrounded by the watchful eyes of the Honor Guard and the Monarch Knights. Every one of the Honor Guard had a spear in hand, and the Monarch Knights—towering men— looked on with hardened stares.

Grey Cloak glanced up. The clouds began to spit cold rain. He could have sworn he saw a dragon wing passing through the clouds. The soldiers shoved him along to the base of the gallows. He was followed by Dyphestive, Jakoby, Than, Zora, and Leena. Honor Guards removed their shackles while other members pointed spears at them.

Over one hundred members of the Honor Guard and Monarch Knights filled the small courtyard set aside for the gallows. It was a private area surrounded by ten-foot-high walls separating it from the rest of the castle. The castle's terraces and spired towers overlooked the courtyard, and the unfamiliar faces of the monarchy filled their windows. Others leaned over the balconies, sipping wine and talking quietly.

As Grey Cloak's hands were bound, he said to his brother, "I don't suppose you have any of that flying potion left on you?"

"Hah. I wish. Listen, brother, I don't blame you for this. You did your best. We did our best," Dyphestive said with a long face. "I am proud of you."

The words moved Grey Cloak's heart. "I'm proud of you too."

"Be silent!" Sergeant Tinison said. "You had plenty of time to say your good-byes in the cell."

Dyphestive looked down at Sergeant Tinison. "What are you going to do, kill us?"

Sergeant Tinison fought back a smile. "Keep moving, losers."

Grey Cloak was the first one up the steps of the boxed-in stage. At the top, six nooses made from stiff rope swayed against the wind. He walked across the groaning stage and looked down. A drop floor below them creaked under their weight. He stood underneath his noose and ran his gaze along the rope. *This is going to hurt.*

The rest of Talon joined him on the stage.

One by one, the high executioner lowered the nooses and tightened them around their necks. It started on the far end with Leena and finished with Grey Cloak. He could feel the abrasive rope burning into his skin. It became hard to swallow, not to mention the high executioner stank badly. "Do you bathe between executions? Or bathe at all, for that matter?"

The high executioner went about his business, tugging on the ropes and seeing to it that they were secure around everyone's necks.

"I'm not ashamed to say it, but I'm scared," Zora said with a sob. "I never thought I'd die. Not this way. I don't deserve this."

"None of us do," Jakoby said. "Especially you."

"I'm sorry, Zora. I'm sorry, everybody," Grey Cloak said. He scanned the faces in the crowd high and low. He didn't see Crane or anyone else that he knew. The faces of the soldiers were hardened. After all, he had embarrassed them. Beak's expression was the only exception. Her face was long, and she couldn't keep eye contact. He kept looking. *Crane, you have to be doing something. And where is Hyrum?*

The soldiers parted in the middle as a woman in a long black gown made her way to the gallows. It was the leader of the High Council, whose name had never been said. Her black robes hid her toes as she headed up the stairs of the gallows and stood on the platform beside the high executioner.

The high councillor spoke, and the low talking diminished. "Today, vermin will be removed from our ranks. Today, we set an example for all society. Today is the day that the wicked will taste the swift sting of justice. Today." She turned and faced the accused. "There will be no speeches, no apologies, and no mercy." She nodded at the high executioner.

The high executioner grabbed the lever.

Grey Cloak summoned his wizardry into his hands, which were tied behind his back.

It's now or never.

Without an object to channel the wizard fire into, his fingers started to burn.

The high councillor gave the high executioner another nod. He pulled the lever.

The floor dropped. Talon dropped. Grey Cloak dropped.

I'm too late!

42

I'M TOO LATE! G<small>REY</small> C<small>LOAK</small> <small>THOUGHT AS THE FLOOR FELL OUT FROM UNDER HIM.</small> He waited for the painful snap of his neck. His feet hit the ground instead. He glanced up. He saw all the members of Talon hanging, including himself, but when he turned his head, they were on the ground with him, and they weren't alone.

A handsome fellow with a razor-sharp dagger was sawing through their ropes. It was Reginald the Razor. "Don't stand there gawking," Reginald whispered. "Climb down into that tunnel, and get moving."

"But how?" Grey Cloak asked as he loosened the bindings around his hands. Up top, Talon was still hanging by their necks while the high councillor watched. He felt an icy touch on his arm and turned. "Tatiana?"

The gorgeous elven sorceress stood with the Star of Light burning in her fingers. Her eyes glowed with starlight. "Wonderful memory. Make haste. My illusion will not fool them much longer."

Talon stood inside the boxed-in stage, hidden from the soldiers, with shocked looks on their faces. Then without hesitation, they vanished into the gap like a rabbit into its hole.

Grey Cloak watched above as a puzzled look grew on the high councillor's face. "I think she's onto us," he said as he swung his legs over the hole.

Yonders gathered above the stage, eyeballing the hanging group.

"We need to go," Reginald urged as he pushed Grey Cloak into the hole. "Go! Go! Come on, Tatiana."

Tatiana jumped down into the drainage tunnel.

The black-clad Razor pulled the grate closed. "We need to run."

The corner of Tatiana's mouth turned up. "One last thing."

THE HIGH COUNCILLOR studied the men and women hanging from the ropes. Her head tilted to the side when the yonders arrived and began flying around the bodies. Her facial features tightened as her gaze dropped. She leaned over the gap, and her eyes widened as a middling dragon erupted from beneath the stage.

"Dragon! Dragon!" the crowd of soldiers hollered as they drew their weapons.

The high executioner dove from the stage, and the high councillor fell backward off it. With the Monarchs shouting in horror at the tops of their lungs, the entire stage buckled and collapsed. The terrifying dragon flew into the sky, chased the yonders away with fire, and slowly vanished.

Down on the ground, Beak exchanged a bewildered look with Sergeant Tinison. He helped the high councillor to her feet. He dusted off her bottom, drawing a sour look from her, and backed away. The shaken woman quickly departed.

Under the sergeant's command, the Honor Guard slowly began picking up the collapsed stage.

They lifted plank after plank, searching for the hanged prisoners inside the wreckage. They didn't find a single body. Beak caught her breath. Talon was gone. A grin flashed over Sergeant Tinison's face as he gave Beak a subtle shrug. He addressed his men, "It looks like a dragon ate the bodies. Haven't we chased all those dragons out of the sewers yet?"

43

Talon scurried through the drainage tunnels underneath Castle Monarch, where they came to a stop at a junction.

"Now what?" Grey Cloak asked as the drainage water trickled over his toes.

"We wait," Tatiana said. The gemstone in her hand offered the only source of light in the darkness.

"Wait for what? They're going to find us down here," he said.

"The only way out of the city is to cross the drawbridge or fly," Jakoby commented. "Unless you can traverse the moat and stay the hunger of the monsters."

Tatiana opened her mouth to speak, but Zora crashed into her. She wrapped the sorceress in a strong hug. "Thank you! Thank you! Thank you! And I missed you!"

"I missed you, too, little sister," Tatiana said as she petted Zora's head and hugged her back. "All is well now, for the moment."

Dyphestive joined in the hug. "Thank you."

"Thanks from all of us, but we need to keep moving," Grey Cloak said. "We can celebrate later, but only if there is a later. Tatiana, you found a way in here, so where is the way out?"

"The same way we came in, over the drawbridge." Tatiana's eyes swept over the stone ceiling of the pipe. "I'd advise you all to keep your voices down. The tunnels will carry sound to the grates in the streets. Follow me."

Talon followed the sorceress from the Wizard Watch without another word. They passed one intersection after another and moved deeper below the surface.

The air became stagnant and rank. They stopped at an intersection where the waters gathered at the bottom. Everyone took a moment to catch their breaths.

"I never thought the stink of the sewers would smell so sweet," Jakoby said with his hands on his knees. "I thought we were finished when he put that noose around my neck." He looked at Tatiana. "Lady, you have my gratitude." He switched his gaze to Reginald the Razor. "You too." He offered his hand. "That's a lot of steel you're packing."

"This is my lighter set," Reginald said with a grin. The energetic youth's brown hair swooshed across the top of his eyebrows. He was dressed in black leather armor. Sharp-edged weapons, some sheathed, some not, decorated his body. A pair of longswords crisscrossed his back, and short swords hung from his hips. A bandolier of knives crossed his chest, and daggers adorned his belt and legs. He had leather bracers, too, with small blades tucked inside. He unsheathed a longsword and handed it to Jakoby. "Take it. Anyone else who needs some steel, help yourself." He raised a finger. "But if you lose it, you buy it."

Zora helped herself to a pair of daggers from his bandolier. Leena eyed Razor up and down and took a short sword.

"What about you, old fella?" Razor asked Than. "Can I help you out as well?"

Than exposed his long fingernails. "These will do."

Razor's lips curled. "Uh, sure, even if it's creepy."

"Is there a way down to get out of here, or do we have to go back up?" Grey Cloak asked.

"I don't think there's another way across the moat. Or at least I'm not aware of one. Using the drainage pipes was only part of the plan." Tatiana smiled. "Be patient."

"They'll send hounds into the sewers," Jakoby said.

"Not if they think that you're dead," Tatiana said. "That was the reason for my illusion. The Brotherhood of Whispers works above in your favor. It has faces that work behind the scenes."

"Is Tanlin here?" Zora asked hopefully.

"No. It's best to assume that he's home safe in Raven Cliff, a far safer place than here," Tatiana said as she watched the ceiling.

"What do you mean, Tatiana?" Grey Cloak asked as he looked at the grim expression on her face. "What is it that you aren't telling us?"

The tunnel quaked. Centuries of grit dropped from the crusty ceiling. The tunnel quaked again. Everyone hunkered down, the whites of their eyes showing in the dark.

"Tatiana," Grey Cloak said with growing concern. "What is going on?"

She faced them. "Black Frost is invading."

44

AS THE GROUND TREMBLED ABOVE THEM, GREY CLOAK RAN UP THE TUNNEL AND climbed through a smaller pipe to a street grate. The courtyard was burning. Soldiers barked orders over terrified screams. A wave of flames washed over the walkways and set the gardens on fire as a middling dragon raced by.

"Riskers!" Grey Cloak said as he dropped back into the tunnel. "It's true!"

"Now is the time to make our escape," Tatiana said. "Follow me!"

"Wait, you knew about this?" Grey Cloak asked.

"The Wizard Watch keeps a close eye on Black Frost's dealings," she said as she made her way up the tunnel.

Grey Cloak grabbed her by her long ponytail and pulled her back. "Hold your horses, Tat! If the Wizard Watch knew about this, why didn't they warn the Monarchs?"

She gave him a heavy look. "We did."

"Disgraceful!" Jakoby spit. "How can the Monarchs do this? Men and women will be slaughtered up there."

"Not if they surrender," she said.

"The Monarchs will never surrender," Jakoby argued.

"Then they'll die."

Grey Cloak didn't waste any more time. He ran up the tunnel and didn't stop until the pipe opened into a storm drain running beneath the castle's walls. He stood against the wall and watched the chaos unfold.

Riskers and their dragons crisscrossed the sky. There were dozens of them, grand dragons and middling dragons alike. The Riskers rode on their backs, wearing suits of blackened platemail armor. Many of them had glowing dragon charms mounted in their chest plates. They passed over the castle's grounds like gusts of wind, spewing white-hot fire from their mouths.

The courtyards, the gardens, the storehouses burned. Black smoke carried over the walls toward the city. On the ground and on the walls, the Honor Guard and Monarch Knights were fighting for their lives and the lives of others.

A squad of twelve dragons streaked over the walls and dropped out of sight into the city. The cries of the citizens could be heard across the moat on the other side of the wall.

"They're everywhere," Jakoby said as he followed the trail of dragons flying through the skies, dropping down, and setting the world on fire. "Everywhere!"

The soldiers manning the towers fired their ballistae at the dragons. The long shafts of metal flew true to their marks, piercing one middling dragon through the neck and blasting a Risker out of the saddle.

A grand dragon swept up from the moat, hovered in the air, his wings beating, and set the tower on fire. Burning men jumped from the tower and crashed to the ground at the base of the wall.

Honor Guard foot soldiers pushed catapults across the grounds. They loaded massive nets into the scoops, pulled back the triggers, and sent the nets spinning skyward. The nets tangled up a middling dragon's wings. It spiraled out of control and nose-dived to the ground.

A Risker crawled away from the wreckage with a glowing sword in her hands.

The Honor Guard cut her down with swords and pierced the dragon with spears. They looked up just in time to see a dragon come roaring right at them. It set the Honor Guards on fire and destroyed a catapult with a single breath.

On the wall above them, the Monarch Knights bravely hurled spears and javelins into the sky. A grand dragon flew right at them with a geyser of flame spewing from its mouth. The top of that section of wall exploded into flame. Burning bodies flew over the side and hit the ground with jarring impact.

One knight rose to a knee with his sword in hand and his armor smoking. Another one didn't move. The knight with smoking armor exchanged a look with Talon, adjusted his helmet, and headed back up the stairs to the top of the wall.

Talon rushed over to the fallen knight, and Jakoby helped her up to a sitting position. She was barely breathing, and her face was badly burnt. "Long live the monarchy," she said with a raspy breath and died.

Jakoby's head sank to his chest. He said a quick prayer under his breath. "They're going to get wiped out by those demons of the air!" He stood and raised his sword. "But not if I can help it!" He ran for the stairs and headed to the top of the wall, his eyes blazing like fire.

From out of the smoking chaos, Crane rode up to them with his horse, Vixen, pulling his wagon. Hyrum sat on the bench beside him. "It's time to roll out. Everyone, get in."

Dyphestive rose. "I'm not going anywhere. The Monarchs need our help."

"We must go," Tatiana urged them. "Even we cannot overcome these forces. There are far too many dragons. Monarch City is lost. They wanted it this way."

"I don't care," Dyphestive said. "Running now wouldn't be right."

Crane reached into the back of the wagon and lifted the war mace, Thunderash. "You'll need this!" He tossed it to Dyphestive, who snatched it out of the air with one hand and flipped it end over end. "What about the rest of you? The drawbridge is down. We can still escape the slaughter."

Grey Cloak stepped up beside his brother. "Where my brother stands, I stand." Streak crawled out of the back of the wagon and scurried toward him. Grey Cloak squatted down and picked up his dragon. "Streak!" Steak's pink tongue licked his face. "I missed you too." He let the dragon crawl over his shoulder and latch its claws into his back. He grimaced. "I don't like that."

"Listen to me," Tatiana said. "As much as I want to stand with you, we must flee. The Wizard Watch has foreseen doom for Monarch Castle. You must come with me. We are the keys to defeat Black Frost. You must trust me."

Dyphestive's eyes scanned the burning battlefield. He shook his head. "I can't stand by and watch it happen."

"You can't defeat them," Tatiana said as her eyes swept over the great dragons sweeping through the sky. "It's impossible."

Grey Cloak patted Streak's head and smirked. "We'll take our chances."

Tatiana's face fell.

"Grey Cloak, you take too many chances," Crane grumbled. "Don't make it a habit."

Hyrum stood up in the wagon. "Then you'll probably need this." He flung the Cloak of Legends to Grey Cloak.

Zora joined Grey Cloak, and he said, "Maybe you should go with Crane."

She shook her head. "I'm not going anywhere."

Reginald filled his hands with steel. "You know me, Tat." He spun his swords around in a blur of bright steel. "I hate to be insubordinate, but I never miss out on a fight."

A new wave of middling dragons flew overhead, carrying a netful of large stones. They opened their claws and released the net.

Stones plummeted to the ground like giant drops of rain.

Grey Cloak shouted, "Everyone take cover!"

45

VIXEN LUNGED FORWARD, JERKING THE WAGON AND ALMOST KNOCKING CRANE OVER the back of his seat. Hyrum shot fire from his hands, blasting the falling hunks of stone to pieces. "Get this wagon out of here before it gets dashed to pieces!" Hyrum said.

Crane flicked his horse whip. Vixen sped out of the way along the wall.

The members of Talon dodged and dove to safety from the free-falling stones.

The foot soldiers spread across the courtyards were crushed under the weight of the large stones. The Honor Guards flattened themselves on the ground. Then on shaky legs, they stood up and shook their fists and shouted at the skies.

Another thunder of dragons flew by, and more stones fell like rain. Bodies were crushed, and hearts stopped beating as the dead and wounded grew in number.

"We have to stop this," Grey Cloak said as he stood rooted, watching the skies above. The Riskers, poised in their dragon saddles, pulled back their bow strings and fired shots of mystically charged arrows that blew up their targets. He kept expecting the Sky Riders to swoop in at any moment. It didn't happen. "Where are they?"

"Where are who?" Zora asked as she huddled beside him.

"The Sky Riders," he said.

"Incoming!" Dyphestive hollered.

Another thunder of dragons rose up from the other side of the wall and released a netful of stone. The company dashed for cover under one of the bridges that traversed the gardens. They watched in horror as the ground troops were pummeled.

"How are we supposed to fight an enemy in the sky?" Razor asked. "They're cowards."

Zora tugged on Grey Cloak's arm. "Look," she said as she pointed at two men sneaking across the grounds. "It's Irsk and Finton. I'm getting my scarf back and killing them." She took off.

"No, wait," Grey Cloak said, but she slipped from his grasp. "Stay here. I'm going after her."

He lost sight of her in the dust billowing across the stone walkways. He dashed through the cloud, past a host of soldiers, and into a clearing. His eyes searched left and right. *There she is!*

Zora darted into a servant's entrance that led back inside the main castle and vanished.

He raced after her and into the servant's entrance leading into the kitchen. He ran right into Airius and stopped just before he plowed him over.

"You're supposed to be dead," Airius said with his snobbish tone and a horrified expression. "Why aren't you dead?"

"Because I wasn't finished with you yet," Grey Cloak said in a dark tone. He showed him his fist. "Where did the half-elf woman go?"

Airius jabbed his finger toward the front exit.

"You better hope I don't see you again, Airius. If I do, I'll feed you to the dragons." He ran after Zora and into the main hallway. Panic-stricken servants raced by.

He pushed past them, down the hall, peeking into chamber after chamber. He saw no sign of Zora or Irsk anywhere. He peeked up the stairs, stopped, looked, and listened. Nothing.

"Streak," he said out of desperate instinct. "Find Zora."

The runt dragon eased down Grey Cloak's body and onto the ground. His tongue flicked over the floor. With his nose to the ground, he moved like a bloodhound. He quickly made his way down the hall, making servants jump when he passed.

Grey Cloak followed. He wasn't sure how he knew Streak could hunt down Zora, but somehow he did. As they wound through the halls, he kept his eye out for danger. Aside from the servants, he didn't see anyone.

Where are all the Monarchs? They must be hiding somewhere, but I haven't seen any of them. He'd felt a strange gnawing in his gut ever since Tatiana had told him that the Monarchs had been warned. *How could they let this happen to their people? It doesn't make any sense. What are they trying to do, get themselves killed?*

Three Monarch Knights ran through one of the castle's intersections. The one in the rear caught a glimpse of Grey Cloak from the corner of his eye and stopped.

Grey Cloak hid behind a support column.

"Hold, men!" The knight that stopped drew his sword and fixed his eyes on Streak. "It's one of those demons from the sky."

The other two knights joined their comrade. The knights were imposing figures, regal and well-built. Their shining plate armor was fashioned to fit their large frames. Their open-faced helms were perfectly sculpted around their chiseled faces. They were all light-haired and light-skinned men. They brimmed with confidence.

Moving as one, they flanked Streak with their swords in hand. The one in the middle crouched. "Kill it."

46

ZORA ZEROED IN ON IRSK AND FINTON AND NEVER LOST TRACK OF THEM. THE SLY
pair navigated the castle passages like they'd been there a hundred times before.
They moved quickly, slipping from her sight a couple of times, but she always
caught back up.

You won't be getting away this time.

Irsk Mondo was nothing short of scum in her eyes. He preyed on innocent
men, women, and children and sold them into slavery. Anyone who stood
against him was beaten and killed. At least that was what Zora thought because
many unruly prisoners had been made an example of and were taken away and
never seen or heard from again.

Zora had spoken out against Irsk once. He'd backhanded her so hard it had
knocked one of her back teeth out. His Iron Devils had used their fists to
pummel the rest of her angry words out of her. But she still had anger, lots of it,
and she was going to turn it loose on him.

She lost sight of the duo in a crowd of servants streaming down the halls.
The women had their black dresses hiked up as they ran, and the men, with
ladles and kitchen knives in their hands, hurried them along.

There they are.

The sinister pair slunk down a corridor, parted the huge set of iron double
doors, and slipped inside. She peeked in after them.

Wooza.

There was no mistaking the chamber. It was Codd's crypt. A huge statue in
beautiful armor stood in the middle, a giant shield in hand. No one guarded the
chamber now, only the stone statues of Monarch Knights long past placed
between the columns.

Finton Slay stepped up onto the huge pedestal, pulling his robes up over his
ankles. He climbed up beside the statue and loosened Codd's stony grip on the

shield. He muttered some mystic words, and the shield came free. He unstrapped the bracers for Codd's forearms and worked on the thigh and shin guards.

Those sacrilegious thieves.

With a quick look around the chamber, she saw no sign of Irsk Mondo, but another archway was open on the other side of the chamber. She slipped inside the crypt, her dagger in hand, and crept toward Finton Slay.

I'll take one then the other. I'll make them both pay.

The door closed behind her with an unseen force. She heard Irsk Mondo's laughter echoing all over the chamber.

Shades! He's using the Scarf of Shadows. Zora stabbed wildly near the door.

"Look at this. My wild butterfly has come to seek vengeance. How adorable," Irsk Mondo said.

Finton Slay turned to face her. His hands glowed with rose-colored fire.

"Zora, Zora, Zora, what in Gapoli were you thinking? Did you really hope to stop us?" Irsk asked.

"I don't hope to. I will."

Something hit her in the back so hard that she fell to all fours. It was followed by what felt like an invisible foot kicking her gut. Her dagger fell from her hand. She crawled after it. Her bare fingers stretched for the dagger and came within an inch. An invisible foot kicked it away.

The next thing she felt was a knee in her back, and an arm wrapped around her throat, choking her.

Irsk's lips touched her ear. "It looks like someone missed me. Too bad I didn't miss you. Pest!"

"Your breath is a pest!"

"Finish her off, and do it quickly," Finton said. "We don't have time for any more distractions."

Irsk jerked Zora off the floor. He pulled the scarf from his face, and his lanky body appeared. "I give the orders, Finton. I'll hold her. You finish her. I don't like to get me nails dirty."

Finton approached with a cold look in his eyes. His hands brightened with mystic fire. "Hold still, woman. This won't hurt a bit."

47

<small>GREY CLOAK CLEARED HIS THROAT AND STEPPED INTO FULL VIEW.</small> "PARDON ME, honorable servants of the crown."

The three Monarch Knights turned their eyes toward him. "You're the man who hanged," the man in the middle said. "What sort of wizardry is this?"

Grey Cloak showed his open hands. "No wizardry involved. I assure you that I am alive and not a ghostly apparition." He glanced at Streak, who'd flattened on the ground and arched his neck to strike. "And that is my dragon. He's not in the brood of Riskers flying around. I swear to you that we're here to aid your cause."

"You were sentenced to death, and we shall carry that sentence out. I'll kill him. You kill the dragon," the leader said.

Grey Cloak rolled his eyes. "I don't have time for this. Smoke them, Streak!"

No sooner did he say it than smoke spewed from Streak's mouth. The knights backed away, fanning their faces and coughing. Grey Cloak and Streak dashed past them. The knights, renowned for their skill and instinct, chopped at them.

Streak squirted between their legs, and Grey Cloak jumped over a blade. He landed on one foot, but a knight grabbed his other ankle and yanked him hard to the ground.

"I have you!"

Grey Cloak kicked the knight in the nose but failed to break the man's grip.

All three of them pinned him to the smoke-covered ground. They landed hard punches with their metal gauntlets and kneed him in the ribs, attacking him like lions.

Time to change tactics before they break every bone in me. He might not have been as big as the strong men, but they were a lot slower in their armor. He poked two pairs of eyes with his fingers and twisted another man's helmet around his face. He jumped away only to have one of the knights snag his cloak and pull him down again. They piled on top of him, but all he could think of was saving his friend. *Zora!*

48

Doubled over in the clutches of Irsk Mondo, Zora made her move, which she'd been planning ever since they'd kidnapped her. They might have gotten the Scarf of Shadows, but they hadn't gotten her Ring of Mist. She'd squirreled it away and hid it whenever they'd searched her. She'd tucked the ring behind her knees, in her armpits, her hair, under her foot, wherever they weren't looking.

It had been her plan to use it when she saw a clear path to escape, but that had never happened. Now was her only chance. She fished the ring out of a small pocket in her pants and pushed it on her finger. She lifted her head and showed them the face of a defeated woman. "Go ahead. Do your best. Kill me. But I'll warn you. Talon will avenge me."

"No, they won't. They'll all be dead," Irsk said. He nuzzled her cheek with his long chin. "But before you go, I would like to thank you for the scarf. It works admirably."

Finton spread the fingers of his burning hands and reached for her throat.

Zora curled her fist upward and rammed the ring right underneath Irsk's nose. The small metal flower opened its petals, and a fine mist sprayed out. Irsk Mondo's limbs turned to jelly. He dropped like a stone behind her.

Finton Slay's eyes burned red. His expression darkened into a snarl. "You won't escape me!"

A dagger flashed down at Grey Cloak's exposed chest. He grabbed the knight's wrist and pushed it back. "I'm on your side!"

All four men rolled and thrashed over the floor. Grey Cloak tried to squirm free, time and again, only to be reeled back into the knot of surging metal bodies.

The Monarch Knights earned their title that day. They were fierce and relentless.

Grey Cloak kicked one knight in the chin. The knight smiled in response through the smoke and licked the blood off his teeth. Grey Cloak popped the man under the chin a second time with his toe, and the knight cried out as he bit his tongue.

"Hold still, elf!" the leader said as he grabbed Grey Cloak by the ankles and held him fast. "We have you now!"

Another daunting figure appeared from the smoky hallway and punched the lead knight in the face with his massive fist. The knight dropped like a rock.

Grey Cloak bounced to his feet. "Dyphestive!"

Dyphestive locked arms with another knight, and they started headbutting one another. The knight still had his helmet on.

"Fool!" the knight said. "I'll crack your head open like an egg." They battered heads like rams butting horns. The knight's legs wobbled. He sank to the ground, muttering, "Impossible," and passed out.

Dyphestive, Tatiana, Razor, Jakoby, and Leena surrounded the last standing knight, who faced off with them, his longsword in two hands. His eyes were as big as saucers. "No matter. I'll finish all of you."

"No, you won't," Tatiana said. With a flick of her wrist, the knight flew upward into the ceiling. He hit his head and crashed back to the ground, knocked out cold.

Grey Cloak and Streak were off and running. "I have to find Zora."

Dyphestive hollered after him. "Grey Cloak, wait!"

Finton Slay lunged for Zora's throat with claw-like burning fingers. He stumbled over the hem of his robes, fell, and struck his chin on the floor.

Zora bounced on his back with both feet and knocked the wind right out of the fragile man. The fire on his fingers went out. She reached for her dagger and clocked him in the back of the head with the pommel. The necromancer lay flat on the stones.

She moved to Irsk Mondo, removed the Scarf of Shadows from his neck, and put it on. Then she put her dagger against his throat. With her chest heaving, she said, "You're never going to hurt anyone ever again."

The doors to the crypt burst open.

Grey Cloak and Streak sped inside Codd's crypt. Zora had a dagger against Irsk's throat. "Zora, no," he said in a calm voice.

She sobbed. "He deserves it."

"I know. I know. But this is not the right way. Not in cold blood." He kneeled down beside her and gently removed the dagger from her grip.

Zora threw her arms around him and hugged him tight. "I hate him. I hate all of them."

"I know. It looks like you really gave it to them. I'm impressed."

She broke her embrace, wiping her eyes, and laughed. "Finton tripped and knocked himself out."

"Really?" Grey Cloak chuckled. "Wizards and their robes. You'd think they'd have learned to wear trousers by now."

"A cloak is little better," she said with a sniff.

"I'll never trip with this one. It's like a part of me." He covered her shoulders with his arm and led her toward the door. "We better move."

"What about them?"

"We'll tie them up and feed them to the dragons." He smirked. "How does that sound?"

"Good."

Dyphestive rushed into the room, leading the others. "Whew, you're okay!"

"Well enough." Grey Cloak searched his brother's eyes after Jakoby closed them inside. "What's going on?"

"It's the monarchy. They've raised the flags of surrender," Dyphestive said.

Grey Cloak couldn't hide his incredulity. "What? I thought the Monarchs never surrendered."

Jakoby spoke. "They don't." The dark-skinned knight was covered with half a dozen wounds. "Something isn't right. We must fight."

"We will fight," Dyphestive agreed. "We can't ever give in to Dark Mountain. What do we do, Grey Cloak?"

Grey Cloak scooped Streak into his arms. "We'll find a way. We'll make the Riskers pay." He searched the faces of his friends and added, "Where's Than?"

WILL Grey Cloak and Dyphestive achieve the impossible and save Monarch City? What happened to the mysterious otherworlder, Than?

PLEASE LEAVE A REVIEW OF MONARCH MADNESS. THEY ARE A HUGE HELP. LINK!

IT ALL UNRAVELS IN BATTLEGROUND: Dragon Wars - Book 7.
On Sale Now at Amazon. US Purchase Link:

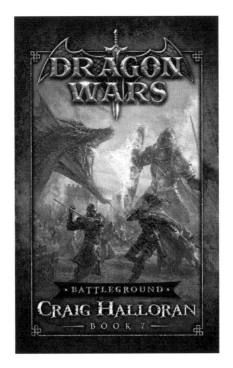

THE FIGURINE OF HEROES/HORRORS – In Book 6 you were introduced to a new character brought forth by Grey Cloak's use of the Figurine of Heroes, Selene. Selene originally appears in the Chronicles of Dragon – Series 1. If you've read the books, well, you know Selene's history quite well, and if you haven't, you might want to check them out. Oh, and Than, aka Nath Dragon, is from The Chronicles of Dragon as well. As I've said in many of my other books, all of my worlds will tie together, in one way or another. That's what makes fantasy fun!

Learn more about Than and Selene at:

The Hero, the Sword, and the Dragon – Book 1

Or

The Chronicles of Dragon Collection – Books 1-10

AND IF YOU haven't already, signup for my newsletter and grab 3 FREE books including the Dragon Wars Prequel.

WWW.DRAGONWARSBOOKS.COM

TEACHERS AND STUDENTS, if you would like to order paperback copies for you library or classroom, email craig@thedarkslayer.com to receive a special discount.

GEAR UP in this Dragon Wars body armor enchanted with a +2 Coolness factor/+4 at Gaming Conventions. Sizes range from halfling (Small) to Ogre (XXL). LINK . www.society6.com

• BATTLEGROUND •

— BOOK 7 —

CRAIG HALLORAN

1

MONARCH CITY

Dragons glided slowly in a circle in the skies above Monarch Castle. Their tremendous wings beat occasionally, keeping them afloat in the stiff wind on an otherwise gray and rainy day. Dozens of dragons had their talons latched onto the castle's walls and battlements. Most of them were middling dragons with black wings, scales like armor, and claws and teeth that shredded metal. Only a few grand dragons were on the grounds.

Grey Cloak brushed his hair out of his eyes. He stood inside the kitchen tower that the elven servant Sayma had taken him to earlier. The small tower gave him a full view of the action in the courtyard. He wasn't alone either. Zora stood by his side, staring out the portal window, shoulder to shoulder with him, her eyes wide.

"I've never seen so many dragons," she said, her voice trembling. "My stomach twists in my belly."

"Don't worry. I'll protect you," he replied as he patted Streak, who was latched to his back underneath his cloak, on the head. The dragon's throat rattled. "I mean *we'll* protect you."

"Huh," she said with a nervous laugh. "If your attempt at humor is to soothe me, it didn't work. Well, maybe a tad."

Grey Cloak smirked. His eyes were fixed on the situation quickly unraveling in the courtyard. Rows of Riskers and their dragons were on the ground. They were face to face with ranks of Monarch Knights and Honor Guard. The soldiers stood in a rigid formation, and they'd laid their weapons down at their sides. They grumbled as the greatly built Riskers, fully armored, wearing their dragon helms fashioned from dark metal, strutted before them. One of the Riskers, a brown-bearded man, had unrolled a scroll and was announcing the terms of Monarch Castle's surrender.

"They should still be fighting," Grey Cloak said as many of the fingertips of Monarch Castle's finest twitched at their sides. "They want to fight."

"Look at all of those dragons," Zora said. "They wouldn't stand a chance against them, would they?"

"They gave up too easily. Bloody Monarchs are making them stand down, just like Tatiana said." His stomach twisted. "How can they betray their own people?"

"I don't know, but it's happening." She peered up at the higher levels of the castles, where men and women in lavish clothing wore stone-cold expressions. "The Monarchs are a strange breed."

"It appears that the Monarchs are only looking out for themselves. That's not strange at all. They are only embracing their selfish nature."

She looked at him with disappointment in her big green eyes and said, "I meant strange looking. It's obvious they are selfish. Look at their gaudy clothing."

He managed a chuckle and said, "It's only a matter of time until Black Frost strips them of that." Grabbing her hand, he started toward the narrow spiral steps. "Come on, let's get back to the others."

"Is that when you are going to reveal your master plan that will save all of us and Monarch City?" she quipped.

"Something like that," he said casually.

"Why don't you tell me now?"

"Uh, I'm still filling in the details. I'll have it ready by the time I'm there."

Zora rolled her eyes. "Sure, if you say so."

Streak nipped his ear as they reached the bottom.

"Ow! What did you do that for?" he asked, rubbing his ear.

Streak stretched his scaly neck toward a kitchen table full of baskets of bread. His pink tongue flicked out of his mouth.

Grey Cloak grabbed a roll and fed it to the broad runt dragon. "Here. And don't bite me again."

Streak gobbled the roll down whole and beckoned with his tongue for more.

He grabbed the basket and fed the dragon along the way. "Save some for Dyphestive. And I mean it—don't bite me again."

On cats' feet, he and Zora stole their way back toward Codd's Crypt, where the others were waiting, without being seen. The halls were empty of servants and soldiers, as they had all gathered near the courtyard to watch their fate unfold.

The two sword masters, Jakoby and Reginald the Razor, stood guard at the crypt door. Jakoby's hard eyes fastened on Grey Cloak's, and he asked, "Is it true? Do the Monarchs surrender?"

Grey Cloak nodded. "The Monarch Knights and Honor Guard are being made to surrender while the Monarchs watch from their high terraces. It's bad, Jakoby. I'm sorry."

Jakoby hung his head. "I might have fallen out with my brethren, but I never would have foreseen this. The Monarch Knights would never surrender. They would die first. Someone is behind this."

Razor grabbed a roll out of the basket, and Streak rattled his neck at him. "I've been doing my fair share of fighting, too, little dragon. I'm hungry too."

Streak flicked his tongue at him.

Razor flicked his back and ate the roll. "If I'm going to die, I'm going to die with a full belly." He glanced at Zora. "And perhaps with one final kiss too."

Zora patted his cheek, smiled, and said, "A full belly will have to do." She opened the door and went into the crypt.

Grey Cloak followed her, leaving Jakoby and Razor stationed outside. They were greeted by Dyphestive, Tatiana, and Leena when they entered. Leena the monk was standing near Irsk Mondo and Fenton Slay, who were sitting propped up against the outer columns, bound with glowing cords of magic. Fenton was out cold, but Irsk was wide awake.

Irsk winked at Zora and asked, "Did you miss me?"

2

"Why didn't you *muzzle* him?" Zora yelled at Tatiana.

The beautiful elven servant of the Wizard Watch cast her eyes down on her friend and said, "He chewed through the rope and swallowed it. He's part goblin, remember."

"He's a fiend." Zora turned her back on Irsk. "I don't want to hear another word out of him."

"Ow!" Irsk moaned.

Leena, a monk with long, cherry-red hair, had started whacking Irsk in the head with her nunchaku. The twin sticks spun quickly as she beat the long-limbed part goblin, part elf like a drum.

"I'll be quiet! I'll be quiet!" Irsk cowered. The beating stopped. The slimy-tongued Irsk said politely, "Apologies, Zora. I'm sorry for all that I've put you through."

"I don't care," she said.

"It seems you do," Irsk replied.

Tatiana spun Zora away from Irsk's creepy gaze and said, "Let Leena handle him. She's good at it." She turned her attention to Grey Cloak as well. "What is going on out there?"

"The soldiers have laid down their weapons. The Monarchy is in full surrender," Grey Cloak replied.

"We can't let that happen," Dyphestive said, gripping his war mace. "Won't they fight?"

"If they fight, they will die," Tatiana warned. "We need to find a way out of here now. I came for you two." She pointed at Grey Cloak and Dyphestive. "We must leave and fight another day."

"I take it Than never returned?" Grey Cloak asked as he scanned the room.

"No," Tatiana said. "We have more important matters to worry about now."

Dyphestive turned his back on Tatiana and stared up at the statue of Codd. "I'm not leaving. He wouldn't leave either. He'd fight."

"You don't know that," Tatiana said urgently. "Listen to me. The Monarchs have chosen their side. We can't change that. Not now."

"They chose the wrong side!" Dyphestive said. He climbed up on Codd's pedestal and started removing the thigh guard of Codd's armor. It was as big as a shield.

Tatiana shook her head. "Grey Cloak, reason with him. We are running out of time." She stared deep into his eyes. "Do you want to win the battle or win the war?"

"I think you should do what she says. I would," Irsk said coolly.

Zora gave Irsk a nasty look. "Leena, can you sew his lips up?"

Leena raised her pointed eyebrows.

"Consider my lips sealed," Irsk said as he scooted away from Leena's fearless gaze. "She scares me."

Tatiana continued her argument. "The longer we wait, the harder it will be to get out of here. We must find a way to get out now," she urged.

Grey Cloak paced with his hands behind his back and thumbs rolling. "If we don't try to stop them now, we might not ever get them out. There has to be a way. There is always a way."

"You know dragons as well as any. Grands that can take out an entire city out there. Do you really think that you can stop them? And the Riskers, some of which are just like you? It's not possible. We must flee."

"I'm tired of running," Dyphestive said. He'd managed to remove one of Codd's bracers and strap it over his arm. "No more running."

"This is not the time and place to fight." Tatiana's cheeks flushed. "And the time will never come if we don't leave now. We need to focus on the Dragon Charms. Trust the Wizard Watch, Grey Cloak and Dyphestive. It's the only way."

Grey Cloak shook his head. "We need to buy time. If we buy time, the Sky Riders will come. I know it."

"Is that your plan? Waiting for the Sky Riders to show?" Zora asked with a huff. "I could have thought up that one."

"They'll show. I know they will. Didn't the Wizard Watch warn them too?"

"You can't count on them!" Tatiana yelled. "You need to trust me now. It's time to quit arguing."

"Of course we can count on them. They are here to protect us," Grey Cloak said adamantly. "They would never let this happen if they could prevent it."

Tatiana clenched her fists, and with fire in her eyes, she asked, "Why won't you listen to me? Why are you so stubborn?"

Grey Cloak eyed her and approached. "What aren't you telling me, Tatiana? What is it? Did the Wizard Watch have a falling out with the Sky Riders?"

"The Sky Riders are dead!" Tatiana shouted. "Black Frost killed them! He killed all of them!"

Zora gasped, Grey Cloak's jaw dropped, and Irsk Mondo's chuckles echoed throughout the crypt.

3

Tatiana took a deep breath and said, "I'm sorry. I didn't want to tell you like this, but you gave me no choice."

Grey Cloak's face had paled. He'd lost feeling in his extremities and barely managed to get out, "All of them? It can't be all of them. How do you know this?"

"I wouldn't say it if I hadn't seen it with my own eyes," Tatiana said quietly as she watched Zora put an arm around Grey Cloak's waist while Dyphestive put a hand on his shoulder. "We were supposed to meet with Justus. He is the one we communicated regularly with. He didn't show. We investigated."

Grey Cloak looked up and met her eyes. "What did you find?"

"There was a great battle—Sky Riders against the Riskers, dragon against dragon. Even the Gunder giants fought. Hidemark was destroyed, all of the Sky Riders and their dragons with them. The entire forest was incinerated."

He responded with disbelief in his tone, "That's impossible. No dragon could have done that sort of damage."

"Even Garthar, king of the giants, was destroyed. Giant skin is resistant to dragon fire, but Black Frost's flame was too hot," she said.

"Black Frost did it?" Dyphestive asked. "He was there?"

"Our spies in Dark Mountain have confirmed it. It wasn't hard to learn, as the Riskers are glad to boast about the great devastation that Black Frost wrought. He stands invincible." Tatiana offered a sympathetic look. "I am very sorry. We all are sorry, but Grey Cloak, you are the last Sky Rider left."

He pulled away from his friends and said, "I can't believe they are gone. Justus, Arik, Mayzie, Stayzie, Hammerjaw, Yuri, Fomander, Hogrim... and Anya? Was she there too?"

"We believe so," she said.

"But she was with me. When did this happen?"

"Months ago, perhaps longer. The crater still smolders like a volcano, so it is difficult to tell."

"Months ago!" He poked his chest. "Are you telling me this happened months ago and I'm only finding out about it now?"

"It wouldn't have made any difference," she tried to say with sympathy, but she had a knack for being cold and direct. "This is why we need to leave now."

"Well, as the fire heats up, the batter thickens," Irsk commented.

Leena clocked him on the head with her nunchaku.

"Ow! You bloody barefooted devil. Quit doing that. I'm a talker."

Dyphestive's mouth hung open, and he shook his head. With deep sadness in his voice, he said, "I can't believe Anya is dead. And Cinder too?"

"Black Frost's flame is unlike anything that we've ever seen before. Again, I'm sorry. I know they were your friends, especially Anya. But we need both of you alive—to help fight Black Frost when the time comes." Tatiana pleaded with them the best that her personality would allow. "You have to trust me."

Zora took Grey Cloak and Dyphestive by the hands and said, "I'm sorry to say this, but she is right. We can't fight them, not now. We need to escape and plan."

"The Wizard Watch told the Monarchs what happened at Gunder Island. I believe that is why they surrendered. They are scared."

"Or compliant," Dyphestive added. He moved back to the statue of Codd with an angry look on his face and started stripping armor from the towering statue's body like a man possessed.

"What is he doing?" Tatiana asked.

"I don't know, but he's been obsessed with Codd ever since he bought that little statue," Grey Cloak said. "Dyphestive, now isn't the time for that."

His words fell on deaf ears, and Dyphestive continued to remove more parts of the polished ancient armor.

"Everyone vents in one way or the other," Grey Cloak said. "Let him be."

Out of the corner of his eye, he caught Irsk watching Dyphestive with avid interest. The leader of the Dark Addler caught Grey Cloak looking and turned away.

With his eyes remaining on Irsk, he said, "Sky Riders or no Sky Riders, we can't stand here and do nothing. We have to inspire the soldiers and fight the Riskers before they dig in."

Jakoby popped his head in the door. He had a concerned look on his face and said, "The soldiers are on the move. Sounds like they are coming this way. We even saw some yonders flying by." His gaze landed on Dyphestive. "What in the other side of the flaming fence are you doing, Dyphestive? Take that helmet off! It's sacred!"

Dyphestive's head was big compared to a normal man's, but it was swallowed up by Codd's helm. He held the bottom rim with two hands and wiggled his head inside. "I almost fit," he said. "Codd really was a big, big man."

"He was an ogre," Jakoby said as he moved deeper into the chamber. "That's why no one else could ever wear the armor. No other knight matched up in size. The legends say he was as big as a giant, but the armor shows otherwise."

"I thought it wasn't the size of the body that mattered," Tatiana commented as she combed her long fingers through her ponytail. "Dalsay told me it's the size of the heart that matters."

"That's true, but his heart isn't big enough to fill that breastplate," Jakoby said, watching Dyphestive try to fit into it. "No one's is."

"It's not very heavy," Dyphestive said as he slipped on one of the gauntlets. He flexed the polished metal fingers.

Razor entered the room and closed the door behind him, smiling at the group. "They are coming."

"We've wasted too much time," Tatiana said as she fished the Star of Light from one of her pouches and faced the door. "We have nowhere to run now. Everyone, come to me. I can conceal us."

Dyphestive said as he watched the gauntlet shrink over his hand, "Grey Cloak, everyone, look—the armor is shrinking!"

Everyone turned and faced Dyphestive and slowly looked upward.

Grey Cloak lifted his eyebrows and said, "Brother, the armor isn't shrinking. You're growing."

4

DYPHESTIVE WATCHED AS HIS COMRADES SHRANK. HIS HELMET BUMPED AGAINST the crypt's domed stone ceiling. With his head tilted at an angle, he gazed upon his gaping friends and asked, "How do I look?"

"Ginormous!" Zora said.

"Glorious," Grey Cloak added.

The whites of Jakoby's eyes were bright. "There is a prophecy of the ancients that has been told and retold for centuries."

"What does it say?" Dyphestive asked in a deep voice.

"The blood of Codd trickles through many rivers and streams, losing itself, only to find itself in the time of need. Codd's blood breathes life into metal. Codd's blood burns like the fires of a furnace. Codd's blood will purify and diminish. Codd's heartbeats are never-ending." With sweat beading on his forehead, Jakoby took a knee. "You are an heir of Codd. I swear my sword to your service. You are the one the Monarch Knights have been waiting for."

"I am?" Dyphestive asked. His blood ran hot as he opened and closed the metal fingers of Codd's gauntlet. The armor fit his body like a glove, and his heart beat like thunder. He stared down at the statue of Codd. "I'm huge," he said in a cavernous voice.

"That's an understatement," Grey Cloak said. "Dyphestive grows and the armor with him. "How is this possible?"

Tatiana held the Star of Light and said, "It is ancient magic that Dyphestive's body has activated, but it won't last forever."

Razor closed the door behind him and sealed them inside the crypt. "Company is on the way, and I don't think our big friend can do much for us from in here. Look at him—he can't even fit back through the door."

Dyphestive began fitting more pieces of armor over his body. He strapped on the thigh and shin guards then added the gauntlet and bracer to his other arm.

After eyeing the sword belt around the statue's waist, he unbuckled it and strapped it to his waist. He also grabbed his war mace and tucked it into his belt. It was little more than a stick to him since he'd become so large. He stood at full height, eyeballed the exit, and said, "I don't need a door. I'll make my own." Bracing his hands against the stone dome above him, he started to push. The seams between the dome and the walls started to crack and chip. Hunks of stone rained down.

"Dyphestive, stop this!" Tatiana shouted. "We need a plan."

"When you're this big, you don't need a plan." Dyphestive's mighty arms were the size of tree trunks, but they still trembled as he clenched his teeth and pushed.

With his hands cupped around his mouth, Grey Cloak hollered up at him, "Use your legs."

Dyphestive glanced at his blood brother and nodded. "Ah, as you say, little brother." His legs heaved under him. "Hurk!"

The crypt's dome popped off at the rim. The red-cheeked Dyphestive shoved the huge lid over to the side, then he grabbed Codd's shield and started to climb out of the crypt.

"Dyphestive, you don't know how long the magic will last," Tatiana said.

"And?"

She gave him an awkward look as she leaned back from his gaze and said, "Be careful."

The soldiers hammered at the crypt's doors.

"These doors are going to give!" Razor said.

The doors crashed open, and well-armed Monarch Knights spilled in.

Razor spun his blades before their eyes. "Welcome to the party!"

The knights stopped dead in their tracks as they stared upward.

"Do my eyes deceive me?" the knight commander, who had a red-plumed helmet, asked. "Is that Codd?"

Dyphestive caught the knight commander's words and saluted. "I'm not Codd, but now I know what it feels like to be him." He rose to his full height. "Who's going to help me take back Monarch Castle from these flying devils?"

The Monarch Knights lifted their swords high. With new fire in their eyes, they let out a unified cheer. "Long live the Monarchy!"

Dyphestive said at the top of his lungs, "Long live the Monarchy!"

The crypt was located on the back side of the castle's outer wall. When he turned, he came face to face with the soldiers manning the wall. Their eyes were bigger than saucers.

"Well, little men, are you going to stand there and gawk or help me fight the dragons?"

The soldiers on the wall started shouting. It spread from one soldier to another as more and more of the Honor Guard joined in. In seconds, all the men and women posted on the castle wall were screaming at the top of their lungs.

Dyphestive set his eyes on the dragons circling in the sky. He shook his fist then reached down and drew his sword and said, "It's thunder time!"

5

Commander Shaw, leader of the Riskers, was overseeing the Monarchs' surrender when the loud cheers from the castle walls began. Though slender in build, the brown-haired, middle-aged warrior was as intimidating as anyone in his black plate-mail armor. He fixed his gaze on the Monarch's Knight in front of him. The knight was older, like him, well built, and had a neatly trimmed black beard. He wore a sea-blue cape with white trim and carried a helmet with a white plume in the crook of his arm.

Lifting an eyebrow, Commander Shaw asked, "What is happening?"

"I don't know," the Monarch Knight commander said as sweat ran down his temple. "We've laid our weapons down. I can't imagine what stirs them now."

"Silence them, or I'll silence you."

The Monarch Knight commander swallowed and said, "I'll quiet them at once."

"You'd better do it at once," Dirklen said. He was standing to the right of Commander Shaw, his father, and was clad in the blackened armor of the Riskers. His wavy blond hair was in tangles from flying on a dragon, and his voice was full of venom. "Or I'll personally stick your head on the battlements."

The Monarch Knight commander dared a look but quickly averted his eyes. "Sergeant Tinison, silence your Honor Guard patrolling the walls!"

The stocky Honor Guard in scale-mail armor stepped away from the ranks of his men, saluted, and said, "At once!"

Dirklen's bright-eyed twin sister, Magnolia, twisted her long blond hair with a finger and eyed the sky. "The dragons see something." She pointed toward the barrier walls. "Something over there has caught their attention."

"That something will die!" Dirklen said.

The ground trembled beneath their feet. *Thooom! Thooom!*

"What is that?" Dirklen asked. He glared at the Monarch Knight commander. "What is that?"

"I don't know, young sire. I swear it!" the Monarch Knight commander answered.

The Monarchs in the terraces above them were bent over the walls and pointing below, watching the activity.

"Father, what is it?" Dirklen demanded.

He gave his son an irritated glance and said, "It's Commander Shaw." He turned his attention to the wall behind the ranks of surrendering Monarch Knights and Honor Guards. "And I have no idea what it is."

The ground trembled faster as the thunderous steps came closer and louder. *Thoom-Thoom-Thoom-Thoom- Thoom!*

The Monarchs screamed as a section of castle wall exploded outward. *Boom!*

A giant knight in full armor burst through the wall like a juggernaut. The soldiers on the walls screamed like their lungs were bursting.

The giant knight stopped and pointed his sword at Commander Shaw. "Leave now, or I'll put an end to all of you!"

Magnolia squinted and asked, "Is that Dyphestive?" Her breath caught. "It is!"

The ranks of knights and Honor Guard started to murmur. "It's Codd. Codd is alive! Long live Codd!" some screamed. They reached down for their weapons.

Dirklen spun on his heel and faced his dragon, who sat on the ground behind him. The towering grand dragon was fully grown, its scales covered in black-and-blue tortoiseshell patterns. Its chest heaved as it glared down at the Monarch Knights.

"Chartus, kill those traitors."

Chartus's chest expanded, and an orange-red flame spewing from his mouth sent the Monarch Knights scattering. Not all of them escaped. Their hair and armor caught fire, and they rolled on the ground while their fellow knights tried to pat the flames out.

"Nooo!" Dyphestive screamed as he charged Chartus. He covered the distance between them in two giant running steps and sliced at the dragon's neck.

Chartus snaked his neck out of harm's way and unleashed another blast of fiery breath. Dyphestive blocked the flame with his shield and hacked at the dragon with his sword. They battled head to head like horn-locked stags. Using his shield, Dyphestive plowed into the dragon and drove it backward. A sword strike into Chartus's side drew a painful roar from him. The dragon squirted away and crouched low.

"Fight me, you moon-faced coward!" Dirklen fired arrows at Dyphestive. He stood side by side with Magnolia, who was doing the same. The glowing tips of their arrows whistled through the air and exploded into Codd's armor.

Dyphestive laughed. "The tables have turned, you little fleas!" He kicked the ground, slinging cobblestones and dirt on both of them.

Dirklen and Magnolia dove and rolled away.

Out of the corner of his eye, Dyphestive caught another grand dragon charging. He spun around and smacked it hard in the snout with Codd's shield. The explosive impact flipped the dragon head over tail and sent it crashing through the gardens.

The more Dyphestive fought, it seemed the stronger he became. Codd's armor seemed to guide him like the spirit of the man that had once worn it. He had a heightened sense of awareness that fueled his extraordinary limbs. *I like it!*

Dirklen was down on the ground, screaming at the top of his lungs, firing one harmless arrow after the other. Commander Shaw fled the resurgence of the Monarch's troop, which had been revitalized by the appearance of the giant Dyphestive.

Dyphestive let out another thunderous scream. "For the Monarchy!"

The Monarch Knights and Honor Guard lifted their voices and charged the enemy.

Chartus lowered his horns and rushed Dyphestive again. Dyphestive braced himself behind the shield.

The dragon's skull cracked into the metal, but Dyphestive held his ground, but then another grand dragon slipped right behind his legs, and he tripped over the dragon and fell backward. Both grand dragons pounced on him.

6

"WELL, I, FOR ONE, AM NOT GOING TO STAND AROUND HERE AND LET THE BIG FELLA get all of the glory," Razor remarked as he headed for the exit. "Let's do it for the Monarch."

"You aren't going anywhere, Razor. You stay with me," Tatiana ordered. "For the life of me, I don't think any of you understand the stakes. We need to have a plan. We need to escape before it's too late. Giant or no giant, there are still dozens of dragons. Dyphestive can't take them all."

Grey Cloak patted Tatiana on the shoulder. "And that's why we are going to help." He gave a devilish grin and said, "To arms." He nodded at his dragon. "Come on, Streak. I'm with Razor. We can't let Dyphestive have all the glory."

The dragon jumped into his arms.

Tatiana hooked his arm. "You need to listen to me. There is too much danger. Black Frost has superior strength in numbers. Now is the time to go."

"I'm not leaving Dyphestive behind ever again." He pulled away from her. "Besides, if the odds are stacked against us, I'll use this." He pulled out the Figurine of Heroes.

Tatiana's body stiffened. "I knew I should have destroyed that when I had the chance."

"But you didn't." He smirked and headed for the door. "Follow that noise."

"Wait, Grey Cloak. What about Irsk and Fenton?" Zora asked.

"You can guard them, or you can come with me. They aren't the biggest problem now," he said.

Zora approached Irsk, gave him a nasty stare, squatted down before him, and said, "Don't ever cross me again, or I swear, I'll kill you."

Irsk waved his fingers at her and said, "I'll try to keep it in mind, fearsome one."

Zora put the Ring of Mist to his nose. The tiny metal petals opened, and pollen spat out. Irsk Mondo dropped like a stone.

Grey Cloak led Talon out of Codd's crypt at a sprint. It was clear by the clamor of battle and the roar of dragons that Dyphestive hadn't wasted any time making his presence known. By the time they hit the outer courtyards, several battles were in full swing.

The dragons attacked the guards on the walls with flames, and their Riskers fired arrows.

Dark Mountain's Black Guard, in their crimson tunics over metal armor, engaged the Honor Guard on the ground.

In the middle of the burgeoning battle scene, among flame and smoke, Dyphestive couldn't be missed. The giant-sized warrior was locked in mortal combat with two dragons trying to tear him to shreds. Grey Cloak had seen his brother in trouble before, but the fight appeared grave. One dragon had its tail locked around his brother's throat, and the other had locked its jaws on his leg. The dragons' claws tore into the armor as they tried to rip away the flesh underneath.

"Dyphestive! I'm coming!" Without thinking, he left the others behind, sprinting to his brother's aid. So small, he wasn't sure what he was going to do. His mind raced. *No potions. No flashings.* He had the Figurine of Heroes but didn't want to use it yet.

Streak squirted out of his arms and dashed away.

"Streak! Get back here!" He pulled his sword and charged, summoning his wizard fire. The sword glowed like starlight. "This will have to do."

Suddenly, Dyphestive twisted out of a dragon's clutches and was on top of it. With the dragon's tail still coiled around his neck, he pounded the dragon in the skull.

The other dragon had a tail with jade-colored scales and swished it under Grey Cloak's feet, but he jumped high over it and sprinted toward the dragon on Dyphestive's back. He'd learned a great deal about dragon anatomy when he trained as a Sky Rider, and he pierced the dragon with his radiant sword right underneath the wing.

The blade sank through the scales and exploded inside the dragon's flesh. The great dragon bucked and jumped away, freeing Dyphestive's neck.

Dyphestive sucked in a mighty breath and dove for his sword. He rolled to one knee just as the dragons attacked as one. His swing caught the dragon with jade-colored scales in the middle of the neck and separated its horned head from the rest of its body. Flames spat out of the dragon's great maw.

Grey Cloak jumped away from the falling head then watched it bounce once and roll to a stop. He waved his hand and shouted up to his brother, "Well done!"

If Dyphestive heard him, he didn't show it. He was locked in a wrestling match with a black-and-blue-scaled dragon. He head-butted the dragon's horns, and the dragon's powerful legs wobbled. He dropped his sword and put the dragon in a head lock. The dragon squirmed and thrashed. Flames blasted out of its mouth and dropped like burning rain on the surrounding troops.

Grey Cloak surveyed the battleground. It was worse than before. The Monarch Knight and Honor Guard were fighting with newfound inspiration, battling the Black Guard and the dragons with deadly vigor, but the dragons came down, spitting fire like burning clumps of hail, turning the courtyard to flame and smoke. Soldiers were dying by the dozens.

Zooks! Even a giant Dyphestive in Codd's armor won't be enough. He fished the Figurine of Heroes out of his cloak pocket, set it on the ground, and took a knee. "Make Tatiana wrong one more time," he whispered. "We need you."

In the midst of a burning sea of chaos, he started to mutter the incantation. The ground exploded beneath him, sending him flying off of his feet. He landed flat on his back and rubbed the grit from his eyes. "What was that?"

"That was us," a familiar voice said smugly.

Grey Cloak groaned when he looked up into the sneering face of Dirklen and the bright-eyed and eerie Magnolia. He hated them both. To make matters worse, Dirklen held the Figurine of Heroes. Without hesitation, Dirklen kicked him hard in the ribs. *Horseshoes!*

7

GREY CLOAK ABSORBED TWO MORE PAINFUL KICKS TO THE RIBS BEFORE MOVING INTO the fetal position.

"Oh look, Magnolia, our old friend Dindae is curled up like a baby," Dirklen gloated. "Imagine that." He kicked Grey Cloak in the back.

"It's not Dindae. It's Grey Cloak," he fired back.

Dirklen tossed his head back and laughed. "Ha! He renamed himself. How convenient." He tapped the figurine on his chin and said, "It makes perfect sense, seeing that you've been hiding for the longest time. I see you even named yourself after a garment. So creative."

Magnolia knelt beside Grey Cloak and brushed his hair from his face. "You have a good eye, brother. It really is him. I'd never forget those handsome eyes. My, how you've grown, Dindae."

Play along. Feign weakness. Then make your move.

"It's so nice to see the both of you. Why, neither one of you has ever looked better," he said as he reached upward. "Ah, I see you've found my statue. Thank you, Dirklen. You were always helpful when you wanted to be." He eyed the dragon and Dyphestive crashing over the grounds. "Now, if you don't mind, I'd like to move on before I'm squished. Great seeing the both of you, though. You look fabulous, all grown up in your armor."

Dirklen stomped on his chest.

"Oof!" Grey Cloak wheezed.

"You aren't going anywhere, worm food." With a haughty expression, Dirklen asked, "Do you really think we would let you go? You are wanted by Black Frost. Oh, how happy he will be to know that we stumbled upon you." He glanced at Dyphestive, who was locked in mortal combat with the dragon Chartus. "Upon both of you."

Grey Cloak offered Magnolia a quick smile. She was staring dead at him with her haunting and probing eyes. She offered no expression.

"What are you talking about, Dirklen? I'm not wanted. All of that fuss was cleared up some time ago. I'd think you would know that, as important as you think you are."

"You still don't know how to bridle that slippery tongue of yours, do you?" Dirklen tossed the figurine up and down. "Tell me, is this of value to you?"

"It's merely a hobby. I've taken up carving since I left Dark Mountain. I find it very relaxing. You should try it sometime."

Dirklen stomped his chest. "How is this for a hobby? Fool!" Dirklen tried to break off the head of the figurine. His pale cheeks turned rose red. "Augh!" he screamed. "What is this cursed thing made of?"

Magnolia giggled.

Grey Cloak whispered to her, "You get me."

"Oh, you think it's funny, do you?" Dirklen's eyes looked like they'd caught fire. "How is this for funny?" He punted the figurine across the courtyard. It landed thirty feet away and splashed in a fountain.

"Nice distance," Grey Cloak said, "but you could have put more leg into it."

Dirklen kicked him again and again.

"Easy, brother. We want him in one piece, I think," Magnolia said.

Grey Cloak curled up and absorbed more punishment. He didn't know whether it was him or the cloak, but he was holding up well, but he played along. "Please, no more! You're hurting me," he whined.

"Good!" Dirklen said. "I'm going to hurt you. All of you!"

A great shadow hung over all of them. Dyphestive stood twenty feet tall, in the perfect image of Codd in his brilliantly polished armor. He had the dragon on his shoulders. The dragon's head was dangling. He looked down at them and asked in a booming voice, "Dirklen, is this your dragon?"

Dirklen sneered up at Dyphestive and said, "Don't you dare hurt Chartus! I'll kill you if you do!"

"Oh, I'm not going to hurt Chartus. Instead, I'm going to hurt you"—Dyphestive pushed the dragon high over his head—"with him!"

Dirklen started to back away, fear filling his eyes. "What are you doing? Put Chartus down! Put him down now!"

"If you say so." Dyphestive tossed the dragon down at Dirklen.

The dragon's huge body landed on Dirklen as he was diving out of the way. Dirklen escaped just in time, but he was pinned underneath the dragon's tail. His fists hammered the ground. "I'll kill you! I'll kill all of you!"

"Magnolia, if you weren't twins, I'd swear that he wasn't your brother," Grey Cloak said.

She caressed his cheek and said, "You were always so clever, Dindae. I missed that. It was quite entertaining." Her eyes glowed with inner fire. "But family is family." She sent a jolt of energy straight from her fingertips and right into him.

Grey Cloak felt like his head would pop, and bright shards of light exploded behind his eyes. "Aaah!" he cried as a painful tingling sensation raced through the entirety of his body. He rolled across the ground, writhing in pain. He couldn't see anything but bright light. "What did you do to me?"

"That was only a kiss from my wizard fire," she said. "Would you like another one?"

"No, thank you," he moaned with his teeth clattering.

Magnolia dropped his head on the ground and moved away.

Grey Cloak blinked repeatedly, and his vision began to clear. He saw a blurry vision of Magnolia pulling her brother from underneath the dragon's tail. Dyphestive was swarmed by middling fire-breathing dragons, and the rest of his friends were nowhere to be seen, but soldiers battled among the smoke and fire all around. Judging by the pained battle cries and the growing thunder of dragons in the sky, even with a giant-sized Dyphestive, they were losing.

Must move. Need the figurine. He eyed the fountain where the figurine lay and started muttering the mystic words of incantation, but his numb lips struggled with the twisting and enchanted words. *Zooks!*

8

THE BLACK GUARD THRUST THEIR FORCES INTO THE COURTYARD, ENGAGING IN battle with the Monarchy's finest. The stalwart troops were terrifying in their crimson tunics over chain-mail armor. A black mountain was embroidered on each of their chests. Their helmets were angular, not rounded, open-faced, with ridge-like spikes on the top.

Reginald the Razor watched the Black Guard and Honor Guard colliding in a ringing clash of steel, and he gripped his swords so tightly that his knuckles were white. He said to Tatiana, "I know that it is my sworn duty to protect you, but I think the side of good could use a hand."

Tatiana gave a deep sigh and said, "No one else is listening to me. Why should you? Go. But don't die."

He was already running when he said, "My gratitude." He'd watched Jakoby engage the enemy until he was about to burst. The older Monarch Knight had proved to be a fine swordsman, but Razor was out to prove he was better. Armed to the teeth with swords and knives, he attacked with the speed of a viper.

The first two Black Guard didn't see him coming. They were sizeable men, chopping away at the Honor Guard, using bastard swords two-handed. Razor stuck one in the chest and the other in the ribs. The men crumpled to the ground, and he used them like springboards and launched himself at the next ones.

"Here comes the Razor!" he shouted.

Steel rang against steel. *Clang! Bang! Rip! Slice!*

The heavily armored Black Guard were no match against Razor's speed and skill. He parried two sword strikes at the same time and countered and filled their bellies full of steel. He blocked, ducked, cut, and killed over and over again.

The Black Guard fell one after the other, but their superior numbers were closing in.

"Fight!" he shouted. "Fight, Honor Guard. Fight! Fight like Codd!"

Razor's words lifted the Honor Guards' spirits. Using sword and spear, they thrust forward and attacked, pushing the Black Guard back toward the wall. Bodies piled up in heaps of metal, and the tide was turning—until a tide of red-hot flame came from the sky.

The Honor Guard stood their ground, battling and burning. Another wave of dragons flew overhead.

Razor screamed, "Get down!"

"STAY WITH ME, Zora, if you want to live," Tatiana said. She was tucked underneath one of the archway bridges that ran through the gardens. "Or not. No one wants to listen to me regardless."

"No need to be so cynical," Zora said as she watched the horrific battle unfolding. The Honor Guard and Monarch Knights fought valiantly, but even with a giant-sized Dyphestive, she could see that it was only a matter of time before the dragons took over. "There's more Black Guard out there, isn't there?"

Tatiana spoke with a faraway look in her eyes. "Dark Mountain's forces come from the north. They have already overtaken the north bridge that crosses the Outer Ring. That is where the Black Guard are coming from. They fill the city." She sighed. "This is what I tried to warn everyone about. There is no winning. The cause is lost. We have to fight another day."

"What are you going to do? Stand here and watch?" Zora said. "Or fight with your friends?"

"I'm a member of the Wizard Watch. I'll serve my purpose. If I must fight, I will fight, but at the moment, I'm trying to find a way out of this madness that Grey Cloak and Dyphestive have caused."

"You can't blame them for trying to do the right thing. They are following their hearts."

"The heart is full of foolishness. That is a weakness." Tatiana shook her head and looked at Zora. "I'm sorry, dear sister, but I know what I am talking about. The Wizard Watch has seen many outcomes. In almost all of them, we lose."

"Almost all?"

"I'll put it in terms that you will understand. Almost one hundred outcomes to one."

Zora's heart sank. As much as she was caught up in the bravery of Grey Cloak and Dyphestive, she felt the wisdom and truth of Tatiana's words. Judging by the burning and bloody battle scene, she knew it would take a miracle to save them. "What do you want me to do?"

"Don the Scarf of Shadows and find Crane. He has the only means to get all of us out of this." She shook her head as she eyed the dragons in the sky. "But even his wagon can't outrun those dragons."

THE MIDDLING DRAGONS were half as big as the grand dragons Dyphestive had faced, but there were many. Three middlings, saddled with riders firing arrows, had latched onto Dyphestive's legs with teeth and claws.

"Get off me!" Dyphestive said as he kneed a dragon in the snout.

A Risker shot him in the nose with an exploding arrow.

"Ow!" He reached down, yanked the man from the saddle, and flung him over the castle wall and into the moat.

A middling dragon flew into the middle of his back, horns first, and knocked him to his knees. Two more dragons latched on. There were five in all, eating away at his armor, trying to strip it off.

"I've had enough of this!" Dyphestive caught sight of Codd's sword lying on the ground nearby. With a loud groan, he crawled to it. He wrapped his fingers around the handle and fought his way up to stand.

The dragons tried to pull him down like slithering angry vines. Flames shot out of their mouths and burned his skin.

He said through clenched teeth, "Enough!"

With a downward thrust, he skewered a dragon. It let out an ear-splitting scream, and its rider dropped out of the saddle. It was a man with a glowing dragon charm shining on his chest. Dyphestive clubbed the man with the flat of his sword, sending him head over heels into the flower gardens.

Dyphestive took another swing and sheared a dragon's tail off. He popped another one in the snout with the pommel then stabbed the other two dragons at his feet. Codd's sword cleaved their scales like a hot knife through butter. Its shiny blade burned brighter with each successful attack.

"Yes!" Dyphestive bellowed. "Yes! I'm going to be wearing a dragon-skin vest and boots to dinner tonight!" The great sword struck with dazzling ferocity. Dragon and rider were torn asunder. "Come, sky devils! Come and die!"

Dragons fell like leaves. He killed them in twos and fours. A dozen lay dead at his feet when the Riskers turned their dragons back into the sky.

"Come, cowards! Fight!" he yelled as he slung dragon blood from his sword. His helmet slipped over his eyes, and when he pushed it back up, he felt a falling sensation. The ground and the dead dragons at his feet seemed to be growing. "What?" he muttered. "Oh no, I'm shrinking."

9

GREY CLOAK RUBBED HIS EYES. HE STILL HAD BLURRY PURPLE SPOTS, BUT HIS VISION was getting better. He crawled to the fountain and peered into the murky water. "Thunderbolts," he muttered as he stared at all the lily pads resting on top of the green-algae-filled water. Then he looked over his shoulder and saw Dyphestive shrinking foot by foot, second by second. "Thunderbolts!"

He crawled into the decorative fountain and ran his hands along the slimy basin. "Where are you? Where are you? Where are you?"

Dragons passed overhead like great shadows. They covered the sky like small clouds.

"How many of them are there?" he asked as he sloshed through the water on his hands and knees. Inky green water splashed into this mouth. "Ugh!" He spat. "That's nasty. Am I talking to myself? Zooks, I am."

He searched through the fountain's muck and cross-examined his decisions.

Perhaps I should have listened more to Tatiana.

We were going to be dead one way or the other.

There is always a way to escape.

How could I stand by and let Black Frost take this city?

Maybe I should have let the Monarchs surrender.

It's not my fault Dyphestive turned into a giant.

Oh my, there are coins in here. Lots of them! I won't die with my pockets empty.

His eyes swept through the smoke and mayhem. *This is chaos.*

His fingers gently seized a rock-hard object, and he jerked it out of the water. It was the slime-covered Figurine of Heroes. "There you are!"

Grey Cloak set the figurine on the ground. At the moment, no one was paying attention to him. Magnolia was still trying to free Dirklen from underneath the dragon. Dyphestive had started running his way, shaking free of Codd's armor as he did so, but he dragged the shield with him.

"Streak! Streak!" *Where is he?*

The runt dragon had vanished, and Grey Cloak could only imagine that he was hiding. If his little friend was safe, he was all right with that. *I'll find him later —if there is a later.*

With a passing glance, he spied Than, of all people, huddled in the gardens, away from the fighting, kneeling with his scaly hands on Streak. The runt dragon flicked his tongue and appeared to nod at Than.

What in Gapoli is going on over there? "Streak!" Grey Cloak called. "Get over here!"

No sooner did his words part his lips than Dirklen's dragon, Chartus, rose back up, freeing Dirklen, and Magnolia dragged her brother away. The grand dragon set his venomous gaze on Dyphestive, stopping him in his tracks, then it took a deep breath and let its scorching flame out. Dyphestive tucked his body underneath the shield.

Without even thinking, Grey Cloak started muttering the incantation to the Figurine of Heroes. The complicated arcane words twisted his tongue and rolled out of his mouth with a life of their own.

The Figurine of Heroes trembled and started to spew inky-black smoke. Grey Cloak fanned his hand in front of his face. He caught a glimpse of Dyphestive facing Chartus, whose flames had died down. Dyphestive's hair was smoking, and his eyebrows were singed off. Chartus stomped on him, smashing him underneath Codd's shield.

"Nooo!" Grey Cloak screamed. "Nooo!"

10

Under the protection of the Scarf of Shadows's invisibility, Zora weaved her way through the sea of chaos. She jumped over the dead and the living, dodged fireballs dropping from the sky, and ducked under a spear that sailed errantly. *Flaming fences! Nowhere is safe!*

With the bodies of men and dragons violently surging against one another, she dashed for higher ground at the castle wall. She couldn't be certain what Tatiana wanted from Crane, but she heavily suspected that she wanted the services of his magic wagon to haul them out of the grounds of Monarch Castle.

She took the steps four at a time and made it to the castle wall then searched from behind the parapets. Though she saw no sign of Crane, there was bombing and bloodshed everywhere. The rallied forces of the Monarchs had lost their wind, and the swarming dragons were taking them down.

Where are you, Crane? She spun around and looked over the castle moat from between the battlements. The drawbridge was down, and more Black Guard were marching into the city. She followed their approach and watched them pass under the castle's massive portcullis and under the gates. That was when she got her first glimpse of her target. *Crane! What is he doing?*

He was sitting on the wagon bench, eating a green apple, as if nothing else in the world were going on. The weird thing was that no one else paid him any mind. *Crazy Crane!*

She raced back down the steps, sliding by a battling Black Guard and Honor Guard on the way down. After jumping the last flight of steps, she hit the ground running, hoping she could reach Crane and rescue the others in time.

GREY CLOAK WATCHED with wide eyes as Chartus ground his brother into the ground. A chill raced down his spine as a dark-gray fog-like smoke rolled over his shoulders. He turned.

Two figures stood within the figurine's mist, which had started to clear away. They were a man and a woman, both human, wearing deep-blue bodysuits like a second skin. The woman had a serious look on her pretty face, and her straight hair was as dark as a raven's feathers. She held a long and narrow contraption with both hands.

The man beside her was a different story. Handsome, strapping, and rugged, he had waves in his dark-brown hair and stubble on his face, and small mirrors covered his eyes. What looked like metal darts were strapped over his brawny shoulders.

They had belts of strange gear on their hips, and they both wore strange laced-up boots, their chins lifted skyward.

The woman asked in a serious voice, "John, what did you get us into this time?"

"It wasn't me, but I like it," John replied confidently. "Those are dragons." He glanced at Grey Cloak. "Are you an elf?"

"Yes."

"Is this world Titanuus?"

"No, it's Gapoli." He straightened his back and said, "My name is Grey Cloak. I summoned you. I really hope you are on my side. It's been a bad day."

"I'm Smoke. This is my wife, Sid, and I think we're here to help," he said casually as he eyeballed the monstrous dragon Chartus. "You seem all right, Grey Cloak. So tell me, is that one dragon the reason you summoned us?"

"John, this had better not be one of your games. I have to pick little John up from school in an hour," Sid said.

"Text your parents," Smoke said.

"Yeah, I don't see any cell towers around here," she replied.

Grey Cloak eyed the strange contraptions that they were carrying. "I hope those are weapons."

"Oh, they're weapons, all right," Smoke said with a small grin. "This is called an M-60 machine gun. It's sort of like a crossbow or a fancy sling, but bullets are a lot, lot, lot better than arrows or bolts. Sid is carrying a 50-caliber sniper rifle. She's the best shot in the family, so she gets the big gun. So which of these dragons is causing a problem?"

"All of them." He pointed at Chartus and said, "Starting with that one."

Smoke fed a belt of bullets into his weapon and said, "I think we might need the blue tips. Those dragon scales look pretty thick."

"You go blue," Sid said as she put the stock of her weapon against her shoulder and aimed for the sky. "I'll go red."

"Works for me," Smoke said as if he had ice water in his veins. "Hey, Grey Cloak, you might better cover those pointy ears. These fireworks are really loud." He aimed at the spiny ridges of Chartus's back. "Let's make some noise."

Grey Cloak stepped to the side, covered his ears, and took a knee.

The muzzle of Smoke's weapon exploded with fire. Blue bullets streaked through the air. The machine gun roared. *Puppah-puppah-puppah-puppuh!* Brass casings spit out of the machine gun like drops from a waterfall.

Chartus reared like he'd been stung by a humongous hornet. The machine gun bullets ripped a hole through his scales and bones. Erratic flames started to spit from his mouth. He wobbled and teetered on his monster legs.

"Zooks," Grey Cloak said with awe as he watched the grand dragon fall down dead with a *whump.*

Dirklen was on his feet and ran to his dragon, screaming, "No! Nooo!"

Magnolia shot Grey Cloak a bewildered look and eyed the machine-gun-wielding warrior raining down death.

Krak-kow! A sound like a lightning strike made Grey Cloak and Magnolia flinch. The jarring sound was followed by a fiery explosion in the sky. Dragon bits, bones, scales, and pieces rained down. A Risker plummeted to his imminent death.

With one eye closed and the barrel pointed toward the sky, Sid fired her massive sniper rifle again. *Krak-kow!* A red missile rocketed through the air in a glowing streak of fury. The bullet exploded inside the chest of a middling dragon.

"Flaming fences! This is incredible!" Grey Cloak watched in awe as the husband and wife tore the skies to pieces in tandem. Dragons spiraled out of control and dropped like rain. The duo from another dimension stuck it to the evil fiends in the sky.

Krak-kow!

Puppah-puppah-puppah-pappuh!

Puppah-puppah-puppah-pappuh!

Puppah-puppah-puppah-pappuh!

Krak-kow!

Puppah-puppah-puppah-pappuh!

Puppah-puppah-puppah-pappuh!

Krak-kow!

"Grey Cloak, what about the guys in armor?"

"Guys?" he replied. "Oh, the Black Guard in crimson are bad. The rest, in sashes, white, and scale mail, are good."

"John, I need cover! They're diving!" Sid said as the dragons came right at her.

"Makes sense." Smoke whipped the barrel of his machine gun around and unleashed his fury. *Puppah-puppah-puppah-pappuh! Puppah-puppah-puppah-pappuh!*

A middling dragon and its Risker crashed to the ground twenty feet away. Bullets ripped another dragon's wing apart, and the dragon spiraled out of control and crashed into a castle tower.

"Crud! I'm empty!" Smoke said as he dropped to a knee and loaded more bullets. "Stay low, Sid. Those butterflies breathe fire, you know."

Sid fired again. *Krak-kow!*

"They eat fire too!" she said as she watched another dragon explode in the sky. "I'm empty! Cripes!"

Smoke fed his bullets into the chamber and charged a small handle on his weapon. His mirrored eyes landed on Dirklen and Magnolia, who approached with glowing swords in their hands.

Dirklen was frothing at the mouth, and his chest was heaving. "You killed my dragon!" Dirklen said. "Now I'm going to kill both of you!"

11

"What about them? Do you want me to waste them?" Smoke asked of Dirklen and Magnolia.

The words were strange, but Grey Cloak caught the meaning. "Absolutely. Waste them!"

Smoke let out a fiery blast that should have cut the wicked brother and sister down like saplings. Instead, they jumped over ten feet high, and the bullets passed beneath them.

"Leaping lizards, they jump like frogs in that armor. Cool," Smoke said.

Dirklen landed right in front of Smoke and knocked the gun barrel aside. Magnolia dropped in front of Grey Cloak and slashed at him. He ducked underneath the lethal blade and leg-swept her from her feet.

"That's the spirit. Sweep the leg!" Smoke said as he danced away from Dirklen's heavy-handed chops.

Magnolia hopped up from being flat on her back and faced off against Grey Cloak again. "You've come a long way since the last time I saw you."

He pulled his sword. "You have no idea, but lucky for you, I'm happy to accept your surrender."

"Ha!" She thrust.

He parried and counterstruck.

She parried and returned her own strike, which almost took off his nose. "I always liked you. It will be a shame to kill you."

"I wish I could say the same," he said.

They went back and forth, blades clashing, twisting and spinning. Magnolia was really good, but all Riskers were. The fire dancing on her blade seemed to make her quicker. Grey Cloak summoned fire of his own and sent it coursing up his blade.

Her eyes widened, and she said, "I see you can use the wizard fire."

"We call it wizardry," he replied as his quick thrusts forced her to backpedal.

"We who?" she said.

He thought of the Sky Riders. Their loss set his veins on fire. "We! Me!" He hit her sword so hard that he knocked it out of her hands. "Ha!" He put his blade to her neck. "Surrender!"

"Or what? You won't kill me. You aren't a killer," the bright-eyed Magnolia said.

Her eerie gaze drew him in, and he said, "I-I what..." He lost his train of thought.

Magnolia whisked a dagger out of her belt and punched at his belly. He twisted sideways, but the blade cut through his side. Awakening from the haze she'd put on him, he lashed out with his sword.

Magnolia backflipped out of his reach. When she stood up, she lifted her arms and winked. "Goodbye, Grey Garment."

A middling dragon soared over head and took her up in its talons. Wings beating hard against the wind, it took her up and away. She climbed onto the dragon's back and waved goodbye.

Krak-kow! Krak-kow! Sid was on one knee, blasting dragon after dragon out of the sky.

Smoke and Dirklen were fighting, and Dirklen knocked Smoke's weapon out of his hands.

"You are finished now, mirror-eyes!" Dirklen pounced at the rangy warrior and brought his sword down hard.

Smoke slid away from the sword with the ease of a cat. He kicked the overextended Dirklen in the hip and knocked him off balance. At the same time, he pulled two smaller handheld weapons from his hips and pointed them at Dirklen. Dirklen turned and rushed in to attack.

Blam! Blam! Blue bullets blasted out of Smoke's weapons and pierced Dirklen's armor. Dirklen screeched like a wounded bird of prey.

A grand dragon dove out of the sky and snatched Dirklen up. The dragon's rider was Commander Shaw.

Smoke fired bullets at the huge dragon as it escaped into the sky. He spun his weapons on his fingers, stuffed them back into the holsters, and snatched up his machine gun. "Honey, how are you holding up?"

Krak-kow! "I'll probably go deaf from a lack of hearing protection, but otherwise, I'm fine," Sid said.

The dynamic pair stood back to back and blasted away into the sky. The dragons retreated to the clouds and circled. *Krak-kow!* Sid blasted a dragon from one thousand feet away.

"You're the best, baby," Smoke said as he lowered his barrel and pointed it toward the Black Guard. *Puppah-puppah-puppah-puppuh!*

Smoke shredded the crimson tunics' ranks. As rows of men fell underneath the lethal onslaught, the bullets started to pass through the bewildered men like ghosts.

"What's happening?" Sid asked. Her and Smoke's hard bodies started to fade.

"It appears that the vacation to the dragon land is over," Smoke replied as his body started to vanish. "Bummer." He eyed Grey Cloak. "Summon us back anytime. And if you ever swing by my world, I'll buy you a milkshake."

As fast as the otherworldly warriors had come, they were gone again in a puff of smoke.

Grey Cloak snared the figurine and dropped it into his pocket. The Riskers' forces continued to circle above but from a very long distance. Meanwhile, the soldiers on the ground were still battling for their lives.

A thought snared him. *Dyphestive!*

12

GREY CLOAK FOUND DYPHESTIVE LYING UNDERNEATH CODD'S SHIELD WITH HIS feet stuck out at the bottom. He pried the shield away from the ground and tossed the shield aside. Dyphestive's body was pressed into the ground. His eyes were as big as moons, and his fingers were wiggling.

"Are you well? Are you well?" Grey Cloak shook him.

"Aside from feeling like I was stomped by a dragon, yes," Dyphestive replied with a crooked smile that revealed a split lip. "Is it gone?"

"Dead," Grey Cloak said as he nodded at Chartus. "Can you move?"

"I've been trying to. I feel like I've been stuffed into a coffin that was too small. Dragons are heavy."

"It's a good thing you are as hard as stone." He grabbed his brother's arm and pulled, rolling him to his side. "Dragons aren't the only things that are heavy."

Dyphestive managed to crawl out of the crevice and sit up with his feet inside. "Whoa, what did I miss? There are dead dragons everywhere."

Grey Cloak patted his cloak and said, "I used the figurine."

"Is that what all of those strange explosions were?"

"That was them."

"Them?"

"Smoke and Sid." Grey Cloak hooked his brother's arm and helped him to his feet. "I'll tell you more about it later."

Dyphestive moved his neck from side to side, cracking it. "I think I can fight." He spun the war mace Thunderash.

"You should be dead. I thought you were dead. I'm glad that you weren't," he said.

"It's good to know that you were worried."

Dyphestive set his eyes on a pair of soldiers that were running his way. It was

Beak and Sergeant Tinison. Their armor was disheveled and their faces scuffed and battle weary.

"What's wrong?" Dyphestive asked.

"It's the Monarchs!" Tinison said it like it was a curse. "They saw what you did, but they want all of you arrested. Again!" he spit. "But we saw what you did too. You donned Codd's armor. There is no crime in that!"

"We came to warn you," Beak, Adanadel's daughter, said. Her left shoulder hung out of its socket, and blood was on her armor. "This is insanity."

Dyphestive pointed at a skirmish along the wall. "There is still a battle going on!"

"It's chaos, I tell you," Tinison said. "The kind that makes you go, 'Augh! Augh! Augh!'"

"The Honor Guard and Monarch Knights are fighting, but they are fighting over who is in charge," Beak said. "The orders on the ground are mixed. The knights fight, inspired by Codd. There is no deterring them. The Monarchs have the Honor Guard's ear, on the other hand. They are being told to stand down."

"But we're winning," Grey Cloak said.

Streak scurried from his garden hiding spot and stopped at his feet.

He picked him up and said, "There you are."

The dragon lifted his eyes skyward. The Riskers were lowering.

"It seems that it's not going to take them very long to get their courage back," Grey Cloak said. Smoke and Sid had taken out at least a score of dragons, but scores more were still left in the sky. He looked at his brother. "At this point, I think we've done all that we can."

"It can't be over yet." Dyphestive jogged over to Codd's helmet, picked it up, and put in on. Then he walked back over to the group. "I don't understand how it works. It won't make me a giant again."

"That's because it's served its purpose," a rough-spoken older man that appeared from the burning gardens said. It was the monarch enchanter, Hyrum. His shoulder-length hair was white and woolen. The robes he wore were pitch black with geometric symbols. He lifted the helmet from Dyphestive's head and tossed it aside. "Now the time has come to move on."

"What? Flee?" Grey Cloak asked.

"The Riskers are descending. The Monarchs do not have your backs. I'm afraid that all of your efforts have been in vain, though I admire them." Hyrum cleared his throat. "Woozah. Too much smoke inhalation. I have to admit, putting all of those dragons down was very impressive. Too bad that figurine's powers are so short-lived." Hyrum shook his fist at the sky. "It sure scared the snot balls out of them!"

A group of yonders flew over them and formed a ring. The bulbous eyeballs with bat wings hovered ten feet over them.

"Look who came to join the celebration," Tinison said with a sneer in his voice. "I imagine our keisters are cooked now."

Grey Cloak had taken every chance he could think of, but he was all out of ideas. As the Riskers lowered from the sky, it appeared it was all over.

"What do we do, Grey?" Dyphestive asked.

"I'm thinking."

The Riskers and their dragons were lowering one hundred feet at a time. They would land in moments. In the meantime, the fighting against the Black Guard in the courtyards had come to a stop, but no one surrendered their weapons. It was an organized standoff.

Crane drove his wagon along the wall. Tatiana was under a garden bridge.

Grey Cloak turned to Hyrum, whispered in the old man's ear, and said, "Get my friends out of here. I'll handle this."

Hyrum nodded. In the bat of a lash, he vanished in a twinkle of star dust.

For several moments, Grey Cloak considered running for the drawbridge and hiding in the city, but Dyphestive wouldn't be able to keep up, and he would never leave his brother.

Time was at a standstill while a host of the Honor Guard encircled Grey Cloak and Dyphestive.

Grey Cloak rose on his toes to try to see what was happening beyond the ring of warriors clad in scale mail. Tatiana, aided by Hyrum, jumped into Crane's slow-moving wagon. Razor, Jakoby, and Leena climbed into the back.

Where's Zora?

Crane put his hand on something on the bench, but the hand was noticeably forced away.

Ah, there she is, invisible.

He caught Crane's eye and nodded.

The old fellow turned the wagon away, slowly leading it toward the castle walls and the drawbridge, while Jakoby subtly waved.

Dyphestive moved to stand by Grey Cloak and said, "There goes our ride."

"Let's hope so," he replied.

13

"Crane, turn this wagon around!" Zora demanded. She was still invisible but didn't hesitate to make her presence known vocally. "We aren't leaving them behind."

His puffy cheeks were flushed, and sweat dripped from his temples. "Patience. I can't run roughshod over the Honor Guard, now can I?" He eyed Tatiana, who was sitting in the middle of the wagon. "What is your call?"

The Star of Light glowed softly in the palm of her hand. Her eyebrows were knitted, and she said, "All of this chatter is going to spoil my concealment spell. They see us as one of them." The wagon was cruising through the ranks of soldiers, and no one paid them any notice. They marched right by them with hardly a glance. "Don't interrupt my concentration. We would all do well to follow Grey Cloak's wish and head out of the main gate before it's too late."

"We can't leave them," Zora said under her breath.

"Do you want to find a noose around your neck again?" Tatiana fired back.

"I know I don't," Crane said, "and I wasn't even on the gallows before."

"No, you were watching," Zora said.

"I was, wasn't I?" Crane eyed the dragons in the sky. "If we move, we need to do it before they land. What is it going to be?"

"Since no one listens to me, I'll be diplomatic and put it to a vote," Tatiana said. "All in favor of escaping with their lives intact, raise their hand." She lifted her arm, but no one else did. Shaking her head, she eyeballed Crane. "What are we waiting for when certain death awaits?"

"You know, I find your grim outlook very charming." With a twinkle in his eyes, Crane grinned. "Lock arms, everyone, and hold tight. It's going to be a hot and bumpy ride." Crane flicked his carriage whip.

Szzz-pop! The whip burst into a tendril of flame and smote Vixen the horse's back. The fire spread down over the horses' bodies and turned them to flames.

Vixen transformed from a fine mare to a nightmare breed of horse from the Netherworld. Her eyes burned with flame, and she breathed hot steam out. The fire spread from Vixen's hooves and over the wagon's wheels.

An otherworldly fire glowed in Crane's eyes as he smiled and said, "Onward, Vixen!" He cracked the whip. *Wupash!* "When my wheels are turning, the world is burning! Onward!" *Wupash!* "Onward!"

The flaming wagon turned in the courtyard, scattering the startled soldiers like rats.

Zora hung on for dear life as she felt her eyeballs pulling from her head.

The wagon surged forward at blazing speed, blasting a hole right through the scrambling Black Guard. Double tracks of flames followed behind the wagon as it set everything and every person that it passed on fire.

As the bewildered soldiers turned to see the source of the hellish commotion, their ranks parted quickly, clearing a path to Grey Cloak and Dyphestive, who stood side by side, eagerly awaiting the arrival of their salvation.

A huge grand dragon, the biggest of them all, dropped onto the ground, blocking the clear passage. His skull was decorated with jagged horns of all sizes. His eyes were bright yellow and burned like the sun. The rigid scales covering his body were also bright yellow. His mouth opened, and orange flames spewed out.

Zora's life flashed before her eyes, and she screamed. Vixen turned hard to the left, making Zora's neck whip to one side. She held on to the back of the bench seat for dear life.

The dragon's flames would have engulfed the wagon, but a shield of mystic energy repelled them. Instead, the fire curled like a cloud above the wagon.

The Star of Light burned bright in the palm of Tatiana's hand. The elven sorceress's eyes were aglow, and her jaw was clenched. "I can only repel the fires so long. Get them!"

Crane blindly drove the wagon through the fire, and they plowed through a regiment of soldiers. "Hang on! I'm going to turn it and make another pass!"

The chaos created an avenue of escape for Grey Cloak and Dyphestive. They sprinted away from the dragon and toward the castle walls.

"There!" Zora said. She pulled down her scarf, revealing herself. "Catch them there!"

Crane cracked the carriage whip, the fiery wheels spun, and the blazing wagon sped after the brothers.

The grand dragon eyed the wagon's path. On its back was a lean, black-haired older warrior. His stern expression showed that he was in command. He made a simple motion with his fingers, and Riskers dropped out of the sky, firing arrows from the backs of fire-spitting dragons. The arrows ricocheted off Tatiana's shield, and the flames rolled over the dome.

"It's getting hot in here!" Razor said.

The wagon was engulfed by the enemy forces. Balls of fire rolled over the wagon. The carriage bumped and jostled over fallen bodies, crushing them.

Zora couldn't see a thing. They were surrounded by flames and dragons. "Where are they?"

"Don't worry. Vixen knows where she is going," Crane stated.

"Hurry!" Tatiana shouted. "I can't hold my shield much longer!"

The wagon sped away from the flames, and a clear view opened up.

"There!" Zora pointed.

Grey Cloak and Dyphestive sprinted down the courtyard roads at an angle that would meet with the wagon. In seconds, their paths would intersect.

"We have them!" Crane said.

Zora stood and waved the brothers on as the wagon slowed. "Jump in! Jump in!"

Grey Cloak raced toward them with Streak cradled in his arms. Razor and Jakoby stretched their arms toward them. Like he had wings on his feet, Grey Cloak leapt into the wagon.

"Slow down. Slow down," Jakoby said, stretching his arms out for Dyphestive.

Razor beckoned with his arm. "Hurry, big fella. Hurry!"

Dyphestive plowed toward them as fast as his thick legs would take him. His fingers had just touched the tips of Jakoby's when a middling dragon plowed right into him and flattened him to the ground.

"Nooo!" Zora screamed.

Grey Cloak grabbed her face, looked her in the eye, and said, "Listen to me! Go! I'll take care of Dyphestive. Go! All of you!"

He jumped out of the wagon, leaving Zora in shock and with tears running down her cheeks as the fire wagon raced toward for the drawbridge. The last thing she saw was Grey Cloak's subtle wave goodbye before he ran for his brother.

"Go, Vixen! Go!"

In a bolt of flame, the wagon sped away, passed under the portcullis, ran across the drawbridge, and destroyed every wicked soldier in its path on the way to freedom.

14

GREY CLOAK HELPED HIS BROTHER TO HIS FEET. "YOU KNOW, IF YOU WEREN'T SO heavy and slow, we might have made it."

Dyphestive dusted the dirt from his chest and said, "I know. You should have gone."

"And let you have all of the fun? Never," Grey Cloak answered as he picked up Streak, who was curled around his feet. He kissed his dragon. "You really should have stayed with the others." He glanced behind him. A path of twin flames burned the ground, starting at the drawbridge. "At least they are safe."

"For now," Dyphestive muttered.

They stood side by side, surrounded by enemies of all sorts: grand dragons, middlings, their riders, the Riskers, and scores of the Black Guard soldiers, who'd made a ring around their leaders.

Foremost was Dirklen and Magnolia's father, the imposing Commander Shaw. He was perched high in the saddle of his grand dragon, Jentak. The dragon's menacing stare could freeze the marrow in an ordinary man's bones.

With Dyphestive at his back, wielding his war mace, and Streak tucked in his arm like a goose, Grey Cloak pointed his sword at Commander Shaw and said, "Are you ready to hear my terms for your surrender?"

Jentak lowered his body to a crouch, eyed Grey Cloak, and ran his black tongue across his giant, razor-sharp teeth. A hot blast from his nostrils steamed Grey Cloak's hair and face.

"Ack!" Grey Cloak said. "Did anyone ever tell you that you have awful dragon breath?"

"Stifle it!" Dirklen screamed.

"Speaking of dragon breath," Grey Cloak said to his brother.

Dyphestive chuckled.

Dirklen and Magnolia were saddled on the back of another grand, which must have been Magnolia's. The grand's thick skin and scales were splashed with pink and white like turtle skin. Dirklen sat behind his sister. He had a leather sling on his arm and was favoring the shoulder that Smoke had shot.

"What are you waiting for, Father? Kill them! Kill them both," Dirklen demanded.

Commander Shaw gave his son a disapproving look. "These are the two that Black Frost is searching for. Are they not? Why would I kill them?'

Dirklen shrank under his father's gaze and whined, "Because they killed my dragon."

"And if you had been more careful, that wouldn't have happened."

"I want him dead!" Dirklen glared at Grey Cloak.

"That is Black Frost's decision, not yours." Commander Shaw turned his attention back to Grey Cloak and Dyphestive. "You would be wise to set aside your weapons at this time. Can't you see that you've cost enough lives already?"

"You are the one costing lives. Not us!" Dyphestive said.

"I'm merely following orders given to me by the ruler of this world. You would be wise to use your talents to do the same." Commander Shaw's tight mouth twitched. "The children of Olgstern Stronghair and Zanna Paydark. I knew your parents. They were the finest of the Sky Riders. I think they would be proud of your effort, even as futile as it may be." His gaze dropped to Streak. "I see you have a runt. How fitting. Now, drop your weapons and surrender. The Monarchs and I have business to attend to."

No matter where Grey Cloak looked, he saw no way out. He considered the figurine, but he didn't think the magic would work again so quickly after he just had used it. *I'll save it for later.*

He dropped his sword and nodded at Dyphestive. "I'm all out of ideas. You?"

"That's not my strong suit." With a heavy sigh, Dyphestive dropped Thunderash. "I hope they don't make me a Doom Rider again."

"I don't think you'll have to worry about that. I imagine that at this juncture, Black Frost has other plans in mind for you—if not agonizing servitude then probably a slow death," Commander Shaw said.

"It sounds to me like you are making a lot of assumptions on Black Frost's behalf. I've heard tell that only a fool would do that," Dyphestive said.

Grey Cloak didn't hide his surprise at his brother's statement. "Clever words from an agile mind. I think I'm rubbing off on you."

The commander climbed down from his dragon and approached. He stood face to face with Dyphestive and gave him a look that could kill. Quietly and with venom, he said, "Drysis was a dear friend of mine. Very dear. I know that you killed her, and I will see to it that you and your friend both suffer for that... greatly."

15

"BLACK GUARD, SECURE THEM," COMMANDER SHAW ORDERED.

Streak squirted out of Grey Cloak's arms.

"Run, Streak! Run!"

The little dragon vanished under Jentak's chest. Jentak curled his head downward, searching for Streak.

"Pay him no mind, Jentak. He is only a runt and, by the looks of him, good for very little," Commander Shaw said. "These are the only two prisoners that I am worried about." He eyed Grey Cloak. "Where is it?"

"Where is what?" Grey Cloak asked as a Black Guard started to tie his hands behind his back.

"The figurine, you fool!" Dirklen shouted. "The one you used to kill my dragon!"

"Yes, the one that you used to kill many dragons—and Riskers, it seems," Commander Shaw said. "Hand it over."

"I can't do anything of the sort with my hands tied, now can I? And I don't know what you are talking about."

The commander looked away for a moment before he crashed his fist into Grey Cloak's jaw. "Search him."

The soldiers threw Grey Cloak to the ground then removed his sword belt and patted him down with rough hands.

His cheek throbbed. "Easy. I'm ticklish in certain places." He giggled. "Oh, that would be a spot."

One of the Black Guard held him still while the other socked him in the belly.

He doubled over and gave a loud "Ooof!"

"Leave him alone. He doesn't have it anymore," Dyphestive said.

"Don't play me for a fool," Commander Shaw said. "Did you find anything?"

The soldier searching Grey Cloak shook his head and said, "No, Commander. He yields nothing."

Commander Shaw's lip twitched. "I know better. I can see it in his eyes." He pulled a dagger from the sheath on his sword belt and fed a charge of mystic fire into it with his hand. The blade swirled with hot, radiant energy. "Lift him up so that I might have a word with him."

The Black Guard hauled Grey Cloak up to his feet. One of them pulled his head back by the hair.

"I only need to return you to Dark Mountain alive," Commander Shaw said and held the point of the dagger under Grey Cloak's eye. "It doesn't matter what condition you are in. Perhaps you would like to keep your eyes in exchange for the figurine?"

"Take his eyes *and* the figurine, Father!" Dirklen said.

The commander cringed at the sound of his son's voice.

With an inward smile, Grey Cloak looked up as he pretended to think. "Hmm... my eyes, which help me to see, for the price of the figurine. I'll tell you what—how about our freedom for this imaginary figurine that you have been talking about? Why, I can whip one up with my fingers right now."

"You are testing my patience," Commander Shaw said.

"Sorry. But that's not what I call a counteroffer. How about the figurine for some beans?"

"I don't have any beans."

"Of course you do. Every man has two of them. They are right there." Grey Cloak kicked Commander Shaw square in the crotch.

The commander's eyes widened, and his knees buckled. His cheeks reddened, and he straightened his back and said through clenched teeth, "I'm going to make you wish you had never been born!"

Jentak gave a strange growl that made Commander Shaw stop in his tracks and look behind him. The grand dragon's head jerked from side to side like he was trying to shake something off.

"What is the matter, Jentak?" Commander Shaw asked, his demeanor suddenly cooled.

Using his hind leg, Jentak scratched behind his ear like a dog.

"Jentak! Stop that!" Commander Shaw said.

The dragon raised his tail and let out an angry roar. Every living person and dragon moved away. Even the Black Guard pulled Grey Cloak and Dyphestive out of harm's way, leaving Commander Shaw facing the dragon alone.

Grey Cloak caught Dyphestive glancing back at him and shrugged. He wasn't sure what was wrong with Jentak, but it was definitely creating a prickly atmosphere. Something in his mind said, *Up here.*

"Huh?" He wondered whether he had actually heard those words. It sounded like a voice in his head, but it was more than that, almost more like a feeling. It was familiar. "Streak?"

"What is it?" Dyphestive asked. His eyes were fixed on Jentak, who looked like he was about to come out of his scales.

Grey Cloak found what he was looking for, and his heart skipped a beat.

Streak was nestled between the horns on Jentak's skull like a tick. His eyes locked with Grey Cloak, who realized that he had been communicating in a language Grey Cloak had never heard but understood. "Fellas, you might want to back up."

The Black Guard securing them backed up farther, leaving Commander Shaw and his dragon.

"Jentak, what is the matter with you? Tell me," the commander said.

The dragon let out a groan as if something were eating him from the inside out. His back paw scratched at his head, but it couldn't go any higher, and the tip of his tail flicked at the top of his head to no avail. Suddenly, his yellow eyes rolled up in his head and turned as white as moonlight.

Commander Shaw stepped back, his jaw dropping, when he saw the white-eyed Streak latched on to the top of Jentak's skull. As Jentak glared down at him, he gulped then said, "Jentak, listen to me—"

A torrent of flames spewed from Jentak's mouth and devoured Commander Shaw's flesh instantly.

16

DIRKLEN AND MAGNOLIA CRIED OUT IN HORROR AS THEY WATCHED THEIR FATHER'S flaming body collapse to the ground. A prolonged silence fell over the courtyard, but it didn't last long.

Jentak tore into his brood. With a swipe of his mighty tail, he flattened rows of the Black Guard and sent them tumbling head over heels. He spit another fiery blast at Dirklen and Magnolia. Their dragon jumped out of harm's way and took to the sky. Jentak let out another fiery blast at the Black Guard ranks, turning the men into molten flesh and metal. The Black Guard, the Honor Guard, and the Monarch Knights scrambled to find cover.

With the heat searing his face, Grey Cloak summoned his fire and let his ignited fingertips burn through his bonds. At the same time, his guards fled the scene. *Gah, that's hot. I have to stop doing that before I burn my fingers off.* He started blowing on them.

Dyphestive twisted around and head-butted one of his guards then kneed the other one in the gut. With a grunt, he tried to snap the ropes that bound him.

"You don't have enough leverage," Grey Cloak said as he picked up his sword belt. He drew a dagger and cut his brother's cords. "If it were metal, you probably would have snapped it."

"I could have broken them." Dyphestive picked up his war mace and asked, "What is happening?"

"We have been endowed with an incredible blessing," he said. "I believe that Streak is controlling that dragon. Come on."

Dyphestive grabbed his cloak and pulled him back. "Wait, what are you doing?"

"We are going to ride that dragon."

"I don't think that is a very good idea."

Jentak snaked toward them and lowered his huge head in front of them.

Grey Cloak felt Streak telling him, *Hurry!* Then he said to his brother, "We are safe. Trust me."

Dyphestive groaned, but he followed Grey Cloak as he climbed onto the dragon's skull and made his way back to the saddle. It was large, made of fine leather, and big enough for two.

"Now what?"

"Hang on to something," Grey Cloak ordered.

"Are you going to fly him?" Dyphestive asked with widening eyes.

"No, Streak is."

Jentak launched himself into the sky. His huge black wings beat the wind like thunder. In a moment, the wind was tearing at their faces, and they were racing through the sky.

"Woohoo!" Dyphestive bellowed.

Grey Cloak looked back at his brother and asked, "You like flying?"

"I think. Don't you?"

"No, I hate it, actually."

"Weren't you trained to be a Sky Rider?"

"Yes, but it's a long story."

Jentak chased Dirklen and Magnolia. The other Riskers were pursuing but not attacking. They were keeping their distance, and it appeared that they didn't know what to do since Commander Shaw was gone.

A glowing arrow whizzed by Grey Cloak's head. Magnolia had fired it.

"Ah-ha, they want a fight. Well, we can play that game. Can you fire a bow?" he asked Dyphestive.

"Of course. The Doom Riders trained me with every weapon you could imagine." He glanced down at the gear hanging on the dragon's saddle—sheaths filled with arrows, two bows, a quiver of javelins, and spears. He grabbed the bow, loaded an arrow, and pulled back the string. "It's going to be odd shooting at something flying away from us."

"Don't aim for them," he said, pointing at Dirklen and Magnolia. "Aim at them!" He pointed at their pursuers.

Dyphestive let loose an arrow that didn't have a glow on the tip. It zinged through the air and bounced off a dragon's horn. "I don't think these arrows are going to do much good."

As the dragons chased one another through the air, Grey Cloak kept his eyes on Magnolia. Her aim was steady, and she was undeterred even though Jentak was pulling away. She fired, and the glowing arrow sailed true.

Grey Cloak plucked the arrow out of the air. "Ah-ha! Look, I caught it!" He handed it to Dyphestive. "Use this one!"

Magnolia's teeth were clenched, and she shook her fist at him. She turned and said something to her brother.

Dyphestive fired the arrow at the nearest dragon tracking them. The shaft exploded in the dragon's face and caused it to veer away. "Taste the thunder!" He elbowed Dyphestive. "Give me another one of those arrows!"

"I don't have any more. No, wait." He slipped an arrow out of the quiver, summoned his wizardry, and charged it with fire. "Here, use this one." He charged up another and another. "And this one and this one."

Dyphestive fired arrow after arrow. Some hit and some missed, but the Riskers stayed at bay. None of them were willing to take on Jentak and his deadly riders.

Grey Cloak grinned. He could see the dragon charms on the chests of most of the riders. They weren't naturals like him and Dyphestive. They didn't have the ability to use the wizard fire, as Dirklen and Magnolia liked to call it. Without the dragon charms, most of the Riskers were ordinary by comparison, if not all.

"I think they're scared," Grey Cloak said, though the winds rushed by, drowning out his voice.

"What?" Dyphestive asked.

"They are scared! Look at them. I can see the white in their eyes and their teeth chattering!"

Dyphestive nodded, fired another arrow, and blasted a Risker clear out of the saddle.

Over a score of Riskers still pursued them, but it seemed that the fire had gone out of them.

"Why aren't they attacking?' Dyphestive asked.

"I don't know, but I'm not complaining."

Dirklen and Magnolia's dragon lifted higher and turned north. Jentak pursued, as did the rest of the Riskers. All of them jettisoned high above Monarch City's north bridge and crossed over the Outer Ring.

Jentak drifted away and downward, and his speed slowed. Led by Dirklen and Magnolia, the Riskers soared away north, back toward Dark Mountain.

"I can't believe it!" Grey Cloak said. "They are running!"

Dyphestive put the bow away and said, "I can't believe it either." He looked over the side of the dragon. "What about all of the Black Guard soldiers on the bridge?"

Grey Cloak shrugged, pointed downward, and said, "Streak, we need to finish them!"

Jentak dove toward the great bridge, which was long and very wide. The Black Guard partially filled it. Jentak opened his maw and turned loose his dragon fire. He ran a trail over a hundred yards long right over the heart of the enemy. Burning Black Guard ran screaming and jumped from the great bridge down into the canyon's water below.

The tide had turned. Monarch City was saved.

Jentak aimed for Monarch Castle and did a flyby past the Monarchs, who stood gaping on their terraces. Grey Cloak and Dyphestive waved triumphantly at them.

"I wonder if we will get a reward for saving the city," Grey Cloak said as they circled high above it. "No doubt we should."

"Victory is reward enough for me," Dyphestive said with a grin.

Streak unlatched from Jentak's skull, spread his wings, and drifted in the sky. Jentak's eyes were no longer white but back to normal.

"Streak, you can fly!" The hairs on Grey Cloak's neck rose. He was face to face with Jentak, who'd turned his head around. The dragon's yellow eyes burned like fire. Grey Cloak reached behind himself and tapped Dyphestive on the shoulder. "Jump."

"What?" Dyphestive asked. He turned, and his eyes grew the moment he saw Jentak's eyes.

"Jump!" Grey Cloak shoved Dyphestive off the dragon's saddle, and they plummeted toward their death.

17

DYPHESTIVE FELL BACKWARD OFF THE DRAGON, CLAWING AT THE AIR AND screaming, "Grey Cloooak!"

"Hang on!" Grey Cloak said. "Well, you know what I mean." He turned his body downward and dove. Freefalling through the sky, he caught up with his brother and grabbed his arms. "I have you!"

Dyphestive looked past his brother's shoulder and said, "No one has you!"

As they plunged toward the top spires of Monarch Castle, the Cloak of Legends billowed out and gradually slowed their fall, but they were still moving fast.

"Zooks!" Grey Cloak said. By himself, in the cloak, he would fall as softly as a feather, but in with another person, it was different. Dyphestive was three times heavier, if not more. They were still sinking like a stone in water. "This might hurt, brother."

"Might hurt?"

"Well, the glass probably won't hurt, but what's underneath it might."

Looking down, they both screamed. "Aaahhh!"

They crashed right through a stained-glass dome, smashing it into shards of scintillating colors, then landed in a bed of silk pillows. They hit hard in an explosion of feathers. "Oof!"

Women's screams surrounded them.

Grey Cloak had landed on Dyphestive's chest, knocking the wind out of both of them. Even with the pillows, Grey Cloak felt like he'd landed on concrete. When he caught his breath, he groaned, "Thanks for breaking my fall."

"Thanks for slowing us down." Dyphestive sat up like he'd woken from a good night's sleep. He tapped his brother's shoulder. "I think we are dead."

"Why do you say that?" Grey Cloak asked.

"Because we are surrounded by angels."

Grey Cloak's eyes popped open, and he immediately sat up. "Hello."

The plush room was filled with satin feather pillows and beautiful women of all races in silky garments. One woman was as good-looking as the next, with curvy figures and long eyelashes. Some of them seemed frightened, but most of them were alluring and playful.

Grey Cloak swallowed the lump in his throat and stood up with the help of his brother. He quietly said to him, "I don't think we are dead. I know what this is. It's one of those harems."

Dyphestive tipped his head back and said, "Aaah. That makes sense."

Clearing his throat, Grey Cloak stiffened as a sharp pain lanced through his back, then he grunted as he straightened and cleared his throat again. "Don't be alarmed, ladies. We are not the enemy. As a matter of note, we are, in fact, the very heroes that saved your fair city. Allow me to introduce myself." He gave a small bow. "I am Grey Cloak, and this is Dyphestive... at your service."

The gorgeous women bathed in perfume let out a series of playful giggles.

"I'm very sorry about your glass dome and your pillows," he said as he shook the glass off of one and gently set it down.

Dyphestive did the same and, without taking his big eyes off them, said, "Yes, you have very nice pillows. Sorry that I landed on them."

The harem giggled playfully again, and gradually, a knot of them crept closer until their enticing silks and bodies brushed up against them.

"You can stay. We won't tell," one of them said. Her voice was a purr. She was a dark-eyed beauty with piles of wavy shoulder-length air. "You are so big and handsome. Stay with me. Stay with us forever."

"Forever sounds like a very long time," Grey Cloak said as a blond elf wrapped her arms around his waist. "But I have time. Don't you, Dyphestive?"

"Uh..." Dyphestive responded as more women trapped him with their bodies.

The double entry doors to the plush room burst open, and Monarch Knights spilled inside. The harem girls scattered like rats. The soldiers surrounded the brothers with a ring of spears.

Dyphestive and Grey Cloak lifted their hands.

"I've got a bad feeling that we are right back where we started," Grey Cloak said and winked at one of the girls. "But this view sure is nice."

18

Dyphestive sat against the wall of the dungeon cell—the same cell they'd been imprisoned in hours earlier—whistling a peppy tune. It was the same song over and over again, and it had been going on for over an hour.

Grey Cloak took his fingers out of his ears and asked, "Would you please stop that?"

"Huh? Oh, the whistling," Dyphestive said. "Sorry, sometimes I forget that I'm doing it out loud. You know that."

"Yes, I remember, but it's been a long time since I've heard it."

"It has been a while, hasn't it?"

"Since Havenstock?"

Dyphestive nodded. "I believe so. Times were much simpler back then."

Grey Cloak begrudgingly agreed, but he didn't show it. If there was one thing he didn't miss, it was the backbreaking work he'd done for Rhonna for three long seasons. In retrospect, he had to admit that it had helped shape him into the person he'd become. He wouldn't mind the moon face of that grumpy curmudgeon again. Even an earful from her would be a treat compared to the last life-threatening situations they'd been in.

"Do you think they are going to try to hang us again?" Dyphestive asked.

"They'll probably try something else, like beheading."

Dyphestive rubbed his neck and grimaced. "Always with the neck." A moment afterward, he managed a boyish smile. "Did you get a good look at me in Codd's armor?"

"Did I ever. I'd never seen or imagined the likes of it. You became a giant. How did you know?"

"I can't say, but a feeling overcame me, urging me to put it on. Do you really think that I have Codd's blood in me?"

"Well, you don't look like an ogre, but if you keep growing, you might be as big as one. The truth is that I don't have any idea if that legend about Codd is true or not. After all, it's only a legend."

Dyphestive lifted his shoulders and bobbed his chin. "Thanks for saving me from falling."

"Thanks for the softer landing." He smirked. "I have to admit that we are getting better at not dying."

"It makes me wonder if we can even die at all."

"I've thought the same thing more than once. Look at what we have withstood—an army and an army of dragons. So far, we are doing good."

"Agreed."

Grey Cloak stood and squinted at the dungeon bars. They were alone, aside from two Honor Guards posted outside. They stood on each side of the cell, holding spears. "Excuse me, but could I get something to drink?" he asked.

The guards didn't move from their posts. At the farther end of the hall, a metal door squeaked on its hinges as it opened and closed.

Grey Cloak stuck his nose through the bars. "Dyphestive, it's your friends Beak and Sergeant Tinison."

Dyphestive rushed over to the cell door and pushed his broad face against the metal. "It *is* them. Over here! Over here!"

"Stifle it, Baby Face. We know you are here. Every soldier in the city knows you are here. No need to announce it," Sergeant Tennison said. His face was battered and bruised, and his hair was a mess. He eyed the other two guards. "You two, dismissed."

"How are you feeling?" Beak asked Dyphestive.

"Me? I'm as well as a well digger."

"A well digger?" She gave him a confused look. "What does that mean?"

"Uh, I don't know." Dyphestive rubbed the back of his head, but he couldn't stop staring at her nose.

Beak had dark rings underneath her eyes, and her dark hair was curled in some places and singed. "My nose is broken."

"Are you sure?" Grey Cloak asked.

Dyphestive elbowed him. "I'm sure it will get better. It looks fine to me."

"If you say so," she said as she gave them both an astonished look that she was trying to hide. "I saw what you both did, but I could hardly believe my eyes. You saved Monarch City."

"Of course we did." Grey Cloak huffed on his fingernails and polished them on his cloak. "I can only assume there is a very, very, very big reward for that."

"Not according to the Monarchs," Tinison said with disgust. "No sooner had you saved the city than the entire castle became divided. Half of them are elated, while the other half fears Dark Mountain's wrath. I know you did the right thing, and as much as it hurts to say this—because I'm not one to be thankful for anything aside from mead and elk ribs—I'm grateful."

"So am I. You were both very brave and oddly resourceful," Beak admitted.

"What now?" Grey Cloak asked.

Tinison ran his fingers through his hair. "Hyrum told us to meet him here. I think he's in the middle of sorting out everything that happened. Who knows what might happen? The Monarchs are a bunch of kooks."

Beak gave Tinison a grave look.

Tinison shrugged. "I don't care anymore. Not after everything that happened today. Let them feed me to the moat monsters. After today, I should have been dead anyway."

"I hear someone coming," Grey Cloak said.

Everyone turned and looked down the hall.

Hyrum approached. Two yonders hung back behind him.

He nodded at Grey Cloak and Dyphestive and said, "I hope you are well."

"We are *so far*," Grey Cloak answered.

Hyrum had a grave look on his face. "I have news. I am ordered to escort you to the throne room of the Monarch King. Sergeant Tinison, open the gate, and I will shackle them."

Sergeant Tinison removed the ring of keys from his belt, opened the door, and said, "It's been nice knowing you both. Now do me one last favor and don't bring my name up."

19

"Do you see that? Do you see that? All of my tiger rosebushes are gone! I've been growing those since I was a boy. Now look at my gardens! They are wiped out!" the human Monarch King said. He was a wizened old man with a sagging face that had jowls that wiggled when he spoke. His robes were golden and glittery with a deep-red trim. A white cape with a leopard-skin collar dragged behind him when he walked. Otherwise, he had nothing extraordinary about him except that he was nearly eight feet tall. "This is a crisis!"

Grey Cloak and Dyphestive exchanged uncertain looks. After Hyrum bound their arms behind their backs with mystic ropes of gleaming fiber, he had brought them to the top of one of Monarch Castle's high towers. It was wider than the rest. From the ground, it was difficult to judge the enormousness of it, but its stone floor was every bit of fifty feet from one side to the other, and a solid-gold throne was in the middle.

The throne wasn't the only thing that was golden either. The Monarch Knights wore gold-plated armor with other weapons and gear to match. They made a ring around the throne, twelve in all, and they were paired with enchanters whose heads were hidden in the hoods of their gold wizard robes.

The Monarch King leaned over the parapet. "Look at the fires. That is dragon fire! I saw the dragons myself, soaring by like buzzing flies." He waved his hand back and forth in aggravation. "It wasn't supposed to happen like this. It wasn't supposed to happen this way at all." He glared down at Hyrum. "Who are these people that have done this?"

Hyrum said, "Your Majesty, let me introduce you to the men that have risked all to save our city. This is Grey Cloak and Dyphestive."

The Monarch King's eyes grew wide. "Saved our city? Does it look like it was saved to you? My gardens are in ruins, my soldiers are dead, and dead dragons are sprawled out everywhere." He clenched his fist in Hyrum's face and said,

"None of this would have happened if they had not interfered. I had it all under control. Now this! Look at my tiger rose bushes. Did you see them?"

Grey Cloak scratched his head and said, "Your bushes will grow back."

The Monarch King froze. With his back turned to Grey Cloak, he said, "Who dares to speak without being spoken to? I should have them tossed from the tower."

Please do. I'd be better off.

The lanky old king spun around, locked eyes with Grey Cloak, and said, "What did you say?"

You heard that?

"Yes, I did!" the king said. "You arrogant little rooster. I've lived one hundred years. I've ruled for eighty. I know people. Hear the thoughts in their minds. That is why I am the Monarch King!"

"You are a mad monarch," Grey Cloak said boldly.

Dyphestive nudged him and asked, "What are you doing?"

"Speaking my mind. After all, he can read it." Grey Cloak looked the old Monarch King dead in the eye and said, "You should be thanking us. We saved Monarch City and perhaps you all that are in it as well. And all that you are worried about are your flowers."

"Fool!" The Monarch King's voice cracked. "Look at you, merely a child yet full of boasts."

"Black Frost would destroy your entire kingdom, but you let him in to exert his will. How long did you think that would last?"

"I had a plan. Do you think I've come to live so long without a plan?" He poked Grey Cloak in the chest with one of his gaudy-jewelry-covered fingers. "I knew Black Frost's plans. I had my own plans. Now you've ruined everything." He grabbed Grey Cloak and Dyphestive by their ears and tugged them along like children then pushed them to the edge of the parapet. "Do you see that?"

They faced the northern bridge. Soldiers were scrambling across the long stretch back toward the city.

"Do you hear that?" the Monarch King asked.

Grey Cloak could clearly hear the sound of hammers striking metal. He nodded.

"That bridge took a decade to build. One decade. And it is ancient, far more ancient than men. Now look at what you have forced me to do."

The northern bridge moved up and down. A terrible sound of metal and stone twisting, popping, and breaking assaulted Grey Cloak's ears. All of a sudden, as if its legs had vanished, the bridge fell into the Outer Rings canyon and crashed with a loud and resounding impact that sounded like the entire city had exploded.

The collapse caused huge waves to flow around the canyon. Smoke and debris rose out of the water-filled expanse.

"Do you mind me asking why you did that?" Grey Cloak said.

"Because you didn't give me a choice, you fool. Monarch City could have lived in peace with Dark Mountain, but thanks to you, now we are officially at war." He gave them both a disappointed look. "The blood of my citizens, my soldiers, is now on your hands. You'd better remember that." The Monarch King turned his back and headed to his throne and sat down. He let out a long sigh.

"Your Majesty, what is your will?" Hyrum asked.

"No doubt Black Frost will want them, but he can't have what I've already killed." He tapped the arm of his golden chair. "Hyrum, you know what to do. See to it that I never see this pair again, ever, for mercy's sake!"

20

It was night, and Zora paced inside Crane's apartment. She wasn't alone. Jakoby and Leena sat on the sofa, while Tatiana and Razor were quietly talking on the balcony. It had been over a day since they had escaped on what Crane liked to call his Wheels of Fire. Since then, they'd seen no signs of Grey Cloak and Dyphestive, or Streak and Than, for that matter.

Tatiana entered the room. Her sheer curtains dusted her shoulder as she passed. "You look worried," she said to Zora. "Why don't you sleep? We will wait."

Zora sat on a stool in the small kitchen and said, "No, I'll wait for Crane to arrive. I'm sure that he'll be back soon."

"Waiting like this isn't going to bring him back any sooner," Tatiana said. "Go rest."

"The more you ask, the less likely I am to do it." Zora yawned. She caught Tatiana's "I told you so" look and said, "Don't say it."

Zora hadn't even napped since they'd made their way safely back to the apartment. From the rooftops, they'd watched the final battle unfold in the sky. With horror, she had watched Grey Cloak and Dyphestive fall from a dragon's back and plummet to their deaths. Her heart had dropped with them, and she shook for hours. Tatiana comforted her the best she could, with soothing words and a shoulder to cry on.

Jakoby did the same. "That was one of the slowest falls that I ever did see," he said. "Something isn't right about that."

All Zora knew was what she'd seen. She couldn't imagine that they'd survived it. In the meantime, the invasion of Dark Mountain had come to an end, and word spread that the Northern Bridge had been dropped into the Outer Ring. The entire city was in shock but thankful.

"How about a cup of coffee?" Razor asked as he stepped into the room. "I make it good and strong."

"All I've done is drink coffee since we came here." Jakoby picked his mug up from the table and handed it to Razor. "And I'll be glad to partake in another pot or two."

Tatiana shared serious looks with Zora.

"We need to discuss what we need to do about Talon. I can't stay here, and I want you to come with me, Zora. I don't think it will be safe for you here either."

"I'm not going anywhere until I know what happened to them," she responded.

"I wouldn't either," Razor said.

Tatiana shot him a look.

Razor shrugged. "What? It's out of respect." He started to fill a coffee urn with water from an upright cistern that sat on four legs. "Oh no, we have a serious problem."

"What?" Zora asked.

"We are out of water." Razor hefted the empty cistern onto his shoulders and said cheerfully, "No worries, everyone. I'll fetch more from the town drinker." He sauntered over to the door and opened it.

Crane stood outside the door with a long face. Razor stepped back and let him in.

Zora hopped off the stool and rushed over to him. "I see that look in your eye. What's wrong?"

Crane massaged his bulging jowls and said, "I'm sorry. I've been outside for a while, trying to find the words to say."

Everyone in the room was standing, and they surrounded Crane, hanging on his every word.

Zora's heart tumbled. She wished more than anything that the blood brothers were still alive, but she'd seen what she'd seen. With her fingernails digging into her palm, she asked, "Say what, Crane?"

The old man swallowed and, with a shaky voice, said, "I'm sorry to say, but Grey Cloak and Dyphestive are gone."

Zora sank back into Jakoby's arms. Tears started to stream down her face.

"I'm sorry, Zora," Tatiana said as she hugged her. "I understand your pain. We all feel it. Grey Cloak and Dyphestive were very, very brave. If not for them, I feel that none of us would still be here today."

Zora buried her head in Jakoby's chest. She wasn't used to crying. She never cried. Wiping her face, she held back the tears. With a loud sniff, she said, "I guess there is nothing more to do but move on."

"What about the bodies?" Razor asked. "Can we bury them?"

"I didn't see the bodies. I was only told that they were taken care of and it was for the best," Crane said. He placed his hand on Zora's back. "Perhaps it's better this way. I don't think you would want to remember them in a dead state."

"You think that I would rather remember them falling to their deaths?" she asked with her voice cracking. "Do you? I want to be alone!"

She stormed out to the terrace and closed the door behind her. She gripped the railing and stared with teary eyes at the sky. "He can't be gone. He can't be."

A small dragon glided into view with the moon in the background. He flew right at her and landed on the railing. "Streak?" She sniffed. "Streak, it is you?" She caressed the dragon's head and neck. "Do you know?"

Streak flicked his tongue out and shook his head.

"You understand me?"

The runt dragon nodded.

"Do you know that Grey Cloak is dead?"

Streak shook his head.

"He's dead."

He shook his head again.

A strange rustle caught Zora's ear, and a sliver of ice raced down her spine. Someone or something was huddled in the shadows of the terrace's corner.

Her hand fell to her dagger. She eyed Streak and said quietly, "Be still."

Streak flicked his tongue out.

Zora spun around and said, "Show yourself!"

21

A SHADOWY FIGURE ROSE FROM A CROUCH. HIS EYES SHONE LIKE SILVER COINS IN the moonlight.

"Grey Cloak!"

He approached with a broad smile and said, "In the flesh."

"Crane said that you were dead!"

"No, he said I was *gone.*" He chuckled and opened his arms. "Aren't you glad to see me?"

She put her dagger away, rushing into his arms, and said softly, "You know I am." Her voice turned hard. "But now I'm going to kill you!" She shoved him off the terrace.

"Zora, nooo!" He fell in slow motion toward the street and made a soft landing on his tiptoes. Looking up at her, he said, "Are you mad at me?"

"Did you think that was funny? Pretending to be dead?" she fired back.

"Well, I did enjoy seeing how much you cared." His fingers found purchase on the stone wall, and he started climbing like a monkey. "I heard how you said, 'I can't believe he's gone.'"

"What? I said, '*they're* gone.'"

"No." He climbed back onto the terrace. "You said *he.*"

"Then *he* was Dyphestive, not you. Why would I worry about a trickster like you?" She shoved him. "And why would you jest about being dead?"

"No one said that I was dead. Crane only said that I, or we, were gone. Come now, Zora." He reached for her hands. "Aren't you glad to see me?"

"I should break your teeth out. I was really upset." She took a deep breath and said, "Give me your word that you'll never do anything that stupid again."

"You have my word, Zora." He took her hand and kissed it. "Never again."

She gave him a funny look and replied, "Why did you kiss my hand?" She pulled it away. "Is that how you guarantee a promise?"

"Er... no?"

She wiped the back of her hand on her trousers. "Then why did you do it?"

With his hand on his neck, he cast a nervous glance about and said, "It was something I picked up in Monarch Castle. A strange custom. I won't do it again." His gaze landed on Streak. "Ah, look who is with us. And he can fly now too." He made his way to his dragon. "Did you see that?"

Zora locked both of her hands on his wrist and pulled him against her body. "I think this is what you meant to do." She gave him a long, passionate, toe-curling kiss.

"Uh..."

She put a finger on his lips. "Don't say anything. Now, where is your better half?"

"I-I, uh..."

A commotion of cheerful voices erupted from inside the apartment.

Zora was the first to reach the terrace doors, and she flung them open.

Dyphestive stood among the group, shaking hands and getting hardy slaps on the back. Everyone inside was jubilant, including Dyphestive, whose smile was as broad as a river. It took a moment before the others realized that Grey Cloak and Zora had entered the room. When they did see them, they rushed over to Grey Cloak.

Jakoby was the first one to shake his hand. "Well done, Grey Cloak! Well done indeed. It's a pleasure to see you standing here in one piece."

"Aye," Razor agreed. "I thought the next time I saw you, I'd be looking at smashed apples."

"This calls for a celebration!" Crane said. "I'll open up my best cabinet of wine!"

Everyone congratulated him in one way or another. The last to speak was Tatiana. She pulled him aside. "You cheated death once again. Congratulations. Everyone but death is happy."

"And you, apparently."

Tatiana raised an eyebrow and said, "Of course I'm happy. Your heroics saved Monarch City for now, but what will you do when Black Frost comes again? Will you gamble with the figurine to everyone's peril? Even with it, it still wasn't enough to defeat the enemy."

"Zooks, Tatiana, I thought we were celebrating, not browbeating." He sat down on the sofa, allowing Streak to crawl into his lap, and petted him. "Go ahead. Get it all out."

She sat down beside him and kept her intense but beautiful eyes fixed on his. "I want you to give me the figurine."

Grey Cloak pulled Streak closer to him. "Why?"

In her rigid tone, she said, "It should be mine, Grey Cloak. It was my love, Dalsay's, and it was given to him by the Wizard Watch. It wasn't created to be used in the hands of the likes of you."

"The likes of me?"

"No offense, but you are a natural. You have abilities people can only dream of. You need to focus on honing those skills and not relying on the Figurine of Horrors."

"Heroes," he corrected. "I've met those people, and so far, they seem pretty nice."

"Regardless, we think it is best that the figurine be returned to the Wizard Watch. Where it came from." She held out her hand. "Please, Grey Cloak. I promise you. It is for the best."

Tatiana's persistence had his intentions leaning in her favor. Her suggestions were very hypnotic, even comforting. He found himself giving in.

It would be one less thing to worry about. But it's saved us all so many times.

Grey Cloak slid his fingers into his cloak, and he summoned the figurine from one of its pockets. He could feel the faceless features of the head. It was smooth like glass and sculpted into a perfect body. He started to pull it out.

Streak's tail wrapped around his wrist. Warmth flowed through the tail, spreading up his arm and into his head.

Grey Cloak snapped out of his daze, and he caught the look of surprise on Tatiana's face. "You don't want this for the Wizard Watch. You want it for yourself."

"That's not true. Listen to me, Grey Cloak. Please, it must be destroyed."

He shook his head and stuffed the figurine into his pocket. *I won't let her have it.* "You think that if you destroy the figurine, you can avenge your brothers. Don't you?"

Tatiana stiffened. "It must be destroyed!" Her loud outburst silenced the room.

"I'm going to keep it," he said.

She stood up and said, "It will be to your peril. I promise you."

"I'll take my chances."

Tatiana glared at him, turned around, and stormed out of the room. "Razor, come on!"

Razor guzzled down his wine and grabbed a bottle from the table. He winked at Crane and ran after her, saying, "Coming."

22

THE CELEBRATION WAS IN FULL SWING WHEN HYRUM DE SOL APPEARED IN THE room and startled the boots off everyone. The old enchanted eyes sparkled under his helmet of woolen white hair, but there was no mistaking the disappointment in his expression.

"Why so glum, chum?" Crane asked as he offered the enchanter a glass. "Try some underling port. It's the very best."

Hyrum gave him a dumbfounded look and said, "You haven't told them, have you, Crane? If you had, you wouldn't still be here."

"I was getting around to it. Have a drink."

Hyrum took the goblet. "Underling port, eh? Why, the last time I had this, well, I was young, and frankly, I can't remember what happened after the third glass." He took a sip. "My, that is good. If we had time, I'd ask how you came to have it, but we don't have time. Should I fill them in, or will you?"

Crane gave his same open-mouthed, surprised expression, shrugged, and drank.

"What is he talking about?" Zora whispered to Grey Cloak.

"The arrangement," he answered.

"What arrangement?"

"I'll tell you what the conditions of the arrangement are," Hyrum said after he'd finished the port and set the goblet down on the table. "My, that's good. Even the Monarchs can't get their hands on that. By order of the Monarch King, in exchange for your lives, you have been banished from Monarch City, from this moment on—well, actually, *that* moment, until the reign of the Monarch King ends. Any record of your existence will be scrubbed from the annals. It will be as if you never existed. But if you return, under any circumstances whatsoever, and are discovered, you will be sentenced to death. Most likely fed to the moat monsters in the dark of night. The Monarchs do that oftentimes."

"Crane! Why didn't you tell us this?" Zora asked.

"I like Monarch City, and I'm banished too. And what about my apartment, Hyrum? I've paid a year's rent in full. Are you going to retrieve my investment?" Crane asked.

"Don't be foolish. You need to go now. The Monarchs are watching." Hyrum pointed out the terrace doors. Two yonders were perched on the walls across the street. "Don't try the Monarch's patience. He has shown mercy and prefers to avoid embarrassment."

"Does this include me?" Jakoby asked.

Hyrum closed the patio doors and pulled the curtains closed. "Yes, you, Leena, Crane, Grey Cloak, Dyphestive, Streak, Tatiana, and Reginald the Razor." Hyrum fanned his hands out in a showy fashion. "Is that all?"

"You left out Than, but he is not here," Grey Cloak offered.

"Find him! All of you must be gone in the dark of night, never to return again. Believe me when I say that the Monarch King has shown you favor. Not only that, but he will convince Black Frost that you are dead, giving you a clear path to do whatever it is that you must do. But you must leave now and never come back. Do you understand?"

Everyone nodded.

"What are you waiting for? Pack your belongings and go!" Hyrum ordered.

"I'd be happy to, but go where?" Grey Cloak asked.

"That's not my problem," Hyrum said. "But you'd better be on one of the three great bridges within the hour." He shoved the doors open. "They are watching!" The quirky enchanter took a bow. "On a personal account, I want to thank you." With the wink of an eye, he vanished into a thousand glittery particles.

"I've never lived anywhere else but Arrowwood," Jakoby said with a long look. "I wouldn't have any idea where to go."

"Well, it won't be north. That's for certain," Crane said, slurring his words. His eyes were watery as he staggered around the apartment. "I really like this place. I'll miss my view of the city. My chair on the terrace. Smoking from my dwarven pipe." He dried his eyes on the curtains. "Nothing good ever lasts when evil exists on every path."

Dyphestive had disappeared into his room. He appeared shortly after with a rough sack on his back, his club and the figurine of Codd under his arm. "I'm ready to go."

"'Go where?' is the question," Grey Cloak said. He'd been so caught up in events in Monarch City that he'd never even considered going somewhere else. He'd been waiting for contact from Tatiana all that time, but she was gone. He knew what he had to do, though he didn't like it. "We need to find Tatiana. She'll know where we are needed best."

Jakoby was standing beside Leena. He asked, "What about us?"

"You are more than welcome to come with us and be a part of Talon," Grey Cloak said. "I'd be honored to have a Monarch Knight join us."

"And a monk from the Ministry of Hoods too," Dyphestive added as he cozied up behind Leena.

She elbowed him in the gut. He grinned.

"I'm not a Monarch Knight anymore, but I gladly accept your invitation."

"Good," Grey Cloak said.

Crane blew his nose on the curtain.

Everyone grimaced with disgust.

"Grab your gear, everyone," Grey Cloak said grimly. "We need to find Tatiana."

ARROWWOOD

ON A RISE IN THE GREEN HILLS OF ARROWWOOD, OVER A LEAGUE AWAY, TALON watched the rising sun shine on Monarch City. From the long distance, the castles spires were starlight-silver teardrops winking in the sun.

Crane sat on his wagon, holding his head and mumbling to himself. "I can't believe we are banished."

Grey Cloak stood on the ground beside Crane. "Is it really so bad? I'd never even been there before."

"Monarch City joins one side of the world with the other. Otherwise, you have to go around." Crane groaned. "I need some water. Does anyone have any water? My tongue feels like it has fur on it."

Dyphestive handed Crane a waterskin and said, "Drink all you want." He gave Crane a hearty pat on the back.

The paunchy, red-faced Crane said, "Oh, don't do that. My stomach is tumbling."

When the company had found Tatiana and Razor, it seemed that Tatiana was expecting them, and they joined up with the minotaur Grunt, who was waiting for them at Eastern Bridge. She told them that they would find better sanctuary in Arrowwood. They rode into the night, by horseback and wagon, and set up camp over a league away from Monarch City.

While the others rested, Grey Cloak patrolled the rolling hills of Arrowwood. The land was rich in woodland and colorful brush that seemed to go on for days. Varmints of all sorts nestled in the trees and scurried over the ground. It was a very suitable climate in which an elf could roam and hunt freely. It was even better when daylight illuminated the land, showing off all the colors and splendors that the wild had to offer.

As Grey Cloak made his way around the camp, helping others pack and rolling up blankets and bedrolls, he caught up with Tatiana. "It was a rough night last night. I say that we bury that hatchet."

She tied her hair back in a ponytail and said, "So long as I don't bring the figurine up again?"

"I'm not parting with it."

"And I'm not going to risk my life, or others', if you insist on using it. Listen, I have to be able to trust you on these missions. I can't do that with so much uncertainty. I'm not going to lie—I hate that object. It is an evil thing."

He loaded a bedroll into the back of the wagon. "For the time being, why don't we change the subject?"

"That suits me."

Grey Cloak eyed the splendid surroundings of the sunny day and said, "Let me guess. You are from Arrowwood?"

"Most elves are, including me." She had a meal bag in one hand and fed her horse with the other. "Arrowwood will give us sanctuary that we desperately need. Not only that, but there are many dragon charms to be found in its forests."

"How many dragon charms do you have?"

"The Wizard Watch won't say. We only retrieve them."

He shook his head. "At some point, we are going to have to use them. But it's going to be a problem if we don't have any dragons. Does the Wizard Watch raise dragons too?"

"No. The Sky Riders do that," she said as she climbed into her saddle.

"But there aren't any Sky Riders."

"There's you and Dyphestive."

Dyphestive tossed him a bedroll, and he dropped it into the wagon.

"First, I failed the Sky Rider course. Second, I have a dragon. And third, Dyphestive has never ridden a dragon or been trained to ride one."

She turned her horse, faced them, and said, "No, but he's a natural, the same as you. We believe that all naturals can ride dragons. If not, we still have the dragon charms."

Dyphestive tilted his head to the side and said, "I can be a Sky Rider?"

"Of course. You are the son of Olgstern Stronghair, a great Sky Rider. Why would you think otherwise?"

Dyphestive scratched behind an ear and said, "I never took the time to think about it." His face lit up. "I could fly a dragon?"

"It's an overrated experience, brother. Trust me," he said.

"You rode on the back of Commander Shaw's dragon, Jentak," Tatiana offered.

"True, but Streak was controlling him," Grey Cloak answered. He hadn't seen Streak all morning, and he scanned the area and spotted his dragon in the shade of a tree. "There you are."

"And we believe that Streak is special and can control many others," she said.

He brushed a strand of hair out of his eye and asked, "Who is we? You speak like there is more than one of you." *It makes me think that you are out of your skull too.* "I don't see anyone else but Grunt and Razor, and I don't get the feeling that they are the decision makers in all of this.

"No, they aren't," she said in her frosty manner. She sat tall in the saddle and carried the beauty of a goddess. "When I say *we*, I mean the Wizard Watch. I use my arcane powers to communicate back and forth with them."

"It doesn't seem like that is the case."

His neck hairs stood on end, and he drew his sword at the same time Dyphestive lifted his club. "Someone is here! Show yourself!"

A ghostly form in robes appeared between Grey Cloak and Dyphestive, the sun shining through it. Grey Cloak couldn't believe his eyes.

Dyphestive exclaimed, "Dalsay!"

24

DALSAY LOOKED NO DIFFERENT FROM HOW HE'D LOOKED THE DAY HE DIED IN RAVEN Cliff. His brown hair was long and wavy, and his beard was neatly trimmed. His features were strong and handsome, and he still wore the same black-and-gray-checkered, gold-trimmed robes. The only difference was that the light passed right through him, and Grey Cloak could see the landscape on the other side.

Leena sauntered over and passed her hand through him. She jumped back and whipped out her nunchaku.

"Those won't do you any good," Dalsay advised her in his familiar stern voice. "My body exists in this world and another. I'm a shade."

"You aren't dead," Dyphestive said, eyes wide.

"The soul and the spirit live forever, but my body is long gone," Dalsay replied.

Dyphestive's shoulders dropped, and he said, "I'm sorry that you died trying to save me."

"Don't be sorry. Neither you nor anyone else could have done anything about it one way or another. We were overmatched that day, but heroes do what they must do." Dalsay walked over the grass and stood before Dyphestive. "What happened had to happen. Do not feel any guilt about it."

"What about Adanadel?" Jakoby asked.

"You are his brother, aren't you?" Dalsay replied. "He's moved on, but trust me when I say that he is in good spirits."

"And Browning?" Grey Cloak inquired.

"The same." Dalsay's eyes were haunting but bright. "Talon's journey is far from over. In death, the same as life, I am here to aid you. I will see to it that you stay the course and battle the enemy. You have come far. Now, you are seasoned and ready for the next step in your journey, the acquisition of more dragon charms. It is the only way."

"That can't be the only way to defeat Black Frost," Grey Cloak said. "I don't believe it."

"Do you have a better idea?"

"No. But I'll think of something."

"Perhaps you'll confront Black Frost yourself and summon the powers of the Figurine of Heroes and let heroes from another world destroy him. Does that scenario sound familiar?"

Grey Cloak couldn't fight back a guilty look and said, "Yes."

"I thought the same thing, but the figurine is not the answer. It is a tool that you learned to use as a crutch. It will become a fatal mistake. I suggest that you turn it over to Tatiana. That is what I should have done long ago. If I had, perhaps her brothers would still be alive today." Dalsay eyed Grey Cloak. "Think about it."

Grey Cloak tightened his cloak around his chest and eyeballed Tatiana. *Something is not right. This has her stench all over it. She's up to something.*

"We will meet again, across Arrowwood's Great River, in the valleys that have no name. It is a long journey. Be well." With a wave of his hand, he vanished.

Crane teetered in the wagon and said, "I don't know about the rest of you, but I'm seeing and hearing things." He cleaned his ear. "Did the rest of you hear and see a wizard?"

"It's very convenient that Dalsay, after all this time, would mention the figurine," Grey Cloak said to Tatiana.

"I don't take your meaning," she said.

"Do you really expect me to believe that was his ghost?" He shook his head. "Nice try, Tatiana. Do it again, and we are going to separate permanently." He got on his horse. "Take us across the river, and if you want to keep me around, don't mention the figurine again."

Grey Cloak brooded for the rest of the day and didn't speak to anyone. Tatiana got under his skin, and he didn't want anything to do with her.

As they crossed the shallow creek and headed over the next rise, Dyphestive caught up with him and asked, "Are you still mad at Tatiana?"

"Mad? Me? Have you ever seen me mad?"

"Oh, you? No, never. Listen, I only wanted to see if you were well. That is all. Are you?"

"I'm alive. We're alive. Why wouldn't I be well?"

"I think you feel guilty about the—"

Grey Cloak shot him a dangerous look.

"I won't say it. So far as I'm concerned, it's yours. You can do what you want with it. Aside from that, is there anything else on your mind?"

"Hmmm... aside from how to destroy Black Frost and save the world, not really. You?"

Dyphestive's stomach groaned. "I could use something to eat. A wild pig and some chicken eggs would go down well right now." He shifted in his saddle. "Do you really not think that was Dalsay?"

"It could have been an illusion. Tatiana would do anything to get *it* back."

Dyphestive nodded. "For a shade, Dalsay appeared genuine to me."

"Who is to say? He's a shade. Can we really trust a spirit from another world? He's not even flesh and blood." Grey Cloak took a backward glance at the others. "I feel that we are wasting our time running around Gapoli, finding dragon charms. We should be doing something else."

"Such as?"

"I don't know. I'm thinking."

"Well, the dragon charms are important, or Black Frost wouldn't want them. I don't see a problem pursuing that."

"Isn't there something else that you would rather pursue?"

"Nothing comes to mind. You?"

"Yes, living on my terms and not someone else's. That's what. Keep this between us, brother, but I feel that they are holding us back."

"What do you mean?"

"We are naturals. They aren't. We can do things that they can't. I'm sorry to say, but I think we would be better off on our own."

"Even Zora?"

"Even Zora," he said sadly. "I don't want her to get hurt."

25

DARK MOUNTAIN

"Dragon's breath," Dirklen cursed, his breath visible in the frosty air. "How many bloody steps are there?"

"A thousand, I've heard," Magnolia answered as she brushed her hair from her eyes.

Since they had returned to Dark Mountain, they had been ostracized from their dragons. The moment they arrived, Black Frost let out a roar so loud that it shook the very rock of Dark Mountain's ridges.

Now, they had been summoned to meet Black Frost face to face, and they had to climb, not fly, all the way to the top of Black Frost's temple, a ziggurat-like structure, wearing their full suits of armor.

The icy wind froze Dirklen's maturing chin whiskers. His fingers and toes were frozen, and the only things burning were his legs. He trudged on, head down, cursing under his breath most of the time, following Magnolia, who'd taken the lead.

His sister looked back at him and said, "Do you think he will kill us for failing?"

"We didn't fail. Father did. But I'd probably kill us."

They were nearing the top, and she started taking two steps at a time. "If he doesn't kill us, what do you think that he wants with us?"

With his usual sneer, he said, "I don't know, Magnolia. Maybe he wants to tell you that your hair looks pretty."

"Is that the best that you can come up with?"

He shoved her in the back and said, "Gum up and go!"

Dirklen had lost his patience long before they were summoned. It had been over a week, and they were banned from flying on dragons. All the Riskers were, per Black Frost's orders. The dragons shunned them and remained in their kennels. In the meantime, the Riskers were put to work doing meaningless military drills and backbreaking tasks. Dirklen and Magnolia had been included in all of this.

Magnolia slowed to a stop several steps from the top and asked, "Are you ready?"

"Of course I'm ready." Dirklen shoved by her and said with a worried look, "Well, come on. I'm sure he would have killed us by now if he wanted." He took the next few steps slowly and peeked over the temple's sprawling platform. He found Black Frost's burning blue gaze locked on his.

"Why do you make me wait?" Black Frost demanded.

The force of his breath sent Dirklen backward, and he started to fall off the steps. Magnolia grabbed his arm and hauled him back up.

He jerked his arm away and marched up the steps to the platform.

Black Frost's monstrous body almost filled the platform from one end to the other. From front horn to tail, he must have been one hundred yards long. Covered in black scales, with splashes of blue on the edges and ridges, he was by far the mightiest dragon, dwarfing all the others that were perched on the temple parapet, facing outward.

Dirklen and Magnolia bowed on hands and knees, trembling.

"Rise," Black Frost commanded.

They complied but kept their eyes on the ground.

"Jentak killed his rider, your father, Commander Shaw. Tell me what you saw."

Dirklen fought the best he could to keep his voice from cracking and said, "A runt dragon latched on to the top of Jentak's skull. Their eyes turned as white as snow. Without warning, Jentak scorched him."

"Scorched Father," Magnolia corrected under her breath.

"It doesn't matter now. He's dead," he fired back.

"What happened after that?" Black Frost asked.

"Majestic one, Jentak chased us," Magnolia said, drawing an angry look from her brother. "We kept our distance, assuming that the runt dragon might be a crypt dragon that could take control of the others. We moved to safety."

"You retreated like cowards!" Black Frost's voice shook the stone platform. "The Dark Mountain does not retreat. Black Frost does not retreat! A lone crypt dragon is not enough to control an army. You failed!"

Dirklen found his courage and argued back, saying, "We lost over twenty dragons and riders! We only regrouped. You called us back!"

Black Frost lowered his head, and his nostrils steamed their faces with hot, rancid breath. "You dare raise your voice to me, flea?" He dragged his paw over and touched Dirklen's chest plate with his claw. "I'll crushed you like a nut and eat you in a single swallow."

Dirklen bit his tongue as he fought the urge to say, "Do it!" Instead, he said something worse. "I don't understand why you didn't level the city yourself the same as you did at Hidemark."

"Who are you to question me?" Black Frost's eyes narrowed. "Your insolent tongue will cost you and your sister." He ran the tip of his claw down Dirklen's left cheek.

Dirklen screamed as if his entire body were on fire. He'd never felt such pain.

Black Frost did the same to Magnolia's right cheek. She fell to her knees, screaming as well.

"This mark is for all to see as a reminder of the price of failure," Black Frost said. "The next punishment will be far worse than this. This is only the beginning. I need leaders of the Riskers that are prepared and strong. The pair of you are not ready, but you will be." He lifted his head and turned away. "Dreadful one, come."

Dirklen couldn't believe his watering eyes, and Magnolia gave a sharp gasp. There was no mistaking the woman walking across the platform toward them. Back from the dead, it was the one and only Drysis the Dreadful.

When she stopped in front of Black Frost, he said, "You failed me in life. Don't fail me in death. Take them."

26

WEARING ONLY HIS TROUSERS, THE DOOM RIDER SCAR CARRIED A HEAVY BEAM OF wood on one shoulder. The muscles of his sweat-slickened body bulged and flexed with every step. He marched right over to the barracks, where Shamrok was waiting with a wooden mallet.

Like Scar, Shamrok had brawny muscles, but damp red hair clung to his shoulders.

They were building onto the barracks where they quartered, and they hadn't been doing anything else since Drysis had died over a year ago. All they did was work and wait.

Scar dropped the beam on the ground. An ax was lying nearby. He grabbed the handle, hefted it onto his shoulder, and brought it down onto the beam with a loud wooden whack.

Together, Scar and Shamrock loaded the beam onto another beam, starting a wall of logs chest high.

Shamrok asked, "What did the dragon say to the sheep?"

Scar didn't answer. He'd tired of Shamrok's musings and phrases months ago.

"Gulp," Shamrok said. He let out a hoarse guffaw. "You really need to loosen your girdle, brother. This won't go on forever."

"It feels like it. It was bad enough that we were shunned before, but now it is even worse without Drysis. At least with her, we mattered." Scar sank the ax into the wood. "Now we're lower than a wagon wheel rut."

"Maybe you, but I'm still floating at the top, if you ask me. It's all a matter of perspective," Shamrok said.

Scar scratched the stubble on his marred face. "I'd think you out of all of us would be more broken, given your relationship with Drysis."

"Women come and go. She moved on, and so will I." His thick red eyebrows knitted. "But if I ever find Dyphestive, I swear I'll end him."

"Not if I end him first." If there was one thing that kept Scar going, it was Dyphestive. He hated the youth more than anything he'd ever known. He'd tried to break Dyphestive, but instead, Dyphestive broke them when he killed their leader. Scar pulled the ax free from the block. "Let's get on with it."

They spent the next few hours notching logs into beams and stacking them ceiling high. As the sun started to fall behind the black rock, they sat down with their backs to the wall and drank from flasks of warm ale.

Ghost walked out of the stables that housed the gourn with a pitchfork in one hand and a plucked chicken in the other. He wore his dye-blue leather skull mask and his full suit of dragon-scale leather armor. His footfalls didn't make a sound as he crossed the grounds.

Scar's eyes followed Ghost until he vanished inside the barracks. "He's a strange one. I don't think I've ever seen him with the mask off."

"Or take a bath. You'd think he'd stink to the heavens." Shamrok's nose twitched. "At least he cooks."

"Yeah..." Scar stood and headed for the stone well on the rise near the outside corral. His boots kicked up dust on is way over. Hand over hand, he lowered the bucket attached to a rope and hauled it up again. Then he doused himself from head to toe with the water. "Ah, that's better."

Scar wiped his shock of black hair out of his eyes and cleaned the water away with his thumbs. When he opened his eyes, he saw Drysis and dropped the bucket. "Kiss my boots!" he cursed.

Drysis was escorted by Dirklen and Magnolia. Imposing, she stood taller than both of them. Her head was bald, her skin pale, and she no longer wore an eyepatch over her left eye. Instead, a blue gemstone eye twinkled inside the socket. The rest of her body was covered in a vest of black dragon-leather armor that she wore like a second skin. She carried no weapons.

Shamrok jumped to his feet and rushed over to her. He slowed to a stop a few feet away, gaping. "Drysis?"

She turned her head, and her cold gaze fell upon him. "Are you glad to see me, Shamrok?" she asked in her distinctive husky voice.

"I've never been gladder to see anyone," Shamrok said. He took a knee and kissed her hand. "I thought you were dead."

Drysis pulled her hand away and said, "I *am* dead. Black Frost resurrected me." She eyed Scar. "I'm not the flesh and blood that you knew."

Scar tried to hold Drysis's iron stare but averted his eyes. She had faint blue veins under the skin on her face and arms. Deep crow's-feet lined her eyes, which were more deeply sunken in their sockets than before. She wasn't the Drysis he knew, even though she looked and sounded much the same. She was an abomination.

"What is with the youths?" Scar asked.

Dirklen stiffened and said, "Watch your tongue, dog!"

"Black Frost sent them here to be trained by us. He feels they are weak and they need to be made stronger."

"I'm not weak," Dirklen stated. "I'll take any one of the Doom Riders apart." He stepped toward Scar. They stood eye to eye, but Scar had a heavier build. "Even though I don't think I can make you look any worse than you already are. I've never seen so much ugly on a face before."

Shamrok let out a hoarse chuckle.

"How old are you, boy?" Scar asked.

"Twenty seasons," Dirklen replied.

Scar nodded. "Twenty seasons, ha. I hope you enjoyed them, because you won't last to twenty-one."

ARROWWOOD

GREY CLOAK, ZORA, AND TATIANA HID IN THE CREVICES OF A RISE OF ROCKS THAT overlooked a river village. Tall, rangy, heavy-shouldered elves wearing nothing but buckskin and furs sauntered through the village. Unlike most elves, their hair was wild, their limbs were thicker, their ears were bigger and longer, and they moved with lumbering grace.

"Are you mad?" Grey Cloak asked Tatiana, but he kept his eyes fixed on the noteworthy elves. "That's a tribe of wild elves. They are practically barbarians. Look at them. If they catch us, they'll rip us apart and eat us."

"They aren't cannibals," Tatiana said. She shifted and got closer to Grey Cloak. "This will be an easy task." She pointed at the village, which consisted of round huts made from stone and clay with straw roofs thatched on the top. "Do you see the one in the middle? That is the one where they worship. The dragon charm will be in there. All that we need to do is sneak in and grab it."

"We?" he asked. "You mean Zora and me." Grey Cloak eyeballed the broad-chested elves with fascination. He'd never imagined that elves could be so big. They were even bigger than Bowbreaker. "Can't you zap the dragon charm from there to here? Wouldn't that make a lot more sense than our getting killed?"

"You're a natural. You can handle a handful of dull-minded savages, can't you?"

"I can handle them," Zora said, her big green eyes glued to the well-built wild elves' glorious frames. "What is the worst that can happen? They catch me and force me to marry into the family."

"They will make a feast out of you," he said.

"As I said, they aren't cannibals." Tatiana gave him a disappointed look. "I'm surprised you are worried about this one. It will prove much simpler than the others. No monsters, ghosts, or poisonous lizards. You'll be in and out in no time at all."

"I thought we were supposed to cross Great River."

"A little bird alerted me to this opportunity. We'd be fools to pass it up." She shoved him in the back. "Go and get after it. They won't suspect a thing while they are preparing for dinner."

"What do you want me to do? Creep down there in broad daylight, sneak inside, grab the dragon charm, and run?"

"You're the thief, not me. You'll figure something out," Tatiana said.

Zora's fingers massaged her black scarf. "I'll use the Scarf of Shadows and go in. Tatiana is right. This should be easy. I'll be back in no time." She started to lift the scarf over her nose.

Grey Cloak grabbed her arm and said, "No, wait."

Zora gave him a funny look. "Wait for what?"

He was worried about her, but he didn't have anything else to say, so he said, "Be careful."

She patted his cheek and said, "I will. I'll see you before you see me." She lifted the scarf over her button nose and vanished.

Grey Cloak's gaze followed her footfalls in the grass until any sign of her vanished altogether. The tips of his fingers tingled as he tried to search out the path that she was taking to the hut in the center of the village. There were two wild elves standing outside the entrance, holding spears. Both of them had prominent overbites.

"You care deeply for her, don't you?" Tatiana said.

"Of course I do, which is more than I can say for you."

"That's a frosty statement."

"Sorry, I shouldn't have said that." He crept farther away from Tatiana and higher up on the rocks. "I almost lost her once, and I'd hate to think that would happen again."

One of the barbaric elves' eyes narrowed, and he let out a grunt and lowered his spear. He scanned the area, and the other wild-eyed elf did the same. After several moments, they settled back into their posts.

Grey Cloak's heart jumped, and he started to rise.

Tatiana snagged the hem of his cloak and held him back. "Be patient. Zora can handle this."

"Says you."

"Yes, says me. You need to remember that Zora and I had our fair share of adventures long before you came along. She is very skilled. Don't worry. She won't do anything stupid. She's as wise as a serpent."

He eased back. "You'd better be right."

"Don't let your heart get in the way, Grey Cloak. This is a dangerous business that we engage in. You have to learn to use your head more than your heart."

"That must be easy for you."

She shook her head. "We have to work together, Grey Cloak. And I don't see any reason why you would hold a grudge against me. I'm only trying to protect you and the others."

"If you say so."

Tatiana's jaw clenched.

One part of Grey Cloak liked Tatiana, and the other part didn't. For some reason, the woman, who was so beautiful that men would bow at her feet, got under his skin. Her intentions were good, or so it seemed, but something about her repelled him.

Dusk fell upon the river valley, and the wild elves gathered wood, started fires, and began to cook hunks of meat.

Grey Cloak had been holding his tongue for close to an hour, but the dam finally broke. "She should have been out of there by now."

"Zora is very careful. Have faith in her skill," Tatiana said as she picked her lip. "There is no reason to be alarmed. No one else has entered or come out."

"Maybe it's not in there."

"If that were the case, she would have come back out."

He nodded, but he was tingling all over. He knew Zora well enough to know that she wouldn't dally.

Something's wrong. I know it.

Just as the thought passed his mind, the two elven sentries rushed inside.

I knew it.

28

Grey Cloak stood up and started to jump down the rocks.

"Hold your horses, big fella."

He swung around. Zora was sitting behind him and Tatiana, tossing an egg-sized emerald-green dragon charm up and down in her hand.

"Zora!"

"Were you worried about me?" she asked, beaming with pride.

"Uh... no."

"Really? You look surprised to see me." Zora flipped the dragon charm to Tatiana, who quickly squirrelled it away in her robes.

"Well done, friend." Tatiana glanced at Grey Cloak. "I never had a shred of doubt."

"I didn't either, but it did take you much longer than it would have taken me," he said.

"Ha!" Zora replied. "You wouldn't have made it past the sentries, who are very smelly, by the way. I didn't expect that, seeing how they have an entire river to wash in."

"Savages don't bathe," he replied, smirking.

He looked over his shoulder. The sentries had come back outside the tent and started hollering for help. An enclave of wild elves rushed over on bare feet.

"Still, I believe that your theft has not gone without notice."

Zora hopped over to Grey Cloak and shared a rock with him. "Well, another guard was inside, and I put him to sleep with the Ring of Mist. My, he woke up quickly."

"The wild elves have an extraordinary constitution," Tatiana said as she crept down the rocks. "It's best that we start moving before they sniff us out."

"What are *those* things?" Zora asked with a strong hint of concern.

"Good question," Grey Cloak said as he fixed his stare on a pack of the biggest dogs he'd ever seen. The dogs had flat snouts, blocky faces, and shiny spotted coats. Their legs were long, and they had brawny necks and shoulders. They sniffed the ground. Saliva dripped from their jaws, and they began to bark and howl.

"Those are wolf hounds!" Tatiana said. "Run! We must run!" She took off down the other side of the rocks at a full sprint, leaving Grey Cloak and Zora standing on the rock.

Grey Cloak's eyes followed Tatiana. "She's pretty fast for a sorceress. Are they normally that fast?"

"She's an elf, isn't she?" Zora tugged on his arm. "Goose feathers, they come!"

By the time Grey Cloak glanced back at the village, the hounds were moving their way quickly. A knot of elves trailed after them. "They're fast! Run, Zora!"

But she'd already taken off after Tatiana and vanished into the trees.

"Oh. I suppose I should go."

Grey Cloak leapt from the rocks and landed on the soft ground of the rise. His long strides carried him into the wood line. He slid through the trees like a ghost, the sound of the wolf hounds charging into the forest following him. *They are closing the gap. Zooks!*

He burst through the other side of the wood line and picked up speed, gaining on Zora and Tatiana. Waving his arms, he said, "Go! Go! Go!"

The other members of Talon waited by a large pond, and they had the horses ready. Jakoby led two horses, and Razor led one horse out to meet them.

They raced down the hill and climbed into their saddles just as the pack of wolf hounds raced out of the woods.

Eyes widened, Jakoby said, "Sweet Monarchy! Those are some big dogs!" He dug his heels into his horse's ribs. "Yah!"

Crane's wagon took the lead on the trail. The wagon wheels rumbled over the dirt and rock. He was hauling Grunt in the back of the wagon. It didn't take long for the other riders to overtake him.

Grey Cloak pulled alongside him and asked, "Can't you go any faster?"

"I have over five hundred pounds of minotaur in the back. Vixen is going as fast as she can go," Crane said.

The wolf hound pack raced after them. Behind the dogs, the wild elves' arms and legs pumped as they sped down the trail, howling, blood in their eyes.

"Turn the wagon into the Wheels of Fire," Grey Cloak suggested.

Crane shook his head. "I can't do that. Enough time hasn't passed. The magic doesn't work like that."

Zooks!

Grunt sat calmly in the back of the wagon with his club across his lap. The bison-faced minotaur stared down the hounds and didn't bat an eye.

What does one say to a minotaur?

Grey Cloak urged his horse ahead and caught up with the rest of the group. "Dyphestive, we have a problem."

Dyphestive looked over his shoulder and said, "I can see that. Are those elves really wild?"

"Yes! They are going to catch Crane. He's too slow, hauling Grunt behind him."

"Those elves are big. There must be scores of them," Dyphestive said.

"I think it's every wild-eyed savage in the village!"

Tatiana's ponytail flew behind her like a banner.

He caught up with her and said, "Give me the charm!"

"No!" she said.

"Look at them. They are going to kill us!"

"There is no turning back now. They will kill us either way!"

Grey Cloak's brow knitted, and he said, "Give me the dragon charm, or I will use the figurine."

"You wouldn't dare!"

"You aren't giving me a choice!"

Tatiana fished the dragon charm out of her robes and stuffed it into his hand. "You'll regret this."

"No, I won't." He slowed until he was at the back of the group and held the dragon charm up high so that all could see. Its emerald facets twinkled in the last light of the day. He hurled it at the elves. "Here, take it!"

The dragon charm tumbled through the air and landed right in the midst of the wild elves. The wild-eyed elven savages' fast footfalls did not slow. With fire in their eyes and crude weapons in their hands, they charged on.

Grey Cloak swallowed. *Oh no, Tatiana was right! I'll never live this down! Zooks!*

29

"CRANE, ARE YOU CERTAIN THAT YOU CAN'T TURN YOUR WAGON INTO FIRE?" GREY Cloak asked.

"I've tried," Crane responded with a flick of his carriage whip. "Believe me, I've tried!" He glanced behind him. "They're going to rip us apart, aren't they?"

"I think so!" At the moment, Grey Cloak was all out of ideas. The only choice was to fight, but in the back of his mind, he knew it wasn't fair. After all, they'd stolen from the savages. They had a right to be angry. On the other hand, perhaps the wild elves were an evil pack of raiders. It was difficult to tell, but they were the scariest knot of men he'd ever seen.

"Log!" Dyphestive screamed. "Log!"

The horse riders in front leapt over a tree that had fallen over the path.

"Oh no," Crane said.

Vixen jumped over the tree, but the wagon wheels burst right into it. The wagon bounced off the ground, rolled over on its side, and crashed but not before Crane and Grunt jumped clear.

Grey Cloak pulled his horse to a halt and drew his sword. The wolf hounds bounded toward Grunt, who shielded Crane with his towering frame. Grunt swung his unique club into two of them, cracking their ribs and sending them flying backward. The dogs bit and chewed on Grunt's mighty limbs. He beat them with up-and-down strokes with the blunt side of his club.

Dyphestive, Jakoby, Razor, and Leena charged the elven ranks on horseback, their weapons primed to strike. They thundered right by Grey Cloak, straight toward the angry throng.

We are going to get slaughtered. There are too many of them. Grey Cloak reached for the figurine inside his cloak.

When they were yards from a flesh-and-bone collision, an eardrum-shattering roar sounded. The horses reared, and the wolf hounds cowered and backed away. The savage elves crouched, and some scattered. Many jabbed their weapons toward the sky, faces full of fear.

"*Roooaaarrr!*"

The monstrous sound was so loud that Grey Cloak wasn't alone in covering his ears. The roar shook the air like a blast of thunder and turned his stomach into jelly. He lifted his eyes to the sky.

A dragon soared through the air with its wings spread wide. A blast of fire spewed from its mouth, lighting up the darkening sky.

The wide-eyed wild elves and wolf hounds ran as fast as their feet and paws would take them. They disappeared into the woodland, big bodies rustling through the branches.

The company fought to control their horses as one final roar carried across the river valley. Everyone's eyes were fixed upward and locked on the dragon. Slowly, it descended and landed in the company's midst.

Grey Cloak couldn't believe his eyes. He slid out of the saddle. "Streak! Did you do that?" He rushed over and picked up his dragon and let Streak lick his face.

The ashen and sweaty faces of the members of Talon regained their color, and warm smiles crossed their faces.

Dyphestive was the first to comment. "That little dragon made that much noise?"

"Apparently so," Grey Cloak said while holding Streak out like a baby. "You're full of surprises, aren't you?"

Streak shrugged his wings.

Zora giggled. "And full of personality," she said.

Everyone from Dyphestive to Leena passed by and patted Streak on the head.

"The little dragon bailed us out again," Tatiana commented. "His timing couldn't have been better. The wild elves are very superstitious people, and that tribe must have had a great fear of dragons."

"Or very loud noises. Wait." He handed Streak to Dyphestive. "The dragon charm!" He sprinted down the trail and stopped at the spot where the dragon charm had landed. He took a knee, and his fingers clawed at the dirt and grass. The dragon charm had been trampled into the soft ground underneath a clump of grass. He dug it out and rubbed the dirt off. He held it up high and jogged back. "Found it."

"Well done," Tatiana said. "I told you that it wouldn't make a difference."

Grey Cloak turned his back and walked away.

Crane worked on freeing Vixen from her harness. His stubby fingers struggled to unbuckle the bit and bridle from her mouth. The horse was lathered up and whinnying. "She's upset."

"Is she hurt?" Grey Cloak asked.

"No. It wasn't the wreck. I think your little dragon scared the manure out of her." Crane petted the dragon's neck. "If you smell something funny, it's because Streak scared the manure out of me too."

With Grey Cloak's help, Crane freed Vixen from her harness, and the horse trotted off.

Dyphestive and Grunt tipped the wagon over as easily as if they were rolling a log in water. Grunt gave Dyphestive a nod and a grunt.

The company made small repairs to the wagon wheels' busted spokes then gathered and strapped down their scattered gear.

"Night has fallen," Crane said with a peek at the starry sky. "We might as well make camp. What do you think?"

"It sounds good to me," Grey Cloak said.

"We will make camp," Tatiana said in a loud and distinct voice, "and leave before first light."

Grey Cloak rolled his eyes and noticed Razor standing apart from the group, staring down the path in the direction they'd come. Fearing the wild elves' return, he said, "We are going to need a lookout in case they return."

"They won't," Tatiana assured the group.

"How do you know that?" he asked.

"I know. Trust me," she said.

"Well, those elves might not be coming back this way, but someone is." Razor pointed down the path.

A figure wearing a full cloak and heavy armor approached, a sword strapped to their back.

Razor drew his sword. "Not to worry. I'll check it out."

30

BEFORE RAZOR MADE IT WITHIN TEN FEET OF THE STRANGER, A SHOCK OF BLUE energy shot out of the newcomer's fingers. Razor dropped his sword and fell to his knees, the hairs of his head standing on end. His teeth clacked together as the stranger walked right past him.

The members of Talon formed a wall on the path and stood armed and ready.

Jakoby pointed his sword at the oncoming stranger and said, "Show yourself!"

Something about the stranger's gait caught Grey Cloak's eye as he moved forward. He tilted his head and asked, "Anya?"

The stranger pulled back their hood, revealing Anya's stern expression but lovely face. She had a white scar on her neck, partially covered by her lustrous auburn hair. She gave a slight smile and said, "Glad you remember me."

Before Grey Cloak realized that his feet were moving, he wrapped her in a warm embrace. "I was told that you were dead!"

Anya stood with her arms hanging stiffly, and without so much as a pat on the back, she said, "You were told wrong."

Grey Cloak broke off the hug and swung his gaze toward Tatiana. "You told me that all of them were dead."

"I was only passing along what was given to me. No one in the Wizard Watch believed that any of them survived." Tatiana came forward with a welcoming smile on her face. "This is an unexpected blessing. Welcome, Anya."

Brimming with fire, Anya said, "Welcome yourself, witch of the Watch, and back away from me."

Tatiana stepped back with a shocked look on her face.

Before they exchanged another word, Dyphestive got ahold of Anya's waist, picked her up like a child, and spun her around. "Anya, it is so very good to see you! I thought you were gone too!"

Anya patted him on the head. "It's good to see you, too, Dyphestive. Will you please set me down so I don't have to jolt you?"

Razor lumbered up the path, using his sword like a cane, and asked, "Is that what you call that kiss you gave me? Oh my, look at you. You are something else, Fiery Red. You can give me a jolt anytime."

Anya looked Razor up and down with disdain. "Who is this lackey? And will you put me down, Dyphestive?"

"Oh, sorry." He set her on her feet.

"I'm Reginald the Razor, the finest swordsman in all the land." He took a bow, swayed, and shook his head quickly. "I'm still tingly from the kiss you gave me."

"It wasn't a kiss," Anya said.

Jakoby stepped forward with a broad smile on his face. "And he's not the finest swordsman either. I'm Jakoby, a former Monarch Knight. It's an honor to meet you, Sky Rider." He took her by the hand and kissed it. "My sword is yours if you ever need it."

"Not likely," she said as she tugged her hand out of Jakoby's bearish grip.

"Anya, where have you been?" Dyphestive asked. "We missed you."

Leena kicked him in the back of the leg and dropped him down to one knee. "What did you do that for?"

With a frown that looked more like a weapon, Leena grabbed him by the ear and pulled him away from the company.

"See you later, Anya? I hope," Dyphestive said.

With an eyebrow raised, Anya asked Grey Cloak, "Is Dyphestive spoken for?"

"'Spoken for' is a funny phrase," he replied then introduced the others. "That's Leena, an outcast from the Ministry of Hoods. Zora. And you remember Crane, of course."

She nodded.

"And that's Grunt, a minotaur from Sulter Slay," he added.

"Yes, I know where minotaurs come from." Anya grabbed his wrist and said, "I need to speak to you privately. No offense, everyone, but I didn't come all this way to meet you. I have business with this one."

Before Grey Cloak could get another word in, Anya dragged him off, out of sight and earshot of the others. They stood inside a grove of dogwood trees whose pink-and-white petals were blooming.

"What is going on, Anya? Whatever you tell me, you can tell them."

"Even the witch from the Wizard Watch?"

"Well, maybe not," he admitted.

She looked him dead in the eye and said, "All the Sky Riders are gone except for us. You need to come with me, Grey Cloak. We have to rebuild the Sky Riders."

He rolled his eyes and said, "Not this again." He checked the sky. "Are you and Cinder going to kidnap me again?"

"Cinder is not here."

Grey Cloak paled. "I'm sorry."

"No, he's not dead. But I couldn't risk him flying here and the Riskers discovering him or me. I had to hunt you down alone."

Streak snaked through the grass and stopped at Anya's feet with his tail slowly waving back and forth.

She picked him up, cradled him in her arms, and said, "Look at how big you have gotten, Streak. And you are as handsome as ever."

Streak licked her cheek.

She kissed his nose and said, "That was a fine job that you did on Jentak, little one."

"You saw that?"

"I was in the city, trying to track you down, when the invasion occurred," she said. "It was a very surprising turn of events. Well done, Sky Rider."

"I'm not a Sky Rider," he said.

"Of course you are. You are a natural, the son of Zanna Paydark. That is what you are meant to be."

He gave her a doubtful look and asked, "What are we going to do, Anya? Do you think that you, me, Streak, and Cinder are going to stop Black Frost? You saw how many Riskers he had, and that probably wasn't all of them. We need help. Tatiana might not be the best leader, but finding the dragon charms is the only way."

Anya stepped toe to toe and eye to eye with him and said, "She is a part of the Wizard Watch. You can't trust them."

31

A SMALL CAMPFIRE MADE OF BROKEN BRANCHES AND TWIGS SURROUNDED BY A RING of rocks crackled at Grey Cloak's feet. He, like the others of the company, sat captivated by the full-blown argument that Anya and Tatiana—standing at opposite ends of the fire—were engaged in.

Anya's fists were balled up at her sides, like she was going to punch Tatiana's teeth out. Tatiana kept her nose up and talked back calmly but with all-knowing smugness. No one in the group dared say a word for fear of having their tongues ripped out.

"Have you ever seen a dragon charm after you turned it over to the Wizard Watch?" Anya argued. "Have you? *Have* you?"

"I don't need to see. I only need to do my duty. You should do your duty as well," Tatiana replied.

"That is the problem with mages. They think they know it all. How do you know that they aren't giving the dragon charms to Black Frost?"

Tatiana brushed it off with a flip of her hand. "They would never do that."

"No, because they never do anything but interfere!" Anya poked her finger across the fire. "What do they do but sit in the towers, supposedly guardians of peace, yet where were they when Black Frost attacked my people? Nowhere!"

"We didn't know where you were," Tatiana said.

"Say the ones that presume to know everything. A funny thing, Tatiana—if the Wizard Watch is gathering stones to rebuild the Sky Riders' dragon forces, then where are they? Hmm? Because the Sky Riders never saw a single one of what you say you recovered."

All eyes fell on Tatiana. She appeared to shrink inside her robes. She had nothing to say. Anya rambled on, keeping the full attention of the quiet audience.

Dyphestive and Razor had Grey Cloak walled in by the fire.

Razor nudged him and said quietly, "I like Fiery Red. She makes me feel prickly and warm all over. She's not spoken for, is she?"

A twinge of jealousy made Grey Cloak's gut flip, and he said, "You might want to talk to Dyphestive. He says that he is going to marry her."

"I did?" He scratched his head. "Oh, I did, didn't I."

Leena, who was sitting beside Dyphestive, threw an elbow into his ribs.

"Will you stop that? I was a stripling back then," Dyphestive said as he covered his ribs with his hands.

Razor grinned. "It looks like the big one has the sort of women problems I'd like to have. Good for him. I have to admit, I like these women. All of them. They have the fire that I admire. And look at the bottom on Red. It's as round as an apple."

Anya stopped midsentence, turned, and glared at Razor. Her fingertips sparked with blue fire.

Razor lifted his hands and said, "Jolt me, please."

Anya's eyes burned a hole in him.

Grey Cloak said, "Perhaps it is time to take a break from this conversation. After all, it is going nowhere." He stood up and ruffled his cloak. "Simply put, the two of you don't like each other. My suggestion is that you avoid all conversation whatsoever."

"Yes, not fighting. Where I come from, the women wrestle when they disagree," Razor offered.

"Hear! Hear!" Crane said and sucked on a wineskin.

"I agree," Jakoby said. "It's the best way to let out your anger and bond."

"No one is going to be bonding with anyone," Tatiana said.

"You foolish men. Shame on your hearts," Anya replied. "Do you really want to see me break this woman into pieces?"

"Excuse me?" Tatiana crossed the fire and bumped chests with Anya. "I'm not scared of you."

Anya seized Tatiana's arm and hip-checked her hard to the ground. In the wink of an eye, she had Tatiana's face in the dirt and her arm twisted behind her back. "Don't ever touch me again, witch!"

Tatiana's eyes glowed white hot. A pulse of white energy shot out of her body and into Anya.

Gritting her teeth, Anya held on to Tatiana. With pain in her voice she said, "It will take more than that to shake me!" She yanked Tatiana's arm backward.

"Aaauuugh!" The fire in Tatiana's bright eyes cooled as beads of sweat built up on her forehead. "Let me go, you brute," she demanded.

"I'll let you up when I'm bloody ready!" She cranked up the pressure, and Tatiana started to kick.

"Enough!" Zora came out of nowhere, plowed into Anya, and drove her to the ground.

They rolled over the grass once before Anya took command on top and held a dagger to Zora's throat. Her chin lifted when her eyes dropped on the small blade that Zora held to her throat as well.

"Ladies, please, drop your blades," came a ghostly voice.

Grey Cloak followed the women's eyes to the shade of Dalsay.

32

Anya lowered her weapon, as did Zora, then Anya helped Zora to her feet and put her dagger in her sheath with a click. She stared down Dalsay and said, as though she'd seen a thousand ghosts before, "Who is this shade? Another trickster from the Wizard Watch?"

"The truth is," Dalsay said, his stern expression making his transparent form appear as real as ever, "that neither I nor Tatiana can say for certain what the Wizard Watch is doing with the dragon charms."

"That's a fat lot of help," Anya said. "And it confirms what I have been saying all along. They can't be trusted. Grey Cloak, you need to come with me and distance yourself from this pack of deceivers."

"Pardon me?" Jakoby stood and said, "Save your javelins for the mages, but don't insult me."

"Or the rest of us," Zora said.

Dyphestive rose. "Grey Cloak won't be going anywhere. Not without me. And we are staying with Talon. We are Talon."

"Son of Olgstern Stronghair, you are a natural, like us, and more than welcome to come along, but the rest will have to go it alone. They cannot fly the dragons," Anya said.

"What dragons?" Grey Cloak asked. "I thought only Cinder was left. Where is he, anyway?"

Anya stiffened and said, "His location is my business, and I won't be revealing it in front of these snakes. As for the others, we will find them."

Zora took a spot beside Grey Cloak and said, "You spent a season with her. I feel sorry for you. But if you must go, I'll understand and support you."

Tatiana brushed off her robes and stood by Dalsay. "This is outrageous. We were on course before you came along. You have brought only chaos."

"Says the enchantress that led them to the wild elf savages. If not for a *dragon*, all of you might have been dead," Anya stated. Her jaw clenched. "But I would have saved you."

"Such arrogance!" Tatiana said.

"I think I could have handled them myself," Razor said as he spun a dagger through his fingers. "If not for the dragon, I'd be wearing a necklace of pointed ears right now."

"Ew," Zora said.

He gave her a wink and replied. "Too much?"

Dalsay lifted his hands and said in a commanding voice, "Listen to me, please. We won't solve our situation by arguing. Tatiana, my dearest, Anya's concerns are not without foundation."

Tatiana's jaw dropped, and she crossed her arms.

Dalsay continued, "Hear me out. I have a strong sense that some of the Wizard Watch are misaligned, though I cannot prove this. I can only say that I have more questions than answers. With that said, I have full faith that the dragon charms are a vital ingredient in engineering Black Frost's defeat. Otherwise, he would not pursue them. As of now, I do what is expected of me, and Tatiana executes what is expected of her. We have no reason to do otherwise."

"Otherwise. Otherwise." Anya paced, a scowl on her face. "You said that you don't trust them. Still, you serve them like slaves."

"I only stated that I have my concerns. This is why Tatiana and I believe it is imperative that you journey to the Wizard Watch tower of Arrowwood across Great River. Perhaps there, more answers to your questions will be revealed. You must ask."

Anya tossed her head back and laughed. "Ask them whatever you want, and they will tell you what you want to hear. The wizardly ones are only using you to serve their agenda. Can't you see that?"

Grey Cloak replied, "You're right. We've recovered the dragon charms, and for what? No one aside from the Sky Riders and us has done anything to fight Black Frost. And what we have done, we have done without dragon charms. Perhaps we are only chasing our tails."

"So you will come with me?" Anya asked.

He shook his head. "No. I'm sorry, Anya, but I'm not going to leave my friends. We are all that we have, and we need to stay together. If anything, I say that you should stay with us."

"Are you mad? I didn't come all this way to join your group. I'm a Sky Rider," she said with her chin lifted high. "And so are you."

"They banished me, remember? You helped me escape."

"I know, but that was different. You are the only one with the training and a dragon. And you are the son of Zanna Paydark. The Sky Riders need you."

"The Sky Riders need me?" He touched his chest and pointed at her. "Or you need me?"

"You know what I mean. Who is it going to be? Us or them?"

"I told you, Anya, I'm not leaving my friends. You're my friend, too, and you should come with us."

Anya walked over to him, put a hand on his shoulder, and said right in his ear, "You're making a mistake." Without another word, she moved away from the campfire and strode into the night.

He called after her. "Anya, wait. Come back."

"Should I go after her?" Dyphestive asked.

"No, let her go," Grey Cloak answered, defeat in his voice. His heart sank as he watched her go. She'd come all that way for him and forced him to choose. "I made the right choice. Don't you think?"

"You made the same choice that I would have made. You chose your closest friends."

Razor joined them, slapped his hand on Grey Cloak's shoulder, and said, "You spurned your first woman. Well done. It will come back to bite you in the behind when you least expect it."

33

DARK MOUNTAIN

Dirklen waddled into the stables with Magnolia trailing behind him. His hand was braced against his lower back, which felt as if it was on fire. From dawn to dusk, they hadn't stopped doing one back-breaking chore after the other, all under the watchful eye of the Doom Riders.

Magnolia collapsed onto a bale of hay. She groaned and said, "My armor is chafing me all over. What did we do to deserve this?"

"Nothing." With a scowl, he started loosening the buckles of his breastplate. He removed it and slung it into the stable's back wall. "Nothing at all. We are naturals, and we shouldn't be taking direction from the likes of them."

"Quit crying, boy," Scar said.

Dirklen's back straightened, and his eyes grew bigger.

Scar stood at the entrance of the stable, which had become their quarters for the duration of their stay. He put a wooden bucket full of water and a platter of boiled potatoes and raw carrots on the floor. "Enjoy your dinner, children."

"Call me a child again, and I'll stuff those carrots into your earhole."

Scar let out a rugged laugh. "Huh-huh-huh-huh. Anytime, boy."

With her knees drawn to her chest like a child, Magnolia said, "We want to see our mother. Adalia. Does she even know where we are?"

"Drysis is your mother now. That is all that you need to know." Scar closed them inside. "Sweet dreams, children. Huh-huh-huh. Sweet dreams."

"I hate him," Dirklen said as he stripped off his sweat-soaked jerkin and slung it over the stable's wall. He was as fit as a young man could be and had a pattern of bumps and bruises on his back and chest. He picked up the tray and set it down between them. "I hate all of them. I hate everything."

"We are being treated like animals." She sniffed. "It's not fair."

"Don't you dare snivel, sister." He picked out a potato and bit into it. "Do you understand me? We'll get through this charade and be riding on a dragon's back in no time." He tossed her a spud. "Now, eat and keep your strength up. We will not give these snake bellies the satisfaction."

"I know," she said. "But we've never trained so hard before."

Dirklen's scowl never left his face as he said, "I know. Father protected us. Thanks to him, Black Frost thinks that we are weak."

"You can't blame Father!"

"Oh, but I can. He's the reason we are here!" His voice started to crack. "If he hadn't died, we wouldn't be here." He slung a potato, and it splattered against the wall. "It's his fault!"

Magnolia rocked back and forth and said, "We are spoiled, aren't we?"

Dirklen picked up a raw carrot and started eating. "It doesn't matter. We are what we are, and we need to be prepared to fill Father's boots before someone else does." He spit out the rough end of the carrot. "He should have prepared us for this."

"I think they were cocky," she said. "Black Frost thought that Monarch City would crumble against our might, but they didn't."

"What are you talking about? They did surrender, according to plan. Codd showed up with Dyphestive, of all people, and ruined the plan. Your friend Grey Cloak didn't make matters any easier. They killed our father and my dragon." He seethed. "I will get them. I will get both of them."

"Perhaps if we were nicer to them when they were younger, none of this would have happened. They would have stayed and become one of us," she suggested.

"You have a strange perspective, sister. I wish you would gum up." Dirklen scooted back into a corner and turned his back to her. The day had been bad enough, and he didn't want to finish it with her babbling. Magnolia wasn't stupid, and he knew that she only spoke to annoy him. Regardless, it still got under his skin every time.

"Brother," she said.

He cringed.

"Does the scar that Black Frost gave you still burn? I only ask because mine does. It wakes me in my sleep. It will go away, won't it?"

He touched the gash on his cheek. It still burned deep, a constant reminder of his failure that would live with him the rest of his days. "Get used to it."

"I won't ever get used to it, I think. It makes me angry."

"It makes me angry too. It's a nuisance, much like your voice."

"Don't be so nasty to me, dear brother. I'm all that you have. And you never had any other friends to begin with anyway."

He looked over his shoulder. Magnolia had made herself comfortable on her bed of straw and closed her eyes. Her words rang true, and they stung. The truth was that he didn't have any friends aside from her and their mother and father. He'd never felt close to any of them either. He remembered years ago, seeing Grey Cloak and Dyphestive laughing with others. He hated them for it. He didn't know why, but he did.

"Magnolia," he said quietly.

"Yes?"

"I wish I had a pillow."

"Why is that, brother?"

"So I could smother you with it."

Magnolia let out a goofy giggle. "I'd like to see you try it."

34

TALON TRAVELED UNMOLESTED TOWARD GREAT RIVER MANY LONG DAYS ON END. They stuck to the back trails, following Tatiana's lead. Grey Cloak used Streak to spy any trouble from the sky.

It was a solemn journey through beautiful countryside filled with every flower and tree imaginable. Groves of incredible oaks stood over five hundred feet high. The deep green and golden leaves were so large that a man could make a blanket out of them.

Being a full elf, Grey Cloak should have appreciated the trip more, but his heart was unsettled. He'd left Anya out in the cold. She didn't have anyone left, and he'd all but abandoned her. He'd been riding in the rear, hood-covered head down, isolated from the others.

Dyphestive rode alongside him. He didn't say anything at first, as he was busy crushing nuts that had fallen from the trees. "These nuts are good. Not very filling but good. Have some?"

"I'll pass, but thanks."

"We haven't talked much, but I wanted to say I'm glad that you wanted to stay with Talon. I wished Anya would have remained, but well, I wanted you to know that I think you did the right thing."

"If I did the right thing, it doesn't feel like it. I spent a lot of time training with her and the others. She'd been with them her entire life." He lowered his head again. "Now, she doesn't have anybody."

"She could have come with us."

"No, she wouldn't stay away from Cinder so long. It must have been hard enough to depart from him to begin with. All on account of me. I feel guilty."

Dyphestive dusted the crumbs off his hands and said, "I feel guilty too."

"Why?"

He shrugged. "We are different, being naturals, and Anya was one of us. I can't explain it, but I feel different from the others somehow."

Eyeing the others, Grey Cloak asked, "Then why are we following them?"

"I don't think that we are following her. We are following you."

"Me?"

"You are the one that agreed to go to the Wizard Watch. If you hadn't, I'm pretty sure everyone else would have followed you elsewhere. Well, besides Tatiana and her henchman."

"Do you really think that?"

"I do."

"Huh." He sat up in his saddle. "I'm pretty sure Zora is mad at me. She hasn't spoken to me since Anya left."

"You haven't spoken to her either. But neither have I. If I do, Leena gets mad. At least, I think she is mad." He lifted his shoulders and gave a perplexed look. "I can't tell because she always looks mad."

"What sort of relationship have you gotten yourself into?"

"I don't know what to call it. How can I call it anything when she doesn't even talk?"

Grey Cloak laughed.

At that very moment, Leena turned and glared at both of them. Dyphestive noticeably shrank in his saddle, like he was trying to dodge her stare.

Grey Cloak couldn't help but chuckle. "Ha-ha, I'm pretty sure she sees you. She's like the little hound that runs the bigger pack. Why are you scared of her? She can't hurt you."

"I don't know. But she does. What do I do?"

"Apparently, whatever she tells you to." He laughed again.

"She doesn't tell me anything, but I'm still doing it." Dyphestive caught her stare. "I'd better get back up there. We'll talk later, when she sleeps. Though I don't even know if she sleeps. I wake up every day with her staring into my eyes." He trotted away.

Zora drifted back from the pack. "It's good to see a smile on your face. I never took you for the kind that sulks. Have you finally gotten over the loss of your woman?"

"My woman? Come now, Zora, you know I only have eyes for you."

"Is that so? Is that why you haven't been speaking to me for the duration of this trip?"

"No," he said as a yellow-and-black butterfly passed by his face. "I apologize for that, but I had the feeling you were mad at me."

"You aren't a complete fool. I *was* mad at you, but I'm over it. I have been for the last few days." Zora's green eyes searched his. "Anya is very beautiful. You care deeply for her. I can tell."

"We have a bond that I'm not going to deny, but it's not romantic in any sort of way. Like you, we've been through a lot together, and now she's alone." He leaned back and stretched. "What can I say? I feel guilty. Wouldn't you?"

"Over her, no. She can take care of herself."

He couldn't hide his surprise and said, "She's lost everything."

"Including her humility, if she ever had any to begin with. She's very arrogant."

"Zora, her entire family and everyone she has ever known was killed by Black Frost. Your horseshoe would be bent too."

She shook her head. "First, I've never known my parents. Second, neither have you. Third, neither one of us acts as awful as she did."

Grey Cloak's shoulders sank. "She might be rigid, but once you get to know her, she really isn't that bad."

"Is that right?" Zora's cheeks turned red, and her expression darkened. "Look at you, making excuses and defending her. Shame on you, Grey Cloak. Where was she when we were fighting for our lives in Monarch City? Where was she when our necks were in nooses? Did she say that she was there? Funny, I didn't see her, but do you know who I did see? I saw Tatiana. She risked her life to save all of us. And there you sit, tall in your saddle, with all of the answers, without so much as thanking her, but instead accusing her of misleading us."

"You didn't really come back here to make up with me, did you?"

"No, I came to talk sense into you."

"Well, you're doing a fine job of it!"

"Good!"

"Good!" She slapped her reins and rode away.

Grey Cloak bobbed in his saddle as he trailed behind the others. He couldn't help but smile and say, "I suppose that could have gone worse."

35

Great River ran from the peaks of the east to the forests of Gapoli in the south, feeding the woodland and farms of the elvish lands along the way. As the gray clouds gathered and a steady rain came down, Talon traveled down grassy slopes toward Great River with Tatiana still leading the way.

"We'll cross the bridge at Doverpoint," she said as she pulled her robes tight around her to protect against the rain, "and travel north to the Wizard Watch, another two days' journey."

Lighting flashed, and thunder began to roll.

"Are there towns on the other side of the villages?" Crane asked as he held his pudgy hand out and caught the rain. "It hasn't rained for the entire journey, and I've become accustomed to staying dry."

"There are," she said. "I'm surprised that you didn't know that."

"I've never traveled to the other side of Great River. I heard it is an untamed land."

"It's not without its savages." Tatiana sat up and stared down into the valley. "That's odd. There are garrisons of elves at the bridge. I'll ride down and see what is happening."

"I'll go with you," Grey Cloak offered.

"There is no need—"

"I insist. After all, we are both elves. I'm sure they'll take a shine to us." He smirked. "Well, me, maybe."

"You and your humor. Come, then." Tatiana trotted down to the riverbank.

They didn't make it within one hundred feet of the bridge before they were surrounded by the garrison.

Grey Cloak had seen plenty of elves in his lifetime but never such a large cluster at once. Most of them were tall and lean, with silky hair hanging down past their necks. They were well dressed and refined looking in soft leather armor that was dyed shades of brown, green, red, and orange that blended into the woodland. They carried bows and feathered arrows, and a longsword and two daggers decorated every hip. He nodded at one of the women. She didn't bat a lash.

An elven soldier with silvery-white hair and a white scar splitting his chin approached Tatiana. "I am Captain Edyrn Silvius. State your name and business."

"I'm Tatiana, and this is Grey Cloak." Tatiana raised an eyebrow. "I have business in West Arrowwood and seek passage across the Doverpoint bridge."

"That won't be possible, Tatiana," the captain said. He unrolled a scroll and handed it to her. "This is from the elven Monarch herself. The quill point is fine, but I'd be happy to summarize it. Currently, the feud on both sides of the river has enhanced." He pointed at his garrison of soldiers and the soldiers on the other side of the bridge. "The West River elves guard our side of the bridges, and the East River elves guard theirs."

Tatiana scanned the scroll. "This is not good. The Monarch Queen has declared the West River elves enemies of the Monarchy. She has stopped all travel and commerce on both sides of the river." She dropped her gaze to Captain Edyrn Silvius and returned the scroll. "This is more than a feud. It's a declaration of war."

"Call it what you will. They're the Monarch Queen's orders just the same. I'm glad to stand by them. The West River elves now keep unseemly company with orcs, gnolls, and other sorts that have trekked over the Green Hills to taint our valleys." He looked like he was about to spit. "Of course, all of this could be avoided if the West River elves will turn over a single traitor."

"All of this over one man? Who?" she asked.

The captain handed her a rolled-up leather parchment. "We are seeking out this elf. Have you come across him in your travels?"

"There are many elves," she said as she unrolled the scroll. "He's distinguished. If I'd seen him, I would remember."

She handed it back, and the captain gave it to Grey Cloak.

"What about you?" he asked.

Grey Cloak's heart skipped. There was no mistaking the hard eyes and strong angular features of Bowbreaker. "I have to say, I'm new to Arrowwood, and I haven't encountered many elves either, aside from today. But this one, I'd remember if I had seen him. I'm curious—how can one elf stir up so much trouble?"

"He threatens the Monarchy. And he is a West River elf, and they harbor him." The captain took the scroll from Grey Cloak and rolled it up. "He is a very bad man."

"If this Bowbreaker is being harbored by the West River elves, why, pray tell, are you looking for him on this side?" Tatiana asked.

"Because there are many conspirators that serve Bowbreaker's brood. That's why I ask everyone that comes and goes. His spies make use of these bridges. All it takes is the bat of an eye when I show them that picture, or perhaps their ears perk up when I mention his name." He swung his gaze up to Grey Cloak. "Just like yours did. Soldiers, seize them!"

36

GREY CLOAK AND TATIANA WERE HAULED OFF TO A SMALL JAIL SET UP NOT FAR from the Doverpoint bridge. The jail was a simple structure, hastily made from wooden logs and rusting iron doors. The roof wasn't well thatched, and rain dripped inside steadily, making the dirt floor pure mud.

"Another fine situation you have gotten us into," Grey Cloak said.

"Me? You were the one with the big eyes at the mentioning of Bowbreaker. Talk about a guilty countenance. A blind man could have seen it." She kept her robes lifted above her boots and tried to avoid the rain in the corner of the room. Drops of water trickled off her shoulder. "From here on out, let me do the talking."

"If you wish." Grey Cloak curled up in his cloak. Despite the sloppy and damp conditions, he was quite comfortable inside the gray garment. "I'll keep my lips sealed. Not a word from me. After all, you are the smart one."

She sighed and said, "You're never going to like me, are you?"

"Let me say that I don't care much for how your kind operates. Anya was onto something when she called you out. I could see it in your eyes. It stuck with me."

"Anya sees what she wants."

"And you don't?"

A long silence followed.

When Grey Cloak had first met Talon back in Raven Cliff, he was fascinated by Tatiana. She was poised, beautiful, and very personal. But since she'd been charged with handling the dragon charms, she'd been nothing short of prickly. Even her beauty couldn't overcome the edge that she carried. Unlike Dalsay, it wasn't well suited for her.

"You aren't the only one that lost much," she said sadly. "I lost Dalsay, my brothers, not to mention Adanadel and Browning. We were close. All of us.

Believe me when I say that it hurts when I think about them. You make me out to be a frosty witch. I am not. Forgive me for trying to do the right thing the best way I know how."

Grey Cloak shifted uncomfortably. He found her irritating but felt sorry for her at the same time. *Maybe she does have a heart.* "Thanks," he muttered.

"What was that?"

"I said thanks."

"For what?"

"Saving me and the rest of us, back at Monarch Castle." He caught her eye. "You saved my neck from the noose, and I'm grateful."

"Thank you."

"I know you are trying, Tatiana, but what I don't know is what we are doing. I'm sorry to bring it up, but you've been gathering dragon charms for how long? Years? A decade? And where are they?"

Shamefaced, she said, "I don't know. If I did, I'd tell you. And I'm not without my doubts either, but my faith in the Wizard Watch is all that I have."

"Perhaps it's time that you put your faith in something else."

"Like what?"

"Your friends."

"If I didn't have faith in you, do you think that I'd risk my life to save you?"

"Good point." He eyed the ceiling, which was still dripping water. "I think we've hashed this out enough. Do you want to get out of here?"

"Yes, but we can't blast out and bring an elven garrison down on us. This is a delicate situation," she said as she watched the water drain from her robes. "Apparently, the situation with Bowbreaker is direr than I realized."

"I know little about him."

"It is said that he is the one destined to slay the evil Monarch Queen. I find it difficult to believe that Esmeralda is evil."

"Perhaps he's being framed."

"Regardless, they will want to peel our skulls open to find out everything we know about him. If we aren't convincing, they'll accuse us of being spies. If that is the case, they'll kill us."

"We shouldn't be punished for knowing him. Perhaps I need to do the talking. I can be very persuasive if you allow me."

"We've both denied knowing him. We have to convince them this is all a misunderstanding. Can you do that?"

Heavier rains began to brew outside, and the muddy floor was overrun with dripping water. He smirked. "Sit back and watch me. I only hope that the others don't try anything silly."

"WE NEED TO GET THEM," Dyphestive said. Talon remained hidden in a grove overlooking the Doverpoint bridge. The rain poured down as they eyed the small jail, which was surrounded by half a dozen elven soldiers. "The sooner the better."

"We can't storm down there and bully them. There are at least a thousand elves in these hills," Crane said. "You might not see them, but they are there. It's their lands. They are everywhere. We need to wait it out and see what they want. Perhaps I can find out."

Dyphestive rubbed his jaw. He wasn't sure who was in charge since Grey Cloak and Tatiana were both gone. Perhaps he was, and everyone appeared to be looking to him. The last thing he wanted, however, was for anyone else to get captured. "Why would they arrest them?"

"That's what we need to find out," Crane said.

"I know that," he said.

Zora pecked him on the shoulder. "I'll use the scarf and go."

Dyphestive wiped the water from his brow and looked down at her. She appeared very small to him. In his heart, he didn't want to risk her getting caught either. He wasn't used to placing others in danger. He put his hands on her shoulders and said, "Do it, but be careful."

"Don't worry. This will be easy. I'll be back before the next raindrop hits your nose." She covered the bottom of her face with the black scarf and disappeared.

Dyphestive wiped a raindrop from his nose.

37

Captain Edyrn Silvius held a disgusting-looking creature in front of Grey Cloak's eyes and said, "This is a river leech, a creature of unique traits. Notice that its slimy, gelatinous body is lean, not full of blood as of yet. But when it eats, believe me, it will drain quarts of blood from your body and swell up bigger than your head."

Grey Cloak's lips twisted, and he pulled his head back. He was secured to a chair with his hands tied behind his back and his ankles tied to the chair legs. And elven soldier stood behind him with his strong hands holding down his shoulders. "Well, my head's pretty big, so that would be something."

"Oh, humor. You will need that to get you through the pain that you are about to experience," the captain said.

"That's good to know, but don't you think this is a bit much? After all, you are accusing us of knowing one elf out of, I don't know, hundreds of thousands."

"Yes, well, there is only one way to be sure if you both won't come clean."

"This is outrageous!" Tatiana was beside Grey Cloak, tied up in the same fashion. "I am a citizen of Arrowwood. You can't torture me."

Captain Edyrn Silvius had come across as a fair-minded elf when they'd first met, but he'd turned sinister. His eyes were cold, and his voice carried a deadly intent. "I have the authority, per the Monarch Queen, to do whatever is required to learn the truth." He swung the foot-long leech over in front of Tatiana's face. "Of course, if you were to admit the truth, we could move away from the uncivilized method of torture."

"You are making a grave mistake, Captain. I'm no ordinary citizen passing through. There will be severe repercussions when my family finds out about this," she said.

"Ah." The captain's face brightened. "So you have close ties to the Monarch Queen. Please tell me, who are they?"

"No, I'll let you hang yourself."

"Hmph." The captain turned his attention back to Grey Cloak. "Do you have any elven family ties that you would like to boast?"

"No." He tilted his head toward Tatiana. "Only her. And between you and me, she's rather difficult," he whispered. "And if you think she's bad, wait until you meet the rest of her family."

The captain chuckled as large drops of rain splashed on his silvery hair. "Given my age and station, I don't think I have much to lose. Also, I'm one of the Monarch Queen's favorite cousins. Ah-ha. Surprise, surprise." He lowered the leech over Grey Cloak's thigh. "Now tell me what you know about Bowbreaker."

In truth, Grey Cloak couldn't have cared less about Bowbreaker. The big elf was solemn and had the personality of a goat. He wasn't fond of Zora's noticeable attraction to him either. He cleared his throat and said, "Do you think that you could torture Tatiana first? After all, her thighs are bigger than mine."

"They are not!" Tatiana said.

Grey Cloak could have sworn that he heard someone else chuckle, but he couldn't say for sure, as it was quickly drowned out by the rain.

However, the captain eyed the room suspiciously. He let out a sigh and said, "If you aren't going to cooperate, then you give me little choice, but I'll offer you one last chance. What do you know about Bowbreaker?"

"Oh yes, now I remember. He is that elf that breaks bows, isn't he?" He glanced at Tatiana. "Remember. I had a bow, and he took it and broke it over his knee. Or wait, was it over his head?"

"Actually, he broke *my* bow on his head," Tatiana said, playing along. "And he broke your bow on your head." She let out a bizarre and unbecoming laugh. "Ahahahaha!"

Grey Cloak and the captain gave her appalled looks.

"What?" she asked. "You don't like my laughing?"

"I'm not sure what that was, but it wasn't laughing or cackling or cajoling," Grey Cloak quipped. He leaned toward the captain, looked up, and said, "We're only distant, distant, distant cousins."

"I'd hope. Enough, however. I've extended to you ample opportunities to come clean, and you've mocked them. I don't like that." He dropped the leech onto Grey Cloak's trousers. "You're going to regret not being more cooperative."

The leech latched on, and Grey Cloak dropped his head for a closer look. The fabric of his pants crinkled. He quickly looked up. "It's going to take forever to press that back out. Well done, Captain Edyrn Silvius. Well done indeed!"

The captain smirked.

Grey Cloak's face puckered as the leech latched through his pants and onto his leg. "Gah!" He stared wide-eyed at his leg. The leech began bulging, and he could feel the blood flowing out of his thigh.

"Now, if you like, Grey Cloak, you can tell me what you know about Bowbreaker, or I can let the leech—or rather, leeches—drain all the blood from your body."

Excruciating pain lanced through his body from the top of his head to his toes. He could feel his heart beating behind his eyeballs. The pain was killing him. He clenched his jaw. *Hang on! Don't give in! You're stronger than him! It's only a leech, after all! And how much blood do I really need anyway?*

By the time he looked back down, the leech had more than doubled in size. *Zooks, I have a lot of blood.*

He glanced at Tatiana. There was no mistaking her horrified expression. She looked as if he was about to die.

"Stop this, Captain! Stop this!" she said.

"Oh, it is quite too late for that. Of course, if you would shed more light on Bowbreaker, then I would be more than happy to help you."

Grey Cloak's voice came out as a pant. "We don't know anything."

Captain Edyrn Silvius whispered in his ear, "We'll know the very truth of the matter soon enough."

38

THE LEECH GREW BIGGER, AND GREY CLOAK'S STOMACH TURNED INSIDE OUT. THE bulging leech was one of the most disgusting things that he'd ever seen, and it was attached to his leg. He became light-headed, and his neck rolled to the side. "Will you stop this?"

"Soon, the blood loss will be so great that you will tell me whatever I want," Captain Silvius said. "It is one of the glorious effects of this rudimentary torture."

"Come closer," Grey Cloak said in a raspy voice. "I want to tell you something."

"Of course." The captain bent over and offered his ear. "What is it that you want to say?"

"I-I..."

"Yes?"

"I really don't like you."

Captain Silvius frowned and rose back up. "This one is very stubborn." He lifted Grey Cloak's chin. "You should have spilled the information by now."

"Let him go!" Tatiana said. "Can't you see he doesn't know anything?" The leech had swollen as thick as an elf's forearm. "You're going to kill him!"

As his blood drained, Grey Cloak's head sank toward his chest. It felt like it was made of sand, and he couldn't lift it.

"Tell me about Bowbreaker, Grey Cloak. I know that you want to tell me. I've been doing this a long time, and I know that you know something. Tell me," the captain urged.

The pain in Grey Cloak's body subsided, and it was replaced by a euphoric feeling. He drooled and smiled. "Oh yes, my friend Bowbreaker." He shook his head. "He doesn't smile." He gave a big frown. "Looks like this all the time. Sort of like you, Captain Leechbottom."

"Now we are getting somewhere, aren't we?" The captain eyeballed Tatiana. "It appears that someone was lying. Well, the truth always comes out, doesn't it?"

With his vision fading, Grey Cloak noticed an indentation the size of a foot in the mud beside the captain. He giggled. "I know someone that likes Bowbreaker."

Pffft! A white mist sprayed under Captain Silvius's nose. His nostrils widened as he inhaled deeply. He tried to jump away from the cloud, but his legs turned into noodles, and he splashed face-first onto the muddy floor.

Grey Cloak was all smiles when Zora appeared. She moved in a blur and struck the elf soldier behind him.

A bright flash and a smell of burning rope followed. Two more elven soldiers were knocked out at his feet.

"Zora?" He practically sang when he said it. "Someone is looking for your boyfriend."

"Bloody horseshoes, he's a mess," Zora said as she stared at the leech. "Uck! It's disgusting. How do we get this thing off of him?"

"I'm not sure," Tatiana said, her brow furrowed.

Zora tried to pry the leech off with her fingers. "Ew, it's so slimy. My hands won't stick to it."

"Don't touch my friend," Grey Cloak said, slurring his speech. "He's not an it. He has a name. Do you want to know what it is?"

"Why not?" Zora said.

"It's Bowbreaker. Ahahahahah!"

Zora rolled her eyes and pulled a dagger. "I'll skin it off."

"No, no, don't kill Bowbreaker," Grey Cloak pleaded. "He's my friend." He sobbed. "A good friend. Slimy but good. Hello, Zora. Are you doing something different with your hair? It looks slimy too. Ouch!"

"This might hurt, but it has to come off. And keep it down."

"Let me try something," Tatiana said. "You cut him loose." Her fingertips glowed white, and she touched the leech.

Popsplurp! The bloody leech exploded all over them.

Grey Cloak's chin quivered. "You killed my friend. You killed my friend Bowbreaker."

Zora wiped the bloody grit from her face and cut him free. "We'll get you another one."

"But I liked that one." He looked at his bloody thigh. "Bye-bye, Bowbreaker."

"Goodness, how much blood did he lose?" Zora asked.

Tatiana gathered their belongings from crude hooks on the wall and held the Star of Light in her palm. "Good, it's all here. It will take some time to get him back to normal. In the meantime, we need to get out of here. How are the others?"

"Waiting for me," Zora said. She helped Grey Cloak to his feet. "Why do they want Bowbreaker?"

"It appears that the Monarch Queen has a bounty on his head." Tatiana bent to one knee and bound the captain. "Help me drag them to the cell."

Zora grabbed the captain's feet, and Tatiana picked him up by the arms. They shuffled toward the cell.

"Why does the Monarch Queen want Bowbreaker?" Zora asked.

"Because he's destined to kill her."

Zora dropped the captain. "Oh."

As they hauled the other two soldiers away, Grey Cloak sat in his chair, neck wobbling, and said, "You ladies are doing a fine, fine job. It's good to see you two working together."

"Can you walk?" Zora asked him.

"Can I walk? Pfft! Of course I can. Watch this." Grey Cloak stood, took a bow, and fell down. He kicked his feet and rolled over to his side. With mud all over his hands, he said, "Zooks, who moved the floor on me?"

Zora and Tatiana exchanged befuddled looks.

"What are we going to do? We can't sneak him out of here like this," Zora said.

Tatiana took a peek out of the jail's front door, which was little more than a flap. It was still pouring with rain. She turned and said, "I have an idea, but we have to act quickly."

39

Zora wrapped the Scarf of Shadows around Grey Cloak's neck and said, "We are going to walk you out of here, but you have to stand. We'll help you."

Grey Cloak gave her a lazy-eyed look, toyed with the scarf, and said, "This doesn't look good on me. Not my style."

"Will you please work with me?"

He made a sour face and said, "I'll try."

Tatiana began putting on the captain's leather armor.

"Oh, look at that. She's already turned traitor. I knew it."

Tatiana rolled her eyes and shook her head. "No one is turning traitor. It's a disguise, you fool."

"Fool? I'm no fool. No fool at all. You are a fool."

"Lords of the Air, what did that leech do to him?" Zora asked as she hauled him to his feet and propped him against the wall.

"Apparently, it damaged his gray matter. We can only hope it isn't permanent." Tatiana relieved Zora and held him steady on the wall. "You have to behave, Grey Cloak. We are escaping, but you must cooperate. Follow our lead. Do you understand?"

He nodded, touched her lips, and played with them. "You have soft lips." He poked them. "I saw an orc with lips like yours. She was a waitress at the Tavern Dwellers Inn. Called Marmie."

Tatiana covered his mouth while Zora slipped on another leather tunic. "I don't have puffy orc lips."

His words muffled by her hand, he said, "Yes, you do."

Tatiana shot a look at Zora and said, "I'm doing this." She covered his nose with the scarf, and he disappeared.

"Where did I go? Help me!" he cried. "I can't see me!"

Tatiana pinched his arm tight. "Be still!"

"But I can't see myself. Oh no! I'm a ghost like Dalsay, roaming the spirit world while still consorting with elven witches."

"I'm not a witch!" Tatiana said.

"Funny, I can feel myself, but I can't see myself. Hmm... I wonder what will happen if I relieve myself. I have to pee."

"Zora, get over here!" Tatiana said as she wrestled to hang on to Grey Cloak. "Grab an arm. We need to go."

Managing to latch onto Grey Cloak's arm, Zora said, "Close your eyes and let us guide you. Remember, you have the Scarf of Shadows on. No one is supposed to see you."

"Ah yes, the Scarf of Shadows. I like it. Where is it?" he said.

"I'm ready," Zora said.

Tatiana filled her hand with the Star of Light. "I'm going to summon my power that will conceal our identities. With the help of the armor and the weather, we should fool the elven soldiers. Let's go."

Grey Cloak stumbled between them with their arms locked around his elbows. They stepped right out of the jail and into the pouring rain.

"My, this is dreary. Am I wet if I can't see myself dripping?"

"Shh!" Zora said.

She took the lead, moving away from the Doverpoint bridge and toward the rise that looked over the river. Grey Cloak half dragged his feet and splashed through muddy puddles. She couldn't see him, but she could see the trail he was making. "Will you stop that?"

"No, because you can't see me."

A trio of elven soldiers was posted along the road that led to the bridge. They cut them off, and one asked, "Where are you headed on a night like this? And why are you walking like that?"

Zora's heart thumped rapidly. She squeezed Grey Cloak's arm, thinking, *Don't you say a word. Please don't say a word.*

"Captain Silvius is not pleased with us. We are to gather wood for the fires. In this!" Tatiana said in a harsh imitation of a manly voice. "Don't ever drop an eyelid on his watch," she added.

"Ah," one of the elves said. "He's as hard as a black walnut. Good luck finding timber that will light in this weather."

The trio of soldiers nodded and moved down the slope toward the road.

"That was close," Zora muttered.

"You have big behinds!" Grey Cloak shouted at the soldiers. "Like ogres!"

Zora and Tatiana hurried up the hill, glancing over their shoulders, but the hard rain must have drowned out Grey Cloak's voice, because elven soldiers marched down the hill without so much as a backward glance.

"You fool, you're going to get us caught," Tatiana said. "From here on out, stifle it!"

"I'm a ghost. Therefore, I can do and *say* whatever I want," he replied. "Ogre bottom."

They continued up the hill, leaving the road to the bridge far behind. They ventured straight to the grove, where Grunt and Razor confronted them.

"It's us," Zora said as she pulled down the scarf from Grey Cloak's face.

"Ah, I'm alive again," he said.

They released him, and he collapsed on the ground. Grunt tilted his head and grunted.

"What's the matter with him?" Razor asked.

"A river leech sucked half of his gray matter out."

Razor's lip curled. "Ew... I've seen that happen before."

Dyphestive rushed over, dropped to his knees, and asked, "What's wrong?"

"He's fine," Zora answered. "Pick him up, and let's go."

Once again, Talon was united.

"Everyone, listen," Tatiana said. "We have to cross that bridge one way or the other before every West River elf in Arrowwood starts hunting us down. I can conceal myself and Grey Cloak in the rain, to some degree, but we have to take our chances now. They are only looking for the two of us." She looked at Crane. "You'll have to use that silver tongue to talk us across. It's the only way."

Crane nodded. "Everyone, mount up. Tatiana, you and Grey Cloak hop in."

Crane took the lead, with Tatiana and Grey Cloak hunkered down in the back of the wagon, Zora rode beside them, and the others rode behind.

"I want to ride a horse," Grey Cloak said.

There was a stir down at the Doverpoint bridge. The garrison of elves had clustered together, and most of them were carrying torches. The moment they spotted the wagon coming, the elves stopped and pointed, and the hard rains let up. Captain Silvius stood among them, mouthing orders.

Zora exchanged concerned looks with Tatiana and said, "We fooled them once. I don't think we'll fool them twice."

The West River elves were coming.

40

CRANE LIFTED HIS CARRIAGE WHIP AND SAID, "I HOPE ENOUGH TIME HAS PASSED."

Grey Cloak reached for it. "Let me do it. I want to do it!"

Tatiana pulled him down into the wagon and covered his nose with the scarf. "Be still!" She eyed Crane. "Do what you will."

Crane flicked the carriage lash, and it immediately caught fire. "Ho-ho!" His eyes burned like the flames of a candle as he cracked Vixen on the back. "Onward, Vixen! Onward!"

The wagon lurched forward and quickly gained speed. Grey Cloak slid to the back and slammed into the gate. He shook his head, grabbed the side, and hung on.

The wheels were spinning flames, and Vixen's hooves were on fire. The wagon roared down the hill.

Behind the wagon, the rest of Talon rode hard. The horses labored to keep up. Arrows zinged through the air and whistled by their heads.

Tatiana rose in her seat and lifted the Star of Light. The gem emanated white light through cracks of her curled fingers. A shield of energy spread out over the back of the wagon, covering the horse and riders.

With the wind tearing at his face, Grey Cloak crawled toward the front. His strength was returning, and he sat up on his knees behind the bench.

A garrison of elven soldiers barricaded the bridge with large spiked beams that were shaped like jacks. The elves were clustered around blockages, some with spears in hand and others firing arrows.

"Can you make it through that?" Grey Cloak asked.

Crane winked and said, "We'll know in a moment."

Grey Cloak's head began to clear. He took one last glance behind his shoulder before they crashed to their doom. The wagon left twin trails of flames behind it. Talon rode between the trails, hunkered down over their horses.

Arrows ricocheted off Tatiana's shield. Grunt thundered down the path in the back. A dozen elves sped right behind him, shooting arrows at his back.

"Hold on!" Crane said.

Grey Cloak whipped his head around in time to see the nightmare horse, Vixen, plow full speed into the elven ranks and barricades. The big-eyed elves hopped out of the way like scared rabbits, fear filling their eyes, as the Wheels of Fire careened through the first blockade. The large timbers popped and cracked.

"Yah, Vixen! Yah!" Crane hollered.

The blockades and troops were three rows deep. Vixen tore through every last one, setting everything on fire and sending flaming elves off the bridge and into the river.

Grey Cloak looked backward and frontward, not believing his eyes. Not only had the wagon cleared the blockades, but Talon had, too, including Grunt, who had a back full of arrows. They were riding hard right behind them.

"Ah-ha!" Grey Cloak exclaimed. "You did it, Crane!"

"It's not over yet!" Crane set his eyes on the road ahead. The East River elves had gathered at the far end of the bridge and formed a tight group. "Should I slow?"

"No. Keep rolling!"

"Roll, Vixen! Roll!" Crane shouted.

The Wheels of Fire thundered over the wooden planks of the bridge, setting the structure aflame.

The West River elves were closing in. At the last moment, they split left and right and passed right by the wagon. In seconds, a full garrison of West River elves cut off the East River elves' pursuit. The coast was clear to the other side of the bridge.

Vixen raced on. The wheels clattered over the wood, and the flames started to die down. At the end of the bridge, Vixen slowed.

"What's wrong?" Grey Cloak asked.

"That's a long bridge. She's whipped," Crane said as the wagon rolled to a stop.

The last flames on the horse hooves and wagon wheels went out. A lathered-up Vixen snorted and labored for breath. In the blink of an eye, Talon, wagon and all, was surrounded by the East River elves five rows deep.

The elves, dressed in leather tunics, stood in the rain, staring at the company with hardened eyes. Their hands were filled with spears and bows and arrows. Every one of them was too close to miss.

Grey Cloak pushed himself up to standing and said, "Excuse me, brethren, but could someone tell us how to get to Breckenridge Dales? We are horribly off course and ..." His head started to swim, the rainy skies spiraled, and the world he knew turned black.

41

Fresh morning air tickled Grey Cloak's nose, and the sun shone through his eyelids. His head lay on a warm pillow of sorts that was comfortable if not odd. He cracked an eye open and found himself looking at Zora, who had a distant expression on her face.

She dropped her stare, and he closed his eye. He was comfortable in her warm lap and didn't have any desire to leave. *No sense in spoiling a good thing. Especially given that the last time we spoke, she was mad at me.*

Zora gently brushed his hair to the side and caressed his face from his forehead to his chin.

This is nice. I knew she liked me.

Her hand cradled his chin and cheeks.

Ah, very nice.

She started to apply more pressure.

Uh, what is she doing? Easy, Zora. My elven features are delicate, after all.

The way her fingernails bit into his skin felt as if a crab had ahold of him.

I'm starting to think that she might not be the best mate after all.

Zora shook his face and said, "I know that you are awake. I saw you looking. Do you mind? My legs are numb from sitting so long."

He sat up and bumped his head into her chin.

"Ow," she said in an irritated manner.

"Sorry."

"It's fine. I'm used to you being a pain."

Grey Cloak got his first look at his surroundings. Crane drove the wagon, Tatiana sitting beside him. Neither one of them looked back at him. To his right and left were East River elven soldiers in forest-colored tunics, marching on foot. Behind them were the other members of Talon on horseback. Grunt still had arrows sticking out of his back.

When Grey Cloak caught Dyphestive's eye, his solemn expression brightened, but it was quickly extinguished when Leena gave him a hard look. He mouthed, "Later," to Grey Cloak.

"What is happening?" Grey Cloak asked.

"Keep your voice down," Zora warned quietly. "I'll explain shortly. How are you feeling?"

"Not awful," he said, even though his head was swimming a little. "How long have I been asleep?"

"Two days."

"Two—"

Zora clamped her hand over his mouth. "I said keep it down. I don't need you to call the river elves a bunch of orc bottoms like you've called everyone else."

"Orc bottoms? When did I say that?"

"In Captain Silvius's jail."

He raised an eyebrow. "I don't remember that."

"What do you remember?"

"I remember the jail and the river leech," he said as he glanced at his thigh, which had a bandage around it. "Gah! What happened?"

"The leech was attached to it." She shook her head. "I need to take a look. There were tiny teeth in your leg that I had to pick out."

"Tiny teeth?" He watched in horror as Zora unwrapped the bandage. That was when he noticed that half of his trouser leg had been cut off. "I need new pants."

"That's not all that you need," she said.

His thigh had a large purple bruise on it and a raised white ring, like teeth marks. "That's awful."

"It was worse when I wrapped it. According to the East River elves, you could have lost your leg if it hadn't been treated."

"I don't remember it feeling that bad, except at first."

"Yes, I don't think you were feeling anything." She wrapped the leg back up. "Can you bend it?"

Gritting his teeth, he drew his leg toward his chest and grunted. "It's stiff, but I'm sure I can walk." He glanced about. They were surrounded by miles of elven countryside that was the envy of the world. "Not that I need to. Where are we going?"

"North, to the Wizard Watch." Zora eyeballed the back of Tatiana's braided hair. "We were fortunate that Tatiana's cousins were among the East River elves when we crossed. They vouched for her, and she vouched for us. Now, they escort us to the tower, however far that might be."

For the first time, Tatiana turned her head and acknowledged Grey Cloak. "I'm glad to see you awake."

"I bet you are," he said. "Are you taking us to the witch tower where you were born?"

Zora giggled. "You're definitely feeling better. Good."

"I really am impressed with the countryside," Crane commented. His eyes were puffy, and his gaze darted about. "So many different trees and birds. It's another part of the world, so unlike the rest. Maybe we don't ever need to go back across the river. I can build a camp and live out the rest of my days here."

"The streams are rich in fish. A single day's outing will feed you for days," Tatiana said. "I spent many years living on the banks in my youth. I miss it."

Crane scooted closer to her until their hips touched. "Perhaps we can make a new life together."

Tatiana jumped out of the wagon and said, "I don't think so. I'm committed to a ghost."

"How long can that last?" Crane asked with a sparkle in his eye as he watched her walking away. "My, she is dazzling, isn't she?"

"I've seen more dazzling," Grey Cloak said with his eyes on Zora.

She shoved his head back. "Stop doing that."

"Do I need to thank you for saving me?"

"Yes," she said with a playful smile on her lips while her fingers toyed with her scarf. "But a simple thank you will do. After all, you saved me too."

"Thank you, Zora." He took her hand and squeezed it.

"It was nothing."

She didn't release his hand, and they both sat back and relaxed.

Tatiana had made her way through the elven ranks and caught up with a soldier in the front. He stood tall and wore a grim expression, and his shock of black hair was short. They engaged in a heated conversation before Tatiana wandered back. Her brow was furrowed more than usual.

Zora broke away from Grey Cloak, slid over to the other side of the wagon, and asked, "What's wrong?"

"My cousin states that they cannot escort us any farther after today. We are on our own from here," Tatiana said.

"Is that bad?"

Tatiana nodded. "The woodland is wild. It isn't good."

<h1 style="text-align:center">42</h1>

TALON MADE CAMP THAT EVENING IN A CHERRY TREE GROVE AT THE EDGE OF A forest. Jakoby dropped branches onto the fire. Crane hummed a cheerful tune as he stared into the fire. Razor was busy digging the last two arrows out of Grunt's back.

"Doesn't that hurt?" Zora asked with a sour face.

"These little arrows hurt Grunt?" Razor said in his rugged but charming manner. "Hardly. His hide is thicker than the Rogues of Rodden. If anything, these arrows help him with his itchy spots." He pulled an arrow out and scratched Grunt's back with it.

Grunt stamped his hoof on the ground and bent a horn over his shoulder.

"See? He likes it," Razor said with a grin.

"I can see that." Zora moved away to where Grey Cloak was waiting by the fire.

He patted a spot on the ground for her. "Care to sit?" he asked, offering a warm smile. He felt closer to her than he ever had, and he liked it. "I won't bite."

"No, your bark is worse than your bite." She sat and braced her back against a log that Tatiana was sitting on. "Do we have far to go?"

"It depends," Tatiana said.

"Depends on what?" Grey Cloak asked.

"On what we may or may not encounter. These are the wilds, and they are full of many dangerous surprises."

He straightened his back and said, "I'm sorry, but I was under the impression that you were born here and that you might have traveled this direction many times before."

"No," Tatiana said as she tightened the cloak around her shoulders.

"Tatiana, that doesn't make any sense. You have been to this Wizard Watch before, haven't you?"

"Yes, of course I have," she said as she stared deeply into the fire.

Many in the company exchanged confused looks with one another.

Grey Cloak started to grind his teeth. "You aren't making any sense, Tatiana, and it's getting under my skin. Do explain."

"I can't," Tatiana replied. "What happens in the Wizard Watch stays in the Wizard Watch."

"What are you talking about?" Jakoby's rich voice rose. "This is not Talagon City that you are speaking of. It's a wizard tower."

Not hiding her irritation, she said, "I'm sorry, but I am not allowed to speak about the Watch. I swore an oath. Our journey would be more pleasant if you would trust me."

"Dirty acorns, Tat!" Zora said. "You never tell us anything."

"Was Dalsay any less vague when you dealt with him?" Tatiana fired back.

"We never had our backs to the wall with Dalsay," Zora replied.

Tatiana sighed and lifted her hands. "I'm sorry. But you have to trust me. I'm certain that your questions will be answered when we arrive at the Wizard Watch. In the meantime, rest well. It will be a treacherous journey on the morrow."

Streak dropped out of the sky and landed beside Grey Cloak, causing Zora to jump out of her seat.

Clutching her chest, she said, "Streak, you scared the nails off my toes."

A field mouse the size of a cat hung dead in Streak's flat snout. He set the mouse down by her toes.

Zora gently nudged it away with her boot. "Thank you, but I'm not hungry. You can have it."

"He likes you," Grey Cloak said as he patted Streak's head. "Perhaps more than me. He's never offered me a rodent before."

"You can have it," she said.

He noticed Grunt's big spacey eyes locked on it. "Streak, why don't you take it over to him?"

"Don't bother," Razor said. "Grunt doesn't eat meat. He lives off vegetation." He passed his hands over Grunt's eyes. "I can't say for sure, but I think the big rat scares him."

Grey Cloak picked the field mouse up by the tail and tossed it over the fire at Grunt, who jumped up and dashed into the darkness of the surrounding woodland.

"I'd say you are right."

"Why did you do that for? Now I have to go find him." Razor stuck the arrows into the ground and followed Grunt.

Dyphestive caught his attention with a wave of his hand. He was sitting beside Leena, who was on her knees, eyes closed in meditation. She was perfectly composed, as still as a statue in her silky black robes with gold trim on the sleeves.

"Excuse me," Dyphestive said to Zora, "but it's high time that I caught up with my brother."

She nodded.

They moved away from the campfire, out of earshot, and stood underneath the ebony tapestry of a star-filled sky.

Dyphestive let out a sigh as he glanced back at Leena. "I'm sorry, Grey. I've been meaning to check on you, but Leena, well, she's possessive."

He glanced at her. "She's no bigger than a wart on a frog's bottom."

"But she hits like a mule kicks."

"Do you like her?"

"I don't know." Dyphestive's big paw of a hand rubbed the back of his neck. "I guess. But she's possessive. What do I do?"

"You're asking me? I don't know. Is this what you brought me over here to talk about?"

"No. Well, yes and no. I only wanted to talk and make sure you are well. How is the leg?"

"I'm a tad gimpy but over it for the most part. How are you?"

Dyphestive shrugged. "As healthy as a horse." He eyed the camp. "What do you think about Tatiana and Anya? Do you believe what Anya said? Can we trust Tatiana?"

Grey Cloak smirked. "I'm not sure, but for now, I'll take my chances."

43

ANYA

"Idiots," Anya said under her breath. "Idiots. Idiots. Idiots."

It was the middle of the night, and steady rain was coming down. She was in the middle of crossing Great River about half a league north of the Doverpoint bridge. Using a log she'd found on the riverbank as a raft, she paddled with the stream, hoping to avoid the ever-alert river elves that patrolled the banks.

Great River's current was swift, carrying her quickly down the wide channel back toward the Doverpoint bridge. She paddled her feet as fast as she could, aiming for the dark, sandy banks on the other side. Her dragon armor, though light, was still more than heavy enough to drag her down into the water. If she let go, she would sink to the bottom and certainly die a watery death. She clutched the log and kicked faster.

"Idiots."

She'd had a change of heart after she departed from Grey Cloak the last time. Tatiana infuriated her so much that she couldn't see straight. Anya had no faith at all in the Wizard Watch brood. She blamed them for the deaths of the Sky Riders as much as any. The Wizard Watch should have known. They should have warned them, but they didn't. It gnawed at her stomach.

At the same time, she didn't have a single friend she could count on aside from Cinder. She'd never been separated from him so long or so far either. He was her rock, and he was as far south as a dragon could be. He was at the Shelf, protecting his and Firestok's fledglings. Firestok, his wife, and her uncle Justus's dragon, had died at Gunder Island, killed by Black Frost himself.

I have to talk some sense into Grey Cloak. He must listen.

As the water carried her swiftly toward the bank, something tugged at her foot, like a fish nipping at a line. *What was that? A little late for fish to be biting.*

Whatever it was came back and swallowed her entire foot and tried to pull her down. She fastened herself to the log and held on for dear life. "Gah!"

Anya fought to hang on to the log as the thing below the surface weighed her down like an anchor. Her grip held fast as both she and the log were hauled down below the surface. She kicked with her free foot, but whatever the thing was would not give.

Up and down she bobbed in the surging water, unable to breathe. Her arms began to tire, and she was hauled down into the blackness of the river. She couldn't see a thing. The only thing that existed was whatever was pulling her down to a watery death. She hit the bottom, and a growing pressure crunched the plating around her calf. *Thunderbolts!*

Anya's well-honed training kicked in. She snatched her dagger free of her belt and filled the blade with a charge of energy. With her lungs starting to burn, she caught her first glimpse of the river monster. It looked like a catfish, as big as a cow and with spiny ridges all over, and tugged her to the muddy bottom.

She struck the burning dagger blade into the giant fish's skull. The first blow sank deep, but the foul creature held fast. She struck it again and again, but its firm jaws held.

Her chest burned, and she wanted to scream. Instead, she caught a glimpse of the wriggling water beast's gills and knew exactly what to do. She lashed out, the dagger exploded in the river monster's side, and its jaws popped open.

Anya kicked and swam away, only to have her armor drag her toward the bottom. With absolutely no sense of direction, she crawled along the bed of the river, praying that she was headed to safety.

Her lungs seemed to catch fire, and she couldn't take another breath. She desperately gasped for air. The black water swallowed her up, and her last breath escaped. Her life flashed before her eyes, her last thoughts of Cinder and Grey Cloak. The water abyss took her in, and she blacked out.

ANYA SAT UP, gasping for air. She was by a warm campfire, covered in dried river grit and trembling like a leaf. She panted. It was pitch black on a cloud-filled night, but at least it wasn't raining. She'd had enough water to last her the rest of her life.

She scanned the surrounding woodland and didn't see a soul. *What happened? Who saved me?* Someone had to have built that fire, but it wasn't her. *Who else could it have been? Did the river elves save me?*

Her sword belt lay by the fire, and she rolled over and grabbed it. She started to stand, but a fierce pain lanced through her leg, and she plopped down on her backside, wincing. A bandage covered the nasty river fish bite. She started to peel the bandage away.

"I wouldn't do that," someone said calmly.

She pulled her sword free of the sheath, glaring around, and said, "Show yourself."

"Why? So you can stab me?" The man speaking stepped away from the shadow of the woodlands and into full view, illuminated by the fire.

He stood tall and rangy. His long hair was rusty brown with streaks of silvery white, and his brown eyes twinkled with gold in the firelight.

"Who are you?" Anya asked, her heart racing.

"I'm a friend." He knelt in front of her and offered his hand and a smile. "Call me Than."

Anya cast a wary eye at him. He had handsome features in his wrinkled face. His brown eyes were as warm as melted gold.

She took his hand. "Than, huh?"

"At your service," he said in a voice that carried strength and kindness. He hauled her up to her feet as easily as a man lifting a child. "A brave thing, trying to swim in your armor. I don't think it is meant to float."

"That wasn't my plan," she said, and more water drained out of her suit. Her first few steps made a squishy sound.

Than chuckled.

Anya removed one boot, poured the water out, and drained the other in the same fashion. Hopping on one foot, she shoved them both back on. "I appreciate the assistance, but I have to go."

"Yes, you have to catch up with your friends, Grey Cloak and Dyphestive. Lucky for you, I'm heading in the same direction."

Her brow furrowed, and her hand fell to the pommel of her dagger. It clicked out of the scabbard. "You have some explaining to do, friend."

Than nodded. "That I do. I'll explain along the journey. In the meantime, we must chase them quickly."

"Why is that?"

"Because wherever they go, trouble follows."

"You can say that again."

With surprising agility, the brawny man took off east.

The move caught Anya off guard. She sprinted after him, thinking, *Thunderbolts, he's fast!*

44

"TATIANA, I'M NOT GOING TO BE ABLE TO DRIVE THIS WAGON THROUGH THAT LAND," Crane said with a poke of his stubby index finger. "What madness overtook you that you would think I could make that passage?"

The Wild was a mass of huge trees and dense brush that barred any passage into the forest. Large insects hummed, and the chirps of loud birds came from within the leagues of leafy branches. The horses nickered and stamped their hooves.

Grey Cloak stood on the forest edge. He broke off a thorn of a rosebush as thick as his finger. It had a dewy drop on the end that he started to touch.

"Don't do that. It's a mild poison, not nectar, that will sting for days," Tatiana said.

"Thanks for the warning." He flicked the thorn away.

The treetops of the forest blotted out the morning sun, casting a leagues-long shadow over them. Whatever creatures were inside the womb of the forest didn't sound good either. The hard buzzing sounded like something drilling in his earhole. It reminded him of the jungle-forest outside of Hidemark but far more unpleasant. He thought of Anya and wished he'd taken her advice.

Crane sat on the wagon bench, rubbing his face. "There has to be another way around."

"You aren't obligated to go," Tatiana said with a stern look on her face. She covered it with a cotton cowl. "You can wait or go around and meet us on the north side of the Wild. You shouldn't have anything to fear from the East River elves. They are well aware of your presence now."

Crane's eyes popped. "Alone? You want me to travel alone. I must say, I've traveled plenty by myself but not in such wild lands. Not alone, ever. I'd prefer that someone went with me." He looked at the forest. "Certainly all of us don't need to go in there."

"I'll stay with you," Jakoby said. He unbuckled his sword belt and tossed it into the back of the wagon. "I admit I'm not fond of bugs of any sort."

"Stay north along the river. We will catch up with you at Staatus. It is a grand city. You will enjoy it," Tatiana offered.

Several horses whinnied, including the nightmare, Vixen.

Razor tugged at the reins of his horse and said, "I don't think we are the only ones with an aversion to the forest. The beasts would rather take a pass as well."

"It's probably better that we travel on foot. It is possible that there will be climbing to do," Tatiana added. She caught everyone's distraught looks. "I'm sorry. This Wizard Watch is heavily guarded by the terrain. That is why few venture these paths."

"Then how do they get there?" Grey Cloak asked.

"This way or another," she said.

"Yes, the other way that you cannot say. Thank you so very much, Tatiana." He dismounted, giving her a disgusted look, and led the horse over to the wagon and tethered it to the back.

"What about you, Leena?" the deep-voiced Jakoby said. "Are you coming along with me or staying with them?"

Seated on her horse, Leena stared down Dyphestive and pointed him toward the wagon.

"Uh, I'm not going with Crane. I'm going with Grey Cloak."

Leena adamantly shook her head. She pointed at the wagon again.

Dyphestive stiffened. "No. I'm not going with Crane."

She pulled out her nunchaku.

"Uh-oh," Grey Cloak said as he backed away toward Zora. "Lovers' quarrel."

"It is not!" Dyphestive whined. "We aren't—well, I'm not even saying that."

Zora giggled as she dismounted. "This will prove interesting."

"Listen, Leena, you can whack me with your little sticks all you want, but it won't change my mind," Dyphestive said as he looked at Crane and Jakoby. "Either you're going with them, or you're coming with me."

Leena tucked her nunchaku back in her belt. She eyed Dyphestive, smiled, and bowed.

As Leena dismounted, Dyphestive mouthed, "Did I win?" to Grey Cloak.

Grey Cloak shrugged.

Jakoby said, "It's settled, then. Crane and I will take the horses to Staatus while the rest of you have all of the fun. Journey well."

"Aye, journey well," Crane said. With a flick of his carriage whip, they were off and rolling north, leaving the others in the grim shadows of the Wild.

Grey Cloak approached Tatiana and said, "Now that you've scared two of the company and the horses off, please take it upon yourself and lead the way."

Tatiana nodded at him and said, "Grunt. Make a path."

Without hesitation, Grunt plowed twenty feet into the thorn-rich shrubs, clearing a path for all of them to walk through. The company had made it into the vine-rich terrain when the steady buzzing quieted. An eerie silence fell across the forest, and it was so quiet that one could hear a leaf drop.

Grey Cloak looked at Tatiana and said, "Well done. *It* knows we are here."

"Are you scared, Grey Cloak?" Tatiana asked.

"No." He glanced upward. Small creatures were jumping from branch to branch. They were like monkeys or squirrels, but they could have been anything. He stood touching shoulders with Zora, feeling like he'd crossed into another world. The trees dwarfed them like ants, and a caterpillar as long as his arms snaked between red ferns taller than a man.

A crunching sound came from down at his feet. Streak was eating a beetle with a horned nose and speckled bright-yellow wings. The loud sound drew everyone's stare.

"Well, that's one less bug for us to worry about," he said in a nervous but cheery voice. "It doesn't look like much daylight is going to shine on our path. Tatiana, why don't you shine some light on our dreary setting."

Tatiana lifted the Star of Light over her head. A soft white light illuminated the dimness, exposing the colorful flora that surrounded them. "Better?" she asked.

"Better." He nodded.

A distant bestial roar echoed through the woodland, scattering the keet birds nestled in the branches.

Grey Cloak eyed Tatiana and asked, "Is that your mother calling?"

45

"Hold still," Grey Cloak said to Zora. A green-eyed fly bigger than a bullfrog was on her back.

Zora froze. "What is it?"

"It's nothing. I'll take care of it." Oversize flies and mosquitos were all over the treacherous forest, causing the alarming buzz that harassed their senses. Quicker than a cat, he batted the fly down and squished it under his boot. "Uck."

Zora sneered as she watched him wipe the bug guts off his boots on a patch of moss. "That is nasty. This place is nasty." Her face was beaded with sweat, and locks of her damp hair clung to her forehead. "The Wizard Watch had better have a place to bathe."

Tatiana passed by both of them. She'd wrapped herself up in her cloak like a blanket and covered most of her face with a cowl. "It will."

"Look at me. My clothes are soaked through with stinking sweat." Zora swatted at some sort of purple beetle that hovered near her face. "Ew... what is that?" She backhanded it away.

"I don't know. I've never seen bugs like this before. Or so big either." He hooked her arm. "Come on, I'll protect you."

Talon had been walking for hours in the sweltering willowwhacks. Along the way, they'd killed more than their fair share of nasty bugs. The only one of them that appeared to enjoy it was Streak, who feasted on almost everything they killed.

Grunt led the way, powering through thick brush where needed. Like Streak, he appeared unfazed. As for the rest of them, they were drenched in their own sweat as they lumbered along with long faces.

Razor walked behind Grunt, Dyphestive and Leena behind them, with Tatiana in the middle and Grey Cloak and Zora bringing up the rear. As bad as the trek was, daylight sometimes spilled through the leaves, and they would take a moment to bask in it before moving on. Otherwise, the Wild remained damp and gloomy, dripping with misery.

"Tatiana, I have to ask." Grey Cloak fanned a mosquito away from his eyes. "How is it that you know exactly where you are going if you've never been this way before?"

"I know. We all know. To our kind, the Wizard Watch is a beacon. I can feel where it is in my bones. A guiding light," Tatiana said.

"I see. It's very strange that the other Wizard Watch I've seen was not hidden. It was in plain sight." He was speaking of his encounter at one of the wizard towers when he first adventured with Talon and they met at a Wizard Watch in Sulter Slay. "Why is this one hidden? Are they all hidden?"

"No." Tatiana pushed tall ferns up and aside so Grey Cloak and Zora could pass. "And this one is not hidden. It was built where it stands, and the Wild grew around it over the centuries. I can't explain it. None can. It is this way."

"Oh, well, that is very helpful. Thank you for that wonderful explanation."

"I cannot control the terrain. I can only control my mouth," Tatiana said.

"Har-har."

Tatiana hooked his arm and brought him to a stop. "I don't know which is worse, the buzzing bugs or your complaintive lips. Grey Cloak, no one made you come this way. It was your choice. I'm guiding you. If you want to turn back now, you can. But I am going forward."

Everyone in the company had stopped and looked at him. They had tired eyes, stooped shoulders, and a growing sense of irritation on their faces. Even the bugs stopped buzzing.

Grey Cloak shooed her with his hands and said, "Lead the way, Tat."

She nodded and went on her way.

Zora nudged him. "It's time you laid off."

"I know, but I can't help myself around her. She irritates me."

"Be the bigger elf," Zora offered, "because all of your complaining isn't very attractive."

He raised an eyebrow. *I'd better remember that.*

They journeyed another hour or so until they came upon a steep climb. Using the vines that snaked over the slippery ground, they hauled themselves to the top.

Trailing far behind the others, Grey Cloak caught the sound of cascading water and exchanged excited glances with Zora. At the top of the hill, brilliant light shone through a break in the trees. He redoubled his efforts, and with a spring in his step, he hurried up while saying to Zora, "See you at the top."

"Not if I see you first." Zora took off right after.

Grey Cloak beat her up the hillside by five strides and met up with the others at the top of the ridge. Every person stood quietly, staring with wonder at a gorgeous watery oasis.

Dyphestive was the first one to strip down to his trousers and jump into the crystal-blue pond. "Waaah-hoo!"

"No, wait!" Tatiana warned.

It was too late. Dyphestive splashed into the water, soaking everyone standing on the rim, but mostly Tatiana.

46

Everyone stripped out of their heavy gear and waded into the serenity of the bubbling pond. Tiny bubbles fizzed to the top when they entered, and red-and-green-speckled frogs jumped from lily pad to lily pad.

Beautiful willow trees grew inside the breathtaking pond, their roots and branches making comfortable nooks to lie upon. Tatiana, Zora, and Leena waded underneath the leafy trees, washing their sweat off with the clean water. Razor and Grunt splashed one another until Grunt practically drowned Razor by creating a huge wave with his arms.

Dyphestive spit a stream of water out of his mouth into Grey Cloak's face. Grey Cloak wiped it away and brushed his damp locks behind his ears. Streak swam toward him, flat head just above the water, tail swishing behind him like a gator. He plucked his dragon out of the water and tossed him back in, splashing the women.

"Stop it!" Zora said, as she rubbed her eyes with her fists. "You got water in my mouth. And it doesn't taste as good as it looks." Her nose crinkled. "It's thick."

He splashed another wave at her. "What difference does it make? You're all wet anyway."

"Will you let me relax?"

He shrugged. "Certainly." As soon as she vanished beneath the leafy willow trees, he ducked under the water and swam after her. He snuck right behind her, popped up, grabbed her, and dunked her.

Zora popped out of the water, gasping, hair covering her eyes, and said, "I'm going to kill you!" She jumped on his back and hauled him down into the pond.

They were both laughing when he slung his hair back and said, "All right, we're even." He offered his hand. "Shake."

"In your dreams," Zora said. She gently splashed him. "Go away."

In the meantime, Dyphestive crept behind Leena. She watched out of the corners of her eyes. The moment he grabbed her, she flipped his manly frame into the water. He rose with her on his back, locking him in a choke hold.

Dyphestive clawed at the air and said in a raspy voice, "It's only a game. Leena, let go."

Leena bit his ear.

"Ow! Did she bite my ear?"

"I think it was a love bite," Grey Cloak said as he shifted, trying to get a better look at Leena. "She might be smiling too. Hard to tell with her wooden expression, but I believe she is having fun with you."

"I hope so." Dyphestive carried Leena on his broad back like a child and waded deeper into the water.

Zora backed into Grey Cloak's arms and had him wrap his arms around her. "This is nice, isn't it?"

Grey Cloak had a catch in his throat as a result of her move catching him off guard and awkwardly said, "Yes?"

She turned her head. "What's wrong? You swallow too much pond water?"

He cleared his throat and gave her a squeeze. "Maybe, or you took my breath away."

"Ha-ha, but I liked it." She sank deeper into his arms.

Grey Cloak wasn't sure what was happening. He was warm all over, and his cheeks were as warm as toast. *This is wonderful.*

Tatiana wandered by without giving them a glance. She moved with the grace and beauty of a swan, and her wet clothing clung to every curve of her figure.

Grey Cloak found it difficult to peel his eyes away from her, though the prickly elf so easily got under his skin. He shook his head and blinked. *I feel so good.*

"Look at the birds," Zora said dreamily as she watched the waterfowl fly from branch to branch. "So amazing."

The sun bleeding through the branches started to fade. Tatiana, who was standing in the middle of the pond, let out a bloodcurdling scream. Grey Cloak thrust his body from underneath the willow trees, tugging Zora along.

Tatiana's mouth gaped as she stood still, looking down on the grime that covered her body. The clear pond water appeared to be nothing more than swamp sludge with slimy beds of algae floating on the top. She trembled as she slung it off of her.

"What's happening?" Grey Cloak asked as he scanned the once-sumptuous cove. Where the sunlight shone, the pond appeared to be a sanctuary of refreshing conditions, but where the shadows hit, a darker appearance was revealed.

The pond turned ugly and muddy. The willow trees' leaves hanging down in the water were withering and dying, choked out by thick vines coiled around the trunk and winding into the branches. Steam began to rise from the water, and a putrid smell caused everyone to cover their noses as they backed into the spots of light.

Everyone desperately started wiping the grime from their bodies. The bright spots of sun were quickly diminishing.

"Grey Cloak, what is this?" Zora asked in a shaky voice as she flicked an ugly toad from her shoulder. "Ew!"

An eight-foot-long ringed snake casually cut through the murk and swam right between them.

Zora hid behind Grey Cloak, shoulders shaking like a leaf. "I hate snakes. We need to get out of here."

"I'm with you." He took her hand and pulled her toward the bank. "Let's go."

"Everyone!" Tatiana called. "Get out of the pond. Move!"

The sunlight was blotted out by treetops that merged on their own, and the beautiful pond was covered in darkness so black that everyone stopped.

Grey Cloak felt Zora's heart beating, and her fingernails dug into his hand. "Everyone, remain still," he said, searching through the darkness.

All of a sudden, several dull lights shone from the pond's bank, illuminating three rawboned men with sunken eyes and oversize pointed ears protruding through their long strands of stringy white-gray hair that hung to their toes. Their flowing beards were long, covering their chests and touching the backs of the great bearded elk they sat upon. They scanned the pond with haunted expressions and carried gnarled wooden staffs in their bony hands. A sour yellow light was nestled in the top of the staffs, casting an eerie light on the company.

Tatiana backed away from the bank and said, "Don't let them touch you. They are the Wizzlum."

"What is a Wizzlum?" Grey Cloak asked.

Tatiana swallowed and said, "Life-draining druids."

47

THE LAST WINDOW OF SUNLIGHT WAS CLOSED OFF BY THE TREES, LEAVING THE company standing flat-footed in the murky, smelly grime.

Grey Cloak's neck hairs stood on end as the Wizzlum lifted the glowing heads of their staffs. "Run!" he called.

His boots stuck in the pond's scummy bottom. He wasn't alone, either, as the others fought and splashed against the icky pond's grip.

"Something has me!" Tatiana cried. Her body was jerked neck deep into the water. Her hand thrashed above the surface. She bobbed violently up and down, gulping in the foul water.

The pond came alive from all directions. Algae clung to their bodies like sweat. The vines in the willow branches dropped, snaked through the water, and seized the company's arms and legs.

A vine coiled around Grey Cloak's wrist. He jerked and pulled his hand free, but another vine immediately entwined itself around his other wrist. "Madness!" He snatched a dagger from its sheath and sawed at the vine. The sharp blade cut but slowly.

Snap! Snap! Snap! Nearby, wading waist deep in the water, Dyphestive and Grunt yanked the vines out of the trees.

Dyphestive plowed through the foaming water. "Tatiana, hang on!"

Her head sank into the blackness of the pond, leaving bubbles behind.

"Get her, Dyphestive!" Grey Cloak called. "Hang on, Tat!"

More vines than he could count sprang out of the water and struck at him like snakes. He grabbed Zora, whose fingers clutched for him. "I have you!"

The vines slithered around their bodies and began to constrict.

Zora gasped. "Guh!"

Every member of Talon was neck deep in the murk. Even the massive Grunt thrashed wildly.

Razor struck out with his blades, chopping off bits of the vine's slimy fibers. "What sort of enemy is this? I fight enemies with swords, not weeds!" The bright steel of his sword flashed repeatedly, until the vines snagged his arms and squeezed. "Filthy weeds!"

The haunting faces of the Wizzlum did not change, and they and their elks did not move an inch. They were the last things Grey Cloak saw before the great vines pulled him under.

Nooo! Grey Cloak's fingers fought for the inner pockets of his cloak. *I need the figurine!*

The unnatural strength of the vines pulled his arms back.

He summoned the wizardry. His fingers caught fire, and he latched them around one of the vines, sending a charge of fire blasting through its fibers. The water boiled, and the vine caught fire. The flames spread up the length of the vine and spread to the branches.

Grey Cloak and Zora burst out of the pond, gasping.

An awful sound followed. "*Skreeeyeeelll!*" The vines twisted, reared, and splashed in the water. They flicked out, attacking like snakes again.

Grey Cloak's hand felt like it was on fire. If not for the water, it would have been burned to a crisp. He desperately unleashed a charge into the vines and glared at the Wizzlum. "Don't mess with me. Let us go."

The stoic druids sat on their beasts, as composed as ever, but the one in the middle said, "This is our swamp, not yours. We do as we please. Tonight, we feast on intruders."

"Not if I have anything to say about it!" Grey Cloak answered.

"Grey Cloak, look out!" Zora said.

He turned around just in time to see a bunch of vines coming at him, and they swallowed his body entirely.

48

TALON WAS TETHERED TO THE BEARDED ELK AND DRAGGED THROUGH THE FOREST, leaves sticking to their grimy bodies. Each of them was bound with thick vines. They were hauled into a dark cave lit by smokeless torches on the walls and abandoned.

After the Wizzlum departed, Grey Cloak pushed himself into a sitting position. "Is everyone well?"

"I am," Dyphestive said. His neck muscles bulged as he strained to break free of the vines. "Guh! These vines are thick! I can't budge them."

"You don't have any leverage," Razor said. He rolled over the ground until he hit the rough cave wall. "Cripes, I can't get out of this cocoon." He eyed Grey Cloak. "How'd you do it?"

"I don't know," Grey Cloak replied as he eyeballed his surroundings.

Everyone was lying on the ground as if they'd been rolled up in blankets. They could only wiggle their fingers and toes. Tatiana and Leena lay facing each other. They looked like they'd been cast aside. Grunt was face-first in the dirt, hooves roughly kicking as he fought to roll over to his back. Zora lay quietly beside Grey Cloak, staring up at the roots that were growing out of the high ceiling.

"Where do you think your cousins went, Tatiana?" Grey Cloak asked.

"They aren't my cousins," Tatiana replied. "I wish you would quit saying things like that. This isn't my fault."

He rolled his eyes. "Of course not."

"What is that supposed to mean?"

"Don't even start bickering, you two," Zora warned. "We need to find a way out of here. Use your energy on that."

"Agreed," Tatiana said.

Leena was giving her a hard-eyed stare.

"Will you close your eyes or at least blink? You're giving me shivers, Leena."
Leena didn't move.

"Grey, how are we going to get out of here?" Dyphestive asked. He writhed and flexed in his bonds. "I can't break them, and Grunt can't either. The vines flex and constrict, like living things."

"I'll think of something," he said. He didn't have any ideas at the moment. Using wizardry might burn the vines, but without water, it might burn his hands too. Shifting his shoulders, he tried to wriggle free. The vines tightened. *Ow!* "Tatiana, what are these druids? Can't we reason with them? After all, they are elves, aren't they?"

"They are the Wizzlum. Don't call them elves unless you want to make it worse," Tatiana said as he managed to roll away from Leena's glare. "They might be elven of a sort but claim to be their own race. We came upon them at the most unfortunate time." She spit a piece of a wet leaf out of her mouth. "They are feeding."

Dread overcame Grey Cloak. "Feeding? This forest is filled with animals. Why would they feed on us?"

"Because they love the wildlife more than men. They consider all of the races evil."

"They are a race too. Who are they to judge?" Dyphestive asked.

Tatiana shrugged. "They do what they do. Regardless, if we don't find a way out of here soon, they will drain us like a spider sucking out bug juice."

Zora cringed. "Ew."

Razor rolled over until he got a good look at Tatiana and said, "Well, isn't that great. Can't you use your magic star to get us out of here?"

"I could if I could reach it," she said. "But as you can see, my hands are fastened the same as yours."

"Coming your way." Razor started rolling toward Tatiana. Determined, he didn't stop until he bumped into her. His fingers wiggled at his sides. "How about this?"

Her eyes widened. "That's not where it is."

"Are you sure?" Razor replied.

"I'm sure. Lower, much lower, at my waist."

Quickly grasping the futility of Razor's attempt, Grey Cloak hopped from flat on his back to his feet. With his thighs bound down to the knees, he baby-stepped toward the exit.

Tree roots and twisting black vines blocked the exit. Grey Cloak bumped up against them, but they were as hard as steel. "Isn't that peculiar," he said.

"Can't you get out?" Zora asked.

He shook his head. "Not without an ax or fire."

"Gah! I can't get it, Tatiana," Razor grumbled. "Those vines squeeze whenever I touch them. "Cursed things. When we get out of here, I'm going to burn them. Burn them all."

The roots blocking the cave's exit parted.

Grey Cloak stood face to face with three Wizzlum. "We were wondering when dinner might be served."

With a gentle motion of his staff, one of the Wizzlum flung Grey Cloak across the room, making him slam into the wall. He bounced off and rolled beside Zora.

"Dinner," Zora said to him. "Really? And you hardly eat."

With a groan, he twisted around until he saw them again. "It seemed like a good thing to say at the time."

The three creepy, long-bearded druids entered the room. Their raggedy earthen robes dragged over the ground as they approached. As their haunting eyes swept over their prisoners, the long-eared leader in the front poked his bony finger at Grunt.

"What are they doing?" Zora whispered.

"I don't know."

The two Wizzlum in the rear waved the glowing tips of their sticks at Grunt. His big body was towed across the floor by an unseen force that sent chills down Grey Cloak's spine. Grunt lay in front of the druids with his head rolling from side to side, his huge brown eyes staring up at them.

Two druids poked their staffs into Grunt's body and pinned him to the ground. The leader knelt behind Grunt's head and lay his staff on his chest. The putrid yellow gems cradled in the staffs glowed brighter. The lead Wizzlum fastened his crooked fingers to Grunt's head, and Grunt lurched.

Razor said warily, "What are they doing to him?"

Grunt started to convulse.

Tatiana looked on in horror and said, "They are draining his essence."

49

WITH HIS FINGERS LOCKED ON GRUNT'S SKULL, THE WIZZLUM LEADER'S EYES started to glow hot white. Grunt's back arched, and he let out quick, painful grunts. His big body twitched and spasmed. The other pair of Wizzlum druids drove the glowing tips of their staffs into him, pinning him fast to the ground.

"What are you *doing* to him?" Razor screamed. "Quit that! I'll kill you for it!"

Hot, pungent air blasted through the chamber the moment the leader of the three Wizzlum opened his mouth. They all muttered as one in a threatening, tense, and garbled tone.

"Do something, Tatiana," Grey Cloak pleaded.

"I can't," she responded. "I'm sorry."

Grunt's body was lifted off the floor by an invisible force. The hairs on his arms stood on end, and his tense muscles began to shrink under his shriveling skin.

"No!" Razor hollered. "Nooo!"

All of a sudden, the Wizzlums' wispy hair started to thicken and turn brown. Their pale skin ripened, and sinew began to build underneath. Their heads cocked back, and their hungry eyes radiated with triumph.

Grey Cloak's skin crawled as he watched Grunt's mighty body begin to shrivel. *I have to do something.* He didn't have the Figurine of Heroes in hand, but he knew the spell-casting words. He started to say them.

From out of nowhere, a small vine coiled around his mouth and silenced the mystic words. *Nooo!*

He caught Zora's wide eyes. He'd never seen such fear before or felt such spine-chilling terror. His heart raced. He couldn't believe the horror he was seeing.

A roar rumbled through the cave. The Wizzlums' deep moaning came to an abrupt stop.

Grunt's body crashed to the floor, sagging inside the vines, unmoving.

The Wizzlum stood. No longer were they hunched. Their limbs were strong and their features far younger and full. They set their piercing eyes on the entrance to the chamber.

Streak crept inside, his tongue flicking.

Grey Cloak bit into the vine over his mouth. He wanted nothing more than to save his dragon from an inevitable life-draining doom. *Get out of here, Streak! Get out of here!*

The leader of the Wizzlum bent a knee before Streak. With staff in hand, the silent killer beckoned the dragon over.

Streak wandered over to the druid, pink tongue flicking out of his mouth, as innocent as a hungry puppy. He stopped a few feet short of the druid.

"Get away from him, Streak! Get away!" Dyphestive called. No sooner had he spoken than finger-thick vines covered his mouth, silencing him.

Before the others could utter a word, twisting vines covered their mouths and silenced them too.

The Wizzlum leader stretched out his long arm and beckoned Streak closer. Grey Cloak swallowed. Tatiana had assured him that the Wizzlum valued creatures over people, but he had no idea whether that included dragons or not. *Run, Streak, run!*

Streak glanced in Grey Cloak's direction, and one of the dragon's eyelids flicked like a wink.

Huh? Is he trying to tell me something?

As if on command, Streak lowered his flat head to the ground in a bowing motion. The leader leaned closer.

Streak, no bigger than a small hound, opened his wide jaws, and his belly filled with air. The leader of the Wizzlum leaned back, and the tip of his staff brightened.

Blue flames spewed out of Streak's mouth and engulfed the Wizzlum's tattered robes and long hair. Streak poured it on, turning the man into burning flesh.

The heat on Grey Cloak's face sent new life coursing through his extremities. The entangling vines loosed their hold, and he started to wriggle free.

One of the Wizzlum crept up behind Streak with his glowing staff poised to strike.

Grey Cloak tried to shout, "Watch out!" But he was too late.

A flashing sword cleaved the Wizzlum's head from his shoulders. Standing behind the falling druid was Anya, a glimmering dragon sword in her hand.

The last druid charged her.

Anya ran her blade straight into his chest. She shoved the dead druid off with her boot and said, "Creepy."

The vines that bound the company began to loosen and fall away.

Grey Cloak flagged Streak over and asked, "Anya, where did you come from?"

"Outside," she said as she wiped her blade off on the dead druid's back.

He cradled Streak. "Another surprise from you, little dragon, but this time, I'm not as surprised as the last."

"Grunt! Grunt!" Razor rushed over and fell on the withered body of the minotaur. "Breathe, Grunt! Breathe!"

Than entered the chamber and caught everyone's eye. He said, "I took care of the rest." He tossed his long hair over his shoulder, knelt by Grunt, and placed his scaly hands on his chest.

"Can you save him?" Razor asked, his voice cracking.

Than gave Razor a sad look and said, "I wish I could, but he's too far gone. I'll help you bury him."

50

"THAT'S ONE BIG GRAVE," GREY CLOAK COMMENTED QUIETLY TO ZORA.

She nodded.

Outside of the Wizzlum caves, in a grove of yellow branch elms, Dyphestive was neck deep in the wide grave, shoveling out mounds of dirt with a somber expression. He'd been digging nonstop for over an hour, taking turns with Than and Razor but still carrying the bulk of the load. His hair was dirty, and he had dried grime from the sludge pond coating him all over.

All of them were filthy, except for Anya and Than, who stood with their toes on the grave's rim. They'd said little since they arrived.

Razor sniffled. He was sitting beside Grunt's shrunken body, wiping his eyes from time to time.

Tatiana hovered behind him with a hand on his shoulder. "I'm sorry," she said once again. "He was a true friend and protector."

"Yeah, I'll miss him." Razor wiped his eyes and stood. Eyeing the grave, he said, "I think that hole is big enough."

Dyphestive nodded, tossed the shovel aside, and climbed out.

Grey Cloak, Dyphestive, Than, and Razor each grabbed one of Grunt's limbs and carried him to the grave. He was as heavy as damp wood, and after a nod from Razor, they dropped him. *Thud.*

An uncomfortable silence followed. Everyone stood around the grave, looking down at Grunt.

Grey Cloak's throat tightened. Guilt built in his gut. Another companion had died on account of their excursions. "Would anyone like to say a few words?"

Razor put his hand over his heart. His eyes watered, and he wiped the tears with his thumb.

Dyphestive cleared his throat and said, "His life was too short lived."

"How old was he?" Zora asked politely.

Razor managed a shrug as his chest and shoulders trembled.

"I don't know," Tatiana said. Her breath hitched as she sighed. "But I was under the impression he was young."

"I hope he's in a better place now," Razor muttered. "May he freely roam the greenest pastures for all eternity."

"Well said," Than added. He bent over, plucked the shovel from the ground, and started digging into the mounds of dirt.

Razor stopped him and said, "Let me do it."

THE FIRST TIME Grey Cloak had laid eyes on a Wizard Watch tower was back in Sulter Slay when he'd first joined up with Talon. It was a great stone tower with unique architecture, standing several stories high. It was in a valley in a field of dragon bones. Its stone walls were blackened by fire, and no entrance showed.

The tower east of Great River was little different. It was another marvel of stone architecture that reached toward the clouds. It was made from large granite blocks and circled by rings of smooth columns. Beams of sunlight leaked through the passing clouds, showing off the stone in the purest elemental white.

In the fields surrounding the tower were deposits of colorful rocks that glowed with vibrant life of their own. They were pink, yellow, bright blue, and emerald green and were roughhewn, jagged but as beautiful as gemstones.

Talon stood on a rise, looking up at the wizardly wonder. Despite the other-worldly design, it was a cold, unwelcoming building with no doorway insight. Additionally, it was surrounded by a ring of thorn bushes taller than men and many yards deep. Black crows and tiny birds flew in and out of it.

Grey Cloak broke a thorn off a bush and eyed it. A dew drop dripped from the thorn's tip. "It looks like you are home, Tatiana."

"Wait here," she replied. She stood in front of the barrier of thorns. Several moments later, the thorns parted and opened up a path. "I'll return... soon."

Tatiana headed down the path, and as she did so, the thorn barrier closed behind her. She emerged on the other side of the path, walking up the hill toward the tower. Her shapely figure diminished the closer she came to the ominous tower, and she vanished before she touched its sleek walls.

Grey Cloak rubbed his forehead and said, "I don't know about you, but my skull isn't aching anymore."

Zora nudged his ribs with her knuckles. "Let it rest. She's gone."

Seeing Zora's exhausted expression, he nodded.

The company made a campfire on the edge of the woodland. All eyes were on the tower as the sun started to set again.

"An eerie place to be," Razor murmured as he poked a stick in the fire.

Dyphestive's belly grumbled so loudly that Leena stood. She shook her head and patted her belly.

"Yes, I'm hungry. I hope Tatiana brings us back something to eat."

Leena pointed at the woodland.

Dyphestive shook his head. "I'm not hunting."

Leena pointed again.

He shook his head again. "Not now."

"It looks like someone is squabbling with their lover," Grey Cloak said.

"Don't say that." Dyphestive looked embarrassed. "She's not my—" He caught Leena's eyes and said, "Never mind." He rose. "I'll try to find something to eat."

"Look," Razor said.

Everyone turned toward the barrier of thorns. It split open again, and Tatiana approached. She was clean from head to toe, without a smudge of sludge on her.

As Zora stood, she crossed her arms and said, "Well, don't you look refreshed."

"The Wizard Watch requires standards when one communes with them," Tatiana said politely.

Grey Cloak stepped forward and said, "That's wonderful for you, but what about the rest of us?"

"I need you and Dyphestive to come with me. The rest of you will have to wait," Tatiana said.

"How long?" Grey Cloak asked.

"The Wizard Watch did not say. They only requested to see you and Dyphestive." Tatiana's demeanor was more wooden than frigid.

Dyphestive stood by his brother's side and said, "If we go, we all go."

Tatiana shook her head. "That cannot be at the moment. I'm sorry. You have to trust me."

"Grunt dies on this trek, and this is the treatment we get? Everyone is left stranded among the thorns?"

Anya walked out of the woodland's edge and said, "This is exactly what you should expect. You don't need to go in there, either of you. You can't trust them."

"You can trust me," Tatiana assured them.

Grey Cloak knelt, gathered Streak in his arms, and stood. "Can I take him?"

Tatiana nodded.

He looked up at Dyphestive. "What do you say?"

"I go where you go," Dyphestive replied.

"Fine. Tatiana, lead the way."

Anya hooked his arm. "Remember who you are." She eyed Dyphestive. "Both of you. And don't forget."

"Forget what?" Grey Cloak asked.

She looked him dead in the eye and said, "I warned you."

Can Grey Cloak and Dyphestive trust Tatiana?
What horror's lie inside of the Wizard watch?

Will the outcome change everyone's lives forever?
Don't miss the next riveting book! Details below!

PLEASE LEAVE A REVIEW FOR BATTLEGROUND. THEY ARE A HUGE HELP! LINK!

WIZARD WATCH: Dragon Wars #8, on sale now!

AND IF YOU haven't already, signup for my newsletter and grab 3 FREE books including the Dragon Wars Prequel.
WWW.DRAGONWARSBOOKS.COM

TEACHERS AND STUDENTS, if you would like to order paperback copies for you library or classroom, email craig@thedarkslayer.com to receive a special discount.

GEAR UP in this Dragon Wars body armor enchanted with a +2 Coolness factor/+4 at Gaming Conventions. Sizes range from halfling (Small) to Ogre (XXL). LINK . www.society6.com

· WIZARD WATCH ·

— BOOK 8 —

CRAIG HALLORAN

1

WIZARD WATCH: ARROWWOOD

Talon had made camp near the Wizard Watch tower in a grove of yellow elm trees that were peppered with burning-orange leaves. The leaves fell like soft rain with the off-and-on breezes. An orange leaf from the midsize trees fell on top of Razor's face. With his eyes closed, the handsome young warrior brushed it away and rolled to one side.

Zora smirked at Reginald the Razor curled up like a child with his face to her campfire. It was midday, chilly, and she warmed her fingers over the flames. It had been three days since Grey Cloak, Dyphestive, Tatiana, and Streak had entered the tower. There hadn't been contact with them since.

She stirred a stick in the fire's coals.

Where are they? Zora glanced over her shoulder. She could see the ominous tower through the branches and shivered. *I hope they're fine. No, they have to be. Don't be wrong. You have to trust Tatiana.*

Needless to say, the atmosphere outside the tower had been nothing short of prickly. She'd been left alone with Razor, Thanadiliditis, Leena, and the frosty Anya ever since. She and Anya weren't speaking. It didn't help that Leena didn't speak either.

At the moment, though cold, things were peaceful in the camp. Anya and Than were hunting. Leena was gathering wood, leaving Razor and Zora alone. It didn't take long to realize that Razor was decent company. He was cocky but good, young, too, somewhere between her age and Grey Cloak's, but he acted like he had the knowledge of a fifty-year-old. All of them did.

"If you keep those eyebrows knitted too long, they'll stick together," Razor said in his charming but rugged voice. He'd caught her staring into the flames, fingering the Scarf of Shadows.

She turned her attention to him. "Is it that bad?"

"Most people worry." Razor rubbed his mouth, stretched his arms out over the grass, and yawned. He sat up. "But I don't worry. Worry creates doubt. Doubt will get you killed." He braced himself against the tree behind him. "I sound like I know all, but I don't."

"It's fine. I'm getting used to hearing that from everyone else, especially you know who."

Razor glanced at the surrounding woodland. "Ah, you're talking about Fiery Red, aren't you? Heh. She's really something, that gal." He nodded his strong chin. "I like her, though. She's up-front about things. And she's a dragon rider. They're an aloof kind, as I understand. Elite. A woman with a dragon is a good woman to have... they say."

"She doesn't have a dragon, just dragon breath."

Razor waved his hand with a growing smile. "Whooo, it's getting hot out here."

"You know what I mean." Zora was squatting and tucked her hands into her sides. "She's mean."

"I can handle that meanness when she's that pretty."

"Are you that shallow?"

"Heh, I like her. She's a fighter, like me. You have to be mean to survive. You've been around the dungeon. You know that."

Zora gave him a straight-faced look. "I thought you were Tatiana's man."

"I wish, but she's in love with a ghost. Don't get me wrong, Zora. I trust Tatiana, too, but I don't fault Fiery Red for mistrusting her." He pulled his dagger out of his sheath and spun it in his hand with a flashy motion. "Fighters like us put our faith in flesh, bone, and steel. Those wizardly things are beyond us. Besides, she's got great hair." The fingers on his free hand grazed his short, feathery brown locks. "Like me."

Zora rolled her eyes but didn't hide her smile. Razor was pleasant to listen to, rough but positive.

Leena appeared out of the woodland and dropped a handful of broken branches by the fire. She sank to her knees and started building a spit from some of the sticks she'd carried.

Zora and Razor exchanged amused glances.

Leena did everything with determination and purpose. Her silky black robes with gold trim contrasted sharply with her long cherry-red hair, which was braided into a tail behind her head. Her long fingers with black nails were quick and dexterous as she bound the sticks together with small vines that she used like twine. Leena caught Zora looking at her and stuck her expressionless face out toward Zora.

Zora looked away.

Razor giggled. "I think someone is missing someone."

Zora couldn't help herself. She addressed Leena. "Do you want to talk about it?"

Leena glared at her.

Razor burst into raucous laughter.

The contagious hilarity had Zora bursting into tears as she clamped her hands over her gut. She fell to one side. "It's not supposed to be that funny. Sorry, Leena."

Leena tilted her head to one side, eyes studying Zora like she'd lost her mind. She removed her nunchakus.

"Bwah-hah-haaa-hah!" Razor fought to spit his words out. "She's going—going to throttle you with her little s-s-s-sticks!"

With tears streaming down her cheeks, Zora rolled flat on her back, laughing her head off. She couldn't contain it. She looked at Leena. "I'm sorry. It's not you, Leena. It's—it's those cute little sticks! Ah-hahahahahah!"

"Stop it. You're going to make me pee my trousers!" Razor said.

Leena suddenly stood up, and her brows knitted together. She wasn't looking at Zora, however. She was looking in the direction of the shadow that had fallen over her.

Razor's laughter was cut short.

Zora's sputtering fell flat as well as she cast her eyes on Anya.

ANYA CARRIED A DEAD YOUNG STAG OVER HER SHOULDERS. SWEAT BEADED ON HER face, and the edge of her wavy red hair was damp. With a thrust of her legs and a heave of her shoulders, she dropped the stag to the ground. "He's young, but his rack has six points," Anya said as she pulled out her dagger and took a knee by the carcass. "So, have Grey Cloak and Dyphestive returned? I don't see them."

Zora ground her teeth.

"Not yet," a wide-eyed Razor said as he climbed to his feet. "You caught that stag? No simple feat, especially with full armor."

Than glided out from between two trees with a smile on his old wrinkly face. "She crept up on it and slew it before it blinked," he said in a scratchy voice. "It was something to behold." Even though Than was older and walked with a slight stoop, the long-haired hermit stood taller than the rest of them.

Using her blade like a hunting knife, Anya cut deep into the stag's belly. "Ah, there's the heart. You should eat that, Zora. It will make you strong... and wise."

Zora's face soured as her belly churned. She'd seen Adanadel and Browning carve up plenty of deer back in the day, but she'd never developed a stomach for it. Tanlin hadn't either. She crept back.

Anya slung a hunk of meat at her. "Don't gawk. Cook. Aren't you hungry?"

"Do you have to be so arrogant?" Zora tried to pick up the slab of meat with a stick.

Leena bent over, snatched up the bloody meat, stuck it on a pointed stick, and took it to the fire.

Anya continued to saw. "Arrogant? That's not a very nice thing to say to the person who brought enough food for you to eat over the next several days. I assume it'll be several days or forever."

"You don't have to stay!" Zora shouted. Her head throbbed, and her heart beat in her temples.

"Look whose nostrils are flaring," Anya said in an annoyed but cool manner. "I'll wait it out. It's worth it to let you know that I'm right."

Than moved between the two women. "There's no need to bicker. We're all on the same side of the battle. You need to remember that."

Zora moved to the other side of the fire, drumming her nimble fingers on her dagger. "Everything was fine until she showed up." She moved deeper into the woodland and sat down under a tree. *I hate her.* From a distance, she watched the others grab a hunk of meat and start to eat.

Razor gushed about the stag. "It's so tender. If we can eat like this, I don't care if we wait for weeks."

It was all Zora could stand. She covered her ears and put her head between her knees.

Since Grey Cloak and Dyphestive had left, it'd taken everything she had to hold herself together. She missed them, and with each passing hour, she carried more doubt about Tatiana. The elven sorceress could be as frigid as Anya, and Zora had no doubt she carried secrets very close to her chest.

I've never felt so alone. Perhaps I should go home, back to Raven Cliff. I miss Tanlin.

It wouldn't have been so bad if Crane and Jakoby were still along. They were easy to talk to, especially Crane. He had a story about everything and had seen so many places.

Than approached. He had a small steaming hunk of meat on the end of a stick. He sat down by Zora and offered it to her. "Please eat."

"I'm not hungry."

"Come now, I heard your belly growl. Eat." He nodded at the campfire. "In spite of Anya."

"Huh." Zora took the stick, peeled off a piece, and chewed on it. The warm meat was very tender. She took another bite off the stick.

"Good, eh?" he asked.

She shrugged. "Could be better." Her eyes lingered on his scaly arms, which looked like shedding snakeskin. His fingernails were sharp and long. She hadn't had many conversations with Than. "Are you a leper?"

Than chuckled. "No. I'm only old and getting weaker by the day." His low voice carried a soothing tone. "They're actually scales."

She lifted a brow. "Does everyone in your world have scales?"

"No, mostly the dragons. It's a long story." He combed his fingers through his stringy red-gray hair. "Very long."

"So, is your world like this one?"

"Very much, or at least it was until Black Frost started to drain it."

"And you've been to other worlds as well?"

Than nodded. "A few."

She sighed. "I wish I could go to another world."

Than put a gentle hand on her shoulder. "There's no place like home. Believe me. And don't let Anya spoil things for you. She's not against you. If she were, you'd be dead."

"That's comforting."

"She's an ally. Believe me."

"Says the hermit from another world."

A moment passed before he added, "I'm a very good judge of character. You're in good company."

She turned toward Than. "What about Tatiana? Do you trust her?"

"She has a good heart, but I fear that she is being deceived." He looked off in the direction of the Wizard Watch. "Tatiana has placed a great deal of faith in the mages in the towers. It's what she knows. We can only hope that she can see the truth for herself before it's too late."

"You don't trust the Wizard Watch either?"

"I know little about them. That's a good reason not to trust them."

Zora chewed the rest of her meat and tossed the stick away. "Thanks. Tell Dirty Red it was wonderful. I think I'll take a nap." Just as she turned her back to Than, she caught a soft white glow out of the corner of her eye. Someone entered the camp. "Dalsay!" She popped up from her spot and rushed over.

Dalsay stood by the fire in a full but ghostly form that she could see right through. He was still in his dark-blue robes, with a head of long, thick brown hair and a beard. His fingers with many rings were clasped together. "I have news," Dalsay said.

"Spit it out, apparition," Anya demanded.

Dalsay nodded. "Grey Cloak and Dyphestive are gone."

3

Anya's dragon blade sliced right through the ghost of Dalsay. "Die, cretin liar!"

"Even your dragon steel cannot harm me," Dalsay said calmly. "And I'm not here to bear ill will. They are safe, only gone, as I understand it."

"We'll see if my blade will cut you or not!" Anya's dragon sword shone blue with dancing fire. The very metal hummed and crackled. She thrust.

Dalsay vanished and reappeared twenty feet away underneath a great oak adjacent to the camp. "I came to tell you to depart north to the elven city of Staatus. Reunite with Crane there and await further instructions."

Anya let out an animallike growl and charged Dalsay. He vanished a split second before she thrust her sword into the heart of the tree. The blade sank halfway to its hilt. She tugged on the steel, which held fast in the tree. Her face filled with strain.

"Need a hand?" Razor offered.

Anya shot him a dangerous look. "Stifle it!" She planted the bottom of her boot against the tree's bark and put her shoulders into it. "Eeeyargggh!"

The sword came free.

Anya's chest heaved underneath her breastplate, and her nostrils flared. "I told you this would happen," she said to Zora. "You never should have trusted that witch!"

"Me?" Zora practically spit when she said it. "I didn't tell them to come here or go in there. They made that decision. Did you ever think that they did it to get away from you?"

Anya's emerald eyes burned like fire. She stormed off in the direction of the tower.

Everyone followed, including Zora.

Anya's right! Tatiana, what did you do to me? Where are you?

Than caught up with Anya. "Where are you going?"

"In there," Anya said without so much as a glance at the tower, but everyone knew what she was talking about.

Anya started hacking into the thorns and bristles towering over the group like a woman gone mad. Her blade ignited with blue fire.

"She's gone plum crazy," Razor uttered under his breath.

Hunks of the thistles burned with new flames. More of the dry wood caught fire as Anya mowed into it like a bull. The path widened as she pressed through the brush, the thorns scraping against her armor. She made it through, but the fiery gap started to close.

"Come on!" Zora said. She raced through the closing thorns.

Razor was the last one through before the thornbush sealed them inside the grounds surrounding the tower.

Anya's face was scraped and bleeding from forehead to chin. That didn't stop her from marching toward the tower. She stomped around the perimeter of it. "Where's the door, you bloody cowards? Where is it?"

All the tower walls were flawless, without the seam of a single door in sight. Even Zora's keen eye picked up nothing.

Anya found a spot on the white granite stone that looked like an archway that had been sealed up long ago. Using her blade, she chopped into it. Chips of stone flew, but the damage was minimal.

Zora stepped back from the tower and looked up. The architecture was brilliant, with separate levels of stone columns encircling it. It stood several stories tall, and the top jutted into the sky like a finger pointing at the passing clouds.

"He said they aren't there," Zora said loudly.

Anya stopped swinging her steel and looked at Zora like she was a fool. "And you believe him?"

Zora felt like an idiot. She'd trusted Tatiana and Dalsay faithfully for years, but when it came to it, she'd started to doubt. She clenched her jaw. *Dirty acorns. She's right.* "I'll climb."

Anya gave her a dirty look. "What?"

"I said I'll climb." She searched for a handhold. "In the meantime, the pair of you can keep trying to chop this tower down. Let's see who gets inside first." Her fingers found purchase on the rough stone of the columns at the bottom, and she started to climb. "See you on the other side."

She'd made it up the first ten feet when she noticed that Leena had joined her. The monk from the Ministry of Hoods crawled the column like a bug and was gaining ground.

"Impressive." Zora sped up her efforts, climbing like a squirrel to the next level.

Down below twenty feet, she saw Razor, Than, and Anya watching her. Anya's hair covered one eye. With her sword in hand, she stood frowning.

"What's the matter? Did you chip your sword?"

Razor hollered up with his hands cupped around his mouth, "Be careful, Zora!"

"Thank you, swordsman obvious! Gah!" She had looked up to see Leena standing on the narrow ledge right beside her. "Don't spook me." She tilted her head. "You go that way. I'll go this way. Look for any opening we can squeeze through."

Level after level, they made their way toward the top. The tower was sealed up as tight as a drum, with only the smallest cracks and creases between the stones. A platform about ten feet wide with a capstone made of steel sat at the top.

Zora took a seat with her feet dangling over the rim. A stiff wind rustled her hair and clothing, and the chill froze her fingers. She blew hot breath into her hand as Leena joined her. "Well, this was a waste."

Whether Leena was hot or cold, one could never tell. Her face remained without expression. All the monk did was lift her fingers and point to a flock of great birds coming their way.

"Great, they're probably going to poop on us," Zora muttered.

Leena shook her head.

"What?" Zora narrowed her keen eyes. The birds didn't have feathers. They had scales. "Horseshoes!"

4

ZORA CUPPED HER HANDS OVER HER MOUTH AND SHOUTED DOWNWARD, "ANYA! We're going to have company! Dragons!"

It wasn't the first time she'd seen dragons in the sky. It wouldn't have been the worst thing, either, if not for the fact that the dragons were flying right at them instead of passing overhead.

"We need to get down. We don't stand a chance up here," she said to Leena.

Leena jumped off the ledge.

"Leena!" Zora cried out. The monk was down on the next level of the tower. Her fingers gripped the columns. She glanced at Zora and dropped down again.

"How in the world is she doing that?" With a glance over her shoulder, Zora saw the dragons bearing down on her.

The dragons were small, like ponies, with long faces covered in hard, bumpy ridges and putrid-green eyes. They opened their jaws wide and screeched like birds of prey.

She eyed the ground, where Anya, Razor, and Than were waiting. Leena was halfway down. "Here goes," she said and jumped as a dragon sailed right over her head.

Zora's fingers skidded against the round column. Her toes hit the rim of the outer ledge and slipped off. She caught hold of the same ledge with the tips of her fingers and held on for her life. Her feet dangled over the ledge as another dragon soared by. "Not good!" She wouldn't make it to the bottom in time without falling or the dragons getting her first. She swung herself onto the tower's balcony and nestled her body behind a column.

Another dragon soared by and let out an earsplitting screech. A fourth followed.

Zora pressed her body deeper into the space behind the column. Her heart pounded in her chest. Her breathing quickened, and her limbs froze.

Again, a terrifying screech blasted through the air. A dragon rose before her from below and fixed its serpentine eyes on her. The dragon landed on the ledge with its wings beating behind its back. It steadied and came at her.

She opened her mouth but couldn't make a sound. Fear took over her mind. Silently she screamed, *Noooooooo!*

ANYA'S EYES locked on the thunder of dragons soaring through the sky. She raised her sword and sneered. "Those aren't dragons. They're drakes."

"Ah, the foul ones," Than added.

"If Cinder were here, he'd tear them to ribbons. They're the vermin of the skies." Anya waved her arms over her head and shouted, "Come, winged lizards! Come and let me introduce you to death."

Leena hopped down the last ten feet of the tower and landed like a cat. Her nunchakus were spinning in her hands. She fixed her eyes on the drakes and joined her companions.

"There's a dozen of them," Than said as he picked up a branch. "Their arrival is very peculiar."

"It's the work of wizards, if you ask me." Anya set her feet in a defensive stance and eyeballed the dragons.

A foursome of the drakes set their eyes upon her and dove.

"Incoming," Than commented quietly.

"Good," she said.

"Time to carve some turkey," Razor added.

The drakes landed and surrounded the small company. They spread their wings wide and hemmed the group in.

Unlike dragons, the drakes had small talons on the ends of their wings. Their bodies were supported by powerful back legs that launched them into the sky, but they didn't breathe fire. Their long tails had spikes on the end and were used for strangling and striking.

"Careful, Leena. They're stupid but very nasty," Anya warned. "Don't let them get their claws on you, or they'll tear you in two." The drake nearest Anya coiled its long neck back and struck with its head. Anya lunged at its face. Her sword skewered its mouth shut. She twisted and wrenched the blade free.

The wounded drake's screech could have shattered glass as it backed away. It wriggled its neck violently. Its eyes burned with primordial hate as it came at Anya again.

Anya set her feet, put her hips into her swing, and let loose.

Slice!

The drake's head came clean off, putting its threatening shrieks to an end.

RAZOR CHARGED with his swords thrust forward. The drake collided with him, horns lowered. Steel clashed with horn as the drake plowed him over. The foul creature sank its teeth into the leather armor and meat of Razor's shoulder. Its back claws raked over his legs, trying to rip him apart.

Overpowered by the savage reptile, Razor let go of his long blades and whisked out the smaller ones. "I won't die on my back." Using the daggers like pointed fists, he punched into the drake's abdomen again and again.

THAN WRESTLED WITH ANOTHER DRAKE. The large hermit had the drake in a headlock. It tried to shake him free. Incredibly, Than held on. "Hold still and die, won't you? I haven't broken a neck in a long time!"

LEENA'S NUNCHAKUS SPUN FURIOUSLY. She busted the drake in the snout six times before it could attack.

Clok! Clok! Clok! Clok! Clok! Clok!

She jumped over its tail, hopped onto its spiny back, and unleashed another torrent of glowing nunchaku power.

Clok! Clok! Clok! Clok! Clok!

The drake's skull cracked underneath the hammering blows. Its body sagged and flattened on the ground, trembling.

Leena jumped from its scaly hide. Her taut muscles eased as she scanned her surroundings. She didn't see the drake's death strike coming. Its spiked tail lashed out and struck her in the belly. Leena sagged.

Anya rushed to her aid and chopped off the drake's tail. She caught Leena in one arm as the speechless woman fell. "Hang on, Leena. Hang on."

Leena's eyes rolled up into her head, and her eyelids closed.

5

"D<small>ON'T DIE ON ME</small>, L<small>EENA</small>," A<small>NYA SAID</small>. B<small>LOOD FROM</small> L<small>EENA'S BELLY STAINED HER</small> hand as she tried to put pressure on the wound. "Be strong."

She heard a loud snap, like a branch breaking.

A drake died in Than's arms. He shoved the dead drake away. Panting for breath, he joined Anya. "I don't think they're after us." He pointed at the tower. "They're after her."

The rest of the drakes nestled on different levels of the tower, crowding around the last spot where they had seen Zora. Their wings fluttered as they sat on their perches, and they let out nauseating shrieks.

"We need to save Zora," he said.

"What about Leena? Can you help her?"

Than placed his scaly fingers on Leena's chest. "Her heartbeat is faint yet strong." He tilted his head. "Very strange." He pulled the nunchakus from Leena's death grip. "I don't know what good these will do, but we need to lure the drakes down here. I'll take a crack at it. Be ready."

Anya rested Leena's limp body on the ground and stood. "I'm always ready. Let it fly."

Than hurled one pair of nunchakus. The small sticks sailed end over end like the blades of a buzz saw and cracked a drake in the back right behind the wings.

The drake's head twisted around. It set its fiendish eyes on Than and shrieked. A trio of drakes jumped from the tower and dove right at them.

Than awkwardly flipped the other set of nunchakus around. "Could you spare a dagger? I'm not accustomed to using sticks."

Anya offered him both of hers. "Have at it, hermit."

As soon as the drakes hit the ground, the battle was on. The drakes lashed out with their tails and teeth. Anya gored one in the belly and hacked into the hide of another.

Than moved like an old panther and pierced a drake behind the wings. He cried out, "Aaaargh!" as the drake chomped down on his forearm. It backed up, pulling him across the ground.

Than planted his feet, sat up, and with a fierce grimace, he jammed a dagger into the top of the drake's skull. "That's good steel." Wheezing, he pulled the blade free.

Anya finished off the last drake with a hard chop into its body.

"Duck!" Than called out.

A drake flew at Anya's back and flattened her to the ground. A second drake came out of nowhere and bit her leg. Her armor saved her leg from getting bitten clean off, but the pressure built like a vise.

"Get off me, drake!" She punched it in the snout.

Another drake landed right beside her. Its tail lashed out and coiled around her neck. Together, the drakes pulled her in opposite directions. They were pulling her apart.

Through clenched teeth, with her face turning purple, she said, "Nasty things..." Anya choked as the pressure on her neck built, making her eyes bulge. Her head felt like it was going to explode. She hacked at the drake fastened to her leg. Her sword swings had a bad angle, and they had no force behind them.

Lords of the Air! They are killing me!

Out of the corner of her eye, she saw Than coming her way. His eyes blazed like burning gold. He opened up his mouth, and a geyser of bright yellow-orange flames spewed out.

Than's dragon breath ate up the drake with its tail coiled around Anya's neck. Its scales shrank to the bone, and it died in its own burning flesh.

The wroth heat of Than's air curled the tips of Anya's hair, making it stink. The flames caught the drake's gaze. It released her and pounced at Than.

With a single gust of breath, Than turned the drake into a living pillar of flame. Its wings beat frantically as it burned to a crisp, staggered on wobbly legs, crackled a shriek, and stumbled over dead.

Two more drakes dropped from the tower. Without hesitating, Than burned them to a crisp.

Anya limped toward Than, who huffed out a ring of black smoke, and said with a raised brow, "Where did that come from?"

Than thumped his chest with his fist. "It must have been something I ate." His legs became noodles. He broke out in a cold sweat and fell down flat on his back.

"Than!"

ZORA COWERED behind the column as a drake clawed and nipped at her. She was wedged far enough back that its long snout couldn't reach her. Its small taloned hand on the end of its wing clawed at her. A talon caught her shoulder and ripped her clothing and skin. She cried out, "Augh!"

The slash from the drake woke her from her fear-filled slumber. She'd become numb to the attack, unable to move or think as the flying reptilian terror rattled her sharp mind. All she wanted to do was run, but she had nowhere to run or hide.

A second drake moved to the other side of the column. They had her pinned in behind the pillars. Their winged claws stretched out, raking at her body. Both drakes let out mind-jarring shrieks.

She covered her ears and squeezed her eyes shut. "Help me. Somebody, help me, pleaaaassse!"

6

Dᴙᴀᴋᴇ ᴄʟᴀᴡꜱ ʀᴀᴋᴇᴅ ᴀᴛ ʜᴇʀ ꜰʟᴇꜱʜ.

"Skrrreeeeeeee! Skreeeeeeeeee! Skreeeee—" *Thuk!*

Zora's eyelids snapped open.

One of the drakes had an arrow sticking out of the side of its head. It teetered on the ledge, turned, and launched itself into the sky.

Thuk! Thuk!

Two black-feathered arrows embedded themselves in the drake's chest. It flung its wings back and beat them once more before it dropped like a stone.

The last drake turned its attention to the danger coming from below. An arrow blasted into its neck. A second arrow struck it square in the chest, and it fell from the tower and smashed into the ground.

Zora crawled away from her hiding spot and looked down. She trembled. Burning drake corpses made black smoke and an awful stink. Than and Leena lay on the ground as if dead. Anya tended to them. Zora scanned the woodland edge but saw no sign of archers.

Where are they?

She envisioned several East River elves coming to their aid, but none could be found. A subtle movement caught her eye. An elf stepped out from the trees with a bow in hand. His hair was long and as dark as raven feathers, and his bare arms were strong and mighty.

Zora's heart leaped. "Bowbreaker!"

As soon as Zora's feet touched the ground, she ran and leaped into Bowbreaker's arms.

The stoic elven archer gave her a rigid hug and patted her back. "You're safe now, Zora."

Tears streamed from the corners of her eyes. "You won't believe how glad I am to see you. I thought I was dead."

"You're wounded," Bowbreaker replied in a firm voice as he eyed the nasty gashes on her arms and legs. "Let me tend to you."

When she got her first look at the blood on her arms, she almost fainted. Suddenly, the wounds burned like fire. "Please, please do."

Anya approached and squatted beside her. "You're very brave. I'm glad to see you survived."

"You are?" Zora asked.

"I would've missed having someone to fight with," Anya said coolly.

"I don't think you'd ever have trouble with that." She glanced behind Anya. "Are they...?"

"Dead? No. Than passed out after breathing fire all over the drakes," Anya said.

Shocked, Zora replied, "He's a fire-breathing hermit?"

"I wouldn't have believed it if I hadn't seen it for myself." Anya's nose crinkled. "The stink might kill us all, however."

Bowbreaker dumped water out of a leather waterskin and into his hands and washed Zora's wounds.

Zora sucked air through her teeth. She couldn't stop shivering. "I'm sorry. You must think me a coward."

"Of course not," Bowbreaker said with a handsome, creaseless expression. "There are few people in the world who could have survived the feat you attempted." He smoothed a hand down her face. "You have a brave heart, Zora."

"Uh... thank you."

Bowbreaker finished treating her wounds with green leaves and a white salve he carried in one of his packs. "This will hold you together for now. In the meantime, don't fight any more drakes."

"I'm not sure about this one," Anya said to Bowbreaker about Leena. "She took a shot in the gut."

"Excuse me." He moved from Zora to Leena and opened Leena's robes. "It's not grave and appears to be healing on its own."

Leena's eyelids snapped open. She saw Bowbreaker and slapped him in the face.

"Apparently you're right." Anya smirked.

Leena closed her robes and sat straight up without wincing. She stared at Bowbreaker for the longest time then put her finger in front of his face, wagged it back and forth, and stood. She moved toward Than and ripped her nunchakus from his fingers. She then wandered off to find the other pair.

Bowbreaker combed his hair behind his pointed ears. "Who is that?"

"Leena. A monk from the Ministry of Hoods. I know little about her," Zora said. "She doesn't speak."

"A rare and admirable quality," Bowbreaker said in a well-mannered voice.

Was that a joke? Zora thought.

One of the dead drakes moved.

In a flash of motion, Bowbreaker was on a knee with his bow ready and an arrow nocked.

Anya's weapons were poised and ready.

The drake rolled over onto its wings, and a bloody man emerged from underneath. "What happened? Did you forget about me?" It was Razor, wounded from head to toe. He looked like he'd been eaten alive and spit back out. "How about some water?"

"SKREEEEEEEEEEEEEEYYAAAAAHHH!"

Everyone lifted their gazes skyward. A lone drake circled above the Wizard Watch tower. It wasn't like the rest of the brood. It was bigger, by three or four times at least.

"What is that?" Zora muttered.

"A firedrake," Anya said sternly. "Very dangerous. It makes the rest of the drakes look like puppies."

Razor finished crawling out from under the pile of dead drake flesh. He stood, using one sword as a cane. "Firedrake as in it can breathe fire?"

At that movement, the firedrake huffed out a mouthful of flames. Its body was armored with rigid scales. It had claws like great scissors. It was a beast, an angry beast with demonic eyes that burned with hungry hatred.

Zora felt the wroth heat from above on her cheeks.

"Tell me steel can pierce its hide," Razor said.

"Sometimes." Anya nodded as her eyes followed the creature's skyward path. She took a deep breath, and her sword started to glow again.

Bowbreaker aimed his bow.

Leena joined them with both pairs of her nunchakus in hand.

Zora summoned her strength and stood with them. "Well, if you've seen one drake, you've seen them all. Let's kill it."

The firedrake dove.

Bowbreaker let loose his first arrow. It skipped off the field of small horns protecting the firedrake's skull.

Every one of Zora's senses told her to run, but she didn't. She stood her ground, facing the fiery winged doom that was about to plow her over with the others.

7

ANYA GROUND HER HEELS INTO THE DIRT. SHE WOULD STRIKE TO TAKE THE DRAGON down before it plowed her over. One perfect strike was all it would take. She concentrated. *I must be perfect.*

The firedrake dropped out of the sky halfway between them and the tower. It pulled up, its wings beating hard, and sucked in a mighty breath.

"Thunderbolts!" she said. "It's not going to attack. It's going to scorch us. Everyone, scatter!"

"You don't have to tell me twice!" Razor darted away from the tower.

A torrent of flames erupted from the firedrake's mouth. The dragon breath blasted into the ground where the company once stood. The flames turned the grass to ashes and scorched the earth black instantly.

Bowbreaker loosed another arrow. The shaft sailed true and jabbed into the firedrake's left eye.

It let out a roar that shook the branches on the trees. Wroth heat blasted out of its mouth in a cone of fire, sweeping in all directions.

Anya dove behind one of the glowing quartz stones that jutted up out of the ground. Fire blasted around her on both sides. "Everyone, scatter! Scatter! Its breath won't last forever!"

"How long will it last?" Razor shouted from somewhere unseen.

"I don't know. Hide!" she said. The firedrakes and drakes were notorious predators that would not give up the hunt until their prey was dead. As for the firedrake's breath, as far as she knew, it could set the entire forest on fire. "Take cover somewhere! I'll handle the drake!"

Anya peeked around the stone after the flames stopped. The firedrake landed on the ground. Its head hung low, and its nostrils flared. Patches of flames burned like campfires in the field before it. It let out another gust of fire, setting the thornbushes ablaze. The flames spread quickly. Suddenly, it locked its eyes on Than lying still in the field of fire. It approached him and opened its jaws wide.

"No!" Anya was on her feet and running at the firedrake at full speed.

The firedrake swung its head around on its long serpentine neck. Its eyes narrowed, and flames spit from its mouth.

Anya covered the gap with long strides. Flames or no flames, she wasn't going to turn back. She ran on a collision course for the inferno.

"Anya, no!" Razor cried out. His words were suffocated by the roar of the flames.

Through the searing heat, Anya kept running.

Whump! Crack!

"Roooooooaaaaaaar!"

The flames evaporated instantly.

A tail swiped Anya out of harm's way. She rolled across the ground and came back up to one knee.

Two titans were intertwined in ferocious battle. The firedrake fought for its very life against a behemoth of a dragon that had landed on top of it.

"Cinder!" Anya shouted.

Cinder dwarfed the firedrake. More than double its size, the powerful Cinder crushed the firedrake into the ground with his front paws. The firedrake blasted fire into Cinder's huge horned face. Cinder shrugged the flames off like the wind. The firedrake's back claws scraped against the armored scales of Cinder's underbelly.

Cinder pinned the firedrake down and bit into its neck. His jaws clamped down like a huge vise. The firedrake's narrowed eyes bulged. The steel-hard bones in the firedrake's neck gave way under the unyielding pressure of Cinder's jaws.

Crack-snap!

The firedrake's taut neck went limp. The fire in its eyes cooled.

Cinder slung the firedrake aside like a rag and sent it flying into the tower's walls. He sat up on his hind legs and let out a roar so loud that it scattered every bird in leagues of the valley. He was mighty, beautiful, covered in scales, hard ridges, and horns, flecked with tortoiseshell patterns of yellow and gold.

Anya ran right at him. "Sssssh! Ssssssh! You bloated bigmouth!" she said with glee. "You can't let the others hear you!" She grabbed onto his big face when he lowered his head. She hugged him tight. "What are you doing here?"

"I missed you," Cinder said sincerely.

"What about the fledglings?" She was speaking of the twelve baby dragons they had saved from Hidemark.

"They're safe. They grow fast." Cinder eyeballed her with his golden eye. "They need attention. Mentors, Anya. You need to come. Did you find Grey Cloak?"

"Yes."

Cinder scanned the others in the company, who came forward with wide eyes. "No need to fear. I'm on your side and quite friendly. Hmm... where is Grey Cloak?"

"In the tower," Anya said dryly. "They've been locked in there for days."

"They?" Cinder asked.

"Grey Cloak, Streak, and Dyphestive."

"I see."

Her lip curled. "The wizards lied to us again. They led them inside and came out and said they were no longer there. I don't believe them. The moment we tried to find a way into the tower, the drakes came." She shook her fist at the tower. "They're liars."

Cinder nodded in a manner that was more human than dragon. If anything, he came across as a wise grandfather. He scratched his chin with his claws. "You can't find an entrance."

"No," she said.

"Hmm... perhaps there's something I can do about that."

CINDER SPENT THE BETTER PART OF AN HOUR USING HIS HEAD AND HORNS LIKE A battering ram, trying to bust the tower walls down.

While Leena stitched up Razor's wounds, Razor said to Cinder, "Watching you is giving me a skull ache. What are those walls made of? Iron?"

"If they were made of iron, I would melt it, but it's stone, hence it won't burn," Cinder replied. "A very clever design by the Wizard Watch, a design to keep dragons out. I fear that I cannot penetrate it. It's not the stone so much as the enchantment."

Zora noticed that whenever Cinder rammed the tower, the surrounding quartz stones glowed. "It's the rocks, isn't it?" She was standing by a pink crystalized cluster of rocks that jutted out of the earth like limestone.

"Most likely," Cinder replied. "Anya, we should return to the fledglings. They need you. They need me."

"I know." She frowned.

"Ugh..." Than fought his way to his elbows. He blinked several times, and his eyes found Cinder. "Hello."

"Hello to you," Cinder replied.

Before anyone could say anything, Than and Cinder were immersed in deep conversation, but it wasn't in any language that Zora understood. She crept over to Anya. "What are they saying?"

Anya had her arms crossed and shared the same perplexed look. It carried in her voice too. "I have no idea. I've never heard it before."

"It's beautiful, whatever it is," Zora said. "It's almost like singing."

Everyone sat down and watched the dragon and hermit talk to one another like a pair of old friends. Even Bowbreaker joined the captivated audience and sat beside Zora. She leaned into his shoulder.

The old hermit, Than, stood before Cinder with his stringy hair hanging down over his shoulders. Frequently he combed his long fingernails through what once might have been fiery-red locks. One shoulder was slumped, and he appeared weaker than he had earlier in the day, but he spoke with a new spring of energy.

Cinder appeared equally enthused. The magnificent beast's great wings flexed out from time to time as they spoke in enchanting gibberish. Cinder seemed to hang on Than's every word. He chortled gleefully from time to time. The conversation was long, and it could have gone on forever had Anya not interrupted well over an hour later.

"Excuse me!" she said on her approach. She stood between them. "I have to ask, what are you talking about?"

"Oh, we aren't talking. We're merely making our initial introductions," Than said.

Flabbergasted, Anya said, "What? All this time and you haven't been saying anything?"

"Well, we've said quite a bit, but our language contains a lot more syllables and song than yours," Cinder said. "It's been so long since I've used it. I thought I might have forgotten the words. We don't use it so much anymore, though, occasionally"—sadness filled his voice—"Firestok and I did."

Zora's knees were pulled up to her chest, and with big green eyes, she asked, "What language is it?"

"Dragonese," Than replied. "Would you like to learn it? I could teach you, but it might take a decade or two."

"We don't have time for that," Anya said, pushing Than away from Cinder. "We need to get to Grey Cloak. Now."

"Why did Grey Cloak go in the tower in the first place?" Cinder asked.

Anya sighed. "Per Tatiana's ceaseless urgings, he went in to find out what's become of the dragon charms that they've been recovering for years. Apparently, the dragon charms have not been relinquished, to the side of good, that is. I suspect they've been giving them to Black Frost all along."

"You don't know that," Zora argued.

"No, but it makes sense. Doesn't it?" Anya fired back. "Look at what happened the moment we tried to enter the tower." She pointed at the dead fire-drake. "Those vermin came. Servants of Black Frost." She turned to Cinder. "You must go."

"We must go," Cinder replied.

"I'm not leaving without Grey Cloak. We need him," she said. "We need Streak too. He's a controller."

Cinder perked up. "My boy is a controller? Hah! I knew he had something special in him. However, I have twelve others to feed, Anya. We need you."

Than spoke in Dragonese to Cinder.

"Not this again," Anya said. "Make it short." She started to wander away when Zora caught her by the elbow. She gave the blond half elf a deadly look.

Zora released her. "You seem very committed to Grey Cloak. Why is that?"

"Because he is one of the last Sky Riders like me. We can't fight Black Frost without riders."

"It sounds to me like you want to stay with us," Zora said.

"Hardly, I can do it on my own." Anya searched the others' weary eyes. "I would think that you'd be tired of my company."

"That's an understatement, but we all want the same thing. To find our friends," Zora said.

"Hah, you don't even know where to start. If they aren't in the tower, where are they?" Anya asked.

"I can't answer that, but I know who can." Zora brimmed with excitement. "Crane can find him."

"How's that?"

"The same way he found Grey Cloak before, using the Medallion of Location."

Cinder cleared his throat. "Anya, can I speak with you?"

With a wary eye, the Sky Rider approached her dragon. "Yes."

"Thanadiliditis and I have come up with an arrangement that should suffice," Cinder said.

Anya raised a brow. "And what might that be?"

"Than can return with me in your stead. He can take part in preparing the dragons," he said.

She eyed Than. The old man didn't look so well, and she could hear a faint wheezing rattling inside his chest. "What makes you think he can train a dragon?"

Than ambled forward. The gold fleck in his eyes sparkled with inner fire. "You saw me," he said in a raspy voice. "I am a dragon." His eyes searched hers. "I speak truth that I am weakening. We would all be better served if I helped out elsewhere, but only with your permission, Anya."

She looked up at Cinder. "And you trust him?"

Cinder lowered his head. "I do, and I trust you to find Grey Cloak, Dyphestive, and my son, Streak. You can do this, Anya, but you can't do it alone. Only holler if you need me."

She kissed his cheek and said with an aching heart, "I will. Be careful, my best friend."

Than climbed into Cinder's saddle and made himself at home. A broad smile broke out on his face.

"Are you ready to ride the sky?" Cinder asked Than.

"It's been too long." He pumped his fist in the air and shouted, "Dragon! Dragon!"

Cinder launched into the sky. The thunder of his wings created a fierce wind. They darted straight for the clouds and were gone.

Zora felt for Anya. Clearly the woman was emotional, as Zora watched the fiery woman wipe a tear from the corner of her eye.

Anya turned and found everyone staring at her. "What are you looking at? Quit gawking. Onward to Statuus."

9

WIZARD WATCH

A FOUNTAIN MADE FROM THE WHITEST STONE WAS THE CENTERPIECE OF THE bottom floor of the Wizard Watch tower. At the top, four huge goldfish spit streams of clear water into the wide basin below. Inside the basin were coins of all sorts, numbering in the thousands, residing below the goldfish that swam above them.

Grey Cloak paced around the fountain while Dyphestive sat on the edge with his fingers in the water. Streak swam among the fish, gobbling them up on occasion. His tail suddenly flipped out and splashed Dyphestive.

"Streak, what are you doing in there?" Dyphestive asked as he wiped the water from his face. "Will you get out of there? You've eaten enough fish already."

Lost in his own world, Grey Cloak didn't pay them any mind. He was too busy studying his strange surroundings. The four walls were over twenty feet high and formed a perfect square, unlike the smooth cylinder of the tower. Each wall had a beautiful archway made of the purest obsidian that shone against the bronze lanterns burning with an enchanted flame of sunlight. More dancing lights, like stars in the sky, illuminated the space above their heads.

Behind each mural was a grand painting of different locations all over Gapoli. One mural showed the towers of Monarch Castle from a distance. Another painting was an aerial view of the burning black volcanoes surrounding Dark Mountain. Many places Grey Cloak had never seen before. A few he had. The paintings slowly shifted and changed from one landscape to another.

At one point, he saw Portham in the far west, and for a moment, he longed for the meager life he'd had on Rhonna's farm. *I wonder how the old crow is doing without us to boss about.*

"Dyphestive, how long have we been here?" he asked.

"I don't know." Dyphestive scratched underneath his tawny locks above his ear. "A few hours."

"Hmm... I can't tell if the moments pass like hours or the hours pass like moments."

Dyphestive looked above him. "It's difficult when you can't see the sky. I'm sure Tatiana will return soon."

"Yes, of course. She's so reliable." Grey Cloak moseyed away from the fountain and closer to the murals. The entire time they had been inside, he'd yet to see another person. Aside from the burbling waters in the beautiful fountain, the expansive room was very quiet and serene. "Do you remember which way she left when she went?"

Dyphestive had a befuddled look as his eyes swept the room. He pointed at the mural in front of him. "She walked that way and vanished into a picture of fields."

"What sort of fields?"

"A pasture of grass, rather."

"Funny, that's not how I remember it. I seem to recall her walking up a flight of steps to a magnificent castle, like Monarch City." He shook his head as he ran his fingers over the painting on the stone wall. The paintings were solid but still moving. "I fear she might have duped us again. Zooks." He raised his voice. "Tatiana, where are you?" His voice echoed once before getting drowned out by the cascading waters.

"Streak!" Dyphestive cried out.

Grey Cloak turned on his heel. "What is it now?"

"He splashed me again."

"You could move," Grey Cloak said.

"I don't want to move. I like watching the fish, but Streak keeps chasing that one and making me wet." Dyphestive reached into the waters. "Get out of there, Streak. You've had enough fish!"

It wasn't like Dyphestive to lose his cool. The brawny youth was even-keeled most of the time. Grey Cloak ambled over to see what was going on.

The fountain's basin was a ring twenty yards wide and at least two feet deep. Goldfish of all colors filled a third of it. Streak knifed through the waters with his tail slithering underneath, propelling him forward.

"Do you see that one?" Dyphestive poked his finger at the water "The big silver one." There was excitement in his voice. "Streak is chasing it, but it's much too quick, even though it's bigger than the other fish."

Grey Cloak fixed his gaze on the silver fish. "I bet I could catch it."

"Huh, even you aren't that quick. Trust me. I've been watching that fish. It's like a hummingbird in water," Dyphestive commented.

"I'll wager that I can."

Dyphestive turned and looked at his blood brother. "I'll wager that you can't. What do you want to wager?"

Grey Cloak sawed his index finger over his chin. "The next time we capture treasure, I'll take your share or you can take mine."

"You never gave me my entire share the last time."

"Of course I did." Grey Cloak removed his boots. Balancing on one foot at a time, he took them both off with ease, revealing his bare feet. He wiggled his toes. "Heh, it's been a while since I've seen you."

Dyphestive pinched his nose. "And smelled them."

"Ha ha." Grey Cloak extended his hand. "Bet?"

Dyphestive took his brother's hand in his crushing grip. "Bet."

10

GREY CLOAK WADED THROUGH THE KNEE-DEEP FOUNTAIN WATERS AND HOVERED over the silver fish. Unlike the fist-sized goldfish, which were spotted with white, gold, and black scales in some cases, the silver fish was the biggest fish of all.

The silver fish was as long as Grey Cloak's arm from wrist to elbow. It had the long whiskers of a catfish and large snow-white eyes. Its small fins flapped and waved in a steady, hypnotic pattern.

I have you, Grey Cloak thought. His trousers were rolled up over his knees, and he squatted deeper into the water. He slipped his hands underneath the clear water and eased them closer to the silver fish. *You're mine.* His hands made a cradle around the fish's body. He grasped at it.

The silver fish squirted away from his fingertips like it had been shot out of a crossbow. It blazed a stream of silver to the other side of the pond.

Grey Cloak slapped the water. "Thunderbolts! That's one fast fish!"

Dyphestive chuckled. He sat on the rim of the fountain with both of his bare feet in the water. "You've been going at this for over an hour. Let me take a stab at it."

"Is that a joke?" Grey Cloak asked.

"No. Just because you can't catch it doesn't mean that I can't."

Grey Cloak jabbed a finger at Dyphestive. "We still have a bet."

"I know." Dyphestive slid his broad frame into the water. "How about this? Whoever catches the fish first wins?"

Grey Cloak considered it and rubbed his chin. "You're on!" He charged through the fountain, splashing water everywhere. Stretching the distance between him and Dyphestive, he scattered the schools of goldfish and dove at the silver fish.

Once again, the silver fish squirted away without him even getting close.

"Zooks!" he hollered.

"I see it!" Dyphestive jumped at the silver fish. It darted right underneath him as he belly flopped into the water. He popped up, soaked from head to toe, and slung his hair out of his eyes. "Horseshoes, that fish is fast! It's like a dart."

Streak swam by Grey Cloak's feet on a path toward the silver fish.

"Oh, no you don't! You aren't getting in on this too," Grey Cloak said. He grabbed his dragon by the tip of the tail and hauled him out of the water. He held Streak out upside down at arm's length. "This is between me and Dyphestive." He wagged his finger at the dragon. "You stay out of this."

Streak shook his bull neck.

"You heard me, Streak," Grey Cloak warned.

The runt dragon huffed out a mouthful of inky smoke. Grey Cloak released him, and the dragon splashed down into the water.

Hacking, coughing, and fanning the smoke out of his face, Grey Cloak said, "That was a dirty trick, Streak!" He moved out of the smoke and hacked a few times. "That's it. Every man, elf, and dragon for himself!"

All chaos erupted in the fountain. Grey Cloak tripped Dyphestive, and a frog hopped over him. Grey Cloak spotted Streak poised to strike at the silver fish, dove at it, and scared it away.

As Streak agilely turned in the water to pursue it, Grey Cloak grabbed his tail again and slung the dragon out of the fountain. "No you don't, cheater!"

Streak landed on his side, rolled to a stop, and popped back up, poised to strike with his pink tongue flickering.

Grey Cloak pointed and laughed at his dragon. "Ah-hahaha, that's what you get, you little bug muncher."

"Gang way!" Dyphestive came out of nowhere and plowed right over Grey Cloak.

The fountain became a battlefield. Within moments, Grey Cloak, Dyphestive, and Streak had tripped, tugged, bumped, tackled, bit, punched, and dunked one another in pursuit of the silver fish.

All of them went at it with a feverish look in their eyes. Water and goldfish flew over the fountain's rim.

The longer they chased the silver fish, the more obsessed they became. The playful punching and tripping became more violent as they clawed their way on top of one another. They were like piranhas hunting for fresh meat.

Grey Cloak found a goldfish in his hand, tapped Dyphestive on the shoulder, and slapped him in the face the moment his brother turned. Dyphestive roared like a hungry bear.

Grey Cloak stuffed the fish in his brother's mouth. "Enjoy your filet." He wiggled by his brother and dove at the silver fish again.

Dyphestive pulled a fish out by the tail. It was a patchwork of black and gold. It wriggled in his mitt. He flung it at Grey Cloak's head. The effort was errant, as it sailed over Grey Cloak, who ducked, and hit Tatiana square in the face.

Tatiana's face reddened as she boiled over with anger and said in an all-powerful voice, "That's enough!" Her voice shook the very fountain's waters, causing it to sputter and spit for a moment.

Grey Cloak, Dyphestive, and Streak stopped in their tracks.

"What are you fools doing?" Tatiana demanded. "Get out of that fountain!" There were several fish flapping and jumping on the wet tile floor. "And put those back in. What is this, a halfling nursery?"

Grey Cloak rubbed his eyes and rolled his neck. His head was light and hazy. He wasn't sure what had come over him, and his jaw was sore. He stepped out of the fountain, dripping water all over the floor, and started helping his brother pick up the fish. He dropped them into the fountain one by one. "Where have you been?"

With a frown and crossed arms, she said, "About."

"Oh." He tossed another fish in the water. "Thanks for filling in all the details."

Tatiana approached the fountain and looked down into the clear water at the schools of goldfish. "You were playing with the silver fish, I see. Many have tried to catch it. All have failed, including me." She managed a wry smile. "It's a tricky fish."

Grey Cloak took off his shirt and wrung it out. "You can say that again." He slung his hair out of his eyes. "That fish made us crazy. I've got a sore jaw thanks to big elbows over there and that fish." He eyed Dyphestive, who was shaking himself like a dog. "What is that fish? It's not like the others."

"No one knows. Perhaps it's an aberration of the goldfish spawn." She dipped her fingers into the water. "Perhaps it appeared by magic. One thing is for certain. No one can catch it."

Grey Cloak grabbed a dagger from his belt on the floor. He charged it with wizardry fire and leaned over the pool. "I have an idea."

Tatiana pushed his hand aside. "Don't you dare. You'll kill the goldfish."

He put the dagger away and sighed. "Fine." He looked her up and down. Tatiana was very beautiful, and her snug wizard clothing only enhanced her handsome womanly figure. He wanted to shove her in the pool. "Is there a reason for your arrival?"

"Yes, you need to come with me." She looked him up and down. "But we need to dry you off first. You must be presentable. Get your dragon."

Streak lingered under the water at the fountain's edge. His eyes were locked on the silver fish.

When Grey Cloak reached into the water to grab him, Streak snapped at him. "Whoa! Streak, get out of there!"

The dragon swam away.

Tatiana shook her head. "Can't you control your dragon?"

Grey Cloak replied, "He'll be fine. Let him play." He gathered up his clothing and gear. "Lead the way, Tatiana. I can't wait to meet your mysterious family. Do they have many horns and extra teeth?"

"Ha ha," she said.

He caught Dyphestive staring into the fountain with a worried expression. "Come on, Dyphestive. He won't come out until he's ready. He's a stubborn dragon."

Dyphestive dropped his long arm down toward the water. "But..."

"But nothing. Come on before he bites your finger off," Grey Cloak added.

"Besides, I think Tatiana is going to feed us something other than goldfish, right, Tatiana?"

"Oh, of course," she said.

Dyphestive finally pulled his gaze away and hurried along.

Led by Tatiana, the trio walked right into one of the murals, leaving Streak and the fountain alone.

11

THE MOMENT GREY CLOAK PASSED UNDER THE ARCHWAY, THE MURAL CHANGED from leagues of flowery fields at dusk to a dreary stairwell made of gray stone. The stone steps were made of black obsidian marble, and they flowed up along the inside of the tower's main wall. The trio was sealed in on both sides.

Tatiana continued to lead the way upward. Her footfalls were quiet, and she breathed easily. They walked nonstop for several long minutes, slowly winding upward toward the top of the tower.

"One would think that wizards would have a more efficient way to travel from one level to another," Grey Cloak quipped.

"Even mages are dedicated to some level of conditioning," Tatiana said as she looked at him over her shoulder. "Do you tire?"

"Not at all. I was more concerned about the length of the journey. I'm not very comfortable with being in close quarters with you for a long time," he said.

"It sounds as if you're growing fond me."

"I'd agree if your mere presence didn't make my skin want to crawl off my bones." Grey Cloak heard Dyphestive chuckle. "But if that's your measure of fondness, then yes, I'm very fond."

The truth was he was becoming fonder of her. Tatiana's beauty was hard to ignore, and it could easily overcome a younger man's impulses. The slight sway of her hips captured his attention on the way up. *She's a witch, remember. Don't let her bewitch you, Grey Cloak.*

To put his mind on something else, he ran his fingers across the stone walls. They were as cold as frost. He cast a nervous look at Dyphestive.

Dyphestive returned his stare with a perplexed look of his own. He touched the wall with his sausage-link fingers. "Chilly."

"Ahem," Grey Cloak said as he fell back a few steps from Tatiana. "But will it be much longer? I feel like I've been in the tower a lifetime, but I haven't aged a day."

"Consider it a blessing." She walked with her robes hiked up over her ankles. "The Wizard Watch does wonders for the aging process. It's a place where you can come, stay as long as you like, and relax."

"I thought this was where you came to train," Grey Cloak said.

"Absolutely. The Wizard Watch accommodates all of our daily needs."

Grey Cloak raised his eyebrows. He wasn't a dwarf, who were notorious for measuring time and distance blindfolded, but he had no doubts that they should've reached the very top of the tower long ago. The laborious walking wasn't as tiresome on his legs as it was on his mind. His back muscles tightened.

Something's wrong.

"Tatiana, seriously, if this is some sort of test or game, it needs to stop. We could have walked to the top of the tower three times over by now." He stopped suddenly. Dyphestive bumped into him. He ignored it and said, "Explain yourself."

Tatiana stopped and turned. "We're almost there." With a nod, she said, "Come and see for yourself."

Grey Cloak and Dyphestive eased their way up the steps. Around the bend, several yards up, was a black obsidian door with two smokeless bronze torches bracketed on each side. Underneath the torches were two figures covered in hooded crimson robes. Grey Cloak couldn't see their hands or faces, but they appeared to hover above the ground.

"Who are they?" Grey Cloak asked.

"Portal Guardians," she said. "We don't have anything to fear from them so long as we have permission to enter the chambers on the other side. Which, I assure you, we do." Her fingers dusted across Grey Cloak's elbow as she resumed her trek. "I hope you understand that it's not my desire to make you uncomfortable. I know the Wizard Watch is foreign to you and very strange to those who are not accustomed to it. Its inner workings are unique, but I assure you that it's for your safety."

"Thanks, Tatiana, that's very comforting," Grey Cloak said as they made it to the top landing. "I feel worse already."

She rolled her eyes and sighed. "Are we ever going to get along?"

"I doubt it, but don't you quit dreaming." He smirked.

Tatiana took center stage in front of the black obsidian door. With her fingertip, she traced arcane symbols on the door. Her fingers left a bright burning trail that slowly faded.

Grey Cloak studied her every move and locked it into his memory as he repeated the motions in his mind.

The black obsidian door faded, and a gust of chill wind blasted their faces.

With the wind rustling his hair, he shouted to Tatiana, "In there?"

She nodded. "I'll go first." She led the way.

The blood brothers followed. The black door re-formed behind them, and the wind stopped. They were outside on a huge stone platform just beneath the passing clouds. The air was as chill as winter.

Tatiana led them up a small flight of steps to the very top of the tower. The girth of the tower top was startling. It was at least one hundred yards long and just as wide. It dwarfed the Wizard Watch tower that they'd seen from the outside.

Grey Cloak's nape hairs stood on end as he locked his eyes on the huge black bulk of scales that almost covered the platform from end to end. It came to life and became the biggest dragon he'd ever seen.

The dragon reared up to its full height and glared down on them with flaming-blue eyes.

"It can't be," Dyphestive uttered as he tightened his grip on his war mace, Thunderash.

Grey Cloak had no doubt in his mind who the all-powerful behemoth was. They were face-to-face with Black Frost.

12

DYPHESTIVE WAS OUT OF THE BLOCKS AND CHARGING BLACK FROST LIKE A BULL. HE had Thunderash cocked behind his shoulder, and as soon as he reached Black Frost's foot, he swung.

The head of the war mace hit the dragon's foot and made a loud *Craaaaack!*

Black Frost, towering several stories above all of them, stood unfazed as Dyphestive clobbered his toes and feet over and over again.

Tatiana stood beside Grey Cloak with the Star of Light burning in her grip.

Grey Cloak's own fingers were locked on the Figurine of Heroes as he stared down inevitable doom. He started to spit the words from his mouth, but in the middle of his summoning, he paused.

"What are you doing?" Tatiana asked with a bewildered look. "Are you going to summon help? Hurry!"

He loosened his grip on the figurine and left it inside the Cloak of Legends's pocket. He narrowed his eyes on his surroundings. Black Frost hadn't made a sound, not even the softest scuffle of talon scraping over stone. No heat or icy cold came from the dragon's body. Instead, Black Frost looked down on them, eyes burning but without recognition.

"Do something, Grey Cloak," Tatiana said. "Use the figurine."

"Funny that you would suggest that given your hatred of the figurine," he said.

"Our plight is desperate!" she said.

Grey Cloak closed his eyes. It was difficult to get a feel for the room, but he wasn't outside. He could tell that much. The chamber echoed with every strike of Dyphestive's mace. The walls reverberated from the sound. He opened his eyes. Black Frost was gone. They were inside with a fountain much like the one where they'd started. Instead of four walls with murals in the archways, this one had eight walls, shaping the room into an octagon. Curtains were drawn in front of each.

"Huh, a grand illusion. I should have caught that sooner," he said.

Dyphestive was still hammering away at the floor. He stopped, gawked, and blinked his eyes. "What happened?"

Grey Cloak whisked a dagger out of its sheath and pointed it at Tatiana. "We've been duped by our dear friend. That's what happened."

Dyphestive rubbed his eyes. "Why?"

"Because they want the Figurine of Heroes, but I don't think they know the words. They wanted me to say them. Isn't that right, Tatiana?"

She shrugged. "If I needed the words, I could retrieve them from Dalsay."

"Oh, put your dagger away, child. There's no need for more discourse. It was merely a test."

Grey Cloak turned and faced the source of the mysterious voice. An elf unlike any he'd seen before sat on the fountain's edge. He had the refined features of elvenkind, but one side of his silky locks was white, and the other side was black. His face was youthful and energetic, and his eyes were dark and spacey. His beard was cropped with silver bands around the black hair. He wore black-and-white-checkered robes and rested his slender fingers on a black wooden cane with a polished silver handle.

"Let me guess. You're Tatiana's father," Grey Cloak said.

"No," the elf said politely. He pushed off of his cane to stand. "I'm Gossamer, the high mage of this Wizard Watch tower." He walked over with his cane clicking on the floor and extended his hand. "A pleasure to meet you."

Grey Cloak shook Gossamer's ice-cold hand. "You're as icy as Tatiana."

"I hope not." Gossamer gave Dyphestive's hand a firm shake. "You *are* a big one."

"Thank you," Dyphestive said with his chin up.

"Eh, first things first. The Figurine of Heroes," Gossamer began. "I noticed that the first item you reached for was the Figurine of Heroes when you were confronted by Black Frost."

"So? It was Black Frost. What else would I do?" Grey Cloak asked.

"Is he that big?" Dyphestive asked.

"According to our sources, Black Frost is every bit as big as that and getting bigger. That bauble"—he eyed Grey Cloak—"will hardly be enough to stop him."

"Then why do you want it?" Grey Cloak asked.

"The Figurine of Heroes is an artifact of unsearchable power. It is property of the Wizard Watch." Gossamer was a smooth talker, but he had a bite to his tone. "If we can understand how it opens and closes portals to other worlds, it might help us put a stop to Black Frost."

Grey Cloak raised a brow. "Are you telling me that you didn't create the figurine?"

"No, we did create it, but magic contains many unpredictable powers. We've yet to master them. Dalsay was allowed to use it to test its properties." Tatiana shot Gossamer a surprised look. "We never foresaw that the consequences could be fatal to our own."

"What else would you expect when you open a portal to another dimension?" Dyphestive asked.

Everyone looked at the hulking youth.

Dyphestive shrugged. "What? I pay attention." He scratched his chin with his index finger. "Why don't you make another one?"

"As much as I hate to confess it, its creation is just as much of an accident as it is of design," Gossamer admitted. "A council of the most prominent members of the Wizard Watch worked in tandem to create it." His expression turned grave. "Several died in the process, and others vanished."

"And you let Dalsay run around with that thing?" Tatiana asked. "It killed all my brothers, who were fetching your precious dragon charms, and to what end? Death!"

Grey Cloak found some relief in the fact that Tatiana didn't know any more about the figurine than he did. *Maybe the batty ole elf isn't so bad.* "It's saved more lives than it's taken since I've had it."

"That was our hope when we sent it out with Dalsay," Gossamer said regretfully. "No one is more sorrowful for your loss than I, Tatiana." He touched her shoulder. "I hope you believe that."

She moved away.

13

GOSSAMER SLOWLY STROLLED AROUND THE ROOM WITH GREY CLOAK AND Dyphestive in tow. He eyed Dyphestive. "You are very insightful for such a brute. What else is rattling around in that thick skull of yours?"

"Well, I was thinking that creating the figurine might have had something to do with opening the portal that Black Frost gains his power from," Dyphestive said.

"Ah," Gossamer commented. "And?"

"Maybe you've come to the conclusion that destroying the figurine might destroy Black Frost," Dyphestive finished.

"Impressive." Gossamer nudged Grey Cloak. "I see you aren't the only bright mind in the tandem. However, the energy source that Black Frost taps into has no direct connection to the figurine."

Good, Grey Cloak thought. He didn't want to have a good reason to give up the figurine. He'd become used to having it. "Where is the source of his power? Why don't you destroy that?"

"We believe the very source of Black Frost's power comes from Dark Mountain." Gossamer approached one of the arches. Forest-green curtains hung inside the archway. With a subtle wave of his hand, the curtains parted.

"Whoa," Dyphestive said.

They were staring at a lifelike mural that showed an aerial view of Dark Mountain's stark terrain. The jagged spires of the black mountain range were peppered with volcanoes spitting out streams of bright-orange molten lava. Gray clouds hung in the sky, blocking the sun, and the highest peaks were covered in frost and banks of snow.

A chill raced down Grey Cloak's spine. If there were ever a place that he hated, it would be Dark Mountain. Raised there most of his life, he only remembered it as a place of misery.

The mural shifted, and the image zoomed in closer to Dark Mountain, as if they were gliding through the sky.

Gossamer pointed at the ziggurat in the top levels of the mountains. The gargantuan stone structure overlooked Dark Mountain's valley. Chiseled right out of the mountain stone, the ominous temple dwarfed any building in Gapoli. As the mural panned in closer, a full view of the temple's top was cast in full light. Dragons were perched on the ledge of Black Frost's temple like battlements. Facing outward, they were the guardians protecting Black Frost and the temple. Dozens stood perfectly spaced along the temple's rim. Both middling and grand dragons were posted on the corners. They were nothing compared to Black Frost.

"Sweet potatoes, look at the size of him," Dyphestive said with awe.

It seemed like an odd statement, considering they'd just seen an illusion of Black Frost earlier, but even Grey Cloak had to agree. Compared to the other dragons, Black Frost was tremendous. It seemed as though an entire thunder of dragons could ride on his back.

Grey Cloak stretched his hand toward the mural that dwarfed him in size. "Is this real?"

Gossamer leaned on his cane. "No, this is a simulation of what we know." He pointed at the mural with his cane. "Long ago, the temple that supports Black Frost's girth was accessible to all. The citizens of Dark Mountain used it as a place to worship the dragons. Decades ago, it was sealed off, when Black Frost gained power after the Day of Betrayal. We believe the power that Black Frost draws upon is inside the temple. People have differing theories, but the most accepted theory is that he and the rebellious wizards opened a portal using the murals, and he was able to tap into another world and drain it."

Grey Cloak and Dyphestive exchanged concerned looks.

"What?" Gossamer asked.

"He's draining Thanadiliditis's world," Grey Cloak said. "Shouldn't you be talking to him?"

"We've tried, but he proves very elusive. We aren't so sure that he can do anything to help anyway. Black Frost is becoming omnipotent. If he continues to feed, how long will it be before he feeds on this world?"

"Won't he become full?" Dyphestive asked.

"One would think so, but that's the problem. Black Frost does not fill. He keeps growing." Gossamer tapped his cane on the image of the temple. "The truth is that we weren't so worried about him at first. So long as he remained in Dark Mountain, he wasn't much of a problem. We relied on the Sky Riders to keep him in check. But lo and behold, he left his roost and all but annihilated them. His breath alone proved to be too much for the valiant fighters of the sky. He even killed the Gunder giants."

Grey Cloak thought about Tontor, the shaggy-haired giant he'd met on the island. "All of them?" he asked.

Gossamer shrugged, staring at the temple. "We planted spies in Dark Mountain to seek out the secrets of the temple. It's been years since we've heard back from any of them."

"They're dead?" Dyphestive asked.

"Possibly, or they joined Black Frost. His popularity has grown quite fashionable of late."

Tatiana stormed over. "Are you telling me that members of the Wizard Watch have joined forces with Black Frost?"

Gossamer arched a brow. "Don't be naive, Tatiana. You know that the Wizard Watch's role remains neutral in Gapoli. We strive to maintain a balance for the greater good, but not all of us see it that way."

Tatiana's fists balled at her sides. "And I take it that killing Black Frost is for the greater good?"

"Of course," Gossamer said politely. "He is a threat to everything that exists. But no doubt, members of the watch have been aiding him. It would be a slip in judgment to assume otherwise."

"Unless you already made the assumption and paid for it," Grey Cloak said.

"Even wizards make mistakes," Gossamer said. He cleared his throat. "I don't deny the error of our ways. We are trying to fix them."

"Some of us are. Some aren't, it sounds like," Tatiana said. "There's no telling who's on whose side, as so many of us come and go from tower to tower."

"So many of who?" Grey Cloak asked. "This tower is huge, and we're the only people I've seen. Where is everyone else?"

"About," Gossamer offered. "Now, if you will, we need some trustworthy allies to enter Black Frost's temple and figure out his secret." He eyed Grey Cloak and Dyphestive. "We want you to do it."

14

"Are you out of your skull?" Grey Cloak raised his voice so loud that it surprised him. "We aren't going back to Dark Mountain. Not now, not ever!"

Gossamer's eyes widened. "Hear me out."

Grey Cloak shook his head and poked a finger at the elven wizard. "No, you hear me out. I didn't come here to do the will of the Wizard Watch. All you've done, in my experience, is send us on a bunch of fruitless adventures. Speaking of which, where are the dragon charms that we recovered? Huh? The only reason I came here was to figure out what happened to them. Well, Gossamer, where are they?"

Gossamer searched everyone's intense stares. "If you agree to go to Dark Mountain, I'll tell you."

Grey Cloak's cheeks flushed, but before he exploded, Dyphestive stepped in front of him. "Tell us about the dragon charms first."

"And if I do, you'll go to Dark Mountain?" Gossamer asked.

Grey Cloak moved in front of Dyphestive. "We'll consider it. But first I want to know how you propose to get us back and forth from there. It will take weeks to travel, not to mention, Monarch City's northern bridge has fallen."

Gossamer clicked his cane on the floor. "We have our ways around that." With a wave of his hand, the other seven curtains opened. Six of them revealed identical views to the fountain chamber they were standing in. It was like looking into a mirror, but their own reflections weren't there. "The Wizard Watch possesses a unique opportunity for travel. We have a tower in every territory, and these separate archways will take you to them."

Grey Cloak rubbed his chin. "Ah, that will save a lot of travel time. But that's not going to get us inside the most heavily guarded temple fortress in the world."

"No, it won't, but we'll aid you the best we can." Gossamer eyeballed Grey Cloak's cloak. "I can see that you're very well equipped as is."

"You do know that everyone in Dark Mountain is looking for us, don't you?" Grey Cloak asked sarcastically. "We've been there most of our lives, and it isn't very easy to blend in, not to mention get close to the temple."

"We've considered all things," Gossamer replied. "You'll be well equipped. We need someone who we can trust, and Tatiana has vouched for both of you."

Grey Cloak slid his gaze her way, but she didn't look at him. *She's full of surprises, isn't she?* "I'm confident that I can go it alone, but I can't do it with this moose tagging along. No offense, Dy, but well, you know, you're big."

"Where you go, I go," Dyphestive insisted in his deep voice.

"Naturally," Grey Cloak said as he spied another mural with the curtains still closed. He walked over to the archway and parted the curtains. As he pulled one side back, the other side parted easily. The huge mural quickly flashed numerous images of different places at all times of the day, all over the world. He stretched his fingers toward it.

"Don't touch that portal," Gossamer warned.

Grey Cloak held his hand out just short of the mural. The entire world was passing by in split seconds.

Gossamer stood beside him. "We opened this portal with the hope that we could travel back in time and stop Black Frost before he acquired his power."

"What happened?" Dyphestive asked.

"I'll tell you what happened. Much like the maligned Figurine of Heroes, we have no control over what happens." Gossamer tapped his cane twice. "What you are seeing is the past, present, and future. You could wind up a thousand years forward or a thousand years back. Everyone who has entered has been lost to us."

"How many have entered?" Grey Cloak asked.

"Three that I know of." Gossamer frowned. "None have been seen or heard from again. We don't know if they survived or not."

"Can you close it?" Dyphestive asked.

"No, the Wizard Watch keeps it open for further study. I can't say I blame them. Times are desperate. We hoped the figurine would provide us with a force that could match Black Frost and his Riskers, but as we all well know, it's unpredictable." Gossamer sighed. "All we can do now is keep looking for answers," he said.

"What about the dragon charms?" Grey Cloak asked. "I'd like an answer to that."

15

GOSSAMER MOVED AWAY FROM THE SCENES FLASHING INSIDE THE MURAL. WITH A wave of his cane, the curtain glided shut, and he approached the fountain. "We have many dragon charms," he admitted as he stared into the waters shining in the fountain's pool. He sat down on the fountain's rim. "The problem is that we don't have as many as Black Frost."

Grey Cloak approached. "Might I ask where the dragon charms are?"

With a wave of his cane, the waters at the top of the fountain began to increase in pressure and burble. In between the three ornamental fish spitting water, a strange object rose.

Grey Cloak and the others tilted their heads to one side.

A warrior's open-faced helmet rose from the spring. It was bright with energy that glowed from the gemstones attached to it. The precious stones shone like rubies, emeralds, pearls, and sapphires. There was no mistaking their uniqueness and flat, oval shapes. They were dragon stones.

"It's beautiful," Dyphestive said, his eyes fastened on the helmet. "It makes Codd's helmet look like goblin craft."

Even Grey Cloak marveled at the object's beauty. He counted ten dragon charms in all fastened to the helmet, which slowly spun in the air. Six stones made a ring around the helmet's rim. Two more were fastened on the cheek plates, and the last two on the back plate that covered the neck. "That's a very surprising configuration, Gossamer. Not to mention, that isn't very many stones. I've seen dozens on the chest of Black Frost's Riskers. Is that all we have?"

Gossamer swiped at the long strands of hair that fell over his eye. "There are a few more, but the rest of the suit is still being assembled."

"Suit?" Dyphestive asked.

"We realize we don't have the same number of charms that Black Frost does.

His dragon riders are composed of *naturals* like the two of you, who lead the other Riskers that rely on the use of the dragon charms."

"So, the more dragon charms he has, the more dragons he controls?" Dyphestive asked.

"An obvious truth, but we believe there's more to it than that." Gossamer stood and eyed the glimmering helmet. "We believe that Black Frost desires the charms because of their ability to control dragons."

Tatiana's face brightened. "He fears that the dragon charms could control him."

Gossamer gave an approving nod. "We theorize that if we can use a large set of dragon stones in tandem, we could control Black Frost."

Grey Cloak stood on the fountain's edge, looking at the helmet, and said, "Have you tried?"

"No. The problem is that we don't have any dragons, and we also feel that this ability would be best suited for a natural. It was our hope to reveal this to the Sky Riders, but that plan failed when Black Frost eliminated them."

"What about Anya? She's a Sky Rider," Dyphestive suggested.

"Oh, I don't think so. She'd rather die than trust the likes of us," Tatiana insisted.

Grey Cloak had the answers he'd been looking for. Gossamer had given him a reasonable explanation about the dragon charms, and as crazy as combining all of their properties at once sounded, it might just work. He made a quick suggestion, "Do you want me to try it?"

16

Everyone looked at him, and Gossamer said, "As I stated, we don't have any dragons to try it on, aside from your dragon, Streak, but you already control him."

"True, and he has the ability to control other dragons," Grey Cloak offered. "Perhaps the both of us could do it."

Gossamer closed his eyes and tapped his cane quietly on the floor. He took a deep breath in and let it out. "Your runt is a crypt dragon, is he not?"

"He's a controller, yes. He took over a grand with little effort."

Gossamer opened his eyes. "I have no way of knowing how this will work without it being tested." He shook his head. "It's too dangerous, and if Black Frost learns of this deceit, he'll be able to turn it against us. Our situation is already dire enough."

"Even if you have more dragon charms, you won't know if the helmet will work or not. Let me test it," Grey Cloak pleaded. "I can at least get close enough to test it out on him. I'll do it."

"And I'll help him," Dyphestive offered.

Gossamer stood. "I'll discuss this with the Wizard Watch. In the meantime, rest." He eyed Tatiana. "Keep them entertained." He walked through one of the archways into an identical room and vanished.

Dyphestive's gaze followed after the black-and-white elf. "Where did that take him?"

"To the Wizard Watch near Loose Boot. Many mages are gathered there in council," she said. "Is anyone hungry?"

"No," Grey Cloak said.

"I am," Dyphestive added.

"I'll have food brought." She looked at Grey Cloak. "You don't eat much, do you?"

"No. Could I fetch Streak? Wherever I'm going, he's coming."

She eyed the fountain. "He should be right where you left him."

"That's not the same fountain, is it?" Dyphestive looked into the water. "The other fountain had two fish, and this one has three fish at the top."

Streak slunk out of the water to the fountain's rim. He spit a stream of water at Dyphestive.

"Will you stop that?" Dyphestive said. "Grey, get your dragon. He's being ornery."

Streak splashed Dyphestive with his tail.

"See?" the brawny blood brother said.

Grey Cloak strolled over and peered into the fountain. It was the same size as the other one and filled with goldfish. He could have sworn it was on the floor below them, however. He glanced at Tatiana. "I'm not even going to ask."

"It's probably for the better," she said.

He hauled the dripping dragon out of the water.

Streak shivered and shed the water. His tongue flicked out of his mouth and licked Grey Cloak's face.

"Someone's acting awfully spry," Grey Cloak said. He lifted the dragon up a little higher. "And feeling heavier too. How many fish did you eat?"

Streak offered an answer with a deadpan stare.

"I see." He let Streak crawl underneath his cloak and latch onto his back. He winced. "Ow."

Tatiana grimaced. "Does he dig those claws into you every time?"

"My shirt is thick, but yes," he answered. "Tatiana, if I didn't know any better, I'd say that you're in the dark about things as much as we are."

"There is much truth to that." Her eye twitched. "I'm really disappointed about the figurine. It has caused more harm than good. They never should've let it out of the towers. We were only an experiment. My brothers were an experiment."

"Do you really trust these people?" Grey Cloak asked.

"I trust Dalsay, and I trust Gossamer." She cast a look at the brothers. "And even though it's hard to say it, I trust both of you. It's probably an error in judgment in your case." She eyed Grey Cloak. "But I have to learn to take risks."

"That's very touching," Grey Cloak said dryly.

Dyphestive gave her a crushing hug that lifted her off her toes. "I trust you too."

Gasping, she patted Dyphestive on the back. "You're crushing me."

Dyphestive let her go. "Sorry. I couldn't have done that if Leena was about." He glanced over his shoulder. "I've wanted to do that for a while."

Tatiana blushed.

Dyphestive waved his hands and fumbled for words. "Not like that. I mean, you're astonishing. It's just, well, you're my friend. I wanted to show you in case I don't get another chance."

She kissed his cheek. "I'm flattered."

A male elf dressed in deep-purple servant's clothing underneath a white apron pushed a cart of food through one of the tower's archways. He pushed the cart halfway into the room and departed in the direction he came.

The cart was covered in silver serving platters and glass carafes full of wine and juice.

Dyphestive lifted the lid off one of the platters. Steam rose from underneath the silvery dome, and he licked his lips. "Cooked venison." He peeled a hunk off and started to eat. "Mmmm. I love venison."

Streak popped his head out from Grey Cloak's cloak and sniffed, his tongue flickering out of his mouth. He slithered down Grey Cloak's back, headed to Dyphestive, and rose up on his hind legs, his tail sweeping the floor behind him.

Dyphestive dropped hunks of meat into the hungry dragon's mouth. Streak's jaws clacked shut with every bite. "It's like feeding those moat monsters back at Monarch Castle," Dyphestive said with a playful grin.

Tatiana poured herself a glass of wine and offered Grey Cloak a sample. "Yes? No?"

"I'll pass." He sat down on the fountain's edge and eyeballed the goldfish. He saw no sign of the silver fish. "This isn't the same fountain."

Tatiana joined him. "They're all the same."

"This is a strange place." Grey Cloak eyed the ominous midnight ceiling that glowed with colorful stars. "I don't think I would like to live here." His nostrils flared. "It smells funny."

She sniffed. "I don't smell anything."

"That's what I mean. It should smell like something aside from a room with eight walls."

Gossamer ran back into the room from a different archway than the one he'd left through. His face was flushed, and his chest heaved. "Time to run. They come!"

17

"WHAT ARE YOU TALKING ABOUT, GOSSAMER?" TATIANA ASKED. "WHO COMES?"

Gossamer hurried over to the fountain with his cane clicking on the floor. He stretched out his hand toward the dragon-charm helm. "We deliberated for hours, but their hearts are as hard as stone."

"Did you say hours?" Grey Cloak asked. "You haven't been gone that long." He looked at Dyphestive. "Has he?"

Dyphestive shrugged as he swallowed another hunk of venison and wiped his mouth with a white tablecloth. "It didn't seem so."

The dragon-charm helm floated into Gossamer's waiting arms. He cradled it to his chest. "Needless to say, they did not like the idea of sending Grey Cloak and Dyphestive to Dark Mountain with the helm." He eyed Grey Cloak. "But they also demanded the Figurine of Heroes."

Grey Cloak gathered up Streak, letting the dragon latch onto his back. "We're out of here. Dyphestive, let's go." He scanned the room. "Tat, how do we get out of here?"

Gossamer shared a grim expression. "That won't be possible. All of the passages are sealed by wizard magic." He tossed the helmet to Grey Cloak. His eyes slid over to the huge mural of flashing images. "There's only one way out, through the mural of time."

Grey Cloak looked at the time mural. "We're not going through there. We'll take our chances elsewhere. Let's go, Dyphestive."

The blood brothers dashed into one of the identical alcoves and found themselves in the same fountain chamber they'd been in with Tatiana and Gossamer.

Gossamer pleaded with him, "I tell you there is no way out except the time mural. You must go."

Grey Cloak and Dyphestive dashed through one strange archway after another only to find themselves in the same room where they'd started. "This is madness." He pointed a finger at Tatiana. "You know how to get us out of here. Get us out!"

Tatiana blanched. "I'm sorry, but I cannot. The Wizard Watch has acted, and only they can let you out."

Grey Cloak faced the time mural. It presented an opportunity to start all over, in the past or the future. *I can't leave my friends behind. That would be wrong.* He handed the helmet to Dyphestive. "Hold on to this." He stood in front of the time mural and faced Gossamer. "We'll wait for the rest of your brood and see what they have to say."

Gossamer shook his head. "A bad spirit stands among them. You should leave now, while you have a chance. Take a leap of faith. I have."

Dyphestive whispered to his brother, "Should we do it? I'll do it if you do."

"We can't leave the others."

"I don't think we have a choice. They'd understand. Tatiana will explain it to them." Dyphestive eyed her. "Won't you?"

"Of course," Tatiana replied.

A host of mages entered the chamber from one of the other archways. All of them wore robes like drapery in an assortment of colors. The tallest of them wore black robes with silver trim and a tall pointed hood over her head. She was human, with piercing-blue eyes, a frosty expression, and flowing silver-blond hair. The others stood behind her.

"I am Uruiah," the tall blond mage said, "highest of the Wizard Watch. You are Grey Cloak, son of Zanna Paydark." She glanced at Dyphestive. "And you are the son of Olgstern Stronghair." She eyed the helmet. "You have something that belongs to us."

Dyphestive held the helmet toward the time mural. "Let us be, or I'll drop it in."

Uruiah tossed her head back and laughed. "Do as you will. We have no use for that." She turned her attention to Grey Cloak. "It's the Figurine of Heroes that we want. It was our desire that you would give it up freely, but you've proved too greedy to part with it. Return it to us of your own free will, and you will be allowed to depart unscathed."

Grey Cloak rubbed his chin. "And we can keep the helmet?"

"No," she said.

"But you said that you had no use for it," he fired back.

Uruiah's eyes narrowed. "Don't toy with me. Hand over the figurine."

"Don't do it!" Gossamer said. "They're in league with Black Frost."

"What?" Tatiana asked. "That can't be."

"Yes, they are. They're traitors to the Wizard Watch. Uruiah is the largest disappointment of all." Gossamer glared at her. "She sold out, the same as the Sky Riders did on the Day of Betrayal. I didn't want to believe it until I heard it from her own lips."

Uruiah smiled. "I made you an offer, Gossamer. You shouldn't have refused. Your refusal shall prove fatal."

A score of soldiers wearing crimson tunics over chainmail stormed into the room from the other archways. They wore the open-faced, hard angular helmets of the Dark Mountain's Black Guard. They hemmed Gossamer and Tatiana in by the fountain.

Uruiah pointed to Gossamer and Tatiana and said to the Black Guard, "Kill them."

18

"No, wait!" Grey Cloak said. He reached inside his pocket for the figurine. "Let them be, and I'll give it to you. Then you let us be."

Uruiah sawed her slender finger over her cheek. "I'm a reasonable person. If they swear allegiance to the forces of Dark Mountain, they'll be spared."

"That's not part of the deal," Grey Cloak said. *Buy time. Buy time. Buy time.* At that point, he had no doubt that Uruiah would kill all of them or turn them in to Black Frost. *I have to figure out another way.* "Listen, be reasonable. Without these objects, we aren't a threat to you or Black Frost. You get the figurine and the dragon-charm helm. Let us go. We'll part ways, and you'll never see us again."

"Take the portal!" Gossamer said. "Don't be a fool. You're making a deal with a demon." A Black Guard knocked Gossamer in the back of the head with the pommel of his sword. Gossamer sank to the ground.

Tatiana rushed toward Gossamer, but two Black Guards seized her by the arms and yanked her away. "Unhand me before I turn you to ashes."

"How delightful. I like you, Tatiana. You always were a fighter." Uruiah's hand glowed. A ball of energy formed in her palm that shone like a ruby rosebud. She tossed it at Tatiana's belly.

The sorceress let out a shriek, and her eyes rolled up in her head. She spasmed violently, and her head dropped down to her chest.

"You witch!" Dyphestive moved forward. "I should pummel you!"

"Ah, but you wouldn't do that, would you, sweet Dyphestive?" Uruiah asked.

"Don't be so sure. I killed Draykis."

Uruiah's eyes widened. "There is no way out. Be wise and surrender."

"Never! You surrender!" Dyphestive argued back.

While the others were engaged, Grey Cloak calculated his chances. *Option one, take the portal to freedom, but Tatiana and Gossamer will still be killed. Option two, fight superior numbers, but at least one of us will die. Option three, use the figu-*

rine, and even the odds. He reached inside his cloak pocket and latched onto the figurine. *I knew it would be option three.* Concealing himself behind Dyphestive, he started uttering the arcane words of summoning.

Tatiana lifted her sagging chin and caught his eye. Her pleading eyes said, *Noooooo.*

Grey Cloak turned an angry stare at Uruiah. "You never should have hurt her." He dropped the Figurine of Heroes on the floor and watched Uruiah's eyes widen. "Say hello to my friend."

Uruiah's jaw tightened, and she and the wizard brood backed away from the smoking figurine. "Fool, we're prepared for your futile attempt." From underneath their floppy sleeves, well-crafted wands slid into their palms. She pointed her crooked wand at him. "I'll see to it that you're finished in the process."

The figurine stood upright as hazy black-and-gray smoke spit out of the top.

Streak popped his head out beside Grey Cloak's cloak for a moment then hid again.

With his fingertips tingling, Grey Cloak watched shadows emerge from the vapors. The smoke cleared, and everyone's gaze fell upon the two strange figures who stood among them.

They were men, of sorts, wearing pitch-black robes with traces of silver patterns delicately sewn into the fabric. Like birds, their heads tilted side to side as they studied their new surroundings. They had shocks of black hair, and their skin was gray and furry like a rat's. They stood nearly as big as men but were smallish in build. Their hands had black fingernails filed to points.

Dyphestive's Adam's apple rolled.

Grey Cloak's skin crawled. He sensed something strange about the smallish men. They were nothing like the others. Their sharp eyebrows and intense stares showed a countenance of evil. His heart skipped the moment they set their eyes upon him. One had silver eyes, and the other gold.

"Verbard," the one with golden eyes hissed. He spoke with cunning and intelligence.

"Yes, brother Catten?" the silver-eyed one with a wider face replied. When he spoke, he revealed sharp little teeth.

"We're back," Catten replied. He set his eyes on Grey Cloak. "What marvelous ears. I take it you summoned us to do your bidding."

He nodded.

Catten's and Verbard's eyes swept through the silent room. Their noses crinkled, and Verbard said, "This chamber reeks of good and evil." He eyed Uruiah. "These wizardlings carry wands. How pathetic."

"I sense our time is short, brother. Whatever shall we do?" Catten asked.

"Make the most of it." Verbard floated off the ground and faced Dyphestive. "I really don't like the looks of this one. I can only hope that we were summoned to kill him."

"Yes," Uruiah said. "Yes, you are. I am Uruiah, leader of the Wizard Watch. You were summoned to serve the will of Black Frost and his wicked causes."

Catten rose a foot from the ground, floating above the floor. "The wizard with the little wand speaks." He nodded. "We are underlings. How is it that we were summoned?"

Uruiah's eyes fell on the Figurine of Heroes.

"I see." Catten needled his chin with his sharp fingernails. "Well, Uruiah, I would like to take a moment to inform you that we are Underling Lords Catten and Verbard." He showed his teeth. "And we don't serve anyone but ourselves."

Before Uruiah could blink, tendrils of lightning blasted from Catten's fingers and into Uruiah's chest. Her skin glowed so bright, the bones could be seen within. A chain of lightning spread from one mage to another. Wands went flying out of their hands.

For a brief moment, Grey Cloak thought they had an ally until Verbard turned on Dyphestive and said, "Let's kill them. Let's kill them all."

Lightning shot out of Verbard's fingertips and blasted straight through Dyphestive's chest. The fiery bolt lifted Dyphestive from the ground, and he flung his arms out. His jaw opened wide.

Without thinking, Grey Cloak charged the smallish man and jumped on him. He got the jolt of his life from his head to his toenails. He landed flat on his back in full spasms with fire running through his veins. *Zooks! These fiends are nasty.*

He rolled over on his side with his extremities cycling through numbness and pain. It hurt to even keep his eyes open. What he saw horrified him. Verbard and Catten were destroying every person in their path, and they set their eyes on Tatiana.

19

DYPHESTIVE SMELLED THE STINK OF HIS SINGED CHEST HAIRS AS HE FOUGHT HIS WAY back to his knees. His chest burned like a brush fire, and he tasted the tang of metal in his mouth. In the back of his mind, he knew that he should be dead. He wasn't. He lived.

With his jaw clenched, he stood with tremendous effort. Every move he made hurt, but it meant he was alive, alive and angry. He set his brooding stare on the visitors.

The moment he'd seen them, he'd known they were bad. He'd never seen such wickedness or natural evil on another creature's face. He snarled. Evil. He hated evil.

The chamber became a battleground with blood in the fountain's waters. The Black Guard and mages who had survived the initial onslaught fought for their lives. Many of them were blown out of their armor by javelins of lightning. Charred flesh smoldered on the tiled floor.

The underling named Catten faced off against two wand-wielding mages. Firepower blasted against firepower. The underling's expression was deadly and gleeful. His lightning shattered their wands and sent the mages flying backward into the walls.

Dyphestive spied his war mace lying on the floor nearby. With his ears ringing, he wandered over and picked it up in his big mitt. He set his gaze on Verbard, who'd turned his attention to Tatiana. "It's thunder time," he muttered. He lifted Thunderash up and charged.

Verbard turned in time to catch the blow of the war mace in his chest. The floating underling soared toward the curtain wall. He stopped before he hit it and sneered nastily. His eyes burned like molten silver as he looked at Dyphestive. "You're dead."

"I'm dead? He should be dead. I hit him with everything I had." Dyphestive stepped in front of Tatiana. "Stay behind me. He's taken his best shot, and I've taken mine."

Tatiana pulled out the Star of Light and formed a shield of white light before them.

Strands of lightning blasted into the shield as Verbard floated back toward them. The blasts skipped, ricocheted, then crackled and sizzled. They made angry hissing noises as they drilled into the dome of light.

Dyphestive squinted as he watched the mystic shield's fabric chip and give way. "Keep it up, Tat!" he hollered.

Her voice cracked as she said, "I'm trying. He's all-powerful. Mercy!"

From out of nowhere, Uruiah rose up behind Verbard. She unleashed the full force of her wand into Verbard's back. The underling's arms flung wide, and he dropped to the ground.

Dyphestive lost sight of Verbard as several Black Guards charged him. Three of them came with drawn swords. He leaned into them and swung. The war mace collided with their fine steel in a loud ring of metal. One blade broke, and the others flew out of the warriors' grasps.

Dyphestive paid the price as a sword lanced the back of his shoulder and pierced him deeply. "Guh!"

Tatiana called out, "Dyphestive!" White fire burned in her eyes. Using the Star of Light, she sent his attacker backward with a jagged bolt of power that exploded from her fist.

Using his one good arm, Dyphestive clubbed his other two attackers with skull-cracking force. Both soldiers fell to the ground dead.

"Your shoulder. It's bad," she said.

"Not bad enough." He spun his club and searched out his enemy, Verbard.

The underling had risen from the floor and had Uruiah pinned down with strands of lightning. Uruiah's hands were flung wide, forming a shield that reflected the underling's energy. She let out a frightful, angry scream as his bolts of power lanced into her entirety. Her body couldn't handle his might. Her skin sank and shriveled. Her body exploded in a plume of ash.

Tatiana gasped. "She was one of the strongest of our kind."

Verbard spun in midair and faced them. "Then the end of your kind is near."

LORDS OF THE AIR! *Who are these underlings? What are these underlings?*

Before Grey Cloak could reach Tatiana, the golden-eyed underling, Catten, fixed his attention on Grey Cloak. Bolts of lightning blasted out of the underling's hands, sending Grey Cloak careening away. Grey Cloak sprang to the side and started running.

Floating in the air, Catten hurled silver javelins at him like it was some sort of game. The lightning blew hunks of floor right out from underneath Grey Cloak's feet. He dove for the cover of the fountain and watched the fish at the top be blown apart.

Catten cackled with evil glee.

Right before Grey Cloak's eyes, he watched the Wizard Watch and Black Guard be devastated. The underlings showed no mercy on their souls as they were blown to bits and pieces. He hid behind the fountain wall.

This has to end. It has to end. The figurine should have summoned them back by now.

But the figurine hadn't summoned the underlings back to the dimension from where they came. They were still present and destroying everything.

Grey Cloak peeked over the rim.

Catten floated toward him. "I see you, rodent. Come on out and die."

A pair of mages rose from among the fallen. They pointed their wands at Catten and said in tandem, "*Sinew eruptus.*"

Catten's body went rigid. His feet landed on the ground as stiff as a board.

The pair of mages, a man and woman in lavender robes trimmed in white, approached. Their brown hair was slicked back, revealing their handsome and scholarly features. They crept toward Catten one more step, and an invisible force ripped their wands from their grips.

Catten caught the wands in his hands.

The mages' shocked faces lasted long enough for Catten to point their wands back at them and say, "*Sinew eruptus.*" The mages exploded.

Grey Cloak sank down farther, his stomach turning into knots. *I'll never use the figurine again.*

20

"Tsk... tsk... tsk," Verbard said to his brother, Catten. "I was really hoping there would be more people to kill, but it appears there are only a few of them left."

Catten floated along by his brother's side. He scanned the archways. "Certainly there are more about. I presume they're cowering. In the meantime, we still have them." He set his golden gaze on the heroes.

Grey Cloak, Dyphestive, and Tatiana clustered together by the fountain, panting. Dyphestive stood tall and made a wall between the underlings and the fountain. "Take your best shot, underling."

Catten and Verbard glanced at one another and barked laughter. "The humans of this world are as arrogant as the humans of our world."

"True, brother. Shall we make another example out of these?" Verbard asked as threads of lightning danced on his glowing fingertips.

Grey Cloak gathered himself on one knee and said underneath his breath, "Buy time. They can't last forever. The figurine will take them back."

"Do you hear that, Verbard? They're conspiring. I don't care for conspirators," Catten said. "Do you?"

Shoulder to shoulder, the brothers floated around the fountain with their long robes dragging over the ground. They faced off with the heroes twenty feet away. Eyeing the bulging muscles in Dyphestive's meaty arms, Verbard said, "I really hate the big one. I think I'll take him apart piece by piece."

"I'll gladly finish off the others," Catten remarked. The dragon-charm helm lying on the tiled floor nearby caught his eye. "What is this?" With a wave of his hand, the helm lifted off the ground and into his hands. His clawlike fingers cradled the brilliant object like it was a child. "How remarkable. It's gaudy but carries within it great power. How significant." He closed his eyes. In a hushed voice, he said, "Ah, yessss."

Streak squirted out from underneath Grey Cloak's clothing and slunk across the floor toward the underlings with his head lowered.

"Marvelous, I've summoned a little dragon," Catten said as his eyelids opened. "Come, little creature, and serve your new master."

"No!" Grey Cloak jumped on top of his dragon as Dyphestive leaped in front of him. Streak's claws scraped over the floor as he strained to make headway toward Catten.

With an upward wave of his hands, Verbard levitated Grey Cloak and Dyphestive from the floor.

Once again, Streak squirted out of Grey Cloak's arms and dropped to the floor. He crawled underneath Catten's feet and sat down.

"Get away from them, Streak! Run!" Grey Cloak said.

Streak sat like a gargoyle.

Verbard twirled one finger, and Grey Cloak and Dyphestive began to spin like tops. "Time to dance."

The blood brothers' airborne bodies slammed into one another.

Running into Dyphestive was like hitting a stone wall. "Watch it," Grey Cloak said.

"I can't help it," Dyphestive offered helplessly. Suddenly his eyes rolled up into his head until the whites of his eyes shone. He lifted his war mace up like a bat.

Verbard grinned evilly. "First, I'm going to let the big one bash the little one into porridge. Then I'll do worse to the big one."

Grey Cloak stopped in midair.

Dyphestive spun like a top, war mace out, and floated straight toward him.

This is madness, Grey Cloak thought. He wasn't a mere mortal with no power of his own. He was a natural, a Sky Rider. *Certainly I can do more than float here and die!*

Dyphestive spun right toward him. Grey Cloak ducked under the fierce swing that would have taken his head off.

Swish!

Tatiana fired an energy bolt from the Star of Light at Verbard. The silver-eyed underling created a small bloodred mystic shield with his free hand and knocked her bolt aside. With a flip of Catten's fingers, Tatiana was knocked head over heels and slammed into one of the archways.

"Finish off the one with the pointed ears, brother," Catten said. "I want to see him bleed."

"It will be my pleasure," Verbard replied. Guiding the spinning Dyphestive with his hand, he launched him in Grey Cloak's direction. "But I need you to hold the lithe one still."

"Not a problem," Catten boasted.

Grey Cloak felt an unseen force invade his body. His limbs stiffened like fence posts. Dyphestive was going to clobber him. *Noooooooooo!* He summoned wizard fire into his hands and blasted a shot out of his fingers into the floor. It propelled him above Dyphestive's lethal swing.

Swish!

"How creative. The one with polished features contains magic too. We'll find out how much after we rip him open," Catten said. He pointed at Grey Cloak. "But first a hard drop."

Grey Cloak's head almost touched the twenty-foot-high angled ceiling. Released by Verbard's power, he dropped into a sudden freefall that would break his bones. The Cloak of Legends billowed out, and he floated toward the ground. "A valiant try, fiends, but it will take more than—*ack!*"

A possessed, spinning Dyphestive crashed into him. His upper-right arm bone snapped against the full force of the war mace. Blinding pain lanced up his arm, through his neck, and into his eyes. Grey Cloak still made a soft landing on the floor, but Dyphestive crashed at his feet.

The young warrior sat up, shaking the cobwebs from his head. He gave Grey Cloak a guilty look. "I'm sorry."

"Forget about it." Grey Cloak jumped in front of his addled brother. He pulled the sword free from his belt and filled it with wizardry. The blade shone with glaring light.

The underlings squinted, shielded their eyes, and Catten said, "Oh no, he's going to blind us with his sword."

"His glowing sword," Verbard mocked.

"That very one."

"How dare he?" Verbard glared at Grey Cloak with eyes that could burn holes in metal. "I'm tired of this." His fingertips heated to a red-hot glow. "Let's finish them, brother. I'm ready to explore our new world."

"As you wish." With the helmet in one hand and lances of lightning in the other, Catten attacked.

Using the sword as a shield, Grey Cloak absorbed his all-powerful firepower, using the training Yuri Gnomeknower had put him through. He took everything that he could. The underling's firepower burned in his sword with a pulsating web of energy. He summoned all he had in him to push them back. "Aaaaaaaaaaaah!"

Grey Cloak's fire burned brighter.

Dyphestive latched onto his wrists and joined him in another desperate howl. "Aaaaaaaaaah!"

With a violent wave of their hands, the underlings snuffed Grey Cloak's wizardry out and sent the blood brothers sprawling to the floor.

Grey Cloak had nothing left. Dyphestive lay on his back, trembling. They watched helplessly as the underlings hovered over them with lances of fire in their hands, their countenances twisted with evil, ready to deliver the death blow.

Zooks.

21

CATTEN AND VERBARD GLOWERED DOWN AT GREY CLOAK AND DYPHESTIVE WITH murder in their metallic eyes. Tendrils of lightning fired out of their red-hot fingertips.

Grey Cloak and Dyphestive twitched and groaned on the floor in mighty spasms.

The underlings' fire sputtered out. They exchanged confused looks and tried to fire their mystic arrays again.

"What's amiss, brother?" Verbard asked with a disappointed hiss. His eyes widened as he studied his brother. "You fade. We fade! It will be the black tomb for us!"

Grey Cloak forced his way up to his elbows. "The visit is over, dung piles!" He wiggled his fingers. "Goodbye."

Catten swung his head around and set his eyes on the smoking Figurine of Heroes. It still stood in front of the flashing images of the time mural.

Grey Cloak read the underling's eyes instantly. He popped to his feet from the flat of his back, dashed for the figurine, and dove.

With a whisper of breath, Catten sent the Figurine of Heroes into the time mural. One image changed to another inside the ominous archway, and the figurine was lost forever.

Holding his broken arm, Grey Cloak turned and watched the underlings' bodies solidify with sheer evil glee on their faces.

"We've cheated death, brother," Verbard said. He shook his fists in the air. "Forever we will survive!"

"Yes," Catten said as his revived glowing fingertips needled the air. "And we have these rodents to thank for it. I'm feeling merciful. Let's kill them instantly." He cupped his hands together. "I can't wait to witness what lies beyond these walls. A new conquest in the making."

The underlings' hands radiated with new power. They sucked the air in hungrily through their small sharpened teeth.

Grey Cloak swallowed. He'd failed. None of this ever would have happened if he'd never used the figurine in the first place. Now, he'd set a new terror loose in the world, and it would never be the same.

He heard a voice in his head say, *Into the time mural. Run!*

At that moment, he watched Dyphestive rise to his feet. He swayed like a punch-drunk boxer and faced the underlings. He lifted his war hammer up and beckoned the underlings to come forward.

With their eyes hungry for death, the underlings let their fire explode from their fingertips. A moment before the lightning cracked into Dyphestive's body, a new ally emerged.

Gossamer appeared from the wreckage of corpses. He stood behind the underlings with his silver-headed cane locked in both of his hands. Purple bands of energy encircled the underlings and constricted them like a great fire snake.

Catten and Verbard let out savage hisses as the coils burned through their robes and into their flesh. The dragon-charm helm slipped from Catten's grip and bounced on the floor.

"Go! Now!" Gossamer yelled at Dyphestive. "Into the time mural. It is your only choice!" He grimaced. "*Have faith!*"

Dyphestive lumbered on heavy feet toward Grey Cloak.

Streak took off and flew like a bird into Grey Cloak's arms.

Tatiana was on her feet again and turning the Star of Light loose on the underlings.

"Tatiana, come with us," Grey Cloak pleaded.

"I belong here. Be well. Be brave," she said as she and Gossamer engaged the underlings in a battle of flame and fire.

Grey Cloak looked into the time mural's flashing array of images then back over his shoulder. "We can't leave them!"

The exchange of wizardly powers looked and sounded like the entire tower was going to erupt. Bright, scintillating light flashed in their eyes.

In a sudden move, Dyphestive caught Grey Cloak and Streak up in his crushing arms. "We'll take our chances." Without looking back, he thrust them all, body and soul, into the mural.

22

"Aaaaaaaaaaaaaaaaaaaaaaaaaaaaaaaaaaaaaah!" Grey Cloak didn't know if he was screaming vocally or mentally. All he knew was that his spirit left his body and came back over and over again with the terrible sensation of falling to his doom.

There was no up. No down. He passed through air like water. He couldn't breathe. He spun through a tunnel of black-and-swirling colors. His past, present, and future soared by his eyes. He swam, but he did not fly.

The ground rushed up to greet him. "Ooooooof!" Grey Cloak found himself on his back, looking up just as Dyphestive came down. He jumped to one side.

Dyphestive landed inches from crushing him like a horse dropped out of the sky. A plume of dust went up from the youth's brawny body.

Grey Cloak rolled over on his broken arm and sucked air through his teeth. "Zooks," he muttered with the sun shining in his eyes. His stomach twisted inside his belly as he shielded his eyes and squinted.

Dyphestive pushed his face out of the dirt. "Are you hurt?"

"No thanks to you. You busted me in the arm with your hammer," Grey Cloak answered.

"I did?" Dyphestive rubbed the dust off his clothes. "I don't remember that. With this?" He held up the war mace.

"Yes, your hammer."

"Thunderash is a mace."

"Whatever it is, you about cracked my skull open with it. I suppose I should be thankful that you didn't and I only have a broken arm to show for it." Grey Cloak stood and did a full turn with the sandy ground crunching underfoot.

They were in a bleak stretch of land that showed nothing but leagues of brown brush and hard-packed earth in all directions. The air was dry, and the wavering heat rose from the ground in plumes. Trees stood, crooked and gnarled, their branches without a leaf on them. A dry riverbed with cattle bones snaked across the land nearby.

Dyphestive stood. "Sorry about your arm. I don't know what happened. I blacked out. I know I was spinning, but that was it."

"It happens," Grey Cloak said. His arm throbbed from the pain. It was broken halfway between his elbow and shoulder. He needed to put a splint on it. "Gah!"

"What?" Dyphestive asked, his eyes widening.

Somehow, Streak had latched onto Grey Cloak's back, and he was crawling out from underneath Grey Cloak's cloak.

Grey Cloak took a knee and pet the dragon's head. "Someone sank his claws too deep, but I'll forgive him." He smiled at the dragon. "I'm glad you're well, boy."

"We better set that arm, or it'll get bad," Dyphestive said as he looked about. "I'll find some wood." He eyed his brother. "Do you have any idea where we are?"

Grey Cloak shook his head with grim eyes. "According to Gossamer, we could be at any time or place in Gapoli." He pinched some dust from the ground and let it fall. "It certainly isn't Arrowwood."

"Agreed." Dyphestive found a small dog tree nearby and began breaking off branches with his bare hands. Using a small knife that he possessed, he skinned the thin bark in long strips.

Much to Grey Cloak's surprise, Dyphestive created a sturdy splint around his arm. "Well done. Where'd you learn that?"

"The Doom Riders."

"Ah, I guess I shouldn't have asked."

"I don't mind." Dyphestive finished setting the splint. "Try not to move it. We'll have to find you some help in the meantime. Grey, do you think that Tatiana and Gossamer survived?"

No, he thought. The underlings would have killed them if they hadn't run, and it was his fault for using the figurine. He should have parted with it long ago, but he hadn't, and now more lives had been lost because of it. "I think it's best that we believe they survived and we have to find them."

Dyphestive eyed the distant sun that was beginning to set in the west. "North, then, until we learn where we are?"

"I'd say that's a wise idea." Together, he, Dyphestive, and Streak began their march northward. "If I were to venture a guess, I'd say that we're in Sulter Slay. We've been there before, if you remember."

"It feels like a lifetime ago," Dyphestive said as he plodded along with one arm swinging and the other arm hefting his war mace on his shoulder. "You know, there's a Wizard Watch in Sulter Slay."

"I certainly do." Grey Cloak managed a grim smile. They had traveled to the Wizard Watch in Sulter Slay when they'd first joined Talon. So many had died since then. Adanadel, Browning, and Dalsay were the first to die at the hands of the Doom Riders. They'd lost Grunt the minotaur too. Now Tatiana might be lost, as well as Gossamer. Death followed them everywhere, it seemed.

They moved at a brisk pace, league after league. There was no brook or stream to be found or so much as a shady tree to shield them from the sun beating down on their faces.

Dyphestive's vest and trousers were damp, and sweat dripped from his brow. The young juggernaut marched on, unfazed by the extreme weather.

Grey Cloak licked his dry lips. For a man who didn't eat or drink much, he was thirsty, more thirsty than he'd ever been. "A breeze would be nice."

Dyphestive grunted, while Streak scurried along like he couldn't be more at home. He chased small bugs and ate them.

"Marvelous," Grey Cloak said.

"What's that?" Dyphestive asked.

"I was thinking we might have to eat bugs. I never would've imagined," he said.

During his time with the Sky Riders, he had been trained on survival techniques. There had been a point where he was supposed to eat bugs to survive on a long outing. He'd refused, considering the act undignified for him, but this time, it was different.

Perhaps all of the excitement caught up with me. I'm starving.

"Are you really hungry?" Dyphestive asked. "I'm a little hungry, but I had some venison before we, well, left. You should have had some, but you never eat. That's not good for you."

"Well, today it isn't. That's for certain." He paused and took a knee. "Let's stop for a moment," he said.

Dyphestive tilted his head to one side and gave Grey Cloak a curious look. "You never stop."

"Well, I am now!" he shouted. Sweat dripped into his eye. He thumbed it away and took a breath. "Sorry, brother, but I don't feel like myself. I feel..." He fell face-first into the sand.

23

Dyphestive rushed over to Grey Cloak and rolled him over. His brother's face had red splotches all over it. He was clammy and covered in a cold sweat. He shook his brother gently. "Grey! Grey!"

Grey Cloak let out a raspy, dry-throated sigh that sounded like he was choking to death. His neck was limp, allowing his head to hang over one shoulder.

"Grey, what's wrong?" Dyphestive asked. He'd never seen his spry brother in such poor condition ever. He placed his hand on Grey Cloak's forehead. "You're burning up."

With no other recourse to consider, he stripped his brother down to his trousers. He fanned Grey Cloak with the Cloak of Legends and used his body to shield Grey Cloak from the sun.

Streak stood by Dyphestive's side, tongue flickering out of his mouth. He nudged Grey Cloak with his snout several times.

Kneeling, Dyphestive said, "I don't know what happened. Perhaps the heat drained him. He needs water. Can you find water, Streak?"

Streak bunched his back legs and launched himself into the sky. He flew like a chubby featherless bird through the air with his stout tail hanging behind him.

The red splotches covered Grey Cloak's wiry frame like giant freckles.

Dyphestive had seen sickness before, including heat exhaustion, back at Rhonna's farm. But he'd never seen anything like Grey Cloak's rash. "I don't know what to do, Grey. I don't know." His thick fingers fumbled and poked over Grey Cloak's rigid body. He even put his ear to his brother's chest and listed to his breathing and heartbeat. Both were shallow and weak.

He fanned Grey Cloak with his cloak and watched the splotches spread. Grey Cloak spasmed.

"Nooooo," Dyphestive moaned as he clutched at the hairs on his head. "Noooo."

Grey Cloak rolled over on his good arm as he foamed at the mouth, kicked, and spasmed. He fell forward on his belly.

That was when Dyphestive saw it. A strange creature had fastened itself to the lower middle of Grey Cloak's back. It looked like a spotted red crab the size of a small hand. Its legs and pincers were deep in Grey Cloak's skin. Its shell was translucent, and blood flowed through it as it pulsed.

Dyphestive swallowed the lump building in his throat. The sickening tick of a creature grew as it filled with blood. He grabbed the thing in his hand and tried to rip it out.

Grey Cloak let out a shriek.

Dyphestive let go the blood-sucking creature. "What do I do?" He wiped the sweat from his brow with his forearm. "Grey Cloak, what do I do?" He eyed the sky, searching for Streak. He needed help, and he needed it now.

Grey Cloak spasmed and spit out more foam. He looked awful. His vibrant skin was pale, and his mouth hung open.

Dyphestive pulled his knife and decided to cut the nasty insect off. It continued to enlarge as it filled with blood, and the hump on its back bulged. He brought the knife's tip to the blood sac and prepared to poke it.

"I wouldn't do that," someone said.

Dyphestive's head twisted around to face a dwarf with sandy-brown hair, a beard tied into a bun below his chin, and sun-browned skin. The dwarf wore desert robes, and he had cold blue eyes. He carried a gnarled wooden staff as tall as him. "Who are you?"

"Your only hope to save him," the dwarf said in a gravelly voice. He looked down at Grey Cloak. His eyes had deep crow's feet, and his hands were leathery. "Your friend was bitten by a desert blood tick. Very rare and fatal. I'm surprised your friend still lives."

"Can you really help him?" Dyphestive asked.

The dwarf eyed Thunderash, which was lying nearby. He rubbed his chin. "For a price." He tapped his staff on the ground two times. "Pick him up, and come with me. We have a very long walk."

Dyphestive put his knife away and did as he was told. He knew very little about dwarves, aside from Rhonna. They weren't like the other races that galivanted about Gapoli like the others. They were more secluded in the south, crafty, unpredictable, and self-serving. Rhonna had shared that much about her people.

"Come," the dwarf said, heading west.

"I-uh..." He scanned the skies.

"I know. You have a dragon. He'll find us. Come. It's a long journey." The dwarf moved at a brisk pace on his stubby legs. "I'm Koll, a druid, if you must know. You're fortunate that I came upon your tracks and fortunate that I am nosy." He thumbed his big snout. "I found your tracks strange."

Holding Grey Cloak in his arms, Dyphestive asked, "You found what strange?"

"Your tracks. Your tracks started in the middle of nowhere. How does that happen?" Koll asked. "Did you fall out of the sky? I've seen stars fall but not men."

"It's a long story." Grey Cloak was as warm as toast in his arms. Dyphestive could see two waterskins that Koll carried. "Do you have water? He's burning up."

"No. Water won't help him either," Koll said as he loosened his waterskin and took a drink. He capped the waterskin without offering any to Dyphestive. "It'll take more than that to save him. Tell me more about how you came here."

"Only if you give my friend a drink."

Koll stopped at a rise among the rocks and tapped his staff twice. "This is my water. Get your own." He turned and walked on.

24

"I can't really explain it. It's called a time mural. We jumped through it and landed here," Dyphestive said.

"Landed on a desert blood tick is what you did. Ignorant thing to do," Koll said. The dwarf never stopped walking west along the winding dusty trails of the south. "Very stupid."

"We didn't have any choice of where we landed," Dyphestive commented. While carrying Grey Cloak in his arms, he'd been telling Koll parts of their journey minus many details. He'd gotten better about keeping his mouth shut over the years, even though it was in his nature to be completely honest. "What would you have done? Those underlings were going to kill us, and well, we didn't have a choice."

"A dwarf would have fought with his last drop of blood," Koll said. He looked back at Dyphestive and wiggled his bushy eyebrows. "Huh, I would have done the same thing, I suppose. I'm no dwarven warrior. I'm a druid, dedicated to knowledge about nature. It will get cold soon, dangerous."

"How are we going to help my friend?" Dyphestive asked. "All we've been doing is walking. Don't you have a village?"

"Village? Hack! Druids don't live in villages. This is where I live." Koll stooped over a small round cactus bush. With his bare hands, he ripped the top off. "You said you wanted water. Drink."

"I didn't want it. I wanted it for my friend." Dyphestive helped himself to the small watery pulps inside the cactus. He squeezed water over Grey Cloak's lips and head. "He feels like he's on fire."

Koll eyed the stars appearing in the sky. "You share strange tales, very strange indeed. I've wandered Dwarf Skull all my life, most of Sulter Slay. I've never been anywhere else. What you say is... entertaining."

"I'm glad you're amused." Dyphestive rolled Grey Cloak over and looked at the desert blood tick. It had blown up to half the size of his hand. "Horseshoes! It's getting worse. How much can this thing drink? Won't it let go?"

"Not until it's finished," Koll said. He tapped his staff twice. "We need to find shelter. In the night are many prowlers. They'll smell our blood. It's too hot to hunt in the day, but in the night, if they find our scent, they will come."

"Won't a fire keep them away?"

"Fire will attract them." Koll wandered over to Grey Cloak and held his wrist. "Your friend is strong. I'm very surprised he breathes. Impressive." He sucked down fluid from his waterskin. "You want to remove the tick, but if you do, it will inject more poison. Poison paralyzes your friend now. Rattle the insect, and it will kill him. Come."

The trek continued upward into the rocky terrain that zigzagged higher and higher. Grey Cloak wasn't particularly heavy, but after such a long walk, even Dyphestive's mighty shoulders started to burn.

I won't let you down, Grey. Hang on.

"If you don't have a village, then where are you taking us? Is there another village with people who can help?" he asked.

"Why do you think dwarves live in villages? Dwarves don't live in huts. They live in buildings, cottages, fortresses, structures. Don't ever call a dwarven home a village, or a hut. It's an insult, not that it matters to me." Koll hustled over some broken stones and vanished on the other side.

Taking long steps, Dyphestive climbed over the rocks, trying to catch up with the dwarf. They were high up in the hills overlooking the sun-cracked plains. The sun had fully set, and the plains had darkened to a black sea. He lost sight of Koll and didn't hear so much as a scuffle.

"Koll," he called out.

"Hush, young fool," Koll said quietly. He'd gathered himself in a cluster of rocks and blended right in. "Come. Look."

Koll was pointing his staff down toward the plains. Keeping his voice low, he said, "Do you see that?"

Dyphestive narrowed his eyes. He saw only blackness at first, but as his vision adjusted, bright spots, like fireflies, appeared in the dark. "Are those torches?"

"Yes," Koll said. He sucked his teeth. "We're being followed."

"By who?"

"Scavengers, most likely. I hoped to avoid them, but they're thick in this barren wood." Koll kept his eyes fixed on the train of torchlight. "There are only three torches, but don't be fooled. That is only the smaller part of a much larger pack."

"Is it stupid of me to ask what the Scavengers are?"

"An assortment of bloodthirsty nomads. They prey on people and kill as they please. As long as they don't interfere with Dwarf Skull's affairs, they are left in peace." Koll hopped down from his hiding spot. "We need to move faster. If they don't catch us by daybreak, they'll leave us be. And the hill rock should slow them down. Let's move. Quickly."

"You never said who the Scavengers were. Are they orcs, goblins, gnolls, *dwarves*?" Dyphestive asked.

"I said they were an assortment. Pray you don't have to see them for yourself. If you do, you'll be too close, and they'll skin you alive." Koll eyed Grey Cloak's limp form. "And him, dead or alive."

Dyphestive hustled after Koll with a lot of questions on his mind. "Why would they kill us? Wouldn't they rob us?"

"Think about it, boy. Did you see fields of farmland and cattle out here? Why else would they hunt the living? Huh?"

"They'll eat us?"

"You aren't as dull as you look, but that took some time. Yes, they will eat us, just like a buzzard that picks away at exhausted flesh." Koll tapped his staff. "They'll use the marrow of our bones to flavor their soup, and you'll watch while they do it."

25

K<small>OLL LED THEM ON A BRUTAL TREK THROUGH THE RUGGED HILLS.</small> H<small>IS FEET WERE AS</small> sure as a mountain goat's, but Dyphestive's weren't. With Grey Cloak on his shoulder, he slipped more than once on the loose rock and cracked his knees. He pressed on.

"I know a spot, a refuge. We can hide there. It's close," Koll said as he drank from his waterskin. He offered it to Dyphestive. "Drink, big fella. There's no sense in being stingy now."

The skin didn't have much water left, but he wet Grey Cloak's lips the best he could and squeezed the remainder into his mouth.

Meanwhile, the surefooted Koll climbed up on the crag. He wasn't up there long before he scrambled back down. "I can see the flicker of their torches. They aren't so far off as I'd hoped. They move quick. Come."

For hours, they snaked their way through the black hills as fast as their legs could take them. It was dark, slippery, and difficult to navigate in many spots, with gullies that needed to be jumped and rises that needed to be climbed. Dyphestive fought his way through all of it. It was even harder with an elf on his shoulder. He used his war mace as a cane on many occasions.

"I don't think we'll make it to tomorrow," Koll commented as they moved onward. "It's hours until dawn, and they won't slow until late morning. I know spots in these hills, good ones. We'll hide in one and wait it out. So long as the basilisks don't sniff us out, we should be fine."

"What about Streak?" Dyphestive asked. "How will he find us?"

"Your dragon? I'm certain he's safer than we are. Be thankful."

They traveled another hour or so until Koll led them into a large burrow nestled in the rocks. It was covered by prickly overgrowth.

Dyphestive slunk underneath the wild brush and duckwalked inside. The burrow was large, more like a cave, and many yards deep. He heard Koll's sandals scuffling over the ground. He followed the dwarf deeper until he bumped into him. "Sorry."

"This is as deep as we go. Now, we wait but first—" Koll crawled by him. "A trick."

Even though it was pitch-black, Dyphestive could make out Koll's rugged form crawling toward the burrow's end. Koll started to chant and mutter in gibberish. Dyphestive's arm hairs stood on end.

At the end of the cave, shades of moonlight bled through the prickly brush. The tangles of vines and thorns grew longer and thicker.

Koll crawled back. "I told you I'm a druid. I have tricks, tricks that have fooled the Scavengers many times. They know me, but they have not caught me." He cleared his throat. "Now, make yourself comfortable, and be quiet. Get some rest, perhaps. I'll stand watch. I sleep little."

"You sound like my friend. This is the most he's ever slept."

"Hush now."

Dyphestive breathed deeply through his nostrils. It had been a long and crazy journey that had started halfway across the world. Now, he found himself in Sulter Slay, trusting a dwarf druid he'd just met, and was being chased by flesh-hungry nomads called Scavengers. To make matters worse, Grey Cloak was down-and-out. Dyphestive was desperate to help him.

And Streak is gone too. If Grey wakes up, he'll kill me. Horseshoes, I don't even know what I'm running from. I bet I could handle whatever's after us. I'll use Thunderash and bash their skulls in. He would rather fight his way out than anything, but Grey Cloak's breathing was shallow. He wouldn't risk Grey Cloak getting hurt or captured, so he waited.

I feel like a bear in his den. He shifted his shoulders, trying to make more room, but there wasn't any. *This is awful.*

"Relax, young fella," Koll whispered. "Trust the night to see us through."

Dyphestive could have sworn that Koll started to hum. It was an easy, earthy tune, and his eyelids became very heavy and closed.

SOMETHING KICKED DYPHESTIVE'S LEG. His eyes opened, and he realized that Grey Cloak had booted him during a spasm. He stretched his head up and bumped into the ceiling. Dirt fell into his hair. He brushed out the dirt and noticed daylight creeping through the brush that covered the burrow. He also noticed that Koll was gone.

"Huh." Leaving Grey Cloak, his war mace in hand, he crawled on hands and knees toward the end of the cave. The thorny brush had been pushed open. He stopped and listened. The morning winds in the high hills whistled through the rocks with haunting effect. He poked his head out into the glare of the sun. He immediately felt the morning heat on his neck. The sun was rising in the east. He pushed out of the burrow in between the wedges of sandy rock.

There was no sign of Koll.

He must be scouting.

Staying low, Dyphestive crawled out of the rocks to a higher elevation. He could see for leagues all around, but there was no sign of the dwarven druid.

Did he abandon me?

He knew nothing of Koll, and it wouldn't surprise him one bit if the dwarf had fled. But Koll was the only guide he had in the barren land. Hidden behind the rock, Dyphestive studied the surrounding plains. He saw no sign of a single soul in any direction. The only living thing was him and the wind.

The hairs on the back of his neck stood up. He closed his eyes and listened. Something scraped over the rocks behind the next rise. A clicking sound came with it. He turned just as a huge lizard head appeared over the rocks. It was a basilisk with a round head like a snake, thousands of sharp tiny teeth, and a black tongue that licked the rock. It was big enough to ride, complete with a harness, but no one rode on its back.

The basilisk fixed its bright-yellow eyes on Dyphestive. Head low, dripping jaws open, it scrabbled over the rocks on a collision course with him.

26

DYPHESTIVE HIT THE GIANT LIZARD ON THE TOP OF THE NOSE WITH A BONE-cracking blow. It didn't stop the lizard from plowing him over. They tumbled down the rocks and over the hillside. He found himself on the bottom of the pile. He had Thunderash stuffed in the basilisk's jaws, keeping its thousands of teeth at bay.

He shoved the monster back and set his legs underneath it. It was the size of a horse and just as heavy. Stuffing his boots in its belly, he pushed.

The basilisk flopped on its side but not without a prize. It tore the war mace out of Dyphestive's fingertips as it rolled over, twisted on the ground, and came to its feet. It charged again.

Weaponless, Dyphestive's large hands instinctively pulled out his knife. He let out an angry growl and charged. He and the giant lizard collided. He brought the dagger down into its serpentine skin and aimed for its eyeball. Steel sank hilt deep into the soft tissue that made up the lizard's eye.

The lizard swung its entire body around and flattened Dyphestive as he continued to stab. He rolled up on all fours and watched the basilisk shake its thick neck and teeter.

Lungs burning, Dyphestive rushed it again. "Raaaaaaah!" He jumped over its snapping jaws and landed on the monster's back. He punched the knife deep into the monster's neck with mighty blows. It gushed blood, and its legs quivered.

The basilisk staggered over the dusty ground. Its feet faltered beneath it as it stumbled and fell.

Dyphestive tore the war mace out of the dying monster's jaws. He filled his lungs with air and let out a gusty breath. The basilisk was dead, but it wore a leather harness made by men. On pins and needles, he resumed his search for Koll.

The search ended quickly as he spied a group of men on the trail. A dozen men of various sizes in desert garb with cowls wrapped around their heads approached him. They wore sword belts on their hips and packs on their backs. Even though their heads were covered, he could see the heavy stares underneath. He recognized one of them, the shortest one in the group, Koll. The dwarven druid's hands were bound behind his back, and he was being dragged down the trail by a rope.

Dyphestive held Thunderash in a white-knuckled grip and cocked it over his shoulder. "If you know what's best for you, you'll let him go and walk away."

The hard-eyed Scavengers stopped twenty feet away. Vultures circled in the sky above.

Koll's beard was full of grit. He rolled to his side. "I'm sorry, Dyphestive." He spat. "I went to scout, and they caught me."

"No need to apologize." He gave the group a hard look. They weren't Monarch Knights or Honor Guards. That much was certain. They carried weapons but wore no visible armor. Their gear wasn't the finest craft either. Their swords were notched, and the tips of their daggers broken. One of them was really big, though, bigger than Dyphestive, and more of them could be close by. He pulled the war mace off his shoulder and tapped it into his hand. "Last warning. Let him go, or I'll do worse to you than I did that lizard."

One of the Scavengers moved behind Koll. He had a rangy build and bright-green eyes. He pulled a curved dagger with wooden finger grips from his belt. He lifted Koll up by the hair and put the dagger to his neck. In a dry voice, he said, "Surrender, or he dies, fool."

Dyphestive swallowed. He was ready to brawl, not negotiate. His gut told him to fight, but the pleading look in Koll's eyes suggested otherwise.

"You don't need to save me, boy," Koll said. "I've lived long enough. Save yourself. I'll be better off in the dwarven mountains of the dead."

With a flip of his war mace, Dyphestive said, "Perhaps we can negotiate. I'll give you all that I have. This war mace is worth more than all that you possess, and it's magic. Take it."

"You killed our basilisk," the Scavenger with the dagger said.

"How much can a lizard be worth?" he replied. He had no idea how much a basilisk was worth. "This could buy ten of them. Twenty!"

The leader pressed the dagger harder against Koll's beard. "Surrender, or he dies. I won't ask again." He gave Dyphestive a warning look. "Drop the weapon."

Dyphestive spun the weapon around one more time, and with a defeated look, he let it slip through his fingers. If Koll weren't in danger, he would have fought them all. Something told him that he could beat them.

"Secure him," the lead Scavenger said as he pulled the knife away from Koll and slipped it into his belt. "Make the bonds tight. He's a strong one."

Two Scavengers slipped in behind Dyphestive and bound his arms behind his back with cords of leather. The cords bit deep into his skin as they looped them around his thick wrists more than once. They patted him down, took away his knife, and stripped him down to his vest, boots, and trousers. With a shove, they put him on his knees.

"Better," the leader said. He bent over and sawed away the cords that bound Koll's hands behind his back.

Dyphestive's heart sank.

Koll gave a wry smile and rubbed his wrists. "You should have trusted your instincts, young fella." He looked at the leader. "Fetch the other one in the cave, and keep an eye out for their dragon."

27

Traveling became a bitter event over the sun-cracked ground of Sulter Slay. Dyphestive was tied to a basilisk, and so was Grey Cloak. In a cruel twist, Grey Cloak was towed behind the lizard like a log.

Dyphestive pleaded with the Scavengers to let him carry his friend. The coldhearted Scavengers cut off his requests by whacking him all over with clubs. He clammed up after the third time, instead opting to play along while casually looking skyward for Streak. The little dragon might be the only hope they had.

Koll took a moment to fall back from the pack and join him. The dwarf didn't seem chipper like he had been before. Instead, he seemed cold and calculating. "Don't feel bad, young man. Men and women more seasoned than you have fallen prey to our traps. I've been doing this a long time. I'm very good at it. Huh."

Dyphestive clenched his jaw. If he ever got his hands on the dwarf, he would break his neck.

"You may speak." He tapped his staff twice on the ground. "The Scavengers won't throttle you as long as you're spoken to first."

Hearing the dwarf's confident tone, Dyphestive decided to play the role of the fearful and downtrodden. *Let them think I'm young and stupid. Get the dwarf talking.* "Are you really going to eat us?"

"Perhaps," Koll said. "We can find many uses for men like you."

Dyphestive purposefully stumbled on a stone and fell to his knees.

The Scavengers stopped and turned.

He scrambled up, and with a worried look, he said, "I'm sorry. I'm sorry." He huffed for breath. "What else would you do with us?"

"That will be decided later."

Dyphestive looked back at Grey Cloak. "Is he going to die from the tick bite?"

"He will if we don't take it off, but for now, it's a foolproof way to keep him incapacitated." Koll fingered his beard shaped like a bun. "We are fortunate that he fell upon it. You might have been more formidable otherwise."

Keep him talking, Dyphestive thought. Koll had given him a hint that the tick might not be as fatal as it seemed, and they were concerned about numbers. It seemed that the Scavengers wouldn't take on a strong group, at least not without numbers. At the present, there were only twelve Scavengers plus Koll. Three of them rode giant lizards.

If I had a suit of armor, I think I could take them. The problem was he didn't have a suit of armor, and he couldn't put Grey Cloak in danger. If he tried anything, they could kill Grey Cloak.

Dyphestive subtly strained against his bonds. His wrists were wrapped so tightly that he couldn't feel his fingers. He imagined them being bloodred. Without any sort of leverage, he had little hope of breaking them.

"Do we have far?" he asked.

"Why, are you in a hurry to die?" Koll replied.

"No."

A DAY LATER, shortly after nightfall came, the Scavengers arrived at a small fortress in the hills long eroded by time. The rocks that made up its foundation still stood, but half of the walls had fallen, leaving gaps around the building. The group sauntered inside, where a large fire burned in the center courtyard.

Women and children with tattooed faces rushed out to greet the men. They were human, orcen, and a mix of the two. All of them looked hard and durable. Within moments, the children were hurling rocks at Dyphestive until Koll and a pair of Scavengers chased them away.

Dyphestive was led into a man-size metal cage, and Grey Cloak was placed in another. They were positioned near one of the walls that was still standing, and he had a full view of the fire, where the Scavengers victoriously gathered.

Koll wandered over after Dyphestive and Grey Cloak were situated. A lone Scavenger with a full battle array that consisted of a short curved sword, a pair of daggers, and a spear came with him. "Don't get jumpy, or my man will skewer you."

Giving the dwarf a heavy look, Dyphestive said, "I thought you were going to skewer me anyway."

"We will hold a council about that, but first we will celebrate," Koll said as he searched Dyphestive's eyes. "Mind yourself, and we'll feed you."

"You keep strange company for a dwarf, don't you?" Dyphestive asked.

"Why do you say that?"

Dyphestive leaned over and looked beyond Koll. "I don't see any other dwarves. I thought dwarves were clannish. Dwarven pride."

"That's not a life for everyone," Koll replied. He looked at Grey Cloak. "He's strong for an elf, but as you can see, his cheeks are sinking. He might make it through the morning, or he might not."

"You have to help him!" Dyphestive demanded. "You said you can."

The Scavenger thrust his spear in Dyphestive's face.

"We will hold a council about it but not until after we celebrate. It's custom." Koll rapped his short staff twice on the cage. "Be wise, and rest. Forget about your friend. His life is not in your hands but ours." He walked away.

The celebration began with the Scavengers dancing wildly around the bonfire. The women flung their bodies into the arms of their men, danced, and cavorted provocatively. They seemed to feel no shame as they peeled off the men's cowls as part of the ceremonial dance.

Like the women and children, the men had colorful tattoos and piercings all over their faces. Their expressions were savage and fierce, and the craftiness of evil men lingered in their eyes.

Dyphestive felt his guts twist the more he watched. He'd never seen men and women act so foul. They smoked from pipes and danced in heated passion. The children joined along in the dark and savage songs. They beat the leather heads of drums.

And I thought it was bad in Dark Mountain. At least there was some decorum.

The Scavenger men jumped and let out shrill screams with children on their shoulders. The women showered Koll with haughty affection as they layered him with wreaths of tiny bones. On and on it went in foul celebration as they praised the sky above them and the ground beneath their feet.

Earlier, Dyphestive had thought Koll had in mind a prolonged servitude as a slave for his imprisonment. That would have given him time to plan an escape, but it was clear that whatever they had in mind would be an act of torment and pure evil.

No matter the cost, I have to escape.

28

THE SCAVENGERS HELD HANDS AND DANCED AROUND THE BONFIRE, CHORTLING with wicked glee. The women's shrieking voices reached a feverish pitch as the men hollered louder and louder.

Women in snug leather skirts strutted toward the blaze and tossed a sandy substance into the fire, which swallowed it up and spit out bright-colored flames. The pyre heaved and moaned like a living thing, feeding on the cold air and growing bigger.

From his uncomfortable position in the back of his pen, Dyphestive leaned forward. Figures twisted inside the flames. The muscles in his back knotted. He broke out in a cold sweat.

A supernatural event was happening, a demon or spirit from another world being summoned.

He saw Koll talking to two Scavengers and pointing at the cages. The Scavengers were towering brutes that had been part of the pack that had captured Dyphestive. They were full-blooded orcs with beady eyes, protruding foreheads, broad noses, and canine teeth. They hustled over to the holding pens, grabbed the ropes tied to Grey Cloak's cage, and dragged them toward the fire.

The Scavengers parted into two rows and chanted for the blood of the fallen elf. Dyphestive watched in horror as the six-foot-high cage was hauled forward by the two rows of chanting people. At the end of the row, before the fire, Koll waited with his staff over his head. His eyes were as bright as flames, and he chanted strange words.

Dyphestive's jaw hung open, and his heart raced as he watched Grey Cloak be pulled toward the hungry flames. *They're going to sacrifice him.*

The bonfire's flames stretched out over the crowd like great arms with long fingers. With haunting effect, the fires swayed through the air. In the center of the fire, at the top, was a head with a face. A burning elemental creature that had been summoned lived inside.

Dyphestive's mind screamed, *Noooooooooooo!*

The brutes unlocked Grey Cloak's cage and hauled him outside. They raised him high in the air for all to see.

The Scavengers erupted with cheers. The hammering of drums grew louder.

I must stop this!

With his blood surging through his veins, Dyphestive strained against the leather cords that bound him. As mighty as his strength was, they flexed but would not give. His hands were so big that he couldn't pull them free.

No! Think! What would Grey Cloak do?

He caught the guard giving him a backward glance. He discontinued his struggles until the guard turned away again. An idea came to him. It was something he'd seen Grey Cloak do before. Instead of breaking his bonds, he found a way to use them.

With his hands behind his back, he pushed them down to the ground and slid them underneath his rump. From there, he brought his hands under his knees. At that point, he was bunched up so tight, he could barely move. His big body didn't make it any easier. He wasn't a little man who could squirm out of tight situations, but given his youth, he was still flexible. Just enough, he hoped.

Almost there. You can do this.

Dyphestive tucked his chin into his chest, pulled his knees in as far as he could, and pushed his hands toward his ankles. The heels of his boots stopped him from freedom.

No. No. No. So close. Do it. Do it or die, Dyphestive!

With his body trembling, he stretched his arms out and heaved. The knots slipped over the heels of his boots, and he brought them over his toes.

I'm free!

He set his eyes on the guard who stood with his back toward Dyphestive. Without hesitation, he got to his feet and thrust his hands through the bars. He grabbed the man's hair and yanked him back. Before the man could cry out for help, Dyphestive trapped the man's neck in his bound wrists and choked the life out of him.

At the bonfire, Grey Cloak was lifted higher in the air and carried toward the flames. At the forefront, Koll chanted louder. The flames and the figure in the fire roared.

Dyphestive reached for the dead guard's dagger, whisked it out, and cut his bonds. He searched the guard's body for a key, but he couldn't find one.

"No, no, no, no, no!" He glanced up at the throng. So in the heat of passion they were, they didn't pay him any mind. He grabbed the bars and pulled. The thick metal groaned and began to bend. Biceps bulging, he pulled the bars back until one bar kissed the inside of another. He did the same to the other bar, creating a gap for him to squeeze his shoulders through.

Even with the rods bent, he didn't have enough space to squirm in between. He made it halfway out and got wedged in the bars. *Not good. I'm stuck.*

29

DYPHESTIVE PUSHED HIMSELF BACK INTO THE CAGE. HE STRIPPED OFF HIS VEST AND tried to squeeze through again. His sweat-slick frame slipped in between the bars. Pushing off with his feet, he popped through.

Freedom. The air tasted sweeter on the other side of the bars.

Grey Cloak's body was only a few feet from the flames. The fire elemental's hands reached out for him.

Dyphestive leaned over and scooped up the guard's spear. From over one hundred feet away, he hurled it toward the clamoring crowd.

The spear sailed silently through the darkness in a perfect arc. It came down and lanced one of the Scavenger brutes holding Grey Cloak through the heart. The orcen Scavenger dropped dead, and Grey Cloak's body fell to the ground.

Dyphestive picked up a sword and dagger as the Scavengers fell silent and turned his way.

"Remember me?" Dyphestive growled. He banged his weapons together. "Because here I am."

Koll strutted to the front of the pack, pointed his staff at Dyphestive, and said with a raised voice, "Kill him!"

The Scavengers, one and all, snatched up their weapons and charged like a hungry pack of wolves. They outnumbered Dyphestive by more than twenty-five to one and came with glazed-over eyes.

He didn't care. They couldn't fight like him, and he was going to prove it. Bare chested, he charged, shouting, "For Grey Cloak!"

"ROOOOOOOOOAAAAAAAAAAAARR!"

The Scavengers stopped in their tracks and collided with one another. They cowered and searched for the source of the frightening sound erupting in the sky.

"ROOOOOOOOOAAAAAAAAAAAARR!"

Dyphestive knew that sound, and he didn't stop his charge. It was Streak. Before the first Scavenger he reached could turn to face him, he took the Scavenger's head off with his sword. A punch with his dagger dropped another Scavenger dead.

The women and children were the first to scatter as they snatched the young ones up in their arms and hustled them away.

The men were far from as fortunate. Streak glided down from the sky, spitting flames. The Scavengers' clothing caught fire, and their skin burned as flames engulfed the evil men.

Dyphestive showed no mercy on the confused brood. His massive arms became windmills, his steel pumping out a bloody death. Scavengers were skewered and gored. They caught the full onslaught of Dyphestive's fury.

Out of the smoke and flame, one of the towering orcs came wielding Thunderash. He charged Dyphestive and swung with great force. Dyphestive blocked the war mace with the blade of his sword. The sword snapped like a dry branch. Without pause, the orcen Scavenger brought Thunderash down.

Dyphestive seized the orc by the wrists, and they shuffled back and forth over the dusty ground. The orc was strong, his limbs as hard as tree roots. He had a lot of fight in him as they wrestled to break one another's grip.

The orc headbutted Dyphestive with his thick skull. Dyphestive sneered and headbutted him back. *Crack.* He busted the orc's nose.

The orc lunged forward. They collided skull to skull and battered one another like rams.

"No one's skull is harder than mine," the orc boasted.

Crack. Crack. Crack.

The orc's knees buckled. His grip on the war mace failed. He swayed, blinked his eyes, and staggered back woozily. He rubbed his head. "Your skull is like iron." A dead body tripped him up, and he fell backward into the heap.

Dyphestive picked up his mace and finished the orc.

Streak soared in the sky, scattering the Scavengers with his flames. They burned and ran. They burned and died.

Dyphestive sought Koll out. The wicked dwarf had set him up and deceived him. He wouldn't let that happen to anyone ever again. Scanning the fort's grounds, he spied the dwarven druid cowering behind the women and children. "Koll! You're mine!"

The women and children ran for their lives.

Koll ran, too, but he wasn't fast enough to escape Dyphestive. At the last second, he spun around and swung his staff into Dyphestive's chest. The blow clapped like thunder. Dyphestive was knocked from his feet and lay flat on his back.

"You should have been wiser than to pursue an old dwarf," Koll said as he lorded over Dyphestive's fallen body. "Now I will feed you to the flames along with your friend. That is the price of vengeance." He lifted his staff, bringing it down with one final and fatal blow.

Dyphestive sat up, grimacing. He snatched Koll's staff, ripped it out of his grip, and flung it away. "Sticks and stones can't break my bones." He seized Koll by the neck. "But I can break yours!"

"No!" Koll shouted in outrage. "Impossible! I struck you down! I struck you down!"

Dyphestive hauled Koll, kicking and screaming, toward the burning and heaving fire. "Hungry?" he asked the elemental figure dancing in the flames. "How about some dwarf for dinner?" Dyphestive hurled Koll end over end into the bonfire. He dusted off his hands and walked away.

The women and children were nowhere in sight.

Every man he and Streak had fought was dead. Bodies burned on the ground. Whatever Streak could burn, he'd burned.

Dyphestive picked up Grey Cloak in his arms and grabbed his mace as well. He surveyed the fort and spoke with a booming voice. "I know you're out there. I know you see me, wicked people. Change your ways, or the same end will come to you!"

Without looking back, he walked out of the fort, leaving the smoke, flames, and death behind him. Following the stars, he resumed his journey north across the black landscape, ready to face any danger he must to save his friend.

30

His legs feeling like anchors, Dyphestive dropped to his knees and set Grey Cloak down. Even his inhuman endurance and strength wasn't enough to take his friend another step. The sun had baked him alive, and his skin was burned red. He licked his cracked lips.

The sun had set on him three times since he'd started walking, and he'd never crossed paths with another soul. He was in the middle of nowhere, and nowhere owned him.

If he fared badly, Grey Cloak didn't fare any better. The elf was still as pale as a sheet, but the clamminess was gone. He breathed in ragged sighs.

Streak landed beside the blood brothers. He studied Grey Cloak with probing eyes and licked the elf's fingers. The runt dragon had been flying off and on for the duration of the journey, flying out of sight before returning hours later. He came back with dead ground lizards, but even Dyphestive couldn't stomach the creatures.

With the sun beating down on his neck, he took a look at Grey Cloak's back. His stomach soured. The desert blood tick was bigger than his fist. Blue veins spidered along Grey Cloak's back in a weblike pattern from where the tick had sunk its pincers in.

Dyphestive dared to touch the blood sac bulging on the tick's back. Grey Cloak stiffened and gasped.

"Horseshoes." He took a breath and eyed the sky. There wasn't a cloud in sight, and there hadn't been for days. All he could do was walk north, but even then, he was uncertain as to where he was. Something felt amiss, and he hadn't drank a drop in days.

"Streak," he said with a dry throat. "If you can find help, find it. I can't go any farther. I'll stay with Grey Cloak."

The runt dragon cocked his head.

Dyphestive shooed the dragon away. "You must go, Streak. Go. I know you can do it."

Streak slunk beside Grey Cloak, licked his face, opened his wings, and flew away.

It took a lot of energy for Dyphestive to lift his head and watch the dragon vanish into the bright sky. Dizziness assailed him, and his vision filled with spots. He flopped face-first onto the desert sand.

DYPHESTIVE OPENED his eyes and found a sea of stars above him. He was moving but not by his own power. He was flat on his back, and a wagon was rolling beneath him, or so he thought.

It was all he could do to keep his eyes open. His limbs were exhausted, and he couldn't move them. Something restrained them. He flexed in a vain effort. He was too weak to fight.

The steady rhythm of the wagon rocking and rolling put him back to sleep.

"WAKEY, WAKEY," someone said.

Dyphestive felt someone tickling his nose with a feather. His eyes cracked open, and he stared at a little man with an impish face. He waved a turkey feather above him. "Ah, you see me, no?"

"Uh…" was all Dyphestive managed to say. It felt like his throat had swollen closed.

The little man with an impish face looked like a gnome. He had fox-like features that gave his face a curious expression. His mouth was big, his eyes slanted, and his nose came to a point. "You breathe. A good thing for you."

The gnome held out a clay jug. "This is water. Drink." He poured it all over Dyphestive's face. "Good, no?" He giggled. "Try not to move. Your skin is peeling, and motion will be very painful, but we shall restore you."

Dyphestive forced himself into a sitting position. His back burned like it was going to split open when he did.

"No, no, no, you should lie down. I have salve. Lie down," the gnome said. He behaved with childlike manners as he patted Dyphestive's forearm. "Rest, rest."

Dyphestive swung his legs off the small cot. "I have a feeling I've been on my back long enough." He spied the room. It was a primitive cottage made out of packed mud walls and branches. The roof was held up by driftwood posts, and the ceiling wasn't very high. The cottage had no door but rather a doorway covered by a heavy blanket. Two steps led down into the main floor, which had been dug out. That was where he sat. It had cupboards and a small table and chairs. The floor was made of tight bundles of grass. He rubbed his feet on the grass. "Where are my boots?"

"Outside," the gnome said, pinching his nose. "They stank very bad. Don't you hurt? Your skin blisters."

"I'll manage." Grey Cloak lay on his chest on a cot in the middle of the floor. He was shirtless, and the desert blood tick was still fastened to his back. Grey Cloak's white and veiny skin looked awful. "Is he going to make it?"

"He breathes," the gnome said as he strutted around in a tattered vest, blue trousers, and bare feet. "I'll try to keep him breathing, but that blood tick has been on him a while."

"What's your name?"

The gnome's face brightened. "I'm Chopper. Friend of the desert, they call me. I've lived here all my life, and I know the ways, the creatures. I can tell one grain of sand apart from the other. I can find the water hidden in the trees and tell you which bugs to eat." He thumbed his nose. "And there is honey in the wood, but one must know where to find it."

"I'm Dyphestive." He looked about for the rest of his gear. His war mace was leaning against the wall by the doorway. He'd trusted Koll before, and he wasn't about to do it again. "Where are we? How long have I been out?"

Chopper rummaged through his cupboards and found a clay jug. "Ah, this will do it. This will help fix your friend." He hurried over to Grey Cloak with a slight limp in his step. "My hip is bad. It aches when it rains. Very little rain these days. He-he."

Dyphestive forced himself across the floor and grabbed Thunderash. "Touch him, and you will die!"

31

BEFORE DYPHESTIVE COULD LUNGE FORWARD TO CUT CHOPPER OFF FROM GREY Cloak, someone—or something—seized him by his hair. "Huh?" Dyphestive grunted in confusion.

All of a sudden, Dyphestive was being dragged outside with his arms flailing.

"Don't you touch Chopper," someone said in a deep, slow voice. "I'll hurt you."

"Not if I hurt you first." Dyphestive spun toward the unseen assailant and whacked him in the knee.

"Ow!" a giant of a man cried as he hopped up and down on his good leg. He was huge, bare chested, and had one eye in the middle of his bald head. He carried a lot of flab over his muscle, and he wore a loincloth. Many of his teeth were missing. He towered over Dyphestive by at least a foot. He reached for Dyphestive's war mace. "Give me that!"

Dyphestive went at the cyclops again and swung.

That time, the sun-bronzed brute caught the weapon in the ribs and trapped it at his side. He punched Dyphestive in the face with a ham-sized fist. Stars exploded behind Dyphestive's eyes. He shook it off and hit the cyclops in the ribs.

The cyclops winced and went down. "Ow! You hit hard for a little man!" He rose up to full height and balled his fists. "Grrrrrrrrr! I'm going to smash you to death!"

Chopper came rushing outside. "No! No! No! Tiny, stop! He's only protecting his friend!"

Tiny the cyclops glowered down at Dyphestive with his huge walnut-colored eye. "He tried to hurt you. I saw!"

Chopper approached with a hand out. "You were snooping, weren't you?"

"No," Tiny said with a guilty look.

"I told you about that. You get yourself into trouble when you snoop. Now, let go of the man's hammer," Chopper said.

"It's a mace," Dyphestive corrected.

Tiny snarled at Dyphestive, but he released the war hammer he'd trapped against his ribs. "I don't like you."

"Dyphestive, I realize that we are strangers, but on my word as a sand gnome, I will help your friend, and the sooner, the better," Chopper said.

Dyphestive slowly tore his gaze away from Tiny, who sat down on a log and began picking his nose. He cocked an eye at Chopper. "The last little fella said he'd help me too. He didn't, and he died for it."

Chopper caught his heavy look and swallowed. "Who might that have been?"

"A dwarf named Koll and the Scavengers."

The gnome's eyes grew to the size of saucers. "Y-you killed Koll? A brown-bearded dwarf?"

"Back at some fort. I killed him and the rest of the Scavenger men." Dyphestive waggled Thunderash at both of them. "If you're anything like them, I'll end you too."

"Please, friend, I promise you we're on your side. Koll and the Scavengers were nothing but a menace. None hated them more than we. They've taken from both of us, Tiny and I, hence we have an alliance."

"I don't believe him." Tiny stood up. He sniffed. "He stinks of lies."

"Do you really want to have another go at it?" Dyphestive warned. "I didn't hit you my hardest before."

"I didn't either!" Tiny shouted. "I'll rip your head off! Liar! You couldn't have killed all of them!"

"Go and see for yourself."

"No," Tiny said.

"We're very far from there, and we will keep it that way. If a warrior such as you says they are dead, then I'll believe it until I see otherwise." Chopper glanced at Tiny. "He doesn't take to many. Don't be offended. It's his nature not to trust."

"You said you could help my friend?"

"Yes. Yes. Come with me. I'm ready."

Dyphestive followed the gnome back inside the cottage and stooped down to keep his head from hitting the ceiling. Tiny stuck his big head in the doorway and sat down, blocking the exit. Dyphestive hadn't noticed it before, but Tiny had small spikelike horns on the top of his skull instead of hair.

Chopper picked up his clay jug and handed it to Dyphestive. "Smell that."

Dyphestive gave the gnome a wary look and took a faint sniff. "Vinegar?"

"Yes!" Chopper said elatedly. "Vinegar. The ticks and a few other creatures hate it." He took the jug from Dyphestive. "Watch this. It works like magic, but it isn't."

"I'm watching."

Chopper poured the vinegar on the desert blood tick, soaking it in the sour liquid. The insect didn't move. The gnome lifted a finger. "Be patient. It will take.

Watch," he said in a hushed manner as he poured more vinegar on the gruesome bug with a bloody hump.

The desert tick quivered. Grey Cloak moaned.

"It's working, no worries," Chopper said.

The desert tick detached itself from Grey Cloak's back. It turned like a crab, left then right, with its bloody hump wobbling.

Dyphestive could see the insect's beady bloodred eyes as it scurried down Grey Cloak's leg to the floor. It made its way across the room. He wanted to stomp its life out, but Tiny had other plans.

"Bloodberry!" Tiny scooped the tick up in his paw of a hand and popped the tick into his mouth. He bit down, and it squished all over. "Mmmmmmm."

Dyphestive's stomach turned inside out. He looked away from the cyclops. "That's nasty."

"Tiny isn't on a restricted diet. As long as it's not poisonous, he'll eat it, though he has eaten poison on occasion. It makes him very flatulent." Chopper winked at Dyphestive. "Don't be in the same room if that happens. It's bad enough as is."

Dyphestive caught a whiff of something foul and fanned his nose. "Yes, I'd say."

Tiny let out a rusty chuckle, took a deep breath, and said, "Smells good."

Looking over at Grey Cloak, Dyphestive asked Chopper, "What are you doing now?"

The gnome was busy rubbing the vinegar into the sore spot on Grey Cloak's back. The area was red, swollen, and pussy, but the web of veins covering his back was beginning to vanish.

"The vinegar will help with the healing. There's poison, but it's not fatal."

"When will he wake up?"

"The fact that he isn't dead is a miracle. I've never seen one go so long without dying." Chopper covered Grey Cloak with his cloak. "Interesting material, this garment. I will care for him, and hopefully he'll awake soon." He moved around the cot to Grey Cloak's head and looked into his eye. "Still glossy. That's good. He must be a strong elf."

Dyphestive nodded. "He is."

32

Grey Cloak remained in a coma. In the meantime, Dyphestive's time was occupied by Chopper and Tiny, who taught him the ways of the desert. It was midday, and the sun's heat felt like a furnace's.

"People die all the time out here and for no reason. The dirt offers plenty," Chopper said on more than one occasion. He said it again just then. "Now, look at this. It's a dead tree, long dead."

Dyphestive didn't know what sort of tree it was, but it wasn't very big, standing about ten feet tall. Most of its branches had fallen off long ago. "Yes, it's dead but good wood for burning."

"Well, that's obvious, but fire is no good if you have nothing to cook," Chopper replied.

"Stupid answer," Tiny added in his gruff voice.

"Show him, Tiny," Chopper said.

Tiny set his tremendous shoulders against the trunk of the tree and pushed. The dry timber cracked, and its root base heaved up. Grunting louder, Tiny put his legs into it and gave a bullish shove. The tree fell flat on the ground, busting several branches beneath it, which snapped loudly.

"Looky here, looky here," Chopper said as he gazed down into the hole the fallen tree had made. "An entire civilization."

Thousands of insects and their larvae lived in the hole.

"What a surprise, more bugs," Dyphestive said. They'd spent a lot of time searching out places with bugs in the ground. "You wouldn't be able to find any meat in the ground, would you?"

"Of course, of course," Chopper said as he stuffed a handful of crunchy bugs into his mouth. "We use the bugs for traps. Mmmm. Very delicious."

Dyphestive eyed Tiny. The cyclops had plenty of meat on his bones for a person who lived in the desert. His hairy belly bulged. "How does this one stay so fat eating bugs?"

"Not fat," the hulking brute said. "You fat, baby face."

Dyphestive arched a brow. "If you say so, donkey skull."

"I don't like you," Tiny said.

"Good to know." Dyphestive turned his back and walked away. He had nowhere to go so long as Grey Cloak was under. It didn't help that Streak had vanished. He'd told the dragon to go for help, and that was the last he'd seen him. He had other troubles on his mind. He had no idea when the time mural had put them. He knew they'd been transported to Sulter Slay, but it was unclear whether they were in the past or the future. "I think I'm going to head back to the cottage."

Tiny beat his chest with his fist. "No hunt. No eat!"

"You can have my share of the bugs." Dyphestive began the long walk back to the cottage with his head hung low. He'd learned enough about surviving the wild, barren stretches to find his way back safely. In a matter of two days, Chopper had filled him with enough knowledge to last him a lifetime. But after all that had happened, he felt empty and lost.

Back at Chopper's homestead, nothing had changed. A small barn, which was more of a shack, housed Tiny. Fencing surrounded the barn and the chicken pens inside, but it held no livestock.

The only livestock they could raise are lizards.

He kicked up dust as he passed a small, rickety wagon that, according to Chopper, Tiny had hauled him and Grey Cloak in. One of the slats in the wagon bed was gone, and there wasn't a bench seat to ride on either.

Thoughts of Crane and the others came to mind. A few days seemed like forever. For some reason, Chopper's bleak homestead made him think of the younger days in Havenstock working under Rhonna. He would love to see her warm, frowning face again. He missed her.

With a sigh, he headed over to the cottage. He wasn't one to complain about anything, the weather least of all, but the sun beat him down. He'd had enough and decided it was time to check on Grey Cloak. He stopped outside the curtain door.

Please be well. Please be well.

He entered the cottage and found Grey Cloak's cot empty. He picked up the cot and slung it aside. "No. No. No. No!"

He spun around the center of the small cottage, his eyes probing for answers, but he found none. Like a ghost, Grey Cloak was gone.

"Chopper!" Dyphestive shouted as he reached for his war mace lying in the back of the room. "Tiny! I knew this was a trick! I'm going to kill you!"

"Who are Chopper and Tiny?"

The voice was very familiar. Dyphestive spun on his heel just as Grey Cloak brushed the curtain door aside. "Grey?" he asked, his jaw hanging. Grey Cloak was dressed in his tattered gear and cloak. Full color had returned to his face. "Is it you?"

"Do you know any other elves who are this handsome?" Grey Cloak smirked.

Patting his belly, he said, "I'm famished. I don't know where we are." His eyes scanned the room. "And the cupboards are as bare as a halfling's behind. Tell me you know where to find food."

Dyphestive charged across the room and swept his blood brother up in his crushing arms. He jumped up and down. "I'm so glad you're back!"

"Easy!" Grey Cloak said. "My arm's still broken."

Dyphestive gently set him down, but he couldn't help but smile. "Sorry."

"All is well, brother." Grey Cloak messed up Dyphestive's hair. "So tell me, what in the flaming fence happened?"

33

GREY CLOAK LICKED HIS GREASY FINGERS. "THIS IS THE TASTIEST MEAT I'VE HAD IN ages." He bit another hunk of seared flesh from the bone. "Marvelous. What sort of meat is this?"

It was early evening, and Chopper was huddled over a campfire, stirring up stew in a metal pot. Grinning from ear to ear, he said, "It's armadillo. Tasty. Now that's a compliment I like to hear." He eyed Tiny, who squatted near the fire, eating an armadillo's head. "This one never says anything kind."

"I like," Tiny commented as he crunched the armadillo skull in his jaws.

"Yes, such a glowing review." Chopper spooned some of his stew into a smaller bowl and handed it to Dyphestive. "Try this. It's seasoned. I have salt and ginger, you know."

Dyphestive had just finished eating a hunk of meat that was like chewing rawhide. He wasn't one to complain about food, but armadillo was awful. He dipped a wooden spoon into his bowl and sampled the stew. "Blech!" He spit it out.

"Too much salt?" Chopper asked.

"I'm not sure what you mean by salt." He swallowed down some water. "Or little."

"Oh, perhaps I overdid it. My salt is very, very strong." Chopper sat down on a large strip of driftwood and started eating.

Dyphestive gave Grey Cloak a suspicious look. "You like this?"

"I told you, I'm famished." Grey Cloak pointed with his leg bone. "Why didn't you tell me food could be so good? You used to eat it all the time."

Dyphestive scratched his head. "I thought you knew."

"I do now," Grey Cloak said cheerfully. "Chopper, more armadillo, please."

The small group finished every bit of the armadillo except its hide. Chopper had other uses for that.

As Grey Cloak licked each and every finger clean, he asked, "Now tell me again, what sort of creature incapacitated me?"

"A desert blood tick. Very dangerous if you don't know how to treat it," Chopper replied. "You had a good friend to look out for you. A blessing."

Grey Cloak nodded. "That I do." He stretched out his arms and rolled them in wide circles as he glanced about. "Where are we?"

"Sulter Slay. Leagues away from Dwarf Skull. At least that's the closest place to here as of now," Chopper said.

"I see." Grey Cloak stood and scratched the side of his cheek. "And how did we get here?"

Dyphestive exchanged a worried glance with Chopper. He'd already told Grey Cloak what had happened twice. For some reason, nothing was sticking with the elf blood brother. He opened his mouth, but Grey Cloak cut him off.

"Oh, I remember." Grey Cloak pointed at Dyphestive. "You said we came through a tunnel."

"No, a time mural," he corrected.

"Ah, yes, a time mural, and it was in a wizard tower." Grey Cloak began to pace around the campfire. When he spoke, he spoke inquisitively. "We were fighting a dragon and fled through the tunnel?"

"No, it wasn't a dragon. It was a wizard, and it wasn't a tunnel, it was an arch-way," Dyphestive argued. "Do you remember anything? Tatiana, Gossamer, the underlings?"

"Do the underlings taste like chicken?"

Dyphestive slapped his forehead.

"What is underling? Tiny want to eat underling," Tiny said.

Dyphestive got up from his seat, walked over to Grey Cloak, and grabbed him by the cloak. He looked him dead in the eye and said, "Tell me you're fooling with me." He shook him. "Can't you remember anything?"

Grey Cloak smirked. "I'm trying."

Dyphestive's shoulders sank, and he let go of his friend. In a soft voice, he said, "You remember me, don't you?"

"Of course I do. You are Festive, my oldest and dearest friend. We've hardly ever been apart." He motioned in circles with his hands. "It's all of these other issues I'm fuzzy about. You mention names. I see faces, but that is all." He patted Dyphestive on the shoulder. "It could be worse, I suppose. It's a beautiful night. I think I'll take a stroll. Don't wait up."

With a heavy heart, Dyphestive joined Chopper by the fire as he watched Grey Cloak wander into the night.

"You seem gravely concerned," Chopper said.

"His gray matter is rattled."

"Elf is dumb like armadillo," Tiny commented with a chuckle.

"Your friend was on the threshold of death. He's still healing. Give him time to come out of it." Chopper glanced over his shoulder. "Perhaps it's a new world to him."

"Well, I had that happen to me before. Bad things happened because of it," he said.

"What sort of bad things?" Chopper asked.

"I killed a few people," Dyphestive said with a deep frown. Even though he was known as Iron Bones and under Drysis's influence, he could still see the images of the halfling men he'd slaughtered. It woke him from sleep sometimes. It was impossible to erase the memory from his mind.

"It sounds like you've killed many. That will change a man as the bodies stack up. Do you fear that your friend will become a reckless killer?"

"No, I fear that I'll lose the best friend I've ever had."

Chopper nodded. "Be patient." He slurped more of his stew. "And eat. It's good for your spirits."

Tiny let out a rumbling fart. "That will keep the spirits away. Hah!"

"Shew!" Dyphestive stood and walked away. "I'll be in the cottage. Keep an eye on Grey Cloak, will you?"

"No worries. He has nowhere to go," Chopper said with a smile. "Perhaps a long walk in the cool air will do him much good. One day at a time, my friend. One day at a time."

"I hope." Inside the cottage, Dyphestive found the cot he'd been using and overfilled it with his big body. "What am I going to do with Grey Cloak and his addled mind? I need him."

Worst of all was that Grey Cloak hadn't even asked about Streak. The elf and the dragon were bonded. Grey Cloak should've at least mentioned him.

Dyphestive lay his head on a dingy cushion and repeated what Chopper had said. "One day at a time. One day at a time." He dozed off.

Chopper woke him later, shaking him hard. "Wake, my friend, wake!"

He sat up. "What is it?"

Chopper gripped a floppy-brimmed hat in his tiny mitts. "It's your friend. I fear we lost him."

34

"Apologies! Apologies!" Chopper pleaded.

Through stiff winds, Dyphestive was carrying the sand gnome in his arms like a loaf of bread. "I don't want to hear it. If you set me up, I'm going to pulverize your bones."

Chopper frantically waved his arms. "We're friends. I swear it. I wouldn't trifle with a slayer such as you. Your friend is fast, very fast like a jackrabbit."

All Dyphestive could do was grind his teeth. He never should have let Grey Cloak out of sight in his condition, but he'd never imagined Grey Cloak would run off without having an idea of where he was going. It was madness.

"Where is Tiny? Is he close?"

"Almost there. He waits." Chopper pointed toward a rocky hillside bathed in moonlight. "Not far at all. I think I see him."

They caught up with Tiny, who stood like a statue on the hard terrain. He wore a large pack between his wide shoulders. He snorted lungfuls of air through his wide nostrils and cast his heavy stare on Dyphestive. "Put down Chopper."

"I don't take orders from you, One Eye. Say please."

"Say what?" Tiny replied.

"Never mind." He set Chopper down but held him by the collar. "Where's my brother?"

"Elf is not your brother. You man, he elf. You speak dumbly," Tiny added.

Dyphestive lifted his war mace. "You're dumbly!"

"Do you still have the scent, Tiny?" Chopper asked quickly.

"Tiny smell the elf. The elf in the Burnt Hills. He not come out. I would know." Tiny spit on the ground and glared at Dyphestive. "Only death in those hills."

"Then why didn't you stop him?" Dyphestive asked.

"Maybe he don't like you," Tiny suggested.

"I'm going to bust your skull."

Tiny leaned forward, showing the small, hard horns on the top of his head. "You try first. I go second."

Dyphestive looked away. "I though you said you lost him."

"We lost him in the Burnt Hills, a terrible place," Chopper said.

"Why is it so terrible?"

"It's haunted."

"What do you mean, haunted? Ghosts? Spirits? Devils? What's in there?"

"I can't say. No one I've ever known who has gone in has come out."

Dyphestive picked up Chopper by the collar. "Today's your lucky day. We're going to go find out what happened to them."

"No, no, please, no!" Chopper begged. His little legs ran through the air. "It's not wise to go in there."

"You should have thought that through before you lost my friend."

Tiny grabbed Dyphestive's shoulder. "Let him go!"

Dyphestive walloped Tiny in the gut with the butt end of Thunderash. Tiny doubled over. "If you're so worried about your little friend, you can come along, too, stinky. But keep your filthy paws to yourself." He marched straight for the Burnt Hills.

"Listen to me. Listen to me, Dyphestive, please," Chopper said in a desperate voice. "I'm a survivor, not an adventurer. I'm not equipped to fight. Look at me. I don't even have a weapon of any sort. If you take me in there, I will certainly die." His little body trembled. "I restored your friend's life. Please, restore me."

Dyphestive stopped and sighed. The last thing he needed to do was drag a gnome who was squealing like a pig into the heart of an unknown enemy's territory. He let Chopper down. "Go. I'll settle this alone."

"I'm sorry, friend, but I live in the burning wild not because I'm brave but because I'm a coward. All I can do is wish you well."

Dyphestive looked down on Chopper's little frame. "I have a feeling I'll need a lot more help than that." He took a knee, picked up a handful of dirt, and rubbed it into his hands. "Thanks for the help, Chopper. But if I find out you betrayed me, I'll—"

"I know, pulverize my bones."

Dyphestive marched over the black and dusty plains toward the Burnt Hills. The wind picked up as he closed in on the stark hill climb. The scent of brimstone lingered in the air, and the rocky spires ahead began to howl.

Even in the darkness, Dyphestive could make out an old path. He hoped to catch a glimpse of Grey Cloak's footfalls, but gusty night winds took any evidence of that away. At the base of the rocky hills, he began his climb into the dark fortress of nature.

Grey Cloak, what are you thinking?

He'd just gotten his friend back only to lose him again. That wasn't the only friend he'd lost. He'd left behind Tatiana, Zora, Razor, Anya, Bowbreaker, and Leena, too, as well as many others—Crane and Jakoby, not to mention Tanlin,

Lythlenion, and Rhonna. He hoped in his heart they'd survived. He hoped, somehow, someway, the threat of Black Frost was gone.

An eerie chill fell over him then went through his skin and into his bones. The wind that whistled through the rocks sounded like living things letting out their last gasps of life. Something was alive in those hills. The scent of death lingered.

Come on, Grey Cloak. Where are you?

35

THE BURNT HILLS WERE AN UNENDING CATACOMB OF ROCKS MADE UP OF JAGGED boulders, gulches, and deep gullies. With his ears peeled and his eyes wide open, Dyphestive traversed the rugged terrain as quietly as he could. He peered into every nook and crested every crag but saw no sign of Grey Cloak, or anything else living for that matter.

His strong fingers found purchase on a rock shelf, and he hauled himself up to one of the higher peaks. His broad body wasn't meant for climbing the narrow ledges, but the strength in his nimble fingertips saved him from falling time and again.

He was more of a mountain goat, surefooted and slow, but could do nothing the likes of what he'd seen Grey Cloak do. Grey Cloak crawled walls like a spider.

At the top of the peak, he stopped and took a breath. He could see the surrounding plains—leagues of nothing that appeared like a black sea. The wind rustled his hair, and his heart beat in his ears. He felt totally alone.

Grey, why would you even come here? Better yet, did you even come here, or am I a lamb being delivered to the slaughter?

Dyphestive had put his faith in a gnome he didn't know. All he could do was judge Chopper by his actions. But the entire series of events had been bizarre. Grey Cloak wasn't himself when he left, but he was alive when he very well could have been dead. Dyphestive was thankful for that much at least.

The howling winds picked up and whistled like a banshee's hollow screams.

A chill raced down Dyphestive's spine as he felt feathery fingers on his neck. He twisted around. Something was there, or something was in the air. *I felt that.*

The eerie howling sounded like a call from beyond, beckoning Dyphestive to venture deeper into the black hills. He resumed his journey into the very heart of the hillside, spiraling downward into the depths hidden from the moonlight.

His eyes adjusted, and he traversed a passage zigzagging through the rocks that was calling out to him. The droning wind sounded like the voices of the dead calling, *Come. Come. Come.*

He went, step after step, deeper into the blackness. He jumped over a narrow chasm with glimmering eyes shining in its depths. He looked again. The bright eyes were gone.

The catacombs ended in front of a cave mouth big enough to swallow a middling dragon.

Come. Come. Come.

Columns were carved out of the rock face, fashioning it like an ancient long-abandoned temple. Yet something lived. He heard it.

Come. Come. Come.

The words were faint and the speech unfamiliar, but he had no doubt about the meaning.

Come. Come. Come.

Dyphestive broke out in a cold sweat as icy fingers tickled his neck again. He spun around.

Grey Cloak stood ten paces behind him. The wind rustled his cloak. His hood covered his head, and his sword and dagger hung in his hands.

Dyphestive couldn't see his brother's eyes. "Grey?" There was no mistaking the height and build, but the stooped stance threw him off. "Is that you?"

The howling winds died down. Silence fell over the black hills.

Grey Cloak took a few slow steps forward. He spun his sword in a circle at his side.

Dyphestive lifted up his war mace and swallowed. "Grey, it's me, Dyphestive. What's wrong?"

The elf came two steps closer. He spun his sword again.

"Grey, what are you doing?"

"I am not he," Grey Cloak responded in a strange, cold voice. "I am me." He pulled back his hood with his dagger hand. His eyes were wide open and pure white. "Who are you, invader?"

"Grey, it's me, Dyphestive." He stepped back toward the cave, his neck hairs standing on end. "Stop fooling around. You need to come with me."

"This is sacred ground," Grey Cloak said. "You—oh man—are an invader." The possessed elf jumped forward.

Dyphestive hopped back, deeper into the cave.

A scuffle of claws over dirt caught his ears. Something charged out of the darkness with its jaws open wide.

Dyphestive swung into the jaws of death. Thunderash crashed into the monster's jaw. A thunderclap followed.

Krak-boooooom!

The monster was a giant eight-legged lizard, and its momentum carried it crashing into Dyphestive, where it came to a stop and died, its tongue hanging out of its mouth.

"Nooo!" Grey Cloak called out in a haunted voice. "You slew my servant." His bright eyes locked on Dyphestive. Grey Cloak came at him with his sword. "You will die!"

Dyphestive's legs were pinned underneath the lizard's massive skull. He pushed out from underneath it and lifted his war mace in time to block Grey Cloak's strike. He swiped at Grey Cloak's feet with his arm.

The elf skipped away. "Invader, you will die!" Grey Cloak came at him again with his blades jabbing.

Dyphestive popped up to his feet. Using the length of his war mace, he kept the attacking elf at bay. "I don't know who you are, but get out of my friend's body."

"This is my body!" Grey Cloak slipped by the war mace and slashed Dyphestive across the shoulder. "Your blood is mine. Everything in Ruunalin is mine! Prepare to die!"

36

IT TOOK EVERYTHING DYPHESTIVE HAD TO KEEP UP WITH THE SPEED OF GREY Cloak's striking blades. He used both ends of his war mace to block the fast strikes. If not for his training with the Doom Riders, he would have been cut to ribbons as they danced in the darkness.

It's times like this when I wish I had some armor. How do I stop him without hurting him?

Whoever had control of Grey Cloak's body wasn't perfect. The sword strikes were fast but wild. It had full control of the elf's fluid frame, but it didn't have the skill, which bought Dyphestive time.

I need to knock him out without hurting him.

It was easier said than done. Grey Cloak hopped out of harm's way as quickly as a jackrabbit whenever Dyphestive reached for him.

I need to get him to the ground.

Grey Cloak was strong, but he wasn't a match for Dyphestive. He only needed to figure out a way to grab Grey Cloak before he could slice his fingers off.

Wait for it. Wait for it.

A sword strike whistled by his ear. A dagger punched at his gut. Dyphestive blocked the next sword strike and kicked at him.

Grey Cloak jumped away like a springing deer. "You will die, invader. Ruunalin is mine!"

Dyphestive changed tactics. "Who are you?"

"I am Elkhorn Blackstone, master of stone."

"Are you a dwarf?" he asked.

"I am the lord of the rock and reaver of invaders." Grey Cloak charged, his weapons flashing. "They all die. You shall die next!"

Dyphestive jabbed his war mace out like a spear and caught Grey Cloak in the shoulder. The hard blow knocked the possessed elf backward. Without hesitation, Dyphestive pounced on his blood brother. He landed on top of Grey Cloak but not before Grey Cloak's dagger stabbed him in the thigh. He dropped his war mace and went after Grey Cloak's wrists.

Grey Cloak squirmed away, but Dyphestive filled his hands with cloak and yanked his blood brother down. They grappled over the hard ground, rolling over one another.

Dyphestive pinned Grey Cloak down by the wrists and wrenched the blades free. "Stop struggling. Grey Cloak, I know you're in there. Listen to me. It's your friend, Dyphestive."

Grey Cloak kicked him in the groin.

Dyphestive grimaced and held fast. "Don't do that again, Elkhorn Blackstone."

"You cannot defeat me! I live forever!" Grey Cloak thrashed about with supernatural strength, pushing Dyphestive back. "I am stronger!" he said with glowing white-hot eyes.

A heavy net dropped from the sky and fell on them.

"Remove these bonds! Remove them at once, invaders!" Grey Cloak shouted.

From the darkness, Chopper approached with a hunk of rock glowing in his fist. The green hue of the stone illuminated his eyes.

"What treachery is this?" Dyphestive demanded.

Tiny's hulking frame moved into view. He had a pouch in his hand.

"Do it now," Chopper ordered.

The cyclops removed sparkling sand from the pouch. He sprinkled it over himself and Chopper. He moved closer to Dyphestive and Grey Cloak and flung the dust over both of them.

"You will pay dearly for that!" Grey Cloak screamed. "I'll take your life, one eye!"

Dyphestive spit the dust from his mouth. "What did you do, traitors?"

Chopper locked his eyes on Grey Cloak and began to chant. The green rock in his hand beat and pulsated. The wind picked up, stirring the dusty ground. The longer he chanted, the stronger and louder his words became.

Grey Cloak cringed and cowered. "Nooo! Nooo!" He shielded his face with his hands, and his voice became evil and deeper. "I will slaughter you, invader! I'll destroy you! Your family! Your homes will rot, and your bones will be fed to the hounds of death! Go away!"

The fierce winds blasted through Chopper's beard and clothing, but he stood as firm as a stone. "Return to the grave, Elkhorn Blackstone! The grave awaits!"

Grey Cloak let out a howl as a ghostly apparition pulled free from his body. It hovered and hissed like a snake. Setting its burning eyes on Dyphestive, it dove at him and bounced off.

"Noooo!" it cried.

The spirit flew at Tiny and bounced away from the sparkling sand on his body. It tried to enter twice more, turned on Chopper, and let out an earsplitting shriek.

Dyphestive covered his ears as he watched the spirit convulse, spasm, and explode into ghostly ashes.

The wind died down. The stone in Chopper's hand cooled. Sweat glistened on his grimy face as he staggered forward, stumbled, and fell. Rolling onto his back, Chopper said, "Well done. We did it."

BACK AT CHOPPER'S COTTAGE, Grey Cloak was as cheerful and bright-eyed as ever. He sipped on tea made with honey as he counted the gold coins in the palm of his hand. "It's a notable score."

"Agreed," Chopper said as he refilled Dyphestive's earthenware mug. "Dwarven tombs are often lavish. We're all very fortunate to have survived that ordeal. The shade of Elkhorn Blackstone was a powerful one. Over the years, I'd only suspected what we were dealing with, but if not for you, Dyphestive, being so brave, we never would have rid ourselves of the menace."

Dyphestive nodded as he sipped his elixir. "I'm glad I have my friend back. That's all that matters."

Chopper toasted them with his mug. "We're blessed. The shade of Elkhorn called out to the elf and caught his ear when he was feebleminded. I apologize that we lost him, but it turned out for the better. The Burnt Hills are free of death, and that treasure will serve us well. We'll be able to supply ourselves for years."

"You can say that again," Grey Cloak said as he filled his inner pockets with gold. He plucked one item free of his cloak, a ruby dragon charm. "Not to mention, we have this. It should come in handy."

"A prize indeed," Chopper said as he teetered through the room.

Grey Cloak caught Dyphestive looking at him. "What?"

"How's your arm?" he asked.

When Grey Cloak had battled him, his brother's arm hadn't given him any trouble at all. It had appeared fully healed.

Grey Cloak rolled his shoulder and rubbed his arm. "It's as good as the other one. You'll have to forgive me, brother. I'm hazy on some details, but my mind clears for the better by the moment." He placed his hand on Dyphestive's shoulder and winked. "I'm back to normal but possibly illuminated."

"What do you mean?"

"It's hard to explain, but I found myself inside my body and out of it. I've been drained by a tick and possessed by a dwarf." He dropped the dragon charm inside his inner pocket. "It changes an elf. Imagine if you had Rhonna living in your head. It was similar to that but much worse."

Dyphestive shrugged.

Grey Cloak eyed the ugly wounds on his brother's arms and legs. "I'm sorry about that. I don't remember anything that happened before the gnome ripped the dwarf spirit from my body."

"It's fine. Chopper stitched me up well." He raised a brow. "What are we going to do now?"

"I suggest you travel to Dwarf Skull. You will need supplies if you're going to journey north again. It takes lots of water."

Dyphestive nodded and headed outside, where the morning sun shone in his eyes.

Tiny had rolled up his net and was stuffing it back into its sack. The cyclops glanced away from Dyphestive as he approached.

That didn't stop Dyphestive from offering his hand. "Thanks for helping out."

Tiny grunted, but he took Dyphestive's hand anyway and tried to break his bones. "Tiny stronger, human."

Dyphestive squeezed back and watched Tiny's eyes widen. "Are you sure about that?"

The cyclops tore his grip away. "Tiny sure. Now go away."

37

CHOPPER AND TINY escorted GREY CLOAK AND DYPHESTIVE TO DWARF SKULL, and it wasn't anything like they'd expected. The brothers stood side by side with their mouths open.

"That's Dwarf Skull?" Grey Cloak asked. He studied the league-long fortified structure built around natural rocks and spectacular pinnacles.

"That's it," Chopper said proudly, as if it were his own. "There's nothing like it in the world, they say, but I don't know. I haven't been anywhere else."

Dwarf Skull sat on a plateau, like Raven Cliff, but was mountainous in size. The structure rested on a sheet of dark stone. It was a solid wall of black rock forty feet high with battle towers spaced evenly all around it. A great pinnacle stood in the middle of the monstrous structure, overlooking everything for leagues. Brilliant flags billowed at the top of the battlements, and dwarven soldiers marched along the top wall with spears and halberds.

"It's as big as Monarch City," Dyphestive commented.

"Er... will they let us in there?" Grey Cloak asked. It might as well have been Black Frost's temple, as ominous and foreboding as it appeared.

"Sure, sure, all are welcome if they pay a tribute." Chopper patted the purse on his hip. "You have more than enough to cover that."

"You're going in with us, aren't you?" Dyphestive asked the gnome.

Chopper rubbed his chin. "Er... as much as we enjoy your company, Tiny and I prefer to move on and conduct our business elsewhere. You've helped us. We've helped you." He thumbed his nose and winked. "And don't mention Elkhorn Blackstone. The less they know, the better. Best to you in Dwarf Skull."

The brothers watched the cyclops and gnome wander toward the distant farms and villages of the bleak surroundings.

"Shall we finish the journey to Dwarf Skull?" Grey Cloak asked. "I'm dying to see what's behind those walls, and I'm famished."

"You're really hungry?" Dyphestive asked.

"I have a newfound appreciation for the finer things in life. It's important that I enjoy them when I can." Grey Cloak glanced up. He'd hoped that Streak would appear, but he hadn't. "Perhaps it's for the better."

"Perhaps what's for the better?" Dyphestive asked.

"Streak is probably safer. I'm glad you sent him for help, but I am worried about him."

"Me too. I'm sorry, but I didn't know what else to do," Dyphestive said.

"Cheer up, brother. You saved me. I couldn't be more thankful. Streak will show eventually." Grey Cloak led the march to Dwarf Skull's entrance leagues away. On their way, they passed villages made up of stone huts and fields of dry farmland. They saw many hardened and dirty grim-faced dwarves who didn't blink or wave. Even the children didn't play.

"Brother, I have a feeling something isn't quite right about this place."

"So do I," Dyphestive said as he surveyed his surroundings. "If you ask me, this place is in short supply of everything."

"There's only one way to know for sure. Beyond those walls, we'll find answers." Grey Cloak picked up the pace and didn't stop until they were at the base of Dwarf Skull's league-long plateau. The cliffs were sheer and hundreds of feet high. Bird nests were scattered along the ledges. Flocks of little birds flew in and out. "I don't see an entrance. Odd."

"I don't either." Dyphestive scratched his head. "Maybe we shouldn't assume the entrance is in the north. Perhaps it's in the south or the east or the west. I'm surprised Chopper didn't mention it."

"I'd say that's why this place is well fortified. It's a mountain, or a sawed-off one at least." Grey Cloak picked up the pace to a trot with Dyphestive huffing along behind him. They jogged over a mile before they spotted a cave opening at the base of the mountain guarded by heavily armored dwarves.

The dwarves were in full battle array, with suits made from plates of blackened iron and full helmets complete with nose guards. Each and every one of them was as stout as a chimney, and they stood perfectly still with a spear or halberd—fitting their size—in hand.

Grey Cloak approached with caution as he eyed the cave backdrop behind the dwarven ranks. A closed iron portcullis blocked the mouth of the cave. He saw nothing but the deeper bowels of the cave on the other side. None in the dwarven ranks moved a muscle as he walked by them as if they were stones.

At the portcullis were several soldiers, and Grey Cloak asked, "May we enter?"

The dwarves didn't bat an eye. They looked straight forward without so much as a nod.

He exchanged a puzzled look with his brother, shrugged, and tapped a dwarf on the shoulder. "Pardon—"

The dwarves moved like a single unit and exploded into action. They surrounded Grey Cloak and Dyphestive with halberds and spears pointed at their chests.

Standing back-to-back, Grey Cloak and Dyphestive lifted their hands in surrender.

Grey Cloak finished his sentence. "—me?"

38

DWARF SKULL

"You weren't supposed to touch them. Why did you touch them?" Dyphestive asked.

"It was a friendly tap. I didn't think it would be misconstrued as an attack," Grey Cloak said as he watched the dwarves wind chain around him and Dyphestive. "You could have run."

Dyphestive eyed the portcullis. "I have a feeling that if I did, they would've poured out of that mountain like bearded ants."

Grey Cloak made another plea from where he sat on the ground. "We came to buy water and food for our journey. We'll pay to enter. We meant no harm." The dwarves' eyes were as hard as coal, and they didn't so much as grunt. "And I thought Rhonna was sour. Do you know if she ever had children?"

"Don't provoke them," Dyphestive warned.

"I think we passed that point."

The dwarves tightened the chains, but one of them vanished in a cleft near the portcullis. Grey Cloak saw the dwarf go. *Ah, a secret entrance. That should come in handy.* The dwarves dropped sacks over their heads. *Or not.*

"I think I fared better when you traveled with a blood tick," Dyphestive said in a muted voice.

"Ha ha. Don't worry. You know I'll get us out of this. I always do." The grinding of greased gears and rattling metal pricked his ears. The portcullis was going up. *Ah, that's where the dwarf went, to let us in.* "See, brother? I have it under control. All part of the plan."

Assisted by the dwarves, they were marched inside the cave. Grey Cloak could hear their bootsteps echoing inside the chamber, and the light dimmed. The air cooled as well, and they moved upward to a higher elevation.

"I love surprises, don't you, brother?" Grey Cloak asked.

"Not as much as you, apparently."

On the trip to Dwarf Skull, they'd discussed using discretion with their names. They had no idea who might be looking for them or at what point in time they had arrived. Of course, Grey Cloak doubted any of that was true at all. It seemed far-fetched that the time mural would move them forward or backward in time. It was inconceivable, yet they'd been teleported from one place to another somehow.

Back in the Wizard Watch, Gossamer had explained how the wizards could move from one tower to another and how the time mural was out of control, but Grey Cloak had never seen it work firsthand until they'd wound up in Sulter Slay.

"It's getting stuffy inside this hood," he commented. "You wouldn't happen to have anything more breathable, like cotton perhaps?"

One of the dwarven soldiers shoved him in the back. He intentionally faltered and landed on a knee. "Easy, it's hard enough to walk when you can't see, let alone be shoved." It wasn't true, of course. Grey Cloak was trying to gauge his captors and location.

They'd climbed steadily up over five hundred steps so far. Even though he couldn't see, he counted eight different sets of dwarven boots marching them deeper into the plateau.

Now might be a good time to turn back and get out of here. The deeper we go, the harder it will be to leave.

He cleared his throat as the strong-armed dwarves lifted him back to his feet.

"See it through," Dyphestive muttered.

That was all the confirmation Grey Cloak needed. If Dyphestive had wanted to turn back, he would have made a comment otherwise.

No turning back now.

They marched another hour through a labyrinth of corridors before they came to a stop in a room flooded in torchlight.

A fireplace crackled, and Grey Cloak could feel the fire's warmth on his fingers. The dwarves undid their chains, and he could hear them clink as they were carried out of the room. All eight pairs of dwarven boots left. A door shut, and they were sealed inside a chamber.

Grey Cloak lifted the sack from his face. He exchanged a look with Dyphestive, who was removing his hood as well. At the same time, they turned to look at the source of the fire.

A stone fireplace as tall as a man burned in the center of the room. A chimney made by dwarven stonework kissed the ceiling of the chamber and vanished. Two dwarven soldiers were posted on each side of the fireplace. They wore full plate armor, and black helms covered their heads. Braided chestnut beards spilled out from underneath. Each of them carried a war hammer, and like the stone, they did not move.

Another figure stood in front of the fireplace with its back to the brothers and its rough hands locked behind its back. The figure's hair had many braids in the back and a bun on top. Most of the hair was gray with shades of brown. The figure wore a dwarven tunic that covered it to its toes.

The brothers exchanged another glance.

Grey Cloak shrugged and cleared his throat. "Nice fire."

The figure answered, "What have you two bent horseshoes done?" The figured turned and faced them.

Grey Cloak's eyes widened.

Dyphestive blurted out, "Rhonna!"

39

Dyphestive didn't make it within ten steps of Rhonna before the two soldiers swooped in and blocked his path. He stopped in his tracks and looked over them to Rhonna. "I was only going to give her a hug."

"By the hammer of the forges, you're bigger than an ox. Stand down," Rhonna said in her rugged voice. "He's a friend."

The soldiers parted, and she moved between them.

Dyphestive took a knee and hugged her. "I never thought I'd be so happy to see anyone."

"I know how you feel." She patted him on the back. "I might be tough as a nut, but you're about to crack me."

Dyphestive let go. "Sorry."

"No worries. I need my bones cracked."

Grey Cloak slipped beside her. He noticed the hard lines on her face had deepened. "I never thought there would be a day when I'd be so happy to see you, Rhonna." He eyed her hair. "Where'd all the gray come from? Did you see a ghost?"

"I wish I had." Rhonna gave Grey Cloak her usual stern look. "Where have you two been?"

"The question is, what are you doing here?" he asked.

"Respect your elder and the one who bailed you out from my kin."

"You first?"

Rhonna's jaw clenched.

Dyphestive stepped in. "Let's not go back to our old ways. Rhonna, we were in the Wizard Watch, east of the Great River of Arrowwood."

"You don't have to tell her anything, Dyphestive," Grey Cloak said. "It appears she's changed."

"It's Rhonna. She hasn't changed." Dyphestive looked about the chamber. "If I can't trust her, no one can be trusted."

"Huh," Rhonna said. She moved away from the fire to a bar with wooden barrels on it. She grabbed a tankard from underneath and opened a barrel tap. A dark walnut ale poured out. "Changed doesn't begin to describe it. And yes, I have changed. I've changed because I'm no longer Rhonna, a blacksmith from Havenstock, but rather Rhonna the Monarch Queen of Dwarf Skull."

"Ah, delusions of grandeur. How convenient." Grey Cloak crossed his arms. "And how did this come about?"

Rhonna drained her tankard and refilled it. "Would either one of you donkey skulls like a drink?"

"Make it two," Grey Cloak said.

The blood brothers sat down at a stone table with benches on either side.

Rhonna sat across from them and shoved a tankard to each. "Drink, maybe that will loosen your tongue."

Grey Cloak took a sip, and his face puckered. "No wonder you're so bitter. Is this what you've been drinking all your life?"

Dyphestive guzzled it down. "I like it."

Grey Cloak took another drink. "I guess it's like you, Rhonna, an acquired taste. Now you were saying about how you came to be the Monarch Queen of Dwarf Skull?"

Rhonna eyed him. "I have to admit, I'm glad *you* haven't changed. You've both grown, but you haven't changed." She drank deeply. "It's as refreshing as dwarven ale after hours on the battlefield."

"We went through a time mural in the Wizard Watch," Dyphestive said to her. "That's how we wound up here."

"Why don't you tell her everything?" Grey Cloak asked sarcastically.

"I will." Dyphestive filled Rhonna in on their last adventure at the Wizard Watch. He explained how they'd come across the dragon-charm helm and used the Figurine of Heroes to summon the underlings, Catten and Verbard.

Rhonna rose from her bench and shook her head. Under her breath, she said, "I knew. I knew in the depths of my belly that you had something to do with it." She eyed Grey Cloak. "You gamble. You take the short path. Do you know what you've done?"

Grey Cloak shrank under her gaze. "I have a feeling that I better have another drink." He drank half the tankard. "Go on."

The wrinkles in the corners of Rhonna's tired eyes deepened. She sat back down. "Do you know how long it's been since I last saw you?"

"Why do I have the feeling that I don't want to know the answer to that?" he asked.

Dyphestive leaned forward. "How long?"

"Twenty seasons."

Grey Cloak spit up his drink. "Twenty seasons? You jest!"

"I wish it were a jest. Believe me, I'd be back in Havenstock, hammering away at the forge, but instead I'm here."

Dyphestive swallowed. He reached over and covered Rhonna's fist in his palm. "You really mean this? It's been twenty seasons since you saw us last." There were two seasons in every year, hence ten years had passed. "I can't believe that."

"Believe it. It's the year sixty twenty-three. Gapoli is under the full control of Black Frost and those underlings." She glared at Grey Cloak. "Whatever you brought here accelerated Black Frost's plans. He's more ruthless now than ever, and with those underlings as his henchmen, he's unstoppable."

Grey Cloak tilted his chair on its back two legs. "So, does this make me twenty-seven years old, or am I still seventeen?" He needled his chin. "Wait, I'm eighteen, or am I twenty-eight?"

Rhonna looked at him. "Do you find this a laughing matter? Do you know how many thousands have died over the past ten years because of your error?"

"Ho, Rhonna, you can't pin the blame on Grey Cloak. He only did what he thought best," Dyphestive said. He shook his tankard from side to side. "Can I get another? I have a feeling I'm going to need it."

40

THE LIST WENT ON AS RHONNA TOLD THE STORY OF THE DEMISE OF GAPOLI. AFTER the underlings had arrived, the world had fallen under a landslide of evil.

Grey Cloak hung on her words, but he feigned distraction even as fear grew in the pit of his stomach. He paced around the table, juggling plates and saucer cups. *It can't all be my fault.*

"I knew that Black Frost was at war with the Dragon Riders and thought, as long as they were defending the skies, he would leave the rest of the world alone —Black Frost would only want a tribute." Rhonna shook her head. "At least that was how the Monarchs saw it in Dwarf Skull, but that wasn't the case.

"Black Frost built up his armies. The Black Guard invaded the smaller towns first and started recruiting more soldiers into their armies. Before we knew it, it was a black wave. They took over Portham and invaded Havenstock. I saw the handwriting on the wall before it happened. I fled."

"How long ago was this?" Dyphestive asked.

"Five years or so," she said as she wiped her mouth. "I came home to find refuge, but instead, I discovered that generations of my family had been slaughtered, generations of Monarchs." Her hard voice softened. "I never told you this, but I'm a Monarch legacy—the great-granddaughter of Ironthumb Warboot. He was the Monarch king of Dwarf Skull. My brothers and sisters were killed in a surprise Risker invasion.

"When I arrived, I was first in line to the throne. Black Frost still has forces here, but he lets me lead so long as I don't cause trouble. Not to mention, he controls the Twin Rivers, which allow our valley to thrive. He dammed them at the Iron Hills. Water flows but only because he lets it. If he wants, he can turn Dwarf Skull into a wasteland."

"This is madness," Dyphestive said. He stood up and punched his fist into his hand. "How can this be? Isn't there anyone in this world who can stand up to him? Him and those underlings?"

Rhonna sighed. "I have to admit that I never imagined anything like this. I thought the Sky Riders would take him down, but when I found out that he killed them, well, my heart turned to wax." She shook her head. "And those underlings. I saw them with my own eyes. I've never seen such evil. I'd hate to imagine a world full of them. They destroy everything."

Grey Cloak cringed. He'd gotten more than an eyeful of the underlings the first go-round. "I can't believe they're still here. They should have vanished into the figurine, but they flicked it through the time mural and stopped themselves from being transported back. It could be in any time or place."

"As much as I didn't care for the elf, Tatiana, she was right. You gambled one too many times," Rhonna said as she refilled her tankard. "It came back and bit us. It came back and bit us all. I don't fault you for it. No one could have seen this coming. I'm glad you're both here and I found you first."

"What do you mean?" Grey Cloak asked.

"They're still looking for you. You, Dyphestive, the figurine, Sky Riders, any enemy that they think can stop them. That's why I'm glad I found you first. When you used my name, word got back to me of your descriptions. I didn't think it could be, but it was. I'm glad."

"Are you telling me that after we've been gone ten years, Black Frost is still looking for us?" Dyphestive asked.

"Most likely. After all, the two of you continue to slip through his claws," she said.

"What about the others?" he asked.

"Others, who?" Rhonna asked.

"Tatiana, Zora, Bowbreaker, Lythlenion," Grey Cloak said, "have you seen any of them?"

Rhonna sadly shook her head. "I've only heard rumors."

Grey Cloak stopped juggling and set down the objects. "What rumors?"

"Every member of Talon is either imprisoned or dead. Worst of all, Bowbreaker has been captured by the elven Monarch queen of Arrowwood, Esmarelda. She aligned herself with Black Frost early on."

"What about Anya? Has there been any sign of her?"

"She was the last Sky Rider. The Riskers were proud to announce during one of their routine visits that they slew her."

"Which Riskers?" Dyphestive asked.

Rhonna sneered. "Two young blondes lead them, older than you. They call themselves—"

"Dirklen and Magnolia," Grey Cloak said. "Are those two windbags leading the Riskers? It figures."

"They'd be thirty years old now," Dyphestive said.

"You know them?" Rhonna asked.

"Oh, we know them. That's how we came to Havenstock, to get away from the likes of them and Black Frost." Grey Cloak couldn't believe his pointed ears.

Everything in the world that could go wrong had gone wrong and all in a matter of days in his time. "I'm going to fix this."

"How?" Rhonna asked.

"I don't know how, but I'm going to try. I broke it. I'll fix it."

"No, brother," Dyphestive said, "we'll fix this calamity together."

Rhonna eyed them. "Since the first day you wound up on my farm, I knew. I knew you were special. I did my best by both of you to prepare you for whatever was coming. That time has come, and now you better be ready because I have a feeling that the fate of the world lies in the pairs of your hands."

41

The inner core of Dwarf Skull was a marvel of dwarven engineering. Similar to Dark Mountain, the city was built in and around the natural rocks that made up the plateau's landscape. Bridges made of iron girders stretched from one pinnacle to another. Some were wide enough for large carts and wagons, and the others were pedestrian walkways.

A network of tunnels weaved through the black rock, twisting and turning from balcony to walkway ledges with slides that led straight back down. Like a hive, there was level after level of cave mouths that led into pods where the dwarves and many others lived.

From the peak where Grey Cloak stood with his friends, he watched the dwarves bustle along like bearded worker ants from workstation to workstation. Their faces were grim, and they spoke little. Among them were many of the other races, keeping busy but with long faces as well. The spirit of Dwarf Skull appeared to be broken.

"It wasn't always this way," Rhonna said as she puffed on a cigar. She was still escorted by two dwarven soldiers in black helms that led them up to one of the smaller peaks overlooking the city. She'd made it a point to use discretion in their travels. She didn't want anyone to know that the blood brothers were there. "My kin are more robust and jollier, on occasion. Fierce fighters when the time comes, always prepared to battle. They enjoy training. When we lost so many of my family, well—" She blew out a stream of smoke. "Their spirits were darkened."

"We'll find a way," Grey Cloak said.

"Yes, well, don't get cocky. You don't have the Figurine of Doodads to bail your elven fanny out anymore. You'll have to use the gifts you were given." She tapped her temple. "And your wit. You have that. Use it. No more shortcuts. The journey will be long, and there is no easy way out." She looked out over her people and shook her head. "Never thought I'd see the day."

With his hands on the iron railing, Dyphestive said, "Has anyone else tried to stop Black Frost?"

"Word of smaller rebellions reaches us from time to time. If they become problematic, Black Frost sends fire from the sky," she said.

"You mean dragons?"

"No small rebellion stands a chance against an army of dragons, which," Rhonna remarked, "is much larger than when you left. It's rumored that Black Frost's forces hold most of the dragon charms and have been enslaving more dragons for the last decade. Now that his army has full control of the skies, he appears invincible."

Grey Cloak's slender fingers drummed the railing as he spied the people down below. They were miserable and scared thanks to Black Frost keeping a thumb on them, and everything had happened because of his gaffe. "All I wanted was to live life on my own terms, and now no one can, all because of one fat-arse dragon."

Dyphestive chuckled.

Rhonna's grim expression brightened. "It sounds like you're ready. I'll give you all the supplies you need for the journey, but I can't come, as much as I wish I could. I have tens of thousands to look after, and we have to be ready for Black Frost to stick his talon in our eye." She blew a smoke ring. "He enjoys reminding us that he's in control from time to time and usually will cut off our water supply. If I could, I'd send some of my finest dwarves with you, but I feel it's best that you travel alone."

"Agreed."

"Where will you go?" she asked.

"I think it's best if I don't say what I have in mind."

She nodded.

"Also, it seems that others don't fare so well in our company," Grey Cloak said. "It seems the farther from us they stay, the better."

"No, you're being too hard on yourself." Rhonna gave him a tight hug around his waist. "As hardheaded as you are, you understand the most important matter."

"What's that?" he asked.

"Freedom and the price you have to pay for it."

HOURS LATER, Grey Cloak and Dyphestive were back out on the dusty trail, heading north with Dwarf Skull fading in the distance. It was the two of them and a pack mule in tow. "Rhonna really went all out for us, didn't she? An entire mule," Grey Cloak said, fanning his nose, "that smells like manure."

Dyphestive scratched the mule behind the ears. "I like him. And look at all this gear." The mule was gray with black-and-brown spots peppering his coat. He had a leather harness and a rope to tie him by and was loaded down with saddlebags, waterskins, and other traveling gear, such as blankets, sacks of dried fruit, meat, and bread. "I think this is the best equipped we've ever been to do anything. Tell me, where are we going? Shouldn't you have told Rhonna?"

"The less she knows, the better," Grey Cloak said. "People think we're ghosts, and we need to stay that way, so we'll have to be very careful, especially since you're as big as a horse. I don't think there's even a haystack big enough to hide you."

Dyphestive let out a jolly laugh. His voice was rich and robust. "I make a great target, but look." He tapped the breastplate on his chest. It had a dark, leathery veneer, but it was made of dwarven iron. "I have this."

"It looks heavy."

"No, not at all. And I don't know how she acquired it, but did you see my sword?" A sheathed two-handed sword was tied down to the pack mule. "It's the iron sword I acquired from the goblin chieftains. I thought I'd never see it again. She said she did some work on it. That's no surprise, seeing as she's a smith."

Grey Cloak's long strides stirred up the dust at his feet. "Well, you can't be hauling that around where we're going, so keep it packed up unless we need it."

"So, where are we going?" Dyphestive asked.

"Where this mess all began."

Dyphestive arched an eyebrow. "Dark Mountain?"

Grey Cloak shook his head. "No, Raven Cliff."

The big youth nodded. "Cliff."

"What?"

"Cliff," Dyphestive repeated. "That's what I'm naming the mule, Cliff." He scratched the mule behind the ears. "Hello, Cliff. How are you?"

Grey Cloak rolled his eyes.

42

It was midday, leagues south of the Iron Hills, and Grey Cloak stood on the edge of a riverbed. The river that once raced through the southern valleys had trickled down to little more than an ankle-deep stream. Dyphestive was bent over, filling the waterskins, while Grey Cloak looked out for enemies. He checked the skies. It had been days since he'd seen Streak, and he was worried.

Dyphestive slung the waterskins over his broad shoulders and loaded them back onto the mule, Cliff, who lapped up water from the river. "No sign of him, huh?" he asked.

"No," Grey Cloak said as he tapped his fingers on the pommel of his sword. "It's not like him either. Whatever help he went for must have been very far away."

"Can he find you?"

Grey Cloak shrugged. "We have a connection, and I think so, but I can't be sure. There's nothing but dead space up here. Nothing thrives, even with the water." He scanned the northern pathway of the river. It flowed straight into the distant Iron Hills. "It's no wonder Rhonna's people are so miserable. Did she say that Black Frost built dams to slow the flow?"

Dyphestive chucked a handful of dry branches into the water. "She did. They need a river flowing again, or they'll starve, won't they?"

"Only if they don't move, and I have a feeling the dwarves will starve before they move." He started north along the Twin Rivers path. "I think we should take a look."

Dyphestive towed Cliff along. "At the dam?"

"Exactly."

Dyphestive grinned. "You want to bust it open, don't you?"

Grey Cloak shrugged. "It's the least we can do for Rhonna after all she's been through. The trick is to do it so they don't blame the dwarves. It will have to look like an accident."

"It sounds dangerous."

Grey Cloak smirked. "I love danger. Don't you?"

Dyphestive gave a firm nod. "It's addictive."

THE BLOOD BROTHERS approached the dam just after nightfall and spied on it from a distance. It was a well-fortified structure made from logs and stone, built right against the backdrop of the jagged Iron Hills.

On the ground, on both sides of the river, were man-made canvas tents, enough to hold a score of troops. Soldiers in Black Guard armor—crimson tunics over chainmail—stood watch along the riverbeds while others ate by the evening bonfires.

The dam itself wasn't the most complex structure. The water followed caves that ran through the Iron Hills. Huge logs dammed up an opening from one side of the river to the other. The river itself was no more than fifty feet wide. The face of the dam was made up of logs stacked on top of logs, with small spaces in between that let the water flow through freely.

"You stay here with your friend Cliff. I'm going in for a closer look," Grey Cloak said.

Dyphestive nodded.

Grey Cloak took off into the shadows of the hills on the east side of the river, flanking the dam. The score of soldiers didn't appear to be a very strong force to guard a key strategical location. *There has to be more here than ordinary men. I could probably take them all out blindfolded—no, most likely—er, definitely.*

He navigated to the base of the hills only a hundred yards from the dam itself and began the climb. It was possible that the Black Guard was supremely confident that no one would challenge them, hence the smaller force, but it seemed unlikely.

Something else must be here.

Using the trees and rocks for cover, Grey Cloak crept toward the back side of the dam.

What do we have here?

Much like a castle, the wall behind the dam had a wooden walkway with another dozen soldiers positioned there. They were armed with crossbows and swords. Behind them, where the river spilled out of the hills, a pool of calm water gathered and swelled to the top of the cave mouth.

Grey Cloak sawed his finger over his chin. *Hmmm... how do I destroy the dam and make it look like an accident?*

He narrowed his eyes and inspected the crudely made structure. Though sound in design, the logs that made the dam's walls were bracketed in by more logs. If any of the logs on the edges gave way, the dam would collapse. The problem was the logs weighed tons, and moving them would be impossible.

He watched the soldiers behind the dam wall milling about. They were an assortment of men, orcs, and gnolls.

And how on earth do I distract so many witnesses?

As quiet as a deer, he slipped back to the hiding spot where Dyphestive and Cliff were waiting. He snuck up on Dyphestive and tapped him on the shoulder.

Dyphestive spun around and chopped a dagger over Grey Cloak's ducking head. "Don't spook me like that. I could have taken your head off."

"Not at that speed."

Dyphestive shook his head gently and sheathed his dagger. "I'm surprised you made it back without creating a commotion. What did you find?"

"There's another squad of soldiers behind the dam wall. Nothing else."

Giving Grey Cloak an eager look, Dyphestive said, "We can take them."

"I know, but we have to make it look like an accident. Like ghosts, we have to get in and out without being seen in case there are survivors."

"How do we do that?"

Grey Cloak's fingertips brightened with blue fire. "I have an idea."

43

WITH DYPHESTIVE ON THE LOOKOUT, GREY CLOAK HEADED BACK INTO THE IRON Hills behind the dam. He crept back to the position that he'd stopped before and crouched in the rocks.

This might be my worst idea ever, but I'll take my chances.

He ran his fingers along the outer seam of the Cloak of Legends. It had been a long time since he'd taken advantage of its powers. Back when he'd been on Gunder Island, Anya had battled Riskers in the sky. He'd fallen into Lake Flugen, but thanks to the cloak's powers, he'd swum underneath the waters and breathed like a fish.

I can only assume it still works. Regardless. Grey Cloak took a breath and held it. From his perch, he dove into the deep pool of dammed-up water blocking the entrance of the cave. His body slipped into the dark waters like a knife without making a splash.

Brrr... colder than I thought.

In a few moments, he made it to the bottom of the pool, where the logs were bracketed in. He looked up where the moonlight shimmered above the waters and waited. He expected to see torches, possibly someone investigating his entrance, but it appeared that no one had caught on to his invasion.

Perfect.

His lungs started to burn, and he let out his breath. Air bubbled up through the water, and he breathed. Not only that, but his vision cleared.

Cloak of Legends, you are amazing.

Life had been so hectic that he'd never had the time to experiment with the cloak's powers. It wrapped him up like a warm blanket. He could breathe underwater and swim like a fish. There were many pockets, and he was able to float to the ground like a leaf. He'd discovered all of those powers out of desperation or by accident.

Now I have to do what I have to do on my own.

He took another look up through the waters. He was at least twelve feet below the surface and underneath the catwalks where the Black Guard was stationed. He called forth his wizardry fire.

His hands ignited in blue flame. The waters began to bubble and simmer.

Yuri Gnomeknower had warned him about the dangers of using the wizard fire without an object. It could burn his hands to a crisp like hers. But by his own inspiration, he'd found that doing it underwater didn't burn at all.

Yes! My fingertips aren't burning to a crisp.

Summoning more mystic energy, he started to burn the underwater brackets at the weakest link.

It's working! Yes, it's working! I wish Yuri were still around to see this.

FROM HIS HIDING SPOT, Dyphestive felt invisible fingers crawling up his spine. Goose bumps popped up on his arms as he watched the pool of black water. He could see a murky blue-green glow deep beneath the surface. A surge of tiny bubbles rose.

Holy Horseshoes, how long can he hold his breath?

But out of the corner of his eye, he caught sight of something long slithering over the surface of the water. It dove deep.

Grey Cloak, look out!

GREY CLOAK SAWED deep into the wooden brackets. The first beam cracked and bowed.

Suddenly, the Cloak of Legends flexed around his body.

He turned and found himself face-to-face with a twenty-foot-long dragon snake. It was a hideous thing with the face of a dragon and fins on its head. Built like a snake, it still had four small legs for crawling. He'd seen dragon snakes in Dark Mountain before, crawling among the rocks.

Hello, hideous one. Grey Cloak blasted fire from his fingertips. It was too late.

The dragon snake rammed him into the brackets and knocked the breath out of him.

DYPHESTIVE RAN toward the pool of water with a full head of steam. He tried to be as quiet as he could, but the blood rushing behind his ears drowned out everything else.

The Black Guard spotted him and started pointing and shouting, "Intruder! Intruder!"

The crossbowmen took aim and fired the first volley just as Dyphestive dove.

A crossbow bolt lodged into the meat of his shoulder a split second before he splashed down and sank like a stone.

THE DRAGON SNAKE coiled its serpentine body around Grey Cloak like a python and started to squeeze.

He wormed his arms out of the watery coils of the dragon snake just in time and drove his burning thumbs into its eyes. With a monstrous spasm, the dragon snake's body flexed, loosened, and tightened again.

Zooks! It's squeezing me to death!

Grey Cloak poured out all the firepower he had left, but his burning hands were extinguished. His ribs started to snap.

Ugh! I don't want to die in a watery grave.

The dragon snake lifted him above the water, where he saw the Black Guard pointing and looking at him. They were all packed on the dam's walkway. *Perfect.* He gave them a wink and wave of his fingers.

The monster plunged him back underneath the water and dragged him to the muddy bottom, where it held him fast. It applied more pressure. Another rib popped. Grey Cloak's vision started to dim, and even with the cloak, he couldn't breathe.

Out of nowhere, a black hulk appeared and locked the dragon snake's head in tree-trunk arms.

Dyphestive!

The brawny youth jammed a dagger deep into the monster's gills. It flexed and released Grey Cloak. Dyphestive held on for his life with one arm locked around the dragon serpent's neck and the other stabbing away.

The bleeding serpent thrashed underneath the waters, slipped free of Dyphestive's grasp, and disappeared into the cave. Dyphestive swam upward and burst through the water's surface.

Grey Cloak swam after his brother with his cracked ribs burning like fire. He popped up out of the water. The first thing he saw was the arrow sticking out of his brother's shoulder. "You're wounded."

"I've had worse." A crossbow bolt sang by Dyphestive's nose and sank into the waters. "Not that I'm inviting any more."

The Black Guard shouted at them with torches in hand and crossbows firing. "Surrender! Surrender!" they shouted.

"Can you hold your breath long?" Grey Cloak asked.

"Longer than you."

"Follow me under. We're going to need your muscle to finish this, and don't forget to use your legs." Grey Cloak dove. With Dyphestive on his tail, he led them to the brackets that held the dam in place. He managed enough fire in his hands to create soft light in the depths.

Dyphestive looked right at him with his cheeks puffed out. Grey Cloak showed him the scarring on the wooden beams he'd blasted into with his hands.

Dyphestive nodded. He grabbed the bracket, set his feet on the base, and heaved.

Grey Cloak gave his brother a thumbs-up the moment he heard the beams pop. He swam back to the surface, waded in the pool, and faced the Black Guard.

"I surrender. I surrender!" he said.

A Black Guard carrying a torch said, "Get out of there, elf!"

One thing was for certain. There was no way they would come to get him, not loaded down with all their heavy armor. Grey Cloak smirked as he counted bodies. Over thirty soldiers were on the dam's platform, and he had no doubt that was all of them. He lifted his hands and waved. "I'm coming." He swam for the bank.

A loud pop exploded beneath the surface. The dam's platform buckled, and the eastern bracket collapsed. From the bottom up, the dam gave way. The platform fell into the rushing waters with all of the soldiers on it. Each and every one of them sank like an anchor and disappeared underneath the waves.

Grey Cloak made it to the bank before the waters swept him away. He wasn't alone either. Dyphestive was crawling for his life up the rocks with the waters rushing over his ankles. They were both puffing for breath as they reunited and watched the waters take the dam's logs and drowning soldiers to a watery grave.

Dyphestive sat on the rocks and pulled the bolt free of his shoulder. "Great plan."

"I couldn't have done it without you." Grey Cloak smiled, clasped his brother's hands, and helped him to his feet. "It was the least we could do for Rhonna. And she shouldn't get blamed. It looks like the perfect accident."

"Like I said, great plan."

The dragon snake's head burst out of the waters and rose above the blood brothers. It came at them.

Dyphestive had his back to the monster as he looked into his brother's eyes. He reached into Grey Cloak's cloak, snatched his sword from its scabbard, and turned his hips in a violent backswing. The blade cut the dragon serpent's head clean off. It flew upward, came down, bounced off the rocks, and was taken with the waters.

Without giving the monster a glance, Dyphestive slid Grey Cloak's sword back into its sheath and said, "Thanks."

Grey Cloak tossed back his head and erupted with jubilant laughter.

44

IRON HILLS

THAT SAME NIGHT, THE BLOOD BROTHERS NAVIGATED THROUGH THE ROCKY woodland of the Iron Hills and made a small campfire. It was a cloudy pitch-black night shaded with great pines whose branches whistled and bent in the wind.

Grey Cloak warmed his hands over the little fire's flickering flames. "How is the shoulder?"

Rolling his wounded shoulder without so much as a grimace, Dyphestive replied, "Not bad. How are your ribs?"

"Could be better." Grey Cloak quickly learned that if he breathed too deeply, it felt like someone was stabbing his chest with a knife. Meanwhile, he chewed on a dried hunk of meat the size of his hand. "You know what I think?"

Dyphestive swallowed a hunk of meat whole. "What?"

"I think we're getting pretty good at being heroes. That's what I think. You took that dragon snake's head off without even seeing it. Impressive."

Dyphestive grinned. "I did, didn't I?"

Grey Cloak nodded. "It was impressive, the work of heroes."

"It sounds to me like you've had a change of heart. What about fortune and glory?"

Grey Cloak lay back on the ground. "As long as I have enough to live on when I'm old, I'll survive. Perhaps we can live like Crane and join the Brother-hood of Whispers. They appear to have it good."

"At the rate we are going, we might not make it to a respectable age."

Grey Cloak propped himself up on one elbow. "Whatever do you mean? Look at us. Ten years have passed, and we haven't aged a day. We look great. Well, at least I do."

Dyphestive stuck his big chin out and nodded. "Grey, I honestly feel like we can do anything. Is that awful?"

Grey Cloak flipped his hand out and said, "I think that comes with being a natural. And remember we aren't the only ones that feel this way. There are others."

"So, you feel the same way too?"

"I've always felt... invincible." Grey Cloak picked up a small branch and flicked it into the fire. "Even when I was young. That's why I hated Dark Mountain so much. At least, that's one reason. I never felt the others, like Dirklen and Magnolia, were any better than me."

"They're ten years older now. Won't they be stronger?"

"I suppose, but we're stronger too. Ten years or no. We can take those pampered worm riders any day."

Dyphestive cracked his neck side to side and managed a smile, but it vanished when he said, "Do you believe Anya's dead?"

"She's too stubborn. I'll believe it when I see it. Listen, brother, we're going to find a way to make it all right."

"I thought we could use the time mural again and go back," Dyphestive remarked. "That would fix everything."

"I've thought the same thing, but it would take a miracle to get near a time mural again. Not to mention, no one has any control over it." Grey Cloak lay flat on his back and stared up at the branches. He'd already thought about using the time mural, but he couldn't see how he could use something that he wouldn't be able to control. "We'll find answers in Raven Cliff. With any luck, Tanlin is still around." He rolled over on one side. "Get some rest, brother. I have a feeling we're going to need it."

"Agreed."

45

THE BLOOD BROTHERS NEARED THE TOP OF THE IRON HILLS, TRAVERSING THE ROCKS and ridges with little problem. The bright sun shone through the leaves while the varmints and birds hustled through the branches.

Dyphestive towed Cliff behind him. The mule's passage had been steady until then. From the higher ground, Grey Cloak looked back and saw Cliff stopped on the trail.

Dyphestive was pulling the pack beast's harness and saying, "Come, Cliff. Come."

"What's the matter?" Grey Cloak asked as he made his way down the hill.

"He won't move," Dyphestive said.

"Well, make him."

Dyphestive looked at Grey Cloak like he was stupid and handed him the rope. "You make him."

"Fine, I'll show you how it's done." He pulled on the mule's rope. "Time to go, mule." His boots slid over the ground as he pulled, but Cliff wouldn't budge. The only things that moved on the mule were his ears and his tail, which flapped at the flies. "This is ridiculous. What did you do to him?"

"Nothing. He stopped." Dyphestive scratched Cliff behind the ears. "Maybe he's tired."

"He's a mule. They don't get tired, at least not after this short of a trip. Pinch him or something."

"I'm not going to pinch him."

"Well, you have to do something. We're almost to the top. It's all—"

"It's all what?" Dyphestive asked.

Grey Cloak lifted his hand to signal for silence. He'd caught a glimpse of yellow eyes in the bushes. It was a goblin. He knew it the instant he saw him. "We're being followed," he said under his breath. "Goblins. I can hear one running through the woodland now. We need to go, Dyphestive. We need to hurry."

A wild cry came up from the hollows of the woodland. It was the savage call of the goblins and their hounds.

"Come on, Cliff. Come on!" Dyphestive pleaded as he pulled on the harness.

Cliff pulled his neck back and brayed.

"Leave him," Grey Cloak said as he started up the hill. "We can outrun them, but we have to go now!"

"I'm not leaving him," Dyphestive said.

"Are you out of your skull? You'll get us both killed over a worthless mule. Don't you remember the last time we crossed the goblins in these hills? They would have killed all of us if not for the figurine, and I don't have that now."

"I don't care," Dyphestive said. "I'm not leaving Cliff behind."

Grey Cloak's eyes grew to the size of saucers. He couldn't believe his eyes. Dyphestive stooped underneath Cliff the mule, and setting his jaw, he lifted the beast onto his shoulders.

"What in the wild, wild woodland are you doing?"

Dyphestive started up the hill with hundreds of pounds of living mule flesh on his shoulders. "Wherever I go, Cliff goes too."

Grey Cloak smirked. "You're crazy."

Up the hill they went at a brisk pace, as fast as Dyphestive's long strides would take him. The mule, loaded down with gear, didn't slow him at all. His sure feet plowed through the low-hanging branches and prickly brush.

"So much for moving with discretion," Grey Cloak said. He could hear the goblin horde coming.

Their shrill voices demanded the blood of the enemy that invaded their forest. Their hungry hounds sped forward, barking and howling wildly.

"Move faster!"

To his surprise, they made it to the bald knob at the top of the hill and raced over the long stretch of grass to the other side.

We might make it. I can't believe we might make it.

He sped out ahead of Dyphestive and came to an abrupt stop at the rim of the hill. Another force of goblins, scores of them, raced up the other side. He pointed east. "That way! That way!"

They made it another twenty yards and stopped.

Zooks!

The goblin horde had hemmed them in from all directions.

46

THE GOBLIN HORDE CONSISTED OF A BUNCH OF DIRTY LITTLE MEN—RANK WITH filthy, greasy, matted hair, covered in furs and skins—who carried crude weapons. Their bright-yellow eyes were hooded by their knitted brows, and their tattooed and pierced faces were visages of evil.

They held their wild dogs by collars and chains, and the slavering beasts barked and howled.

Dyphestive lowered Cliff to the ground while Grey Cloak drew his swords from their sheaths. They stood back-to-back beside the mule, listening to the goblins' wild howling.

A loud voice rose above the noise. "Silence!"

The goblins fell silent, and a knot of the grungy little men parted and took a knee.

A huge goblin that towered over the others approached from the other side of the hill from where Grey Cloak and Dyphestive had come. It was the goblin chieftain, similar to the one they'd met before but bigger. His shock of hair was shaved on both sides, and iron hoop earrings hung in a chain from his ears. His nose was broad and flat. Coarse black hairs covered his oily body. He was deep chested and had a barrel of a belly. Muscles bulged beneath a healthy layer of fat. On his shoulder, he carried a wooden club with metal spikes driven through the head.

"He looks reasonable," Grey Cloak said. "Let me do the talking." He cleared his throat. "Ahem. Mighty chieftain, we desire safe and peaceful passage through the Iron Hills and would be very grateful if you granted it."

The goblin chieftain's nostrils widened, and his chest heaved as he locked his eyes on Dyphestive and his sword. "You!" he bellowed. "Where did you get that sword?"

Dyphestive glanced at Grey Cloak and whispered, "Should I answer that? Because I don't think he's going to like the answer."

Grey Cloak shook his head and turned his attention to the hulking goblin chieftain. He was very much the same as the goblin that Venir the Darkslayer had slain years ago. Scores of goblins had died that day. Perhaps it was the right time to remind them of it. "Over ten years ago, I traveled with a group that had a run-in with two goblin chieftains. They carried tremendous clubs, similar to what you carry. As a matter of fact, I believe that club is the very same."

The goblin chieftain dropped his club from his shoulder with an uneasy look. He sneered at Grey Cloak. "One of those chieftains was my father." He twirled the massive club over his wrists with ease. "I saw the carnage. I smelled the blood. I kneeled over my father's corpse and vowed vengeance—if I ever found the man, or elf, who did that to my people, I would kill him." He pointed his club at Grey Cloak. "And now, you admit this crime to me." He lifted his club high overhead. "I am Jubax! I call for blood! I call for vengeance! By the word of Jubax, goblin chieftain, king of the Iron Hills, I will have it! We will have it!"

The goblins erupted in wild howls.

Grey Cloak backed toward his brother.

Raising his voice above the crowd, Dyphestive said, "Maybe you shouldn't have told them that we killed his father."

"You think? I was trying to intimidate him." He rummaged through his pockets.

"What is the opposite of intimidate?" Dyphestive snapped his fingers. "Incite! Are you sure that wasn't what you were trying to do?"

"Gum up!" Grey Cloak pulled out one of the carvings he'd made of the Figurine of Heroes from one of the Cloak of Legends's many pockets. He placed it on the ground for all the goblins to see and lifted his hands like a great wizard.

Jubax and the goblins dropped their eyes to the face of the figurine and fell silent.

Grey Cloak shouted, "I warn you! By the power of my figurine, all of your filthy brethren were destroyed. I will use it again, and even more of you will perish." He pointed at them one by one. "You! You! You! And you!"

The goblins stepped back and cowered.

"What will it be, Jubax?" Grey Cloak asked. "Will you take another treacherous step and eradicate the goblins from these hills forever, or will you be wise and back away?"

Jubax's chest heaved, and his nostrils flared as his forehead wrinkled in many layers. His gaze switched between Grey Cloak, the iron sword, and the figurine. "I gave my word as a son, now as a king. I won't break it whether you summon your witchcraft or not." He glowered at Grey Cloak and lifted his club. "Prepare to die!"

As the goblins moved in, Grey Cloak snatched up the false figurine, charged it with wizardry, and hurled it at Jubax.

Jubax swung his club at the figurine and hit it squarely. The figurine blew up, and it knocked Jubax backward as he stumbled and fell over his feet.

Grey Cloak joined his brother. "That could've gone better."

"Two bad bluffs. Do you care to go for three?" Dyphestive asked as he tightened his grip on his sword and swung at the nearest goblin. The blade sliced the fiendish man in half.

"I had to try, and you didn't have any ideas at all that I can recall." Grey Cloak's two quick sword strokes felled two more goblins.

"You didn't give me a chance." Dyphestive stepped forward and lanced two goblins with his sword. He pushed their bodies free with his boot. "But I didn't have any better ideas. I thought yours were really good."

Jubax climbed back to his feet, and with a murderous look in his eye, his shouted, "I want their skulls! Kill them!"

Launching powerful, arcing swings, Dyphestive hewed ranks of goblins down in threes and fours.

Grey Cloak charged his swords with wizard fire, turning the steel into bright-blue flames. Dancing, dodging, and striking, he pierced the goblin enemy, one heart after the next.

The wild foes piled up, but they kept on coming, spurred on by their chieftain, Jubax.

"Kill them! Kill them!"

"There's only one way to do this," Dyphestive said as he skewered a goblin and flung it off his sword. "Go after Jubax!"

"Agreed," Grey Cloak said as his blade bit deep into the neck of a goblin. He stabbed another in the heart with his short sword. "But there are waves of them." Grey Cloak made as quick work of the goblins as he could, but more and more of them rose up over the hills. It took every ounce of skill and strength he could muster to fend off the filthy minions. "There're too many! Any ideas?"

Dyphestive replied as he busted a goblin's teeth with his fist, "Do you remember what Venir the Darkslayer said?"

"No!"

A goblin jumped on Dyphestive's back and tried to crack his head open with a leg bone. Dyphestive grinned as he dropped his sword and flung the goblin into the horde. "Fight or die!"

47

THE GOBLIN FORCES POURED OVER THE BLOOD BROTHERS LIKE A WAVE OF ANGRY ants. They didn't have skill, but they had numbers.

Slice! Pop! Glitch! Stab! Chop! Thunk! Slice!

The unfettered horde chased after Grey Cloak as he slid to freedom and brought quick death, time after time. His sore ribs burned like fire, and his arms became heavy. The glow in his swords dimmed, and he fought on, brawn against brawn.

A pack of goblin war dogs knifed through the surge and pounced. Their bodies crashed into Grey Cloak's. He slipped and went down.

Zooks!

A dog bit down on his arm. Another tore and yanked at his cloak with slavering teeth. He kicked one dog in the jaw.

"Get off me!" He let go of his swords and switched to his daggers. A war dog yelped when he cut into its ribs.

The goblins came, reckless and wild-eyed, to pile on.

A blaring dragon roar exploded in the sky that put a halt to everything.

"ROOOOOOOOAAAAAAAARRR!"

The cowering goblins dared a skyward look.

Fire from the sky came down with a mighty wrath. Dragon fire burned their dark, oily bodies to crisps. Burnt hair and scorched animal skins brought the sweet aroma of death. Goblins burned, dropped, and rolled.

Grey Cloak pushed out of the pile of panic-stricken fiends. "Streak!"

The runt dragon landed on the ground, spitting a geyser of flames. He wasn't alone.

"Eeeee-yaaaaaah!" an army of quarry gnomes screamed. They poured out of the woodland with hammers and picks in hand. The stocky miners—with pointed beards, leather aprons, and metal caps—blasted into the shocked goblins' ranks.

JUBAX SHOOK WITH RAGE. "No! No!" He brained a gnome with his club and turned his wrath loose on another.

Smash!

The quarry gnome, shorter than a goblin but stouter, was pulverized.

The goblin chieftain dropped his club and slipped a pair of iron knuckles over his fingers. He pointed at Dyphestive. "I'll have my family's sword back."

Dyphestive stabbed the sword into the ground. "Come and take it!"

Jubax strolled across the battlefield. Towering over Dyphestive, he said, "You killed my father. You killed my uncles." Jubax slammed his huge fists together with a *clang*.

"I didn't kill any of them, but on behalf of the warrior who did—" Dyphestive balled up his fists. "Let's dan—"

Jubax punched him in the jaw so hard it spun him around.

Dyphestive's knees wobbled, and he fell to a knee, his ears ringing. He rubbed his jaw and spit blood. "Let's try this again."

The goblin chieftain rained down hammering blows, his big fists colliding with Dyphestive's body. He pounded the big youth down like a hammer driving a spike. "You will die! You will die!"

Dyphestive absorbed all the punishment he could take. He turned into Jubax's body and socked him in the ribs. The crack of bone followed, and Jubax fell backward like a tree. The goblin was dead.

Dyphestive looked at his fist and muttered, "I only hit him once."

"Don't flatter yourself." Grey Cloak wiped his bloody sword off on Jubax's body.

"You killed him?"

"A quick jab to the pumper. We don't have time for you to dance with the goblins." Grey Cloak sheathed his sword. "So of course I killed him. We have things to do."

Dyphestive shook his head in disbelief. He wanted to fight, but the fight was over. With the death of Jubax and the arrival of the quarry gnomes, the remainder of the goblin force scattered like rats. He caught sight of a quarry gnome saluting him with a hammer. He was the last of the living that vanished into the woodland.

As quickly as the battle had started, it ended, leaving a field of food for the crows, some still roasting.

GREY CLOAK FOUND Streak perched on Cliff's back, licking the mule's ears. How the mule had survived, he didn't know, but he was elated to see his dragon again.

"Streak! You couldn't have shown up at a better time!" He hugged the thickly built dragon and started to pet him. "Where have you been?"

"Getting help, like Dyphestive told me to," Streak replied in the sly but polished manner of a well-spoken child. "Good help is hard to come by these days."

"You can say that again," Grey Cloak said. His heart was still racing, and he caught his breath. He noticed Dyphestive looking at Streak with wide eyes. "What?"

Approaching the dragon and mule, Dyphestive fingered his ear. "Did Streak speak?"

Grey Cloak stiffened. He and Streak had a connection that allowed them to communicate, but it wasn't vocal speech, rather more like a sense of understanding. "You heard that?" he asked Dyphestive.

"My ears are ringing so loud, I'm not sure."

"Streak," Grey Cloak asked the dragon, "did you speak?"

Streak's pink tongue probed the mule's ears. He licked his nose and Grey Cloak's cheek. "Who is this fellow?" he asked, eyeing the mule. "I don't recall him being a part of the group. I bet he's tasty."

Wide-eyed, Grey Cloak snatched Streak off the saddle and held him at arm's length. "Streak, you can talk?"

As stiff as a board, Streak eyed Grey Cloak. "Of course I can. Which is more than I can say of this mule." He nodded. "How have you been?"

Grey Cloak nodded excitedly. "Better."

"I'm glad to see that you are well. I was worried about you, and I went for help"—he turned his thick lizard neck in Dyphestive's direction—"as your brother insisted. On my journey, I had a delay."

"What sort of delay?" Dyphestive asked.

"A deep slumber overcame me. I can't really explain it, but I think it had something to do with that silver fish that I ate. I'll tell you, I've felt fabulous since I consumed it." He exchanged glances with both men. "You remember the silver fish, don't you?"

"The one in the Wizard Watch fountain?" Dyphestive asked.

"The very one. I got him." Streak smiled, revealing a mouthful of sharp teeth. "Needless to say, the rest did me some good, and I immediately tracked you down. That's when I discovered the quarry gnomes and found my tongue. You should have seen their faces when I spoke to them. They fell down and worshipped me. Literally, but I bade them to follow orders and attack the goblins who were on your trail. Hence here we are."

Grey Cloak and Dyphestive exchanged uncertain looks.

That was when Grey Cloak noticed a few details about Streak that he'd overlooked. Small horns had popped up on the dragon's face, and the ridges on his back had hardened, not to mention he was noticeably bigger. He pet his dragon with a happy look on his face. "So now I have a talking, and flying, fire-breathing dragon. What more could an elf ask for?"

"Stick around," Streak said. "I'm full of surprises."

48

RAVEN CLIFF

IT WAS POURING RAIN BY EARLY EVENING WHEN THEY ENTERED THE CITY OF RAVEN Cliff. The cobblestone streets ran with water. Citizens dashed from porch to porch, seeking cover, while others trudged along the streets, submitting to the pounding rain.

Water flowed down from the steeply slanted roofs of the buildings and made huge puddles. Refuse floated underneath the porches and flooded into the grates in the alleys.

A group of children chased a boat made from a block of wood down the road, their bare feet splashing in the water. The boat came to a stop at a soldier's feet, where the water pooled around his boots. He was a Black Guard in full gear. He bent over, picked up the boat, and chucked it down the road.

The children scattered.

Grey Cloak and Dyphestive avoided eye contact with the harsh-looking soldier and moved along.

"Zooks, there are Black Guards everywhere. What happened to this place?" Grey Cloak asked.

"Ten years of Black Frost, I suppose," Dyphestive commented.

Grey Cloak had liked Raven Cliff the first time he'd come there. It had been a thriving city, bustling with excitement and adventure. The people had been forthcoming and amiable, and there had been plenty to do and see. It was where he'd chased Zora down and become a member of Talon. It was also the place where Dalsay, Adanadel, and Browning had died. It was where he'd lost his brother to the Doom Riders too. It appeared that the dark times had become darker.

A dragon shrieked above the streets.

The citizens cowered.

A middling dragon perched on one of the rooftops. It launched into the sky and shrieked again.

"Zooks, where there are dragons, there are bound to be Riskers," Grey said as he pushed Streak's head down into the bundles Cliff carried. "Keep low. We can't let anyone see you."

Streak flicked his tongue out and sniffed. "Something smells good."

"Agreed," Dyphestive said as he patted his stomach. "They have great meals here, and I'm tired of dried meat. I want something fresh, plates of butter-baked bread, strips of bacon, turkey legs, potatoes."

Grey Cloak hungered himself. "Let's find a place to stay. Come on. I remember a few places that should be suitable."

He found a run-down tavern on the edge of town and stabled Cliff. "What do you want to do, Streak? You might be too big to go unnoticed now."

"I'll keep Cliff company. Besides, I saw some juicy barn cats prowling about. I think I'll venture out and meet them," Streak said.

"Low profile," Grey Cloak warned.

Streak flicked his tongue out.

The inside of the rickety tavern had more chairs than customers. Water ran down the chimney stack, but a fire was burning. The blood brothers took a table in the corner with full view of the front door.

A robust waitress approached. She had tired eyes and messy hair, and her apron was marred with food stains. "What can I do for you?"

"We need a room, two beds, a growler of ale, hot bread, a bowl of that stew I smell, and a plateful of your finest meat," Dyphestive said.

The waitress looked him up and down. "You'll need a big bed. I'll make it happen. I fix the food, and it might even come with an extra side of me." She walked away with her hips swaying.

"Try not to fall in love," Grey Cloak said. "We still have to locate your wife, Leena."

"She's not my wife." Dyphestive showed a weary look. "Do we have to find her? I hate to think of what she'll do to me after disappearing for ten years. Maybe she forgot and moved on."

"Maybe she's dead."

"Don't say that." Dyphestive dried his damp face with a cloth napkin. "When are we going to see Tanlin?"

"*We* aren't going to see Tanlin."

Dyphestive gave him a puzzled look. "What do you mean? That's why we're here, aren't we?"

"I'm going to find Tanlin by myself. We can't barge into his store and catch up on old times. First, we need to see if he's there, and second, there might be spies keeping an eye on him, and I'm not going to take any chances."

"But you always take chances."

"You know what I mean." The waitress returned with a growler of ale and moved back to the kitchen. "I'll exercise more caution this time. At this point, we can't trust anyone, Tanlin included."

49

The first thing Grey Cloak picked up on outside of Tanlin's Fine Fittings and Embroidery was the numerous Black Guard in the area. They were thickly gathered in one of the most active merchant streets in the entire city and staring at struggling citizens with hawkish looks.

It was morning, one of the busiest times of the day, and the hard rains had leveled down to a steady drizzle. Across the street, Grey Cloak peered out from an alley where he squatted down by a rain barrel, covered in his cloak.

Rain steadily dripped from the porch over Tanlin's store, splashing into the potholes in the deteriorating roads. The doors to Tanlin's store were closed, but fine clothing on mannequins was on full display in front of the windows.

Squeezed in between an eatery and a shoe shop, Tanlin's store drew a constant flow of passersby. A woman in a big hat decorated with flowers stood outside Tanlin's door, tapping her foot and peeking in the window.

Where is he? He should be open by now. He always opened early before. I bet he's in the back working. Maybe I should check.

Finally, the front door opened inward, and Tanlin came into full view. He'd changed little. He was clean-shaven, with soft brown sculpted hair. He wore a pressed white button-down shirt, black slacks, and a purple scarf around his neck. Tanlin greeted the woman with a warm smile and stepped aside.

That was when Grey Cloak noticed the limp in Tanlin's stride and the cane the man carried in hand. Tanlin's face grimaced when he walked.

What happened to him?

Grey Cloak kept his eyes glued to Tanlin's store for the next few hours. Customers came and went, and he was careful to move from his spot and walk the streets with the crowd from time to time. The only person that stayed in the store with Tanlin was a pudgy woman who wore a knit cap on her head. Other than that, little changed.

Grey Cloak couldn't fight the feeling that something was amiss. The Black Guard hovered near Tanlin's store and kept a watchful eye through the window. They even sauntered in from time to time. One of the soldiers knocked a pile of shirts onto the floor and stepped on it.

The portly woman was quick to pick it up after the Black Guard left. Grey Cloak could see her bickering with Tanlin now and again.

Hmm, maybe he remarried.

Dusk came, and soon after, the doors to Tanlin's Fine Fittings and Embroidery closed.

Grey Cloak stole his way around to the alley behind the store, but something was still eating at him that he couldn't put his finger on. Rather than steal down the dark alley, he opted to climb to the rooftops instead. He glided over the slanted roofs and waited across the street.

Tanlin exited and locked the door behind him. His assistant was with him, her arm hooked in his, as he hobbled down the alley, cane clacking on the ground.

Grey Cloak was just about to follow when something flew out from underneath the building's eaves. His blood froze. *A yonder!*

The strange eyeball creature hovered in the air on bat wings for a moment then sailed silently after Tanlin.

Zooks, they're watching him! Why?

He followed Tanlin all the way to a small apartment complex only a few blocks from the store. Tanlin entered on the first level of the three-story building and vanished. The yonder floated outside then flew upward, stopping level with the top apartments. It attached itself to the building wall across the street and turned to stone.

He-he-he. I might not know what's going on, but I know exactly where Tanlin lives. Now, for some patience. Well played, Grey Cloak, well played.

GREY CLOAK CHECKED in with Dyphestive and Streak and headed back to Tanlin's apartment the next day. He entered the apartment building, took the stairwell to the third floor, and put an ear to Tanlin's door.

All is quiet. Just the way I like it.

Scanning both sides of the hallway, he removed his thief's tools—two metal picks—and started picking the lock. He raked the small tumblers with one pick while applying pressure to the locking mechanism with the other.

I should have known it wouldn't be your standard lock.

One of the apartment doors down the hall opened.

Grey Cloak stopped picking the lock and casually acted like he was looking for a certain door. A fluffy white cat slunk out of the other apartment, and the door closed behind it.

Ah, close call.

He squatted down and said, "Here, kitty, kitty."

The cat with bright-green eyes sauntered over and rubbed up against his leg. It started to purr.

He picked up the cat. "You don't want to come home with me. My little dragon will make a meal of you." He set the cat down. "Now, hurry along before I change my mind."

The white cat scampered away and vanished down the stairwell.

Checking both ends of the hall, Grey Cloak resumed his lock picking. A few moments passed, and the latch popped. "There we go." He opened the door a crack, listened, and entered. When he closed the door behind him, he noticed a small dove feather lying on the floor. "Clever."

The feather was an old trick Tanlin had taught him. The feather was placed at the top of the door, inside the seam, after the door was locked. If someone entered, the feather would fall unnoticed, but Tanlin would know if someone was inside before he went in because the feather would no longer show in the door's seam where he'd placed it.

Grey Cloak put the feather back in place and made his way around the quaint and well-furnished apartment. Velvety burgundy curtains were drawn in front of the bay window. A single bedroom held twin beds, neatly made with blankets folded on the end. A comfortable sofa as well as tables and chairs for dining occupied the living room. The kitchen had cupboards mounted on the wall and a wardrobe that was too big for the small bedroom.

He put his hand over the coal-burning stove and felt the warmth rising from the metal plates. A half-filled canister of tea sat next to the stove with small china cups beside it.

I bet if I thoroughly searched this place, I'd find a heap of treasure. He eyed the nooks and crannies but thought better of it and moved to the curtains. Through the slit in the middle of the curtains, he could see the building across the street where the yonder had nestled the night before. It was gone. *A good thing.*

Grey Cloak stared out the window, waiting for nightfall.

Hours later, the same as the night before, Tanlin and his companion ambled down the back alleys. A yonder appeared and nestled under the building's eaves across the street. He tucked himself into the kitchen, out of sight from the exit.

A key fumbled at the lock. The latch popped, and the door swung open.

Grey Cloak peeked around the corner.

Tanlin entered, cane in hand, with a shorter woman filing in behind him. He closed the door, bent over, and picked up the feather. The woman hung their cloaks inside a small open closet beside the door. She took his cane and hung it by the handle on a peg. Together, they wandered inside. They froze the moment Grey Cloak slipped in front of them with his dagger blades on their throats.

"Shhhh," he said as he watched their eyes widen. "Shhhh... Zora?"

50

EPILOGUE

THERE WAS NO MISTAKING ZORA'S BEAUTIFUL EYES. HER CHEEKS WERE BIG AND HER face as round as a pie, but it was her, curves and all. Her petite build was gone, replaced with a fuller figure.

Grey Cloak wasn't the only one gawping. Tanlin and Zora looked at him with stupefied expressions, as if seeing a ghost. Their jaws hung open, and their eyes were wide with amazement. They appeared weary too. Tanlin's distinguished features had begun to sag, and he carried a fatigue about him. Zora, still beautiful, didn't have the same energetic luster in her eyes that she used to.

The tired-eyed Tanlin broke the silence, glanced at the blade on his throat, and said, "If you'll please, Grey Cloak."

"Oh, zooks, sorry." Grey Cloak tucked his weapons away. "I was being cautious."

"You broke into my place. Well done," Tanlin said with a thin smile.

"I learned from the—*oof*!"

Zora tackled him onto the sofa and peppered his face with kisses. She hugged and squeezed him tight. "I thought you were dead!"

"I'm not," he said quietly, "but keep your voice down. We're being watched."

Tanlin limped over to the curtains and peeked outside. "I know, a yonder. Bloody thing watches us like a hawk." He looked at Grey Cloak. "Are you sure it didn't see you?"

"Positive."

Zora still straddled him and kept him pinned down when he tried to stand.

He poked her chubby cheek. "What happened?"

She frowned. "My human side has gotten the better of me the last decade. Needless to say, I've found my only pleasure in eating since you've been gone."

"Are you saying I made you fat?" Grey Cloak asked.

"Yes." She grinned.

"Zora, stop playing games," Tanlin said as he ambled into the kitchen. "Let me put on some tea while we get caught up on past and present matters."

"Why are they watching you?" Grey Cloak asked as his hands settled on Zora's waist.

"They're watching for you and your brother," Tanlin said as he prepared the tea. "Is he alive?"

"He's fine. Hiding at the moment, at least I hope he is. Why are they looking for us? We've been gone a decade."

Tanlin spun a kitchen chair backward and sat down. He tapped his nose. "I'm still tapped into the Brotherhood of Whispers. As we understand it, you're still perceived as a threat. They want the Figurine of Heroes. It's those invaders, Catten and Verbard, who desire it. Tell us, what happened in Wizard Watch over a decade ago?"

"Well, it hasn't been so long for me. Not even a couple of weeks. But this is what happened." Grey Cloak told them every detail, from the battle inside the Wizard Watch to his meeting with Rhonna at Dwarf Skull. With a long face, he said, "I never would have imagined that I could make matters ten times worse than they were."

Zora climbed off him as he finished, but she still held his hand. "It's not all your fault. I mean, most of it is, but not all of it."

"Thanks, Zora. That makes me feel better."

The teapot whistled, and Tanlin hustled over to the stove.

Grey Cloak could see pain in the old man's tired eyes. "What happened to your leg?"

Tanlin prepared the cup and saucers of fine china. "A warning from Black Frost and his minions. The only reason Zora and I are still alive is because we've agreed to spy for them. Otherwise, we'd be imprisoned, the same as the rest of them." He handed Grey Cloak a cup of tea. "I should inform them that you're here, but I won't. We won't, of course." He sat back down.

Grey Cloak's back straightened. "Are you telling me that you work for Black Frost?"

"We serve the Brotherhood of Whispers, not Black Frost. Black Frost thinks we serve him, but we don't." Tanlin sipped his tea. "I have an arrangement that keeps us safe. It's with Baron Dorenzo, the ruler of Raven Cliff in name only. He's merely a puppet of the Black Guard now, but I check in with him for information. It keeps the Riskers off our backs."

"Riskers?"

Zora nodded. "Riskers and their dragons occupy every major city. They maintain the order throughout Gapoli. Grey Cloak, your arrival gives me hope, but I don't know if there's much that can be done. Black Frost's army has been growing for ten years. They've overtaken everything. The world is overrun with evil."

"Rhonna was right on most accounts of what she shared with you," Tanlin continued. "Black Frost controls most of the countryside. The underlings have overrun the Wizard Watch. There are more dragons in the sky than ever before. Each and every one of them is a Risker. There are no Sky Riders, no quests to acquire dragon charms. Talon and like groups that served the Wizard Watch have been completely abandoned. Black Frost owns all and rules all."

Grey Cloak's jaw clenched. "He might own the rest of the world, but he doesn't own us. Now tell me, what happened to the rest of Talon?"

Zora's expression turned bleak. "It's a long story."

"We have all night, and I'm not going anywhere."

"Some are imprisoned, and others disappeared," Tanlin added.

"We're going to find them. We're going to free them." Grey Cloak tapped his index finger on his temple. "Because I have a grand idea."

Did any other members of Talon survive the last ten years?

How will Grey Cloak and Dyphestive defeat the underling threat?

Can the heroes trust Tanlin and Zora, or do they serve a darker master?

Grab your copy of *Dragon Wars: Prisoner Island – Book 9*, On Sale Now! Click here! See pic below.

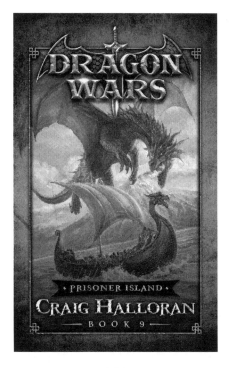

DON'T FORGET to leave a review for Wizard Watch: Dragon Wars - Book 8. They are a huge help! LINK!

THE FIGURINE OF HEROES: The silver fish is a magical creature that first appeared in *The Darkslayer Omnibus - Series 1*. My Book Check out this series and learn more.

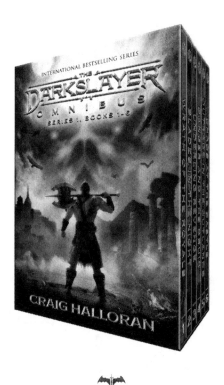

AND IF YOU haven't already, signup for my newsletter and grab 3 FREE books including the Dragon Wars Prequel.

WWW.DRAGONWARSBOOKS.COM

• PRISONER ISLAND •

— BOOK 9 —

CRAIG HALLORAN

1

RAVEN CLIFF

Several days had passed since Grey Cloak reunited with Zora and Tanlin, and he hadn't seen them since. The risks were too high for him to visit day after day, so they'd set a day for them all to meet, and it had come.

To burn time, Grey Cloak walked Raven Cliff's streets on another damp and dreary day, passing many long faces unnoticed. He'd been scouting the city, making his rounds, and getting a feel for the place.

The warm and robust people of Raven Cliff were long gone, replaced by cross looks and harsh stares. Depression and poverty were thick. Beggars laced the streets. Black Guard ran them off, only to see them quickly return. Children extended their dirty hands and gave pitiful, hollowed-eyed stares. No cheerful troubadours on the corners could be found.

Grey Cloak crossed Lovers' Lane, the bridge that overlooked a great chasm in the cliffs. It was there that he'd evaded the Doom Riders many years ago. It was there that his life had changed forever and he dropped into the deep gorge and fell like a feather, thanks to the Cloak of Legends. He'd survived. But so had the enemy.

The shadow of a dragon and its rider passed overhead. He glanced up in time to see a Risker in black armor riding on the back of a middling dragon, soaring above the city. The evil team drew terrified looks from the people on the streets, who scurried for shelter the moment the dragon let out an earsplitting shriek.

Grey Cloak cringed, and he closed his hood tighter over his face. The Riskers made his stomach turn. Over the past few days, he'd observed them making their presence known time and again, keeping the citizens on their toes. The monstrous dragons shrieked in the day and all hours of the night. Nobody could get a full night's sleep... or at least no one who wasn't deaf.

The dragon circled the city before finally settling on a building's rooftop. Its hawkish eyes scanned the streets while the Risker remained in the saddle, observing.

I've had my fill of them, Grey Cloak thought. *I detest them.*

He'd seen more than enough of the Riskers and the Black Guard to last him a lifetime. The Black Guard were as thick as flies, and they relentlessly bullied the people on the ground. The three that Dyphestive had counted so far shamelessly made their presence known at the most unpredictable times of the day. There was nothing timely about their coming or going. They came and they went as they pleased.

It started to drizzle. With a heavy heart, Grey Cloak resumed his path over the bridge and made one more pass through the city. He took random streets and alleys, taking his time, moving like a ghost, so as not to draw a wary eye. He'd crisscrossed every alley and street but hadn't found what he was looking for.

Zooks.

He headed back toward the Rusty Nail tavern, where he and Dyphestive had been staying since they returned. Zora had agreed to meet them there. Behind the Rusty Nail was a barn with stables, where Streak and Cliff had been staying.

On one of the back streets, behind the barn, an old crone with bright-yellow hair called for her cat. She wore a pink-and-white-striped cotton robe, carried a bottle of wine, and had fluffy wool shoes on her feet. "Patches!" she hollered with a high-pitched voice that carried over the wind. "Patches! Come home!"

Grey Cloak hurried toward the barn but not before the old woman caught him crossing.

"You! You! Have you seen my cat? He's black with a ringed tail. Named Patches!" she said as she stepped into a mud puddle. "Donkey dung!"

By the time she looked up again, Grey Cloak had gone into the barn and was hiding behind a post.

The old crone's eyes scanned the area. "I know you know where my cat is, cat stealer!" She teetered away and resumed her irritating yelling. "Patches! Patches! Come home, Patches!"

Grey Cloak dropped his hood and ambled over to Streak and Cliff's stable. Cliff the mule was standing, and Streak was nowhere to be seen.

"Streak," he whispered.

A dragon tail dropped and hit Grey Cloak in the face. "I'm up here." Streak was nestled on one of the rafters. "Is that woman stupid? I ate her cat two days ago. You would think that she would have given up by now."

Grey Cloak brushed the tail aside and said, "Stop eating the neighbors' cats. It will draw attention to us. If you want food, I'll get it."

Streak looked down at him with bright eyes, yawned, and said, "But cats are so delicious. And they are difficult to catch. I'm bored and need a challenge. Besides, Cliff isn't very much for conversation. None of these pack animals are. I need stimulation."

"Take a long nap, will you?" Grey Cloak eyed him. Streak was bigger than an average dog and appeared to still be growing. His small horns were becoming more prominent, and his dark tan scales were thickening. "And hide better before someone sees you."

"*You* didn't see me."

"I wasn't looking. You were supposed to be in the stable." He looked about. "And I don't want anyone to see me talking to a dragon either. In," he ordered.

Streak gave him a lazy look, arched his back, crawled over the beams, and dropped down into the stable. "Happy?"

Grey Cloak nodded. "Stay put."

Streak vanished into the bed of straw.

Satisfied, Grey Cloak left and entered the back door of the Rusty Nail.

2

THE RUSTY NAIL COULDN'T HAVE HAD A BETTER NAME. THE FLOORBOARDS groaned underfoot, and the place had a musty smell that always lingered. During a hard rain, water ran down the stones of the chimney stack, and there was never a fire. If you ran your hand along the walls, you would probably get a splinter. But Grey Cloak picked his way through the greasy kitchen and entered the smoky tavern behind the black oak bar.

It was late in the day, and over a dozen patrons had filed in and taken their places on chairs that groaned and sat behind wobbly tables. They huddled over bowls of steaming stew, and their clothes were sticky with sweat from another backbreaking day.

No one looked up when Grey Cloak entered. They didn't care about anything, not even judging people by appearances.

Dyphestive was sitting at a table beside the fireplace, looking out of a smudged window. His knee bounced.

Grey Cloak smiled. His brother couldn't wait to see Zora. He had barely been able to contain himself since Grey Cloak caught up with them.

As Grey Cloak slipped up to the table, he said, "Bad news. Zora isn't coming."

Dyphestive's large head snapped up. With a disappointed tone, he asked, "Why?"

Grey Cloak pulled up a chair and sat down, the wood creaking. He held the armrests of the wooden captain's chair, looked from side to side at the floor, and said, "I'm really surprised you haven't broken more of these."

"I use the same one. The owner found it for me. She likes me." Dyphestive leaned over his bowl of stew and asked, "Zora really isn't coming?"

"I'm only jesting. She's coming, so far as I know." He peered through the window. "I was hoping she'd be here by now." He scanned the room and found nothing but a bunch of grumbling hard faces, but a halfling woman with bright-green eyes and golden hair climbed onto a stool on stage and started to sing. Her voice was awful. "I hope that doesn't scare Zora away."

Dyphestive's foot was still bouncing, and he bit his fingernails.

"Brother, you seem rattled. That's not like you."

"I don't know what it is. I only want to see Zora." He leaned toward the window until his nose touched it. "Is that her?"

Grey Cloak shook his head. "She is plump, not ginormous. And that's a half orc."

While they were both looking out the window, a sweet but spunky voice said, "If I ever look like that, run a dagger through me."

"Zora!"

Dyphestive jumped out of his seat and banged his knee against the table. It knocked his bowl of stew off the table, but Grey Cloak caught it before it made a mess.

Swallowing her in his arms, Dyphestive said, "I've missed you!"

Even though Zora had packed on a few pounds, she was still little more than a child in his arms. She patted his back and grunted, "I might be pillowy, but I still have bones that can break."

"Oh, sorry." Dyphestive gently released her and grabbed her a chair. "Please, sit down. You look wonderful."

Zora flipped up her brown traveling cloak, which was damp from the misty rain. "I look like a mushroom in this thing."

"Now that's an exaggeration," Grey Cloak said. "As a matter of fact, I think you are as fetching as ever."

She rolled her eyes. "Spare me the compliments." Her nostrils flared, and she lifted an eyebrow. "Are you really staying in this stink hole?"

"They make great stew," Dyphestive said.

With his elbows on the table, Grey Cloak added, "It's a great place for discretion."

"Agreed." She flagged down a barmaid and gestured for a drink. "How's the wine?"

"Better than the water," Dyphestive said.

"Anyway," she continued as she put her hand on Dyphestive's bare forearm. "Tanlin sends his regards. He'd be here if not for the utmost need for discretion. The yonder follows him more than me. And since I run most errands for the shop, it doesn't often tag along, so long as I don't act suspicious." Her fingers slipped away from Dyphestive, and she turned toward Grey Cloak. "So, any news from either of you? I was hoping you'd elaborate on this grand idea of yours."

Grey Cloak's brow furrowed. "I'm sorry to admit that I haven't had the fortune that I hoped for."

"Which is?"

Keeping his voice low, he said, "I hoped that I could find the Figurine of Heroes. Or at least its location."

"Here?" she asked as the somber barmaid swung by the table and set down a goblet of wine. "Why would it be here of all places?"

Dyphestive dug his wooden spoon into his stew.

"When I first came to Raven Cliff, I encountered Batram's Bartery and Arcania. That's where I pawned the dagger that you stole from me and later acquired this cloak and a few other items. But..." He lifted a finger. "Batram only appears when he wants to appear. The entire store of his will vanish after an exchange. However, I have been to one in Loose Boot and Monarch City as well."

Zora finished a long drink of wine and said, "It sounds like a long shot."

"That's why I've been combing the streets, hoping that he'll appear. Think about it." He poked his index finger on the table. "If anyone knows about the Figurine of Heroes, it will be him. And if Tanlin's sources are correct, and they are searching for the figurine, it means they don't have it, and I bet Batram will know where it is."

"This is your grand idea? Finding a magic broker that vanishes as he pleases? I was hoping for a better plan than that."

"Can you think of a better idea?"

She guzzled down the rest of her wine, lifted the goblet in the air, and said, "No."

3

With his meaty forearms resting on the table, Dyphestive asked, "What happened after we entered the Wizard Watch? Where did all of you go?"

Zora combed her fingers through her lustrous red hair and said, "It's been an age, but I'll tell you, nothing went well. All of us headed to Staatus, the elven city, north of the tower. If you remember, we were to meet with Crane and Jakoby." She huffed. "Needless to say, Anya... or Fiery Red, as Razor likes to call her... didn't wait. She was furious when no one came out and blamed all of us, especially Tatiana. The truth is that I was glad for her to be gone. But I haven't seen Tat since. I thought she'd be with you, since you went into the tower together. It's sad that she didn't make it."

Dyphestive and Grey Cloak exchanged uneasy looks.

Grey Cloak had told Zora and Tanlin about the battle against the underlings in the tower and how the wizard Gossamer helped. His throat tightened as he thought about it. He squeezed Zora's hand and said, "She gave her life to save ours."

Zora wiped her eyes. "I know. Anyway, without Tatiana and the both of you, there was no quest for the dragon charms or any leadership either. None of us really knew what to do without a guide, and Crane wasn't much help. For the time being, we all agreed to separate or return home and wait. And that's what we were doing for the first few years.

"It wasn't long before the Black Guard crept into the lives of everyone and dragons and their Riskers raced across the skies. That was when I knew that something had gone very wrong. Tanlin reached out to the Brotherhood of Whispers, but even so, a great deal of mystery surrounded the recent events. There were rumors that the Sky Riders had perished, and we all but knew that. Monarch City and Arrowwood quickly came underneath Dark Mountain's influence. Cities collapsed like dominos without anyone to defend them. They didn't even fight. The Monarch surrendered, and anyone that resisted the Black Guard was hanged. That was when word from the Black Guard came in person to our very doorstep. Tanlin and I were taken to see Baron Dorenzo. He informed us that our *colleagues*, as he put it, were imprisoned and that Black Frost was looking for both of you. Given the nature of our talents and Tanlin's relationship with Baron Dorenzo, we were able to strike a deal. We would be spies, or we would perish." Zora's hand trembled.

Grey Cloak squeezed it. "You have nothing to be ashamed of."

"But I do. I sold out. Tanlin sold out. There are others that we ratted out. We had to cast shadows away from us and on others." She wiped the corner of her eye. "I'm ashamed."

"You did what you had to do to survive," he said.

"Would you have done the same?" She glanced at Dyphestive. "Or you?" She took a drink. "I'm sorry. I'm blubbering like a fool. It's not fair for me to ask." She took a deep breath into her goblet and said, "About a year or so after that, we were contacted by Crane. We never knew where the others were imprisoned, but he told us that he learned that they were taken to Prisoner Island, at the Inland Sea, by Harbor Lake. According to him, dragons guard the water, making it all but impossible to escape. He also told us that Bowbreaker had been captured by the West River elves and was the prisoner of the Monarch Queen, Esmarelda. All of us, except for Anya, if you count her, are accounted for." She sniffed. "Do you really want to try to rescue the others?"

"Of course," Grey Cloak said with an absentminded look. "I was hoping to acquire the Figurine of Heroes first. My gut tells me if we can get rid of the underlings, our task will be far easier."

"They are holed up in the towers like rats, our sources say," she said.

Grey Cloak pulled one of his carvings of the Figurine of Heroes from one of his many pockets and set it on the table. "And why wouldn't they be? If they cross the real figurine again, they'll be sent back to where they came from, and the Wizard Watch will control the towers again."

Dyphestive pushed his bowl aside and said, "I've never heard of Prisoner Island."

"The islands have always been in the inland sea. They were remote and used for fishing and seasonal escapes. A sanctuary for the wealthy, some said. But Dark Mountain's forces took them over. In an act of mercy, Black Frost's enemies were banished to the island for a lifetime and left to fend for themselves. The only way to freedom is to cross the dangerous water or find a way to survive on your own. The others have been there at least seven years. No one knows if anyone lives or dies. Once the ship takes you in, you don't come back out, unless you can swim like a fish."

"The wait is over." Dyphestive banged his fist on the table. "We have to go and rescue them now."

"We don't know if they are alive or dead," she said.

"I don't care. One way or another, we are going to find out," Dyphestive replied.

"Ah, you miss Leena, don't you?" Grey Cloak smirked.

"No," Dyphestive replied with a guilty look. "Fine, I miss her. I miss all of them. And we are going to get them."

"No argument from me. I don't see any reason to wait here any longer. It's time to move on. What about you, Zora? Are you coming along?"

She glanced between the two of them with a shamefaced look and said, "I'll have to ask Tanlin." She eased out of her chair and kissed each of them on the cheek, finishing with Dyphestive. "It's been great seeing you again, but I'd better move on so no one gets suspicious. Let's meet back here in two days, same time."

Grey Cloak nodded, and as soon as Dyphestive waved, she vanished out of the front door.

"What do you think?" Grey Cloak asked.

Dyphestive shrugged. "I don't know. For some reason, I can hear Rhonna in my mind, saying, 'Time changes everything, especially people.'"

"Those are the exact same words that I hear rattling around in my skull. I never thought any of what Rhonna said way back when would ever sink in, but it did." Grey Cloak twisted his finger inside his ear. "That and that halfling squawking over there. She's awful."

Dyphestive stared at the halfling and tilted his head. "Maybe she is deaf and can't hear herself singing."

"Might be."

"So, what do you want to do about Zora? Do we still trust her?"

"Until we have any reason to believe otherwise, I'll take my chances."

With a nod, Dyphestive said, "Me too."

4

DYPHESTIVE LAY IN HIS TAVERN ROOM BED WITH HIS HEAD ON HIS PILLOW, LOOKING up at the dingy, cracked ceiling. Drops of water slowly built up in the corner behind his head and dripped to the floor behind the headboard.

Five hundred sixty-two.

With nothing better to do, he'd been counting the drops ever since Grey Cloak departed. He was making his rounds through Raven Cliff again, hoping that he would have a run-in with Batram's Bartery and Arcania. In the meantime, he told Dyphestive to stay put. Apparently, because of his size, he drew too much attention to himself.

Five hundred sixty-two. No, five hundred sixty-three, I think.

"Drat it." He swung his legs over the side of the bed, which wasn't big enough to hold him, and put his boots on the old rug. "I'm not sitting here all day while he gets to stroll all around the city."

A small window, marred with soot, was on the other side of the room. Grey Cloak had closed it before he left, but Dyphestive opened it. A cool breeze kissed his face, and he stuck his head outside. A chilly rain came down in a fine mist. "Ah, that's better."

The citizens sauntered down the road, where many horse-drawn wagons were rolling. People shouted and hurried by one another. Fresh scents of baked bread and spicy sizzled meats hung in the air. Dyphestive's stomach growled. He'd been eating the same stew for days. It was the most palatable food at the Rusty Nail, but it wasn't enough to satisfy his tremendous appetite.

"Seeing how we are leaving soon, I think I should sample more of the local fare." He grabbed his coin pouch and traveling cloak, left his sword and war mace behind, and hustled downstairs.

Without a glance from the tavern's patrons, he covered his head with the hood and went outside. The first thing he did was stretch his long arms. His fingertips could reach from porch post to porch post. He jumped off the porch and onto the street and started walking.

A distinct, mouthwatering scent wafted through the air, widening his nostrils. It led him farther down the street with his shovel-sized hands swinging. His belly growled and caught the attention of a pair of ladies in wicker bonnets, who giggled as they passed him. He gave them both a warm smile when he nodded at them.

"He's handsome," one of the women said. "I'm telling my oldest daughter about him."

"Not if I tell mine first," the other woman said. "She's becoming an old hen, but if I was younger..."

Their voices trailed off while Dyphestive continued to mosey down the road. It felt good to stretch his legs. He'd been cooped up inside the stinky old tavern long enough, so long that the foul smell had become normal.

"Shriiieeek!"

Most people jumped or ducked, while the horses whinnied and nickered as a Risker flew overhead and vanished. But other hardened souls still plodded along, because they'd heard the awful dragon sound hundreds of times before.

Dyphestive's heart raced. He'd grown up around dragons, but it was more about being spotted than the awful sound of their voices. He dared another glance at the rooftops, where another Risker landed on a chimney. He drew his cloak tight.

Maybe I should go back.

His belly rumbled. The smell of spiced meat was stronger than ever. A line of people bent around a tavern corner. A huge metal grill was outside, scented smoke billowing out and tempting the tongue.

No, I should eat something first.

He waited in line until he had a full view of the cooker. An older man and woman wearing aprons were busy behind it, slapping on racks of ribs and slathering them with a rich brick-red sauce. Sweat dripped from their faces, but they were all smiles and laughing.

Alongside the grill was a younger woman taking orders and payments. She was a freckle-faced dirty blonde in a tight leather jerkin that enhanced her ample bustline. She talked up the men, doubling their orders, and several Black Guards were in line, flirting.

Dyphestive kept his head down. *Horseshoes.* He'd been so caught up in hunger that he hadn't even noticed the soldiers. It was a small group of the imposing men, and they weren't shy about flaunting their status.

"You are a cute one," a soldier with a hooked nose said as the young woman gathered his order. "When you can spare a moment, why don't you come over to my table and sit on my lap."

The other soldiers sniggered.

The young woman smiled back and said, "I only wish I had a moment, but we'll see."

"See you around," the soldier said in a rugged voice. He winked and moved along.

When the time came for Dyphestive to order, he was starving. The smell of roasting meat had consumed him.

"What would you like?" the young woman asked.

"Uh, a rack of ribs and a turkey leg. Make that two of each." He looked over his shoulder and could see that all the tables were full and most of them with Black Guards. "Er, can I take it home with me?"

The young woman gave him a smoldering look and said, "Only if you take me with you, cutie."

"Huh?"

"I haven't seen you here before. New in town?"

"Sort of, I guess."

She offered a warm smile. "I'm Amber." Suddenly, she hollered at the top of her voice, "Two full racks! Two legs! Make 'em spicy!" She lowered her strong voice to a more soothing level. "You like spicy, don't you?"

He nodded eagerly. "Yes, very much."

Amber rose on her toes, leaned closer, and looked him over. "You really are something. Tell you what... Wait over there, by the tavern post, while they get your order ready. I'll bring it over personally."

He started digging into his pouch and asked, "How much do I owe you?"

Amber winked at him and said, "It's on me."

Blushing, he plucked out a gold coin and pressed it into her hand. "No, I insist, Amber. I'll be over there."

She lifted her eyebrows as she eyed the coin. "I'll be right over."

Dyphestive walked backward toward the tavern entrance, giving the fetching blonde a nod as he did so. He walked into a wall, or so he thought, but he turned, and his hood fell down as he came face-to-face with a muscle-bound brute that was as bald as an onion and every bit as big as he was. The man had just walked down the tavern steps into him. The sloe-eyed bruiser was picking his teeth with a toothpick. His eyes widened, and he said, "Watch where you are going, fool."

Dyphestive froze as he and the towering man locked eyes for several moments. He knew the man. It was Bull, a member of the Scourge, a group led by Sash. They'd crossed long ago when he was with the Doom Riders.

Bull leaned forward and asked, "Don't I know you?"

"No," he answered quickly as he turned his shoulders away.

Bull grabbed Dyphestive by the arm and spun him around. He glared into his eyes. "I've seen you before, but where?" He glanced up and to the right, as if he were trying to remember.

Dyphestive balled up his fist and said, "You're mistaken."

"Bull doesn't forget a face. You're—"

He slugged Bull in the jaw. *Whop!*

Bull fell like a tree and crashed into the porch deck.

The Black Guard rose from their tables.

Dyphestive stole a glance at Amber, winked, grabbed a hot turkey leg from the grill, and ran like the blazes.

5

Grey Cloak slipped into the tavern room in the early evening and found Dyphestive peeking through the tattered window curtains. "Looking for me?"

"No," Dyphestive said as he took a seat on his bed. "But I have been waiting for you."

He shed his cloak and put it on the peg on the back of the door and said, "So, if you weren't looking for me, then who were you looking for? Zora? She's not meeting us until tomorrow."

Dyphestive rubbed the back of his head and asked, "Are you sure it wasn't today?"

Grey Cloak took a seat on his twin bed and noticed a turkey bone lying underneath Dyphestive's bed. "Have you been eating in the room again?"

"A little."

He eyed his brother. Dyphestive wore a guilty expression like a new suit of armor. "You left the tavern, didn't you?"

"I might have taken a little stroll." He stood. "Look, it's too cramped in here, and the singing is awful down there. I had to get out."

"It was only another day. And you could have gone into the barn for some fresh air." He leaned over, fluffed his pillow, and lay down. "What did you do?"

"I ordered some food. Turkey and ribs, but I forgot the ribs. Er... did you find Batram?"

"No." He stared up at the ceiling, which was made from slats of wood. "Honestly, Dyphestive, it's not a matter of grabbing a bite of food. The issue is not being recognized. So, as long as no one saw you, no worries. Besides, we only have one more day of this."

An uncomfortable silence hung in the air.

Grey Cloak sat up like a dead man rising and turned toward Dyphestive. He locked his eyes with him and asked, "Who saw you?"

Dyphestive held his hands out and said, "Well, don't jump to conclusions. I was seen, but I don't know that I was recognized. It was a very brief encounter."

He put his feet on the floor and leaned forward. "Who saw you?"

"Do you remember Bull from the Scourge?"

He nodded.

Dyphestive gave a sheepish grin and said, "I bumped into him. But..." He raised his index finger. "I don't think he remembered me. If you remember, we only met briefly, and I don't think he's very smart."

"Was he alone?"

"I didn't see any others. I took my food and hurried along, and I've been here ever since." He pointed at the window. "I haven't seen any interest either. I was very far away from this spot when it happened. And it's been over ten years since he saw me. I imagine I've changed."

Grey Cloak recalled his last encounter with the Scourge at Daggerford. The Doom Riders had been there too. It was the place where Dyphestive had killed Drysis and was rescued. They were chased afterward and finally escaped to Monarch City. He rose and grabbed his cloak.

"Where are you going? You should stay in. I'm sure all of this will blow away with the wind."

"The streets were thick with Black Guard when I returned. They were looking for someone but operated very discreetly about it. There was a lot of door knocking and questions." He pulled his cloak on. "And they were coming this way. What exactly happened with Bull? Tell me everything."

"Well, he said he thought he knew me. I said he didn't. And just when he was about to say who he thought I was, I busted his jaw and ran." He gave a sheepish grin. "I hit him pretty hard. He might not remember anything ever again."

Grey Cloak smirked. "I wish I could have been there. Now, grab your gear. We have to go."

6

"Zora, are you telling me that you had no idea that the Scourge was in town?" Grey Cloak asked. He'd snuck back to Tanlin's apartment and met up with the both of them.

"There are tens of thousands of people in Raven Cliff," Zora said as she loaded a shoulder pack. "The last census was near one hundred thousand. I wouldn't have noticed them any easier than I would have noticed you if you hadn't reached out." She slung a bandolier of daggers over her shoulder. "We've been keeping our heads down, you know?"

Tanlin paced the floor, and with his fingers needling his chin, he said, "We shouldn't be so surprised. According to the Brotherhood of Whispers, the Scourge is still in the business of recovering dragon charms for Black Frost. We haven't had any run-ins with them for over a decade, but it still turns my stomach to think they are so close. Were there any others?"

Grey Cloak shook his head. "Dyphestive only saw Bull."

Tanlin shrugged. "Perhaps he is alone. It wouldn't be uncommon for a member to be cut loose or move on. I'll keep an eye out. In the meantime, the sooner you move out, the better." He eyed Zora. "I'm not sure this is the best move that you go. The timing will be very suspicious if Bull indeed remembers Dyphestive. He was always a lout. I'm surprised that he remembers anything after all of the hits he's taken to the skull. I'll cover."

"The Black Guard is on the move," Grey Cloak said as he watched Zora pack. "No doubt they've questioned the dwellers at the Rusty Nail by now. I'm sure it won't be hard for them to identify an overly handsome elf and an oversized farm boy if anyone asked." He winked at Zora. "That's why I left the innkeeper a little something before I left."

Zora smirked as she slung her pack over her shoulder. "Good thinking. I taught you well."

"Ha."

"Tanlin, are you sure that you can cover for me?"

The older rogue clasped her hands and said, "You know I'll think of something."

She gave Tanlin a kiss on the cheek and hugged him. "Be well."

"I will. Best to both of you on this journey." Tanlin moved to the stove and lifted the tea kettle. "I'll do what I have to do to throw any possible pursuers off."

"Thanks, Tanlin," Grey Cloak said.

Tanlin filled his teacup and raised it. "You're welcome."

With catlike ease, Grey Cloak and Zora hurried out of the apartment and into the night and stole their way down the streets.

They caught up with Dyphestive on the northern edge of town where the road dropped toward the plains and farmlands. He was sitting on a tavern porch, and Cliff was drinking from a trough. It was still early evening, and people still combed the street and actively went in and out of the tavern.

Zora gave Dyphestive a quick hug.

"Did you see anyone?" Grey Cloak asked.

"Not a soul I recognized, not that I would. We are pretty far from where we started." He glanced at Zora. "You're coming?"

"I don't plan on ever letting either of you out of my sight again." She pointed at her eyes with her two fingers then at both of them. "Never again. Harbor Lake awaits. Shall we?"

Grey Cloak scanned the streets one last time and said, "Lead the way, milady."

They moved at a brisk pace but not so fast as to make it obvious. Every so often, they heard a dragon shriek, and the longer they walked, the more those terrifying shrieks faded away. They were at least a league away from Raven Cliff before Grey Cloak looked back again. A bright moon hung over the stark city. He blocked the city from view with the tips of his fingers.

"It looks like we made it out of town without being noticed. Thank goodness." He walked backward. "I'm all for walking through the night and putting as much distance as possible between Raven Cliff and us."

"Agreed," Zora said as she labored up a rise in the hill. "Oof!" She stopped at the top and arched her back. Her face glistened. "I'm ashamed to say it, but I'm not in the best shape. I can't remember the last time I walked so much." She leaned on Cliff. "I might need to rest."

"There's plenty of room. Hop on," Streak said.

Zora screeched and jumped into Grey Cloak's arms. "Did the donkey say that? You have a talking donkey?"

"No, no," Grey Cloak said with a chuckle. Zora's fingernails dug into his ribs as the silhouette of Streak's head rose from among the packs of Cliff's saddle. "That's Streak, remember?"

Zora clutched a hand over her chest. "My heart is pounding. Feel it." She put Grey Cloak's hand over her breast.

"Uh..." He swallowed. "Indeed."

"You don't have to be shy. I don't bite—well, not you, Zora," Streak said as his flat head caught the moonlight. His tongue flicked out of his mouth. "Come on over and say hello."

She gave Grey Cloak a flabbergasted look and said, "He talks? You failed to mention that."

He shrugged. "More than me sometimes."

Zora's heavy breathing eased, and she said, "That can't be a good thing." She approached Streak with her hand out and petted his flat head. "It's been a while, young fella. How are you?"

"Better than ever," Streak replied coolly. His tongue licked her face. "You?"

Zora cupped Streak's head in both of her hands and said, "I feel better than I've felt in a long time, thanks to the three of you."

HARBOR LAKE

THE SALTY BREEZE FROM THE INLAND SEA COULD DRY A TONGUE IN MOMENTS. GREY Cloak rubbed his eyes. He'd never been to Harbor Town or encountered its salty people before. Unlike Raven Cliff, Harbor Town was vast, stretching along the southern shore for leagues in a network of stone buildings and wooden shanties.

Dyphestive towed Cliff down the wharfs that ran along the Inland Sea. A flock of pelicans flew overhead, and Streak hissed. Dyphestive stopped and hung the reins over the railing then eyeballed all of the ships that had pulled in along the docks. He gaped at Grey Cloak. "I've never seen the likes of them. Have you?"

Grey Cloak shook his head. It was the first time that he'd ever seen sailing ships. They were long wooden craft with tall masts and bright-white sails. There were sailors, merchants, and soldiers—Black Guard—busy on the wharfs and the docks. They moved crates up and down ramps and hefted barrels on their shoulders while rolling other barrels down the ramps.

"Have you ever been here before?" he asked Zora.

"I've made a few trips here over the last several years. Tanlin buys a lot of silks and linens from Harbor Lake. It's fantastic, isn't it? Perhaps too big, but if you enjoy fresh seafood, you couldn't be in a better place. They have crabs and lobsters."

Dyphestive gave her a funny look. "Crabs and lobsters?"

"It will be evening soon," she said. "I know a fine place to dine and check in. You are both in for a treat." She looked at Grey Cloak. "Well, maybe not you if you don't eat."

"No, I eat," he said absentmindedly as he stared out over the choppy water, which glinted against the bright sun. "You'd be surprised. I've changed."

"Good." Zora looked over the sandy beaches and stood shoulder to shoulder with him. She rose onto her toes and pointed out to sea. "That's Prisoner Island. You can only get there by ship. They take a group of prisoners there every week, and they never return. I shudder to think of what our friends have been through. I hope they have survived."

Grey Cloak nodded. "Me too. But what about Than? Was he taken to the island too?"

"Not that I'm aware of. The last we talked, if you remember, he was headed south to the Shelf to train the dragons. But there has not been any word of them since."

"So, we have to take a boat to the island," Dyphestive said.

"Yes, but you have to become a prisoner first," she said. "That's the easy way in."

"There has to be a better way than that," Grey Cloak said with a frown. "I can get there on my own."

"You can't swim it. The dragons will see you," she said.

"Not if I'm underwater."

"You aren't going over there without me," Dyphestive stated. "We can't separate again. I like Zora's plan."

"We'll be stripped down to nothing," Grey Cloak argued. "We won't have any gear or weapons. It's too risky."

"I'll hang on to your gear and weapons," Zora offered.

Grey Cloak gave her a surprised look and asked, "You aren't going?"

"Someone needs to stay on this side of the shore and make sure that you return. If you don't, I'll have to go for help," she said.

"From whom? Tanlin?" He locked his hands behind his back and walked away. "I need to think about this. Let's get a room."

LATER IN THE DAY, after they settled in and had piles of buttered seafood, they headed back to the docks.

"*Shriiieeek!*"

A Risker flew over the buildings, circled, and flew back over the sea. Unlike the people of Raven Cliff, the folks in Harbor Lake didn't startle easily. They moved along, covered up in loose clothing, with their heads down, without saying a word to anybody. Meanwhile, the sailors unwound from a long day of backbreaking work, carrying wine jugs and singing arm in arm.

Grey Cloak, Dyphestive, and Zora crept along the docks, stealing their way along the massive boats to a middle-sized black craft at the end of the dock. It had a huge red skull with flaming eyes on the figurehead. There was a single mast for the one sail, and it had rows of benches with oars resting on the floor.

"This is the prisoner galley," Zora said as she watched the unmanned boat rock against the docks. "The prisoners row to the island, and the Black Guard sail it back." She touched the figurehead. "It's called a death's head. Sounds fun, doesn't it?"

"A sheer delight," Grey Cloak said. He inspected the craft with a studious eye. Shackles were attached to the floor, and racks of spears were at the fore and aft of the ship. A large kettledrum stood at the rear. He pointed at it. "What is the drum for?"

"To keep the oarsmen in rhythm. It will be a backbreaking quest over the choppy water, but I'm sure you two young men will manage." She looked at Dyphestive. "I bet you could row it yourself."

"Perhaps, but I'd rather sail it. What do you think, Grey? Are we going over together or not?"

Grey Cloak had many ideas racing through his head and said, "Let's find out when it departs next. In the meantime..." He offered a warm smile. "We should sleep on it."

Dyphestive and Zora exchanged puzzled looks as they watched Grey Cloak walk away.

8

"Psst. Psst." Grey Cloak was alone in the tavern barn and stepped inside Cliff's stable. "Streak, where are you?"

Streak's head popped out from underneath a bed of straw. "Where else would I be but here? I'm not allowed to go anywhere else." He inhaled deeply into his flaring nostrils. "Did you bring me any cooked fish? Or cold fish? Any fish will do."

"No, you can eat later." Grey Cloak sat down beside his dragon and pulled him over his lap. "Listen, the prisoner boat leaves tomorrow, and I've agreed to depart on it. I want you to stay here and keep an eye on Zora."

"Protect her? Not a problem."

"Well, yes and no. Spy on her too."

"Really?" The runt dragon nodded. "I wouldn't suspect anything of her, but who knows... she wouldn't want to be suspected, would she."

"I don't have any idea how long we'll be searching that island, but at some point, I'll need you. If we aren't back in a few days, come. You can swim, right?"

"I can fly too."

"True, but I don't want the other dragons to see you. Stay underwater and find me on the island," he said.

"It won't be a problem. Five days. Take a long swim. Find you. Oh, and spy on Zora." Streak winked.

"Good." He rubbed his dragon's head and exited the stable. "I appreciate you."

"Then bring me some fish!"

DYPHESTIVE WAS CRACKING open a lobster when Grey Cloak arrived inside the seafood-serving tavern. Unlike the greasy smell that he was used to in other taverns, it had an overwhelming scent of fish. He took a seat at the round table with a barrel for a base, joining his brother and Zora.

"Did you and Streak have a nice talk?" Zora asked as she petted his forearm. "Did you tell him you'd miss him?"

"He said he's looking forward to spending more time with you. Try to keep him out of trouble, will you?" He eyed the plate of seafood delicacies and picked up a white nugget of sea flesh. He'd seen giant crabs at Thunder Island's shore but not the other plethora of shellfish creatures. "Hmm... what are these?"

"Those are scallops," she said.

Dyphestive crushed a red boiled lobster claw in his hand, and with a mouthful of buttery meat, he said, "Eat them. They're good!"

Grey Cloak popped a scallop into his mouth and chewed. He raised his eyebrows and said, "That is marvelous." He helped himself to a few more and washed it down with sweet wine. "It's no wonder that Harbor Lake is a very popular place."

"You should see it during the hot season. The women comb the beaches and streets half-naked."

Dyphestive choked and asked, "Really?"

"Let's say they leave little to the imagination," she said as she nibbled away on a crab leg. "You know what skimpy means, don't you?"

Dyphestive nodded feverishly.

"Perhaps we'll stick around until the seasons cross," Grey Cloak said as he consumed another scallop. "I tell you, the demeanor in Harbor Lake is warmer than Raven Cliff." He heard the faint sound of a dragon screeching over the robust crowd. "Why do you think that is, Zora?"

"I think the people in Harbor Lake embraced Black Frost's authority sooner. They aren't as rebellious toward their new leader. Every place is different. The people of Harbor Lake live in the moment."

Right after she said that, a woman let out a delighted squeal and a cackle.

"See what I mean?"

"I do." Dyphestive craned his neck toward the cackling woman. In a low voice, he said, "The people here are loose, aren't they?"

Zora nodded and patted his hand. "They aren't the kind you want to spend your time alone with too long." She turned her attention back to Grey Cloak. "So, have you come up with a way to gain passage on the prisoner ship? I see you are dressed for the occasion." They were down to cloaks and clothing and hadn't packed weapons. "You look like prisoners to me. All we need to do is add some chains and a few bumps and bruises."

He leaned back in his chair and said, "We need to get arrested. But what sort of crime, aside from murder, will get us on the island?"

Zora wiped her mouth and fingers on a napkin and said, "The funny thing is that the island is filled with violent criminals, but it has its share of those who struck against Black Frost. Traitors. You don't have to kill anyone, but if you assault the Black Guard, it's considered an assault on Black Frost himself. That's the best way to get yourself in."

Grey Cloak searched the room for the Black Guard. They traveled in packs and were always in the most popular places. He spotted four men wearing tunics with mountain crests and spikes of lightning. The hawkish soldiers filled a table and had sultry women on their laps. "It looks like I found our boarding pass."

Dyphestive looked over his shoulder. He crushed another lobster claw and set it down. "Let me go first." He scooted his chair back and walked over to the soldiers' table.

"Oh my," Grey Cloak said as he got to his feet. "I'd better get over there. Keep your distance, Zora. I need you here, not where we are going, inevitably."

"Be careful," she said.

"I heard that the Black Guard are a bunch of donkey skulls," Dyphestive said as he dragged a chair over to the table and sat down with the group.

The Black Guard across from him with a prim and proper haircut and manners gave him a cross look and asked, "What did you say, oaf?"

"I said, I heard that the Black Guard were a bunch of donkey skulls." Dyphestive glared at the man. "It's a question. Is that true?"

The soldiers shoved the women away from their laps and pushed away from their tables. They exchanged confused looks with one another.

Grey Cloak interrupted as he arrived behind his brother and said, "Apologies. Apologies. I fear my dear friend has had too much to drink, and his loose tongue has become brazen. Come on, Gilly," he said, trying to shove Dyphestive from his chair. "Let's go pester the sailors, not this bunch of donkey skulls."

"What did you say?" the eldest of the group by appearance asked. "Did you call us donkey skulls?"

In a pleasing manner, Grey Cloak responded, "Well, yes. As a matter of fact, I was telling my friend Gilly earlier about how stupid the Black Guard were. It was no surprise there were so many orcs and halflings among their ranks, because, well, you know." He raised his palms in a gesture of surrender. "They are all stupid."

Every Black Guard rose from the table.

"I will have your tongue!" their leader said.

"Why?" Grey Cloak asked. "Because you are too stupid to use your own?"

"Seize them!" the leader shouted.

Dyphestive flipped the table like a giant coin. He punched out two Black Guards before they could draw their swords.

Grey Cloak quickly kicked the leader in the nanoos before the man came fully to his feet. The fight would have been over before it started, but a host of Black Guard from outside poured in, piled on, and brought them down.

Holding his crotch, the red-faced leader said, "Take them to the dungeon! The dungeon, I say! I'll deal with them myself."

As they were dragged out of the tavern, Grey Cloak caught Zora's worried expression, gave her a thumbs-up, and winked.

She gave him a quick wave goodbye and vanished into the crowd.

9

THE PRISONER SHIP CUT THROUGH THE CHOPPY WAVES LIKE A KNIFE TO THE STEADY beat of the tom-tom. Grey Cloak and Dyphestive sat on the same bench, chained to the oars, which dug deep into the green water. Grey Cloak's back burned like fire before he even began to row. The Black Guard had whipped the tar out of them the night before in the dungeons. Without any rest, they'd gone to the ship just before daybreak.

With the morning sun shining in his eyes, he said to his brother under his breath, "Lords of the Air, this might have been the worst idea I've ever had. I swear my back is in flames. How is yours?"

"It itches," Dyphestive said dryly.

"How rich for you." He stole a look over his shoulder, searching for the island, which sat leagues away. They'd rowed for hours, and the deadly island retreat didn't appear any closer. "I could have swum faster."

"Silence!" a Black Guard said. He followed it up with the crack of a lash. The Black Guard on the ship weren't the same as the ones in the city. They were bare-chested and wore crimson hoods instead of helmets. They were a burly and brawny sort, eight in all, four on each end, including the drummer. "No more words! Only silence!"

Grey Cloak mimicked the man under his breath. "*No more words, only silence.* Idiot."

The comment drew a chuckle from Dyphestive.

The soldier with the loud mouth quickly strode down the middle plank and whipped both of them across their backs. "Don't talk! Row, fools!"

Grey Cloak's back muscles spasmed as he arched forward. Fighting the pain, he pulled the oar in rhythm with Dyphestive. Luckily for him, Dyphestive was doing most of the work.

Zooks, this is awful. They'd better be on that bloody island.

To make matters worse, his cloak had been taken. All of the prisoners had been stripped down to the waist, and their shirts and cloaks were piled up at the front of the boat. At least the cloak was close, but the problem was that he wasn't sure he would get it back.

Aside from that, he and Dyphestive weren't alone. Every bench had a haggard-looking man pulling on the oars, and there was one woman, an orc, who still had most of what was left of her clothing still on. She sat in the back near the drummer, and strong muscles bulged in her arms.

"I wonder what she did," Grey Cloak whispered.

"You like to get whipped, don't you?"

"No, but I like conversation. And I'm starting to get accustomed to this burning sensation. Perhaps I'm tougher than you."

"Could be," Dyphestive said with a quick look over his shoulder. "We are at least halfway there. Only a few more hours."

Grey Cloak rolled his eyes. "Yes, only a few."

There were fifteen other prisoners aboard, and most of them didn't appear to be fit enough to heft a spear. But a couple were sailor types whose skin was rich with colorful tattoos. There were at least a few fighting men among them.

We could take the Black Guard if we had to, Grey Cloak thought. *One more crack of that lash on my back, and I just might do it.*

A wave blasted over the ship, soaking everyone aboard. The salty water burned Grey Cloak's new stripes.

Zooks! I hate this! He spit the salty water out of his mouth and wiped the wet hair from his eyes. *Awful.*

"Honestly, I don't see what is so impossible about escaping from the island. I haven't even seen a dragon since we departed," he muttered under his breath. "What's to stop us from taking the ship once we arrive on shore?"

Dyphestive shrugged his monstrously large shoulders. "It's your plan."

A shadow like a huge cloud passed over the ship, followed by a bone-rattling "*Roooaaarrr!*"

A grand dragon with scales so dark that it was almost black soared overhead. It was bigger than Cinder and didn't have a rider on its back.

Several of the prisoners started to tremble, and many prayed for mercy as the great behemoth glided over the waters and roared over them again. It flew for the island with its long thorny tail trailing behind it.

"That was one big dragon," Dyphestive said.

The Black Guard at the front of the ship let out a wicked laugh as he pointed at the dragon and said, "Prisoners, meet your new warden. We call him Thunderbreath."

10

PRISONER ISLAND

THE BOTTOM OF THE PRISONER SHIP DUG INTO THE SANDY SHORELINE AND CAME TO a stop. The Black Guard undid the prisoners' chains and forced them off the boat and into the water by spear point. One by one and two by two, the prisoners splashed down into the salty water and lumbered toward the shore.

"Enjoy your stay, miscreants!" the Black Guard captain of the vessel said. "A certain death awaits!"

Using the oars, the other Black Guard pushed the craft off the beach, through the surges and breaking waves, and raised the small sail. In a final effort, they tossed the prisoners' clothing into the water.

"Take what will be yours!" the captain said. "It's every man"—he sneered at the orc woman—"and orc for themselves now."

Grey Cloak was standing knee deep in the tide when the pile of clothing dropped into the green surge. He saw his cloak floating on the surface, but the orc woman with long braided hair was closer than he was. Their eyes met, and both of them started swimming for the garb.

The orc woman arrived chest deep at the pile of floating clothing first. Her long fingers locked on Grey Cloak's cloak. He arrived a moment later and grabbed it. "This is mine!"

"You heard the guard! Every man for himself!" She yanked the cloak, but his grip held fast.

He smirked and said, "You're strong but not as strong as you th—"

The orc woman socked him hard in the jaw with a blinding punch and tugged the cloak free of his loosened grip then wrapped it around her shoulders.

With blurry purple spots in his eyes, Grey Cloak rubbed his sore jaw and shook his head. She had knocked the crap out of him. He set his eyes on his cloak and said, "Use your own clothing. That garment is mine!"

"I don't have any other clothing. I need something to cover myself," she fired back. "And this will do perfectly fine."

He grabbed handfuls of wet clothing and threw it at her face. "Sew this together!" He jumped on her the moment the clothes covered her face and wrestled her down into the water.

She kicked, kneed, and punched like a woman gone mad, hammering him with wild blows. Grey Cloak's offensive assault quickly became a defensive effort composed of ducking and dodging. Whoever the orc woman was, she proved that she was strong. Dodging her wild swings, he backed away with the tide lifting him up and down and said, "Let's work something out." He offered a smile. "I'm Grey Cloak. And what is your name?"

She snarled at him and said, "Come closer, and I'll tell you, little elf." She tilted her head. "What is the matter? Are you scared? Don't you want to stab me with your pointed ears?"

Dyphestive crept behind her. "It's his cloak. Let him have it. We'll make it right."

The orc woman was tall, but she still looked up at Dyphestive and said, "Come one step closer, and I'll be feeding your nanoos to the fish. It's every man and woman for himself here. What is mine is mine, and you'll have to kill me to take it." She gave them both a quick once-over. "And I can see by those soft eyes that neither one of you is a true killer like me."

On the beach, the rest of the prisoners had gathered around the rest of the clothing that had floated toward the shore. They fought like wild men over the garb. One of the sailors had a slab of driftwood in hand and clobbered another man over the head. The brutal scene turned bloody.

"I must insist, for your own good, that you return the cloak to me. It's only a cloak, after all. I promise to fashion something suitable for you."

"I'm no fool. You only want to set your hungry eyes on me. I promise you this... you'll wind up as dead as the defiling Black Guard I killed."

"As fetching as you might think you are, I promise I have no interest in violating your dignity." He offered a sincere expression. "The cloak is very sentimental to me. A gift from my mother."

"I spit on your mother story, liar!" She started to distance herself from them and made her way toward the shore. "Stay away from me! Or I'll kill you both."

"I'll get her." Dyphestive strode through the water, making a beeline for the woman, and caught up with her. "Don't make this so difficult. Let us have the cloak back, and we'll protect you."

"From whom?" she snarled.

Dyphestive pointed at all of the rest of the men gathered on the shore. "From them and whatever other horrors lie in those dark hills. We can help one another if you let us."

"Stay away from me," she commanded. "I can handle myself."

He lifted his hands over his head. "Fine." He crept closer. "But it would be better if we made a pact and worked together."

She narrowed her eyes as he came closer. Suddenly, her expression softened, and she let him come closer and said, "Fine. What do you have to offer, Big Chin?"

"Well, I was thinking—*oof*!"

From underneath the water, the orc woman kicked him in the beans and hustled away.

Dyphestive sank chin deep into the water with his face as red as a beet.

Grey Cloak passed by him and said, "Well done, genius. I'll handle this."

"Be careful," Dyphestive warned. "She kicks like a mule."

11

GREY CLOAK SLIPPED UNDERNEATH THE WATER AND LAUNCHED HIMSELF AT THE ORC woman's legs. *I've fooled around long enough.*

He called forth the wizardry, locked his fingers on her kicking ankles, and sent a jolt of wizard fire up her legs.

The woman bucked like a mule and violently spasmed. She sank into the water with her eyes closed.

Grey Cloak rose out of the water just as a wave splashed over him. He grabbed the orc woman, who floated facedown in the water. He rolled her over and cradled her in his arms.

I hope I didn't kill her.

Dyphestive waded over and asked, "What did you do? Is she dead?"

Her chest rose and fell.

"No, I used a charge and knocked her out. She'll live, unfortunately."

By the time they made it back to the shoreline, the group of men had scattered. But two of them were dead in the sand.

Standing over the dead with the orc woman in his arms, Grey Cloak said, "So, the fun begins."

"I'll bury them," Dyphestive said as he picked up their shirts.

"With what?"

Dyphestive looked at his hands and said, "Good point." He slapped the sand off of his shirt. "I'll let the sea take them."

Grey Cloak scanned the area. The island was made up of tall hills with rocky peaks jutting toward the sky. The woodland flourished with tropical green terrain. It was paradise with a vicious dragon hidden somewhere in its peaks. "Come on. Let's head into the wood before that dragon swings back around."

"Good idea."

Grey Cloak carried the orc woman over his shoulder as they ventured into the surrounding wood. They were met by the beautiful sounds of tropical birds that darted from tree to tree.

A little more than a hundred steps in, Grey Cloak set the woman down in a clearing. "My, she's heavy."

"I could have carried her," Dyphestive said.

Grey Cloak started to unfold the cloak wrapped around her body. "I bet you'd like that. After all, she does have a marvelous build."

"That's not why."

"Sure it isn't." As Grey Cloak peeled away the cloak, he quickly caught an eyeful of the damp shreds of clothing barely covering the orc woman's body. "Brother, I think it would be proper if you lent your new lady your shirt. Here, help me get her out of my cloak."

Dyphestive got his first full look at the woman, blushed, and covered his eyes. He handed over his shirt. "You do it."

"She's not that naked." He started tugging the cloak off. "Only mostly naked, sort of."

The orc woman's eyelids snapped open. She caught Dyphestive in the jaw with an elbow but not before Grey Cloak took his cloak back. They engaged in a tug of war.

"It's mine!"

"No... it... isn't!" Grey Cloak pulled hard with both arms, but the orc woman reeled him in. "Bloody horseshoes, you're strong. Even for an orc. Especially for a woman."

"It runs in the family!" The taut muscles in her shoulders and arms bunched up as she rocked backward. "You will both pay for trying to defile me."

"We aren't trying to defile you, Sleeping Beauty," Grey Cloak said through clenched teeth. He wasn't about to let go of his cloak—not now, not ever. "I only want my cloak! I couldn't care less about the rest of you."

With her nostrils flaring, she replied, "That's what they all say! But I won't be fooled again."

Dyphestive tackled her. "Sorry."

The move didn't break her strong grip on the cloak. "It's mine! It's mine! It's mine!" Wrapped up in Dyphestive's arms, she cocked her head back and busted him in the nose with her forehead.

"Stop that before you get hurt," Dyphestive said.

She kneed him in the beans.

"That's it!" Dyphestive's eyes burned like flames. "You want to fight dirty, so be it." He filled his hand with her braided locks and walloped her in the gut with his fist.

"Ooof!" The orc woman doubled over and released the cloak. She started to cry. "Why did you hit me? Can't you see I'm a woman trying to protect herself?" She let out a wet sob. "I'm all alone. What did you expect me to do?"

Dyphestive dropped his guard and stammered, "I-I'm sorry. I didn't mean to hit you so hard. Sometimes I don't know my own strength. Let me help you." He stretch out his hands and leaned toward the sobbing woman.

She took his hands, twisted under him, and slung him to the ground, then she rolled on top of him, pinned him between her thighs, and started pounding his face with her big-knuckled fists.

Watching the brutal scene unfold, Grey Cloak casually swung his cloak over his shoulders and said, "Brother, have you ever seen an orc cry before? I saw that move coming a league away." He reached into one of his many pockets and fished out a dagger then slipped behind the vicious woman and stuck the tip to her back. "The fun is over, unless you really, really want me to run you through."

She froze, her body tensed.

"Ah, ah, ah," he warned her as he pressed the tip of the dagger harder. "I know exactly where the heart is, though you don't appear to have one. Raise your hands."

She lifted them halfway.

"Higher!"

She complied. "Are you going to have your way with me and kill me after?"

"Ettin's ears, woman, could you be more obsessed with yourself?" He leaned over and asked Dyphestive, "Are you well?"

Dyphestive wiped a dab of blood from his nose and said apparently without realizing he was ogling the woman straddled on top of him, "Couldn't be better."

She glowered at him.

"Oh no, sorry, not like that, I mean."

"Do you mind if I stand?" she asked. "I swear I won't attack. An orc's word."

"Oh, that's so very valuable, but please, rise," Grey Cloak said.

She backed off of Dyphestive and slowly moved away. "You really aren't after me, are you?"

"Not at all. As a matter of fact..." Grey Cloak moved away and picked up his brother's shirt. "We truly want to help. At least for now." He tossed her the shirt. "But this will have to do instead of my cloak, dearie. Now cover up your modesty before my brother drools all over himself."

"I'm not drooling. Will you stop saying things like that?" Dyphestive whined as he made a point to look away from her.

She caught the shirt and pulled it over her body. It was a little big but fit her well. Her many long braids hung over her shoulders. "My name is Gorva. How did you acquire that dagger?" Her eyes widened, and she snapped her fingers. "It was hidden in the cloak, wasn't it?"

Grey Cloak shrugged. "Something like that."

She swung to face Dyphestive and asked, "And how is your face not broken?"

Dyphestive pushed himself up to his feet and said, "Don't take it personally, but I have a really hard head. But you can punch with true power. I'll give you that. I felt it."

Gorva put her knuckles on her hips and said, "So, you two really are good ones, huh?"

Grey Cloak tucked his dagger away. "We try, but things haven't been going our way lately, as you can see."

"Well, you know why I'm here, but why are you here?" she asked.

"We had a run-in with the Black Guard as well." It wasn't a completely honest answer but honest enough. He was careful with what he said, because Gorva didn't come across as someone that was easily fooled.

Her expression soured. "I hate the Black Guard. I hate Black Frost. I hate them all."

They raised their eyebrows.

"You sound like an old friend of mine," Grey Cloak said, referring to Anya the Sky Rider. "If it gives you any comfort, we hate Black Frost too."

"*Roooaaarrr!*"

Thunderbreath's bellowing was distant but loud enough to scatter the birds.

"Perhaps we spoke too loudly," Dyphestive said.

"I'd kill that dragon, too, if I were able. I've killed dragons before," Gorva said. "I've killed lots of wicked things."

"Killing a dragon is no small feat. How did you pull that off?" Grey Cloak asked as he caught her glare. "Only curious. I'm not questioning if the story is true or not."

"It was a middling, on the shores of Lake Flugen. I journeyed to find my father, Hogrim, a Sky Rider," Gorva said.

Grey Cloak cut her off. "Excuse me, did you say that your father was a Sky Rider?" He knew very well who Hogrim was. He was one of the Sky Riders he'd trained with at Hidemark on Gunder Island.

"What I say is true!"

"Easy, Gorva. I believe you. Truly, I do." He produced the dagger and tossed it end over end to her.

She snatched it out of the air with saucer-sized eyes.

"I knew Hogrim too."

12

DᴙᴘHᴇsᴛɪᴠᴇ ᴘʟᴏᴡᴇᴅ ʜɪs ᴡᴀʏ ᴛʜʀᴏᴜɢʜ ᴛʜᴇ ᴊᴜɴɢʟᴇ ᴡɪᴛʜ Gʀᴇʏ Cʟᴏᴀᴋ ᴀɴᴅ Gᴏʀᴠᴀ in tow. Grey Cloak had filled her in about his relationship with her father during the journey. Gorva hung on to his every word, listening intently with her mouth half open. She teared up on more than one occasion.

"It was Anya, the niece of Justus, that discovered Black Frost's surprise attack. She said that everything in Hidemark's crater had been turned to ash. Even the giants burned by the power of Black Frost's breath. They didn't stand a chance."

"Don't say that," Gorva said as she swept a leafy branch aside. "My father always stood a chance. He was strong, the strongest Sky Rider of all."

"No arguing there," he replied politely. "I can see his strength in you."

"I get it from my mother's side," she said, managing a small grin, "but she is dead too. Killed by Black Frost's forces. We all fought, my brothers and sisters. I was the last of the Hogrims to survive."

"I'm sorry," Grey Cloak said.

"So, you are a Sky Rider?" she asked.

"Yes and no. They kicked me out when I went to rescue Dyphestive. It's a long story."

"You have the rest of your lifetime to tell me," she said.

Dyphestive pushed through a thicket of berry bushes and faced a clear lagoon. A waterfall hundreds of feet tall plunged into the lagoon. "Fresh water!" he hollered.

Grey Cloak hooked his arm. "Do you remember the last time we refreshed ourselves in a lagoon? We almost didn't make it back out." He hunkered down. "Let's wait it out and see what happens."

Dyphestive nodded and crouched back with him. He felt Gorva's warm breath on his neck and moved several inches away and sat down. "Gorva, we aren't here by chance. We are looking for our companions."

"Sky Riders?" she asked.

"No, but every bit as durable. I'm going to need them if we hope to defeat Black Frost."

"How can you defeat Black Frost without Sky Riders? My father told me that only the Sky Riders can defeat the likes of him." Gorva thrust her finger at him. "And if I had a dragon, I'd be a Sky Rider too. I was only a child, but my father promised to train me. He took me on his dragon once. It was an experience that I will never forget. There is nothing better than riding the skies."

"If you ask me, it's overrated." Giving Gorva further study, he realized that she wasn't much older, or any older, than they were. And given the nature of her deep strength and lineage, it was highly possible that she could be a natural too. "So, the goal is to find our companions, hopefully alive, and find a way off of this island."

"I am very surprised that you would risk so much to save your friends," she said. "Not many would do such a thing."

"Everyone needs a hobby," he said.

She stiffened. "A hobby? You call this a hobby?"

"It sounds better than saying I have a death wish."

Dyphestive duck-walked backward through the brush and talked with his voice down. "The lagoon has visitors."

A pack of people, a mix of wary-eyed men and women, were on the other side of the lagoon. They wore modern garb that was in poor condition and carried crude weapons made from wood and stone. The group hurried along the edge of the lagoon, casting glances over their shoulders. A pair of dwarven men, one with a spear and the other a stone hatchet, stood watch while the others filled waterskins in the waterfall.

The entire process of filling the waterskins didn't take long. The group slung them over their shoulders, exchanged silent hand signals, turned their backs on the lagoon, and hurried toward the bush.

A young man at the rear of the group slipped on the muddy bank and dropped his waterskin. He snatched it up and slung it back over his shoulder then took a moment to scan the water. His eyes swept over the brush Grey Cloak and the others were hiding behind, and they narrowed.

Under his breath, Grey Cloak said, "Nobody move."

The youth took a step toward the lagoon.

A giant crocodile the size of a horse burst from underneath a bed of lily pads. Its massive jaws clamped down on the young man's legs. The young man gave a horrific scream. The whites of his eyes clearly showed as he stabbed the lagoon monster with his spear.

The others of the group came running but not before the great crocodile pulled the young man into the water and vanished beneath the bubbling surface.

A young woman ran into the lagoon, screaming at the top of her lungs, "No! No!"

The others grabbed her by the arms and hauled her kicking and screaming out of the water. The young man was gone, never to come back.

With frowns and deeply creased faces, the pack carried the sobbing woman away and disappeared back into the wood.

Placing a hand on Grey Cloak's shoulder, Gorva said, "We should stay out of the water."

Grey Cloak looked over his shoulder, smirked, and said, "Thank you, Gorva. I'll cancel my plans to take a refreshing dip."

"Are we going to follow them?" Dyphestive asked.

"No. I am going to follow them, and the both of you are going to follow me. Quietly."

13

It had been a long time since Grey Cloak navigated through jungle terrain. The dewy leaves dripped as he passed through them. Small insects skittered away from his feet. The colorful birds let out gusty calls and chirps while large-ringed snakes slithered down the trees.

He moved on cat feet, following the telltale signs of the passage of the others. The pack of people he was following were careful to not leave any tracks, but they were far from perfect. They still moved quickly, leaving partial footprints in the soft ground and twisted leaves behind.

Dyphestive and Gorva brought up the rear, moving their big bodies through the tight folds of the jungle with surprising ease. If Grey Cloak had his way, he'd go it alone, moving much quicker, but the burly pair, like hilltop barbarians, had little trouble keeping pace.

He came to a stop and squatted. A vine ran across the faint path and stretched from tree to tree. It was pulled tight like a bowstring.

Dyphestive leaned over Grey Cloak's shoulder and said, "A trap."

"Or an alarm." Grey Cloak glanced above him and searched the branches. Nothing was suspended, and there wasn't any sort of net on the ground. He dropped his gaze and looked for any imperfections in the natural pattern of the jungle. There were many red and yellow ferns with their leaves turned over. Quietly, he said, "It's a trip vine. Simple but effective. Be careful where you step."

Back in Gunder Island, the elven sisters Stayzie and Mayzie had trained him to make and detect traps and snares. The trip vine was a simple way to bring a pursuer down while making a lot of noise. It could quickly turn the hunter into the hunted.

He envisioned the unforgettable elven beauties in his mind. Their time had been cut short by Black Frost.

Dyphestive caught him absentmindedly staring and gave him a nudge. "What are we waiting for?"

"Be patient. I'm thinking." Grey Cloak stepped over the trip vine and watched to make sure the other two didn't hit it. "Let's go."

It didn't take him long to find the trail of the pack. The deeper into the jungle they went, the sloppier they became. He had a feeling the distraught young woman had held them back, judging by the dragging heel marks in the dirt. In the meantime, he paid extra-special attention to the ground, looking for more trip vines.

Another hour later, he spotted another trip vine, and only a few dozen yards past that was another. He faced the others and said, "I have a hunch about something. Wait here."

Dyphestive nodded. Gorva distanced herself from Dyphestive and scowled. He shrugged helplessly.

Grey Cloak stole his way through the jungle, and as he'd expected, he discovered several more trip vines encircling the area. He hurried back to the others and said, "Evening is falling. I think they are setting up camp and have the trip vines set up to warn them."

Gorva pushed forward with the dagger Grey Cloak had given her and asked, "What are we waiting for?"

"It's a spy mission. All we want to do is watch and listen. If they catch on to us"—he tapped his chest—"let me do the talking. After all, they should be reasonable to talk to. We are all in the same situation, right?" He eyed her dagger. "But caution before bravery."

"After you," Gorva said.

With the last moments of daylight fading behind the great hills, Grey Cloak led them deeper into the jungle. Trip vines were scattered all over the jungle floor, and he had a hard time imagining so many. He started picking his way down a path that avoided them entirely.

The muffled sound of voices reached him. He stopped and touched his ear and pointed ahead.

The voices were so low that he couldn't make out any words, but they belonged to men. Branches snapped, and the smell of wood burning lingered in the air.

Together, they crept closer and stopped in the cover of huge ferns.

Grey Cloak split the ferns apart with his fingers as Dyphestive's and Gorva's bodies pressed against his shoulders. He gave them an irritated glance and turned his attention back to the pack of people.

The young woman who'd screamed earlier crouched in front of the small fire and stared, while an older woman started cooking dead lizards on spits. She talked to the younger woman in a soothing tone, but the younger woman only showed a face of stone.

Grey Cloak didn't see any of the others. Aside from the two women, the small camp was abandoned. The hairs on the nape of his neck rose. He turned and looked behind him. A giant-sized tarantula—camouflaged in the natural colors of the trees—silently dropped from the branches. It had a dwarven rider.

Dyphestive and Gorva spun around and caught a blast of sticky webbing shooting from the spider's spinnerets in the face. Grey Cloak sprang away but not before the webbing caught his legs. In a moment, a blanket of webbing sprayed over all of them.

"Bloody bones!" Gorva roared as she stabbed the webbing with her dagger. The more she struggled, the more she stuck. The gooey web held her fast.

"Zooks!" Grey Cloak exclaimed as he vainly tried to slip the sticky bondage. "Dyphestive, can you break it?"

With his bare shoulders, chest, and arms knotted up and bulging with cords of muscles, Dyphestive replied, "I'm trying, but there is too much!"

One by one, the eight-eyed tarantula, with stiff black hairs raised all over its hideous body, rolled them up in cocoons.

Grey Cloak helplessly watched himself being log-rolled over the ground. His stomach became queasy, and he started to retch. "And I thought flying was awful."

The monster tarantula lifted them onto its back and hauled them deeper into the darkening jungle.

14

Stuck inside the mouth of a cave and left for dead, Grey Cloak, Dyphestive, and Gorva had plenty of time to bicker at one another.

"It's pretty simple. I watch the front. The two of you watch the rear," Grey Cloak argued. "I mean, how in the world did you miss a ginormous spider?"

Dyphestive squirmed in his bonds and said, "You missed it, too, brother."

"How many times do I have to explain it? I'm surveying the front and the ground, and you two donkey skulls should be guarding the rear." He was propped up against the cave wall and wriggling with all of his strength. His web-made cocoon shifted, and he slid down the wall and landed with his nose on the ground. "Thunderbolts!"

Gorva let out a gruff laugh. "You talk too much. Serves you right."

Grey Cloak turned his lips out of the dirt and said, "And what assets have you brought along to the party aside from your big mouth?"

She blanched. Somehow, she managed to hop on her hind end toward him, teetered over, and landed across his back.

Grey Cloak let out an "Ooof!" Red-faced, he said, "Will you get off of me, you ogre?"

"I'm not an ogre," she said as she pushed harder on him. "I'm an orc. The daughter of Hogrim!"

"More like the spawn of Hogrim, you fat heifer!"

"I'll kill you for that!" Gorva rolled over him like a rolling pin flattening bread. "Ignoramus elf!"

"Ignoramus, hah! I'd like to hear you spell that!"

Gorva put her weight on him with every letter and spelled it out.

"I!"

"Oof!"

"G! N!"

"Oof!" he said. "Get off of me!"

"O! R! Uh..."

"I told you that you couldn't spell it." He turned his face toward his brother. "Didn't I say so? You heard me!"

"O!" Dyphestive blurted out.

"Oof!"

"Thanks, Dyphestive," she said. "R! A! M! O! U! S! E!"

Grey Cloak burst out laughing. "It's M-U-S, stupid, not M-O-U-S-E!"

Gorva bounced off of his back and came down hard.

"Ooof!" he wheezed.

She rolled off of him and lay on her back beside him. "Who cares. I don't think spelling is going to get us out of here."

He caught his breath and said, "It's interesting that the outside of the webbing isn't sticky like the inside. Maybe we can roll out of here."

"And down the side of a cliff!"

"That's why I was going to let you go first," he offered.

"I'll roll you out of here," she fired back.

"Grey, can't you burn your way out?" Dyphestive asked.

"Oh, certainly. Why not. I'll burn my hands off while I'm at it. No, thank you," he said.

Gorva eyeballed him and asked, "Is that how you shocked me? With power? My father had that. Why can't you use it again?"

Grey Cloak sighed. He didn't want to reveal why but said, "It works differently in water."

Soft footfalls caught their attention, and they turned their heads toward the cave entrance. A stocky dwarf with a full head of gray hair and a chest-long beard entered. It was the same dwarf that rode on the back of the spider. Both of his eyes were missing, and the scar tissue around the sockets showed that they'd been gouged out. He carried a small walking stick with a fist-sized river stone on the top.

"The three of you are a mighty wind. Always blowing. Squabblers. Children. Especially the elf," the stern dwarf said. "No man survives on the island long without practicing caution. Your saucy talk might get us all killed. I should have gagged you."

Grey Cloak cleared his throat. Before he could utter a syllable, the blind dwarf stepped over Gorva and gently clubbed him in the head with his staff.

"Gum up, elf. I talk. You don't." The dwarf spun his staff around. "I'll bust all of your jaws if I must. I am called Thatcher. To be clear, I am the leader of a small clan of survivors on the island. All of us have seen many come and go. Most don't make it as far as you did." He tapped his stick on the ground. "But there is strength in numbers. If we come by men and women of good salt, we offer them a chance. If not... we send them on their way."

Grey Cloak battled the urge to speak. That last thing he wanted was another painful knot on his head. Luckily, Dyphestive spoke for him.

"I am Dyphestive, and we can—"

Thatcher smashed his staff across Dyphestive's skull. "Don't talk."

Dyphestive's eyebrows knitted. He continued, "And that's Grey Cloak and Gorva."

Whack!

"You can hit me all that you wish, but my head is harder than that stick of yours," Dyphestive stated defiantly. He stuck his chin out.

Whack! Whack! Whack!

Dyphestive grinned at the blind dwarf.

Thatcher ambled closer to Dyphestive and ran his grubby fingers over Dyphestive's face. He felt his lips and teeth. "Goat turds. Are you smiling?"

"Sometimes I can't help myself."

"Interesting." Thatcher set his stone-headed staff aside and withdrew a dagger with a razor-sharp black blade. He held it against Dyphestive's eye socket. "Let's see if I can't bring a bigger smile to your face."

15

THATCHER'S BLACK-BLADED DAGGER CUT THROUGH DYPHESTIVE'S COCOON LIKE A hot knife through butter.

"You're freeing us?"

"Not exactly," Thatcher said in his gruff voice. "No one is really free on this island. But I am satisfied that you aren't the sort of trouble that we seek to avoid." The blind dwarf moved over to Gorva and cut into the cocoon.

"How are you doing that?" Gorva asked as she peeled off the sticky cocoon shell. "You don't have any eyes."

"Just because I'm blind doesn't mean that I cannot see." Thatcher turned his back to her and headed for Grey Cloak. "Now for the big mouth."

Grey Cloak watched with widening eyes as the dwarf cut into the cocoon with unfaltering precision. It was still sticky, but the strands of webbing on the inside quickly dried up and faded away. Pulling webbing off of his hands and balling it up in his palms, he said, "Thank you."

"Huh. Thank yourself. All of that griping and bellyaching you did told us all that we needed to hear. You're stranded here the same as us, trying to survive." He lifted his other hand and showed them Grey Cloak's dagger. "Not sure how you smuggled this onto the island, but I'll keep it on me for now. It's a true treasure. Come." He walked out of the cave.

They exchanged surprised looks as they followed after him. They exited the cave mouth, which overlooked a drop-off to another level. Thatcher led the way down a narrow ledge that was a little wider than his shoulders.

Grey Cloak marveled at the blind dwarf's surprising agility. He didn't move fast or with the nimbleness of a squirrel, but he was surefooted and steady as he led them down the rocky hilltop. When they bottomed out at the base of the hill, they were met by the rest of Thatcher's gang. They were the same weary-looking group they'd seen at the pond. Their eyes were hard, and their jaws were set.

Each of them carried a crude weapon, a spear or a club, made from sticks and stone. Behind them was the giant tarantula.

Dyphestive waved his fingers at them and said, "Hello."

The pack returned stone-faced stares. Aside from Thatcher, there was another dwarf, younger, deep chested and with a curly brown beard, and four humans, two men and two women.

Thatcher marched by the wary-eyed group and stood underneath the massive spider. "I'm not one for introductions, but this is Itchee." He pointed at the spider's head. "He's my dog—*our* dog and protects us all. You can get to know the others later. For now, let's camp and fix something to eat."

Dyphestive, Gorva, and Grey Cloak joined the pack in another spot nestled in the lower caves, where prying eyes couldn't see. Bushy Bull, the other dwarf, stood watch, while the humans prepared food and Thatcher talked. The humans said little, as they seemed more concerned with cooking lizards and horned rabbits than anything else. The women served them, giving them small charred bits of meat on sticks.

Grey Cloak chewed on lizard meat and gave the woman who served him a thankful smile. She had pretty eyes and looked away. It was the young woman who'd lost her partner earlier in the day.

"Strength in numbers is the only way to survive here," Thatcher said, and he whittled on a rabbit horn with Grey Cloak's blade. "We are a small pack and should be bigger, but too big is bad. We've survived thanks to our wits and Itchee." The giant tarantula was nowhere to be found. "I control him because of the sacrifice I made."

"Your eyes?"

Thatcher nodded. "I'm from a long line of druids that thrived in these hills for centuries. When Thunderbreath came, he slaughtered the whole lot of us. All good in the island was destroyed by him. I did what I had to to protect us."

"How many people are on the island?" Dyphestive asked.

"Thousands at least." Thatcher propped his beefy forearm on his knee, leaned forward, and asked, "You came from Harbor Lake, correct?"

"Yes," Grey Cloak said.

"That's one prisoner ship, but there are four in all. They come at different times of the day or night from the north, south, east, and west." Thatcher turned the rabbit horn into a sharp little stick. "You are fortunate that you didn't encounter the beach devils when you arrived. They are a nasty pack of men turned cannibals that feast on the newcomers."

Grey Cloak shook his head and gave Thatcher a perplexed look. "I'm confused. If Black Frost is sending his enemies here, wouldn't the island be filled with good people?"

Thatcher responded with a rusty chuckle. "You are young and naïve. It's no surprise that you would think this place would become a paradise, but here, the strong survive. Do you really think that Black Frost would banish his enemies to a suitable retreat? No, he is as sly as a fox. He imports evil."

They leaned closer to the fire, and Gorva asked in her gruff manner, "What do you mean?"

"First," Thatcher said, his face near the fire, "all men carry evil in them. A place like this, remote and dangerous, will let it out. Second..." He spun the dagger in his hand. "Black Frost sends people whose hearts were black before they arrived. We call the black-hearted tormenters Ministers of Evil. They serve Thunderbreath and sow nothing but discord from one side of the island to the other."

"How do we know that you aren't one of them?" Grey Cloak asked.

Thatcher tossed the dagger to Gorva and said, "You don't."

16

Gorva snatched the dagger out of the air.

"A man's heart speaks through his actions. And..." He lightened his tone. "Most of them have black tattoos on their faces. That makes it easier." He started in on a leg of rabbit and tore the flesh from the bone with his teeth. "It's good. Juicy. They are the biggest rabbits in the world."

Dyphestive licked the rabbit-meat grease from his fingers and asked, "Has anyone ever escaped the island?"

"I wondered when you'd get around to asking that. It's the first question that comes to anyone's mind. Escape." Thatcher spit. "Puh! We don't spend our time keeping track of who comes and goes. We have a hard enough time fending for ourselves. We've crossed paths with others over the years, but none have ever shared about a path of escape. Of course, we've heard plenty of tales of those who died trying.

"If you were a fish, you might make it, but no craft or swimmer will escape Thunderbreath's notice." Thatcher cleared his throat and drank from a water-skin. "Your life is on this island now. Keeping moving to survive and make the most of it."

"Well, that isn't the plan, Thatcher. We are on a rescue mission."

Thatcher spit out a mouthful of water, and the others in the pack stopped eating. "Say that again?"

"We are on a rescue mission. Searching for friends of ours," Grey Cloak replied.

Thatcher's jaw dropped. "You came here on purpose? Are you mad?"

"No, only loyal," Dyphestive replied. "We hoped that you might be able to help us."

"I haven't seen a face in years, but I know names. We know names," Thatcher said with a look of disgust. "People are scattered all about. The burrow. They hide. Like us. Who are you looking for?"

"They would have come to the island several years ago. Two men, Jakoby and Reginald, who calls himself the Razor. And a woman, Leena, from the Ministry of Hoods."

Thatcher grunted. "They sound like fighters. Is that so?"

"Fierce fighters," Dyphestive said. "The very best."

"How can you be certain that they are here?" Thatcher said.

"We have friends that told us," Grey Cloak said.

"And you believe them? Hah!" Thatcher tossed his waterskin aside and said, "Most men and women that come don't last very long. Often, a few weeks at most. But if your comrades are true survivors and can carry weight, it's possible they still live."

"You've managed to survive," Grey Cloak commented.

"Yes, because of Itchee. Without him, we'd all be dead. He keeps intruders away. No one wants to cross him." He sighed as he rubbed his hands on his knees. "I've never heard of such a fool's errand in my life. But the best place to look is on the northern face of the island. The dragons destroyed most everything that was here before, but one town still stands. Braykurz. It's a den of wolves ruled by the Minister of Evil and their minions. It operates like a fishing town well enough and has hovels stretching into the high hillsides. Be careful, but you can ask around there. Nothing but trouble. Nothing but death." He looked in Grey Cloak's direction. "Tell me. How do you hope to get off of this island if you even find them?"

"A good question." Grey Cloak smirked. "We haven't figured that out yet."

"Yet something tells me that you have something stuck up your sleeve." Thatcher grunted. "Hoy! We'll take you to Braykurz. The journey isn't long, but it will be slow on account of all the devils about. But I want something in return."

"What might that be?" Grey Cloak asked.

"I'm not worried about me so much, but if you can find a way off of this island, I want you to take them with you." Thatcher eyed the pack. "They deserve a second chance."

Grey Cloak sat up and said, "I can't promise that, Thatcher. All I can promise is that I'll try."

Thatcher nodded. "That will have to do. We leave in the morning."

"Would you be offended if I conferred with my comrades in private?" Grey Cloak asked.

"Do as you will."

They huddled out of earshot in the cover of the leafy branches. "We can go it alone or trust them, but I wanted to hear your thoughts."

Dyphestive's face was grim when he said, "I've been burned by a dwarf before. Koll was a druid, too, and he twisted a knife in my back. I trusted him wholeheartedly like a fool."

Grey Cloak nodded. "I had similar thoughts." He gazed at Gorva. "You?"

"If it's on the other side of the island, we can walk around the ring of beaches," she offered.

"True, but he says devils comb those beaches day and night," he replied.

"That's only what he is telling us," she said. "We don't know that it's true."

He glanced at the dagger in her palm. "I think giving you a weapon is a fair sign to trust him. I'll take my chances but only if you agree."

Dyphestive nodded. "The situation is different, and I believe we can handle ourselves at the first sign of trouble."

Gorva shook her head, looked up, and said, "And I won't let that giant spider get the drop on us again."

Grey Cloak smiled. "Good. It's settled then. The rescue is underway."

17

HARBOR LAKE

Zora carried a bucket of crabs along the dock toward the heart of Harbor Lake. Her shoulder ached underneath the weight of the wriggling crabs. She switched the bucket from one hand to the other. "The things I do for dragons," she said.

It was late in the evening, and a gusty, chilly breeze came from the lake, stirring her hair. Goosebumps popped up on her neck.

I should have worn my cloak, she thought.

She'd trimmed down a good bit since they departed Raven Cliff. Her arms and legs were slimmer and firmer. She'd avoided all of the sweetcakes and wine she used to fill her emptiness. Now, she had a purpose. A mission. She wore smaller, tighter clothes to show for it.

With her head down and her back to the wind, she cut through an alley, scattered a den of cats chasing sewer rats, and crossed the next street. She checked over her shoulder before she ducked into the next alley. Only a few people walked the streets at night, and they moved quickly. The Black Guard was nosey, and they questioned everyone, it seemed.

Zora remained vigilant to avoid them, but she always felt as if she was being followed.

"*Screeech!*"

The sound of a shrieking dragon flying overhead rattled her spine. She crouched but kept her feet moving. *I hate those things.*

She stopped at the end of the next alley and looked both ways. The streets were clear of patrolling Black Guard.

"*Screeech!*"

Zora instinctively ran her finger over the Scarf of Shadows. It was the only protection she had besides the Ring of Mist on her finger. She twisted the ring on her finger and crossed the street, but she couldn't shake the feeling of eyes on her back. She stole a glance over her shoulder. In the alley she'd left, a shadowy figure moved along the darkness of the walls.

Uh-huh. I thought so.

Even though Harbor Town was run by the Black Guard, it didn't mean that it didn't have its share of murderers and thieves. It could be anyone following her. She squatted behind a rotting storage barrel, lifted the Scarf of Shadows over her nose, and vanished.

Try to catch me now.

She didn't stick around to see who was following her. Prowlers were more than common at that time of night. Instead, she used the power of invisibility to finish her journey to the barn where Streak and Cliff were stabled.

The icky smell of hay and manure tickled her nose as she made her way to the stable gate. Cliff chewed on a mouthful of straw while she opened it. She called for the runt dragon and rattled the bucket of crabs. "Oh, Streak, I have a delicious treat for my little friend." She lowered the scarf from her nose and reappeared.

"I can see that."

Zora's heart skipped, and she snapped her neck back and looked up. Streak was nestled in the rafters.

"You didn't have to do that," she said, clutching her chest. "My heart is racing enough."

"Really?" The end of Streak's tail curled in and out. "You were that excited to see me? How flattering."

She dug a live crab out of the bucket and tossed it up to Streak's awaiting jaws. "Don't flatter yourself."

Streak's jaws clamped down on the crab, cracking the hard shell and squirting out the juices on Zora.

"Ugh ... be careful, you scaly slob." She wiped her squinted eye. "Don't you have better manners?"

"Crunchy and delicious," Streak said as he pulverized the crab with hundreds of sharp little teeth and swallowed it. "I'll have another, please."

She pulled one off of the top and dropped it on the ground. The crab crawled over the hay. "Feed yourself. I bought you an entire bucket, after all."

Streak flicked his pink tongue out and said, "And I appreciate you. Besides, I either ate or scared off all of the cats in the area."

"I saw a few in the alleys on the way over here," she said.

Streak's serpentine eyes brightened. "Really? Whereabouts?"

Zora slid down the stable wall, sat, and sighed. "Just eat your crab, will you."

He pinned the white crab down with his paw, and a front crab claw latched onto the end of his snout. "Uh, a little help here. I think it got me."

Zora managed a laugh, crawled over, and ripped the crab claw off of his face with a grunt. "They are better cooked, you know." She fed the crab claw to him. "And that way, they can't bite you."

Streak crunched the crab. "No, thank you. As raw as a wriggling worm is fine with me."

Zora's lips twisted. "Ew."

"Is everything well, Zora? You appear to be distressed. Is watching over me that dull of a task?"

"No." She leaned back against the wall and crossed her legs. "Aren't you worried?"

"I don't believe it's in a dragon's nature to worry."

"That must make life easy for you."

"When you have a beautiful half-elven woman fetching crabs for you, yes, life is easy enough." He grinned like a toothy crocodile and nudged some crab toward her feet with his nose. "Won't you have some?"

She held out a hand. "I'm plenty full." With a huff, she blew a curly strand of red hair away from her eye. "I'm tired. I'm tired of always watching my back. I wish I could be more like you, Grey Cloak, and Dyphestive. All of you are so confident."

"Hm... I never really thought about it." Streak held his nose over the bucket. "These crabs are very interesting." He gently bit a crab claw and pulled. All of the crabs started to lift out of the bucket. He let go. "See that? One tries to crawl out, but the others latch on and pull it down. People are much like that, aren't they? Always dragging one another down."

She gave an agreeable nod, eyed him, and asked, "Are you saying we are crabs?"

"Crablike. It's your nature to drag one another down."

"Or," she said, "we are safer in a group."

"Have it your way if it makes you feel better. You look tired, Zora. Get some rest. I'll be fine. I have Cliff to protect me."

Zora reached over and rubbed his bumpy skull. Two small horns with thin black rings were developing on his head. "It sounds like good advice. I'll swing by in the morning." She had the urge to kiss him like a person but resisted. "Good night, Streak."

Crunching another crab, Streak absentmindedly said, "Good night."

Zora left the barn and headed for the Greasy Horn, another shoddy tavern she'd holed up in. It was a lot easier navigating the salt-mired streets without a bucketload of crabs in her fist. Sticking to the shadows and avoiding the pools of light offered by the oil lamppost, she managed to navigate her way back to the tavern only a few blocks away.

She went through the kitchen entrance and was slapped in the face with the overwhelming scent of spilled ale and seafood. Orcs worked the kitchen, wearing smocks covered in grease. The black hairs on their bare arms were matted and sweating. They smoked cigars, too, and ashes dropped into stew pots and were stirred in. Zora almost vomited in her mouth.

Never eat at this place. Yuck.

Outside of the kitchen, the robust crowd's carousing was in full swing. She quickly navigated through the smelly bodies pressing against her. She made it to the stairwell and hurried up the steps as quickly as a cat and entered her room.

She closed the door behind her and stood with her back against it, catching her breath. The door did little to mute the tavern's rambunctious clamor, but at least she had walls and a door between them.

Who can rest in a place like this? I should have stayed in the loft in the barn.

Zora allowed her eyes to adjust to the darkness. An oil lantern on the night-stand beside the bed showed the slightest flame. She took one step forward then froze as another floorboard inside the room groaned. Something hit her hard in the back of the head. Stars exploded in her eyes, and down on her knees she went.

18

"HELLO, ZORA," SOMEONE SAID IN A WARM BUT DEVILISHLY RUGGED VOICE. "IT'S been a while."

The flame of the oil lantern was turned up, and an all-too-familiar face came into view. It was the fish-eyed warrior Sash, the leader of the Scourge. The rugged-looking man wore his dyed-black leather armor, and ribbon-like black sashes hung from his arms and legs, and one was wrapped around his waist like a belt. He had long, pointed sideburns and short hair.

Zora reached for her dagger, but it was gone from the scabbard. She felt something sticking in her back.

"Lift those hands up, pretty," a woman with a scratchy voice said. "And take a seat on your comfy bed."

Blinking the spots from her eyes, Zora complied and turned toward the rodent-faced Squirrel, who had messy hair and a smallish build and wore a fur-collared cloak. "Look what the cat dragged in."

Sash barked with laughter. He grabbed her chin and said, "Oh, how I missed your quick wit, Zora." He put his boot on the bed beside her and leaned over her. "So, how have you been?"

She looked him dead in the eye and asked, "What do you want?"

"That's an interesting question—a question for a question." Sash back-handed her across the face. His tone darkened. "I ask. You answer."

"I'm fine! Happy!"

He nodded. "Better." His knuckles cracked when he balled up his fist. "Tell me, why did you leave Raven Cliff and come here?"

"I have business."

"What sort of business?"

"Nunya," she fired back.

Sash popped her again and knocked her onto the bed. He grabbed her scarf, squeezed it tight around her neck, and lifted her back up. He got nose to nose with her and said, "That's not what Tanlin said. No, he had a lot more to say when we questioned him. We beat the snot out of the old man, but he's still breathing... for now."

Zora busted him in the nose with her forehead. "You dirty murderer! You killed his wife, and now you beat him! Can you go any lower?"

Sash wiped his bloody nose, picked her up, and threw her into the wall. "I can do a lot worse than that. And I didn't kill his wife. It was an accident. And if it makes you feel any better, Bull put the hurting on him, not me. You might say I have a soft spot for him. Besides, you and Tanlin are spies, so don't pretend you are innocent. We enforce the dirty little tidbits of information you share. That's right. We all lie in the same bed. The same as we did before."

"Never!" She swung her hand around, bringing the flower-shaped Ring of Mist to bear. The tiny metal petals opened, and a fine pollen-like mist sprayed into Sash's face.

He gently coughed and grinned. "We didn't forget the ring, girl. Honzur prepared a protection spell. The only one that is going to sleep is you." The black sashes on his arms and legs came to life like snakes and slithered onto her body. The silky fabric tendrils squeezed her wrists together and entwined her ankles and legs. The last snakelike sash circled her mouth. "Look at you." He patted her face with his hard hand. "As quiet as a mouse. Just the way I like you."

She wriggled and strained against her bonds. The black cords stiffened like iron and cut her circulation off.

Sash lifted her like a child onto his broad shoulder. "The more you squirm, the tighter they become." He slapped her on the rump. "Behave yourself, or they'll cut your life off."

19

"WELL, ISN'T THIS A DELIGHT?" HONZUR SAID. THE BALD WIZARD HELD A GLOWING fingertip under Zora's eye. He was a mysterious older man adorned in wizardly robes that hung loose on his scrawny body. A nasty jagged scar crossed his right cheek, his fingers were covered in ornamental rings, and tattoos decorated his hands like a painting. "It's so very nice to have you in our presence again, Zora. It's been a long time."

"I can't say the same," Zora replied as he pulled her head away from his burning finger. She was bound to a chair by black ribbon-like sashes in a damp room in the corner of a dungeon. Water trickled down the walls and formed small puddles on the floor. Sash and Squirrel stood nearby, and they were joined by another member of the Scourge, Katrina.

Katrina was a warrior with tomboyish good looks and green hair tied back in a long braid. She wore a suit of leather armor dyed black like Sash's and sported a pair of swords on her hips. She had a strong athletic build and wore a confident look on her face.

Zora's fingernails dug into her palms. The Scourge had caught her flatfooted, and they were onto Grey Cloak and Dyphestive's return but didn't know why. She clammed up.

Wait and see. Let them do the talking.

Honzur moved behind her and put his bony hands on her shoulders. "Zora," he whispered. "We have so much catching up to do. Tell me, how have you been?"

She looked out of the corner of her eye and said, "Get on with it, you old vulture. I don't have time to entertain your cryptic conversation."

Katrina smirked. "She still has some fire. I like it."

Honzur started to stroke Zora's hair. "Play nice, Zora. Or the more painful the process will be."

Sweat built up on her forehead, and a drop ran down her cheek.

The older wizard's fingers probed her skull and attached themselves around the temples. "I want you to see what I see, Zora. Open your mind, but don't concentrate. Let me do the work."

Honzur's hands started to glow, creating a soothing warmth that spread out of his fingers and into her skull. She gasped.

"Easy. This won't hurt a bit if you don't resist," Honzur said as his fingers softly needled her skull. "Open your mind. See what I see."

Zora tried to resist the invasion, but it was unlike anything she'd encountered before. Energy flowed into her mind, and she had no idea how to stop it. Her eyes opened wide, and the images of the other people in the cell started to fade and were replaced by something else. She gasped again. "Tanlin."

As clear as day, Zora could see Tanlin sitting inside his apartment, bound with rope and sagging in his leather chair. His swollen face was bruised, and his lip was busted. She'd never seen him in such bad shape. "What did you do to him?" she exclaimed.

"I didn't do it. Bull did. You are seeing through Bull's eyes. We are connected. Bull, wriggle your fingers."

Bull's fingers didn't appear, but his line of sight moved around.

"Idiot, hold your fingers up where I can see them."

Bull's hands passed his face and rose over his head.

Honzur sighed. "In front of your eyes. Put your fingers in front of your eyes."

Finally, a pair of scarred meaty hands appeared with wiggling sausage-sized fingers.

"That will do, Bull. You may drop your hands now," Honzur said.

Bull complied.

"Now, Zora, I want you to know that we mean business. And if you can't be completely honest with us, Tanlin is going to pay for it."

"It looks like he's paid enough for it already," she said. "Leave him alone."

"I'm more than happy to comply, so long as you are more than forthcoming." Honzur massaged her skull. "Breathe easy now. Very easy, and this won't hurt a bit."

She could still see Tanlin, but she couldn't hear inside the apartment. Tanlin was searching Bull's eyes. It was as if he were looking right at her, but he was hundreds of leagues away. She wanted to call out to him.

Tanlin, I'm so sorry.

"First, an easy question. Do you love Grey Cloak?" Honzur asked.

Zora heard sniggering but said, "No." A jolt of energy spread through her mind, piercing her right behind the eyes. "Gah!"

"Well, that was a lie. Bull, show Zora how we deal with liars."

She watched in horror as Tanlin's eyes widened a moment before Bull's fist crashed into his face. "Stop it! Stop it! He's an old man. This is low, even for you!"

"I'm guilty of actions far lower than this. I do what I must do to accomplish the mission. You would do the same as well," Honzur said. "Now, are you going to work with us or not?"

With her damp hair hanging over her eyes, Zora's shoulders slumped, and she nodded. "Don't hurt him anymore."

"That's all up to you." Honzur pressed his fingers harder into her head. "Tell me, where are Grey Cloak and Dyphestive?"

"Prisoner Island."

"Interesting," Honzur replied.

"I'll say," Sash agreed. "What are they doing there?"

Zora felt so weak and ashamed for answering. She could take the pain and die if she had to, but the hapless form of Tanlin slumped in his chair got to her. "Rescuing old friends."

"Ha! That's the dumbest thing I've ever heard," Sash stated.

"I wouldn't expect you to understand. Any of you. You aren't good people," she said.

"Zora," Honzur continued, "do they possess the Figurine of Heroes?"

"No."

"Where is it?"

"It was lost in the Wizard Watch at Arrowwood." She swallowed. "They don't have any idea where it is."

"She tells the truth," Honzur said. "If that is the case, we don't need to concern ourselves with Grey Cloak and Dyphestive."

"Good, because I wasn't planning on taking a trip to Prisoner Island," Sash said. "That's where I draw the line. Ask about the dragon."

"Huh?" Zora said.

"Yes, the runt dragon, Streak. Where is it?" Honzur asked.

Zora felt the pressure building in her mind. "What do you want with a little dragon?" she asked.

"Bull! Break some of Tanlin's fingers," Honzur ordered.

"No, wait!" Zora pleaded. She couldn't bear the thought of Tanlin being hurt. "The dragon is in the barn here in the city."

"Bull, stop." Honzur stroked her hair. "You stole a dragon from us once. A crypt dragon that can control others. I've since learned that Streak has the same power. Now the time for payback has come full circle. The runt dragon will be mine. Now tell us exactly where the dragon is. We'd like to pay it a visit."

Sagging in her bonds, Zora revealed the location and sobbed. She'd never felt so ashamed, but she had to protect Tanlin. Honzur released her head. The image of Tanlin was replaced by the workers of evil in the room. She hated them, one and all.

"Stay with her until it's finished," Honzur said to the others. He removed an oval egg-sized dragon charm that swirled with mystic colors and had the appearance of an eye. "Sash, you come with me. It's dragon-catching time."

20

STREAK HAD JUST FINISHED OFF HIS LAST CRAB WHEN HIS NOSTRILS TWITCHED. "Lord of the Air, Cliff, what have you been eating?" He fanned the air with his tail. "Don't answer that. I don't want to know."

Cliff the mule tooted again.

"I'm out of here. There's only so much even I can take." Streak wormed his way through the thick layers of straw and started climbing the back stable wall like a lizard. His sharp claws clung to the wood, and up he went to the top, where he switched over to a support beam that led into the rafters.

He took his time slinking across the rafter beams to his favorite spot, where the Inland Sea breeze passed through. He kissed the salty air with his tongue and said, "Ah, that's much better." From his lofty position, he clung to the wood and leaned his head over one side. It was the perfect spot to wait out curious cats that ventured into the barn. He licked his lips and thought, *Come, furry meat-filled delights. Come. I have plenty of room for more.*

The sun had set three times since Grey Cloak departed, and even though Streak didn't worry, he was still eager to venture elsewhere. Dragons weren't ones to be bored. They were more than comfortable remaining in a cozy burrow of some sort. But even a dragon could be curious. And swimming across the Inland Sea sounded like a fantastic adventure.

Would it be so bad if he didn't make it back and I had to rescue him? I like it.

A white long-haired cat crept into the barn.

Oh my, what do we have here? A pretty succulent kitty.

The fluffy white cat silently crept through the barn, moving past stable after stable, nose in the air.

That's it, my whiskered delight. Keep your nose pointed in that direction.

Streak had consumed most of the crab but not all. He'd left a few hunks behind the stable. He watched the cat stick its nose between the gap in the stable planks. The white cat squeezed through.

Perfect.

He snaked over the top beam as quietly as a mouse and stopped right over the cat. Streak licked his snout with a hungry swipe of his pink tongue.

A late-night treat all for me.

The cat gobbled up the crab meat bit after bit, taking large swallows.

Streak coiled his body, leaned over the beam, and prepared to drop. His eyes fastened on the cat.

Perfect. So perfect.

The cat's hackles rose. It pounced away, squeezed through the gap in the wooden stable gate, and darted out of the barn.

He glared at the mule. *Cliff, you stunk it up, didn't you?*

Streak sniffed. Cliff's foul odor didn't linger, but the soft scuffle of feet caught his earhole. He swung his thick neck around. Two men entered the barn.

Ah, those are the culprits that spooked my furry treat. I should flame them. I should —oh my, what is that? So... pretty...

One of the men held a beautiful gemstone that sparkled with many vibrant colors in the palm of his tattooed hand.

Streak could not tear his eyes away, nor did he want to. The beautiful stone called to him, its warm colors drawing him deeper and deeper into its enchanted womb. His neck swayed from side to side, and he was in a hypnotic state that bathed him in comfort and warmness.

Ah, I feel so good. The stone is so beautiful. I must have a closer look. His mouth opened in a wide yawn. *Mmm... I love it. I love that stone. It is my moon. My sun. My friend.*

Numbness fell over his extremities. His claws loosened their grip on the wood. The weight of his head dragged him from his position in the rafters. To him, he fell like a feather, with a soft golden bed waiting to catch him. He hit the ground with a loud thud that he didn't notice and lay flat on his back.

So beautiful. So precious.

The stable gate opened. Two men entered and stood over Streak. The only thing he noticed was the dragon charm, which glowed like a cozy fire in his eyes.

My friend. I love my bright and shiny friend.

The gemstone called out to him in a soft and soothing voice. *Sleep, young dragon. Sleep, and we'll be together forever.*

Streak's eyelids became heavy. He sank deeper into the golden bed of hay and let the dragon charm take him away.

21

"Open those little fingers up, girlie," Squirrel ordered Zora. She was trying to pry her balled-up fist open. "I'll have that Ring of Mist."

Zora squeezed her fist tighter. "Do your worst, you moth-eaten hag!" She jerked her hand away and head-butted Squirrel in the chin.

The scraggly-haired woman stumbled backward, holding her chin. Her bony cheeks reddened, and she snaked out a dagger. "I'll cut them off if I have to."

Katrina stepped between them. Towering over Squirrel, she asked, "What makes you think that you get the ring?"

Squirrel's mouth hung open. Her eyes narrowed. "What? Why would an anvil like you get it? It's a thief thing!"

"The ring can be used by a warrior or a rogue," Katrina said. Her eyes slid over to Zora. "Right?"

"I acquired it from a dead fighter," she admitted, even though it was a lie. *Perfect. Keep them at each other's throats.* When Honzur and Sash had left, the warrior's magic sashes went with him, and Squirrel bound her up with new ropes. She'd tied Zora's wrists together and bound her waist to the chair. Luckily for Zora, she still had enough padding on her body to make the ropes look tight when they weren't. "And the ring will magically—"

Katrina gripped Zora's hair and pulled. "Magically what?"

She played nervous and swallowed. "Nothing."

"Dirty acorns, Zora, haven't you been smacked around enough?" Katrina walloped her in the belly. "Magically what?"

Zora gasped and said, "Fine." She spit and sputtered, really overdoing it. "It will fit any finger. Even big ones like yours or Bull's."

"Like Bull's?" Katrina's lips twisted into a snarl. "Aren't you the jester? Hah, well, I suppose that I would be, too, if I knew I only had an hour or so to live."

Zora stiffened. "What do you mean?"

"Once Honzur has the dragon, he won't have any need for you or Tanlin. You'll both be dead."

"But we are Black Frost's spies. You can't kill us."

Katrina patted her head. "Accidents happen. Of course, it doesn't hurt that you were aiding known fugitives. We caught on and hunted you down. I bet I will receive an accommodation for it."

"Good for you, Katrina." Her eyes slid over to Squirrel. "And you, too, rodent. Perhaps they'll gift you with another ring like mine and you won't have to fight about it."

"Yeah, about the ring... I want it," Squirrel said. Dagger in hand, she stood toe to toe with Katrina but was little more than chest high. "I need that sort of protection. A big woman like you doesn't."

"A big woman like me doesn't take orders from scrawny little women like you." She bumped Squirrel with her chest. "Back off, Squirrel."

Zora seized the opportunity. *That's it, girls. Keep bickering.*

Katrina turned her back and blocked Squirrel from her view. An expert in escaping ropes, Zora twisted her hands free just as Katrina glanced backward at her. She kept her hands and loosened ropes in place.

Squirrel pushed back on Katrina. "Don't try to bully me. You think because you share a bedroll with Sash, you're a boss, but you ain't."

"I might as well be." Katrina shoved Squirrel back to arm's length.

Squirrel had murder in her eyes and the point of the dagger at Katrina's throat. "It's only a ring. Is it worth dying over?"

"You wouldn't dare. Honzur and Sash would kill you for it." Katrina shoved her back. "I'll flip for it."

"No, I'll flip for it!" Squirrel said. "I have a coin right here."

"I know better than to let you use your two-faced coins and those oily fingers."

"I'll do it," Zora offered.

"Gum up!" Katrina said as she plucked a coin from a small belt pouch on her girdle. "I'll flip. You call the face on the ground."

Squirrel's brow furrowed, and her thin lips pursed. "I don't like it, but I'll do it. Flip, step back, and watch it fall."

Zora loosened the knot of the rope that fastened her to the chair, but the rope was still coiled around her waist. She weighed her options. They didn't know about the Scarf of Shadows, only the ring. She could turn invisible and try to slip out, but the bolt to the outside was locked with a key. Katrina had it on her neck. Then there was the Ring of Mist. She could only use it once a day, and the day might not have turned yet. Not to mention that Squirrel and Sash were already protected against its effects. Katrina probably was too.

Fear gripped her heart. She'd failed so many times before. *I have to do something. I must save Streak and Tanlin.*

Katrina flipped the silver coin. "Call it."

"Tail end," Squirrel grumbled with her beady eyes fixed on the flipping coin.

The silver coin spun end over end, reached the top of the arc in the air, and dropped. It bounced on the damp stone floor, rolled toward Zora, and fell. She hid it under her shoe.

Katrina and Squirrel crowded around her with faces filled with fury.

"Move your foot," Katrina ordered.

Zora looked them both dead in the eye. *What does Grey Cloak always say that I hate so much? Oh yes, "I'll take my chances." Here goes.*

She slipped her hand free of the loose cords and stuck her Ring of Mist in Katrina's face. "You want this? You can have it!" The tiny petal on the ring remained closed. Nothing happened. She gave a sheepish grin.

22

"Who are you trying to fool? Why are your hands free, you little sneak?" Katrina asked. "Trying to escape, huh?" She shot daggers from her eyes at Squirrel. "Next time, I'll tie the kn—"

A cloud of mist puffed out of the ring into Katrina's face. *Sphizzz!*

Katrina inhaled a mouthful and choked. One hand went for her sword, and the other hand covered her mouth. She had murder in her eyes as she pulled her blade free, but then she collapsed onto the ground.

Zora swung her attention to Squirrel. The hag-like rogue backed away, covering her mouth and wiping her eyes. Zora slipped free of her bonds and dove for the key hanging from Katrina's neck.

"No, you don't!" Squirrel said. The wiry woman filled both her hands with daggers. She had a crooked grin on her face. "Your little trick didn't work on me. I'm still protected." She advanced. "And now I'm going to carve you up!"

Zora scrambled away and popped to her feet on the other side of the dungeon cell. She beckoned to Squirrel. "Come on. Carve me up, then."

"Fool." Squirrel wiped her sleeve across her button nose and spun her daggers in hands. "I'm the best close-quarters fighter in this company. You'll be dead before you can count to three." She charged.

Zora crouched and swept out her leg.

Squirrel hopped over it and laughed. "Nice try, fool." She stabbed and sliced with alarming speed. "But you have nowhere to go."

Zora evaded her. She ducked, jumped, slipped, and twisted away from the deadly strikes. They circled the square room as if it were an arena, sizing each other up.

Squirrel offered a crooked smile and said, "You're bleeding."

Zora hadn't even noticed, but her forearm had been cut open. Her blood ran down her elbow and dripped to the floor. "I'll live."

"No, you won't." Squirrel slunk closer with her twin daggers held high.

Zora did a back handspring and vaulted over the chair then landed smoothly right behind it. She picked up the chair and held it out like an animal trainer.

Squirrel laughed. "Nice chair. I'll be sure to bury you with it."

The snide comment sent a hot streak of fire right through Zora. She'd been beaten on long enough, and she wasn't going to take any more. She unleashed a furious roar and charged like a raging bull.

Squirrel's eyes widened. The flat-footed woman turned to slide out of the way, but she collided with the chair first. Zora drove her back and pinned her against the wall and kept ramming the chair into Squirrel with jarring impacts.

"What are you doing?" Squirrel dropped her daggers and tried to push out from behind the chair. "Stop it!"

"Shut up, varmint!" Zora let loose. Using the chair like a cudgel, she beat the shocked Squirrel senseless. *Whack! Whack! Whack!*

Squirrel fell to the ground, wincing in pain. "Stop, please!" Two chair legs broke over her back. She let out a groan. "Stop. I'm sorry. Stop!"

Zora didn't let up. She wasn't about to let Squirrel trick her by playing possum. She kept hitting her until the bones in her hands broke, then she kicked her in the gut. To finish it off, she picked up a broken chair leg and clubbed her in the head. Squirrel didn't move, but she was still breathing.

Zora grabbed the key to the dungeon from the chain around Katrina's neck, grabbed her gear, locked both women inside, and left. She raced up a stairwell that led to the tunnels below the streets and found her bearings. She was still several blocks from Streak's barn.

I can make it. I have to.

The first few blocks were fine, but after that, her legs burned like fire, and her thighs ached.

Horseshoes, I'm in awful shape.

Holding her side, she jogged as fast as she could handle, sticking to the shadows and trying to avoid prying eyes. She hustled across one street and caught the eye of a trio of Black Guard on patrol.

"You! Stop there!" one of the soldiers called.

She waved and said, "I'm being chased by a madman!" She pointed down the alley. "He killed a Black Guard, and now he hunts me." She raced into the next alley, feeling like her lungs were going to explode.

I hope that bought some time. Guh! I'm never going to eat so much again.

Finally, she made it to the barn and caught a glimpse of Honzur and Sash standing inside. Honzur's dragon charm was full of vibrant light, and he approached the entrance to Cliff's stable.

Sticky with sweat, Zora tried to quietly catch her breath and devise a plan.

Be smart. Think of something quick. Sultans, I'm winded.

She stole her way into the loft and got a bird's-eye view of the whole scene. Honzur was standing over Streak. The small dragon's eyes were aglow and locked on the charm. Honzur went so far as to kneel and touch the dragon's face and pet him.

"He's all ours," Honzur said. "The dragon charm has him. Grab a sack, and we'll haul him off."

The rangy sword fighter gave a disappointed nod and asked, "Where am I going to find a sack big enough for that dragon?"

"It's a barn. Find something," Honzur fired back. As Sash moved away, Honzur started to lead the hypnotized Streak out of the stable. "Come, little friend, come."

Zora scanned the barn. She was no match for the likes of Honzur or Sasha. Squirrel and Katrina were weaker than them, and she'd had the jump on them.

I have to try something.

A heavy-looking wooden pulley hung from the rafters, suspended from a wooden beam. It was designed to lift heavy objects from the ground to the loft.

Zora unhooked the head of the pulley and hook and aimed it at Honzur. If it worked the way she hoped, it would swing right over the ground and blast into him.

This might be the worst idea I've ever had, but here goes.

She released the pulley. As if in slow motion, it swung silently toward the unsuspecting target.

It's going to work.

The hook and pulley flew right over Streak's head and blasted Honzur out of his slippers. The mage skidded across the barn floor, and the charm slipped free of his fingers.

Sash rushed over to Honzur. The wizard was out cold.

He pulled his sword free and searched the barn. When he spotted Zora lurking in the loft, he sneered. "You're going to die!"

23

"Not if you can't find me," Zora replied. She lifted the Scarf of Shadows over her nose and disappeared.

Sash's eyes widened at first, then he squinted and searched the rafters. "That won't do you any good." Using the burlap sack, he knelt and covered Streak, who still sat in a dreamlike state. He picked the sack up and slung it over his shoulder, keeping his sword in his free hand. "If you want your scaly friend, you'll have to come and get him."

Zora was already on the move, going to the back of the loft. She jumped out of the loft opening into the street. She landed as silently as a cat, stole her way around to the other entrance to the barn, and entered.

Sash stood in the middle of the corridor of stables. His head turned from side to side, and he shuffled around in a slow circle. His fishlike eyes were narrowed, and in his rugged voice, he said, "Come out, Zora, and I promise I won't kill you. But if you don't, I promise you will die." His eyes scanned right over her. "What do you say? Huh? There is no need for you to get yourself killed. And believe me, I know a lot about killing. I've killed scores of foes far more formidable than you. Visible and invisible. Huh-huh-huh. You don't want to underestimate me."

No doubt you'll keep your word. Liar.

Zora didn't have any doubt that if she got too close to Sash and he sensed it, she might wind up dead. She had to think of another way to get Streak away from him. As she searched for an opportunity in the barn, something caught her eye, and an idea came to mind.

It's crazy enough that it might work.

Zora snuck into Cliff's stable and cozied up to the mule. She whispered in his ear, "Easy, friend. Easy." She pulled her scarf down from her nose and let out a loud sneeze.

Sash swung over to the stable and blocked the exit. "Well, well, well, it sounds like someone's nose is ticklish." He nodded Zora over. "Come on out, and I'll make this easy. And you'll need my help, because when Honzur wakes, he won't be very happy with you. I can protect you."

"You're a liar, Sash. Only a fool would trust you."

He raised his eyebrows and said, "I keep my word to my people. Join the Scourge, and I'll keep my word to you." He eased into the stable. "Apparently, you are more resourceful than I imagined. Did you kill Squirrel and Katrina?"

Zora pressed her body to the back wall, faked a nervous head shake, and said, "No."

"You should have. After this foul-up, I might have to kill them anyway." Sash crept forward another full step and lowered his long sword from his shoulder. "You're trapped, Zora. In a few more seconds, it will all be over, unless you change your mind and work with me."

Sash had her hemmed in, and she had nowhere to go. A quick thrust would skewer her. Zora shook her head. "Never!" She yanked hard on Cliff's ear.

The mule bucked. His hooves slammed square into Sash's chest. His sword went flying, and he landed in the corridor, flat on his back.

"Thank you, Cliff." Zora headed out of the stable.

Sash's eyes were closed. She pulled out her dagger. *I should kill him. I should kill them both.*

Streak stirred inside the burlap sack that lay at Sash's feet. Zora knelt, took her eyes off of Sash, and opened the neck of the sack.

Sash's black ribbons came to life and seized Zora around the wrist. Another ribbon snaked around her body and coiled around her throat, constricting.

She clawed at the black ribbon on her neck. She felt her eyes bulge in their sockets and watched in horror as Sash sat up with a pained expression.

Sash clutched his ribbons and said, "Clever. You broke a few ribs and even stunned me, but you made one fatal mistake." He fought to his feet while his sashes lifted her from the ground. His eyebrows knitted. "You should have killed me when you had the chance."

Zora clawed at his eyes.

Sash snaked a dagger out of his sword belt and grinned. He stabbed her in the stomach. "How about that?"

His ribbons released her, and she lay on the ground, clutching her bleeding stomach.

"Dying hurts, doesn't it?"

From out of nowhere, a blacksmith hammer smote Sash in the temple. *Whop!*

Sash dropped like a rock.

Zora's belly wound burned. She looked at her blood-covered hand. Wooziness assailed her as she focused on the hooded figure that stood over Sash. Whoever it was was big. She coughed and asked, "Who are you?"

Hammer in hand, the cloaked figure rushed right at her.

24

SOMEHOW, ZORA FOUND HER DAGGER IN THE GRIP OF HER NUMB FINGERS, AND SHE slashed at her attacker. An iron grip locked up her wrist and held her fast. She jerked and tugged, but the figure's grip was strong.

"Let go of me."

"Easy," the figure said in a deep and soothing voice as he dropped his hood. "You are wounded. I can help, Zora."

Her eyes widened. "Lythlenion?"

He dropped his hood, revealing his handsome orcen face. His warm smile revealed his lower canine teeth, which jutted out. "It's good of you to remember, but be still. This is a grave wound." He had rough hands with thick, sharp, short nails on the end. He nimbly fished a small vial out of one of his many belt pouches then pulled the cap off the vial with his teeth. "This is going to burn, but try not to scream."

Zora lay back on her elbows and said, "It's good to see you."

He poured a milky flame-orange liquid onto her belly wound.

"Guh!"

"Shh, shh, shh. The Black Guard are sure to hear if you squeal like a pig."

Zora panted and groaned. "Well, it really does burn. Is it helping?"

"It will sear your innards, and you'll be sore for some time, but you won't bleed out." He offered her his hand. "Can you walk?"

The stabbing pain in her belly made her grimace as she slowly came to her feet. "I will run if I have to."

"Good, because we need to move on from here quickly," Lythlenion said. "Very little escapes the Black Guard's notice."

Streak crawled out of the sack and shook his thick neck. "What happened to me? I felt like I was flying on a silky pillow, and now this?"

"The dragon charm!" Zora walked quickly over to Honzur, where the dragon charm lay on the ground. She picked up the stone and showed it to Streak. "Honzur charmed you, Streak. They tried to kidnap you."

"They did, huh." On all fours, he walked over to Honzur. "I can't let that happen again. Stand back."

Zora took a couple of steps back and asked, "What? Why?"

Streak shot a stream of flame out of his mouth, setting Honzur on fire like a log. Bits of dragon fire splattered off the body, and the flames spread all over the immediate area.

"I probably should have given this a little more thought." Streak shrugged his wings. "Oh well, flame happens."

Lythlenion eyed Zora. "I see the dragon talks. Interesting."

"And he thinks for himself. And he's not the best at it," she said as he started opening the stable gates and herding out the animals.

The flames spread fast, and white smoke began filling the barn.

Lythlenion grabbed her wrist. "We must go now, Zora! The Black Guard and the Riskers will be all over this place in moments!"

Streak led Cliff out of the stable, jawing as they went. "You should have seen it, Cliff. It was dragon heaven. Fluffy cats that tasted like chicken everywhere. Pure bliss, I tell you."

Zora had an idea and grabbed Streak by the tail. "We need to hide you." She picked him up, set him on Cliff's back, and tossed a blanket over him. "Be still." She turned to Lythlenion. "Lead them out. Act like you are helping and move on. Some of the guards have already seen me." She lifted the Scarf of Shadows over her nose. "Go!"

Lythlenion hurried out of the barn, towing Cliff along behind him. He coughed and pointed at the Black Guards that were charging his way. "There is more livestock in there. This is all that I could save," he said to them and gave a loud cough.

Flames spit out of the loft, and a pure-orange blaze burned inside the barn doors. The entire barn, from top to bottom, was consumed.

By that time, people had woken and were running down the street. A chain of buckets of water started from a nearby well.

Zora hid on a porch across the street and watched Lythlenion creep away from the distraught onlookers.

"*Shhhrrriiieeek!*"

A Risker and his dragon dropped out of the sky into the street, scattering the startled crowd. The middling dragon lowered its head and blasted out another piercing shriek. It shook its black wings in a showy display of superiority, pressing the people back into the alleys and porches. Then it folded its wings behind its back and lowered itself to the ground.

A Risker sat tall in the saddle, wearing custom black armor and an open-faced helmet with small black wings on the side. He stood up in the saddle and stared into the flames. His dark eyes swept over the crowd and Zora.

A chill went through her. She'd never seen the Risker before. She wanted to see if Honzur and Sash were found but wasn't going to stick around with a Risker about.

If they're dead, they got what was coming to them.

She hurried away and caught up with Lythlenion a few blocks away. He was taking his time leading the donkey through the streets.

Zora uncloaked herself, hugged his arm, and said, "I wanted to thank you, Lyth."

"No need," he said, walking proudly with his broad chest out. "It's a blessing that I found you in time. It was meant to be." He shoulder-nudged her. "You handled yourself quite well back there."

"I was lucky."

"You made your own luck." Lythlenion stole a look over his shoulder. "Best we get as much distance between them and us as possible. You can come with me. I have a nice safe place along the shoreline where you can stay."

"After tonight, I could use a place to stay, but I still have to save Tanlin," she said.

"Come. We will find a way to save him together."

25

LESS THAN A LEAGUE FROM HARBOR LAKE'S MAIN STREETS, ZORA AND STREAK were gathered on the Inland Sea shores with Lythlenion's wife, Sara, and their young daughter, Lylith. Sarah was a beautiful woman with braided hair and a warm smile. Lylith was a pie-faced, half-orcen youth who giggled uncontrollably as she chased Streak over the sands.

Lythlenion and Sarah held hands as they spoke to Zora. "Are you certain that you need to return to Raven Cliff? I'm well acquainted with Tanlin. Not so much as you, but don't you think that he can handle the likes of Bull?"

"I can't risk it. You didn't see what Honzur showed me. I've never seen him so helpless," Zora said. She walked along the sands with her hand placed over her belly. It still burned, and it hurt when she walked. Sash would have killed her if Lythlenion hadn't come along. "Will you wait for Grey Cloak and Dyphestive for me? I swear that I'll return."

"Of course we will," Sarah said. Her hair was sun-bleached, and she wore a flowery home dress. She clasped Zora's hand. "You have our word, but I hate for you to go it alone. It's a long journey."

"I can make it. I've made the trip several times before." The sea winds blasted her hair into her face, and she brushed it aside. "I'm not sure what the Scourge was up to. They were more interested in Streak than they were Grey Cloak and Dyphestive. I think they wanted him to control other dragons."

"Streak can control dragons?" Lythlenion asked with a raised eyebrow. "It's no wonder that Black Frost would want to acquire his services. He wishes to control all of them, which I believe he does. Perhaps he fears Streak. He's independent."

"I don't know. A part of me had the feeling that the Scourge wanted Streak for themselves," she said.

Lythlenion and Sarah exchanged looks. "Possession of such a dragon would come in useful for the likes of them. Maybe they have other plans."

Lylith came running up the beach with Streak in her arms. She was dressed like her mother but had a stronger build and was taller. "Can I keep him?"

"He's not a pet," Sarah said as she patted Streak on the head. "He's a person."

"Can he live with us?" Lylith insisted with a cheerful voice.

"He can stay as long as he likes."

Lylith spun Streak around in the air, screaming, "Yaaay!"

"Slow down, Lylith. You're going to make me vomit," Streak said.

Lylith spun down into the sand and crashed on top of Streak.

"She's an orc. She plays rough," Lythlenion commented with a grin. "But she gets it from her mother."

"Tell me, Lyth... how did you find me?" Zora asked.

Sarah's pretty face paled, and a guilty look crossed Lythlenion's face.

"What?" Zora asked.

"Come with me," he said.

He led Zora back to his seaside stone cottage, which was surrounded by a bounty of flower-rich gardens.

Inside, he took her to a small wardrobe in the bedroom. "Open it," he said.

Zora gave him a wary look, grabbed the brass handle, and complied. Hanging inside the wardrobe was a maroon Black Guard tunic with the embroidered symbol of lightning on the mountaintops. She gasped and backed away. "What is this?"

Lythlenion held up his hands and offered a sorrowful look. "It's not what you think. I am a Black Guard but not in spirit. I'd never risk so much for you if I was."

Her hand went for her dagger. "I've had my fill of liars."

"Look around, Zora. Search your heart. You know that I bear you no ill will. Please, let me answer your questions."

"You'd better talk fast."

"I serve on the prison ship. I was there when Grey Cloak and Dyphestive were taken to the island. It took all that I had to contain my excitement when they appeared. I felt the change in the wind that has been missing these past ten years."

"Can you get them off of the island?"

"All I can do is hope that I am present at the right moment. Do you believe me?"

Zora looked about. The tidy cottage was as warm and cozy a place as she'd ever been. She clicked her dagger back into the scabbard and said, "You know that I do. And who am I to call the kettle black? I guess we did what we had to do." She gave him a big hug. "I trust you. So, what did you mean about the wind?"

"Black Frost may have won the battle, but the war has only begun." He led her back outside by the hand. A full view of the island could be seen in the far distance. "I've seen it in my dreams."

"I wish I could see them too. Come over here. I forgot to show you something," she said. The night before, she'd gathered their gear before they headed for Lythlenion's cottage. It was late at night when they arrived, and Lythlenion stowed it all in one of his garden sheds. Dyphestive's iron sword leaned against the wall in the corner. An object was wrapped in a blanket. She handed it to Lythlenion. "This is yours, isn't it?"

With a curious expression, he unwrapped the blanket and gasped. "Thunderash. I feared I might not see it again." He hugged it, stroked the weathered wood with his fingers, and kissed it. "I've missed you. Thank you, Zora."

She nodded. "My pleasure."

They headed back to the beach. Lylith was pulling Streak by the tail and dragging him away from the surf. His paws were clawing at the dirt. "He's trying to leave!" she screamed.

Zora ran over, her feet splashing through the low tide. "Streak, where are you going?"

"To the island. It's been five days, and that's how Grey Cloak and I planned it." He turned and faced Lylith and licked her face. "Let go of my tail. I promise..." He lowered his voice and said, "I'll be back."

26

PRISONER ISLAND

A HARD RAIN CAME DOWN ON THE COMPANY OF MEN LED BY A DWARF DRUID, Thatcher, riding on the back of a giant tarantula that led the way through the tropical terrain. The ten-foot-tall spider's footfalls were silent, and it moved like a ghost through the network of jungle trees. It was eerie watching the tarantula navigate as its body shifted colors like a chameleon and blended in with all that it passed. Each of its legs was taller than any man, and it moved along at a brisk pace.

Grey Cloak kept his distance, but never once did he let the spider out of sight. He marched on with Dyphestive and Gorva bringing up the rear and the rest of Thatcher's pack among them. Along the way, he picked up small rocks and stones and dropped them into his pockets, thinking that he might use the wizardry to charge them with wizard fire. He kept the powers of his cloak to himself for the moment. There was no need to fully trust Thatcher's group. As amiable as the dwarf might be, for all Grey Cloak knew, he could be leading them right into a trap.

Several steps behind him, Dyphestive lumbered along, rivulets of rainwater washing over his bare shoulders and chest. His soaked hair hung over his eyes, and if he could see, Grey Cloak wasn't sure how.

The water beaded off of Gorva's braids, and Dyphestive's old shirt clung to her rain-soaked body. She carried a grim look on her face and had a dagger in her hand, and her strides were long and easy.

They were the perfect picture of a durable group that had survived a shipwreck.

It had been a hard-paced journey. They'd stopped in the evening only long enough to let the others get some rest. Thatcher's pack were hardy, but their eyes were tired, and they yawned often, except for the dwarf named Fulton. He carried a stone hammer with a wooden handle and never said a word.

In the meantime, the Cloak of Legends shed water like a duck, and Grey Cloak was as dry as a bone underneath. Only his hair and boots were sopping wet as he climbed up the ravine wall after Thatcher. The blind dwarf only glanced back every so often. Otherwise, his trek remained as steady as a stone.

"*Roooaaawwwrrr!*"

Thunderbreath's dragon call made the bright-winged birds scatter from the trees. The grand dragon made his presence known all over the island several times every day. The booming call had become something the hardened band was used to, and no one faltered a step.

But Grey Cloak couldn't shake the tingle from his fingertips that had hung with him since late in the morning. The trees were full of critters with bright eyes, but something else was lurking among them. From time to time, he'd searched the leafy branches, prompted by the feeling of a new set of eyes on him, but he saw nothing. The jungle, thick with vines and rising mist and pouring rain, made it difficult to see anything more than several yards away.

Even with Grey Cloak's keen vision, Itchee the tarantula wasn't so easy to track. Deep in his bowels, he had a feeling that if it weren't for the tarantula, they'd have been attacked already. The wooly insect beast made a fine deterrent, and it made perfect sense why Thatcher's pack had survived so long in the dangerous fringes of the jungle.

Two older men from the pack cut their way through the forest in front of Grey Cloak, carrying crude but effective spears. One pushed back the leaves of a giant red fern and let the other pass through. After a quick comment, they chuckled.

It was the first sign of mirth Grey Cloak had seen from any of the group. It warmed his spirit.

Then the world came crashing down. From the higher branches of a knotted tree, a furry beast dropped like the rain and crushed both men under its weight then vanished behind the ferns.

Grey Cloak called, "We are under attack!" He sprinted after the fallen men and burst through the other side of the ferns.

Both men lay dead on the ground with parts of their bodies torn off. Their blood fed the ground along with the rain, but their attacker was gone.

Dyphestive and Gorva were the next to come through the dense brush. The whites of their eyes showed when they gazed at the mutilated men.

"What did this?" Gorva demanded.

"I have no idea." Grey Cloak's eyes were narrowed down to slits as he searched through the pouring rain. Whatever it was that had struck had come and gone. "It dropped out of the trees. A muscular hulk bigger than any two of us. I didn't get a look at it before it was gone."

The rest of the pack rushed over. The three remaining women dropped to their knees around the men and started wailing.

Out of the gloom, Thatcher and Itchee appeared underneath the dripping branches. His hollow-eyed stare fixed on the dead.

"What did you see?" Thatcher demanded. "What did you see?"

"I didn't see much of anything. It was a blur. A powerful figure that dropped out of nowhere, killed, and was gone."

Thatcher's tone was somber when he said, "That's what I was afraid of."

27

Thatcher tapped his staff on Itchee's side and started barking commands. "Women, get under Itchee and stay low. Men, stay close to his legs. That creature you saw, I fear, is a manticore, a fearsome beast built like a lion and as strong as a bull."

"Isn't it scared of your giant spider?" Gorva asked.

"A manticore is not scared of anything. They hibernate and hunger, then they hunt flesh and feast like kings." Thatcher's stubby fingers clawed their way through his beard. "And they don't hunt alone."

"There's more than one of them," Grey Cloak said as he looked left and right. The critters that called out in the jungle had fallen silent, and the rain had come to a stop too. The strange silence was haunting. "I only saw one."

"The monsters will take us out one at a time and drag all of our dead bodies to the den later. It is their way," Thatcher said. "Our only hope is to stay close and move together."

One of the older women cried out, "Thatcher, we cannot leave our dead."

"Would you rather join them?" he replied in a sharp voice. "There is nothing we can do now but flee. We must be in the midst of their hunting grounds."

A roar carried through the twisting and vine-rich woodland. The women gasped and huddled under Itchee.

Thatcher began to murmur. The head of his staff came to life with blue flames. That same fire burned in his eye sockets. His head twisted from side to side, and he tapped on Itchee again. "Move along. Quickly."

Itchee's long legs moved at a brisk pace, and the sobbing women were momentarily left behind. Two of them scrabbled ahead, but the last one, an older woman with graying hair, ran back to her dead husband.

"Get back here, you fool!" Gorva said as she watched the woman race down and join her husband. "I'll go for her."

A blur of musclebound fur blasted out of the bush and plowed into the woman. It had a humanish, lionlike face and a wild mane encircling a huge skull. Its fur was black, but it was also covered in patches of scales and had feet with claws like a dragon. A long tail with a ball of spikes on the end swung around from its back and bashed the older woman in the chest. Then the creature's mighty jaws opened, and it bit her head off of her shoulders.

Blood rushed in Grey Cloak's ears. He'd never seen the likes of the monster before. It was an ugly, terrible thing with cold dead eyes, that feasted on the living like a wild dog. And it was almost as big as a horse and as fast as a dragon.

The manticore swung its gaze on the group. Drool mixed with blood dripped from the monster's slavering jaws. A distinct popping and crunching came from its mouth as it chewed the woman's head.

Grey Cloak's fingers fished through his inner pockets, and he filled his hands with small stones. *I knew I should have brought more weapons. Only a dagger. What was I thinking?*

So as not to draw attention to himself, he'd left many necessities behind. He never imagined they would be battling for their lives in the wild.

Perhaps this wasn't the best idea after all. He started to walk backward and almost bumped into Dyphestive. "Stay with the group," he muttered. "It might fear strength in numbers."

Dyphestive's fists were balled up at his sides, and his broad chest heaved. A storm brewed in his eyes, and his nostrils flared.

"Brother, what are you think—"

Dyphestive charged the manticore like a raging bull.

Zooks!

The manticore's humanish face wore a clever expression as it braced for the attack.

Out of the corner of his eye, Grey Cloak watched a second manticore hidden in the brush erupt from the foliage. It hit Dyphestive with the force of a ram and knocked him down.

Grey Cloak sped toward the attacking manticore. Without even thinking, he filled a stone with wizard fire and hurled it at the foul beast. The glowing stone exploded against the manticore's shoulder, sending ripples down its black fur. It shot a look at Grey Cloak, revealing a womanish face. *Ew!*

Dyphestive cocked back and blasted the first monster in the jaw. He struck again in the meat of the manticore's face, and it bit down on his arm. Its jaws locked, while Dyphestive delivered furious and futile punch after punch with his other arm.

From out of nowhere, Gorva came flying in, jumped on the female manticore's back, and plunged her dagger into its side. She stabbed its meaty flesh again and again.

"Duck!" Grey Cloak shouted.

The female manticore's spiked tail whipped around. He jumped, grabbed the tail, and latched on. It writhed like a snake in his arms and beat him against the ground.

"Ow!"

The male manticore came to savage life and jumped into the fight. With its clawed paw, it swiped Gorva clean off of the other manticore's back. It set its eyes on Grey Cloak and opened its mammoth jaws wide.

Grey Cloak twisted around and guided the female manticore's tail into the snapping jaws of her counterpart. The male manticore chomped down hard on the mouthful of spikes. The tail snapped off, and both manticores let out frightful howls of pain.

"How's that for a mouthful!" Grey Cloak said as he slid away from the vicious beasts and joined his brother.

Dyphestive's forearm was openly bleeding, and Gorva helped him back to his feet. His arm dangled at his side.

"That's bad, isn't it?" Grey Cloak asked.

Dyphestive's eyebrows knitted, and he picked up a stone and said, "Not too bad."

The manticores butted heads and exchanged angry roars. The female tenderly used her paws to pluck the end of her tail from his jaws. The male licked the wounds on the female's back, then both turned and faced Grey Cloak, Dyphestive, and Gorva.

"I don't think we scared them off," Grey Cloak said as he gathered more stones. He looked about and didn't see any signs of Thatcher, Itchee, or the others. "I think we've been left for dead."

Gorva's blade was wet with blood, and she said, "I stabbed it several times, and it shrugged it off like a mosquito bite." Her lips twisted into a sneer. "I've never seen such nasty things. How do we kill them?"

The male manticore spoke, his wrinkled, lionlike face making the ugliest expression. "We've lived five hundred years. We'll live five hundred more. We'll drag your carcasses to our den, where you'll forever join thousands of bones."

28

"Did it talk?" Grey Cloak asked Dyphestive, who cradled his bloody arm.

Dyphestive nodded. "It did."

Shoulder to shoulder, the manticores slunk closer.

The female said in a husky voice, "This is where you plead for your life. Please, oblige us. Your fear makes flesh all the sweeter."

They exchanged glances and Grey Cloak smirked.

"Fear? Of you two ugly beasts? We've raced the skies on the backs of dragons. We've slain giants and titans. Great cities have fallen under the spell of our hands." He turned the stones in his hands to flames. "If anyone is going to feast tonight, it is we who will dine on the sour hides of the manticore." He leaned over and looked at his brother and Gorva. "I believe their beautiful black manes would look fantastic over those broad shoulders. Don't you?"

"The fur will definitely keep the evening chill away," Dyphestive replied.

Gorva flipped her braids and added, "And I look fantastic in black."

The male manticore stamped his paws and said, "Insults! Mockery!" He threw his mane back and roared like thunder. "In five hundred years, I've never seen the likes of it!" He paced in front of them a dozen yards away. "Never!"

"What are you thinking, dear?" the female asked. "They destroyed my tail. Certainly we will kill them."

"Your tail will grow back," the male manticore said. His feline nostrils flared, and his furry forehead wrinkled in a very human fashion. He came nose to nose with Grey Cloak and towered over him. "Why are you here?"

The smell of the manticore's hot, fetid breath could knock over an ogre. Grey Cloak fought off the urge to fan the foul air and offered a truthful answer. "I have friends in Braykurz. We've come to take them home."

Both manticores barked with laughter.

"Thunderbreath will kill you," the female said and slunk forward. "Nothing escapes his notice. Not even the likes of us."

Grey Cloak shrugged. "Nothing ventured, nothing gained."

The female crept up on Dyphestive and said, "Hold out your wounded arm." Dyphestive complied.

She licked it. Her whiskers twitched, and her green eyes brightened. "His blood is sweet and tastes of iron." She eyed her mate. "Not to mention that his arm is still attached after I sank my teeth into it. He is a natural."

"Interesting," the male manticore said. "That explains their bravery, but even the naturals can die." He glanced up into the trees. "Come down, insect rider, or I'll feast on you first."

Thatcher and Itchee dropped down from their camouflaged spot in the branches. The two women and Fulton the dwarf were with them.

The male manticore eyed Thatcher and said, "It's wise that you didn't attack. I would have ripped off your pet's legs and fed them to you, stubby one. I am Ebonthrak, and this is my mate, Jessel. We were the kings of the wild until Thunderbreath came with his minions." He paced around the group with his spiked tail dragging behind him. "I'll let—"

"We'll let," Jessel corrected.

"Yes, we'll let you live if you complete a quest for us," Ebonthrak continued.

"What do you mean, let us live?" the younger woman spoke up. She was sitting on the back of Itchee, behind Thatcher. "You've killed three of us."

Ebonthrak lifted his voice and said, "These are our hunting grounds. All who pass are game. This is where the strong survive, you bony morsel. And I'll have you know that I'll take the whole of you out if you don't fulfill my quest. Look at you." His eyes swept over them all. "You have no weapons of might. No spider silk can constrain us. This elf's fire is little more than a prick. At this juncture, you have no choice."

Grey Cloak didn't have any problem believing what Ebonthrak was saying. They were outmatched, and even if they tried, more of them would die. "What is it that you want?"

"You say that you are going to Braykurz." Ebonthrak cast a longing look at his wife. "We have a child there. Our son, Karzak. Thunderbreath took him from us when he was young. He wanted to show us, *show us*, who was in charge." His throat rumbled. "You will bring him back, or the ones that you leave behind will die."

"Leave behind?" Grey Cloak asked. "Who will we leave behind?"

"The dwarf and the rest of this pack will stay," Ebonthrak said. "And if you fail our quest, all of them will die."

"Where are we supposed to find this son of yours?"

"He is a manticore. The greatest of all beasts. He won't be hard to find."

Grey Cloak looked Ebonthrak dead in the eye. "You have my word that we will return with your son."

Ebonthrak started to turn away and said, "We'll see."

29

"How is your arm?" Grey Cloak asked Dyphestive. It was bound with green leaves, but his hand and fingers were swollen and black and blue. "It looks awful."

"As much as I hate to admit it, it feels awful." Dyphestive grimaced. "But Thatcher's salve helped. These leaves he treated it with are helping too. The truth is that I'm surprised I still have my arm. Jessel bit clear to the bone."

Gorva looked squeamish. "I saw it. I can't believe you still have your limb either. I've seen wild hogs smaller than those manticores bite off the hands of orcs bigger than you. It seems impossible."

"Not if you knew his namesake," Grey Cloak said as he led the way through the jungle thickets, which hummed and buzzed irritatingly with life.

Gorva's long legs traversed to the top of the next rise, and she caught up with Grey Cloak, leaving Dyphestive behind. "What does that mean?" She glanced over her shoulder. "Is he cursed?"

"No, of course not." He flicked a mosquito away. "Zooks, I hate those nasty bloodsuckers. As for Dyphestive, they used to call him Iron Bones, but no one took it literally. But over time, I've realized that seems to be the case. I think it's one of his gifts as a natural."

"Do you mean to say that his bones are made of pure iron?"

He shrugged. "Without actually seeing them, I can't be sure, but I'd say that they are as hard as iron. He's like an ox and very durable."

Gorva frowned at Dyphestive. "He's an ox for certain."

Grey Cloak smiled at her and said, "I saw you jump in to save him. I think you like him more than you admit."

"That was instinct! My blood rises at the first sign of battle. I can't control that," she said.

He lifted his hands in apology and said, "No worries. I understand. He's spoken for anyway."

"Spoken for by whom?" she demanded.

Grey Cloak fought off the urge to laugh. He decided to play it up. "Leena. She's the woman we are going to rescue. An unrivaled beauty and a sheer delight in conversation. Not to mention a matchless warrior. Yes, my brother has been quite stricken by her ever since they met. They were attached at the hip until the tragedy happened at the tower."

"This woman, is she big?"

"Let's just say she's big enough to conquer him."

Gorva glanced back at Dyphestive. "Humph."

Not wanting to needle her into complete embarrassment, Grey Cloak changed the subject. "Your father, Hogrim, would have been really proud of the way you fought yesterday."

Gorva's face dropped, and her voice softened. "I'd do anything to see him again. I miss him. My father was a great warrior. A Sky Rider." She lifted her gaze to the sky. "He still rides the clouds forever now."

"And no doubt he's watching you from above," he said.

She nodded at him and swept her braids over her shoulders. "Sometimes I can feel him. A warm breeze is like his kiss on my neck. He would tickle me in that manner when I was a child."

"Oh, so you are ticklish, huh?"

"Don't you dare try it. I'll cut your elven fingers off and stuff them up your—"

"I won't. You sure are touchy for an orc."

"I don't like being tickled, especially by a man or an elf."

Dyphestive hustled up the rise and caught up with them. "What are you two talking about?"

"I was telling Gorva about your betrothed."

"My betrothed?" Dyphestive's puzzled expression turned to irritation, and his cheeks flushed. "Leena is not my betrothed. Will you stop with that?" He pushed past both of them and headed down the other side of the rise.

Gorva's gaze followed him. "Whoever this Leena is, she draws the fire from him."

"You can say that again," Grey Cloak said.

Dyphestive turned around and walked backward. "You can both stop saying anything. She isn't my betrothed. I only hope that she lives—Razor and Jakoby as well." He eyeballed Grey Cloak. "Do you really plan to bring the manticore's son back?"

"I gave my word."

"That's what worries me. I don't get the feeling that that manticore can be trusted. I'm not so sure about Thatcher either." Dyphestive slipped, grabbed a branch with his free hand, and caught his balance. He winced and said, "It seems strange that they'd let all of us leave."

"I agree," Gorva said in her husky voice. "Why would Thatcher and the big bug stay back if they could help us?"

Grey Cloak shrugged and flicked away another mosquito that had landed on his shoulder. "First, I don't think Thatcher would let his own people die. Second, he said we are close to Braykurz. Head north, and we can't miss it. Third, those manticores would have killed us. What choice did we have but to buy time?"

"How are we going to find our friends and save a manticore?" Dyphestive asked. "It seems to me that we have our hands full enough as it is. Not to mention that dragon, Thunderbreath. How are we supposed to slip by him?"

"Well..." Grey Cloak smirked. "It might be a problem for the two of you, but it won't be a problem for me." He wrapped himself in the Cloak of Legends. "I'm sneaky."

Gorva shoved him. "Not that sneaky."

He grinned. "I'll take my chances."

30

BRAYKURZ

"*Roooaaawwwrrr!*"

Standing on the edge of the jungle, which overlooked the sea, Grey Cloak checked the bright sky. Thunderbreath soared, circling the highest rocky spires of the mountaintops, then vanished on the other side.

Grey Cloak wasn't the only one staring at the winged terror. Dyphestive and Gorva stood with their chins up, shielding their eyes from the bright sun.

"I've never seen a dragon so big," Gorva said with awe. "Even Father's was not so ... tremendous."

"I take it that you've never seen Black Frost?" Grey Cloak asked.

"No," she replied. "They say that he is the size of a city, but I believed that was an exaggeration."

Grey Cloak pointed at the massive hills. "It's not exaggeration. His body would blanket the top of that mountain."

Gorva's jaw dropped. "He sounds too big for this world. That's not natural."

"Next time we see him, we'll be sure to tell him that. Maybe he'll leave." He set his eyes on the Inland Seas. "Come on. I think we've finally arrived."

They approached from the heights of the tropical land after a half-day-long climb upward and stood in a garden of massive stone pinnacles with flora and greenery sprouting all over them. Below, the sandy beaches and Inland Sea waited, and not so far off was a city.

A warm sea wind ruffled their hair, and they made their descent away from the suffocating jungle. The seabirds drifting over the breaking waves were a welcome sight after a days-long march while fighting tiny bugs and mosquitos.

"Perhaps this won't be so bad. After all, there is some sort of civilization ahead," Grey Cloak remarked as he combed his hair back with his fingers. "The two of you are awfully quiet."

"What are we supposed to do? Walk into this strange place and say, 'How do you do? I'm Gorva'?"

"We'll figure it out. Remember, let me do the talking." He caught Dyphestive's and Gorva's worried glances. "I saw that. Listen, whoever is in Braykurz is in the same situation that we are in. At least most of them. And if Thatcher wasn't lying, the Ministers of Evil shouldn't be hard to identify by the black tattoos on their faces. All we have to do is avoid them and blend in with the others. Follow my lead."

"If you say so, brother," Dyphestive said.

"How is the arm?"

"It's getting better."

A stony natural ledge weathered by time ran along a path above the beaches. A crag jutted out over a one-hundred-foot drop, creating an overlook.

Grey Cloak stood on the farthest edge and pointed. "That looks like Braykurz to me."

It was a seaport city complete with docks, buildings, and fishermen's wharf that was nearly a league long. The buildings were little and made from stone, and thousands upon thousands of seashells decorated the roofs. The place was much smaller than Harbor Lake and looked more like a small getaway for visitors than anything else. The streets were narrow, and people hurried along like busy ants. There were shanties all over, beginning at the edge of the city and peppering the overlooking mountainside, and caves in the stark rocks with people ambling in and out.

Grey Cloak felt eyes on his back and glanced at the ominous hillside that overlooked the small fishing town. Thunderbreath was perched on a pinnacle stone. His eyes burned like the flames of a fireplace as he glowered down at the city. "Let's keep moving, shall we?"

The stony ledge dropped down to a gently used path that took a steep downward turn toward the heart of Braykurz. It wasn't long before they were on the outskirts of the seaport, walking along the narrow winding roads surrounded by caves and shanties. Malnourished people huddled in their doorways, peeking outside. Their clothing appeared motheaten or in tatters.

Many small fires were set in rock pits where small fish cooked on spits. In the caves back in the hills, small children could be heard crying.

"They are looking at us like our heads are on fire," Grey Cloak said under his breath. He looked back into the eyes of an old man who was crouched and unblinking. One of the elder's eyes was milky. "These people are pitiful."

Dyphestive waved at a group of women who were covered in old blankets and said, "Hello."

They returned his greeting with stone-cold stares.

Gorva's nostrils flared, and she said, "They carry a stench." She covered her nose. "I've never smelled people who stank so badly."

"I don't think it's them," Grey Cloak said. The wind shifted course and blew a foul yellow smoke into their faces. "Maybe they are burning their clothes."

"You don't think it's people, do you?" Dyphestive asked with a sniff. "I smell burnt hair."

"I don't know. Keep going."

Covering their noses, they headed down the road toward the city. A small woman appeared in the smoke. She was accompanied by a group of smallish men, and they all blocked Grey Cloak, Dyphestive, and Gorva's path.

Grey Cloak fanned the thick smoke in front of his eyes and got a better look at the short-statured people. They were halflings. The tallest was a woman wearing a tall hat with a buckle on the middle of the brim. She wore a long maroon coat with brass buttons. Long black hair spilled out of her hat, framing her round face.

He took a knee and asked, "Are you the welcoming committee?"

"Are you a fool?" she replied in a gravelly voice.

Gorva chuckled.

"What is so funny, Ugly?" the halfling woman asked.

Gorva's hand fell to the dagger she'd tucked into her belt. "What did you say, half person?"

The halfling woman's eyes were as hard as coal. "I said, 'What is so funny, Ugly?'"

"Get out my way before I turn you over my knee like a child," Gorva threatened.

Grey Cloak turned his head toward Gorva and asked, "What did I say about letting me do the talking?" He held out a hand. "I'll handle this."

Gorva grunted and said, "Half person," under her breath.

He offered an apology. "Very sorry."

"Don't be. Orcs are idiots," the halfling lady said.

The male halflings sniggered behind her back.

"Elves are fools." She rose on her toes and looked behind Grey Cloak at Dyphestive. "And humans are worse than the two of them put together."

"I'm sorry, have we done something to offend you?" Grey Cloak asked.

"Yuh," she said and crinkled her button nose. "You showed up, and now we have to report you."

31

THE BROOD OF HALFLING MEN WHO ESCORTED THEIR FEMALE LEADER SPREAD OUT and surrounded them. Most of the men were bare chested, but some wore vests. All of them wore well-stitched trousers with pockets and a few sewn patches over the knees. All in all, the tiny group appeared formidable and bore serious looks, arms crossed over their chests, but they didn't carry any weapons.

Grey Cloak studied the group and asked, "Er, who do you have to report us to?"

"The Ministers," the halfling woman said. She fished a smoking pipe made from animal horn out of a side pocket in her coat and stuck it into her mouth. "What did you think? That you could stroll into Braykurz and make yourself comfortable? You'll be newcomers. You have to pay your dues."

He exchanged glances with Dyphestive and Gorva and said, "You're speaking about the Ministers of Evil, eh?"

Her eyes widened. "How did you know that?"

"It's not a secret, is it?"

She tilted her head to one side and eyed him. "I suppose it isn't. But I know all who come and go, and I've never seen the likes of you three before. I'd be curious to know how you came to be here."

"We came on the prisoner ship from Harbor Town," he said.

"And crossed through the jungle, but someone out there told you about Braykurz. How else could you have known?" She rubbed her dimpled chin. "Interesting. Not many make it this far." She touched his cloak and felt the fabric. "Interesting. And that one holds steel." She poked her horn pipe at Gorva. "A priceless treasure in these parts. I can't believe you were about to stroll into town like you've been there all of your life. This is not civilization as you know it. This is a place where you survive or die. And a quick death would have descended on the three of you."

Grey Cloak extended his hand. "I suppose we owe you a great deal of thanks for stopping us."

"How much are three lives worth?" She shook his hand. "My name is Deeann. And your thanks does me little good."

He started making up false names in his head and said, "Well, Deeann, our names are—"

"Grey Cloak and Dyphestive," she said.

"Well, Deeann, it appears that you have us at a disadvantage." Grey Cloak could hear Dyphestive and Gorva bristle behind him. He raised a hand. "I hope to goodness that you weren't searching for us."

"Never in a thousand years. Your secret is safe with us. But that doesn't change a thing. I still have to turn you in. But walk with us. It's the safest route for now." Deeann spun on the heel of her boot. "Come on, boys." The team of halfling men fell in behind her.

Grey Cloak decided to trust his gut. He didn't know who Deeann was, but she appeared to be looking out for them. He gave Dyphestive and Gorva a nod, and with uncertain looks, they followed with him.

Deeann let the pack of halflings take the lead and drifted back to Grey Cloak. "I'm sure you are wondering how I know you."

"You read my mind," he replied.

She smiled. "I worked with Zora at Dark Mountain when they were searching for your big friend that was taken by the Doom Riders. I'm close to Crane and Tanlin."

"You're part of the Brotherhood of Whispers?"

"Yes, or what's left of it. Black Frost's minions sniffed us out and all but eradicated us years ago. We were found out and exiled to this island." She motioned to her fellow halflings. "This is what is left of my crew. Only ten of us left, but there used to be more."

Grey Cloak felt those guilty butterflies fluttering in his chest. "I'm sorry."

"Don't be. It's not your fault."

"I'd like to think not, but I'm not so sure."

Deeann gave him a funny look and said, "I'm not sure what you could have done that would have caused the world to fall apart."

"You'd be surprised," Dyphestive commented.

"Nothing surprises me," she said. "I have to admit that I'm sorry to see that you've been captured and that you're stranded here like the rest of us, but I'll do what I can to get you through it. Be wise and listen to me. It won't be easy, but over time, life will be manageable, and I'll show you how to avoid trouble."

Grey Cloak stopped. "Deeann, there is something I need to tell you."

"There will plenty of time for that later."

"No, you don't understand. We weren't captured. This is a rescue mission."

The halfling crew began murmuring to one another with surprised looks on their faces.

Deeann stopped in her tracks with a slack-jawed expression and said, "Now that surprises me." She removed her hat and started beating Grey Cloak with it. "Are you mad? No one escapes the island. I mean no one. And now you're telling me that this is a rescue mission? That's the craziest mission that I've ever heard of."

"We've been known to do worse," Dyphestive said.

"What is with the comments?" Grey Cloak fired back. "You must be feeling better."

"I was never feeling that bad."

Deeann straightened her hat and jammed it onto her head. Her pipe rolled from one corner of her mouth to the other. "Who are you here to rescue? Us, I hope?"

"Well..." he said with a guilty look. "Not exactly."

32

GLOOMY CLOUDS NUDGED OUT THE SUNLIGHT, AND A SPITTING RAIN STARTED coming down. Grey Cloak and Deeann continued walking and talking the whole way but at a slower pace.

"I know the three that you are speaking of," Deeann said of Jakoby, Razor, and Leena. "But you aren't going to like what I have to say. They serve the Ministers of Evil now."

"What?" Dyphestive exclaimed. He pulled Grey Cloak back by the shoulder and dropped to a knee in front of Deeann. "They would never do such a thing. Tell the truth. I know you're lying."

Deeann shook her head. "You'll see for yourself. Listen, all of us have done what we must do to survive. I spy for the Ministers of Evil."

"The same way Zora and Tanlin spy for the Black Guard," Grey Cloak added.

"I'd die first," Dyphestive said.

"You would eat those words if you walked in their boots. Don't be so quick to judge," she said. "This place brings out the worst in all of us."

"Then we'd better not stay around very long." Dyphestive shoved Grey Cloak forward. "Let's get on with it."

"Easy, brother. We can't rush headfirst into the fire."

"It never stopped us before." Dyphestive marched ahead.

"He must really care for Leena," Gorva said as she pushed by Grey Cloak and Deeann. "I'll stay with him."

Deeann snagged the dagger from Gorva's belt and said, "Not with this, you won't." The dagger vanished into her coat. "Don't worry. I'll take care of it." She turned her attention back to Grey Cloak. "I have to introduce you to the Ministers of Evil. I suppose it's best that you stay with false names. You don't want to take a chance that they've heard of you. I'll handle it. After that, you'll be taken to the proving grounds."

"Proving grounds? Like the Honor Guard in Monarch City goes through?" he asked.

"You wish. No, you'll be taken to the quartz mines until they see what is best suited for you. It's the place where they break you."

He nodded. "It sounds delightful."

"Sure, keep telling yourself that. You'll sleep better—if they let you sleep at all," she said. "I have to ask. How in the wild world are you planning to get your friends off of this island if you can't get yourself off?"

Grey Cloak smirked. "I'll think of something."

Deeann shook her head. "Great plan."

"Try not to stare at her," Deeann warned as she walked them through the dreary seaport town.

"Her?" Grey Cloak asked. "What sort of *her* is she?"

"High Minister Helsa is very unique, to say the least."

She approached a stone lodge that was one of the larger buildings in the city. Two brutish lizard-man guards holding clubs were posted outside the wooden double-door entrance. They had a lazy look about them and stepped in front of the door.

"I have newcomers," Deeann said.

The taller of the two lizard men pushed Deeann back with the head of his club. He spoke in a hissing voice. "Wait here, halfling." He opened the double doors and vanished in between them, and they quickly closed behind him.

The shorter lizard man barred the doors with his squat body.

Deeann rocked on her heels. "Nice day, isn't it?"

The lizard man leaned against the door and said, "Gum up."

The doors opened, and he fell backward into the unsuspecting arms of the other lizard man. Both of them crashed to the floor and quickly popped up again.

The taller one shoved the shorter one outside. "Be careful, fool!" He glared at Deeann. "Minister Helsa awaits."

Leaving the rest of her crew behind, she said, "Thank you."

Grey Cloak, Dyphestive, and Gorva followed the halfling into the lodge. It was a simple two-story building with a fireplace burning on each of the side walls. Water dripped from the wooden rafters, making small puddles on the floor. It smelled of burning wood, mold, and mildew.

Deeann stopped a few feet inside the door and took a knee. "Get down," she ordered under her breath.

They complied.

"Minister Helsa, I bring three newcomers!" she shouted to the figures on the far side of the room.

Grey Cloak kept his head down and his eyes up. By the far wall were several men wearing steel helms with chain-mail faces that hid everything but the eyes. Each one was also geared up in dyed sea-green leather tunics with longswords and daggers on their hips. He counted six in all, and they appeared to be guarding a throne-like chair positioned against the back wall. A very burly woman unlike any woman that he'd seen before was seated on the throne. She had a pudgy face stamped with a black tattoo like a tick, and her hair was slicked back and golden blond. Like the guards, she was a real bruiser. She had a big chest, and she wore a dark tunic that revealed arms bigger than Dyphestive's. Her lips were wet and puffy. She sat behind a small table with a platter of food, and she gnawed a piece of flesh off a wide turkey leg and belched.

"Deeann!" the high minister said in a commanding voice. She smacked her lips and licked the grease from her fingers. "Rise! Tell me about these newcomers!"

"Yes, of course," Deeann said and stood. She quickly bowed. "They arrived from the south side of the island. I came upon them when they wandered out of the jungle. One is an elf, one is a man, and the woman is an orc. Very young. Ready to serve your will."

High Minister Helsa tossed her turkey leg over the back of her chair and said, "We'll see about that."

She nodded at her guards. Two of them hurried over and moved the table away from her. She stood, fully revealing the monstrous form of a full-blooded ogre, but she was shorter than one. Her yellow eyes matched her yellowish skin. Iron jewelry covered her thick neck and wrists. Many earrings pierced her ears.

"Come closer. All of you. Approach!"

Grey Cloak couldn't help but steal another glance. Something about Helsa felt familiar. *Who does she remind me of?* Then it hit him. Helsa reminded him of Orpha, the ogre that he'd met at Monarch City. Orpha worked for Dark Addler. She wasn't just an ogre but part orc and a lot of other things as well, and she was a very memorable woman, to say the least.

"I see you looking at me, elf," High Minister Helsa said. She flipped her greasy hair over her brawny shoulders. "Are you admiring my beauty?"

Deeann took her hat off and said, "High Minister, I advised them not to speak."

"Is that so? Do they take orders from you or me?" the high minister asked.

"You, of course." Deeann knelt.

Grey Cloak could feel Helsa's warm, turkey-smelling breath on his face. Her thick hands clutched his ears and began to twist.

"Who is this, Deeann?"

"Uh, he calls himself Graysun."

"Cute. Graysun, were you admiring my beauty?" Helsa asked.

"There are countless things I admire about you," he admitted. *But not your beauty or your breath.*

"Clever." Helsa snorted. "I'll be sure to follow up on all of those *things* that you admire later." She made her way to Gorva. "And who is this?"

"Gorza," Deeann said.

"Gorva," Gorva corrected.

The high minister tugged on Gorva's braids. "Strapping and spirited. It's been a long time since I've had guests with the meat still left on their bones. So many have been so fragile."

"Agreed," Deeann said nervously. "Uh, the last one calls himself Duugun."

High Minister Helsa was taller and broader than Dyphestive, and her hungry eyes were all over him. She slapped him hard on the rump. "I like this one." She stroked his arm with her fingers and squeezed the muscle. "A very impressive human specimen. And young." She faced him and leered into his eyes. "I like young."

Dyphestive swallowed.

"Is there anything else I can do for you, High Minister Helsa?" Deeann asked. "I'd be more than happy to assist in prepping them for the mines."

The high minister kept her yellow eyes fixed on Dyphestive and said, "Oh, they won't be going to the mines. It's been a long time since the Ministers of Evil entered new blood into the arena." She ran her fingers through Dyphestive's hair. "But this handsome one stays with me."

33

Separated from Dyphestive, Grey Cloak and Gorva were marched into the hills and locked inside a cave that was sealed with steel bars.

Gorva tried to pull the corroded metal bars apart. Her taut muscles flexed in her arms and back, but the bars didn't give. She banged her head against them. "Gah! How is your plan working out now, *Gray Sun*?"

"I think it's Graysun." Grey Cloak wrapped his cloak about him, leaned against the bars, and looked out over the sea. "One step at a time."

"Don't try to make it sound like you know what you are doing," Gorva said. She slid down with her back against the bars and took a seat. "Because you don't!"

"Sure I do. We need to know what we are dealing with. We are dealing with Helsa. We can handle her. And look at this view. We can see the entire city. Count the people. Get a feeling for the guards and their routines. I couldn't have planned it better myself, even though I did."

"And what about your brother?"

"For someone that doesn't claim to like him, you certainly show a lot of concern."

"More than you, obviously."

Grey Cloak rolled his forehead against the bars and watched the guards that patrolled the dungeon-like caves. "Dyphestive will be fine. He's been through a lot worse."

Gorva looked up at him. "Leena is worse than that ogre?"

"She makes a strong case for that. It all depends on what you find tolerable and detestable."

She gave a squeamish look. "This Leena sounds like a bad person."

"Again, it's all a matter of perspective, but I think that you would like her." He noticed a pair of the minister's soldiers approaching. They were fit men, rich in muscle, one light skinned and the other dark. "We have company."

Gorva turned her head and said, "Good for them."

The two soldiers stared Grey Cloak dead in the eye.

"It's not polite to stare," he said.

"It is if you haven't seen someone in over ten years," the lighter-skinned man said in a familiar rugged and uniquely accented voice.

Grey Cloak's hands locked on the bars. "Razor! Is that you?"

"I wanted to ask you the same question when you showed up at the throne. I almost leaked down my trousers when you and Dyphestive walked in," Reginald the Razor said. He clasped hands with Grey Cloak. "It's great to see you."

"Don't get so mushy, and keep your voice down," the other soldier said.

Grey Cloak didn't have any trouble recognizing Jakoby's voice. "I can't believe that I didn't notice before."

"Helsa is very distracting. She sucks up all of the attention," Razor said. "Goy, ten years. I never knew what happened to you. What did happen?"

"It's a long story, but I'm here now. We came to rescue you."

Jakoby and Razor gave each other serious looks before they erupted in laughter.

"Why does everyone laugh when I say that?" he asked.

"Because it's idiotic," Gorva said, rising. "Any fool can see that."

"Are you telling me that the reason you are here is to rescue us?" Jakoby said. "And be honest."

"I am being honest. We have to find a way to stop Black Frost, and we can't do it alone. And it's probably my fault that you are in this pickle. I have to make it right," he said.

Jakoby nodded. "I would do the same thing, but getting off of this island is impossible. Thunderbreath watches the water like a hawk. Nothing comes and goes without his notice, not even the fish."

"What about the Ministers of Evil? How many of them does Helsa control?" he asked.

"Helsa is in charge of Braykurz," Jakoby said, "and there are dozens at her beck and call. Hard to miss, given the black tattoos. They are enforcers, a step above bodyguards like us," Jakoby said.

"So you serve Black Frost?"

"It's a real dung-heap detail," Razor said, "but it's better than the alternative of begging for scraps. We do what we do to survive."

"What about Leena?" he asked.

"Er, well, she's around," Razor said, rubbing the back of his neck. "We haven't seen her about in a while."

Grey Cloak noticed Razor's eyes sliding toward Jakoby. It was obvious they weren't telling him something. "What happened to Leena?"

Jakoby sighed. "She's one of the Ministers of Evil now."

34

Gorva gave Grey Cloak a pat on the back and said sarcastically, "Poor little Dyphestive will be heartbroken."

"Speaking of Dyphestive," Razor said, "he has bigger matters to worry about than Leena. Helsa put her hooks in him, and she won't let him out of her sight. Not when she fancies him. More than likely, they'll have a ceremony. Probably tonight at the arena."

"What sort of ceremony?" Grey Cloak asked.

Razor gave him a funny look and said, "A wedding ceremony, of course."

"What?" Gorva exclaimed. "She will marry him?"

"Dyphestive would never do that," Grey Cloak said. "He'd die first."

"And that is exactly what will happen if he refuses. She'll kill him, the same as the others who refused," Jakoby said.

"How many men has she married?" Gorva asked.

Razor started counting on his fingers, shook his head, and said, "I lost count, but don't worry. All of them are dead now." He nudged Jakoby with his elbow. "So Dyphestive won't have to share her."

Grey Cloak slapped his head and stepped away from the bars. "Zooks, can matters get any worse?"

"Well, you could be in Dyphestive's boots," Razor said. "Listen, mate, there's always a silver lining in everything."

"There is? What?"

Jakoby cleared his throat and said, "The arena is a proving ground, a place to impress Helsa. Battle well there, and she'll keep you around as one of her personal Black Guard, like us."

Grey Cloak didn't hide his irritation. He glowered at them and said, "And that would mean swearing loyalty to her, like you two."

"She has our words, but she doesn't have our hearts. It was this or death, and we can't help you stop Black Frost or save our friends if we're dead," Jakoby said. "The truth is that deep down, I never thought our battle was over. I've been hanging around, waiting for that final battle." His reached his hand through the bars. "This is the moment we've been waiting for."

Grey Cloak shook his hand. "It's a moment all right."

Razor moved over to Gorva's side of the bars and said, "So, love, I've been thinking that you are the moment I've been waiting for."

"Come closer," she whispered.

Razor leaned forward and said, "As you wish."

Gorva grabbed him by the collar of his tunic and pulled him face-first into the bars. "This is as close as you'll ever get. Keep dreaming, human." She shoved him back.

Razor straightened his cock-eyed helmet and said, "I love a challenge." He lifted his veil and blew her a kiss. "See you around, gorgeous."

"Grey Cloak, dealing with the Ministers of Evil is one thing, but getting off of the island is another. Thunderbreath couldn't care less what men on the island do, but no one leaves unless they go through him." Jakoby patted the pommel of his sword. "Our weapons are useless against his steel-hard scales. He can turn Braykurz into cinders with a single breath. Tell me you have dragons coming or something."

"I don't have dragons, but I do have this." He reached into his cloak pocket and pulled out the dragon charm that he'd found at the Burnt Hills of Sulter Slay and showed it to Jakoby.

Gorva raised her eyebrows. "What is that?"

The shiny orange gemstone was egg-shaped but flatter, like a river stone. It glinted with bright little fires in its center.

"That's a dragon charm, isn't it?" Jakoby asked.

Grey Cloak nodded. "When the time comes, I'll use it on ol' Thunderbreath, and getting off of this island will be easy."

"We still need a boat to get off of the island," Gorva said.

"I'm working on that."

"Do you know how to use a dragon charm?" Jakoby asked. "I thought only wizards could use them."

"Wizard, schmizard. I'll figure it out," he said, palming the smooth stone with both hands. It was warm to the touch and pulsated.

"He doesn't know how to use it," Gorva said. She reached for it. "Give it to me. I'll figure it out."

Grey Cloak pulled it away. "It's mine. And don't worry. I'm a natural. We have a gift for using these sorts of things. Trust me."

"*Roooaaarrr!*"

The dragon charm burned hot in Grey Cloak's hand. A shadow fell over the mountainside followed by the sound of dragon wings beating. *Wump! Wump! Wump!*

Jakoby leaned back, the whites of his eyes showing. "Put it away!" he whispered. "He's coming!"

Grey Cloak stuffed the dragon charm into his pocket. His palms were as warm as toast. He rubbed them and watched Thunderbreath sail by. The dragon's eyes were burning orange flames that stole his breath. His heart jumped as the dragon looked away and flew on. "What just happened?" he muttered.

Gorva punched him in the shoulder and said, "I don't know, but don't take that rock out again until we need it."

35

THE ARENA WAS A NATURAL ROCK FORMATION NESTLED IN THE HILLS NEAR THE beach. The rocky surface made a massive bowl in the ground that was over twenty feet deep and three times as wide. Grey Cloak and Gorva were marched down a natural ramp onto the arena floor with their hands tied behind their backs. The soldiers that escorted them cut loose their bonds and moved back up the ramp, where a grate of iron bars was lowered, sealing them inside.

Rubbing his wrists, Grey Cloak studied his new surroundings and said, "Interesting place."

"Indeed."

A crowd started to build in the surrounding rocks that overlooked the arena. They were the citizens of Braykurz, hapless in expression, disheveled, and weathered, with deep wrinkles in their sun-browned skin. They pushed along the rim of the arena, shoving their way to the best spots.

More soldiers were positioned along the top of the wall. They were Black Guard, like Jakoby and Razor. They stood between tall torch stands whose orange fires reflected dully on their steel helmets. In addition to their belts of weapons, each carried a spear in a firm hand.

Centered over the arena, with their backs protected by the rocks, and facing the waves breaking on the shore, were the Ministers of Evil. It was a small group of eight men and women with black tattoos like spiders covering their faces. All of them had shaved heads and wore black robes and belts of daggers around their waists. The four men stood to the right of High Minister Helsa, who was sitting, and the four women stood to her left. Their faces were cold and expressionless.

Dyphestive sat at Helsa's feet with a frown on his face. His big fists held up his chin, and a collar with a chain had been attached to his neck.

Grey Cloak waved his fingers at his brother. His gesture drew a scowl. He leaned over to Gorva and said, "He seems to be having a good time."

"Yes, he wears it well," Gorva replied.

HIGH MINISTER HELSA tugged on Dyphestive's chain and said, "Soon, you will be my groom, Duugun." She ran her rough hands through his hair. "And it will be a night that you'll never forget."

Dyphestive's stomach flip-flopped. He pulled away.

She jerked him back into her lap. "Now, now, don't be difficult. You'll get used to me."

"And what if I don't?"

Helsa pulled his collar tighter and whispered with her big lips touching his ears, "Then you'll be dead!" She shoved him forward and cackled. "Now, fetch my wine. The high minister is thirsty, and I need to wet my lips. You should sweeten yours as well before our first kiss."

Dyphestive crawled away, using the full length of the chain, wishing he could wrap it around her neck. *I couldn't kill her, could I?* he thought. He picked up a clay jug of wine that sat on a small serving table and started pouring it into a metal chalice. The purple wine had a sour smell. A tug on his neck caught his attention, and he spilled the wine on the rocky terrace.

"Bring me the entire jug. I'm very thirsty." Helsa glared at him. "And put a smile on that pretty face of yours! It's our wedding day. You will be happy!"

Wedding Day? Horseshoes, this is really happening, isn't it?

He caught one of the Ministers of Evil smirking at him. It was a woman, human, with bright-blue eyes that shone like the stars. She caught him looking and sawed her finger across her neck. He stared at her as he took the jug of wine to Helsa.

"Sit down, Blondie! I can't see in the arena!" Helsa snatched the jug of wine and tilted it to her hungry lips. The wine spilled over her chin and ran down between her bosoms. She gave Dyphestive an ornery smile. "I saw you looking."

He turned his head away, caught Grey Cloak's eye, and shook his fist.

Helsa hauled him back by the chains and pinned his back between her knees. "Stay put, young fella. The early show is about to begin. You'll like it. Gets the blood flowing from head to toe. And look, there is a full moon tonight." She let out a howl.

Dyphestive tried to pull away, but Helsa held him fast with an iron grip. Being an ogre, she was naturally as strong as an ox and far more intelligent than most. Cunning and shrewdness lurked in her beady eyes. As for the other Ministers of Evil, they were far less prominent in stature. Some of the men even had soft bellies.

I could take them. I could take them all.

Helsa let out a loud belch. "Ah, that's better."

Dyphestive pinched his nose. *For you maybe, but not for me.*

The high minister rose from her chair and lifted her arms high. The crowd's murmuring fell silent when Helsa stepped up on a dais for all to see.

"Citizens of Braykurz, it has been too long since blood was shed in the arena. It's been too long since I've wed. But tonight, I promise, will be a festive celebration!"

The silent crowd blossomed into raucous cheers.

Helsa's voice rose above the excited throng. "Tonight, two *newcomers* have come into our midst, seeking refuge. An elf! An orc! Strapping and healthy. They survived a dangerous trip crossing the harrowing jungles, but can they survive" —she pumped her fist into the air—"the *arena*?"

The feverish audience shouted a resounding "Nooo!"

36

"Apparently, these slack-jawed miscreants don't know who they are up against," Grey Cloak said as he made a slow circle around the inside of the arena. "And to think, I'm here to save them."

Gorva bared her teeth and flexed her arms at the crowd. "Tonight, they will learn what the daughter of a Sky Rider is!" She pounded her chest. "Bring the pain, wretches!"

Somewhere, a gong sounded. *Booonnng!*

The jawlike gate where they'd entered was lifted by the soldiers. It was impossible to see above the arena wall, but Grey Cloak could see the ramp. The soldiers shoved a motley bunch of barefoot people with clubs down the ramps. There were a score of them, and many were hunched over and malnourished. They shuffled on their dirty feet and exchanged nervous glances with one another.

"This is the doom that awaits us? A bunch of vagrants?"

"What would you rather have? A bunch of lions?" Gorva asked.

"Good point."

High Minister Helsa stood over the arena wall. She pointed at Grey Cloak and Gorva. "Destroy them, and you will eat like monarchs for the rest of your life!"

"You have to be jesting!" Grey Cloak shouted. "They are pitiful."

"Desperate people will surprise you, elf. Destroy them and feast!" Helsa commanded. "Destroy!"

The motley attackers raised their clubs over their heads and came all at once.

"This is ridiculous." Grey Cloak waited for what seemed like forever for the first man to take a swing. He twisted the club out of the man's hands and popped him in the jaw with his fist. The man fell down and lay at his feet, out cold. "Easy-peasy. Who is next?"

Not all of the attackers went down easily. Their hungry bellies groaned, and they fought out of desperation.

Grey Cloak tried his best to be merciful. Using the club like a sap, he evaded their desperate swings with the ease of a cat and socked them with a club to the jaw.

Whap! Crack! Pop! Smack!

The hungry throng fell at his feet like rain. He kicked another club up with his foot and turned to find more attackers. They were running right at him with terrified looks on their faces.

Gorva shouted at the top of her lungs, "Look at them! They wilt under my thunder!"

The crowd was on their feet, pumping their fists and shaking their arms wildly.

"Fight, ravenous cowards! Fight!" She swung her club full force, pounding men to their knees. *Whop! Whop! Whop! Whop!*

The attackers ran for their lives in all directions.

Grey Cloak watched the sea of would-be attackers race right by him, back through the gate.

Gorva chased them down, shouting, "Come back! Come back!" Her chest was heaving. "Come back!"

Soldiers with their spears lowered walled her off. She growled at them and backed away, stepping over a field of unmoving bodies.

Grey Cloak counted fourteen men that were down. Most of them appeared to have broken bones and were bleeding. "You didn't have to be so hard on them," he said.

Gorva glowered at him. "Have you ever met an orc before?"

"Point taken."

The Black Guard soldiers continued backing them toward the wall with their spears while the bodies were dragged out of the arena. The soldiers cleared out and stole their way up the ramp. The arena jaws were closed.

Grey Cloak noticed a pair of soldiers on the top of the wall, looking down at him. It was Jakoby and Razor.

"Well, did we prove ourselves?"

"Ha! That was only a crowd teaser," Razor said with a grin showing through his chainmail veil. "The next bit will be a crowd pleaser."

"What sort of crowd pleaser?"

"It could be anything—an ogre, a minotaur, bears, or sea devils. Helsa likes surprises," Reginald said.

"Is that so?"

Jakoby seemed oddly silent. His stare was fixed on the doors of the arena.

"What are you thinking, Jakoby? Ogre or minotaur?"

The former Monarch Knight and brother of the deceased Adanadel shrugged. "It could be anyone. Anything."

The gong sounded again. Grey Cloak and Gorva, with clubs in their hands, walked to the middle of the arena.

The crowd erupted in howls and cheers as the doors lifted and a new opponent sauntered down the ramp. She was dressed in the dark garb of a Minister of Evil. A spiderlike tattoo covered her face, and she carried a long black stick in each hand. She was no bigger than an average woman.

Gorva tilted her head to one side and commented, "She's very small. This should be easy."

"This isn't easy," Grey Cloak said as his throat tightened. "That's Leena."

37

Dyphestive let out an audible gasp the moment he laid eyes on Leena. There was no mistaking her long red ponytail and splendid build. His heart raced. The ugly black tattoo on her face caught his eye, and his thundering heart saddened. She was one of them now, a Minister of Evil.

What has she done?

He crept up behind Helsa to get a closer look. The high minister lathered up the crowd by pumping her fists in the air and shouting wildly. He tried to catch Leena's eye, but her stone-cold stare remained fixed on her opponents.

Dyphestive caught Grey Cloak looking at him and mouthed, "Don't hurt her."

Grey Cloak waggled his eyebrows and nodded at Gorva.

Horseshoes. He'd just watched Gorva beat a bunch of defenseless people senseless. She would show less mercy on Leena. He inched toward the wall.

Zzzt!

A jolting shock that felt like fire blasted through Dyphestive's neck. He fell down, clutching his neck and groaning. The shock stopped, and he found Helsa standing over him.

"Did that sting, my love?" She petted his face and lifted his chin. "That iron collar you wear will shock you on command. I have to make sure that you don't get out of line." She kissed his head. "And that you do as I say when I say." She tapped an iron necklace studded with onyx stones. "Don't ever forget who is in control. Now, have a seat. I'm looking forward to watching the most lethal Minister of Evil in action once again."

Dyphestive took his place at Helsa's throne, where she took her seat and joined him. His hand trembled, and his wounded arm burned like hot coals. He sank his hands between his legs and breathed deeply.

Helsa lovingly stroked his head with her calloused hand. "That's it, my dear.

Be a good boy. I will take care of you. I will take care of you the rest of your life so long as you let me."

GREY CLOAK and Gorva spread out.

"So, this is Leena, huh?" Gorva asked.

"In the flesh," he replied.

Gorva gave him a wary look and said, "If she knows who you are, won't she tell Helsa?"

"Luckily for us, she doesn't speak. She was a member of the Ministry of Hoods and took a vow of silence or something." Without taking his eyes off of Leena, he shuffled toward her. "Let me talk to her first. I'll let her know what is going on. Hopefully, we can work together."

Gorva spun her clubs and said, "She looks pretty committed, if you ask me."

"That's why I didn't ask you."

The crowd's roaring for blood kept their conversation away from prying ears. With his guard up, Grey Cloak ventured toward Leena. "Remember me, your old friend Grey Cloak? Listen to me. I am here to rescue you. Me and Dyphestive. I know you remember him."

Leena didn't bat a lash. Her stern gaze cut right through him.

"Come now, Leena. I know that you didn't forget us. Don't you remember all of the good times we had? Er... for example—"

"Fight, you stupid donkey skulls! Fight!" Helsa shouted.

Grey Cloak took his eyes off of Leena for a moment.

Bap! Crack! Pop!

The next thing that he knew, he was on the ground, with bright blurry spots in his eyes and the taste of blood in his mouth. He propped himself up on his elbows and shook his head.

The crowd roared.

Zooks, what hit me?

Several feet away, Gorva and Leena were engaged in mortal combat. Gorva swung her clubs with skill, but Leena dodged them easily. It looked like Gorva was trying to swat a fly that buzzed away at the last moment. Her strikes looked slow and clumsy.

Leena darted inside Gorva's swings, ran up her body, kicked her in the chin, and did a backflip.

Gorva's arms flailed at her sides, and she lost her footing and landed hard on her backside. Before she could wink, Leena drummed her sticks on her head several times.

"It looks like someone has been doing a lot of practicing over the past ten years." Grey Cloak twirled his sticks around. "Let's try this again."

Leena charged.

Wood rattled against wood as Grey Cloak parried her flurry of attacks. She was quick but not any quicker than he was, and he started to catch on to her style.

"Leena, listen to me. We don't want to hurt you."

The intensity in her eyes deepened. She faked an attack, drawing his guard, and countered with a side kick to his groin.

Grey Cloak went down in a heap. "Uuuh! What is it with you and busting the acorns?"

The masses exploded in shouts and danced in their seats.

"That's it!" Gorva returned to her feet with her nostrils flaring. She banged her clubs together. "I'm not holding back on the little woman this time!" On speedy long legs, she propelled herself at Leena.

Leena stood her ground. With a twist of her wrist she turned her sticks into a pair of nunchakus.

Gorva slowed. "What are those things?"

Grimacing, Grey Cloak said, "You don't want to know."

Leena's sticks whirled to life, and she hit the hesitant Gorva all over. In the knee. *Clok!* Across the jaw. *Clok!* The other knee. *Clok!* The back of the skull. *Clok! Clok! Clok!*

Gorva crashed down beside Grey Cloak and gave him a bewildered look.

"I told you she was mean," he said.

With wild, bloodthirsty chants filling the arena, he grasped Gorva's hands, and they helped one another to their feet.

"Let's do this together. You go high. I'll go low. We have to get her down on the ground."

Gorva rubbed the knots on the back of her head. "She's going down, one way or the other."

DYPHESTIVE'S NAILS dug into his palms, and he ground his teeth. It was killing him not being able to jump into the arena and put a stop to the madness. Leena was like a buzz saw. She was beating Grey Cloak and Gorva to death.

If they keep holding back, she's going to kill them.

Behind him, Helsa was on her feet, cheering as wildly as the rest. She beat her chest and slung her jug of wine all over.

Dyphestive sneered. Helsa was an obnoxious lummox. *I have to get away from her.*

He watched the iron necklace bounce off of her chest. It was made of many links and had a large medallion in the middle along with several smaller ones. His fingers flexed.

Helsa caught him looking and wagged her finger at him. A shock sent ripples through his neck.

He cried, "Gaaah!"

38

GETTING LEENA DOWN TO THE GROUND PROVED AN EVEN MORE TROUBLING TASK than Grey Cloak imagined. He dove at her feet only to see her jump away time and again, and Gorva was too slow to catch her.

"She's like trying to catch a greased chicken," Gorva said. "She slips right through my fingers!"

Leena whacked her hand with her sticks.

"Ow!"

Grey Cloak was even more embarrassed. He prided himself on being quick, but Leena remained one step ahead. Not to mention that she was a dangerous close-quarters fighter the likes of which he'd never seen. He had never been much of a fist fighter. "Come on, Leena. You can let up now. Remember, we're friends."

Leena jumped and tried to kick him.

He ducked, letting her sail overhead, and snagged her by the back leg. "Got her!"

She landed hard on the ground, rolled to her back, and kicked him in the face with her free leg.

She got his cheek, but he held on. "No, you don't!"

Leena kept kicking him in the face.

"Gorva!" he called. "A little help!"

"I'm coming!" Gorva came out of nowhere and dropped an elbow on Leena. "How does that feel, little woman?" She straddled her and clamped her hands over Leena's throat. "Now I have you where I want you!"

"Don't kill her!" Grey Cloak said.

"What am I supposed to do? Let her kill us?"

"Hold her down."

Grey Cloak wormed his way around Gorva and tried to grab Leena's arms. She was still beating Gorva in the face, but Gorva wouldn't let go.

"Submit, Leena. Submit. We'll figure a way out of this." He grabbed a hand, wrenched a nunchaku free, and cast it aside. "There, only one more to go."

Leena bucked like a mule under Gorva, but she held her fast.

"You aren't going anywhere. Be still before I break your neck," Gorva warned. "I think I can put her out in a choke hold. Help me twist this little squirmer around."

Leena squeezed her eyes shut. Her little nostrils flared.

"What are you doing? You're choking her to death," Grey Cloak said.

"I wish. Her neck muscles are like steel."

Leena balled up her fist, and bright-blue veins burned beneath the skin.

Grey Cloak caught it out the corner of his eye and said, "Uh-oh."

"What does that mean?" Gorva asked.

"Look out!"

It was too late. Leena launched a fiery punch that blasted Gorva hard in the middle of the chest. *Pow!*

Gorva's body sailed across the dusty arena floor and slammed into the wall. Her body lay limp.

Grey Cloak stared. Leena turned under him and flipped him away. He rolled over the ground and slowly got up.

That time, his nostrils flared. "Leena, now you're starting to twist me off!"

Leena stood across from him with one fist pulsating with blue veins and the other filled with spinning nunchakus.

The crowd was on its feet, screaming so loudly that it drowned out the sound of the crashing tides.

Grey Cloak had had enough. Deep inside of him, something started to burn. It wasn't the wizardry either. It was something else, something deeper, stronger, and yearning to come out. He wiped the blood from his lip and stared at the red on his fingertips. For some reason, everything he'd been through came to mind. It all came together. He was a natural. He was the son of a Sky Rider. He focused.

I am Grey Cloak.

He marched right at Leena. She came right at him and swung with her nunchaku. He caught the stick with his fingers and snatched it away.

Leena punched, and he evaded. Using his cloak, he tied up her hand and held her fast.

The pace of the melee quickened. She kicked at his groin, and he blocked with his knee and head-butted her in the face.

Leena rolled over his back and twisted her fist free then kicked him in the back.

Grey Cloak stumbled forward, gathered his balance, and crouched as she sailed overhead with a flying kick. But when she landed, he leg-swept her. She landed on her back and hopped up again. Her blood-filled fist popped him like a striking cobra. Sharp pain exploded in his chest, and he faltered, going down to a knee.

The wild crowd's cajoling filled his ears. They wanted blood. They wanted his head. He stood and waved Leena toward him with a fluid motion of his wrist.

Leena furrowed her bow and attacked with an onslaught of fury. She tore into him with a combination of kicks and punches. Grey Cloak dodged and ducked everything she threw at him.

The bright veins in her fist cooled. He didn't.

Grey Cloak didn't know what had gotten into him, but he transferred it to her. His fists moved faster than he could think. Her blocks were slow and sluggish. He burst through her defenses and scissor-kicked her in the jaw.

Leena went down. She was out.

The throng fell silent. They all stared at him, wide-eyed and slack-jawed. Even the Ministers of Evil's dark faces showed signs of dismay.

Grey Cloak turned and faced the high minister's stand. He tossed his cloak over his shoulders, crossed his arms over his chest, and asked, "Who's next?"

High Minister Helsa slowly dropped her arms and moved to the edge of the arena wall. Looking down at him, she said, "I've never seen a man move so fast before. That was astonishing. It concerns me too." She rubbed her chin. "I can't take any chances." She lifted her voice. "Send in the manticore!"

39

THE BLACK GUARD OPENED THE DOORS TO THE ARENA, AND A MANTICORE WALTZED in. He was built the same as Ebonthrak and Jessel, only younger and bigger. It had to be their son, Karzak. He had the same humanish lionlike face and black hair and mane, and he had dragon scales on his legs and body. He dragged his tail behind him, and the spikes clawed the dirt like a plow.

The enthusiastic crowd quieted as they watched the great beast enter, and the arena's groaning doors were closed. A quiet, awe-filled *ooh* escaped their lips as they watched the monster prowl about with its orange eyes burning like flames.

Grey Cloak wasn't entirely positive what had overcome him earlier. Whatever it was, it felt good, but as he came face-to-face with another manticore, his confidence was visibly shaken. Fighting a 130-pound woman was one thing. Brawling with a savage beast that weighed half a ton was another.

He hollered into the stands, "I don't suppose you'd be willing to equip me with one of those spears, would you?"

Helsa leaned over the wall and said, "Why, of course not. I want this over quickly. I have a wedding to attend."

"Well, don't you think that your groom will want a best man to see him off?" he said as he backed away from the manticore.

"My sweet young man will be fine." Helsa reached back and tickled Dyphestive's chin. "Won't you, darling Duugun?"

Dyphestive shook her off.

Grey Cloak focused his attention back on the manticore. "Listen to me, Karzak. I'm here to rescue you. I was sent by your father and mother, Ebonthrak and Jessel. I'm going to free you."

Karzak's eyes widened. "How do you know my name?"

"Your parents told me."

"My parents are dead!" Karzak pounced with his front paws spread wide.

A single swipe from his talons would rip Grey Cloak open. He dove under the monster's jump and skittered away.

The manticore's tail lashed out. Grey Cloak skipped away before the spikes impaled the ground.

The crowd shrieked in delight, almost drowning out the manticore's angry roar.

Grey Cloak picked up a club and threw it at the manticore. It bounced off the creature's wide nose. "Now that I have your attention... your parents aren't dead!"

Karzak charged forward with his paws ripping up the dirt and creating a cloud of dust. Grey Cloak sprinted along the outer circle of the wall. As the manticore bore down on him, he sped up, stretching the distance farther and farther. His toes barely touched the ground.

The onlookers and soldiers leaning over the wall, hooting and hollering. They were witnessing the fastest footrace they'd ever seen.

With his cloak billowing behind him, Grey Cloak turned on the speed again. Before he knew it, he was right on Karzak's tail and had to slow down.

The manticore lost sight of Grey Cloak but was still running. Finally, it turned its stare back over its shoulder and spotted Grey Cloak jogging behind him. Grey Cloak waved.

Karzak skidded to a halt right under Helsa's stand.

Grey Cloak raced up Karzak's back, jumped off of his head, and slapped Helsa hard across the face. "Tag! You're it, fatty!" He made a soft landing and started running again.

Karzak was back on his heels, but Grey Cloak raced ahead and kept his distance.

Hollering over his shoulder, he said, "Karzak, you have to listen to me. Your parents are very much alive." He stopped and turned. "I swear it on my life!"

Karzak slid to a stop. Saliva dripped from his jaws, and he had murder burning in his eyes. "You are either a liar or a fool," he said. "My parents were killed by Thunderbreath. Helsa spared me."

Grey Cloak shook his head. "Look into my eyes. I do not lie. They live. If you don't believe me, ask Helsa yourself. You'll know the truth when you see it."

Karzak turned to look over his shoulder. "I'll ask," he said out of the corner of his mouth, his black whiskers twitching.

He approached the stand, rose, put his paws on the wall under Helsa, and asked, "Are my parents alive?"

Helsa sputtered and fidgeted with her necklace. "Of course not. When you were a cub, they were slaughtered by Thunderbreath. I spared you and raised you myself."

"You lie!"

"Oh, what difference does it make? You are mine now!" Helsa's meaty hands squeezed the medallion on her necklace.

Karzak bucked like a mule and let out a painful roar.

"Now kill that elf!" Helsa ordered. "Or I'll kill you!" She sent another shock-wave through the manticore.

Karzak lay on the ground in convulsions and spasms.

A red-faced Helsa shouted at the top of her lungs, "Kill that elf, or my collar will burn your head off from the neck up! Bring me that elf's body as a wedding present!"

The manticore rolled from his side to his feet and kept his body low like a predator ready to pounce. He eyed Grey Cloak and said, "I must do what I must do. Prepare to die, elf."

40

DYPHESTIVE BRISTLED. HIS EYES COULD HAVE BURNED A HOLE CLEAR THROUGH Helsa's back. She stood over the wall, shouting, mocking, and gloating. She was everything he hated, an abusive, controlling monster the same as the Doom Riders. He grabbed his iron collar and stood.

Helsa turned. "What are you boiling about? Sit down, Duugun!"

"Duugun isn't my name, Cow Lips. Call me Dyphestive!" He started forward. A painful shockwave surged through his extremities. He trembled from head to toe, and his muscles rippled. His knees started to buckle, but he stood tall. "Keep it coming. I like it!"

Helsa's eyes became as big as saucers. "What? What are you doing? Impossible! Sit! Be still!" She backed against the wall. "Ministers of Evil, stop him!"

Dyphestive lowered his shoulder and tackled her over the wall. They tumbled one over the other and landed side by side. The shockwave came to a stop, but Helsa didn't. She punched him in the face, not once but three times. *Wap! Wap! Wap!*

"You're ruining my wedding day!" she cried. "Men ruin everything!" She grabbed her necklace.

Another jolt passed through Dyphestive's body. He wasn't the only one twitching. Karzak was as well. He tried to undo his collar and shouted, "Grey Cloak, get that collar off of Karzak. We both have one!"

"Grey Cloak!" Helsa said. "Dyphestive! Yes, I've heard those names." Her eyes lit up as if she were a pirate finding buried treasure. "Black Frost wants both of you! And I have you both! Ah-hah-hah!"

"No." Dyphestive muttered as more shocks bored their way through his system. "Nooo!" He launched himself at Helsa and plowed her over.

They wrestled over the ground, fighting like starving bears. Helsa bashed his face with fists as hard as hammers. He rolled over her and kneed her in the ribs.

"You are strong!" she said, pushing his face back. "But not as strong as an ogre." She kicked him off of her. "We are the strongest race of all!"

Dyphestive sat up with a smile and said, "But you aren't as strong without this." He held up her iron necklace.

Helsa's face dropped, and she clutched at her chest and said, "No! Give me that back!"

"Over my dead body," Karzak said.

Helsa spun around and faced the manticore. "Listen! Listen to me! I only lied to you out of love! Please, don't eat—"

Karzak bit Helsa's head off. *Chomp!*

The citizens of Braykurz looked on in stunned silence. Even the Ministers of Evil exchanged bewildered looks.

Finally, a voice rose out of the silence. It was one of the Black Guards, Jakoby. "The high minister is dead!" He tore off his helmet and threw it into the arena. "Death to the Ministers of Evil! This is our island now!"

A Black Guard attacked Jakoby with a thrust of a spear, but Jakoby batted the spear aside with a flick of his sword and ran the man through. "Rebellion!" he shouted. "Rebellion!"

All of a sudden, the citizens—good men and women who had long been downtrodden—rose from their seats in the rocks and swarmed the Ministers of Evil. They weren't alone, as Jakoby and Razor joined the slaughter.

Dyphestive jerked away from someone helping him to his feet. It was Gorva. "Oh, sorry."

"No worries. I like how you handled yourself." She grabbed his collar and unlocked it. "Your skin flapped like birds' wings. It was an ugly sight, and I thought you were going to die."

"It sure did feel like it." He spied Leena lying on the ground and ripped the necklace apart and flung it away. "Excuse me." He hustled over to Leena and picked her up.

"I don't think I killed her," Grey Cloak said. "But don't wake her too soon, because I'm sure she'll try to kill me again."

Karzak approached and said, "I am in your debt."

"You'll find your parents deep in the jungle where you left them. If you will, tell them to free our friends. They'll know who you mean," Grey Cloak said.

Karzak nodded. "It will be done." He turned his back, ran, and leaped clear out of the arena. He mauled two Ministers of Evil on his way out and vanished into the hills.

Grey Cloak smirked in the sea of chaos.

"What are you smiling about?" Gorva asked.

"I'm enjoying watching my perfectly executed plan in action," he said. "I've rescued my friends, freed the manticore, saved my brother from an ill-timed wedding, and liberated the seaport city. What more can you ask for?"

Gorva slapped him on the shoulder and said, "A way off of the island."

"Oh, don't worry. I have a plan."

"Which is?" Dyphestive asked.

Searching the skies and hillside, Grey Cloak said, "I don't see any sign of

Thunderbreath. If what they say is true, he doesn't care about life down here, but I suggest that we move on. For a dragon that supposedly notices everything, he's bound to notice this."

Jakoby and Razor raised the doors to the arena and waved their swords, saying, "Come on!"

Grey Cloak, Dyphestive, and Gorva made their way up the ramp, where Gorva grabbed sword belts for herself and Dyphestive and buckled them on.

"Don't get any ideas," she said as she strapped his belt on.

He grinned. "You brought it up, not me."

"Huh!" She took off after Grey Cloak, who led the way.

They made a beeline for the shanties in the mountains, where they were cut off by Deeann and her crew of halflings. She huffed smoke out of her pipe and said, "That was something. Now all you have to do is find a way to get all of us off of this island, because we're coming too."

"We can't take them too. That's too many," Gorva said.

Using his finger, Grey Cloak did a quick head count. "Only eleven more, and they are tiny. It won't be a problem because—"

"We know," Dyphestive and Gorva said in unison. "You'll think of something."

41

THE INLAND SEA

THE PRISONERS' OARS DUG INTO THE WATER OF THE CHOPPY INLAND SEA. A heavyset orc at the stern of the craft supplied a steady drumbeat. The Black Guard prisoner ship knifed its way through the waves, making a straight line for Prisoner Island underneath the morning sun.

The prisoners, shackled to their benches, groaned with every effort. A woman, no more than twenty, sobbed and shook all over.

One of the Black Guard, bare chested and crimson hooded, walked down the middle of the ship and took a leather lash to her back. *Wupash!*

The poor woman let out a scream. Her hands fastened to the oar, and she started pulling again.

"That's it, girl. Put your back into it!" the guard with a loud mouth said. Like the others, he had a black cloth hood over his head and was well-knit. His gaze swung around, and he lashed another man across the arms. "What are you staring at?"

"Ow!" the man cried. He was older and had slicked-back black hair and a long beard. He was an orc, too, but not the burly sort. Instead, he was lean and scholarly. He didn't appear to have done a day of hard work in his life. His hands were soft and his skin smooth. "I'm sorry. I'm sorry. Don't hit me again." He rowed harder.

"Heh," the guard grunted. "Not much of an orc, are you? One of those bookish types." He snapped the lash. The rowers jumped or cowered. "You won't last a day on the island. None of you will!"

Lythlenion's grip tightened on his war mace. He'd been part of the Black Guard for years, doing what he had to do to survive. It ate at him every day, leaving him with nothing but shame. He told himself that he did what he did to protect his family and keep them safe, but deep down, he knew it wasn't right.

He had been about to lose all hope when Grey Cloak and Dyphestive showed up and changed everything.

Eight Black Guards were on the prisoner ship, four posted on each end, including the tom-tom drummer. Their crimson hoods covered their faces, and their bare chests were bronzed by the sun. They never wore armor to prevent them from drowning, except that day, Lythlenion did. He wore the breastplate that he'd recovered from the Dust King over a decade ago when he traveled with Talon. It fit him perfectly and brought with it an air of invincibility.

The loudmouthed guard with the lash joined him at the stern of the ship. He eyeballed Lythlenion's war mace and said, "That's not standard-issue equipment. That chest plate isn't either. What if you fall overboard?"

Lythlenion looked deep into the burly loudmouth's eyes and said, "What makes you think that I'll fall off of this ship? Besides, I'm the captain. I'll wear what I wish."

The loudmouthed guard said, "Seems foolish to me. Perhaps you'll find a watery grave at the bottom on the sea."

"Perhaps you will as well."

The guard moved to the other end of the ship.

Good, Lythlenion thought. He hated the loudmouth. He hated almost all of them. The Black Guard he knew had irredeemable characteristics, and it was a marvel that he'd survived among their kind for so long. He got away with it thanks to his orcen size, and he was big enough that no one crossed him. Still, he had a peaceful heart and was truly a fish out of water.

A group of sea birds gathered in the air alongside the ship and were diving for fish in the water. The prisoner ship closed in on Prisoner Island.

Lythlenion caught the prisoners casting nervous glances over their sunburnt shoulders. There were only twelve that time, and he could see the fear building in the whites of their eyes. Each and every one was tormented. On the one hand, they wanted to put an end to the agonizing rowing. On the other, they didn't know how they would survive the unknown. Already, he could see evil lurking in the eyes of what had once been considered good men. They probed one another for weakness.

It would be a sad demise. As soon as the ship raised its sail, the prisoners would be at each other's throats, fighting for supplies, when they needed to focus on staying together.

"Land ho!" a guard at the front of the ship called. He was standing on the back of the ship's dragon figurehead. "Keep those oars rowing! Prepare to beach!"

It wasn't long after that the ship dug into the soft sand and came to a stop. The loudmouthed guard started tossing the prisoners' clothing over the ship. Among the clothing was a chest full of supplies. "There's some goods in that chest worth fighting over. Whoever can attain it wins! Ha-ha!"

One by one, the Black Guard unlocked the prisoners from their chains then shoved or tossed them overboard, where they splashed down into the breaking waves. All of them went for the chest like a school of piranha. But not all wanted to leave the ship.

The young woman hung on to her oar for dear life. "Please! Please leave me! I'll do anything! Don't throw me in with those jackals!"

The loudmouthed guard started beating her with his lash. "Get off of my ship!" When the woman didn't let go, he grabbed her arms and peeled her away from the oar. He backhanded her and flattened her on the bench. Grabbing her by the hair, he hauled her to her feet. "At least this one has some fight in her." He dragged her to the port side of the ship.

"Let her go," Lythlenion commanded firmly. He spit into his hands and rubbed them together.

The loudmouthed guard looked at him and asked, "What?"

Lythlenion rested Thunderash on his shoulder and said, "I said, let her go. I'll handle this."

Toying with the woman's hair, the loudmouth said, "She's fetching, eh? And here I thought you were soft for a Black Guard. Have a little fun and toss her overboard."

Lythlenion took off his hood, revealing his receding white hair and well-trimmed beard. "Oh, I'm going to have some fun."

The young woman's eyes grew like saucers.

The loudmouth stepped aside and said, "She's all yours."

Lythlenion look at the woman then back at the loudmouth and said, "Here, hold this." He turned his shoulders into his swing and blasted the loudmouth in the chest. The blow sent the man sprawling over the deck and into the water.

The Black Guard sprang to life. They drew their swords and advanced on Lythlenion from all directions.

42

Lythlenion's next swing clobbered two men and made a sound like a thunderclap. *Boooom!*

The Black Guard were knocked out of their boots as they went flying over the deck.

"Ah, it's good to have you back, Thunderash!" He spun the club like a windmill. "Come and taste my thunder, fools!"

Three guards down only left four on deck. He could see the whites of their eyes behind their hoods as they attacked.

A sword tip smashed into his chest and skipped off the breastplate. Lythlenion punched the man in the belly and whacked him in the head.

As long as he wore the mystic breastplate of the Dust King, no ordinary blade could pierce his skin. Lythlenion let loose his inner warrior, which had been bottled up for way too long.

Whop!

Crack!

Thuk!

The Black Guard were powerless without any armor to protect them. They squealed in pain as Lythlenion bashed arms, legs, ribs, and jawbones.

Thunderash pulverized the devilish men and sent them limping across the deck and diving for the water.

Only one was left standing unscathed. It was the drummer, a hefty beast of a man, carrying a long machete. Judging by his bloated girth, Lythlenion thought he had at least a two-hundred-pound advantage on him.

"What are you waiting for, Biggun?" Lythlenion asked as he spun the flanged head of his mace faster and faster.

The beefy Black Guard dropped his machete, pinched his nose, and cannonballed off of the back deck.

Down in the water, the Black Guard waded toward the shore with bad limps and drooping shoulders.

Lythlenion waved his war mace at them. "Keep running!" he said in a savage voice. "Or I'll finish all of you off!"

A feeble voice caught his ear.

"Thank you," the young woman said. "Are you going to take us back now?"

He found a blanket in a chest on the floor, covered her shoulders, and said softly, "No, dear. Not yet, at least. Stay here." He dropped anchor and jumped into the water. With the chest-deep waves washing over him, he watched the other prisoners run for the beaches and scatter like crabs. He shook his head. "I'm not that scary, am I?"

The gritty sand clung to his boots as he marched his way onto the shore. He wiped the water out of his eyes and peered into the leagues of wild jungle.

Grey Cloak and Dyphestive could be anywhere.

He shook his head and muttered, "Should I stay, or should I go?"

"SLOW DOWN, SLOW DOWN," Razor said as he ducked underneath some low-hanging tree branches and fell to the jungle floor. He panted hard, and his face was covered in sweat. "I haven't run this far this fast in—" He panted. "Forever!"

Deeann and her crew agreed. "Don't forget our legs are half the length of yours." She fanned her face with her hand. "Phew!"

"Agreed." With sweat dripping from his chin, Jakoby took a knee. He sucked in lungfuls of air and asked, "Do we even know where we are?"

Grey Cloak wasn't winded at all and said, "This is the way we came from. We're heading back to the south shore."

"And then what?" Jakoby asked.

"We wait for another prisoner boat to show up, take it over, and sail it back," he replied.

Gorva gave an approving nod and said, "That isn't a bad idea."

"I told you I'd think of something."

With a groan, Jakoby forced himself back to his feet. "How about we march at a brisk pace until we catch our breath? It's been a long time since we've seen any action."

"I second that notion," Razor said as he rolled over to his belly and tried to push up. He collapsed again. "I can feel my heart exploding in my chest." He looked at Dyphestive, who was carrying Leena. "Hoy, big fella, do you think you can handle another bundle?"

"I can, but I won't," Dyphestive answered. "Not even if she wakes up."

Leena came to life, twisted free of Dyphestive's arms, and landed on her feet. She crouched into an open-handed fighter's stance and stared down her enemies.

"The sleeping princess awakes. Great," Razor said.

They surrounded the wary-eyed Leena.

Jakoby held his hand out and did the talking. "Leena, listen to me. You are safe now. We are getting off of this island and want you to come with us."

Leena's brow knitted. She slowly turned, staring each and every one of them down.

"It's me, Dyphestive," he said, opening his arms and offering a hug. "I came to rescue you."

"You might want to cover your acorns," Grey Cloak quipped. "If you haven't learned by now what's good for you."

"She's one of them," Gorva said. She had a dark bruise under her eye from one of Leena's hits. "Let her walk."

"Let me do the talking," Jakoby said. He approached her in a cautious manner, crouched and with his palms out. "I know you hear me. The Ministers of Evil are defeated. You are the last one left from Braykurz. You can go back if you want, to nothing, or you can leave the island with our old friends. What do you say?"

"She doesn't say anything," Razor reminded him.

Leena's hard eyes scanned the group once more. The last face she searched was Dyphestive's. He returned a sheepish smile. She jumped back into his arms and gave him a full kiss.

"This is touching," Gorva said to Grey Cloak.

"*Roooaaar!*"

"That's Thunderbreath." Razor came to his feet. "I'd say he's onto us, and he sounds angry."

The next roar sounded even closer.

"*Roooaaar!*"

Razor started shoving everyone in their backs. "What are you waiting for? Run!"

43

GREY CLOAK STARTED TO RACE AFTER THE OTHERS, BUT HE NOTICED DYPHESTIVE standing still and still holding Leena in his arms.

"What is the matter? Are the pair of you needing some alone time?"

Dyphestive shook his head and said, "No, that's not it. Didn't that roar sound familiar?"

"It sounded like a dragon roar, but come to think of it, it was very close and familiar," Grey Cloak said.

"Boy, I was wondering if you donkey skulls were going to figure it out."

Grey Cloak looked up into the trees. A small dragon was nestled in the branches.

"Streak!"

The dragon swung down from a limb but hung upside down like a bat. "And the golden chalice goes to... wait for it... Dyphestive. Sorry, Master Grey Cloak, but that roar zinged right over your head." He released the tree limb and floated down like a feather. "So, how are things?" His yellow eyes fixed on Leena. "I see you found Chatty Cathy."

Grey Cloak squatted and picked up his dragon. "Anvils, you are getting heavy."

"I'm big-boned." Streak's pink tongue flicked out of his mouth. "You look awfully surprised. Did you forget about me?"

"No," he said sheepishly.

Gorva crept up on them. "Yes, he did. He never mentioned anything about having a dragon."

Streak ran his gaze from Gorva's toes to her head. "Allow me to introduce myself, gorgeous. I'm Streak."

"And I don't care."

"Ew, why are all of the women in this company so frosty except for Zora? Lighten up, ladies. It's me. It's Streak."

Jakoby, Razor, and the halflings returned.

"Hey, halflings. I like halflings." Streak wriggled out of Grey Cloak's arms and went straight to Deeann. "Tell me, sunshine, do you like to party?"

Deeann bent over and pinched his lizard cheeks. "All night long."

"That's more like it!" Streak cozied up to the crew and let them pet him. The black stripes on his back flared like a dog's hackles. "That's it. Scratch right behind the earhole. Those little fingers are perfect."

"Streak, we still need to get off of the island," Grey Cloak said.

"Why?" Streak's tongue flicked out, snagging a monarch butterfly. He munched it up, smacked his thin lips, and swallowed. "This place is paradise."

"*Roooaaar!*"

Everyone's eyes lifted skyward.

"That wasn't me," Streak said as he looked at Grey Cloak. "Not that you'd know. Anyway, I think Zora and Lythlenion worked something out, and he's going to bring a prisoner ship back to the island."

"Lythlenion!" Dyphestive said. He dropped Leena. "Where'd he come from?"

"Well," Streak said, "when two orcs fall in love, they make babies, even though I think coming from an egg is far more fashionable."

"Enough of that, Streak," Grey Cloak interrupted. "How did you cross Lythlenion?"

"He helped Zora save me from the Scourge."

"The Scourge!" Grey Cloak couldn't believe his ears. He looked at his brother. "They must have followed us from Raven Cliff." He turned his attention to Streak. "Is Zora safe?"

"Of course. She killed them all," Streak said.

Dyphestive and Grey Cloak exchanged looks of surprise.

"Really?" Grey Cloak asked.

"Well, not all of them. Two of them, at least. I had a little hand in it after she rescued me." Streak flexed his wings and settled into story-telling mode. "You see, one of them, a wizard with tattoos all over his arms and an ugly scar, used a dragon charm on me. A really dirty trick. Well, he and his fish-eyed goon are ashes now."

It was a startling revelation to Grey Cloak. He sorted through his thoughts as Streak continued to entertain his captivated audience. He'd doubted Zora and feared she'd changed for the worst. He felt ashamed.

He interrupted his dragon. "And she's well?"

"She's going to save Tanlin, and Lythlenion is coming to save you. I might not have ears, but my hearing is super good," Streak said.

Gorva had her arms crossed and said, "This dragon has a very funny way of speaking words. Do more dragons talk like this?"

Streak winked at her. "Just me, baby doll. It's a dragon thing."

"I think his skull was scrambled in the time mural. Ignore him," Grey Cloak said.

"*Roooaaar!*"

Jakoby's eyes lit up. "That sounded closer."

Razor and the halflings were off and running again.

"Let's go," Grey Cloak said. "Streak, stay close to me."

"Of course. Where else would I be at a time like this?"

Grey Cloak rolled his eyes. "Hard to say. The rest of you, follow me."

He raced through a net of vines hanging from the trees, trying to catch up with the others, when he heard a series of wild screams. Several footfalls later, he came upon Razor and the halflings. They were trapped in spiderwebbing that covered the area. He stopped himself and the others behind him. "Wait."

"Cut me out of this gunk," Razor cried. The more he wiggled, the more entwined he became. The halflings were doing the same thing. "Ugh, this stuff is awful."

"Everyone, be still," Grey Cloak said. "You're only making it worse."

"Worse? How can it be any worse?" Razor complained.

"I've seen worse," Streak commented.

"No, you haven't," Grey Cloak said. "Dy, do you see our old friend?"

Dyphestive searched the trees, but he shook his head. "No."

"What old friend are you talking about?" Razor demanded.

A giant tarantula eased its way out of the jungle behind the cords of webbing.

"Ah!" Razor screamed. "Where in the flaming fence did that thing come from?"

"That's our old friend I was talking about." He caught sight of Thatcher sitting on top of the giant spider Itchee. "The question is, whose side is he really on?"

44

"I SEE YOU MANAGED TO ESCAPE, GREY CLOAK," THATCHER THE BLIND DWARF SAID. "Very impressive. You even saved the manticore as well. But there is an order to all matters. Matters that are meant to be and matters that aren't." He patted his hand with the head of his staff. "The order is simple. No one leaves the island."

Grey Cloak took his place in front of the group and said, "I take it that you are here to stop us? We are many."

"So are we," Thatcher said. He gave a sharp whistle.

From the dark corners of the jungle came low and hungry growls. Three manticores hemmed the company in, making them huddle together, swords drawn, with their backs against one another. It was Ebonthrak, Jessel, and Karzak. All of them were bullish in size and slavering at the jaws.

"I take it that your group was on the same side all along," Grey Cloak said, not hiding his disgust. "You didn't think we'd survive, did you?"

"No," the hollow-eyed dwarf said, "and I still don't. As I said, no one leaves the island. Not unless you can vanquish Thunderbreath."

"Wait. What do you mean?" Grey Cloak asked.

Jessel the manticore came forward. As tall as a horse, she stood face-to-face with Grey Cloak. "Now that you've saved our son, it's only a matter of time until Thunderbreath hunts us all down. Our only hope is strength in numbers."

Grey Cloak's back straightened. "You're here to help?"

"Only because we don't have any choice in the matter," the deep-voiced Ebonthrak added. "Of course, we could save face by killing you and bringing your bodies to Thunderbreath's feet. But we'd still be at his mercy."

"*Roooaaar!*"

"He knows we are here. He only waits," Thatcher said as he scratched Itchee's head. "Thunderbreath knows that we must eventually go to the water. He'll be waiting for you there, but he won't be expecting us."

"Are you suggesting a sneak attack?" Grey Cloak asked.

"I prefer to call it a surprise attack, but yes," Thatcher said with a nod. "That is the plan."

Grey Cloak stepped out of range of Jessel's rotten breath and asked, "Then why the webs?"

"To stop you from waltzing straight into Thunderbreath's trap. What did you think that you were going to do? Swim across the sea?" Thatcher asked.

"No, we were going to overtake a prisoner ship."

"Elf, if I had eyes, they'd be rolling in my skull right now," Thatcher said. "That's been tried and has failed a dozen times before."

"I have a plan," Grey Cloak said, deciding to keep the secret of the dragon charm to himself and his company. "Now free my friends. We'll take our chances."

"Suit yourself, but we're coming too." Thatcher rapped Itchee on the head with his staff. The sharp nodules on the giant tarantula's legs cut through the webbing like knives, freeing Razor and the halflings.

Razor fought to peel the sticky webbing away from his body and said, "I hate spiders."

Itchee squatted and put his head down in front of Razor.

"But not you, naturally. You're adorable." He shot Deeann a scary face and sauntered away with his back to the spider.

"Everyone, gather around," Grey Cloak said. He searched their determined and tired eyes. "Listen, we are going to get off of this island, one way or another." He put his hand in the middle of the group. "We are Talon. Who's with me?"

One by one, the hands stacked up, one over another, including one of Itchee's eerie legs.

Gorva's nose curled. "Creepy."

Dyphestive started to chant. "Tal-on! Tal-on! Tal-on!"

Everyone shushed him.

Leena covered his mouth with her hand.

Grey Cloak grinned. "Let's go."

THE COMPANY HAD VASTLY EXPANDED from what was originally planned. To start, it was Grey Cloak and Dyphestive saving Jakoby, Razor, and Leena, but they'd since added Deeann and her crew of ten halfling men, Thatcher's group of two women, a dwarf, and a giant spider, and three manticores. In most circumstances, Grey Cloak would have loved those odds in a fight, but the obstacle they faced was no ordinary creature. It was a fully grown grand dragon the likes of which he'd never seen. A blast from its fiery breath could easily lay waste to them all.

Leading the way as they cut through the gloom, he kept the dragon charm ready to go in his pocket. Using the dragon charm against Thunderbreath was plan one. Using Streak to control the dragon was plan two.

"Are you sure that you don't want me to handle this?" Streak asked. The small but growing dragon had attached himself to Grey Cloak's back and was talking quietly in his ear. "You've seen me do it before."

"If the charm doesn't work, I'll have you to back me up. No sense in showing all of our cards. Besides, I have a good feeling the charm will work. But you stand by and be ready. Don't let him see you. I doubt he'll let you get within an inch of him if he does."

"Good point." Streak's tail drummed Grey Cloak's head. "That's why you're the brains of this outfit."

"Don't forget it, and stop messing up my hair."

"Duly noted."

Grey Cloak sighed. "Where do you come up with this jargon?" He felt Streak shrug his wings. A moment later, he came to a stop and signaled to the others. The sound of waves crashing against the shore caught his ear, and daybreak had broken through the tree line.

"Do you want me to go take a look?" Streak asked.

"Stay put." He reached back and tapped Dyphestive. "We'll take a look."

Dyphestive followed after him, as did several others.

"I said to stay put!" Grey Cloak whispered sharply. "What's wrong with you? Are your ears filled with cotton?" He took off toward the shoreline, quickly distancing himself from the others. The trees and brush were thick where the jungle met the beach. The salty sea breeze rustled the leaves and warmed his cheeks. A foul smell caught his nose.

Streak's tongue flicked in the air. "Do you smell that?"

Grey Cloak nodded. "There's no mistaking the smell of brimstone and flesh cooking."

45

THE SEA WIND CARRIED BLACK SMOKE ACROSS THE SAND INTO THE TREE LINE. GREY Cloak covered his mouth and nose, but there was no avoiding the foul stench. Dragon fire cooking flesh down to nothing but ashes and oil was something one would never forget.

He picked his way along the inner edge of the tree line until he spied the source of the smoke. Three fires were spread out on the beach. Dragon flame was still eating the flesh from the bodies that had collapsed in the sand. One of them appeared to be crawling away with his mouth hanging open from one final scream.

"Brutal," Streak said.

"I don't see any signs of Thunderbreath. Do you?" Grey Cloak asked.

Streak shook his head. "I don't hear anything either. He's been awfully quiet for a dragon named Thunderbreath. Do you think he's named that way because he's really loud or because his dragon breath is awful?"

"No offense, but all dragon breath is awful."

Farther up the shore, the prison ship floated in the water. The anchor line held it in place. It appeared abandoned.

Grey Cloak pointed. "There."

"I see it. Shall I check it out?"

"As much as I hate to say this, stay put." An awful thought occurred to him. His gaze swept over the burning bodies. "Oh no."

"What's wrong?"

"One of those men could be Lythlenion."

Streak's tongue flicked in the air. "There are orcs among them. I'm sorry."

Grey Cloak perished the thought. "Many of the guards were orcs."

"True. Keep those positive thoughts. We're going to need them," Streak said.

"Remind me to have your skull checked."

"Why?"

Grey Cloak made his way farther up the tree line until he was looking straight across at the prisoner ship. The crimson sail was wrapped tight around the lone mast, and it appeared to be in perfect order, aside from missing a crew. He peeled Streak away from his body, set the dragon on the ground, and poked his snout. "Stay here while I go and take a look."

Streak nodded. "Holler if you need me."

The wind shifted and carried the smoke right over Grey Cloak and the ship. Like a stinking fog, it gave him a little cover. Unable to fight the eeriness that settled over the shore, he hurried toward the ship, taking several glances over his shoulder and fully expecting someone or something to advance out of the sky or woodland. Only the crashing tide came as he waded into the water and stood alongside the ship.

Where is everyone?

He ran his hands along the ship's hull, and it didn't appear to have any sort of damage. He looked back at the edge of the jungle and saw no sign of Streak.

At least he's listening.

With the early-morning sun shining over the breaking water, he hauled his body over the rim of the ship, fully expecting to see attackers lurking among the benches. The gently pitching craft was empty, but something caught his ear. As the sea water drained from his clothing, he walked across the benches to where he heard someone sobbing.

Nestled underneath the planks, a woman trembled like a leaf. He bent down and touched her.

"Eek!"

"Shh! Shh! Shh! I'm here to help. Please don't scream. You are safe now."

The woman turned her head and showed him a frightened stare. Her matted and tangled hair covered an otherwise attractive face. She shook uncontrollably.

Grey Cloak sat on the bench, offered her a warm smile, and took her hand. "You are freezing." A blanket sat nearby, and he covered her. "I'm Grey Cloak, and I'm here to help. Can you tell me what happened?"

Her jittery eyes searched the bright sky. "D-D-D-Dragon came." She cowered. "Big dragon."

He rubbed her hand, trying to settle her. "You're safe now. The dragon is gone. Can you tell me what happened to the prisoners and the crew?"

"G-G-Gone. They fled into the jungle."

"They fled when the dragon came?"

She shook her head. "No. One of the Black Guard attacked the other Black Guard. He was nice."

"Was he an orc?"

She nodded quickly. "With a white beard."

"Lythlenion," he muttered. "Where did he go? Did the dragon kill him? Was he among the dead on the beaches?"

"I don't know. Men were coming back, and-and-and the dragon came and burned them. I've been hiding under this bench ever since." She jerked away from him and covered her ears. "I'll never forget that sound, that awful sound. The roar and the screams of burning men. I want to go home."

He tried to pet her, but she recoiled deeper into the benches. He stood and sauntered over the deck. There were small equipment chests, coils of rope, and a few crimson hoods that had been cast aside. He turned his eyes toward shore.

At least I have hope that Lythlenion is out there somewhere.

Grey Cloak was about to head back to inform the others when the boat rocked under him. "Eh?" He made his way to the stern of the craft and stared out at the water. There weren't any rocks jutting out, but a dark and shadowy bed of rock was under the waves. He leaned over the stern.

How'd they row the ship over those rocks?

The rocks appeared to slowly rise and come to life. Grey Cloak's body tingled all over.

Those aren't rocks!

He backed away from the stern, heart pounding, as he watched the monster rise from the sea. A dragon's head rose first. Rivulets of water ran down its horns and over the bumpy ridges of its skull. Its eyes burned like torches, and its hot, smoky breath reeked of death. It continued to rise, revealing the dark steel-hard scales that armored its body. Its smoldering gaze turned Grey Cloak's bones to jelly.

That's Thunderbreath!

46

Up close, Thunderbreath was the ugliest and biggest dragon he'd ever seen. Cinder was big for a grand dragon, but Thunderbreath was even bigger. With a stare that could kill and one busted fang jutting out from the bottom of his mouth, the rocky beast looked like he had been birthed from a volcano.

Heat emanated from the dragon, and the water cascading down his body started to steam. Thunderbreath eyed Grey Cloak and spoke with a raw and deep voice. "Going somewhere, worm?"

Grey Cloak swallowed and tried to catch his breath. He finally found his wits and said, "I'm not much of a sailor."

"Is that so?" Thunderbreath lowered his head and glowered down at him. "Then what are you doing on this ship?"

"Er… investigating, mighty one." He casually inched his fingers into his cloak, searching for the dragon charm. "I was merely looking for morning crabs when I saw the fires and noticed the ship. I didn't think it would hurt to poke around. Strange that the guards are missing."

"Don't toy with me, elf. I've seen your face in Braykurz. Every face I see, I remember. You have a sneakiness about you. You seek to fool me. Many have tried. All have failed. Your best chance for survival is honesty."

Grey Cloak offered an agreeing smile and said, "I see." He cleared his throat, buying more time as he attempted to butter the grand dragon up. "I speak honestly when I say that I have abandoned the Ministers of Evil in Braykurz. To put it bluntly, I'm ambitious, and I didn't care to be one of their servants. So I left. But I didn't imagine that I'd come across an abandoned ship."

"There is treachery afoot. Always treachery with men," Thunderbreath said as his eyes searched beyond Grey Cloak to the jungle line beyond the sand. "I find it amusing. But I have one task. I see to it that no one, man or beast, leaves the island. I was given this charge by my brother, Black Frost."

"Oh, you are *brothers*? That is fascinating. Though I find it hard to believe that you are a servant of his."

"I am no servant!" His hot breath ruffled Grey Cloak's hair. "We come from the same nest! I hatched before him! I only help my brother as a favor."

Grey Cloak nodded eagerly. "I see. It doesn't sound very challenging for a dragon as grand as you. But what do I know about dragons and their pecking order?"

Thunderbreath tilted his head. "You are full of guile, aren't you, elven worm? Do you take me for a fool? I am well aware of the failure at Braykurz. I'm well aware that the manticore was freed. And I'm well aware that you played a *grand* part in it."

Grey Cloak locked his fingers around the dragon charm. "You are very knowledgeable. Only a fool would seek to fool you."

"I see all. I hear all. I know all on the island," Thunderbreath warned. "Nothing escapes my notice. Not you. Not your fellow worms in the bush. None of it."

Grey Cloak's heart skipped as the blood ran out of his body.

"Yes, I know they are out there, wide-eyed and watching. And they arrived just in time to witness your death." Thunderbreath's chest plates began to glow bright orange.

As the air heated around him, Grey Cloak regained his composure and smirked. "You don't know all." He held out the dragon charm, which bathed his hand in golden light and warmed his fingers. "You didn't see this. Withhold your fires, Thunderbreath, and obey my command."

Thunderbreath's eyes lingered on the glowing stone. His chest plate's color began to cool.

I've got him. It's working.

Grey Cloak slowly moved the charm from side to side. Thunderbreath's eyes and head followed the burning light.

Oh, now what do I do?

He had the dragon right where he wanted him, but he'd never thought about how he would handle it after that.

Do I drown him? Try to kill him? No, he'd defend himself. He snapped his fingers. *Ah, I'll send him far, far away or take him to his nest and put him down for a long sleep.*

With his eyes locked on the dragon, great pressure built in his head. In his mind, he heard Thunderbreath's strong voice say, *Only a worm like you would think that little bauble would work on me.*

The corners of Thunderbreath's mouth turned up into an evil smile. His chest glowed red hot, and his mouth began to open.

Zooks! Grey Cloak was a split second from diving overboard when he remembered the woman cowering at his feet. *Oh no!*

The dragon's mouth was opened wide, and a geyser of flame started to stream out. Grey Cloak jumped over the woman and covered her, and the flames engulfed them.

47

Dyphestive's nose crinkled. He snorted in the smoke, which was tickling his nose. "Do you smell that?"

Jakoby nodded. "Aye. A foul burning lingers."

"I say we check it out," Razor volunteered. "Frankly, I'm tired of hiding in this dewy place. It's creepy." He eyed Itchee, who lingered in the jungle only a few feet away. "Speaking of creepy." He stepped away and moved alongside Dyphestive. "Get me away from that thing, will you?"

"We wait for Grey Cloak," Dyphestive said, but he wasn't entirely sure why. He trusted his brother, but the awful smell raised the hair on his arms. "That's hair burning, isn't it?"

Gorva took a deep breath. "I'd know that smell anywhere. I smelled it when my family was killed. It's dragon fire and flesh." She unsheathed her sword. "It could be anybody. Even Grey Cloak."

"Horseshoes!" Dyphestive looked over the company and said, "Don't anyone try to be a hero and follow me." He took off in the direction Grey Cloak had departed.

The company didn't listen and followed anyway. The smell and smoke grew stronger. It wasn't long before the bright light of a new day broke through the branches, casting sunlight on their faces.

They came to a spot where the jungle and the beach met, and they stayed hidden from the shore. As they walked along the inside edge, they cast nervous looks at the bodies burning on the shore. The halflings covered their noses, and Deeann fanned her face with her hat.

"That's far enough, Dyphestive," Streak said. The dragon had climbed ten feet up the trunk of a palm leaf tree.

"Where's Grey Cloak?" Dyphestive asked.

"Keep your voice down." Streak nodded toward the ship. "He's over there, making friends."

With Leena hovering over one shoulder and Razor behind the other, Dyphestive peeled back the foliage and looked through.

All three of them gasped at once.

Grey Cloak stood on the stern of the prisoner ship, facing Thunderbreath.

"What in the world is he doing?" Dyphestive asked.

"I told you—he's having a conversation." Streak swung his tail beneath him. "It appears to be going well."

Grey Cloak held out a dragon charm that shone like a golden medallion in the sun. He had the dragon's full attention.

"Shiny," Streak uttered. The charm's reflection shone in his eyes. "So shiny. I like shiny."

"Quit babbling, Streak," Dyphestive said. "Can you hear what they're saying?"

"Not with all of the background noise the waves are making, but if you could calm the sea—uh-oh..."

The dreamy-eyed Thunderbreath's stare hardened, and his chest turned red hot. A geyser of dragon flame poured out of his mouth and blasted into Grey Cloak.

"No!" Dyphestive hollered. He launched himself out of the brush. "Nooo!"

Razor dove at his legs. "No, mate! No!"

Dyphestive shoved Razor to the ground and kept going. The dragon was still heaving out breaths of fire, and the entire ship went up in flames. Steam rose from the boiling water, covering the dragon in mist. Thunderbreath rumbled with laughter as he dragged his girth out of the sea.

Dyphestive stopped in his tracks and hurled a spear. It broke apart on Thunderbreath's rack of horns.

The dragon faced Dyphestive and said, "Why, if it isn't another worm to cook." He eyed Dyphestive like he was nothing more than an insect. "I'll wait for the others." His voice rose. "Come out, worms, that I might feast on your bones!" He inhaled a great breath. "Ah, I smell manticore." He perked up. "And I smell dragon. Interesting."

Dyphestive jabbed his finger at Thunderbreath and said, "You're dead! I swear, you are dead!"

"The worm speaks but does not know what he says." From out of the water, Thunderbreath's thorny tail lashed out and knocked Dyphestive clear off of his feet. "No need to waste my glorious breath on you."

Dyphestive lay in the sand, choking. He'd never been hit so hard before. He couldn't breathe. The thorns in the dragon's tail had torn up his chest. Blood dripped into the sand. He fought his way up to his hands and knees, grunting. "Guh!"

From his position, he watched the company file out of the jungle. Jakoby, Gorva, and Razor were armed with swords. Leena carried her nunchakus. Blades and spears filled the halflings' tiny hands. The three manticores formed a row beside them.

Deep down, Dyphestive's frustration mixed with agony. The company didn't stand a chance against the grand dragon, and he knew it. Not without a special weapon or a dragon of equal size and power. Covered in sand and grit, he hauled his battered body up to his feet and balled up his fists. "I'm not finished with you."

If Thunderbreath heard him, he didn't show any signs of it. His attention was set on the manticores. "My dear friends Ebonthrak and Jessel. Look at you, rising up to fight your tormentor. And you even have the boy." He huffed out a stream of fire that sent the halflings running for the branches. "This will be delightful."

"It will be delightful when we dance on your bones!" Ebonthrak charged and jumped at Thunderbreath's throat.

Thunderbreath unleashed his fiery wind, setting Ebonthrak's hair on fire. The head of the manticore family latched on to the dragon's neck and sank his teeth into the scales and flesh.

In the wink of an eye, Jessel and Karzak pounced. Jessel's slashing claws tore into Thunderbreath's wings. Karzak went for the dragon's eyes.

Thunderbreath flicked the young manticore off with his horns and batted the mother away with his tail. "You are cubs. I am the lion!" he roared. "None can stand against me!" Using his claws, he raked Ebonthrak's flaming body away from his neck and slammed him onto the sand. "Your infantile efforts amused me, but now you will face my wrath!" He let loose another blast of volcanic flame on Ebonthrak.

"Father, nooo!" Karzak roared as he watched his father's body vanish in a plume of hungry flames. "Nooo! Nooo!"

Dyphestive stood in awe as he watched the senior manticore being burned into waste. Without a weapon in hand, he reached down and grabbed the dragon's tail, screamed at the top of his lungs, and yanked it as hard as he could.

Thunderbreath's flames went out. His serpentine head twisted around, and his eyes fastened on Dyphestive. "You again. Humph." Using his tail like a whip, he flicked Dyphestive toward the sea, but impossibly, Dyphestive held on. "Enjoy the ride, pest." Thunderbreath used his tail like a hammer and beat Dyphestive into the ground as if he were beating a drum.

48

A<small>T THE LAST MOMENT</small>, G<small>REY</small> C<small>LOAK DROPPED DOWN OVER THE WOMAN AND</small> shielded her from Thunderbreath's flame with his body and cloak. The suffocating heat of the dragon fire stole Grey Cloak's breath, and he felt as if his back were boiling. Underneath the roaring flames, the woman kicked and tried to scream.

Impossibly, shielded in the folds of the cloak, they survived the first devastating moments, and the dragon flame no longer beat them down.

Surrounded by hungry bright-orange flames, Grey Cloak dared a look from underneath the Cloak of Legends. The entirety of the ship was aflame. The wood popped and crackled. Plumes of smoke were rolling. Through the clouds of thick smoke, he got a glimpse of Thunderbreath. The dragon's attention had turned elsewhere.

Grey Cloak hauled the terrified woman into his arms, stood among the searing heat, then jumped overboard into the water. They sank beneath the waves.

The woman sputtered and writhed in his arms like a fish caught in a net. He lifted her head above the water and said, "Take a breath," then he dunked her again.

He waded underneath breaking tides, staying out of sight of Thunderbreath. The dragon's gaze passed over them once before he moved on toward the shore. Grey Cloak lifted the woman and broke the surface of the water.

Gasping and coughing up water, she slapped him across the face. "Why are you trying to drown me?"

"I'm not," he said loudly enough that he could be heard over the roaring flames. "Hmm... we're going to need another boat." He gathered the woman in his arms.

"Thank you for saving me." She kissed him on the cheek and passed out.

"I'm not so sure that it was me," he said as he carried her toward the shore, his mind racing.

I should be dead. We should be dead.

It was another strange bit of fortune that had befallen him. A surge had filled him with impossible speed in the arena only a day ago, and now he'd shrugged off a dragon's breath.

It must be the cloak.

Dripping with water from head to toe, he marched onto the shore with weary limbs. He set the woman down in a safe spot and looked toward the sounds of monsters, men, and dragons engaged in battle. His heart jumped. *Oh my!*

Dyphestive had the end of Thunderbreath's tail in a death grip. The dragon beat him on the sand like a drum.

Two manticores pounced on the scaly hide of the dragon, while a third was on fire and fleeing for the water.

Jakoby, Razor, and Leena seemed to be looking for a weakness to attack, while the halflings hurled coconuts at Thunderbreath.

A swipe of Thunderbreath's tail sent Jakoby, Razor, and Leena tumbling head over heels.

"Zooks!" Grey Cloak ran toward the fray.

The manticores got their claws under Thunderbreath's scales and ripped them away from the flesh. Thunderbreath let out a pained roar and spit fire everywhere.

"You hurt him!" Dyphestive said. "You hurt him! Keep doing that." Thunderbreath's tail slammed him face-first into the ground. "Umph!" He lost his grip, rolled, and came to his feet. As he wiped the sand from his eyes, he didn't see the thorny tail coming back down.

Grey Cloak tackled him out of the way.

"Who in the—Grey Cloak! You're alive! Ah-ha!" He wrapped him up in a bear hug.

Grey Cloak patted him on the back. "And intact. I'd like to keep it that way."

"Sorry." Dyphestive pulled Grey Cloak down as the dragon's tail passed right over him. "How are we going to kill him?"

"I'm working on it."

The company and the manticore attacked the dragon from all directions like stinging hornets, but their efforts did little harm. It was only a matter of time before Thunderbreath wore them all down. He scattered them time and again with his tail, claws, and flame.

All of a sudden, a sound like a giant locust caught Grey Cloak's attention. Streak flew out of the jungle on a path for Thunderbreath.

"Ah, there you are, little runt," Thunderbreath said. "I was beginning to wonder if you were going to join the dance."

"I never miss a party," Streak said as he hovered with his back to the ocean, "and I wouldn't want to miss your funeral either."

Thunderbreath spit flame at Streak, but he slipped away. "I know what you are, runt. I know what you try to do. I know all."

"Let's be honest. No one knows everything." Streak sent his own blast of fire at Thunderbreath, but it barely tickled the mighty dragon's nose.

"Fool!" Thunderbreath shook the manticore off of his back like a dog shedding water. "Do you seek to mock me?"

"That's part of the equation. Look behind you, and you'll see the other," Streak fired back.

"I won't fall for that ploy!" Thunderbreath said.

"Suit yourself, but don't say that I didn't warn you."

Grey Cloak had gotten so caught up in the situation that he almost completely missed the giant tarantula Itchee creeping out from the jungle's edge.

Like a crab, the riderless Itchee sped over the sand and launched himself at the back of the dragon. His eight legs pierced the dragon's wings. Gobs of sticky webbing shot out of his spinnerets, coating the dragon's body.

"How dare you? Insect!" Thunderbreath flexed his wings, and the web strands began to snap. His neck strained against the web cords that bound him, and his superior strength won out. He clamped his jaws on two of Itchee's front legs and ripped them off. "No one can defeat me!" He blasted the spider with flames. "No one!"

Itchee turned into a ball of flame with six legs, fighting to the very end.

Grey Cloak watched in horror as the company's hopes for victory went up in a plume of smoke.

49

THUNDERBREATH BUCKED ITCHEE FROM HIS BACK AND BURNED A RING OF FIRE ALL around him. He chortled in victory. "All of your efforts have been in vain! Prepare to die, worms!" He set his eyes on Grey Cloak and Dyphestive. "The pair of you aren't worms but roaches. You won't escape my wrath a second time." Suddenly, his eyes rolled up, and his neck stiffened.

Streak had cradled himself between the dragon's horns. His eyes were as white as snow, and Thunderbreath's eyes turned white as well.

Grey Cloak tapped Dyphestive. "Look. I told you I had it all figured out."

Thunderbreath's tail swished over the dirt, putting out the flames. He started to speak with Streak's voice. "I have control of him." The huge dragon shook like he was shaking off a fly. "For now. His head is hard." Thunderbreath shook his neck. "Oh boy, he's fighting me. Stay clear!"

As the others gathered around Grey Cloak, Lythlenion came dashing out of the jungle.

"Lyth!" Dyphestive exclaimed.

At the same time, Ebonthrak wandered out of the water and joined his family. All of his black fur was gone, and where he didn't have scales, his skin was pink. Jessel licked him behind the ears.

Thunderbreath bucked like a bronco. His voice changed back to normal. "Get out of my head, worm!"

Before Lythlenion reached the group, Thunderbreath's tail dusted across the sand and hit him in the legs. He cried, "Aaargh!"

Grey Cloak and Dyphestive rushed to his aid.

"Are you hurt?" Grey Cloak asked.

"My knee is shattered. It is still a fine reunion, old friends. If only we can survive this." He fed Thunderash into Dyphestive's grip. "Take this." He glanced at Thunderbreath, who used his back leg to scrape Streak from his skull. "Call the thunder. Hurry!"

Dyphestive rose, covered in sand and his own blood, and set his smoldering eyes on the dragon. "It's Thunder Time!"

"Streak!" Grey Cloak hollered. "Get control of that dragon. Get control now!"

"I'm trying! He's a stubborn one!"

Dyphestive set his jaw and started his advance.

Grey Cloak hooked his arm. "Aim for the earhole."

"Don't worry. I won't miss."

Thunderbreath got his back claws under Streak and ripped him away like a tick. "You're dead now! You're all dead now!"

Streak buzzed across the sky and said, "Not if you can't catch me." He twisted Thunderbreath's neck around and made a beeline for Dyphestive. He led Thunderbreath's fiery jaws toward the man, soared right by him, and said, "It's your turn now."

Dyphestive timed his swing, and he put everything he had into it. The war mace connected with the earhole as Thunderbreath's lowered head passed by. Thunderash released its power. *Kapow!*

The war mace snapped in half, and the blowback from its power hurled Dyphestive backward and to the ground. He looked at the broken handle in dismay.

Thunderbreath, on the other hand, was stopped stone cold in his tracks. His tongue hung out of his cavernous mouth, and the side of his face had caved in.

Streak's wings fluttered like a small bird's as he landed on the dragon's horns and said, "Yeah, he's dead."

Razor pointed his sword in the air and said, "Waaahooo! We did it." He marched over to Thunderbreath, climbed onto his head, planted his boot on the horns, and stuck his sword tip in the top of the head. "Remember this day. I'm going to have it painted."

Gorva came out of nowhere and gave Grey Cloak and Dyphestive hugs. "You have the worst plans ever, but somehow, they work." She kissed Grey Cloak on the cheek and started in on Dyphestive, but Leena blocked her. Gorva lifted her hands in surrender and said, "You can kiss him for me."

While they were sharing hugs and celebrating, Grey Cloak broke away from the pack and ventured over to Thatcher. The blind dwarf stood beside the burning husk of Itchee's body. The awful stench forced Grey Cloak to cover his nose. "I'm sorry about your pet... er, friend."

"We all have to make sacrifices." Thatcher sniffled. "I wish I still had my eyes so I could shed my tears. Itchee was special. But he would do anything to protect the pack. He would do anything for me." Looking toward the flames, he continued, "You and Itchee had a lot in common. You risked your life to save a friend. I didn't think you would go through with it. I'm pleased you proved me wrong."

"Well, if you don't have friends, you don't have enemies. Where's the fun in that?"

Thatcher clawed at his beard and chuckled. "You are unique. Will you still take my pack to the shore?"

Grey Cloak turned his gaze toward the prisoner boat. "Uh, well, in case it escaped your notice, the boat is on fire, and I don't see any more available."

Thatcher tapped him with his staff and said, "I'm sure you'll think of something."

Grey Cloak rocked on his heels and smirked. Thunderbreath was dead, and he'd beaten the odds again. "Yeah, I will, won't I."

50

EPILOGUE

THE INLAND SEA WIND FILLED THE CRIMSON SAIL, AND THE PRISONER SHIP CUT through the water toward the main shore.

Thatcher had been wrong when he told Grey Cloak that he would *think of something*. He didn't, but the hobbled Lythlenion did. The recently retired Captain of the Black Guard suggested they wait for another prisoner ship on the east side of the island. A day later, when the prisoner ship arrived, they raided it, cast off, and left the disposed-of Black Guard behind.

Now, Grey Cloak sat with the warm wind in his hair at the ship's fore, studying the weary faces of the passengers that filled the benches.

Dyphestive sat with Leena, and she made sure that no one shared a bench with them. Lythlenion and Gorva chatted quietly. Jakoby and Razor were in good spirits, chuckling away, while the jubilant crew of halflings, led by Deeann, kept them entertained. The rear passengers consisted of Thatcher's pack and the female prisoner that Grey Cloak had saved. He hadn't even had the energy to ask for her name.

Only Streak wasn't immediately accounted for. The dragon had taken to the water and had been swimming alongside the ship. Grey Cloak had lost sight of him hours ago, but he wasn't worried. He and the dragon had a bond, and Streak would show up when he wanted to.

For the first time in a long time, Grey Cloak took a deep breath and exhaled. *We did it. We really did it.*

As Prisoner Island diminished in the distance, so did the harrowing events that had occurred there. It was only one obstacle in a very long journey whose end was nowhere in sight. He created a checklist in his mind.

I have to find Zora.

Secure Tanlin.

Find the Figurine of Heroes.

Oust the underlings.
Destroy Black Frost.
Sigh. I'll think of something.

Lythlenion was sitting closest to him and said, "The Black Guard will come looking for the ship, and when they can't find it, they'll notify the Riskers. The good thing about ships is that they don't leave a trail in the water. We'll take this ship downriver and abandon it in the wood."

"Thanks, Lyth. I hadn't even thought about that," he said.

"I could see the heaviness on your brow. It helps to have one less thing to worry about," Lythlenion replied.

"What? Me, worry?"

Lythlenion smiled. "I had a friend, Alfred—he used to say that all of the time." He shifted in his seat and grimaced.

"How is the knee?" Grey Cloak asked.

"I'll be walking with a cane for a while, but I can mend it. I'm getting old, and I don't bounce back like I used to."

"Are you planning on coming along?"

Lythlenion shook his head. "No, I have to take care of Sarah and Lylith. Best we move on and quickly."

"I know someone who would love to see you, and you'd be safe."

Lythlenion tilted his head. "Who?"

"Rhonna. She's the Monarch Queen of Dwarf Skull now."

Lythlenion stroked the wiry hairs on his chin with a grin and said, "I'll be."

MOST OF THE company parted ways when they hid the boat along the river. Thatcher's thankful pack was quickly underway with little more than a word, and they took the women Grey Cloak had rescued with them. All of the others, Deeann's halflings included, headed to Lythlenion's cottage by the sea, where they were introduced to a worried Sarah and Lylith. She embraced them all, made them comfortable, and fed them.

As the group cooked fish over a campfire on the beach, Grey Cloak unveiled his plans.

"I'm heading back to Raven Cliff to check on Zora and Tanlin. We're going to need to run into Harbor Lake to stock up on supplies if all of us are coming."

Deeann was smoking her pipe when she stood. "Me and the crew are going to head south with Lythlenion. But you have our thanks." She eyed Dyphestive. "That was a brave thing you did, both of you."

Dyphestive reached over and gave Deeann a hug. "It was our pleasure."

All of the little men piled on top of him.

He started laughing. "Stop tickling me, please, ahahahaha!"

"Tell Zora hello for me," Deeann said as she shook Grey Cloak's hand. "If we ever cross paths again, I hope you know you can count on us."

"I know."

With his hands on his hips, he said, "Well, it looks like Talon is back in business."

"What's Talon?" Gorva asked.

Dyphestive stood up with the halflings hanging all over him, raised his fists, and shouted across the sea, "We are Talon!"

AT THE CRACK of dawn the next day, Talon ventured into Harbor Lake, split up, and gathered supplies from separate lists. Dyphestive and Leena, with Cliff in tow, were tasked with gathering water, rations, and dry goods. Jakoby, Razor, and Gorva went to fetch horses, and Grey Cloak went to purchase new clothing. They planned to meet half a league down the road at the bridge that crossed a small brook and head south to Raven Cliff.

Instructions in hand, all of them went about their business.

A sharp dragon shriek cut through the air, and a Risker and his middling dragon soared toward the sea. On the other side of town, another dragon could be heard shrieking, and another Risker whizzed over the river.

Grey Cloak quickened his pace. No doubt Thunderbreath's dead body had been discovered.

I was hoping for later rather than sooner, but it should take a long time before they sort out what happened.

He hopped up on the porch and headed for the nearest general store. As he passed an alley between the buildings, a bright-red door caught his eye. He stopped in his tracks. A small, rickety building was wedged in the alley, connecting the buildings. A chill swept through him as he read the wooden sign hanging from chains over the door: Batram's Bartery and Arcania.

He rubbed his eyes. A chill wind rustled his hair, and the red door swung inward.

I-I can't believe it.

Grey Cloak hurried inside.

The door slammed shut behind him, and the gravelly voice of the boar's-head rug on the floor said, "Welcome! Don't forget to wipe your feet."

Grey Cloak complied.

The rug responded, "Ah, that feels good."

WILL Talon save Zora and Tanlin from the Black Guard in time?

How will Dirklen and Magnolia react when they learn Grey Cloak and Dyphestive have returned?

Are the Doom Riders, led by an undead Drysis, back in the picture?

Find out in book number 10, which is on sale now! Details below!

Don't forget to leave a review for Prisoner Island: Dragon Wars - Book 9. They are a huge help! LINK!

Grab your copy of *Ruins of Thannis – Book 10*, On Sale Now! Click here! See pic below.

And if you haven't already, signup for my newsletter and grab 3 FREE books including the Dragon Wars Prequel.
WWW.DRAGONWARSBOOKS.COM

TEACHERS AND STUDENTS, if you would like to order paperback copies for you library or classroom, email craig@thedarkslayer.com to receive a special discount.

GEAR UP in this Dragon Wars body armor enchanted with a +2 Coolness factor/+4 at Gaming Conventions. Sizes range from halfling (Small) to Ogre (XXL). LINK . www.society6.com

• PERIL IN THE DARK •

— BOOK 10 —

CRAIG HALLORAN

1

BATRAM'S BARTERY AND ARCANIA

THE ARCANIA HADN'T CHANGED OVER THE TEN YEARS SINCE GREY CLOAK HAD LAST set foot inside. White candles with golden flames illuminated the murky interior of the hovel. A chandelier of candles hung high overhead, corroding brass sconces held more, and others flickered on candle stands on a black mahogany countertop.

Grey Cloak set his eyes on the glass case and rested his hands on the tall counter. Inside the glass case, on crushed-velvet sheets, were gorgeous sparkling treasures worth a fortune. It held necklaces with pink pearls, earrings with rubies as big as his knuckles, and a rapier with a diamond-encrusted handguard. Ancient scrolls were bound and stacked in one corner, and a gold hand mirror that didn't show a reflection rested near them.

"Where does he get all of this?" Grey Cloak muttered. He lifted his eyes and scanned the quiet room. "Batram?"

His voice carried for a moment, echoing down the deep corridor of drawers and shelving behind the countertop. Large brass-handled mahogany drawers, each big enough to hold a large body, made up the bottom of the shelves. As the web-covered drawers stacked up toward the top, they became smaller, and they didn't stop until they reached the top of the old building. Spiders of all sorts crawled along the shelves and stretched webbing from one drawer to another.

Grey Cloak cupped one hand to the side of his face and called again, "Oh, Batram! You have a customer!" He eyed the boar-head rug. "Where's your boss?" It didn't bat an eye. "Look at me, talking to a rug." He gave a nervous laugh. "Glad no one is around to see how silly I am." He turned his attention behind the counter and jumped ten feet backward. "Oh my!"

"Welcome!" the rug said as he landed right on top of it. "Don't forget to wipe your feet!"

Batram stood behind the counter in his monstrous spider form. He had the head of a tarantula, stood over ten feet tall, and wore a red-and-white striped coat. Sticking out of his sleeves were eight spidery legs with sticky fingers on the ends. His eight eyes were bright green, and he had stringy blond hair hanging over half of his eyes. His lower set of hands drummed on the counter. *Tickety. Tickety. Tickety.*

Grey Cloak clutched his hand over his pounding heart. "Is this how you greet all of your customers?"

"No," Batram replied in a coarse voice, "only you."

"Why doesn't that surprise me?" He approached the counter and gazed at the towering monstrosity. Rubbing his fingernails on his cloak, he asked, "So, how have you been?"

Batram leaned his big body over the counter and said, "Look at me. I'm the picture of health."

Grey Cloak rolled his eyes. "If you say so. Regardless, it's good to see you. You're a hard man... er, whatever to find, and I've been seeking you for some time."

Batram gave a smile full of tiny sharp teeth. "Have you, now? And why would that be after these many, many years?"

"Well, it's only been ten years in your time. Not mine—it's only been a year or so for me."

Batram swept his oily locks away from his eyes with his top hand and said, "That's a very interesting bit of information. How can that be? Did you travel through time?"

"You know about that?" Grey Cloak asked with a look of surprise.

Batram instantly turned into the form of a halfling and stood on the counter. His hair was curly and almost white, and he still wore the striped coat with a yellow flower. With eyes as big as saucers, he asked in a warm, excited voice, "You really traveled through time? I thought you were dead or locked in a dungeon." He rubbed his dimpled chin. "I never imagined this. Interesting. How did you do it?"

As relieved as Grey Cloak was to see Batram back in halfling form, he said, "I don't have time to explain all of the details. I'm in a hurry."

Batram started smoking a black-horn pipe that appeared from out of nowhere. He tapped his foot and said, "And I'm in no hurry. Please, share your story. I have to know. Besides, you aren't going anywhere."

Grey Cloak looked behind him. The red door was gone, and so was the boar-head carpet. Batram had played the same trick on him the first time they met, but the door was black then, not red. "I'm trying to save the world, you know."

"All the reason to be more thorough." Batram eyed him with his big blue eyes, tapped his foot, huffed out a smoke ring, and said, "Out with it."

He sighed and spit out a brief version of his encounter with the underlings he'd summoned from another world using the Figurine of Heroes. He finished it off by saying, "And that's why I came here. I need to find the figurine. I hoped that you might have it."

Batram let out a rusty chuckle. "So you are the one that let those terrors loose. Hah!" He spewed out a stream of smoke that made the room misty. "I should thank you, I suppose. Thanks to you, my business has boomed. Why, I've had every mage, wizard, and sorcerer from one side of Gapoli to the other in here. There have been knights and the finest swordsmen, each of them looking for a weapon to destroy the underlings. They've given me everything they have to beat them, yet the underlings thrive. And now you think you can defeat them?"

"If I have the figurine, I can send them back."

"Ho-hah, so you think it will be so simple. They will see you coming from leagues away. Certainly, they have prepared for it." Batram chewed on the stem of his pipe. "Over the years, I've gathered bits and pieces of information. Wizards love to talk. The ones from the Wizard Watch, the ones that survived, have fled. Those underlings have killed all who cross them, and the ones they didn't kill now serve them." He gave a chilling cackle. "As if Black Frost weren't enough to deal with. Now he has two invincible henchmen who control the Wizard Watch."

"They aren't invincible," Grey Cloak said. "I know how to beat them. The figurine will send them back. One word, and they are gone. I need your help, Batram. That's why I've been looking for you. The figurine is bound to have turned back up over the past ten years."

"And what makes you think that the underlings don't have it? Or Black Frost, for that matter? Hmm?"

"I don't know if they have it or not. That's why I'm here to ask you." He looked Batram dead in the eye. "Do you have it?"

Batram raised his bushy white eyebrows. "It is smart of you that this is the first place you would look. As you well know, I've acquired many rare antiquities over the centuries." He placed his arms behind his back and started to pace over the glass panes of the countertop. "I like you, Grey Cloak. I do. You are scrappy." He shrugged. "You are trouble too. After all, you are the one that unleashed this terror on our world."

"It sounds to me like you know where the figurine is."

Batram spun on his heel and locked his intense eyes on him. "I do know where it is. But..." He lifted a stubby finger. "That information will cost you... dearly."

2

THE WAY BATRAM FINISHED HIS LAST SENTENCE MADE THE MUSCLES IN GREY Cloak's lower back bunch. The halfling was up to something. He was always up to something.

Grey Cloak played along. "So, you do know where it is?" He cast his stare into the shelves behind the little man. "Is it *here*?"

"That would be your wish, wouldn't it?" Batram wagged his finger at him. "I've dealt with my share of slippery tongues, and you would dupe me into revealing an answer without paying for it."

"So, the figurine is not here?" Grey Cloak asked, hoping to catch Batram twitching, glancing, or doing something revealing.

"Didn't I just tell you? I won't be duped!" Batram said. All of his facial features, except for his mouth, were gone. But the disturbing image of the halfling continued to speak. "Do you really think that I'll reveal anything to you? Try to be so clever, Grey Cloak. It will cost you."

"Fine."

He reached into his inner pockets and fished out a small pouch of gold coins. He'd acquired a lot of treasure in his working days in Monarch City. He tossed the purse to the eyeless Batram, who deftly snatched it out of the air.

"How'd you do that?"

"Just because you can't see my eyes, it doesn't mean that I don't have them." Batram shook a coin into his chubby palm and bit down on it. "Gold is one of my favorite flavors. Now, what was your question?"

"Do you have the figurine here?"

"No."

Batram pitched the sack of coins toward the top drawers. A small drawer pushed its way through the loose webbing, and the purse dropped inside. A pair of tarantulas with red-and-white stripes on their backs shoved the drawer closed.

"Next question."

Frustrated, Grey Cloak asked, "Was the figurine here... recently?"

Batram flexed his fingers repeatedly. The rest of his features appeared on his face. "That will cost you."

Grey Cloak groaned and asked, "Don't you even care what is happening out there?" He flung his hand in the direction of where the door used to be. "With all of this, you could help."

"That's not my purpose. Your purpose is to figure it out."

Grey Cloak tapped his head on the counter and gritted his teeth. He couldn't spend the entire day bartering with Batram. The others would be waiting for him. "Fine." He placed another pouch of gold on the table. "Where is the Figurine of Heroes?"

Batram's belly jiggled when he laughed. "That pittance isn't going to retrieve the answer you seek." He hung his gaze on the Cloak of Legends. "I told you it would cost you dearly."

Grey Cloak clasped his cloak about his neck and stepped away from the counter. The cloak wasn't some ordinary garment. It was a part of him and had saved his life more than a few times already. Most recently, it had saved him from becoming a pile of ashes from Thunderbreath's fire. "You don't want this. It won't even work for anyone else. You said so yourself."

"It won't work for just anyone, but it will work for others of a rare breed such as you."

Grey Cloak smirked for a moment. Batram had answered a question without payment. It wasn't what he wanted to hear, but it was helpful.

Perhaps he is not as clever as he thinks he is.

He gave a Batram a pouty look and said, "I can't part with this. I'll be defenseless. How can I fight the underlings, then?"

"You have your friends, a dragon, wizardry—the list goes on. Don't try to fool me." Batram tapped his temple with his index finger. "You need to rely more on your wits than your weapons. Give it up. Make a sacrifice. No good thing comes without sacrifice."

Grey Cloak's mind started to race as he clasped the cloak tighter. Sweat built on his brow.

Maybe I don't need the figurine.

I can stop the underlings without it.

There is more than one way to skin a cat.

I'll take my chances.

He swallowed the lump building in his throat.

Why does Batram want the cloak so badly, anyway?

He wants everything—the cloak, the figurine. It's mine. Why should I give it all to him?

"You are thinking too hard about this. The answer should be easy if you want to save the world."

"Well, that's easy for you to say! You never even leave this shack!"

"Oh, that will cost you. And to think that I was going to be reasonable." He pointed at the red door, which had reappeared along with the boar-head rug. "Perhaps it's time that you shopped elsewhere."

Grey Cloak cast nervous looks between the door and Batram. "No, no, I apologize." He tried to smooth things over. "Can you blame me for being irritable after all I've been through? This cloak..." He smoothed the fabric with his palm. "And I have been through a lot together."

"And perhaps you can redeem it."

"Redeem?"

"Yes. After all, this is a bartery. You can buy back what you have lost. But..." He huffed out a ring of smoke. "As I said, it will take a sacrifice on your part."

An idea sprang to Grey Cloak's mind. "Wait, wait, wait!" He reached into his pockets and removed the dragon charm he'd acquired in the Burnt Hills of Sulter Slay. Shaped like a flat egg and as smooth as a river stone, the precious jewel twinkled in his palm with an orange inner fire. He lifted it before Batram's eyes. "I have this!"

Batram planted his fists on his hips and tossed his head back with laughter. Finally, he regained his composure, wiped a tear from the corner of his eye, and said, "And I have no use for that whatsoever."

3

GREY CLOAK'S JAW ALMOST HIT THE FLOOR, AND HIS SHOULDERS SAGGED. "IS THIS A jest? You can't use a dragon charm?"

Batram said flatly, "No. And why would I want one? So I can sell or trade it and have it tracked back to me and have Black Frost breathing down my neck? No, thank you."

"How can he track you down if you disappear all the time?"

"That's *my* problem." Batram puffed out a ring of smoke, but he seemed to be having a hard time keeping his eyes off the beautiful charm. "Uh, get that thing out of my face. We are dealing for the cloak, unless you have something better to offer."

"Better to offer? This is a dragon charm. Don't you get it? You can control a dragon with this."

"Some dragons but not all. It depends on the user. Again, it's a problem that I don't want to have."

Grey Cloak wasn't going to take no for an answer. "Surely there is someone that could use this charm, eh?" He smiled at Batram. "Worst case, you can hide it in your drawers. Keep it safe from trouble."

"My drawers are fine." Batram ambled to the end of his counter and grabbed an hourglass made from copper. It was a large object, half as tall as he was. He brought it over and placed it before Grey Cloak's eyes. "You're on the clock now."

Grey Cloak's eyes widened as he watched the sand at the top rapidly slide through the hourglass's neck and build up on the bottom. "That's a very fast hourglass."

"Yes, it is. Now, are we going to deal or not?"

"I'm thinking."

"You've had enough time for that. Once the last grain drops, you're out of my shop, and who knows—it might be another ten years before you come back."

Grey Cloak's fingers dug into his palms. Batram had him right where he wanted him. "Fine!" He slapped the dragon charm on the counter and said, "But I'm keeping everything in the pockets." He unloaded several bags of gold and silver coins and placed them on the counter. There were three figurines carved from black onyx he'd made and two potion vials with corks waxed on the top. He pulled a dagger and a sword free from the inner folds and stuck an emerald and a gold coin into his pants pocket.

"Oh my," Batram said, rubbing his chin and marveling. "What else does it do?"

"I lost track," Grey Cloak said, slapping down item after item. He pulled out a gold necklace with small emeralds, a stuffed mouse, a pair of scissors, a spool of string, two dove feathers, a figurine of Codd, and a small five-pound anvil. "That's Dyphestive's. And you will tell me everything about the figurine's where-abouts. Who has it

and what to expect? I want details," Grey Cloak continued. "Agreed?"

"Of course. I will tell you everything that I know."

"You'd better. No games." By the time he finished emptying the pockets, a small trove of treasure and trinkets had piled up on the counter. "And I need something to carry all of that in."

Batram waved a hand. A pack of tarantulas hauled a leather sack across the floor behind the counter, climbed up the side, left the sack, scurried away, and vanished.

"You're running out of time," Batram said. The hourglass was halfway drained.

Grey Cloak started shoveling his objects into the sack with his arm. He slowly peeled the cloak away from his body, and a chill fell over him and made his arms break out in goose bumps. He held the cloak out toward Batram's outstretched fingers but pulled it back. "No tricks."

"No tricks. That wouldn't be good for business."

Grey Cloak handed the garment over. The hourglass only had a quarter of the sand left in the top. "Out with it."

"Gladly. The Figurine of Heroes is guarded in the Ruins of Thannis, which lie below the Iron Hills. You can gain entrance where the Inland Sea's waters spill into Monarch City's Outer Ring."

"What guards the figurine?"

"Thannis was a wicked city swallowed up by its own evil. It is said that the undead still thrive there, waiting for warm flesh to cross the darkness to satisfy their ravenous hunger. It is a wicked place. The living don't belong there."

Only a fingertip's width of sand was left in the top of the hourglass.

"Who put the figurine down there?"

Batram rolled the cloak up in his arms and smiled as the last grain of sand fell. "You did."

The red door opened wide and bathed the room in daylight. The rug said, "Come back soon!"

A powerful wind lifted Grey Cloak from his feet and started to whisk him toward the door. In the nick of time, he grabbed the sack of his goods. As the unseen force pulled him toward the door, he caught a glimpse of Batram in spider-monster form, cuddling the cloak and waving at him.

"Batram, you liar!"

Batram shrugged and said, "Lies are often a matter of interpretation. Good luck finding the figurine." He waved the right side of his strange arms and hands. "Bring me the Sword of Chaos, and I'll return your cloak to you. Bye-bye!"

Grey Cloak's body sailed through the door, and he skipped across the road and slammed hard into a water trough. He heard a door slam shut, and by the time he looked up, Batram's Bartery and Arcania had vacated the narrow alley.

He rose, ignored the early-morning onlookers, and headed down the street with only one thing to say. "Zooks."

4

SUNLIGHT PEEKED THROUGH THE GREY CLOUDS, SHEDDING LIGHT ON THE DEWDROP-covered beds of wildflowers gathered alongside the muddy road. The morning fog lifted, revealing a clear path of small rises over one hundred yards out. The morning birds sang as they darted from bush to bush and streaked across the sky. The hooves of trotting horses made sucking sounds as they were pulled out of the mudholes.

Jakoby, a dark-skinned bear of a man, sat tall in his saddle, leading the way. His steady gaze remained fixed on the road ahead. Riding beside him was Reginald the Razor, a much younger man with short, tawny hair. He was dressed in black leather armor and wore his many blades like a suit of clothing.

Right behind them was Gorva, a young and strong orcen woman with a build that could have been cast in iron. Beside her was Leena, wearing black robes trimmed with gold. Her long cherry-red hair bounced off her back. They set their eyes against the wind and didn't look around.

Dyphestive and Grey Cloak guarded the rear, keeping pace. Dyphestive's mule, Cliff, loaded with gear, trailed behind them.

Aside from the thunder of hooves splashing through the mudholes, the journey had been quiet. The company rode for hours at a steady pace, straight for Raven Cliff. They had done so on Grey Cloak's orders, but at the moment, Grey Cloak wasn't speaking. Since they'd departed Harbor Lake, he had been quiet.

"Where's your cloak?" Dyphestive asked for the third time that day.

"We'll talk later, I said!" Grey Cloak replied. His voice drew a backward glance from Gorva. "Nothing to see here. Keep riding."

"Well, aren't you edgy? Will you tell me what is going on? And I'm not taking no for an answer. Where is your cloak?"

Grey Cloak gave his brother a steely gaze. "Can't an elf brood and not be bothered?"

"No, I want to know what is bothering you. It affects us."

"Not as much as me!"

Dyphestive frowned. "It must be bad. I think you'd feel better if you talked about it."

"I don't need to be consoled. I need time to think."

"About what?" Dyphestive asked.

"I'll talk when I feel like it. In the meantime—"

Jakoby and Razor brought their horses to a stop at the top of the next rise. Their horses nickered, stamped their hooves, and whinnied.

"We have a situation," Jakoby stated in a strong voice.

Farther down the road was a covered bridge guarded by troops of lizard men.

Dyphestive leaned over his saddle and squinted. "What in the world are they doing?"

"It looks like they are barring passage across the river," Razor quickly retorted. He poked his finger in the air and counted out loud. "One, two, four, eight, twelve... we can take them."

Gorva sat up in her saddle. She'd discarded her tattered clothing for a more suitable suit of leather armor that showed off her sinewy frame. "I agree."

"What do you want to do, Grey?" Dyphestive asked.

Grey Cloak's nostrils flared. "Obviously, we should ride down there and kill them."

"Those are Black Guard banners flapping in the wind down there," Jakoby warned. "I can see the mountain and thunderbolts. We could slay them, but I doubt it will stop with them."

"He's being sarcastic," Dyphestive said. "Right, Grey?"

"Who can tell the truth from a lie?" Grey Cloak replied.

"Boy, aren't you in a cryptic mood."

"That's putting it mildly."

Razor pulled the reins of his horse, turning the beast to face them. "I'm all for turning lizard men into fancy boots but not if we aren't all in. What's it going to be? Are we going to go through them or around them? Certainly, we can cross farther down the river."

"We won't be crossing on horseback. That river is too fast and deep," Gorva said.

"Do you think they are looking for us?" Jakoby asked.

Razor pulled his sword from its scabbard. "Well, if they are, they aren't taking me without a taste of steel first. I've been a prisoner for ten years, and I'm not going back to the island."

"Will you put that away?" Jakoby pushed Razor's sword down. "The lizard men aren't blind. They can see us."

Grey Cloak's brow furrowed, and he had a spacey look in his grey eyes, like he wasn't listening.

Dyphestive nudged him in the shoulder with his fist. "Are you thinking?"

"Of course I'm thinking. I'm always thinking." Grey Cloak's cross look swept over the group. "For you and you and you and you."

"Not for me!" Gorva fired back.

Leena gave him a stern frown.

"Stay here. I'll return," Grey Cloak said as he led his horse toward the bridge.

"What are you going to do?" Dyphestive asked.

"I'll think of something."

Dyphestive scratched his head as he watched Grey Cloak trot his horse toward the troops of lizard men, who had gathered in front of the bridge with spears. "He'd *better* think of something."

"Our friend is in a sour mood," Jakoby said. "What do you think is eating him?"

Dyphestive shrugged. "I don't know. I've never seen him like this before. He's been very chipper of late."

"He's an elf. Elves are moody," Gorva said.

Everyone in the company gave Gorva a doubtful look.

"What?" she asked. "They are."

"Said the pot to the kettle," Razor replied.

At the base of the hill, where the road met the bridge, Grey Cloak was surrounded by half a dozen lizard men with spears pointed at him. He lifted his arms and locked his fingers behind his head.

"Horseshoes," Dyphestive uttered as the muscles in his jaws clenched. "I don't like this."

5

"I<small>F WORSE COMES TO WORST, WE CAN TAKE THEM OUT</small>," R<small>AZOR SUGGESTED</small>. H<small>IS</small> horse, a black stallion with a white spot above the nose, snorted. "See, my fella wants to get in on the fight too."

Grey Cloak's fingers remained behind his head as he talked to the lizard men. He nodded back toward the company.

"What's he saying?" Gorva asked.

"I don't know," Dyphestive answered.

"I can read lips," Razor said. "He says, 'If you don't let us pass, we are going turn Razor loose on you. He's not only the finest swordsman in the world but very handsome and charming too.'"

"You can't read his lips if you can't see them. You are making lies," Gorva said.

Razor chuckled. "You caught me, angel. But I wasn't lying about what I said."

"Huh, finest swordsman, my big behind," Jakoby said with a grunt.

"Come now, Jakoby. You're too big to be as quick as me. I'd poke you three times before you got a nick on me," Razor said.

Jakoby's broad shoulders bounced when he laughed. "Keep telling yourself that." He leaned forward and set his gaze on Grey Cloak. The lizard men crowding him brought their spears dangerously close to his skin. Jakoby's hand locked around the pommel of his sword. "They are about to skewer him. We need to ride."

Dyphestive pulled his long sword halfway out of its sheath, and he led his horse forward. "Everyone, be ready."

Grey Cloak dropped his hands, and the lizard men backed away. A purse was exchanged between him and one of the lizard men.

"Everyone, settle down," Dyphestive said.

The lizard man emptied coins from the leather purse. He said something to

Grey Cloak, and Grey Cloak twisted around in his saddle and waved the company down the slope. Dyphestive took a breath and shoved his sword back into its sheath. "It looks like my brother has it all taken care of."

Razor returned his weapons to their scabbards and said, "That's a shame. I needed some exercise."

"Jakoby, lead the way," Dyphestive said. "And don't eyeball the lizard men. Keep your eyes down and go."

"Aye," Jakoby agreed. "We might want to put a hood over Razor."

"Even better—I'll slay them all blindfolded."

"Where did you find this one?" Gorva asked Dyphestive.

"He's a present from Tatiana."

"Present?" Razor lifted his shoulders and nodded. "Yes, I am a gift, aren't I?"

The company met up with Grey Cloak and the lizard men soldiers.

Grey Cloak did the talking. He had an irritated look on his face. "There is a toll. It seems that Dark Mountain's reach is expanding, and they are charging for passage at all of the bridges. Fortunately, I scraped up enough to pay the toll for all of us. You're welcome."

The lizard men sauntered through the company, eyeballing everything that they carried. All of them were strapping brutes, thick in muscle that bulged behind their scaly green-brown skin.

"These are fine horses," the lizard man that had taken Grey Cloak's coins said. He had a hiss in his voice when he spoke. "And your group carries well-crafted weapons. What is your business?"

Grey Cloak's jaw tightened. His steely gaze narrowed, and he muttered something under his breath.

"What was that?" the leader of the lizard men demanded.

"Get your claws off me!" Gorva warned.

"What happened?" Dyphestive asked.

Gorva growled at a lizard man soldier that hovered by her legs. "This one put his hand on my thigh!"

"Can't say I blame him," Razor remarked.

"Sergeant, what is this about? I've paid the toll," Grey Cloak said.

"That was before I had a better look at your crew." There was no hiding the greedy look building in the lizard man's eyes. "You have fine weapons and fine beasts. We'll take them. But you can keep the mule and the rest of your gear."

"That's outrageous!" Grey Cloak said.

"No, that is the privilege of being a Black Guard. You'd be wise to join us. Perhaps you might get your gear back." The lizard man gave a hissing chuckle and waved his arms at his soldiers.

The lizard men surrounded them with spears pointed toward their guts.

"Get your hands up!" the sergeant demanded.

"I told you we should have gone with my plan, but no, you didn't listen," Razor said mockingly.

Not a single member of Talon lifted a hand.

Dyphestive's fingertips tingled. Judging by the scowls growing on everyone's faces, he knew a fight was coming. Not to mention the dark look in Grey Cloak's eyes, which were burning a hole in the sergeant.

If we fight them, we'll have the entire Black Guard coming after us. There has to be a better way to settle this.

He was used to Grey Cloak doing all the talking, but his brother was acting strangely, making him uneasy. He cleared his throat and said, "We are mercenaries who serve the Doom Riders. We are on a mission for them."

"The who?" the sergeant asked.

Horseshoes.

Dyphestive straightened his back and stuck to his story. He lowered his voice and didn't hide his deadly intent and summoned his darker side, Iron Bones. "Don't let your greed blind those beady yellow eyes of yours. Everyone knows who the Doom Riders are. They have slain and slaughtered from one side of the world to the other. I'll tell you what—you can have our gear and our horses, and when we arrive on foot at their camp, and they ask where all of our horses and gear went, I'll send them back here for you to answer."

The lizard men's yellow eyes blossomed in their sockets, and they exchanged nervous glances with one another.

Finally, the sergeant humbly corrected himself and said, "Oh, *those* Doom Riders."

He stepped out of the way, and his men moved along with him.

"Apologies. It's been a while. Give them my best." He approached Dyphestive and gave him the purse of coins. "A thousand apologies. We never saw you." With a wave of his hand, he shouted at his troops guarding the bridge. "Get out of the way!" He bowed and added, "Dragon speed to all of you."

6

THE MOON NESTLED BEHIND THICK CLOUDS THAT BLANKETED THE SKIES. TALON SET
up camp in the woodland, far from the road.

Razor lay on his back near a small campfire, rumbling with laughter. "Oh-
ho-ho-ho! I'd never seen a lizard man's eyes turn so round as when you told that
tale about the Doom Riders. I swear their tails curled underneath their legs." He
elbowed Gorva. "Did you see that?"

"Don't do that," Gorva said.

He propped himself up on his elbows, and his laughter started to subside.
"The big fella scared them. You about scared me, too, with that deadly look you
gave them. Where'd you draw that up from?"

"I thought about how much I hated the Doom Riders, and I don't know—it
surfaced," Dyphestive replied as he chewed a portion of dried meat. He was
sitting on the ground with Leena at his right hip. He allowed himself a smile. "I
did scare them, didn't I?"

"Scared the scales off of them," Jakoby said as he stoked the fire with a stick.
"It was a good move. Well done. I thought we were going to be in a scrap."

"I hoped for it, but seeing you make them shiver was worth me missing out
on some practice," Razor added. "You've got an ugly side. It's gritty. I like it."

Leena put her hand on his knee. As usual, she hadn't said a word and stared
at the flames. They created shadows on the black arachnid-like tattoo on her
face, giving it movement like a living thing. It wasn't a pleasant thing to see, and
Dyphestive felt sorry for her.

On the other side of the fire, Grey Cloak squatted, rocking back and forth on
his toes. He wore a new riding cloak but appeared to be shivering.

"Since we've all settled down for the day, I think it's high time you told us
what is going on," Dyphestive said. He picked up a twig and tossed it at his
brother. It hit him in the head. "Grey Cloak?"

"Huh?" Grey Cloak blinked. "What?"

"You tell *us* what. You looked like you were going to kill the lizard men back at the bridge. What has gotten into you?" Dyphestive asked.

"Are you cold? It feels cold."

"It's chilly but not unbearable," Razor commented. He scooted toward Gorva. "I'm getting warmer."

Gorva stood and moved across from Razor and sat by Grey Cloak.

"Where are you going?" Razor asked.

"Away from you before I kill you," she said.

With a playful grin, he said, "You know, most women find me irresistible."

"Include me in the camp that finds you detestable."

"Ouch, that hurt. Well, no roses for you." Razor lay back down and closed his eyes. "See you in the morning."

Gorva gave Grey Cloak a stiff shove and said, "Out with it, moody elf. What has happened to you? You have the look of a devil since you lost your little cloak."

Grey Cloak sighed. "I didn't lose it, and it's not little." He glanced at his brother. "I had a run-in with Batram."

"You gave him the cloak?"

"I didn't give it to him. I traded it for information," Grey Cloak replied.

"Who is Batram?" Gorva asked.

Grey Cloak scratched the smooth skin on his cheek and said, "Uh, that's hard to explain."

"He's a merchant that lives in a magical store and appears and disappears," Dyphestive said. He'd only been in Batram's Bartery and Arcania once, when he'd first gone to Raven Cliff, but he'd never forgotten the memorable trip. "Grey Cloak sees him more than I do."

Razor chuckled with his eyes closed. "A magical store—now I've heard it all."

"It's true. Anyway, I traded the Cloak of Legends for information about the Figurine of Heroes," Grey Cloak said as he tightened his cloak over his shoulders. "And I've regretted it ever since. I feel like I lost a part of me."

Gorva nodded. "Ah, the cloak had powers. It saved you from Thunderbreath's fire, didn't it?"

"That's not all it did. And without it, my skull aches," Grey Cloak replied.

Jakoby broke his stick and tossed it into the fire. "Well, what did Batram say about the Figurine of Heroes? Where is it?"

Grey Cloak eyed the campfire. "He said it's in a place called the Ruins of Thannis."

Razor sat up like he'd risen from the dead. "Say that again."

"The Ruins of Thannis."

"That's what I thought you said." Razor lay back down. "It's been nice knowing you, and thanks for the rescue, but I'm not going there. Ever."

Grey Cloak perked up and asked, "What do you know about it?"

"Yes, I've never heard of it," Dyphestive said.

"Me either," Gorva said.

"I'm not talking about. It's bad luck to talk about it." Razor curled up. "I'm not going to be turned into a zombie."

Dyphestive noticed Jakoby's glassy stare and asked, "Do you know this place?"

Jakoby nodded. "I have. It's no secret. Thannis is a city filled with the undead buried ages ago. It was a flourishing city of great wealth that rivaled Monarch City. Perhaps it was greater. For centuries, men and women have made the trek into the bowels of the world to snatch its glory." His heavy stare swept over his audience. "Some survived, most didn't, and the ones that made it were never the same. They lost everything and went insane."

"Or became zombies that are dancing in the depths as we speak of them," Razor said. "Pipe it up, already."

"How in the world did the Figurine of Heroes wind up down there?" Dyphestive asked.

"That's where Batram's information becomes interesting," Grey Cloak said. "He told me that *I* put it there."

Dyphestive's jaw dropped. "But that's impossible."

Grey Cloak smirked and replied, "Is it?"

7

PRISONER ISLAND

THE RISING MORNING TIDE CRASHED AGAINST THUNDERBREATH'S DEAD BODY. THE island guardian's body had sunk a quarter way deep into the sand, and his spiked tail floated over the water when they passed. He was surrounded by men and women wearing the black suits of armor of the Riskers. Several dragons were among them.

Commander Dirklen stood in front of Thunderbreath's skull, staring down at the defeated beast. A man of remarkable good looks, he wore a black suit of plate-mail armor perfectly fashioned to fit his well-knit frame. His sun-bleached hair was blond and wavy, and he had the chiseled facial features of a Monarch. An ugly scar ran down the side of his left cheek. Black Frost had given him the scar as a painful reminder of his past failures.

"Look at his skull. It's caved in," Dirklen remarked as he moved closer to the dragon and pointed. Slimy ooze drained out of the fist-sized earhole. He gave his twin sister, Magnolia, who stood nearby, a disgusted look. "What sort of weapon could have caused this sort of damage? Who used it?"

"That is what we are here to find out, isn't it, brother?" Armored like Dirklen, Magnolia was an athletically built beauty with curious playfulness lurking in her eyes. She touched the ugly scar on her right cheek. "Perhaps a giant hit it."

"There aren't any giants around here. If there were, Thunderbreath would have killed them." He rubbed his well-groomed beard. "Something else did this. We'd better find it fast. Moray!"

A Risker in black armor hoofed it over, sand kicking up behind his heels. Moray was a big fellow whose broad face looked like it had been stuffed into his dragon helm, and the rest of his body bulged beneath his armor plates as well. He saluted. "Yes, Commander Dirklen."

"I thought this island was a prison camp," Dirklen said.

"It is, Commander."

Dirklen scanned his surroundings and asked, "Then where are the prisoners?"

"Most of them are confined to Braykurz, the city on the other side of the island. The Ministers of Evil watch over them," Moray said.

Dirklen grabbed Moray by his shoulder armor and pulled him toward the beach. "Then why don't you hop on your dragon, fly over there, and find out if they know anything?"

"Uh... er..." Moray saluted again. "Yes, Commander." He sloshed his way through the tide and headed to his middling dragon.

"And take two more Riskers with you!" Dirklen shouted.

There were eight Riskers in all, each on a middling dragon. Only Dirklen and Magnolia had grand dragons, which sat on the beach.

"I know a quicker way to find out what caused this," Magnolia said as she moved out of the tide and joined her brother.

He rolled his eyes and said, "Fine, let's hear it."

"I can use my wizardry on Thunderbreath, and we can see the last thing he saw." She gave an all-knowing grin. "Who better to tell us what happened than him?"

"Your practice of wizardry is more like witchcraft, but if it will save us time, do it." He bowed and swung his arms at the dead dragon. "The beast is yours to manipulate."

"Why, thank you, and you really need to stop talking to me like I'm your subordinate. You have enough people that don't like you. I don't think you need any more." She waded knee-deep into the surge and hovered over Thunderbreath's good eye. With a grunt, she grabbed his horn and tilted his head farther over. "Thanks for the help."

Dirklen crossed his arms and said, "I didn't want to disrespect you."

Magnolia lifted Thunderbreath's eyelid, revealing an orange eye that was as big as her head. She removed a small dagger from her belt, pulled the eyelid over the upper rim of the eye, and pinned it up with her dagger. Then she glanced over her shoulder and said, "Don't worry. It doesn't hurt. He's dead."

"Ha-ha," Dirklen said dryly. "You do know that he's Black Frost's brother. I'd be careful about not defiling him."

"Don't worry. I'll be ever mindful." She placed both of her hands over the dragon's eye, closed her eyes, and uttered unintelligible words.

The hairs on the nape of Dirklen's neck rose as he watched the golden locks of his sister's hair rise. Her hands began to brighten with rose-colored mystic energy. Thunderbreath's head started to move. Dirklen stepped back, his jaw dropping, as his hand fell to the pommel of his sword.

Magnolia spread her arms out wide, and she moved them as if she were gently and slowly conducting a symphony. Thunderbreath's head lifted clear out of the water and turned to face her. He stared into her eyes as if hypnotized.

She rested her hands on the horn of his nose and made her way around to his eye. In the sweeping, haunting words of a siren, she said, "Oh, great Thunderbreath, the marvelous creation that you are, show us the final moments of your life."

The dragon huffed out a blast of cold breath. His tail rose from the water and lashed up and down.

"Is he alive?" Dirklen asked.

"Of course not. He's not even undead, only a shell of himself. But he's a shell with memories. Come, join me and gaze into the dragon's eye."

Dirklen joined his sister and stared into Thunderbreath's eye. Small images of a battle taking place on the beach came to life. There were manticores and men, though none that he recognized until the dragon glared down at Grey Cloak and Dyphestive. "No, no, that's not possible! They are dead. Gone!"

A wide-eyed Magnolia leaned closer to the image and asked, "And they are still so young? How can that be?"

"Who cares how old they look? They can't still be alive!" He saw a runt dragon being chased and a war mace crash into Thunderbreath's face. The image died.

Dirklen beat the dragon's eye with his mailed fist, shouting, "No! No! No!"

8

RAVEN CLIFF

A DUO OF RISKERS SOARED OVER THE STEEPLY PITCHED ROOFS AND TOWERS OF Raven Cliff, toward the sun, which was fading behind the distant hills.

"Skreee!"

Grey Cloak and Gorva entered the city on foot, leaving Dyphestive, Leena, Jakoby, and Razor on the northern outskirts of the once robust and cheerful town. Both of them donned traveling cloaks and kept their hoods up, shielding them from drizzling rain and prying eyes.

"Have you ever been here before?" Grey Cloak asked Gorva.

"When I was a girl, my family passed through here a few times to load up with supplies," she said as she stepped over a puddle in the messy cobblestone street. "This place was in much better shape back then, and the people didn't wear the long faces that we see now."

"Skreee!"

A dragon and its rider buzzed a bell tower fewer than two blocks away, circled, and landed on the tower's roof. It was a middling dragon, a dark-scaled beast with pitch-black wings. Its rider wore black plate armor and the open-faced helm of a Risker.

Grey Cloak caught Gorva staring at the Risker and said, "Keep your eyes off of them. Their sight is keener than you think. The last time I was here, I saw a woman and her child snatched from the ground for looking."

"What happened to them?"

"They were dropped off outside the city."

Gorva pulled her hood down and said, "That is evil. How can men be so evil?"

"Men? It was a woman Risker," he said.

"You know what I mean."

"Dark Mountain raises the Riskers to be cruel and merciless," he said as he picked his way through the citizens that were traveling home from another day of work. "The Riskers don't have parents to nurture and love them. When they are children, they are separated from all of that attention. They are taught that it makes them weak."

Gorva gave him a sad look. "And you were one of them?"

"Dyphestive and I both."

"How come you didn't become like them?"

He shrugged. "I guess they couldn't beat the good out of us. Heh. Not that I'm that good. If I had my way, I'd prefer to be doing something else. That's what got me into this mess in the first place."

A squad of Black Guard wearing crimson tunics with Dark Mountain's insignia over chain mail marched down the middle of the street toward them. The citizens scattered, and Grey Cloak pulled Gorva by the hand toward the open end of an alley and pressed her back against the wall.

"What are you doing?" she asked, twisting her wrist out of his grasp. "I know how to take care of myself."

The Black Guard marched by, and he said, "Sorry, I wasn't thinking."

She slapped him on the rump. "It's fine, elf. I'm only teasing you."

He smirked. "That's good, I think."

He took a step toward the street, and she pulled him back. "Tell me more about Dark Mountain."

"Now?"

"You seem to be feeling better, and I want to know more about you."

He rubbed his head. The truth was that he *was* feeling better. Even though he missed the Cloak of Legends, he'd begun to overcome his withdrawal from it and was starting to feel more like himself. "I was raised in Dark Mountain, and no one told me any different about right and wrong, but in my heart, I knew. Well, not exactly, but I didn't like not having any choice in my life. That... bothered me."

"And Dyphestive too?"

"He never talked about it. I did all the talking. I think since I was the only friend he had, he followed along with my plan." He raised his eyebrows. "I can't really explain his motivations. I don't understand them myself."

"He had faith in you, and you are his friend. He is loyal to you. What else is there to understand?"

"Why would anyone want a friend like me?" He flashed a grin. "I'll only get you into trouble."

Gorva offered him a smile and said, "I like trouble. Now tell me more about Zora and Tanlin."

He peeked around the corner and pointed. "Another street down is where Tanlin's Fine Fittings and Embroidery is located. I have no idea if he's still alive or not, but Zora went after him. They are a smart pair, but they are watched by the Black Guard and a yonder."

"A yonder?"

"It's a giant eyeball with wings. It keeps tabs on Tanlin and Zora."

"Why?"

"I think because they're still looking for Dyphestive and me. Anyway, the yonder keep to the back alleys. The Black Guard hovers in the streets near the front." He turned and pulled his hood down. "I think they know what to look for with me, but you, they haven't seen before. I'll be close by, but you are going to have to be the one to go and contact Tanlin and Zora. Be discreet." He placed a small purse of coins in her hand and gave her a wink and a goofy smile. "Buy yourself something real nice."

She stuffed the purse under her cloak and gave him a doubtful look. "And what if something goes amiss?"

"Then run like a bat out of the netherworld."

9

"Can I help you?"

Gorva shook the rain off her cloak at the threshold of Tanlin's store and eyed him. As Grey Cloak had described, Tanlin was an older slender man with kinky hair, high cheekbones, and dark circles under his eyes. His white shirt was neatly pressed, as were his trousers. His warm smile and soothing voice were very welcoming.

She cleared her throat and said, "Yes."

"My name is Tanlin, the same as the name on the shop." He extended his hands and added, "Let me help you with your cloak."

She shed her cloak and handed it to him. While he hung the cloak up on a peg behind the door, her gaze swept over the room. The store was filled with neatly organized racks of hanging clothing. The outer walls were covered in box-shaped shelves filled with shirts and trousers.

Gorva sauntered deeper into the store, and her arms brushed against fancy and well-made dresses. She plucked one from its hanger. It was a long white gown with pearly beads embroidered into the chest and shoulders.

"Are you looking for something formal?" Tanlin asked. His hands were hidden behind his back, and he kept the same easy smile on his face.

"Uh, no," she said. "I was thinking about something for everyday wear."

Tanlin looked her up and down. "Please don't take offense, but your leather armor screams warrior. Would you like to switch to something more casual?"

"Maybe, but I like my leather armor."

"I see." Tanlin began plucking clothing from the racks. Among them were several tunic dresses. He held them up. "How about you try on one of these? They might be snug, as I don't have many customers with your strong build. No offense. There is a dressing room over there in the corner."

"Are there any other helpers that might give me an opinion? A woman, perhaps?" she asked.

Grey Cloak hadn't told her as much about Tanlin as he had Zora. He wanted Gorva to find out if both of them were alive. Streak had told them about Zora's run-in with the Scourge and how Tanlin was in danger. Since Zora had gone to rescue him, it seemed odd that Tanlin was doing fine.

Tanlin wagged a finger at her. "Ah, you want a second opinion. Well, that can be arranged." He clapped. "Zora!"

"Coming!" a woman hollered from the storeroom.

"Apologies." Tanlin gave a polite bow. "I don't keep as much help on hand on dreary days such as this. Business is slow."

A very pretty half-elf woman with short auburn hair appeared from behind the curtain that led into the back of the shop. Her green eyes widened when she caught sight of Gorva. Dressed in a white blouse and a blue skirt, the mildly obese woman hurried to Tanlin's side and asked, "What can I do to help?"

"Our friend would like your opinion on some more fashionable casual wear." He offered Zora the clothing he had draped over his arm. "I thought these would be a good start."

"Yeah, well, these might fit until she bends over to lace her boots and rips the back open." Zora giggled. "Sorry, but we don't have many gals with your burly build."

"I'm not burly," Gorva said. "I'm an orc."

"Don't be offended. We have plenty of clothing fit for orcs in the store and in the back. The truth is that we haven't been selling much at all lately, except to the Monarchs and the Black Guard families. They are the only ones with money to spend these days." Zora tossed the tunic dresses into Tanlin's awaiting arms. "Stay right here. I'll be back."

Gorva wasn't in the mood to try on dresses. Zora and Tanlin were there, and it was time to declare her intentions. "No, wait."

Zora stopped and turned. "Yes?"

A dripping-wet Black Guard entered the store. He was a big orc, taller and broader than Gorva, bald on top, with thick sideburns and a beard that were well trimmed. On the other side of the door and windows, more soldiers waited.

"Excuse me," Tanlin said as he spun on his heel and made a beeline for the Black Guard. "Sergeant Slot, how is life treating you today? I have your men's tunics ready."

Gorva noticed Zora stepping in front of her, shielding her from Sergeant Slot's watchful gaze. It didn't do any good. Sergeant Slot had already caught her eye. The corner of his lips turned up, and a hungry look built in his eyes. He shoved Tanlin away and approached Gorva and Zora.

"Who do we have here?" He took Gorva by the hand, brought it up to his lips, and kissed it. "I'm Sergeant Slot. Twenty seasons with the Black Guard. I'm honored to make your acquaintance."

"I bet you are." Gorva pulled her hand away. "I'm in the middle of something. Do you mind, Sergeant Slot?"

He seized her wrist and said, "Indeed, I do. You see, it's my job to get to know the people who come and go in my district. And I've never seen you before. I'm certain to have remembered a beauty like you." He gave her the once-over. "You are dressed like a warrior and carry a dagger."

"Would you expect anything less from an orc? Look around, Sergeant. I'm in a clothing shop, looking to dress down my attire. If you would do me a service, let me go about my business, and you can go about yours."

Sergeant Slot stuck his broad chin out, shook his head, and said, "I give the orders, not you. Tell me your name and where you come from."

"I'm Gorva from Portham," she said.

"And what brings you to Raven Cliff?"

"A feud between me and my... current mate?" she said.

"Ah." He gave a devilish grin. "Having a falling out, and you want to get away. I'll tell you what." He hooked her arm and led her toward the door. "My shift is over. Let me show you around Raven Cliff. It would be my pleasure."

She caught Tanlin and Zora's concerned looks. "That's not necessary."

"I'm not giving you a choice."

10

Gorva pulled her arm away and said, "At least let me change into an outfit more pleasing to your eyes. After all, that is what I'm here for."

"I like what you have on," Sergeant Slot said.

"Please, I look like rabble in this."

He kissed her hand again. "I like rabble."

Gorva broke away from Sergeant Slot and said to Zora, "Come with me, girl. Find me something fetching, and find it quick." She practically shoved Zora behind the curtain. "Don't go anywhere, Sergeant Slot. I'll return shortly."

Sergeant Slot leaned one elbow on the counter and gave a smile as broad as a river. "I'm not going anywhere."

Gorva passed through the curtains and pushed Zora farther back into the storeroom.

"Easy!" Zora said.

She clamped her hand over Zora's mouth and pinned her against the wall. Then she felt a prick against her belly. Zora held a dagger against her stomach.

Keeping her voice low, Gorva said, "There is no need for that, Zora. I'm a friend. I'm with Grey Cloak."

Zora's eyes widened. She lowered her dagger and gently pulled Gorva's hand down from her mouth. "How do I know that?"

"When you see him for yourself."

"So, he escaped Prisoner Island?"

Gorva nodded. "All of us did."

"'All of us' who?"

"Dyphestive, Jakoby, Leena, and Razor. There were some others, but you don't know them."

Zora let out a relieved sigh. "I can't believe it. I was so worried."

"You didn't seem worried, as you are here, going about your business. I thought Tanlin was in danger."

"Don't worry. We handled the problem."

"Gorva!" Sergeant Slot hollered from the front of the store. "I don't like to be kept waiting. Don't make me come in there and shackle you."

"Be patient. I'm worth it!" She turned to Zora. "Find me something to wear quickly."

"You aren't really going to go with him, are you?" Zora rummaged through more outfits on the storeroom shelves.

"I can handle myself."

"Are you sure? Sergeant Slot is dangerous. They all are. This is not a safe place."

Gorva peeked through the curtain. Sergeant Slot was receiving a package of bundled tunics from Tanlin. Some of his soldiers had sauntered into the store. "I can see that, but don't worry about me. I can handle them. You need to rendezvous with Grey Cloak. Will that be a problem?"

"Me, finding Grey Cloak?" She tossed Gorva a crimson-and-gold tunic dress. "No problem."

GORVA WAS LED out of Tanlin's Fine Fittings and Embroidery by a small host of Black Guard. Grey Cloak watched with big eyes from across the street.

No. No. No. No. No.

He moved out of the alley and took to the crowded porches, where many citizens were avoiding the rain. From a distance, he kept his feet moving and his eyes on Gorva. An orc Black Guard had his arm around her waist and hurried her along down the rain-slick streets.

How did this happen?

Grey Cloak caught several glimpses through the store window of Tanlin, who'd been addressing the Black Guard from behind the merchant counter. Grey Cloak's stomach had knotted when he saw the orc escort Gorva out of the building.

Traitor. It was the first word that came to mind when Gorva was hustled away by the soldiers. Obviously, Gorva had revealed herself to Tanlin, and Tanlin turned her in.

Everything is peachy in your life, isn't it, Tanlin?

He jumped off the end of a porch, crossed the alley, and leaped onto another porch, bumping into a portly man who staggered out of a tavern.

"Watch where you're going," the man slurred. He took a clumsy swing at Grey Cloak, lost his footing, teetered off the porch, and splashed into a water trough. He came up gasping.

"I think it's you that needs to watch where you're going," Grey Cloak muttered as he kept following Gorva.

The orc Black Guard stopped in the road and dismissed the other soldiers, who moved on.

Grey Cloak hid behind a porch support beam. *What's this?*

The orc Black Guard kept his arm around Gorva and led her down the street, talking her up with every step that she took. They finally vanished through the swinging doors of a tavern with a corner entrance a few streets down.

Grey Cloak's nimble fingers needled his palms.

This is odd. He scratched his eyebrow. *He's an orc. She's an orc. Maybe they are acquainted. Maybe they are too acquainted.*

Several potential tragic scenarios crossed his mind.

If Tanlin knows I'm here, perhaps he's trying to trap me, and Gorva is bait. Hmm... They could slip out through a back exit. He looked down both ends of the street and checked the rooftop for yonders. *All clear. Maybe too clear.*

He pinched his cloak by the neck and lowered the hood over his eyes. Cold and damp, he missed the comfort and warmth that the Cloak of Legends had brought him. He'd shed water like a duck, and even his toes never became damp or cold. He gritted his teeth and started to venture across the sloppy street toward the tavern.

Donkey Skulls. I'm going in.

11

GREY CLOAK DIDN'T MAKE IT HALFWAY ACROSS THE STREET BEFORE A FAMILIAR voice caught his ear.

"I wouldn't do that if I were you. She's a big orc. She can take care of herself."

He spun around. A figure stood in the shadows of the alley.

He changed direction and approached. Peering through the misty rain into the alley, he asked, "Zora?"

She stepped into full view. "Who else makes sneaking up on you look so easy? I've been tailing you for blocks."

He got boot to boot with her. "I knew you were there."

"No, you didn't." Zora wrapped her arms around him and gave him a fierce hug. "Thank the good dragons you're well! I was worried sick!"

"You don't look sick." He caressed her cheek and tickled her earlobe. "I've missed those pretty eyes of yours. Prison changes an elf."

"Are you wooing me?"

He looked from side to side and said, "I don't see anyone else to woo aside from leaky downspouts."

"You're a little young for me." She moved his hand away from her face. "And seeing how you haven't aged in ten years, it only makes matters worse."

"You aren't going to hold that against me, are you?"

"There are more important matters at the moment." She turned him around to face the tavern. "Your friend said that she could handle herself. She's very charming."

"She's something, all right. Gorva shared the prisoner galleon with us on the trip to the island and proved to be a very worthy ally." He stood on tiptoe and craned his neck. "What is she doing in there?"

"Sergeant Slot asked her to have dinner. She didn't have a choice and played along. But I'm not so sure that she can handle the likes of him. He's no one to fool with. He's dangerous and hasn't been bashful about putting his paws on me a time or two."

"All the more reason to get her out of there," he said. "Let's go around back and make sure they don't slip out."

He crossed the street and ducked into the next alley over, avoiding a puddle of muck, and covered his nose from the stink.

"I promise when we finally have dinner, I'll take you to a place that won't smell so bad."

"How thoughtful of you," she replied as she hopped over a puddle and nearly landed on a black cat, which screeched and bounded away. "Eek! I didn't see that cat. Speaking of which, how is Streak? I take it he found you."

"He's about," Grey Cloak said. "No worries."

"I hope he's not too close. There are Riskers everywhere. Even the runt dragons the citizens own are accounted for. The farther away he is from here, the better."

The end of the alley joined a narrow street that ran along the back of the tavern. Grey Cloak stopped and shielded Zora behind him. Several men were outside the tavern's back door, smoking cigars and moving out waste bins. A Black Guard stood nearby. It wasn't Sergeant Slot, though. It was another man who was smoking a pipe.

"Do the Black Guard hang out here often?"

"They are like flies. They are everywhere." She pulled him back into the alley. "Don't let them see you. They are as nosy as old cranes too."

"Keep your ears open."

He eased back into the alley and put his back to the wall. Zora stood across from him.

"So, I hear that you killed Sash and Honzur."

Zora's eyebrows rose. "It was an awful moment. And I had some help."

"You risked it all to save Streak. I'm grateful, but wasn't Tanlin in trouble? That's why you returned, isn't it?"

She nodded. "Tanlin had it under control by the time I made it here. Once Bull lost contact with Honzur, well, as Tanlin explains it, Bull, not being so smart, was lost."

"Where is Bull now? Dead?"

"You know we aren't killers. It wasn't easy, but Tanlin used his connection with Baron Dorenzo to have Bull taken to prison. He set the entire scene up as a robbery, and Bull was hauled off like a commoner."

Grey Cloak tilted his head over his shoulder and said, "That worked out nicely. What about Squirrel and Katrina? Any word from them?"

"No. As far as I know, they are still in Harbor City. What's wrong, Grey Cloak? You don't sound like you're convinced. Do you doubt me?"

"No, no, of course not." He opened his hands in a peaceful gesture. "I'm elated. You battled the Scourge and survived. Both you and Tanlin are alive and well. I couldn't be happier, really. You know that."

She leaned her head over her shoulder and said, "I'm not convinced you believe me."

"I'm not feeling myself, Zora. Not since I lost the cloak."

"Don't make excuses." She crossed the alley and poked him in the chest. "You don't think I could take down the Scourge by myself, do you?"

"Of course I do. It was a brave thing that you did, but—"

"Don't 'but' me! I risked my life for you and your dragon. I raced back here to save Tanlin, and you doubt my intentions."

"Keep your voice down."

"Don't tell me what to do!"

A Black Guard appeared at the end of the alley. "What is the problem? This isn't a place for lovers' quarrels. Scoot your boots, both of you, or I'll haul you to the magistrate's court."

"So sorry," Grey Cloak said. He quickly turned his back to the soldier and pointed Zora the same way. "My lady has had too much to drink. I'll take her home now."

Zora threw him an elbow. "Too much to drink! I ought to—"

Grey Cloak covered her mouth and said, "Now, now, watch what you say. It could be held against you in court." He gave the Black Guard a head shake. "So sorry. Er, enjoy your evening."

Zora broke away from him at the end of the alley at the tavern's corner entrance. "You really have a way with women, don't you?"

"Can you blame me for being careful? And you shouldn't be any different. These are dangerous times that we live in."

Zora leaned against the wall, put her hands on her knees, and sighed. "I guess you're right. I don't mean to be so sensitive, but times have been hard the last ten years—well, even longer, since before I met you."

"I'm glad you came to your senses."

She shot him a dangerous look.

He offered his hands in surrender. "Only teasing. You know I can't help it."

"Funny."

He moved beside her and looked behind him up into one of the windows. The people were enjoying themselves with song, hot food, and wine. "I bet Gorva is having a good time."

"At least one of us is."

He nudged Zora with his elbow. "Come now, you know I'm fun. Right?"

She gave him a stiff elbow in return. "I'm glad you're back. So, where is the rest of Talon?"

"In the south side of the city, Cemetery Hill, waiting. I'll take you there once Gorva slips free."

"Sounds good. I can't wait to see Dyphestive." She gave him a worried look. "He's well, isn't he?"

The window above them shattered. Sergeant Slot flew over their heads and crashed into the alley.

"Better than him." He looked up and saw Gorva climbing out of the window. She wore a tomato-red-and-gold trim dress. His mouth dropped open. "Problem."

"Problem?" Gorva hopped down into the street. She kicked Sergeant Slot in the ribs, but he was knocked out cold. "He needs to learn his manners."

"Yes, well, we don't have time to teach them now," Grey Cloak said.

The Black Guard at the end of the alley was running their way. More Black Guards hung their heads out of the window, and others spilled out of the front of the tavern.

He pointed back down the alley. "That way! Run!"

12

GORVA TOOK THE LEAD, LOWERED HER SHOULDER, AND PLOWED OVER THE BLACK Guard coming their way.

"Well done," Grey Cloak said as he raced ahead.

He came to a quick halt at the end of the alley. Behind them, half a dozen angry Black Guards shouted at them to stop.

Grey Cloak looked left and right down the narrow street. "Decisions, decisions."

"This way," Zora said after a quick tug on his elbow.

They broke left and sprinted down the rain-slick street. Despite carrying a heavier build, Zora still moved with natural elven grace and agility. She turned right, jumped over waste bins like a cat, and turned left.

The Black Guards' shouts carried down the alley.

"They are calling for reinforcements," Grey Cloak said.

"I know," Zora replied. "They call for reinforcements on everything. Don't worry about that and keep up."

"No problem there," he said. He glanced over his shoulder to see that Gorva was right on his heels, but her stride was short. "Why are you running so funny?"

"Have you ever run in a dress before? This one is too tight!" Gorva shouted at Zora.

"It's the only one I had that would fit you," Zora said. She skidded to a stop and looked down one of the main streets then pointed at the other side of the road. "Let's go."

The moment they crossed the street, Black Guard spilled into the road another block down.

"There they are!" one of them shouted.

Another guard pulled out a small horn made of bone and blew it.

They didn't stand around and wait for more soldiers to arrive. Instead, they renewed their sprint and raced down the next alley.

"Do you have a hiding spot or not?" Grey Cloak asked.

"I do."

"Is it in this city?"

"Har-har," Zora replied.

Black Guard horns could be heard echoing down the alleys and streets. They were smart soldiers, using the horns to guide one another. It would only be a matter of time before the number of troops cut off all their avenues of escape.

"There!" Zora pointed ahead.

They were in the trade district, where all the stonemasons and woodworkers exercised their craft. It was a dead area at that time of night, with plenty of places to hide. She led them into a lumber mill, stirring up the sawdust as they passed.

They hid behind a stack of logs piled eight feet high. Zora sat down, chest heaving.

"This isn't an ideal hiding place. Perhaps for children," Grey Cloak said.

"Gum up. I need to catch my breath. I feel like my lungs are going to burst," Zora said.

"Do you want me to carry you?" Gorva offered. "I'm very strong."

"It's true. She is very strong," Grey Cloak agreed. "And you don't look that heavy."

Zora narrowed her eyes at him. "Watch it. I might not be as fit as I used to be, but that doesn't mean I can't handle myself."

The Black Guards' horns sounded closer.

"They are right on top of us," Gorva said. "We need to keep moving."

Grey Cloak helped Zora to her feet. "Where is the hiding place?"

Panting, Zora said, "We need to keep going north." She gasped. "There's a cathedral that houses the diseased. They won't go there."

"You're joking, right? That's your hiding spot? An infirmary of the soon-to-be dead? No, thanks. Everyone, follow me. We'll keep running until we wear them out and they give up. We can do it. How bruised will their egos be after a bad date?"

Zora took a sharp breath and regained her composure. "They won't stop. It's all a game to them. They use horses and bring dogs."

"Skreee!"

All three of them looked up through the wood mill's skylight and watched a winged shadow pass underneath the dark clouds.

"And dragons, apparently," Grey Cloak said. "It must be a slow night. It seems they don't have anything better to do. Now they can see us from the sky. Great." His gaze swept through the wood mill. "We need to find another way out of here."

"And if we don't?" Gorva asked.

Grey Cloak shook his head. "We'll be dragon food."

13

THE BLACK GUARD CREPT INTO THE WOOD MILL AND SPREAD OUT. THEY MOVED quietly between the stacks of wooden planks and logs of the huge structure. Their chain mail armor clinked, and their metal weapons scraped out of their sheaths.

Grey Cloak took the lead and headed away from the host of soldiers. They kept their heads low, letting the materials hide their path. The darkness gave them excellent cover, but the soldiers lit hooded lamps.

"Zora, use the Scarf of Shadows and get out of here. Go tell Tanlin what's happening, and we'll all meet up at the cemetery where Browning was buried," Grey Cloak whispered.

"I'm not leaving you," she said.

"You have to. Gorva and I will handle this."

He peeked over a pile of planks. Several soldiers were navigating their way toward them.

Squeezing Zora's hand, he said, "Go. Please go."

"I'll get help," she said. "Don't get yourself eaten. It was nice meeting you, Gorva." She lifted the scarf over her nose and vanished.

"That was a useful trick."

Grey Cloak nodded. "Tell me about it." He glanced into the rafters and saw several spots that would be safe to hide in. "Can you climb?"

Gorva nodded.

They moved like cats to the back of the mill, lengthening the distance between them and their cautious pursuers. A ladder on the back wall led up into the storage loft. They climbed the ladder and found that the loft was loaded with shop tools and pieces of scrap wood.

Twenty feet below, the soldiers prowled through the mill, some using lanterns and others navigating the shadows. They were making a thorough search of every nook in the building.

There was a six-foot gap between joists. Grey Cloak took a giant step from one rafter to the next.

"What are you doing?" Gorva whispered.

"We are going to get behind them and slip out," he whispered back. "Make sense?"

She gave a quick nod and started walking across the joists. Her feet scraped away the wood dust, making it trickle down and land on a man's shoulders. He let out a loud sneeze.

Grey Cloak and Gorva hurried across the joists, racing beneath the rafters, which supported a ceiling that was over one hundred feet long. They were halfway across when the soldiers they passed turned their lights toward the ceiling. The funnel of light started at the end, where they climbed up and began to work their way down.

Grabbing Gorva's arm, Grey Cloak said, "Faster."

He continued running across the joists, knocking more sawdust to the ground. Gorva stayed on his heels. As the beams of light swept over the rafters and closed in, they dropped, hit the ground, and rolled forward. When they came to their feet, they sped out of the wood mill, evading the soldiers.

As they exited the lumber yard, he saw horse soldiers coming down the opposite end of the street. Hiding from view, they let the horse soldiers pass, then they dashed into the alley across the street.

"I think we made it," Grey Cloak said as he walked quickly toward the far end of the alley. "It should be a piece of cake getting out of the city now."

A Risker on the back of his middling dragon entered the far end of the alley.

Grey Cloak's blood froze in his veins. "Go back, go back, go back." He turned and bumped right into Gorva. Her eyes were fixed on a second dragon and rider that blocked the alley where they'd entered.

At the same time, both dragons let out ear-splitting screeches. The sound grew louder and turned Grey Cloak's legs to noodles. His knees buckled, and he landed on them and covered his ears.

Gorva was in the same shape he was. The tight confines of the alley amplified the dragons' harrowing shrieks.

"It's days like this I wish I'd never left Havenstock," Grey Cloak muttered.

The Riskers squeezed deeper into the alley, the dragons still shrieking.

"Skreee! Skreee!"

The jarring sound froze Grey Cloak's limbs. He couldn't move or think. *What is happening?*

"We have to get out of here!" Gorva said.

"I know!" He fought his way back to his feet in time to see the chest plates of the dragons glow the color of fire. "It looks like they are going to roast us, thanks to your bad dinner date!"

"I wasn't the one that was bad!"

The shrieking stopped.

"Surrender or be incinerated!" the Risker saddled on the dragon facing Grey Cloak called.

Grey Cloak hollered back, "I believe there has been a grave misunderstanding." He was buying time. The only way of escape was up, and he couldn't fly, and he was pretty sure that Gorva couldn't either. If they tried to climb, the dragons would torch them. "You see—"

"Silence!" the Risker yelled back. "Get on your knees and place your hands on your head."

"I don't see any way out of this," Grey Cloak admitted. If he'd had the Cloak of Legends, he could handle the dragon fire, but without it, trying anything at all would only get them killed. "We can surrender and live a little longer or run and be turned into charcoal. Do you have a preference?"

Gorva dropped to her knees and said, "We'll fight another day."

"Take off your sword belt, elf, and toss it toward me," the Risker said. "And keep your hands where I can see them."

Grey Cloak loosened his belt and tossed it at the dragon's feet then placed his hands on his head.

"That will do." The Risker sniggered and said, "Let's torch them anyway."

14

THE EYES OF THE RISKER'S DRAGON WERE LIKE BURNING RUBIES. SMOKE BEGAN TO flow over its teeth and out of its mouth.

Grey Cloak and Gorva both came to their feet.

"If we are going to die, we'll die standing!" Gorva said.

"Have it your way!" the Risker said. He patted his dragon on the neck.

The dragon took in a breath. A glowing dragon charm appeared at eye level between Grey Cloak and the dragon. So did the woman holding it.

"Zora!" Grey Cloak said.

The dragon's gaze locked on the stone.

"Where did you get that?" the Risker demanded. "Give it to me!"

"Grey Cloak," Zora said as her hand trembled, "I don't know what I'm doing."

He and Gorva moved closer to her.

"Keep it before the dragon's eyes. Don't let anything distract you," he said.

The second dragon approached from the opposite end of the alley. Its eyes were locked on the dragon charm as well.

Grey Cloak felt something burning a hole in his pants pocket. "Zooks, I forgot all about it." He'd been so obsessed with losing his cloak that he'd forgotten entirely about the dragon charm he'd found in the Burnt Hills. When he fished it out, it glowed like a star. He held it toward the other dragon, stopping its approach.

"Give me those stones!" the Risker demanded.

"What do we do?" Zora asked.

"I've never used one before. Tell them to stay back, but don't ask them to do something they wouldn't like or that would make them hurt themselves," he said, recalling his training at Hidemark. There, he'd learned about the dragon charms and how they could be used. Riskers that didn't bond with dragons the same way as naturals like Grey Cloak could use them. "Let me try something."

While Zora kept her dragon at bay with her charm, Grey Cloak approached the other. The middling dragon was a female. He could tell by the lighter scales on her chest plate. "Easy, girl. I bet you don't like that nasty man on your back. Why don't you throw him off?"

The dragon tilted its head and made a rattling sound in its throat.

"Don't listen to him!" The Risker hit the dragon on top of the skull with his mailed fist. "You obey me!"

From behind the dragon, a tail rose like a cobra. It slipped around the Risker's waist, jerked him out of the saddle, and slammed him into the alley wall. *Smack!* The Risker was either dead or knocked out.

Grey Cloak didn't care, but he did notice a dragon charm mounted in the man's chest plate. "Gorva, get that dragon charm!" He rushed over to Zora and put his charm beside hers. They burned brighter. "Tell the dragon to toss his rider."

"Toss your rider!" she commanded.

The dragon didn't budge, but its rider stood in his saddle, holding his stone. "You have no power over me! This is my dragon! My dragon!"

Grey Cloak offered encouraging words. "Envision what you want the dragon to do. Bond with it."

She nodded.

The dragon bucked like a mule, tossing the Risker head over heels into the air. Before the man landed, the dragon's tail whipped out and batted the Risker into the wall. It whipped the Risker several times, busting the man's bones inside his armor.

Zora gasped. "Did I do that?"

"I don't think your new friend cared for his rider." Grey Cloak hurried over to the dead Risker and took his dragon charm from him. When he turned back, the dragon was nuzzling Zora. "I think you made a new friend."

The dragon licked her with his long black tongue. Zora cringed and said, "Now what do I do?"

Grey Cloak placed his hands on her shoulders and said, "The first thing you can do is accept my apology for ever doubting you."

"I'll think about it."

"Second..." He pulled the Scarf of Shadows over her nose. "Bring Tanlin up to speed and meet us at the cemetery, the same as before."

As she faded into invisibility, she said, "How are you going to get out of here? The Black Guard will still come for you."

"Don't worry about us. We'll take the dragons," he said, patting the dragon she'd charmed on the cheek. "If he'll have us."

"You take your own dragon!" Gorva hollered down the alley. She'd climbed into the saddle of the female dragon and gripped a dragon charm. "I'm taking this one."

Grey Cloak felt a soft kiss on his cheek and heard Zora say, "See you soon, Grey Cloak."

"Soon won't be soon enough," he replied as he grabbed his sword belt and climbed into the dragon's saddle.

The Black Guard blocked off the ends of the alley and had begun to creep in. He and Gorva turned their dragons back to back.

Gorva grinned as she locked her fingers around the reins. "I can't wait to fly. Don't you love it?"

"I hate it," he said and wrapped his fingers in the reins.

"Really?"

"Really." He rubbed his dragon's neck and said, "Let's see what you can do. Take us out of here, and feel free to use your flame."

Like charging chickens, the dragons sprinted down the alley in opposite directions. Nearing the end, they spit geysers of flames out of their mouths.

The Black Guard scrambled for their lives, racing away from the flames, which set their boots on fire. The burning men rolled across the ground and dived into water troughs.

Grey Cloak's dragon ran down the street, beating his wings and sending terror-stricken citizens running over one another to get out of his path. The dragon lifted off the ground and soared upward into the sky. Raven Cliff diminished beneath them, and Gorva and her dragon flew alongside.

"This is wonderful!" Gorva shouted with the wind tearing through her braided hair. "I love it!"

Grey Cloak's stomach turned inside out, and he said, "Good for you!"

15

Surrounded by the dawn sun shining down on foggy rolling hills, tombstones, and dandelions, Grey Cloak and Dyphestive stood over their old friend Browning's grave. The tombstone had the salty old warrior's name chiseled at the top, and the saying beneath it read: Dirty Acorns, I'm Dead.

Dyphestive took a knee and started scraping away the grit that had built up over the tombstone's lettering with his fingers, then he pulled out a few weeds and tossed them aside. He sniffed and said, "Of all the ones we lost, I think I miss him the most."

"He had a way about him, didn't he?" Grey Cloak added.

"Yes, he did. Very memorable." Dyphestive grabbed the tombstone, which was slightly askew, and straightened it. "That's better."

Cemetery Hill was covered in overgrowth. When they'd first come, it was in far better shape. The grit on most of the tombstones had been cleaned away, and flowers were planted near the graves. The flower beds had all run wild. The caretakers that oversaw the grounds appeared to have moved on, leaving the dead to be covered in overgrowth and forgotten.

"I can't believe how much this place has changed in only ten years. It looks like a jungle," Grey Cloak said. "Will the rest of the world look like this if we don't take care of it?"

"The weeds will take over if you don't pull them out by the root," Jakoby said. He was sitting against a gnarled, rotting tree. "They choke the life out of everything but feed themselves until there is nothing left to feed on."

Razor chopped at the tall grasses with his sword. "Even if you cut them, they still come back. You have to kill them." He stared at the sheer cliffs that Raven Cliff rested on. "How long are we going to wait here?"

"Until Zora comes, however long that will be," Grey Cloak said. "She'll be along. Shortly, I'm sure."

Gorva paced the grounds with a scowl on her face. She hadn't cracked a smile since they landed and set the dragons free per Grey Cloak's instructions. She kept muttering with her fists bunched at her sides. "What is the point in having a dragon charm if you can't use it?"

Grey Cloak turned his attention to her and said, "You have to let it go, Gorva. We can't run with the dragons. Black Frost will come after them. The farther away they are from him and us, the better."

"A dragon would be useful," she stated.

"Not if the dragon is dead. And no thanks to you, we have the Black Guard searching for us."

Gorva crossed her arms and glowered at him. "What is that supposed to mean?"

"You threw Sergeant Slot through a window. All you needed to do was slip out the back."

"He tried to kiss me," she said.

Razor chuckled. "I'll make a note that you don't like being kissed near windows."

"It's not funny, fool."

He bowed and rolled his wrist. "A thousand apologies."

"The point is, Gorva, your actions could have gotten us killed. No one faults you, but we have to be smart about how we act. We can't draw attention to ourselves, or all of Black Frost's forces will be after us. We have an edge while he still doesn't know that we're alive. The longer he thinks we're dead, the better."

"Well, one thing is for certain—we are in a great place for dead people," Gorva said. Her nostrils flared, and she let out a sigh. "I miss my dragon."

Grey Cloak tossed his charm in the air and caught it. "At least we have two more charms that we can use. They should come in handy like they did today."

"How come we were able to get the dragons to respond to our charms over the Riskers?" Gorva asked as she eyed her gemstone.

"Huh, I think we surprised them. That and the fact that I don't think the dragons like their riders. I learned about dragons and the charms from the Sky Riders at Hidemark and at Dark Mountain too. A rider with natural gifts can bond with a dragon without the charms. Like me and Streak. Those riders are naturals and have unique powers." He wiggled his fingertips, and tiny blue strands of lightning danced on them. "But these other riders, they aren't all naturals. They need the charms to control the dragons, and they have to be trained. Dragons have minds of their own, the same as horses but stronger. They'd rather be wild and free, but they can be tamed or broken. I think the choice between us and their riders was easy for them. Ultimately, they wanted to be free, like you and me."

Gorva nodded. "That's what this is all about, isn't it? Freedom."

Looking off into the distance, he said, "Freedom to live and choose as we please. At least, that is what drives me." He moved to a rise among the graves and spied someone coming. He recognized Zora's stride. "It's Zora."

Jakoby and Dyphestive rose and stood with Grey Cloak.

Zora was panting when she jogged up to them, pulling a small sled behind her. She stopped and put her hands on her knees.

"Are you well?" Grey Cloak asked, eyeing the sled.

"We need to go. They are looking for us everywhere, and it's only a matter of time before they come here."

"They should be more preoccupied with finding the dragons than us. It should buy us some time." Grey Cloak could hear more dragons shrieking from the roofs of the city. He shook his head. "All of this over a bad date?"

"No," Zora said, picking her pack up again. "All of this because you flew off on two dragons and two Black Guard are dead." She took a knee by the sled and removed the blanket that covered it. It was loaded with Grey Cloak's and Dyphestive's gear, which she'd taken from Harbor Lake, including Dyphestive's two-handed iron sword. "Well, grab your gear. I'm not going to drag it anymore."

Dyphestive picked up his sword and squeezed and twisted the leather grip. "I've missed my old friend."

"Good," Zora said. "You can have it."

16

IRON HILLS

THE SOUTHERN PLAINS OF WESTERLUND ENDED WHERE THE IRON HILLS BEGAN. Endless leagues of tall rocky hilltops created the perfect border between Sulter Slay and the Westerlund territories. The Iron Hills' rugged terrain was notorious for countless dangers such as avalanches, pitfalls, and ambushes from goblin raiders.

Talon traveled along the base of the Iron Hills, keeping its eyes on the skies for any pursuing dragons. They'd made a clean escape from Raven Cliff and kept moving nonstop on horseback toward their next destination.

Grey Cloak and Zora shared a saddle. She leaned with her cheek against his back and her arms around his waist. She talked, but it was more of a mumble.

"I mentioned the Ruins of Thannis to Tanlin to see what he knew. He said only a fool would venture in there without a sorceress or a priest. 'Dark magic thrives in those pits. Be wary.'"

"Lucky for us, I have some magic at my disposal." Grey Cloak massaged the air with his right hand. "We'll manage. Besides, we are only going in to take a look, in case Batram sent me on a wild goose chase."

"We need a priest or sorceress like Tatiana. Someone from the Wizard Watch, Tanlin said. Do you remember the ghost we met, Bella Von May, in the hills of Crow Valley?"

He nodded. "Yes, she almost killed you. Killed us."

"Well, Tanlin says that the Ruins of Thannis will be filled with spirits like her and even worse."

"Has Tanlin ever been there?"

"No."

"Well, he could be wrong."

"And if he isn't?"

"I'll take my chances."

JAKOBY STOOD on the banks of the Inland Sea River, watching the water disappear into the plunging depths of the Outer Ring. He was joined by the others, who stood beside him, marveling at the great expanse between them and the edges of Monarch City.

"Home never looked so far away," he said.

A stone overlook vast enough to hold the entire group was wedged between the river and the rocks of the Iron Hills. They moved out onto it.

Razor looked over the edge and asked, "Grey Cloak, do you even have any idea where to find this place? All I see is a giant watery pit. How are we supposed to find a city that is buried? I don't see an entrance."

"No, but we know that there have been expeditions there before," Jakoby said.

Razor shook his head. "No, we've *heard* that there have been expeditions. But how do we know if we weren't on one?"

"Don't be a fool. It is well-known that men ventured into Thannis and never came back. How else can you explain so many people that are missing?"

Razor pointed down into the Outer Ring and said, "Maybe they fell down there!"

Jakoby gripped the pommel of his sword. "I tire of your petty comments."

"Go ahead and draw, big fella," Razor replied as his fingers drummed on the pommels of his swords. "I'd love to see how good you really are."

Dyphestive stepped between them. "Enough squabbling. If either one of you wants to fight, you're going to have to go through me. I suggest you settle your egos."

Razor waved him off. "All is well. Only bickering." He patted his belly. "Besides, I'm getting hungry. I wouldn't mind a plate of hog chops and eggs. A flagon of ale wouldn't hurt too. There is a small town north of here. They make a good biscuit."

Grey Cloak moved along the rim of the stone overlook. "It's not a bad idea. Someone in the area must know something if other expeditions have passed through as you say. It wouldn't hurt to ask. Make camp, and I'll head into town with Zora and ask some questions."

"I'm coming too," Razor insisted.

"I want to go," Gorva said.

"Hold your horses. It's a small town. We can't all show up and spook them. Let Zora and me handle that."

"There won't be any need for any of that."

"Really?" Grey Cloak asked as he spun on his heel and faced the source of the objection. "And why is that—you!"

Several members of Talon gasped.

The ghostly form of Dalsay stood among them. He hadn't changed since the last time Grey Cloak saw him. His eyes were intense and probing, his beard was neatly trimmed, and he wore the same black-and-grey checkered robes with golden trim on the sleeves and hem.

Gorva drew her sword. "A spirit!" She rushed Dalsay and chopped right through him.

"He's a friend, Gorva," Grey Cloak said. "At least, I hope he is." He looked Dalsay dead on. "Are you?"

"I serve the Wizard Watch, the same as I always have," Dalsay replied in a haunting voice that carried.

Grey Cloak's skin prickled. "Then why are you here?"

"I came to warn you. Do not enter Thannis the Fallen. A certain death awaits."

17

GREY CLOAK ROLLED HIS EYES. "STOP BEING CRYPTIC AND VAGUE, DALSAY. FACING death is what we do. It's how we came to be here. Are you here to help us or spook us?"

"I am helping," Dalsay answered. "By telling you not to go into Thannis."

"The only way I'm not going in there is if I know for certain that the Figurine of Heroes is not in there. Do you know where the figurine is?"

"I do. It's in the Ruins of Thannis," Dalsay replied.

"Great! How do I get there?"

"*I*, you say. Very troubling. Why do you insist on using the figurine? Is it for your gain or for the gain of others?"

Feeling his company's eyes on him, Grey Cloak pointed at his chest and said, "It's not for *me*. I need it to get rid of the underlings. They killed Tatiana. I'd think that you'd want to be rid of them too."

"Tatiana is not dead," Dalsay stated.

Zora's face lit up, and she asked, "She lives?"

"Indeed," the wizard replied.

Grey Cloak gave Dalsay a doubtful look and said, "She's not a ghost, is she?"

Dalsay shook his head. "No, she is very much alive but is enslaved by the underlings now. She's been searching for you all these years, or at least I have, for her benefit."

Tatiana and Grey Cloak had had their differences, but it warmed his heart to know that she was still alive. She'd risked her life in the towers so that he and Dyphestive could escape.

"Well, this is easy," Dyphestive said. "If we get the figurine, we can free Tatiana. We owe her that much."

"No," Dalsay said. "Tatiana sent me to find you to warn you to let this matter play out. The Figurine of Heroes is too dangerous. It took death for me to understand why, but finally, I agree with Tatiana. Leave the figurine be. The underlings, Verbard and Catten, are more preoccupied with controlling the Time Mural and leaving for their world than staying on this one."

"Are you telling me that those fiendish men are going to leave of their own accord and let us be?" Grey Cloak asked with an incredulous look. "Certainly you know better than that, Dalsay. They serve Black Frost, don't they? He won't let that happen. He needs them."

Dalsay shook his head and said, "No, he doesn't. The Wizard Watch is all but destroyed. Our craft is abandoned. The underlings saw to that in exchange for working on the Time Murals. Tatiana aides them in hopes they will soon depart. She is close."

"She is a fool, Dalsay!" Grey Cloak poked his finger through the ghost's face. "And you are a fool too. If anything, you are doing the underlings' bidding by trying to talk us out of it."

"I don't serve the underlings! I serve the Watch!" Dalsay fired back.

"No, you serve yourselves. Anya warned me about your kind, and I'd have been wise to listen. If I'd never entered that tower, the last ten years never would have happened. We wouldn't be in the mess we're in." His cheeks burned. "Tatiana took me in there, and look what happened."

Dyphestive placed his arm over Grey Cloak's shoulder and led him away. "Easy, Grey. I think Dalsay is trying to help in his own... well, mysterious way."

"Every time they stick their noses in our affairs, the worst happens."

"That's not true. You know they've been there for us."

"Really, Dyphestive? You think so? I don't." He slipped away from Dyphestive and placed his attention square on Dalsay. "Will you show us the way to the ruins or not?"

"I will, but I must warn you—"

"I know. Death will come. Show us the way."

Dalsay nodded. "You'll have to leave the horses. And most of your gear. The trek is dangerous." He walked across the overlook and into the air as if he were on an invisible bridge then turned to face them and pointed down at the rock. "There is the path."

Grey Cloak leaned over the overlook and craned his neck. A narrow ledge with handholds could be seen on the face of the drop-off. It zigzagged back and forth over one hundred feet and vanished underneath the waterfall created by the Inland Sea River. He shook his head, leaned back up, and said, "I hope everybody likes to climb."

The entire group took a long look over the edge.

"Ah, I see it," Gorva said. She'd suited back up in her leather armor, which Zora had returned to her. "I've climbed worse."

Razor whistled and said, "I haven't. Looks like we're going to need a really long rope." He caught everyone looking at him. "What? I'm a swordsman, not a mountain goat. What about you, Jakoby? Do you think you can climb down that like a squirrel?"

Jakoby shook his head. "No, I'll be using a rope."

Dyphestive had already started tying a rope to his horse's saddle. He threw the rope over the rim and gestured to Jakoby and Razor. "After you."

"Great," Razor said as he lifted the rope from the lip. "I'll go first."

"What about the horses? Who is going to stay with them and our gear?" Zora asked.

Razor stopped his descent and said, "Well, they are going to need protection. And seeing how I'm the best protector, I'll volunteer to stay."

"Zora, I was hoping you would stay," Grey Cloak suggested.

"If you are going to steal something, you're going to need a thief." Zora lowered herself over the rock and started to climb down. She winked at him. "See you at the bottom."

Leena slipped in right behind her, followed by Gorva. They traversed down the sheer climb, using the small handholds and narrow ledges like they'd done it one hundred times before.

Razor elbowed Grey Cloak and grinned. "You know what they say—ladies first. And it looks like I'm staying on the deck."

18

WIZARD WATCH

Tatiana lugged a golden jug filled with wine down the corridor. Her shoulders sagged, and her tattered wizard robes hid chains that linked her bony ankles and dragged across the floor. Her hair was a mess, and dark circles were under her eyes. She yawned and moved on, dreading her next stop in Verbard and Catten's chambers.

The towers of the Wizard Watch had been her home most of her life, and they had turned into a place of death and disaster. They had changed from being a sanctuary of beauty and splendor to a crypt with no hope for escape.

She passed a beautiful fountain whose waters had long gone dry. All the fish that had thrived in the pool were long dead. The air was stale and reeked of rotten flesh.

Life had been awful since the underlings arrived. In a matter of minutes, the devious pair took over everything. They killed Uruiah, the highest-ranking wizard of the Watch, and destroyed her evil brood. Uruiah and her wicked brood had joined forces with Black Frost and betrayed the Wizard Watch by coming for Grey Cloak, Dyphestive, and the Figurine of Heroes. They came to kill them all.

Tatiana never saw it coming. Her faith in the Wizard Watch was shattered.

But that wasn't the worst of her troubles. Against her objections, Grey Cloak had used the figurine to bail them out. Instead, two horrors from another world arrived and turned the tables on Uruiah. With power the likes of which Tatiana had never seen, the underlings toyed with the Wizard Watch and blasted them out of existence. But the victory for good was short-lived. As the underlings started to fade, they sent the Figurine of Heroes through the Time Mural, allowing their essence to stay. Grey Cloak, Dyphestive, and Streak fled into the mural and were lost, and Tatiana was trapped.

The underlings spared her and her mentor, Gossamer. But the life she'd known would never be the same.

"Hurry along, elf woman," Catten called as she passed through an archway and entered their chamber. It was same chamber where the Time Mural was hidden from view with curtains. "I swear, you become slower by the day. Pick it up. I thought elves were supposed to be quick."

Tatiana hurried into the room.

Verbard and Catten sat side by side on two pewter thrones fashioned for them. They were small in build and had grey skin and fine rat-like fur. The hair on their heads was coarse and black, their teeth were sharp, and the pointed tips of their fingernails needled the armrests of their chairs. Both of them wore pitch-black robes with traces of silver patterns in the lining. The only features that set them apart were their eyes. Catten's irises were pure gold, and Verbard's were as polished as silver, but the latter's head was rounder.

Verbard sat to the left of Catten, and he twirled a black cane with a silver ball tip that had once belonged to the former high wizard of the tower, Gossamer.

The chains binding Tatiana's feet moved with a life of their own and tripped her. She stumbled and fell, hitting her knee hard on the ground as the carafe of wine bounced off the floor and spilled all over.

"You clumsy fool!" Verbard said. "We demand wine, and you spill it all over. What is wrong with you, elf woman? Why can't you keep your feet?" He tapped the cane on the floor. "Answer me!"

"I'm sorry." Tatiana pushed up on her trembling bony arms. "I-I tripped. I'll clean it up right away." She set the golden carafe upright and started wiping up the spilled wine with her robes. She kept her eyes down and said, "I'll fetch more."

Verbard leaned forward and said, "Listen to her, brother. She speaks to us as if she is an equal."

"No, master, I—"

Whack! Verbard hit her across the back with his cane. "I am not your master. I am Lord Verbard. He is Lord Catten. How ignorant are you?"

Tatiana sobbed. "I'm sorry. I am weary. I forget... Lord."

Whack!

"Aaauuggh!" she cried and collapsed onto the floor.

"Why do you torment her so much?" Catten asked. "If you break her back, she won't be able to serve our purposes."

"I like to hear her scream. It's delightful. And her shrieks have a special ring to them. They're music to my ears." Verbard leaned back and made himself comfy in his pillowed chair. "Up, elf woman. Fetch us more port from the wine cellar. I'm tired of your watery wine. I need something stronger."

Tatiana rose, kept her eyes down, and said, "As you wish, Lord Verbard. I'll hurry."

She had more marks on her back than she could count, but she didn't care. The more vulnerable she seemed, the greater trust she could gain. Ever since the underlings had taken over, she played the part of a feeble sorceress, all but help-less without the Star of Light, which Lord Catten wore around his neck. Her plan had allowed her to live thus far. Others that showed defiance or joined the underlings were tormented and oftentimes killed quickly.

Gossamer entered the room. The last ten years had worn the formerly young-looking elf's face. Crow's-feet were in the corners of his eyes, and he had burn marks on his cheeks from the power in Catten's clawed fingers. His long hair, which had once been neatly parted with strands of white on one side and black on the other, had grown out and mixed together. His black-and-white checkered robes were worn and frayed at the hem. Chains rattled underneath his robes when he walked farther inside, politely bowed, and made an announcement. "Lord Catten and Lord Verbard, we have visitors that seek your audience on the roof."

Catten asked, "Who is on our roof?"

"It is the leaders of the Riskers, Commander Dirklen and his sister, Commander Magnolia. They seek your audience."

"Who?" Verbard asked his brother.

"Humans, the ones who ride the dragons," Catten replied.

"Oh," Verbard said as he waved Gossamer on. "They'll have to wait."

19

THE WINE CELLAR IN THE BOWELS OF THE TOWER FILLED AN ENTIRE FLOOR. RACKS of wooden shelving started on the outer ring of the circular room and surrounded a smaller ring, creating wine rack after wine rack toward the center, where only one small ring of wine bottles remained.

Tatiana navigated through the maze of wine racks, which towered above her. The shelves were filled with wines from cities in every one of the nine territories, collected over the centuries. Some bottles were over a thousand years old and had labels written in a language that was long forgotten.

She removed two ancient bottles of port and wiped the dust away from the green glass with a towel. The sound of rattling chains caught her ear, and she turned. "Gossamer, you shouldn't be down here."

"I wanted to see how you're doing. I saw what Verbard did to you."

"My skin's thick. I can take it." She navigated back toward the exit, where a drinking lounge was located, then grabbed an empty crystal carafe from one of the bars and emptied the bottle of port into it. "They like crystal. They won't break it. Do you know why the Troubled Twins have arrived?"

"No," he said, sweeping his long hair over his pointed ears, "but I find it humorous that the underlings are keeping them waiting. They have little regard for anyone in this world at all. Anyone else would be rolling out the red carpet to let them in."

"That's why I want to be up there when they are given an audience. I want to see what they have to say." She brushed by Gossamer and briefly embraced him. "Stay strong."

He nodded.

Tatiana went back to the Time Mural chamber and filled the underlings' goblets to their rims.

Verbard sipped his goblet halfway down before Catten even touched his.

"You'd better drink, brother. You know how wordy these humans can be." His eyes slid over to Tatiana, who stood nearby with her arms behind her back. Gossamer was in the room with her. "I see you brought a second bottle, but it won't be a gift for our guests. No, their gift is an audience with me."

"Yes, Lord Verbard," she said.

"Hmm," he grunted. "Life is so much better than death, except for times like this. Shall we see them in and get this over with?"

Catten fiddled with the Star of Light. The diamond twinkled in his fingers. "Agreed. Bring them in. And see to it that they are properly examined. There is always a chance they are imposters stowing away the figurine."

"As you wish, Lord Verbard." Gossamer hurried away and vanished through the archway.

Verbard's fingernails needled his metal armrest, making tiny divots in the metal and creating a sound like rain on a roof. "The sooner we depart this world, the better. Imagine, a world without underlings. How miserable."

Catten took his first sip of port and said, "Patience, brother. It's only a small matter of time until we master the Time Mural, then we'll be reunited with our family."

Verbard bared his teeth and replied, "And vengeance will be ours."

A few minutes later, Gossamer announced the arrival of Dirklen and Magnolia, who stormed into the room and stood before the underlings. They were a handsome pair with wavy blond hair down past the shoulders. Tatiana had seen the pair on and off over the years. They towered over the underlings.

"How dare you search us, underlings?" Dirklen poked his finger at both of them. "We are not commoners! We are the rulers of this world, your allies, and you treat us like the enemy! Apologize!"

Verbard cocked his head, tapped his fingertips together, and said, "I don't know the meaning of the word."

Dirklen pulled his sword free.

Verbard's fingertips danced with lightning. "One more step, human, and I will cook you inside and out."

Dirklen's long sword flared with mystic fire. "Don't trifle with me, underling. One poke from my steel, and I'll end you. And I'll feed you to my dragon too."

"Enough of this puffery," Magnolia said as she pushed Dirklen's sword down. "We'll make Black Frost fully aware of this insubordination. If they don't want to cooperate, I'm certain he'd be glad to tear the top off this candle they hide in and let them fend for themselves."

The fire on Verbard's fingertips died, and he cowered behind his hands. "Oh no, please don't abandon me in the world full of inferior people that I can destroy with a thought." His smug look returned. "Are you finished letting your feelings be hurt, human?"

"It's Dirklen!"

"Dirklen, human... all of you look the same to me." Verbard swallowed the rest of his port. "Ah, now, will you put away your sword and share your business? You are interrupting very important work."

Magnolia and Dirklen glanced over their shoulders as the curtains drew in from the Time Mural and shook their heads.

"Yes, you appear to be very busy in this very empty room," Magnolia said.

Dirklen sheathed his sword, but the prickly atmosphere remained. "We have news. A common enemy has resurfaced after all these years."

"Common enemy? Interesting. I didn't think we had any," Verbard replied. "And who might they be?"

Tatiana's back straightened. Out of the corner of her eye, she noticed Gossamer slightly turn his ear. Her heart leapt when she heard Magnolia say, "Grey Cloak and Dyphestive have returned."

20

VERBARD OFFERED CATTEN A PUZZLED LOOK AND ASKED, "WHO IS THIS HUMAN talking about, and why should we be concerned?"

"Do you remember when we arrived?" Catten turned his gaze on Magnolia. "I believe the human is referring to the elf that summoned us. He is the one called Grey Cloak, is he not?"

"Precisely," she said.

Verbard's back straightened. "Does he have the figurine?"

"Ah, *now* you're interested in what we have to say. My, how the tables have turned, underling," Dirklen said while offering a cocky smirk that drew a deep frown from Verbard and Catten.

Tatiana tingled all over. She'd hoped that Grey Cloak and Dyphestive had survived and would reappear again. The fact that they had was nothing short of a miracle. She'd been able to communicate with Dalsay in secret, and he'd been searching for years for the brothers. At least she could tell him they were out there, if he had not found them already.

Finally, we have a chance against these fiends.

She'd given Dalsay orders to tell the brothers to stay away from the Wizard Watch. The underlings would see them coming from leagues away. As long as the underlings remained inside the towers, the evil brothers were protected from the figurine's powers. It was imperative that the figurine didn't make it within the tower's arcane walls.

But that wasn't the only reason Tatiana wanted the brothers to stay away. The underlings were brilliant magicians with great minds and were testing the Time Mural's powers and learning how to control it. If they mastered the Time Mural and returned to their home, it was possible that she could use the Time Mural to defeat Black Frost once and for all. She needed that knowledge, and she would do anything to get it.

The underlings rose from their chairs and floated, glowering down at the twins. The hems of their robes hung inches above the floor, but their feet could not be seen. They moved toward the twins.

Dirklen and Magnolia stepped back.

Verbard stuck his nose down in Dirklen's face. "Where are these nuisances?"

"Oh, now you want our help, I see," Dirklen said as he returned a smile. "The truth of the matter is that I don't know exactly where they are. I only know where they have been."

"Don't toy with me, human," Verbard warned. "I'll fry your grey matter with a thought."

Dirklen's jaw muscles clenched, his nostrils flared, and he leaned into Verbard's face. "Listen to me, Port Breath. We have an alliance. Your purpose and our purpose is one, and you are only here because Black Frost allows it. He has a vested interest in you and this portal. Do your duty, and we will take care of ours."

"We can't do our duty if the elf shows up with the figurine, human," Verbard said. His right index finger glowed red-hot like metal in a forge, and he held it by Dirklen's face.

Sweat beaded above on the Risker's brow.

"Put an end to these people."

"Rest assured that our finest hunters are tracking them down as we speak. It's only a matter of time before we catch up with them, if we haven't already." Dirklen brushed the underling's hand away from his face. "And if you ever stick that finger in my face again, I'll cut it off and feed it to you. Come on, Magnolia. We have better things to do."

As quickly as they arrived, Dirklen and Magnolia departed, with Gossamer trailing after them.

Tatiana hadn't smiled in years, but she smiled on the inside as a warm feeling washed through her. *They're rattled. Who better to do it than Grey Cloak and Dyphestive? Like halfling beggars, they keep showing up.*

Verbard wrung his hands. "Brother, we need to accelerate our efforts."

"I couldn't agree more." Catten waved his open hands in a smooth circular motion, and the curtains parted, revealing the archway of the Time Mural.

The ominous archway had a continuous series of images that changed in the wink of the eye. It showed green fields, stark mountains, lagoons, and battles raging on other worlds.

Tatiana rubbed the goose bumps on her arms. Every time she viewed the Time Mural, a thrill went through her. More than once, she'd toyed with the idea of jumping into the mural and making a hasty escape, the same as Grey Cloak and Dyphestive had done. She had a duty, though, to the Wizard Watch and, more importantly, to her friends. Diving into the portal would be the easy way out.

Catten floated across the room to a pedestal the underlings had erected. He removed a silk blanket that covered the pedestal, revealing a square top filled with large gemstones in a variety of colors spread out evenly like they were part of a game board.

The underlings had worked tirelessly on the Time Mural pedestal and its pieces. They'd invested a great deal of time enchanting each and every gemstone they recovered from the Wizard Watch's vaults. The vast majority of the gemstones were carefully embedded in the archway stones of the Time Mural. Diamonds, rubies, emeralds, amethysts, jade, moonstones, and garnets the size of eyeballs accompanied finger-wide bricks of gold, silver, and copper that filled the gaps between the arch's stones.

Catten plucked a diamond the size of his finger from the pedestal then rolled it between his palms and said, "Are you ready to try again, brother?"

Verbard's slender fingers massaged his chin. "I've been meditating long enough. It's time to conquer our destiny." His eyes slid over to Tatiana. "Elf woman, come here. Your day has come."

21

RUINS OF THANNIS

BEHIND THE WATERFALL CREATED BY THE INLAND SEA RIVER, A CAVE-LIKE PASSAGE was burrowed into the rock. Led by the luminous form of Dalsay, the members of Talon began a slow descent into darkness over one hundred feet below the ground.

They'd been walking for hours through the narrow passage, which was barely three shoulder breadths wide. At the front, Dyphestive and Jakoby walked with their necks bent and their shoulders hunched.

"You wouldn't happen to know how much farther it is, would you, Dalsay?" Grey Cloak asked. "It's not as if my feet are sore or anything, but the scenery is very bleak."

"The edges of Thannis stood leagues away from the edge of the Outer Ring before the Iron Hills swallowed it," Dalsay replied without looking back. "At this pace, it will be hours longer."

"Huh, I don't suppose there are any tavern stops along the way," Dyphestive quipped.

Without a word, Dalsay continued his brisk pace. Even without a solid body, he still walked through the passage as men did.

Grey Cloak caught Dyphestive looking back at him and gave him a shrug, which Dyphestive returned. He knew what Dyphestive was thinking. Dalsay was a cryptic sort, and he kept the true intent of his missions tight to his chest. Grey Cloak hadn't liked that when they first met him, and he still didn't. Members of the Wizard Watch, like Dalsay and Tatiana, had played games then and were still playing them.

"Tell me, Dalsay, how is it that you know that the Figurine of Heroes is hidden in these depths?" Dyphestive asked.

"Good question," Grey Cloak agreed.

"My answer isn't going to change the situation," Dalsay said.

"I don't like him," Gorva, who carried a torch, said quietly to Zora. "He's misleading."

"Most wizards are," Zora replied.

"Now isn't the time to build mistrust, Dalsay!" Grey Cloak said. "We've all been through enough. Tell me, tell *us*, how you know for certain that the figurine rests down here... somewhere."

"What makes you think that it is down here?" Dalsay replied.

"If you aren't going to help, why are you here?"

"I didn't come to help. I came to warn you." Dalsay stopped and turned. "If you insist—"

"I do," Grey Cloak replied and caught approving looks from his comrades. "We all do."

Dalsay nodded and said, "I know the figure is here because you told me."

"That's impossible. You're repeating the lie that Batram gave me," he said. "It couldn't have been me, because I've been with Dyphestive ever since it was lost. We're going to need a better explanation than that, Dalsay."

"I don't have a greater explanation to give you. It was you that told me it was here." Dalsay turned and resumed his trek.

Grey Cloak caught everyone looking at him. He threw up his hands and said, "It wasn't me. I swear it. I think. Dyphestive and I haven't been apart since we jumped through the Time Mural. Right, Dyphestive?"

"You haven't been out of my sight." Dyphestive wiggled his eyebrows. "Maybe the Time Mural made another one of you." A whimsical smile crossed his face. "Maybe it made another one of me."

"Two Grey Cloaks?" Zora rolled her eyes. "As if one didn't get us in enough trouble."

"Goy," he said as Zora pushed by him and smirked. "You'd be lucky if there were two of me. You all would."

The company moved as one, leaving Grey Cloak talking to himself in the dark.

"Two of me... huh, now that would be interesting."

OVER A LEAGUE of nonstop walking came to an end where the passage bottomed out in an endless black cavern with a huge field covered in glowing dandelions with floating white seeds.

Zora bent over and plucked one. "It's beautiful." She blew the white floaties away, and they drifted in the air. "How can they live in darkness?"

"Where there is death comes life," Dalsay said. "Such is the way with seeds. There is life in the soil here. Follow. We must be close."

The wizard passed right through the dandelions without disturbing a single one. Dyphestive and Jakoby walked right behind him, kicking up bright seeds by the thousands and clearing a path for the others.

Dyphestive had a huge grin on his face as he blew the seeds away from his face and gave a hearty chuckle. "I wonder why they aren't like this on the top side of the world."

"Who knows," Zora said while catching the floating seedlings. "But I wish they were."

The seeds' light lasted for several seconds before it died out and the seeds landed on the ground again.

"Ah," Dyphestive said.

Grey Cloak followed the group from the rear, taking note of the black path they left behind between the shimmering fields of strange dandelions.

Zora drifted back beside him and asked, "Isn't it the most wonderful thing you ever saw?"

"It's taking all I have to contain my excitement," he admitted.

"I'm sure it is." She reached down and held his hand. "My tummy is telling me that we need to make the most of it. I imagine this delightful walk through the fields won't last that long." She caught him glancing over his shoulder. "Why do you keep looking back?"

"I'm wondering if we've reached the point of no return."

"Don't say that." She squeezed his hand. "I have faith in you. You'll think of something."

Grey Cloak tightened his grip. "I know."

As he walked, Dyphestive spun around, looking upward, and said, "It looks like the night sky without stars. There is no top to it. Why hasn't the world above fallen in on the world below?"

"Gapoli is rich in leagues of great tunnels and caverns in the earth, more than the races could explore in a hundred lifetimes," Dalsay said. "Fortunately for us, we are only looking for one spot in the bowels of the earth." He pointed his ghostly finger outward as everyone stood in a row beside him. "And there it is. There, my friends, is Thannis."

In the open field among the dandelions were huge piles of rubble, rocks, and ruins. Most of them were covered in green moss that glowed like the dandelions and outlined the surviving structures of the fallen city.

"It's so quiet," Zora said as she rubbed her nose. "Almost peaceful, but I have chill bumps all over me." She swallowed. "Are we going in there?"

The grim-faced Dalsay slowly nodded. "But from here on out, exercise silence."

"I thought you said this place was filled with the undead," Grey Cloak said. "But we haven't seen anything but flowers."

"The dead slumber, but remember this. Wake up one, and we wake them all and become one with their armies," Dalsay warned.

22

ZORA WASN'T THE ONLY ONE WITH CHILLS AS THEY WADED INTO THE RUINS OF THE fallen city. They broke out all over Grey Cloak.

Get it together, elf. Get it together. You don't need the cloak.

The Cloak of Legends had become a crutch for him over the years, and he felt naked without it. It gave him protection and a feeling of invincibility like he'd never felt before. Now he only had his skin and bones to protect him.

To make matters worse, he had to rely on his friends more to see the mission through. That meant putting their lives at risk, which was the last thing he wanted to do. *If I had my way, I'd do it all by myself.*

With Zora shadowing him, he crept along strange ridges and structures that had been long buried by time. The faint outline of old streets made a rough-hewn pattern through the city in some spots. Strange vegetation aside, there wasn't any sign of anyone, living or dead, aside from them.

It's hard to believe someone couldn't find their way out of this. There's nothing here.

Everyone walked the grounds, looking for an entrance to something, and that was the problem. They'd been searching through the piles of rubble and fallen pillars without finding anything. Even Dalsay had a perplexed expression on his long face.

Nearby, Dyphestive and Jakoby sat on a pile of rocks, sharing a canteen of water. Leena hovered behind Dyphestive's broad back.

Grey Cloak scratched behind his ear and shrugged at Zora.

She mouthed, "There isn't anything down here. Dalsay is crazy."

She might not have been too far off the mark. Perhaps Dalsay wanted them out of the way, and he'd led them to a trap. After all, many of the Wizard Watch had turned and served Black Frost. Grey Cloak approached Dalsay, only to see him vanish inside a fallen structure half-buried under stone.

He did that on purpose. I know he saw me coming.

They'd been combing the area for hours without finding any evidence that would lead them to the Figurine of Heroes. Grey Cloak held his chin and tapped his cheek with his index finger. *If I had been here before, where would I hide the figurine? Wouldn't that be something if I was here before? Could there really be two of me? And if there were two, could there be three or possibly four or more? Oh my, I'm getting giddy.*

Grey Cloak traipsed toward a pile of rocks that had crushed what looked like a wooden barn. He'd been past it a dozen times before.

I've hidden plenty of things, and often, the best place is in plain sight. That's what I'd do.

He peered at the pile of rubble and noticed that several of the planks were still intact and lying side by side in a neat row. There were several stones the size of a man's head resting on top of them. Moss covered them, and dandelions grew among them. The odd thing about the stones was that they were shaped almost like horseshoes, and he hated shoeing horses.

"What are you staring at?" Zora whispered in his ear.

He pointed at the formation of stones and made a U-shaped pattern in the air. "For some reason, that seems oddly familiar. What do you think?"

"I think those stones look too heavy for you to lift," she said.

"Funny." He stepped onto the mossy planks and felt them slightly bow. He picked up a stone and said, "Help me out," to Zora.

She took the stone from him and gently set it on the ground. He continued to pull the stones away from their mossy nests and hand them to Zora, who groaned as she cradled each and every one and set them down.

"Next time, use your brother for manual labor." She placed her hands on the back of her hips and arched backward. "These things are killing my back." She caught him looking at her chest, furrowed her brow, and asked, "What are you looking at?"

"Me? Nothing." He smirked as he knelt on the planks. "Only it's a shame your back hurts. Next time, I'll remember to use smaller stones."

She playfully smacked him in the back of the head and said, "Get to work."

He scraped away the moss with his fingers until he found the outlines between the individual boards. Then he wiggled one in the middle free and peeled it away from its home in the dirt.

"Did you find something?" Dyphestive asked.

"Shh," Zora said.

Dyphestive lowered his voice to a whisper and asked, "Sorry, did you find something?"

"Perhaps," Grey Cloak said. He grunted as he struggled to pull the next plank of wood up. It was wedged firmly in the ground.

"Here, let me help." Dyphestive bent over, grabbed the board with one hand, and started to lift it from its grave.

"Easy!" Grey Cloak warned.

The wooden plank made a loud sound as it rubbed against the others and came free. The ground slipped at the top of the plank, and a small boulder rolled into the pitch-black gap. Stone smacked against stone as it plunged into the darkness. *Clack. Clack. Clack.*

Grey Cloak looked up at his brother and said, "Well done, Dyphestive. Well done. Now the dead will know that we're here."

Dyphestive leaned over the gap. "What makes you think the dead are down there? It's only a hole in the ground. It's probably noth—urk!"

A mossy tendril spotted with thorns came out of the darkness, coiled around Dyphestive's neck, and yanked him into the pit.

"Dyphestive!" Grey Cloak shouted into the gap. His voice echoed back. "Dyphestive, I'm coming!"

23

GREY CLOAK STARTED TO JUMP INTO THE GAP, BUT JAKOBY HOOKED HIS ARM AND hauled him back. "Don't be a fool. You don't know what lies down there. Exercise some discipline, or we'll all be dead."

"Let go of me. The longer we wait, the farther it gets away," he said, yanking his arm out of Jakoby's grasp.

Dalsay stood over the pit, hovering in the air, and said, "Jakoby is right. We must exercise caution. I'll go forward and see what has befallen him. It cannot hurt me."

But Leena jumped right through Dalsay and vanished into the dark hole.

"Oh no, she's not going to rescue my brother before me." Grey Cloak jumped in after her and landed on a rock several feet below. It created a crude staircase that led into the depths of the fallen city.

He hurried after her and caught up dozens of feet below. "Wait, Leena."

Dalsay dropped between them. His ghostly form created a dull illumination that revealed a passage made of broken walls and dirt. There were drag marks on the ground that followed the passage.

Grey Cloak drew his sword and dagger and said, "I'm not standing around and waiting for the others to get down here."

He and Leena made their way down the passage.

Dalsay soared by them, turned, and asked, "Will you let me lead this expedition? As I said, they cannot harm me. Wait here and give me a moment to find him."

"If you find him, you can't help him," Grey Cloak said. "Whatever took him is strong and fast. You'll need our help to fight it."

Dalsay glared at him. "Whatever sort of creature took him won't be alone either. I warned you about the need for silence. Listen to the clamor."

Grey Cloak could hear the others making their way down the rocks. There was panting, heavy breathing, footsteps scuffling on rock, and the rattle of Jakoby's armor. He stormed back down the passage and whispered through his teeth, "Stay put. Dalsay, Leena, and I will go forward."

"You don't have a torch. I have a torch. I should lead you," Gorva said.

"Dalsay is our torch, and I have other methods. We'll return shortly," he said.

Zora gave him a worried look and said, "You have an hour. Hurry."

He caught up to Leena and Dalsay, who had moved farther down the passage.

We're coming, brother. We're coming.

THE TENDRIL PULLED Dyphestive into the inky depths and kept going. He bounced off stone landing after stone landing and hit the ground, still being dragged by the neck.

Whatever had ahold of him moved fast and had great strength. The strands coiled around Dyphestive's neck and squeezed hard. The thorns dug into his flesh, sinking deeper and deeper. They would have broken the neck of a lesser man and snapped it like a twig.

Dyphestive was a natural and no ordinary man. He flexed his bull neck and sank his head deeper into his shoulders. One hand remained locked on the handle of his sword. The other hand was free.

Whatever you are, you won't have me today. This isn't the first time I've been dragged.

The Doom Riders had put a rope around his neck once and dragged him behind a dragon horse called a gourn. He was reminded of that day, and the thought of it turned his blood to fire.

Using his free hand, he grabbed the thorny tentacles and squeezed. The sharp thorns pierced the skin and muscles of his palm. He kicked, trying to catch a fixed object that would slow him. The toes of his boots skipped over rough rocks that tore up his trousers and busted his knees.

He tugged on the tentacles, which were dragging him as fast as a galloping horse, and twisted over onto his belly. Though he couldn't see a thing ahead of him, he could feel the ground scraping the skin from his chest. He envisioned his hand locked around the tentacle. *Don't cut your hand off, Dyphestive.*

He lifted the iron sword from the ground, aimed for the tentacle above his hand, and brought it down hard. *Chop!*

Steel cut cleanly through the tendril, and he rolled to a stop.

Farther down the corridor, the creature let out an ear-splitting screech.

A sound like thousands of tiny feet stomping over the ground echoed down the passage and stormed toward him.

Dyphestive groaned and came up to one knee. Lost in the dark, he faced the unseen enemy charging toward him. It sounded like thousands of buzzing bees. With the painful tentacle still attached, he grabbed his sword with both hands and closed his eyes. His vision was useless in the dark. He would have to rely on his other senses, the way he'd been taught by the Doom Riders when he leaned to fight in the dark.

The creature stormed closer.

Dyphestive timed his attack, cocked his elbow, and lunged.

24

A TERRIFYING SHRIEK ECHOED THROUGH THE EXPANDING LABYRINTH OF MISSHAPEN passages and caught Grey Cloak's ear. He raced straight through Dalsay's body, with Leena on his heels, only to see Dalsay sail back through both of them.

"Follow me, I implore you," Dalsay said as the tips of his toes dusted over the ground and sped through the tunnel. The passage bent left and right, sloping up and down. The stone structures that held the ceiling in place looked as if they might cave in at any moment. Dalsay jabbed his fingers out from under his robes. "There."

Dyphestive knelt in the middle of the passage, grimacing. He'd begun to peel away the thorny tendril buried in his hand.

Grey Cloak rushed to his aid. "Brother, are you wounded?" He caught his first glimpse of the monster that had reeled Dyphestive into the depths and stopped in his tracks. He brandished his blades.

"It's dead," Dyphestive said in a hoarse voice. "But this is the first look I got of it. Yuck. A nasty beast."

Blocking further passage was one of the ugliest creatures Grey Cloak had ever seen. It had thousands of legs underneath a massive wormlike body with black hair that was sharp and spiny. Oversized green eyes loomed over a gaping, oozing mouth filled with hundreds of sharp and jagged teeth. The iron sword was sunk hilt deep between its eyes. Pus from the wound leaked down its face. On its back were spiny ridges and long thorny, slimy tentacles thicker than rope.

Dyphestive pulled the tentacle out of his bloody hand and chucked it aside.

Grey Cloak grimaced. "Doesn't that hurt?"

"Yeah, but only on the inside and everywhere else." With the help of Leena, Dyphestive uncoiled the gooey strand choking his neck. It peeled away and took some skin with it.

"Ouch," Grey Cloak muttered. He watched Leena pluck black thorns from Dyphestive's thick neck. "Glad it was you and not me."

Dyphestive picked a few more thorns from the palm of his hand and said, "You might not have made it. I plowed over more rocks than I'll ever remember." He rubbed his shoulder and cracked his neck. "And I felt every one of them."

Leena dangled the severed tentacle in front of her sour face and flung it away.

Dyphestive planted his foot in the monster's face and pulled the iron sword free. "Dalsay, do you know what that thing is?"

"A cavern creeper. Very deadly. It's a wonder that you are alive," Dalsay commented. He passed through the creeper and disappeared to the other side.

Dyphestive looked like he'd been dragged behind a wagon for a league. He had cuts and scrapes all over him. His trousers were shredded. He checked his woolen vest, which was in better shape than the rest of him, and said, "Will you look at this? After all of that, the stitching still held. Remarkable, isn't it? I couldn't have stitched it better myself."

"Are you sure you're well?" Grey Cloak asked.

"Would it make any difference if I wasn't? We're still here, aren't we?"

Gorva approached quickly with a torch in one hand and a sword in the other. Wide-eyed, Zora and Jakoby were right behind her.

"What happened? We heard a shriek," Gorva said.

Dyphestive pointed at the cavern creeper. "That happened. Don't worry. It's dead now."

Zora let out a sigh. "Thank goodness. But are you well?"

"Why does everyone keep asking me that?" Dyphestive asked.

"Because you look like that monster chewed you up and spit you out." Jakoby poked the monster with his sword. "A cavern creeper. I've heard about them but didn't believe they were real. Hopefully, you killed the last of them." He hacked into its body several times with his sword and said, "You can never be too sure." He slung the gore off his blade. "Yuck. It smells worse than it looks."

For the rest of the trek, Grey Cloak let Dalsay lead the way through the passages. The last surprise had almost gotten his best friend killed, and he couldn't let that happen again.

The next time one of those cavern creepers appears, let it wrap its tentacles around Dalsay. I don't think I'd mind seeing that. I'm starting to believe wizards are nothing but trouble. I miss Anya.

Chink. Thud. Chink. Thud. Chink. Thud. Chink. Chink. Chink. Thud.

The company exchanged startled looks.

Dyphestive said, "That sounds like digging."

Dalsay picked up the pace and moved straight toward the source of the sound. The passage emptied out on a rise that overlooked an entire ancient city resting underneath a dome of stone. He clawed at his beard and said, "Welcome to Thannis."

"Dragon's breath, it's almost as big as Raven Cliff," Zora uttered. "How can this be?"

Grey Cloak shrugged.

Thannis sat under a ceiling of rock filled with quartz that glowed like starlight. It cast light on a deteriorating city of weathered buildings that had withstood the test of time. The strange light shimmered on the glassy surface of a lake between them and the city. A backdrop of rocky climbs and tunnel entrances stood behind the city. Small bodies moved along the ledges, pushing carts and carrying hammers and picks.

"Are those gnomes?" Dyphestive asked.

Many people wandered along the outskirts of the city and the streets within. But the hammering and shoveling were definitely coming from the hills.

"There's only one way to find out. *I'll take a closer look.*" Grey Cloak took off before anyone had time to object. He raced down the slope as quietly as a deer and made his way around the edge of the lake. Paths had been worn in an odd mossy grass, and he followed them toward the city.

A pair of people walked toward him at a slow gait. He crouched behind a pile of rubble along the road and hid. It was a man and a woman wearing moth-eaten clothing. Their skin had deep creases beneath the cheekbones, and their eyes were almost hollowed out. Flesh had fallen from their bones. They moved slowly on their rickety limbs, holding hands with fingers that were missing.

Grey Cloak's heart started to race. He slunk farther away from the pair and scanned the grounds. The undead were everywhere—in the fields, on the streets, living out their routine lives, fishing, hammering, walking, and eating.

His skin crawled. He turned to head back up the hill to his friends and found himself face-to-face with zombies.

25

WIZARD WATCH

"GO AHEAD, ELF WOMAN, PICK ONE UP," THE GOLDEN-EYED CATTEN OFFERED. HE stood on the far side of the pedestal of precious stones. "Choose whatever stone that will connect you."

Tatiana, who stood near the thrones, hesitated before making the slow trek to her destination. The underlings were notorious for calling her forth, only to turn the tables and torment her.

What games are these fiends up to this time?

She passed by the silver-eyed Verbard and caught a whiff of his fetid port breath.

He rapped her on the behind with his cane, sending a painful jolt through her limbs, and said, "Get moving!"

She shook, and her legs bowed. Though she started to stumble, she fought to stay upright and lifted her chin as if nothing had happened then made her way to the pedestal of precious stones.

Catten's eyes, burning like two golden coins, locked on hers. "Pick one," he said.

She'd been in the presence of the underlings since they created the pedestal and had a strong understanding of what the mystic mechanism was all about. The stones were used to control the Time Mural.

The beautiful arrangement of colorful gemstones pulsated with inner light, casting a rainbow of colors on her face. She stretched her fingers over the stones and could feel arcane power caressing her bones.

She lifted her stare to Catten, who returned an approving nod.

Here goes. He'll probably burn my fingers off.

A square-cut amethyst, one of many in the grid of stones, caught her eye. She slowly picked it up. Its touch warmed her hand. She tightened her fist around it and started to ask, "Now what?" but bit her tongue.

"Face the Time Mural," Catten ordered.

Image after image flashed in the Time Mural. Some barely lasted a moment, others a second or two, before shifting to another picture. She saw places all over the world, many she recognized and others she didn't. The jagged black peaks of Dark Mountain appeared. The windswept grasses of Westerlund were in full view. Valley Shire was a beautiful land with forests laden with spectacular trees that were one of a kind. Each and every picture was as captivating as the last, and some stole her breath away.

Catten floated along one side and Verbard along the other, pinning her between their shoulders.

"We want you to try something, elf woman. When you see an image you feel strongly about, use your connection with your stone, and hold that image," Catten said.

Tatiana swallowed. She'd watched some other wizards from the watch attempt the same challenge, only to have their minds turn to goo as drool spilled from their lips. Her time had come. It could be her death.

She nodded and said, "As you wish, Lord Catten."

"Good." Catten drifted back behind to the pedestal and held his hands over the stones. "We'll be trying something different this time. During my meditations, I had an epiphany."

"Is that so, brother?" Verbard asked as he spun and faced him. "When were you going to share this information with me?"

Catten started rearranging the stones in the pedestal. "I was curious to see if you would figure it out yourself. I'm surprised you didn't. Certainly, you recall the time when we summoned a demon from another world to dispatch of one of our fiercest foes?"

"Ah." Verbard's silver eyes brightened. He scratched his cheek with his pointed black fingernail. "That does bring back memories. A painful reminder of the past." He caught Tatiana looking at him out of the corner of her eyes and poked her ribs with Gossamer's cane, sending a jolt through her. "Stop staring!"

"Guh!" she gasped, dropping the gemstone and falling to the floor. The amethyst bounced off the floor and stopped a few feet from the Time Mural.

"Brother, will you stop tormenting the elf woman? We are conducting an experiment, and she'll need all of her fortitude to survive." Catten sighed. "Elf woman, fetch the stone. Hurry!"

She picked herself up, gritting her teeth. Her body spasmed, and she fought through the painful sensation coursing through her limbs and picked up the stone. Staring into the ever-changing abyss of images, she allowed a gentle bend in her knees. There was still plenty of elf left in her. *I should jump and end this.*

"Elf woman," Catten said, "don't stand so close. You might be tempted to do something stupid."

Verbard had crept up on her and pressed the end of the cane into her back. "And that would force me to blast you into little pieces. You don't want to wind up like so many other members of your pathetic Wizard Watch, do you?"

"Of course not, Lord Verbard. Lord Catten." She inhaled deeply. "I hope to fare far better than them."

"Good." Verbard rapped her on the head with the silver ball handle of his cane. "Now, let's see how much energy your grey matter can hold."

26

TATIANA GRIPPED THE GEMSTONE AND STOOD IN FRONT OF THE OMINOUS ARCHWAY, which was so large that it dwarfed her. Image after image flashed, revealing living things of all sorts and dark and beautiful places.

The enchanted gemstone pulsated in her palm. Like the Star of Light she'd once possessed and Catten now carried, she summoned its magic and became one with it. It was part of her sorcery, which the Wizard Watch taught her, and the mastery of other magical objects.

Along the rim of the Time Mural's archway, the other gemstones brightened with their own majestic light. The array of colors flashed and flickered, bathing the chamber in pools of swirling light.

"Good, good," Catten uttered. "Bond with the portal. Use your stone and bend it to your will!"

Tatiana had seen others attempt to freeze the time portal before, only to witness their quick and ugly demise. They were never the same afterward. Like her, they hadn't had a choice. She lifted the stone, called forth the wizardry, and channeled it through her. Power that felt hot as coals coursed through her blood.

An image of a green pond surrounded by tall willow trees appeared in the mural. She'd spent her time there as a child. A wave of strong memories surfaced in her mind—her first kiss; the use of magic; an untimely death.

Lock it!

Matching amethysts mounted in the archway burned brighter than the other stones. Rays of light burst forth from the stones and joined with the stone in her hand.

Tatiana's eyes were as wide as saucers, and her mouth hung open. The vision of the pond didn't change. It remained in place.

"Hold it, elf woman. Hold it!" Catten demanded.

Verbard drifted closer to the Time Mural. He passed his cane through the amethyst's light and gave a victorious grin.

A dull pain started in her mind and began to quickly build. Tatiana's arm started to tremble. It carried into her body.

"Hold it! Hold it!" Catten shouted.

Tatiana focused on the image. It was a place that she would not let go—a place she knew strongly. *I won't let go! I'll hold it!*

A great pressure built in her mind and became more intense by the moment. The amethyst burned like a bright star in her hand. The image in the Time Mural began to warp and twist.

"A little longer!" Catten cried. "A little longer!"

Tatiana screamed, and her knees buckled. She collapsed to the ground, and the smoking amethyst rolled free of her blistered fingers. Shaking like a leaf, she lay on the ground, lips sputtering and tears running from her eyes.

Verbard hovered over her, pointed the cane at her, and asked, "Should I put her out of her misery?"

"No." Catten floated alongside his brother and glared down at her. "She fared far better than the others. She held the Time Mural in place at length. Unprecedented."

"I suppose if she can still fetch port, she can be serviceable." Verbard poked her with his cane. "Can you crawl, elf woman?"

Tatiana's teeth clattered. She managed a feeble nod.

"Crawl, then!" Verbard commanded.

"Why don't you lend her a hand, brother?" Catten suggested.

"I'm not touching that hideous thing. Where's an urchling when you need one? I never would have imagined I'd miss my physically maligned brethren." Verbard made a rolling gesture with his cane.

Tatiana tumbled over the floor and bumped into the bases of the underlings' thrones.

"I'll give you a brief amount of time to prove you can pour my port. If you can't do it in the time I've allotted, I'll feed you to..." Verbard looked about. "Well, some sort of abominable creature."

"Will you quit trolling the elf woman, brother? We have more important matters to attend to. Our little experiment was nothing short of a success." Catten waved his brother to the pedestal. "Come. See."

Verbard joined him. The hawk-nosed men leaned over the pedestal and started speaking to each other in another language that sounded like the chittering of birds. Catten spoke and pointed at the stones, while Verbard rubbed his chin and nodded.

Tatiana rubbed her shivering shoulders and tried to shake the burning fog from her mind. She'd never felt such raw power like what she'd felt from the Time Mural. She'd held its might in her grasp for a moment, and it hadn't killed her. It fed her.

The underlings paid her no mind as their chittering conversation began to heat up. They'd spoken often in their underling language before, and she'd picked up bits and pieces of it.

I've never heard them so excited. They must be getting close.

She crawled over to a small serving table and picked up the crystal bottle of port. Her bony arms continued to tremble, and she spilled port on the ground.

"Stop wasting it, or I'll waste you!" Verbard said.

"Will you ignore her? She's not harming anything," Catten said. "Pay attention!"

"She's harming my port. It's the only thing worth having in this world," Verbard replied as he turned his back on her.

Tatiana continued to pour. Her teeth no longer clattered, nor did her arm tremble. What little strength she had returned to her tingling limbs.

Ah, I'm still serviceable, rodents—more serviceable than I'm going to let on.

She finished filling the goblet and wiped the spilled port away from the goblet's rim. With a painful groan, she rose. Keeping her head tilted slightly to one side, she made the trek across the room toward the underlings.

"Your port, Lord Verbard, as requested," she said with a thick tongue.

Verbard floated around in a half circle and faced her with glaring eyes. "Did you interrupt our conversation, elf woman?"

"But Lord Ver—"

With a stroke of his cane, Verbard sent Tatiana sailing across the chamber and slamming into the wall. "I said you need to pour it, not serve it!"

"Stay focused on the task at hand, brother," Catten demanded.

Verbard looked at the shattered crystal on the floor and seethed. "She spilled my port. She's going to have to pay for it."

27

RUINS OF THANNIS

THE GROUP OF UNDEAD PEOPLE LOOKED AT GREY CLOAK LIKE A ROCK THEY'D SEEN a thousand times before and shuffled on.

He held his hand over his chest, and his heart thumped underneath his fingers. *Zooks.*

Grey Cloak walked backward toward the other side of the underwater lake where he'd come from. He didn't take his eyes off the undead as he did so and watched with avid curiosity as the undead trove of people gathered at a break in a knee-high stone wall and started filling it in with stones.

They're working, but why? How?

It didn't make sense that the mindless, deteriorating men and women were working as if they were living. Perhaps they only knew the life that once was.

Maybe Dalsay will understand what is going on.

He hurried up the slope to where his friends were gathered. All of them were glaring at him, either with their arms crossed or brows knitted.

"A welcome back would be nice," he said.

Zora stepped on his toe. "Don't do that again."

"Ow. Zooks, Zora, it's better that I risk my neck than the rest of you."

"What did you discover?" Gorva asked.

"I'll tell you what I discovered. A group of the undead looked right through me and kept going. Nearly scared me out of my boots. That's what I discovered." He gave a nervous chuckle. "I don't think they care that we're here. I don't think they care about anything."

Dalsay intervened and said, "That's because they are zombies. They don't have the ability to care about anything or anyone, living or dead."

"They were walking around like normal people, except they smell like they haven't bathed in a thousand years, and parts of their limbs had fallen off," Grey Cloak said. "But much of their clothing had held up well."

"Creepy," Dyphestive uttered. He ventured forward. "I want to go see them."

"Bear in mind that all who have entered have not come out," Dalsay warned. "We must proceed with great caution. I sense a great evil lurking within, luring us into a trap. Follow me and stay close."

The company made the short trek to the border of Thannis and entered the fallen city.

Zombies wandered the streets and didn't pay them any notice.

Zora wrapped her arms around Grey Cloak's and whispered, "My skin is crawling. Don't they see us?"

"I guess, but perhaps they don't care, or perhaps we're dead already."

"Don't say that." Zora's nose twitched. "They smell awful."

"Uh-huh," Grey Cloak replied as he took a closer look at his surroundings. It appeared that many fallen buildings had been rebuilt. Several structures made from blocks of differently shaped and sized stones towered. The buildings' lines were askew in most places, but somehow the leaning fortifications stood.

"How in the world is that standing?" Zora asked. Then she crushed Grey Cloak's arm. "Eek!"

A herd of tarantulas the size of large hounds scurried across the road, up the buildings, and over the rooftops and vanished.

"Those spiders are huge. I've never seen them so big," Zora said.

"It's a good thing you weren't with us on Prisoner Island," Grey Cloak said.

"Why? Were there giant spiders?"

He nodded. "Big enough to ride. So, Dalsay, should we split up and look for the figurine? I don't think the zombies will have a problem with us poking around."

Dalsay stood with his arms by his sides and his eyes closed.

Dyphestive was on the other side of the wizard, looking right through him. "I think he's concentrating." He passed his hand through Dalsay's neck. "Huh, that made the hair on my arms stand up. Come over here and do this, Grey." He continued to pass his hand through Dalsay.

Leena grabbed his hand and pulled it away.

"Never mind," Dyphestive said.

Dalsay opened his eyes, surveyed the group, and said, "There is strong magic running through the veins of this city. We need to find its source, and that is where we will find our answers."

"I hope you aren't sensing more giant spiders," Zora said with a shiver.

"You mean a spider sense?" Grey Cloak quipped.

"I like the sound of that," Zora said. "Seeing spiders before they creep up on you. Or I could hunt them down and squish them."

"Why would you want to do that?" Gorva asked. "Spiders eat all the bad bugs like mosquitos and those annoying moths."

"I don't like spiders, and I'm free to dislike as I please," Zora replied.

Grey Cloak's mind wandered off. *If I was here before, where would I have put the figurine? There are thousands of places to hide it. And did I bring it here? Why would I do that? Did I do that to hide it, or did I do it so that only I could find it?* He smirked. *My, I'm a complex elf. It's good to be me. Nothing like excitement mixed with mystery.*

Zora nudged him. "What are you smiling about?"

He twirled his index finger around his ear and said, "Only entertaining some thoughts. Dalsay, I think we should split up into two groups. You lead one, and I'll lead the other."

"We should stay together," Dalsay said. "Splitting up now would be foolish against these numbers."

Grey Cloak touched his chest and said, "If I hid the figurine here, more than likely, I'll be the one to find it. And I don't think marching into the heart of danger is the best idea."

"Haven't you made enough foolish decisions?" Dalsay retorted. "You need to learn to trust others."

He stood nose to nose with Dalsay and replied, "Watch what you say, wizard!"

Dyphestive interrupted them both and said, "Friends, I'd like to draw your attention to something."

Grey Cloak's ears were heated. "What?"

Dyphestive pointed down the street.

A mass of zombie soldiers in full armor marched straight toward the company.

"Huh," Grey Cloak said. "This might be a problem."

28

THE ARMORED ZOMBIES APPEARED FROM ALL DIRECTIONS. THEY WORE TARNISHED bronze helmets with purple plumes, matching bronze breastplates, and leggings with thigh and shin guards that rattled when they walked. They took determined shuffling steps, one step after the other. The sinew and skin of their limbs hung from the bone in many places. Their slack jaws were portals to small abysses.

Jakoby drew his sword, and Dyphestive cocked the iron sword over his shoulder.

"No!" Dalsay said. "Lower your weapons. So long as their weapons are not drawn, neither should yours be."

"Are you mad?" Jakoby asked. "Those things will rip us apart."

"We need to run," Grey Cloak said, but he didn't see an avenue for escape. The streets and alleys filled slowly with zombie soldiers. He pulled both of his blades halfway out of their sheaths. "And now, while we can still carve a path through them."

"Agreed," Gorva said.

"I told you not to come here, but you insisted," Dalsay replied. "There is no choice but to see it through. This is the path you have chosen."

"What do we do, Grey?" Dyphestive asked.

He glared at Dalsay and stuffed his swords back in their sheaths with a click. "You'd better be right about this, wizard."

The zombie soldiers were six deep when they surrounded them. With Talon crammed between their ranks, they marched deeper into the city.

"Phew!" Jakoby said. "And I thought long marches with the Monarch Knights smelled bad. These things reek, but they are wearing the finest crafted armor I ever saw."

Dyphestive agreed. "Look at the pommels of their swords. Those handles are pearl. Zombies or no, they are worth a fortune."

They couldn't have been more right. The zombies might be deteriorating, but their armor had held up very well. Even their sword belts and scabbards glimmered with precious stones.

Zora held onto Grey Cloak with one arm and covered her nose with the other. "This stinks."

"Literally."

Gorva couldn't hide her disgust and asked, "How do the dead live? It's not natural."

"Only the strongest and darkest magic can reanimate the dead. They are not living things, as we know one another, but instead, they are flesh golems given temporary life by another being or beings," Dalsay said. "I admit that I am very eager to meet whoever or whatever has executed this massive incantation."

"I have a feeling you're going to learn the answer to that question soon enough," Grey Cloak said as they turned down another block.

At the end of the road was a massive square cathedral with tall ivory towers topped with golden spires on the corners. A wide stone staircase led into the towering double doors, which opened from the inside. The zombie soldiers lined up along both sides of the staircase, forming a passage that led inside.

Grey Cloak moved to the front, beside Dalsay and Dyphestive. The three of them were the first to cross the threshold, and the doors immediately closed behind them, sealing their friends outside.

Dyphestive spun around, dropped his sword, grabbed the door handles, and started to pull.

The others pounded on the door from the other side. Their voices were muted.

"Urrrgh!" Dyphestive moaned as he set his foot against one door and pulled the iron handle of the other. "It won't budge."

"Use more leg!" Grey Cloak demanded.

Knots of sinewy muscle bulged in Dyphestive's huge arms. His cheeks turned bloodred.

Pop! The handle came off the door, and Dyphestive went flying backward. He landed on his behind and rolled flat on his back. He held up the long twisted iron handle and said, "Not the outcome I was hoping for."

"Who dares enter my temple and defile my property?"

The haunting voice came from the opposite end of the temple. Down the aisle, which was filled with wooden pews over one hundred rows deep, a lone figure waited in the shadows created by torches bracketed on the walls and huge metal chandeliers that burned with flickering green flames.

Dyphestive stood and chucked the handle aside. "We do."

"Let me do the talking," Dalsay demanded.

"Come forward, interlopers," the figure said.

Grey Cloak and Dyphestive fell in step behind Dalsay.

"Did that sound like a woman to you? It did to me," Grey Cloak said.

"I think you're right," Dyphestive replied.

"In that case, I should do the talking. Women like me better," Grey Cloak whispered back.

"They do not. They like me as well as you."

"First off, they don't, and second, you are spoken for."

"Will you stop saying that? I'm not spoken for. Leena and I are only friends."

Grey Cloak smirked. "Tell her that."

"Silence!" The figure lingered inside the swirling black fog on the stage. The fog began to dissipate, revealing a tall, ugly woman with burning ice-blue eyes and a crown of gold. Long strands of white hair hung over her bony shoulders, and skin had rotted off her face. She wore drab, frayed, and moth-eaten robes, and her hands and fingers were all bone. She had no lips. "I am Mortis, Queen of Thannis."

Grey Cloak slipped behind Dyphestive, pushed him in the back, and said, "You can have her."

Dyphestive shook his head. "No, you can have her. I insist."

"At least this one has a tongue that works." Grey Cloak kept pushing. "Think about the benefits. She can probably whistle and hum. Wouldn't that be nice?"

"Silence!"

A shock wave knocked Grey Cloak and Dyphestive off their feet.

Grey Cloak stuck his fingers in his ringing ears, patted his brother's back, and said, "Maybe you should stick with Leena."

29

QUEEN MORTIS LAUNCHED INTO A TIRADE ABOUT THE HISTORY OF THANNIS, including its triumphs and failures. "Our armies never lost in battle. Streams of silver filled our coffers. No heights could not be reached. Sacrifices cost the lives of the living. No man ever touched a hair on my head."

"Dalsay, what is she?" Grey Cloak asked in a low voice.

"She is a lich, an omnipotent undead creature who carries astounding power. Shh, stay silent, and we may learn something."

"You listen all you want. I'm going to take a look around." He nudged his brother. "Let's go."

"But I want to hear what she has to say. It's interesting," Dyphestive said.

"Lap it up, then. I'll be about."

Dyphestive groaned. "Fine, I'll go. It's not as if I can't still listen."

"Precisely."

For some reason, Mortis spoke at length without the slightest concern for what they were doing. So long as they didn't interrupt her speech, the lich appeared content to let them do what they would. Grey Cloak navigated through the pews, searching for anything that might be helpful.

Dyphestive searched another row beside him and asked, "What are we looking for?"

"The figurine. I could have put it anywhere, knowing me." He ran his hand underneath the benches and peeked under each and every one of them.

All the while, Mortis continued talking.

"The world swallowed our city, but it didn't ingest our spirit," she said. "We are more than tile and stone. More than flesh and bone. We live forever."

"Her speech is lasting forever," Dyphestive said.

"Apparently, she doesn't have anyone to talk to and has centuries of catching up to do," Grey Cloak replied. "Listen, you search the pews on the other side. I'm going to take my chances on the stage."

"Don't get too close her... or it," Dyphestive said.

While Dalsay held audience with Mortis, Grey Cloak hurried onto the temple stage and began to look around. There were tables with serving platters covered in dust and dirt. Several high-backed wooden chairs with torn velvet cushions were lined up against the wall in the back. But in the middle of the stage, several feet away from Mortis's back, was an altar chiseled out of pure jade and covered in bloodstains.

Grey Cloak's stomach turned at the thought of the sacrifices that must have been made in the name of evil. Resting on the slab was a foot-long dagger with a very curious design. The gilding around the handle was pure gold, and an oversized emerald was fastened into the bottom of the handle by tiny claws. The blade itself was the most unique design Grey Cloak had ever beheld. It had four blades in a conical shape that came to a point at the top. The purpose of the design was obvious. To stop the bleeding from a puncture wound from that dagger would be nearly impossible.

Murderers.

His hand hovered over the dagger as he stared at the talking lich's back.

I could pick it up and put an end to her, but she's already dead. Zooks. How do you kill someone that's dead?

Something about the dagger held his gaze. It called out to him in a sinister velvety voice, *"Take me in hand. I am your friend. I will show you what you need."*

Wide-eyed and heart pounding, Grey Cloak lowered his hand over the handle. His fingers started to close on the grip.

A strong hand seized his wrist. He tried to twist out of it.

"Grey Cloak, what are you doing?" Dyphestive asked. "Don't touch that instrument of evil. It's cursed."

He blinked and stared back at his brother. "How... how do you know that?"

Dyphestive shrugged. "I don't know how, but I do. Did you find anything else?"

He gave a feeble nod, but Mortis's tirade caught his attention.

Her head twisted over her shoulders and faced them. "Whoever enters Thannis stays in Thannis. You are one of us now. Destined to join my growing army. We vow to return to the surface and take over a world that is rightfully ours." Her burning blue eyes fastened on the dagger. "Use it. End your life. The life of your companions. In death, there is no worry. There is no pain. There is only victory."

An uncomfortable silence followed as Mortis stood before them without saying a word.

Grey Cloak wasn't shy about breaking the silence. "You aren't going to kill us outright?"

Mortis offered a wide smile of missing teeth and said, "No, you will be dead soon enough. There is no food or water you can drink. It's only a small matter of time before you are at each other's throats." She tapped her bony fingers together. *Click. Click. Click.* "And I will delight in your misery."

Grey Cloak raised a finger. "But to be clear, you aren't going to kill us or try to kill us now?"

"Unless you do something foolish, the pleasures Thannis has to offer are yours to enjoy," Mortis said.

"Can you define 'something foolish'?"

"Don't try to leave. My army will slay you. Don't raid the coffers. It will seal your doom. Century after century, treasure hunters seek out the riches of Thannis, only to find their doom. They are soldiers in my army now. Soon, so will the rest of you be."

"Great! I wanted to make sure there wasn't any misunderstanding. Can we leave now?"

"The temple, yes. The city, no."

The front doors to the cathedral opened wide.

Not a single soul stood in the entrance.

"Goy! Where'd our friends go?" Dyphestive demanded.

Mortis laughed.

30

RAZOR

Over one thousand feet above Thannis, a drizzling rain started coming down from the cloudy daylight sky. The horses whinnied and nickered as a stiff breeze picked up and bowed the smaller surrounding trees.

The green leaves turned upside down, and Reginald the Razor muttered, "Great, a storm is coming."

With one eye on the sky, he watched a flock of geese soar overhead toward the southwest.

"I wouldn't mind some cooked goose about now."

One of the bigger horses, the one that Dyphestive rode, let out a loud snort and stomped his hooves.

"Hold your horses," Reginald said in his rugged voice. He shook his head. "That must have sounded stupid."

He made his way over to Cliff the mule and prepared a feed bag. "They're down there having all the fun, while I'm up here playing with the animals. Lucky me." He fastened the feed bag on Dyphestive's horse, scratched it behind the ears, and said, "There, that should keep you quiet."

A couple of other horses snorted and wiggled their necks in his direction.

"You'll have to wait." He pointed at the river. "Go get a drink from the river if you're thirsty." He walked to the end of the overlook and watched the white mist of the waterfall plummet into the water of the Outer Ring. Over one hundred feet below, the falls cascaded in front of the spot where his friends had vanished. "I should have gone."

Razor might not have been a fan of climbing, but he was no fan of missing out on a fight either. Staying behind with the horses felt cowardly. He tested the rope that hung over the overlook and peered over again. It was a long plunge if he fell into the watery gorge that formed the Outer Ring. He let go of the rope and said, "They're probably on their way back. In the meantime..." He drew two daggers that were sheathed below his ribs on both sides and spun them in his hands then stuffed them back in their sleeves.

Razor carried twelve blades at all times, at least where permissible. Twelve was his number of fortune, and he saw to it that he carried it with him, in one way or the other, preferably in the form of edged weapons, at all times. Two long swords were crisscrossed over his back. A pair of short swords dressed his hips. Below his black leather armor were two daggers. Two more daggers were strapped to his thighs, matched by two more strapped to his shins above his boots. Behind his back was another pair of daggers hooked into his belt, making twelve in all.

He closed his eyes and took a deep breath. One by one, he drew each blade, stabbed an unseen opponent, and sheathed the weapon again. He'd practiced the same routine over a thousand times in his lifetime, pressing to be quicker every time.

New sweat mixed with the light drizzle, and he launched into another routine.

Razor pulled two swords from behind his back.

Jab, step, slice. Jab, step, chop.

He sheathed them again then exercised the same routine with each pair of blades while creating different combinations.

Razor's action grew into a blur of steel. He finished his routine, leaving a long sword in his right hand and a short sword in his left. A monarch butterfly with burnt-orange wings floated by. He chased it. The butterfly's erratic flight pattern made it a perfect target for practice.

His short sword flashed. He shaved one wing off the butterfly. Then he sliced through its body before it hit the ground.

He wiped the sweat from his brow with his forearm, sheathed his blades, and grabbed a skin of water that hung from his horse. He chugged the water in big gulps, then something caught his eye.

"What do we have here?" he asked as he corked the waterskin.

Far away on the trail that ran along the base of the Iron Hills, a group of riders approached. They were only the size of ants from that distance, and they disappeared underneath the next rise, only to reappear again a few minutes later, growing in size.

Razor wiped his mouth and put the waterskin away. Talon's camp was far off the beaten path. There wasn't anywhere to go but over the cliff, which made for an unlikely journey.

"Whoever is coming is coming for a reason." He grabbed the rope and spooled it over his shoulder, then he tossed it aside in the high grasses near the rocky base of the hills. He flexed his fingers. "So much for boredom."

The clouds darkened. A light rumble of thunder was accompanied by flashes of lightning. The drizzle became a steady rain, obscuring Razor's vision.

He grabbed a blanket, covered himself, and found a spot in the hills to hide that gave him full view of the trail.

Look at me, hiding in the bushes like a coward. At least there isn't anyone around to see.

Only one rise was left on the trail between them and the river's drop-off. The small group had disappeared from view and hadn't appeared again.

Razor ran through scenarios of what might be coming.

Could be bandits. I could handle them.

It might be soldiers. Again, I could handle them.

There is no telling who might be tracking us.

Maybe it's allies—not likely but possible. I could definitely handle them. Perhaps it's a group of beautiful women seeking my hand in marriage. Lucky them. Here I am.

Through the rain, he saw four riders come into view over the final rise. They came forward at a slow gait, on the backs of the biggest horses he'd ever seen. They were no more than one hundred yards away, but the long strides of the beasts moved them faster than common horses would.

With no more than fifty yards between them, Razor got his first good look at all of them. Big rangy men rode tall in their saddles. Behind the tallest horse was a bald woman with an eye patch covering her left eye.

Instead of horses, they rode on extraordinary beasts that were built like horses but covered in scales and with the heads and horns of dragons.

Razor tightened his blanket over his shoulders. Nearby, the horses' snorts and nervous nickers grew louder. He swallowed the lump building in his throat and said under his breath, "Bust my acorns, those are Doom Riders."

31

THE DOOM RIDERS WANDERED INTO CAMP ON THE CLAWED FEET OF THEIR GOURNS. Smoke huffed out of the gourns' nostrils and mouths. Like horses, they had hooves on their back legs, but their front feet were like lion paws with sharp claws that dug into the soft dirt of the riverbank.

Two of the riders swung their legs out of their saddles and dropped to the ground. Both of them wore worn, blackened leather armor that was fashioned like dragon scales. One of them wore a dyed-red leather mask resembling a skull. The other man's mask was dyed blue.

Like Razor, both men had long swords crisscrossed across their backs. They eased their way through the camp, checking the horses and the gear that they carried.

That left the other two riders sitting tall in their saddles, observing. The man wore a green mask, and red hair spilled from underneath it and touched his shoulders.

The bald woman wore an eye patch instead of a mask. She was armored the same as the others but wore a chain mail sleeve on her left arm. Unlike the men, she wore her sword belt on her hip, and over her back was a crossbow unlike any crossbow Razor had ever seen. It had bolts loaded into a cylinder.

Razor's jaw clenched. He'd been in several conversations about the group before but had never seen them in person.

Red is Scar. Blue is Ghost. Green is Shamrok, and that must be Drysis, but I thought she was dead. And here they are, getting into my business. Bloody biscuits. It looks like the day I've been waiting for has come. It's going to be a battle royale.

Wrapped in a wet blanket, Razor wandered out of his hiding spot in the bushes.

The Doom Riders, gourns included, turned and faced him.

"Can I help you with something?" he asked.

Drysis spoke in a strong but brittle voice, her lone black pupil searching his face. "Is this your camp?"

He faked a cough and said, "It is."

"You have a lot of horses and a lot of gear for one man," she said.

"That's my business."

The other three Doom Riders began to spread out and surround him.

"Ah, I see. You are bandits come to rob me."

Drysis shook her head. "We are not bandits. We are a search party, looking for... old friends. Perhaps you have seen them."

"I've seen a lot of things in my life but never old friends. I like the young ones."

"What is your name?" she asked.

"Reginald." He had to bite his tongue to keep from adding the Razor part, though it killed him not to do so.

"Reginald, do I appear to be someone you can take for a fool?"

He studied her hard jawline and the blue veins on her pasty face. "I'm not sure what I take you for. Any of you. I see scary masks and scary horses, and I can't help but wonder what festival I missed out on."

Scar said, "The only thing missing is going to be your head if you don't start talking."

"Is that so?" Razor asked as he bought time and continued to size them up. All of them were well-knit, above average in size and build, with eyes as hard as iron. "Don't get too cocky. You see, whoever you are looking for, well, I killed them. Chopped them down and pitched them into the ring. Their horses and gear are mine now."

"And you accomplished this feat all by yourself?" Drysis asked.

"I did. My skills are notorious in these hills. They call me the Lone Blade." He took a bow.

Scar and Shamrok broke out in gruff laughter.

"Drysis, let us finish off the mule thief," Scar suggested. "He's only wasting our time."

"I believe it's the other way around. You interrupted my day. I didn't interfere with yours," he said.

"Where are the others?" Drysis demanded.

"I told you. Their bodies float on the waters of the Outer Ring."

Drysis narrowed her eye on him and said, "I tire of this. Bring him to me."

Razor dropped his blanket and drew a long sword and a short sword in the wink of an eye.

Scar's head tilted, and he said, "Lords of Steel, how many blades are you carrying, mate?"

"I carry twelve. Do you think you can handle them?"

Shamrok chuckled and said to Scar, "It sounds like someone is overcompensating for something. A real fighter only needs one."

Razor spun his swords on his wrists and said, "We'll see about that."

Shamrok started to dismount.

Drysis lifted a hand and said, "No, stay put."

"You can't see me grinning under this mask, but I have a beautiful smile all over my face," Scar said. He reached behind his back and drew both of his long blades. "This is going to be a dance to remember."

Drysis shook her head at Scar. "No, not you either." She turned her frosty gaze to another Doom Rider. "Ghost, I'll let you take this cocky little fighter apart. But keep him alive. Once it's over, I'll have questions."

32

THE RUINS OF THANNIS

THE STREETS OF THANNIS WERE CLEAR—NO ZOMBIE SOLDIERS, NO AIMLESSLY wandering citizens, and no members of Talon. The town was abandoned.

Grey Cloak jogged down the stairs and asked, "What is the meaning of this? How could they be gone?" He spun around. "All of them are gone?"

"We were in there a long time," Dyphestive stated. "Long enough for them to move on."

"Dalsay, go inside and ask your new friend what happened to our old friends, why don't you?" Grey Cloak said.

"It appears that Mortis has moved on. I don't see her," Dalsay replied.

Grey Cloak picked up a hunk of stone and chucked it across the street. It smacked against a building, bounced, and clattered down the street. "Well, isn't this fantastic? Why in the world would I ever come here in the first place?"

"You can't be certain that you *have* been here. That might have been a lie," Dyphestive said. He walked down the steps with his sword resting on his shoulder. "We'll find them."

"Dalsay, any brilliant ideas?" he asked.

"Obviously, Mortis enjoys playing games. I suggest we separate and look for them. I can travel faster without the two of you, as passage through obstacles won't slow me."

"Well, what are you waiting for, Ghost Man?" Grey Cloak shooed him away. "Get going."

"Aaaiiieee!"

The scream echoed down the street.

"That was Zora! I'd know that scream from anywhere!" Grey Cloak started running toward the source of the sound. "Come on!"

When he was five strides into the run, the air whistled by his ears, and his cloak flapped behind his back. He heard another high-pitched scream.

"Aaaiiieee!"

The sound echoed from another direction. He skidded to a halt and scanned the surrounding buildings.

Dyphestive caught up with him and said, "Horseshoes, you're as fast as a jackrabbit."

"I'm faster than that. Be silent."

Zora's scream faded into the distance.

"I don't have any sense of direction of where that sound came from," Grey Cloak said. "It sounded like it came from over there." He pointed down an alley. "Then it came from down that way." He pointed in the direction Dyphestive had come from. "Zora!"

The sound of his voice carried down the streets and echoed back to him a moment later.

"Zooks, this is madness!"

Dyphestive put a hand on Grey Cloak's shoulder. "We'll find her." He closed his eyes. "We only need to concentrate."

Grey Cloak trusted his eyes and ears. The only thing he heard was his own heart beating.

Then came another distressed scream. It came from all directions, echoed, and faded away once more.

He slowly shook his head.

If I can't trust my ears, I'll have to trust my other senses.

His nostrils flared, and he took in a deep draw of air.

The rotting city carried a musty scent like garbage after the rain. The suffocating smell stayed with you everywhere you went. The only thing worse was the reek of the zombies.

"Aaaiiieee!"

Grey Cloak's nose twitched.

"I wish I had Streak. Where is my dragon when I need him? He'd lick her scent right up, but my tongue's not going to touch this pavement."

Dyphestive took in short bursts of air through his nostrils. His nose crinkled, and he asked, "Doesn't Zora wash with lavender?"

"Come to think of it, yes." Grey Cloak's nose twitched like a bunny's. Elated, he said, "I smell it. Ew, and not only that."

"Sorry," Dyphestive said with a guilty look.

"That was you? Oh, that's awful. I'd forgotten how rotten you could be."

"My stinks are worse when I'm excited. It happens." Dyphestive took off down the street. "Hurry while her scent is still strong."

Grey Cloak followed Dyphestive with Zora's scent lingering in his nose. When he'd trained at Hidemark with the beautiful, honey-haired elven sisters, Mayzie and Stayzie, they conducted survival tests with him in the wild. They told him being a natural gave him heightened senses beyond those of ordinary men. He was taught to walk blind through jungle terrain and learn to rely on his other senses. The problem was that he'd learned to rely more on the Cloak of Legends more than his own instincts.

"Aaaiiieee!"

Zora's scream might have been echoing from all directions, but it was getting louder.

"This way!" Dyphestive said.

They raced down an alley and angled into a wider street. They sniffed again.

"Aaaiiieee!"

Grey Cloak pointed. "There!"

On the opposite end of the road, two blocks down, Zora dashed across the street with a pack of dog-sized spiders on her tail.

He took off at full speed and closed the distance on the alley she'd vanished into in a few seconds. Three spiders blocked his entrance. Zora was trapped in a dead end with spiders closing in.

"Help!" she shouted.

Without slowing, Grey Cloak leaped over the web-spitting spiders and drew his blades. He landed on the back of an ugly tarantula and gored its body with steel. "Hang on, Zora! I'm coming!"

"Hurry!" she cried. Her dagger flashed downward, butchering the face of a tarantula. "I can't hold them off!"

The spiders backed her against the wall and began shooting webbing. A blast of gooey spider silk pinned her dagger to her body. She groaned.

Grey Cloak sliced off the legs of one spider and buried his blade in the side of another. He chopped and hacked at anything that moved. Spiders collapsed in heaps of their own goo.

More spiders appeared from above. They came from the roof and climbed down the wall, shooting parachutes of webbing that came down like a slow rain.

"That's a problem." Grey Cloak carved a path through two spiders in an effort to evade the webbing dropping over his head. A strand of spider silk latched onto his boot and yanked it off. "Dirty acorns!"

"Hurry, Grey Cloak!" Zora was covered in strands of webs. "They're covering me up!"

"Coming!" Grey Cloak chopped a path through the spiders toward Zora until he was elbow deep in spider guts. "Almost there!"

The webbing parachutes covered his head and shoulders, fastening his limbs together so he couldn't move. He was only a few feet from Zora and surrounded by spiders. "Zooks!"

33

Dyphestive plowed into the alley, swiping the iron sword from side to side in broad strokes, crying, "Die, insects! Die!"

The iron sword ripped through three spiders at a time, spilling their guts all over the alley.

"Ha! Taste my iron, Eight Eyes!"

The eight-legged fiends let out odd shrieks and propelled their nasty black-haired bodies at Dyphestive.

Glitch! Dyphestive skewered two spiders with his great sword and shoved their wriggling bodies over his shoulder.

Spiders descended the wall, spitting clouds of cottony web at him.

"What's this?" He stabbed them one by one as they came down the wall. "There are so many! I like it!"

"Dyphestive, watch out for their webs!" Grey Cloak warned. The spiders had half covered him in webs. The more he wiggled, the more he stuck. "They're strong."

A spider came at him with its small mouth of sharp teeth wide open. It aimed for his bare foot.

Grey Cloak pulled his foot back and hopped away then forced his sword through the sticky webs and drilled the spider in the face. "Take that!"

Another spider snuck across the alley and sank its teeth into his ankle.

"Ow!" Grey Cloak called. He thrust his dagger at the creature, but the webbing clinging to his arms stunted his reach. Above, clouds of webs fell all over. "Zooks! Dyphestive, we've got trouble!"

"Grey Cloak!" Zora hollered in a muffled voice. Her face was half-covered in webbing. "Do something!"

"I'm thinking!"

"Think faster! Use your magic or something!"

A flame of a thought brightened in his mind. "Good idea!" He summoned the wizard fire and pushed the force into his blades. The steel glimmered with radiant blue flame. Every strand of webbing it touched peeled away. His limbs were freed, and he sliced right through the sticky strands. He started butchering the spiders again. "That's more like it!"

"Slay them, brother!" Dyphestive hollered. He stomped a spider into goo. Half-covered in sticky strands, his powerful muscles ripped through the webs. The iron sword went up and came down with force, tearing spiders open and splattering their goo.

Grey Cloak fought his way to Zora, sending spiders by the pair to their graves. Using his dagger, he sliced her bonds away. "Stay close to me. We're getting out of here!"

"How? They're everywhere!"

Webs continued to rain down, and spiders scurried down the walls.

"We can take them." He plunged his hot blue steel into another one. He pushed an added charge of wizard fire into the blade. The spider exploded.

"Whoa!" Zora said. "You did that?"

He smirked. "Impressive, isn't it?"

"Well, it was only one. There must still be a score left."

A spider jumped off the wall toward them. Zora covered her head and screeched.

Grey Cloak swung her away and gutted the spider open.

"Get me out of here! I hate spiders!" Zora screamed.

"I'm trying! Dyphestive, make a hole!"

Dyphestive was covered up to his hips in webbing. Spiders attacked him from all directions. He twisted from side to side, arms pumping, sweeping his blade through them one by one. "I'm trying, but I can't move my legs."

Grey Cloak cut through the strands as fast as he could, but the thick webbing piled up all around them. The street became sticky with webbing, and his feet stuck to the ground. "This is a problem. Watch your step, Zora. We need to find a clear path out of here."

Her lips were curled back over her teeth as she searched the ground and said, "It's sticky everywhere."

Grey Cloak stabbed a spider in the side. "There has to be a better way." He gave Zora his sword. "Use this!"

"It's not my style, but fine!" She swung the sword back and forth, keeping spiders at bay. "What are you doing?"

Grey Cloak fished a handful of coins out of his pocket then summoned his wizardry and filled them with wizard fire. "I'm doing this!"

He flung the coins at the spiders and on the ground.

Boom! Boom! Boom! Boom! Boom! The coins exploded, blowing up the spiders and clearing a path to Dyphestive.

"Well done, brother!" Dyphestive roared. The muscles in his neck bulged and strained. "You inspire me! I'll rip though this!" He started tearing out of the cocoon of webs. "Eeeyargh!"

Spiders pounced on him. Their hairy bodies covered his head and shoulders.

"Dyphestive!" Grey Cloak shouted. "I'm coming!"

Leena burst into the alley with her glowing nunchakus spinning with lethal fury. She tore through the webbing like it was made of rose petals, and the spiders practically exploded.

Chok-tum! Chok-tum! Chok-tum! Chok-tum! The crack of her wood killed them on the spot. They flattened out on the ground and stiffened.

"Tear them apart, Leena!" Dyphestive shouted as he tore out of the cords.

Leena made every spider that came within two feet of her burst open. Her weapons moved with blinding speed. *Chok-tum! Chok-tum! Chok-tum! Chok-tum!*

The alley fell silent. Not a single spider moved. The path to the main street was cleared.

"Lords of the Air, thank the dragons that is over," Zora said as she picked her way through the dead bodies with Grey Cloak's sword gripped in her shaking hands. "Can we get out of here, please?"

A shadow fell over the group at the end of the alley. It was a towering spider the size of Itchee from Prisoner Island. It blocked their exit with its massive body. Its eight eyes burned like coals.

Dyphestive stepped in front of the group. "I'll handle this." He raised his sword and charged. "It's thunder time!"

34

THE GIANT TARANTULA REARED ON ITS BACK FOUR LEGS AND STABBED ITS POINTED front claws at the charging Dyphestive.

The iron sword came down. *Slice!*

The metal sheared through the ends of the spider's front legs, which spit ooze. The sword's tip cut into the spider's open mouth and hung on the bottom row of its teeth. He shoved the sword into the meat of the spider's skull, piercing its small brain.

It gave an inhuman shriek, which was cut short. Its legs flattened out, and it hit the street with a thump.

Dyphestive wrenched his sword free of the spider's body and slung off the gore. Then he turned and faced his friends. "I told you I'd handle it."

"ZORA, WHAT HAPPENED?" Grey Cloak asked as he led the group through the city.

"The moment you went into the temple, the zombie soldiers departed. The streets cleared. It was the oddest thing," she said. "We planned to wait, but the spiders came."

"There are more spiders?" he asked.

"Oh yes. Too many to fight. We thought it would be safer to split up and divide their force," she said as she rubbed her scarf. "I used the Scarf of Shadows, but those bloody spiders could still see me. I guess eight eyes are better than two."

"Bloody biscuits, they could be anywhere, and we have to find them," Grey Cloak said. "At least the spiders are gone for now."

"They might have a lair," Dyphestive suggested. He walked with his arm hanging on Leena's shoulder, and she had her small arm around his waist. "We only have to find it."

"That's assuming the spiders have them." Grey Cloak's gaze drifted to the distant cave-riddled hills. They reminded him of the dragon kennels in Dark Mountain. Small bodies were still moving along the ledges, and he could hear the faint clamor of hammers and shovels. "That might not be a bad spot to hide."

"They are not there."

They spun around and found themselves face-to-face with Dalsay.

"Where have you been?" Grey Cloak asked.

"Searching for the others," Dalsay said. "And I have found them."

"All of them?" he asked.

"Are they alive?" Zora added.

Dalsay nodded. "At the moment. We must hurry. Follow me." He moved into the old buildings and vanished from sight, leaving Dyphestive scratching his head. Dalsay reappeared a moment later on the porch of an ancient tavern. "I'll stay on the road, but some doors you are going to have to break."

They jogged through the empty alleys and streets, with Dalsay's ghostly form leading the way. Several blocks away, he came to an intersection where four roads met. A knee-high of neatly stacked stones stood in the center of the intersection. Dalsay hovered over a twenty-foot hole in the ground.

"The arachnids took them down there," Dalsay said as he pointed downward.

The four members of Talon leaned over the wall and peered into the darkness.

"It looks like a giant well," Dyphestive said.

Grey Cloak pointed at the stone steps that spiraled down along the well's inner wall. "Since when do wells have staircases?"

Dalsay floated downward and said, "I'll see you at the bottom."

Grey Cloak slung his leg over the wall and asked, "How deep in this world do we have to go? All the way down to the Flaming Fence?"

"If we have to," Dyphestive said.

Zora grabbed Grey Cloak's arm. She shivered like a leaf and said, "Don't go, please." She averted her eyes from the well. "I-I can't go down there with all those spiders. I can't. Stay with me."

He gently laid a hand on hers and said, "You know I must go. They're our friends. It's fine if you stay up here. The zombies won't harm you. Mortis said so."

"Let Dyphestive and Leena go. You stay with me!"

He tucked her damp strands of hair behind her slightly pointed ears and said, "You'll be safe with us. Come and stay close to me."

Zora shook her head.

Grey Cloak shared a desperate look with Dyphestive.

"Time is ticking!" Dalsay hollered from below.

Leena cut between Grey Cloak and Zora and pushed him back with the palm of her hand then put her arm around Zora's waist. She gave Grey Cloak and Dyphestive intense looks, and with her right hand, she beckoned for them to go.

Grey Cloak searched Zora's eyes. She gave him a nod.

"We'll return soon," he promised. "All of us."

He and Dyphestive descended the spiral staircase into an underworld of total blackness. They were greeted at the bottom by Dalsay. His soft illumination revealed a wide sewer tunnel large enough for men to walk through. It smelled of rot and waste.

Dyphestive found a torch bracketed on the wall and pulled it free. He swung it toward Grey Cloak and said, "Hit me."

"Hit you?"

"Use your wizard fire. Light it up."

"Huh, I never thought about using it like that before." He drew forth energy and pushed it into his dagger. The blade glowed blue, and he jabbed the tip of the torch and drew fire. The flame warmed his face. "I don't think I've ever appreciated a flame more than I do now."

"Agreed," Dyphestive said.

Dalsay led the way down the grimy tunnel. They were sandwiched in a pressing darkness that clung to their light. "I almost feel like the blackness here is a living thing."

"Perhaps it is," Dyphestive agreed.

"As if we didn't have enough troubles." Grey Cloak noticed another torch bracketed on the wall. "That's promising."

Dyphestive lit the torch then repeated the process every twenty or thirty steps.

From far ahead, the sound of rushing water echoed.

"Do you hear that?" Dyphestive asked.

"It sounds like a river," Grey Cloak said.

They hurried down the tunnel, racing toward the sound of the water.

The tunnel ended on a ledge that overlooked a wide current of water cutting through the belly of the earth.

Suddenly, a foul breeze whistled into the tunnel and blew all the torches out.

35

"So much for torchlight." Dyphestive tossed his torch aside. "At least we have Dalsay's glow."

"And my fire. Pick up your torch. I can still light it," Grey Cloak suggested.

Dyphestive bent over and picked up the torch.

Grey Cloak lit it again with his dagger. "See?"

"I wonder where that breeze came from," Dyphestive said.

"Does it really matter? Will you get us out of here?" Gorva shouted from somewhere in the blackness.

Grey Cloak looked upward. The ceiling of the river chamber was as black as a coal tunnel. There was nothing to be seen above. He called, "Gorva, where are you?"

"Up here!"

"I can't see a thing from here."

"Let me see if I can shed my light on it." Dalsay's feet left the ground, and he floated higher. His body illuminated the outline of a ceiling.

Grey Cloak's upper lip curled. "Ew."

The ceiling was covered in pockets of webbing and dog-sized spiders crawling among the dew-dripping stalactites.

"That's a lot of spiders," Dyphestive commented.

"Over here, wizard!" Gorva hollered again.

Dalsay drifted under the stalactites and stopped below Gorva.

Her body was in a cocoon of webbing and hung from the ceiling by its strands. She wore a frown as deep as a river.

"Don't gawk. Do something!" she said.

"I don't have the means," Dalsay said. "Where is Jakoby?"

Gorva replied, "He was with me, but they took him. He shouted, then his voice was gone." She wiggled in her bonds. "Now, will you get me out of here?"

"Easier said than done," Grey Cloak said under his breath. "Any ideas, brother?"

Dyphestive shook his head. "There are so many webs. How do we get her without sticking? She's trapped."

"Not to mention that the moment we touch a strand, a spider will come running. Probably all of them."

"Let me try something." Dyphestive moved along the ledge that overlooked the river. Webbing coated the walls in several spots. He put the torch fire against the webs and watched them curl away. "My flame and your power should handle the stickiness."

"True, but we still have to climb up there. And fight the spiders. Dalsay, is there anything that you can do aside from nothing?"

"I can watch and advise."

Grey Cloak let out a sarcastic chuckle. "That's great. You've been so very helpful so far."

"At least he provides a light source," Dyphestive said.

"Yes, but we seem to be doing fine without him," Grey Cloak answered, holding his glowing dagger in front of him. He'd never imagined so many webs in his lifetime. "Zora would jump out of her skin if she came down here. It's a good thing she didn't come." He noticed a natural stone bridge that crossed the river and vanished into the darkness on the other side. "Huh, I wonder where that goes."

"I know how we can find out." Dyphestive climbed down the steep bank of stones that led to the river.

Grey Cloak followed him.

"Where are you going?" Gorva shouted. "Get back up here!"

"Dalsay, make yourself useful and stay with her. We're going to take a look at something," Grey Cloak said.

The steeply pitched stone bridge arced over fifty feet of rushing black water then knifed into another tunnel in the rock and vanished.

Dyphestive dipped his fingers into the water. "Icy."

"Hold your torch over the water," Grey Cloak said.

The torch flames shone through the ebony stream, revealing a shallow depth on the bank that quickly deepened.

"That's quite a current," Grey Cloak said. "Not likely that a creature lurks in the depths of its waters, but keep an eye out. Let's cross."

"Human! Elf! Get back here and free me!" Gorva demanded.

Grey Cloak started across the shoulder-width bridge and said, "We're going for help!"

"Well, you're going the wrong way!"

They made it halfway across the slick bridge and stopped. A foul breeze sent new chills down Grey Cloak's neck. The torch flames flickered.

Dyphestive leaned over Grey Cloak's shoulder and asked, "What are you waiting for?"

"I can't see where the bridge ends. Our light has too small of a radius." He crept forward and said, "Watch your step."

The bridge was as slick as wet river stones, and it descended at a steeper angle. Grey Cloak wore only one boot, and his feet began to slide. The blackness closed in. "Zooks."

A glance over his shoulder revealed Dyphestive with his arms stretched out and balancing with a sword in one hand and the torch in the other. He started to slide.

"Gangway!" Dyphestive hollered.

Grey Cloak turned toward Dyphestive's body. "Stop, you oaf!"

"I can't!"

Grey Cloak lowered his shoulder into Dyphestive's chest and tried marching up the ramp. His feet slipped over each other and kept sliding downward. "Zooks, you are a load!"

Dyphestive's body gained momentum, and the speed of their slide increased. "I told you to watch out."

"Where was I to go? In the water?" Grey Cloak dug his feet into the rock, hoping to find a foothold in the smooth surface. Even his flexible toes couldn't find purchase.

Down they went, into the darkness waiting to swallow them.

They crashed to the ground, with Dyphestive landing on top.

"Will you get off me?" Grey Cloak asked.

"Sorry." Dyphestive rolled over and lifted his torch. They sat on a rocky bank. "Huh, this side is no different from the other."

Grey Cloak tugged his boot off and slung it down the bank. "I don't know why I even bother to wear boots. They're so restricting."

"You wear them because you don't want to cut your feet on the rocks."

"Impossible when they are that smooth." He started climbing up the riverbank.

"What's going on down there?" Gorva hollered.

"Nothing!" he shouted back.

"Watch out!" she warned.

Grey Cloak turned. "What is it?" He expected to see spiders dropping out of their nests, but there was nothing.

Dyphestive rose then bent over and picked up his sword. A wave washed over his feet, and a white crab the size of a horse with a luminous shell burst out of the water and clamped its huge pincer down on his ankle.

"Eeeargh!"

36

DYPHESTIVE RAISED THE IRON SWORD OVER HIS HEAD AND BROUGHT IT DOWN ON the head of the crab. *Snap!* The iron sword's blade snapped off at the hilt.

"Horseshoes!" he shouted.

The white crab's legs dug into the rock, and it began towing Dyphestive into the icy water of the rushing river.

Dyphestive clawed at the rocks and fastened his strong fingers in a stony groove. "Grey Cloak, some help would be nice!"

Grey Cloak battled the giant crab with sword and dagger. "I *am* helping, I think." He stabbed at the crustacean's free pincer, which jabbed and snipped at him like a striking snake. "That thing is fast!"

"And strong! It broke my sword," Dyphestive said as he held on to the rocks for dear life. "It's pulling my leg off!"

"Hold on!" Grey Cloak turned up his power and unleashed his speed. He struck the crab's attacking claw in a flurry of burning blue steel. Chips of shell and small hunks of flesh started to fly. A quick strike from his sword sliced the smaller snapping bottom pincer off. "Yah! That's progress! Only a hundred more strikes, and you should be free!"

"A hundred more, and we'll both be dead!" Dyphestive pointed toward the river. "Look!"

Several more white crabs crawled under the water toward them.

"That might be a problem," Grey Cloak said.

Dyphestive groaned. His body slid closer to the river. He clung to the rock by the tips of his fingers. "I'm losing my grip. Hurry!"

The crab used its broken pincer like a club to beat Grey Cloak. He leaped over the claw, did a somersault in midair, and landed perfectly on the crab's back. Using both hands, he plunged his burning steel into the crab's brain. The shell cracked, and mystic fire burst through its limbs. Its efforts to drag Dyphestive into the chilling depths stopped.

Dyphestive sat up and started prying open the pincer locked on his leg. "Sweet Gapoli, it's like a vise!"

Nearby, the crabs crawled out of the water and scurried onto the beach.

Grey Cloak started hacking at the bottom of the dead crab's pincer. "Dirty acorns, these things are tough!"

"You don't have to tell me!" Dyphestive latched his fingers on the lower pincer and heaved. "Urk!"

"Put some muscle into it, brother!" Grey Cloak said as he saw mounds of muscle and veins pop out on his brother's arms, neck, and temples.

The crab pincer cracked and split away from the husk of the main claw. Dyphestive pulled his leg free and crab-walked up the bank and away from their pursuers.

Grey Cloak helped his brother to the top of the bank. "Can you walk?"

Dyphestive stared down at his bloody ankle. "As long as I have both feet, I can walk."

The other giant crabs didn't show any interest in pursuit and slunk back into the water.

Grey Cloak shook his head. "Spiders and crabs and zombies, oh my."

"What is going on down there?" Gorva shouted. "What are you standing around for?"

"We're going! We're going!" Grey Cloak noticed another tunnel like the one they'd entered from on the other side and said, "That must be where the spiders took Jakoby."

"After you," Dyphestive said.

"Here, you're going to need this." He handed Dyphestive his long sword. "You really need to take better care of your equipment."

"Don't remind me. I found myself attached to the iron sword. I'm going to miss it." Dyphestive spun the long sword on his wrist. "It's small, but thanks."

"Small. Ha, you're too big." Grey Cloak led the way into the tunnel, which had the same dimensions as the last one. Torches were bracketed to the wall, and at the tunnel's end was a flickering burning light like one would see in a fireplace. "Well, it's clear that men made these tunnels at some point in time, but who?"

"Perhaps Thannis collapsed on another subterranean city," Dyphestive suggested.

"That would mean that something else lived down here before, and aside from spiders and crabs, I see no other evidence of that."

The end of the tunnel opened into a circular-domed chamber that was perfectly built from the rock. Strands of webbing and spiderwebs decorated the better part of the room. Giant ruby-like stones in the outer wall glowed with their own fire. A golden glint immediately caught Grey Cloak's eye, and he looked down at the floor. He tapped his brother's shoulder and said, "Look down."

Dyphestive dropped his stare.

The chamber floor was covered in treasure from one end to the other. Among the tremendous piles of ancient coins were precious stones, gold and silver chalices, plates and flatware, weapons, armor, and the bones of many skeletons.

"This sort of place would make Batram drool," Grey Cloak said as he wiped his mouth. "It's making *me* drool." He bent over and reached for a small golden jewelry box lying near his toes.

Dyphestive grabbed him, pulled him up, and said, "I wouldn't do that if I were you."

Grey Cloak narrowed his eyes.

Spiders nested in the webs extended their legs, which they had balled up into their bodies. They began to crawl and climb over the webbing.

"I think I'm getting sick of spiders," Grey Cloak said.

"*You're* getting sick? How do you think I feel?" Jakoby said. He was in the back of the room, covered in webbing and fastened to a throne-like golden chair. Two spiders were latched on top of him, their fangs fastened to his limbs. "In the name of the Monarchy, get these things off me!"

37

coins in their wake.

Grey Cloak arrived at Jakoby's chair first, slid across the treasure, and stabbed a spider in the side with his dagger. The spider detached from Jakoby and scurried away. Dyphestive skewered the second spider, lifted it off with his sword, and flung it away.

The spiders burst into activity. They crawled down the walls and shot down the webbing.

"Get this off me!" Jakoby demanded.

"There's no time!" Grey Cloak said.

The spiders closed in from all directions.

"Dyphestive, catch!" He tossed his dagger to his brother, who snatched it out of the air.

"What are you going to fight with?" Dyphestive asked.

Grey Cloak knelt and filled his hands full of ancient coins. He fed his power into the metal and knit his brow. "Watch and see!" He slung a handful of glowing coins into the oncoming wave of spiders. The metal cut into them and blew away their limbs.

"I like it!" Dyphestive's arms started pumping steel deep into the spiders' bodies. *Glitch! Gurk! Slice! Gorch!*

"That's it, Dyphestive!" Jakoby roared. "Stomp the spider goo out of them!"

Grey Cloak moved like the wind, slinging coins and blowing spiders to pieces.

What Dyphestive didn't stab, he stomped the life out of with his boots. A spider dropped on his back and sank its teeth into the back of his neck. He turned his back to his brother and said, "Grey, hit me!"

Grey Cloak flicked a coin and blew a hole in the spider. It sprayed goo and dropped dead on the floor.

Another wave of spiders raced toward them. They were fast, but Grey Cloak proved faster. He scooped up handfuls of more coins and wrought havoc. "You've tasted my thunder. Now feel the burn!"

Boom! Boom! Boom! Boom!

The quicker, stronger, and more powerful Grey Cloak and Dyphestive outmatched the small horde of spiders and mutilated every last one of them.

Dyphestive's sword and dagger hung at his sides. He was up to his elbows in spider gore.

Grey Cloak wiped bug splatter from his face and said, "That was easy." He retrieved his dagger from his brother and used it to cut away Jakoby's silky bonds. "Are you well?"

Jakoby rubbed the bite marks on his forearms. "My head is light from the blood they sucked out of me, but I'll live." He dropped a heavy hand on Grey Cloak's shoulder. "Thank you both. The truth is that I didn't think I would make it, like Dalsay said."

"Well, what does he know?" Grey Cloak sheathed his dagger and began to mosey through the treasure chamber. "Look at all of this. Fantastic!"

"More than we can carry—that is for certain." Dyphestive kicked a dead spider out of the way and began to wander around the room. "Have you ever seen so much treasure, Jakoby?"

"Monarch City has several vaults such as this that I guarded when I was younger. It wouldn't surprise me a bit if this was one of many," he responded.

"Several?" Dyphestive asked.

Jakoby nodded. He made his way over to a suit of plate armor that lay on the ground and knelt. A skeleton was still inside it. "Lords of Thunder, this man wears the seal of a Monarch Knight. I had a suit the same as this once. He must have been part of the expeditions. It seems we've made it as far as they did, but they didn't make it out of here."

"No, but we will. After all, we've made it this far." Grey Cloak stood beside a stone table with treasure piled on top. There were tiaras, crowns, bracelets, and necklaces lying among the coins. He picked up a jewel-encrusted crown and set it cockeyed on his head. "How do I look? Could I pass for a Monarch?"

"Only if you come from Monarch blood or marry into it," Jakoby said. "Or you can buy your way in if you have enough. This vault would be enough."

"I like that idea."

"But why would you want to be a Monarch? They are a very detached society. Believe me, I've seen it."

Grey Cloak dropped the crown back onto the table. "We have more important matters to worry about than being rich, I suppose. We still have to save Gorva and destroy the lich and her army of zombies." Cold metal coins slid underneath his steps. "It's best we take it one evil minion at a time."

Jakoby unfastened a sword belt from the corpse and buckled it around his waist. "Impressive. There is corrosion on the metal, but the leather's still pliable. I wonder what took this man. His weapons weren't drawn. There is no major scarring on the armor." He drew the sword. It came out of the sheath with a ring of metal. The blade shone like daylight, and with wide eyes, he said, "Lords of the Monarch, what a sword!"

"I wouldn't get attached. According to Mortis, we won't be able to keep any of this," Grey Cloak said. "But we might be able to use it." He picked up a coin from another table. Everything in the piles was covered in a fine green grit. He rubbed it off on his fingers. "It must be the dampness."

"What was that?" Jakoby sheathed his sword then drew it again in the wink of an eye. "Beautiful."

"I was curious about all the grit, but why should I expect anything different in a damp spider lair?"

"Uh, Grey, you might want to come and take a look at this," Dyphestive said from the other side of the room.

He picked his way across the room, avoiding the dead spiders and the skeletons that had been picked clean by the spiders, he assumed. "Yes, what is it?"

Dyphestive pointed at a standing suit of armor propped up in the corner.

Grey Cloak gasped.

38

"I CAN'T BELIEVE MY EYES," GREY CLOAK WHISPERED. "CAN IT BE?"

Draped over the standing suit of armor's shoulders was a broken-in grey cloak.

He eased his fingers toward the fabric. "It must be a trick." Two fingers brushed over the soft fabric, which felt unlike anything he'd ever felt before. He glanced at his brother. "This is it."

"The Cloak of Legends?"

"I'd know it anywhere," he replied.

Jakoby cleared his throat, caught their attention, and said, "There is something oddly familiar about these dead bodies on the floor." He poked at the air. "But I can't put my finger on it. This sword belt, for example, fits my hips perfectly."

Grey Cloak returned his attention to the cloak and rubbed his jaw. "How could I have been here before and done this? Do you think I did this?"

Dyphestive shrugged. "Someone did. It looks intentional." He stared hard at the great sword gripped in the hands of the suit of full plate armor. The metal gauntlets' fingers were wrapped around the hilt of the sword, which was pointed toward the ground. His head leaned farther over his shoulder as he studied the crusty sword. "It looks like the iron sword," he said.

Grey Cloak tore his eyes away from the cloak and looked at the blade. "It does look the same as the iron sword. The handguard and pommel are the same, but look at that." A square gem was built into the sword's cross guard on the right, below the blade. He scratched the grit away with his finger. The gemstone twinkled with bloodred fire. "I think it's magic, maybe."

Jakoby tapped them both on the shoulders and said, "I thought the spiders made my skin crawl, but I think I found something worse. Come." He led them through the chamber, taking note of the bodies he came across. "This one is a knight like me." He moved away. "Not much left of this one, but look at the teeth. Orcen. Over here is a man, I believe. Look at his leather armor and all the blades he once carried." He pointed. "And there." He hurried over to a set of bones and knelt then lifted a sash wrapped around a very small waist. "Leena wears robes such as these. Don't you agree?"

Dyphestive's face paled.

"It has to be a coincidence. It can't be her." Grey Cloak's eyes swept through the room. Jakoby's theory had accounted for every person in their party except for Dyphestive, Grey Cloak, and one other. A smallish skeleton woman in familiar clothing lay against a table. "Zora!"

The skeleton wore a pair of tall boots, and a black scarf was tied around her neck. "This is impossible. It can't be them. It must be some sort of a trick. An illusion. It must be the doing of Mortis."

Dyphestive sat on both knees, holding what could have been Leena's long ponytail. "It feels real, but where are we, brother?"

"I don't know." Grey Cloak marched over to the suit of armor, gathered his cloak, and put it on. A familiar warmth spread through his extremities. "We need to move." He started peeling the gauntlet's fingers away from the iron sword. A black staff, four feet long, fell from behind the blade. He caught it in his right hand. "What's this?"

"A cane?" Dyphestive asked.

"It's too long to be a cane. It's more of a walking stick. But why would I put it here?" He spun it around in his hand. "It looks more like something your woman would carry." He eyed the dead body that they thought could be Leena. "Not that one, naturally. But who could be absolutely certain, seeing how neither one of them speaks?"

"Grey Cloak," Dyphestive said with a growl in his voice, "that's not nice."

"No, I don't suppose it is," he said, running his gaze along the staff. He noticed runes and symbols carved along the length of the polished wood. "It must be here for some reason. Nevertheless, we need to get out of here."

"What about the figurine?" Dyphestive asked.

Grey Cloak gave a nervous laugh. "Forgive my excitement. My reunion with my cloak got the best of me, but I didn't see it anywhere in this chamber."

"No offense, but we haven't been looking that long," Dyphestive said. "We need to keep looking."

"Agreed," he replied.

"I'm not going to spend the rest of my life down here like the rest of them," Jakoby said. "My bones are itching. We need to hurry."

As Grey Cloak waded through the treasure trove, a thought came to mind. *No, it couldn't be that easy. Could it?*

He started patting himself down and reached into the inner pockets of the cloak. A familiar object filled his hand. He pulled out a black figurine of a faceless man. It was as smooth as polished onyx or black jade. His smile could have filled the room. He cleared his throat and caught the others' attention. "Look what I found."

Dyphestive stared at him with disbelief. "You found it? Where was it?"

"In my cloak pocket."

"Are you certain that's it?" Jakoby asked.

Grey Cloak polished the figurine on the sleeve of his robes. "Oh, this is it. I can tell by the surface and the heft. There is nothing like it in all the world." He recalled the word of power.

Osid-ayan-umra-shokrah-ha!

The figurine stayed cool to the touch.

Will it work, or will it not? That is the question.

He hid the figurine back in his cloak. "Grab anything that might be useful. We're still going to have to fight our way out of here." He found some potion vials, a scroll, and some other trinkets and fed them into his pockets. He hugged himself. "I'm so glad to have my cloak back."

Water began to spill into the chamber from the mouth of the tunnel and rose like a creek. It covered their feet in seconds.

"The chamber is flooding!" Jakoby hollered. "We need to go now!" He headed up the steps that led out of the chamber. A tide waist high knocked him backward. "Monarchs!"

"Grey Cloak," Dyphestive said. He wore a huge gold necklace with a cross on it. "I don't think we're going to be allowed to leave here with the treasure."

"And this explains what happened to the others—they drowned," Jakoby added. The water flooded in so fast that it was up to their knees. "We're doomed!"

"No, we aren't!" Grey Cloak knew the cloak would allow him to swim underwater, but that wouldn't save the others. He waded toward the tunnel.

A tremendous figure dropped from the shadows in the ceiling and blocked his path.

"Zooks!"

39

THE MONSTER BLOCKING THE TUNNEL WAS TWICE THEIR SIZE. IT STOOD ON TWO powerful legs and had a head like a bat and four pairs of eyes. Sets of feathery gills flexed on its neck. Its body was covered in fishlike scales, and it had four muscular humanoid arms and four spider legs in between.

"What sort of abomination is that?" Jakoby asked.

"I don't know, but we have to get past it!" Grey Cloak said. Without thinking, he summoned his wizard fire. The end of the four-foot staff he carried blossomed into the tip of a fiery spear. "Whoa! That will do."

The monster opened its slavering jaws. Drool spilled over its sharp fangs and down its chin. It flexed its arms and webbed hands and let out an ear-splitting roar.

Grey Cloak pinched his nose. His eyes watered. "If we can survive that smell, we can survive anything."

Dyphestive raised the iron sword. The gem in the cross guard glowed like a red-hot coal. "It's thunder time!" He stormed the monster.

Grey Cloak and Jakoby flanked Dyphestive and ascended the watery steps.

The monster made a rattling sound with its mouth. It pointed its spider legs at Dyphestive and shot long quills out. The quills stuck into Dyphestive's flesh as if he were a cushion, but it didn't slow his advance.

Grey Cloak jabbed his spear at the monster and asked, "Dyphestive, are you well?"

"We'll see!" He chopped at the monster's leg and tore through its thigh. It bled green.

"Rawr!" The monster punched Dyphestive with two of its fists and knocked him back, making him splash into the water.

Jakoby knifed his way up the stairs and stabbed the creature between the ribs. It twisted at the hip and backhanded him, knocking him into the wall.

"Get back!" Grey Cloak poked at the creature's webbed hands, keeping the sharp talons of its fingers at bay. "Back!"

"Grey Cloak, you must shut off the water! You need to hurry!" Dalsay said. He appeared in front of the monster, whose claws passed right through him.

"Oh, now you show up!" Grey Cloak ducked under the monster's outstretched hands. "What am I supposed to do?"

"The river has been dammed. You need to open it. Follow me, and I'll show you what to do," Dalsay replied as he waved him toward the tunnel.

"Easier said than done, wizard! In case you hadn't noticed, there is a small obstacle in the way!"

"I'm sure you'll think of something." Dalsay vanished down the tunnel.

Dyphestive rose from the water with a determined look on his face. Knees pumping, he went after the monster. "Grey Cloak, we'll distract it. You go!"

"I'm not leaving you behind!"

"Go, Grey Cloak!" Jakoby shouted from the other side of the steps. "Your brother and I will handle this monstrosity!"

They rushed the monster and thrust their steel into its flesh. It belted out a roar.

Grey Cloak snuck behind the monster and dove into the rising water. The tunnel had filled above his shoulders, and the water pushed him back toward the chamber. He dipped his head under. *Here we go, cloak. Do your thing!*

The Cloak of Legends took over the same as it had in Lake Flugen. It propelled him under the surface, and he swam like a fish.

He popped up on the other side of the tunnel and treaded water. Dalsay hovered over the surface with his arms crossed over his chest. The river water had risen over the bridge.

"Well?" Grey Cloak asked.

"This way!" Dalsay led him downriver to where the water flowed through the rock. "The opening is dammed. I watched as a trap door fell and sealed it shut."

"What am I supposed to do about it?"

"There has to be a release that will lift the seal back up. Find it! And hurry, or everyone will drown."

"Yes, I'd figured that much out." He sank into the water and saw the huge stone seal that blocked the tunnel. It was surrounded by giant crabs.

40

"My sword is sharp, but this monster feels no pain!" Jakoby said. He ducked under the claws of a webbed hand and stabbed the monster in the stomach. "Die! Curse you!"

Dyphestive fared little better. He chopped off two spider arms and gored the monster in the chest, but it still kept coming. "I feel your pain!" He pushed out of the chest-high water and executed an awkward overhead chop. The blade sliced through the monster's forearm and bit through the bone of its shoulder.

The monster brought two fists down like clubs and slammed them into Dyphestive's shoulders. The jarring blow drove him under the water. *Bloody Biscuits!*

The fight went on, back and forth. The monster struck, then Dyphestive and Jakoby let steel cut into its abdomen and limbs. All the while, the water continued to rise, making it impossible for them to keep their footing.

"Keep swinging! It has to die eventually!" Dyphestive hollered and gave a sword thrust that pierced bone.

Jakoby spit out a mouthful of water and replied, "Not if we drown first."

The monster ducked beneath the water and vanished.

"Where did it go?" Jakoby asked. His head was bleeding, and he gasped. "And I'm standing on my tiptoes! Are you?!"

Eyeing the water, Dyphestive nodded. He was a little taller than Jakoby, but it wouldn't be long before they were both completely submerged. "I think we hurt it. Now it's waiting for us to drown to finish us."

"That's what I'd do," Jakoby said. "We aren't going to float carrying this steel either. We need to kill it and—*ulp!*"

Jakoby was jerked under the surface. His arms waved above the water then vanished.

"Horseshoes!" Dyphestive took a deep breath, dropped his sword, and dove into the water. Two bodies thrashed. He swam like a frog toward the melee. The monster had Jakoby in a stranglehold. Jakoby whacked at its side with his sword.

Dyphestive swam underneath the monster's legs and snuck behind it. He bunched his legs under him and launched. With a mighty effort, he climbed onto the monster's back and put it in a headlock and squeezed.

The monster thrashed from side to side. Its shoulders and hips twisted violently, and it stormed through the water.

With one arm around its bull neck and the other hand locked to his wrist, he yanked back. The muscles in his arms knotted up, and he squeezed the bat head and crushed it like a vise.

His lungs started to burn, but so did the fire within. *Die, monster! Die!*

He spit out air bubbles and let out his own watery yell.

The monster's strong limbs trembled. It spasmed and jerked. The hard muscles in its neck caved against the pressure. Its spine snapped. *Pop!*

Dyphestive paddled to the surface and, gasping, came face-to-face with Jakoby. "Are you—*eeyah!*"

The monster floated up between them. It was on its back, and its neck was bent, a dagger stuck in it.

Using the monster for a raft, Jakoby pulled the dagger free. "We did it," he said, panting. "I don't know how, but we did."

Dyphestive nodded.

The water continued to rise, and they floated ever closer to the ceiling.

"We need to swim out of here," Jakoby said.

"There's nowhere to go," Dyphestive said. "If it's flooded on this side, it will be flooded on the other side too. It's in Grey Cloak's hands now."

GREY CLOAK THRUST his spear into a giant crab, searing it inside and out. It floated down into the watery depths, and three others came forward.

Great! At least I can swim like a fish!

The Cloak of Legends's unique powers lent him the ability to breathe, see, and swim fast underwater. Using his superior maneuverability, he weaved through the slowly swimming crabs and gored them individually.

Finally!

Using his spear for light, he searched the seal in the tunnel. It was made of tons of rock and was impossible for him to move.

What did Dalsay say? Look for a trigger or a release.

Grey Cloak ran his hands along every nook and cranny near the seal. He didn't see a lever or handle of any sort. He swam back to the surface and shouted, "Dalsay! I don't see anything! Do you?"

"I'm looking!"

"Someone must have set it off. Did you see anyone?"

"No one is here but us," Dalsay replied.

"And me!" Gorva yelled. "Find it or we are going to drown!"

The chamber was three-quarters filled.

Grey Cloak spun around as he treaded water, searching the ceiling. He tried to understand the trap. *The purpose is to flood the chamber. Once the chamber is flooded, the trap needs to be set again, and it needs to be drained. No one could swim down here. Hence, it must be triggered by something.*

Half-hidden in the webbing, mounted in the ceiling, was a bronze plate with three wavy lines.

"Aha!" he said.

"What?" Gorva asked.

He swam underneath the plate. "I bet my pointed ears that's a pressure plate. Except I can't reach it. Hold on." He dove deep in the water, turned, and swam upward, gaining speed, then burst out of the water like a fish. He hit the bronze plate with his staff and pushed. The pressure plate clicked.

Grey Cloak clung to the ceiling, using the webbing to hold him fast.

Below the water's surface, stone ground against stone. The water bubbled and started to churn. A whirlpool formed beneath them.

"Will you free me?" Gorva demanded.

"Do you want me to free you now? You'll drop into that whirlpool."

"As soon as it's finished, you get me out of these webs," she said.

"I will." He glanced about. "Where are the spiders?"

"They aren't foolish," she said. "They scurried out of the tunnel the moment the water started to rise."

41

THE UNDERWATER RIVER DRAINED, AND GREY CLOAK FOUND TWO SOAKING-WET men back inside the flooded tunnel chamber. He gave Dyphestive a bear hug, even though he had a hard time wrapping his arms around him. "Brother, you are well! I'm elated!"

Dyphestive thumped him on the back and said, "Thanks to your efforts. It came down to the final moments, though."

Jakoby poured the water out of one of his boots and said, "You have my thanks as well. I've envisioned myself perishing by the sword many times but never water. A watery death would have been far worse."

The deeper section of the treasure chamber was still flooded. The coins and gems shone beneath the calm water, and the monster floated on top.

Gorva stormed down the tunnel with Dalsay in tow. Her gaze passed over the men and set on the floating monster. Her lips twisted, and she asked, "What is that thing?"

"We were hoping you would know," Dyphestive said.

She gave him a serious look. "Why would you think I would know?"

The men chuckled.

Gorva waded deeper into the room and said, "Your humor is sad. Great dragons!" She rushed into the water below the tunnel then dove in and came up with her arms full of dripping treasure. "Look at this hoard!"

"That's the reason we almost died," Grey Cloak said. "We can't take it with us."

"We can take some." Her big eyes reflected the gold she held. "It would be a waste not to."

Dalsay stood at the tunnel's entrance and said, "We have more important matters to worry about than treasure. We have a lich and her zombie army that need to be dealt with. Find a weapon to fight with. You're going to need it."

"That won't be a problem." Gorva waded through the water.

Grey Cloak caught Dalsay studying his staff. "What?"

"Those are some interesting items that you have acquired," Dalsay said. "Did you find the figurine?"

Grey Cloak hadn't even had time to think about it. He considered not telling Dalsay but opted for the truth. "I have it."

Dalsay nodded.

"Did you know all these items were here all along?" he asked.

"I only knew of the figurine. And nothing has changed. We still don't have a prayer to escape Thannis—at least *you* don't—but you made it this far. There is a sliver of hope." He approached Grey Cloak, and a whimsical smile crossed his face. "Life never ceases to amaze me."

Grey Cloak twirled the staff under his arm. "What do you mean by that?"

"There isn't enough time to explain. But that staff you carry, I've seen it before, long ago. It's called the Wand of Weapons."

"Where did you see it?"

"As I said, we don't have time."

Gorva emerged dripping wet from the water. She carried a spear and had a sword belt crossed over her back. "I'm ready to get out of this spider-infested sewer." She walked right through Dalsay. "I'm not waiting anymore."

They hurried through the exit tunnel, crossed the bridge, and made their return trip to the heart of Thannis. Everyone's boots squished with every step, except for Grey Cloak, who was barefoot.

Water dripped from the ceiling, and the flood water continued to drain. Their footsteps splashed over the slick surface. No spiders appeared. Nothing slowed their trek.

Grey Cloak sped ahead as they neared the well they'd entered. He thought of Zora.

I hope she's there.

The top of the huge well loomed above like a skylight. He jumped over the rocks and hurried up the spiral stairs. The once-empty streets were busy again with the wandering dead. The pavement surrounding the well opening was covered in water. There were no signs of Zora or Leena.

Zooks!

He climbed out of the well. The undead paid him no mind and went about their business. He scanned the area as the others climbed out.

"Where's Zora?" Dyphestive asked.

"I don't know. I'm looking," he said without hiding his irritation.

"Judging by the new activity, I believe our enemies think that we're dead," Dalsay said. "This could be a good thing."

"Nothing could be good if Zora is missing." Grey Cloak felt a tap on his shoulder. "What, Dyphestive?"

"Huh?" his brother asked from the other side of the well.

The scent of jasmine caught Grey Cloak's nose, then Zora appeared and threw her arms around him. "You're alive! Thank goodness you are alive!"

"Thank goodness *you* are alive," he said. "Are you well? What happened?"

"Where's Leena?" Dyphestive asked with concern.

Zora pointed at the entrance to an old tavern. Leena sat on the end of the porch with her legs kicking.

Dyphestive smiled and hurried over to her.

"I thought you were dead, but we waited," Zora said. "What happened down there?"

"What happened up *here*?"

Zora broke off her embrace and said, "I'll tell you what happened. My heart almost burst. We heard a roar of water inside the well. Without warning, more spiders scurried out. I thought I'd die. But they didn't attack. They came and kept going. Shortly after that, water bubbled over the rim of the well, soaking the streets." She clasped his hand and kissed it. "I thought for certain you were all gone. Still, we waited. Shortly after the flood, the undead returned to the streets. The same as before, they looked right through us."

He turned his attention to Dalsay. "If they think we're dead, we can slip out of here, can't we?"

"That's unlikely."

"Why?"

Dalsay's wide sleeve hung low from his bony arm as he pointed. Thannis's zombie soldiers marched down the street, making a beeline for the company.

"They know we're here," Dalsay said.

"What do we do?" Zora asked.

"There's only one way out of Thannis alive," Dalsay said. "We must kill Mortis."

The slow march of the zombie soldiers turned into a run.

"To the temple!" Dalsay ordered. "Everyone, run!"

42

RAZOR

"Little? Who are you calling little?" Razor watched the man called Ghost dismount. He wore a worn leather mask dyed blue and moved over the ground without a sound. "And what is the situation with the masks? Are all of you as ugly as you sound?"

Ghost reached over his shoulder and drew his long sword from his scabbard. The blade snaked out of its sheath without a sound.

"One sword, eh? Against my two? You might want to reconsider, fella," Razor warned. He stole a glance at Scar and Shamrok, who let out rusty chuckles. Their voices made his skin crawl. "You fellas have quite a sense of humor, seeing how your friend is about to die."

"He's not the one that's going to die." Shamrok leaned back in his saddle and crossed his arms over his chest. "I'll bet my life on that."

Razor fixed his attention on Ghost. Unlike the other men, his eyes were black pits. "At least you don't flap your lips like the others."

Ghost stormed forward and swung. Metal kissed metal in a ring of steel. Razor caught his attacker's blade between both of his. The jarring impact rattled his arms to the elbows.

Bloody biscuits, he's strong! But is he fast?

He spun away from Ghost and unleashed a backhand swing at the Doom Rider's thigh. Ghost blocked the strike and countered with a stab at Razor's throat.

Razor snaked his head aside and brought both of his swords up to bear. Ghost hammered away at him with both hands on the handle of his sword. Razor shuffled backward.

He's fast!
Clang!
And strong!

Bang!

He parried for his life.

He's not a man. He's a force!

Razor had faced the finest swordsmen in the land and never met his match, but they weren't men like that one.

Ghost's sword snaked through his defense and clipped him across his cheek.

"First blood!" Scar hollered. "That didn't take long!"

"Let him catch his breath, Ghost!" Shamrok said. "Don't end it quickly. We haven't had this much fun in days."

Warm blood ran over Razor's cheek.

Hold it together!

He paced back and forth, eyeing his enemy.

I can beat him. This is the fight I've been waiting for.

"Uh-oh, it looks like someone is getting mad. You'd better be careful, Ghost. He might bleed tears all over you," Scar said.

"The only one that is going to bleed is you, Red Face." Razor spit and squared off on Ghost.

I know how fast he is. I know how strong he is. I know how skilled he is.

He grinned.

But I haven't shown him how good I am.

He beckoned Ghost over with his short sword. "Let's keep dancing."

Scar guffawed. "Look at the bow in this young man's back. I like it."

Ghost set his shoulders and came right at Razor.

Razor went on the offense and met the Doom Rider with spinning steel. His arms pumped out lightning-quick strokes. Ghost stood his ground, parried, shifted from side to side, and shuffled his feet. The damp air filled with the chorus of the ring of steel.

The Doom Rider fought off every attack, so Razor turned up the heat. *Clang! Bang! Chop! Hack! Slice! Stab!*

He snuck that last strike between Ghost's defenses and buried his short sword deep in the Doom Rider's chest. "You didn't see that coming, did you?" He shoved the blade clean through.

Ghost let out a raspy sigh of cold fetid breath.

"Ooh," Razor said, "what was your last meal? Rotten fish?" He pushed the man away and slid his sword free. His gaze switched between Scar and Shamrok. He could see the whites of their eyes hidden in their masks. "Which one of you sack faces is next?"

They sat on their gourns and didn't say a word.

"That's what I thought." He sheathed his blades and swung his gaze toward Drysis. "We're finished here. It's best that you be on your way," he said.

Drysis returned a cold gaze, leaned forward, and said, "You are mistaken, Razor. Your fight isn't over." Her gaze passed over his shoulder.

He turned and found Ghost standing and looking right at him. "Impossible. You're dead."

Ghost's arms shot out, and he locked his fingers around Razor's throat then lifted him off the ground by the neck.

"There's a reason we call him Ghost, you fool!" Scar said. "He's already dead."

Razor's eyes bulged in their sockets. He chopped at Ghost's rigid arms with his fists. Ghost walked him across the ground.

He dropped his hands to his sides and took two daggers from his hips. He jammed them into Ghost's ribs. Ghost only squeezed harder.

Die, blast you!

He kicked and kneed the undead man. In the background, he could hear Scar and Shamrok laughing.

"Don't kill him, Ghost. I don't want him dead. I want him broken," Drysis ordered.

Ghost slammed Razor hard into the ground then pinned him by the neck and started punching him in the ribs.

"Hit him for us, Ghost!" Shamrok said. "Hit him hard!"

43

GHOST BEAT RAZOR LIKE A DRUM. HIS RIBS CRACKED, AND HE BEGAN TO WHEEZE.

Razor jammed every small blade he had into the Doom Rider's body, but the blows kept coming.

"Enough!" Drysis said.

The Doom Rider stood over Razor. Daggers were stuck in his ribs, leg, and abdomen, but he didn't bleed.

Razor spit out a tooth and asked, "What's the matter? Are you getting tired?"

"He might not fight well, but at least he has spirit," Scar said with a nod. "Respect."

"You know where you can stick your respect." Razor rolled over to his hands and knees. Pain lanced through his body. His lungs burned. He tried to stand.

Ghost stepped on his back and pushed him down.

He let out a painful gasp and said, "Fighting with your feet, eh? That's low, even for a worm-eater like you." With one arm extended and the other hidden under his gut, he got ahold of his short sword's grip. "Where are we going with this? What do you want to know?"

"Ah, we have cooperation. I like the sound of promise," Drysis the Dreadful responded. "Tell us who you're traveling with."

"Yuh, Lone Blade, spit it out!" Shamrok said.

Ghost removed his foot from Razor's back.

One way or the other, they're going to kill me. But I'll keep it interesting. To the end.

He tightened his grip on his sword, started to rise, and slumped down again. *Need to sell it.* He let out a painful gasp.

"That sounds bad," Scar said. "I bet he has a cracked rib or two."

"I'd say four or five. I'm pretty sure I heard them snap," Shamrok commented.

"Why don't you come over here and count for yourselves!" Razor sucked air through his teeth. "Lords of Steel!" He fought his way up to his knees but kept his head down and slumped over.

"We're waiting," Drysis said.

"Give a fella a moment to catch his breath, will you?" He closed his eyes and took a deep breath through his nose. He envisioned Ghost's position and exactly where he was going to strike. He tilted his head back, took a breath, and said, "Now, what was the question?"

Drysis groaned. "You're wasting time. Who do you travel with?"

Razor pulled his sword and twisted at the hips. He put all of his strength and momentum into the swing. The blade whistled through the air. *Slice!*

Flashing steel bit clean through Ghost's knee and severed it from the leg. Ghost wobbled.

In the same moment, Razor rose and hacked Ghost's sword arm off at the elbow. Limb and steel fell flat on the ground.

Razor was in the zone. He moved with alarming speed without thinking. He zeroed in on Ghost's neck. His short sword rose and started down. *Clatch-Zip!*

A javelin of fire ripped through his right shoulder and spun him around. He faced Drysis with a bolt in his shoulder, and his sword fell from his fingers. She pumped the handle of her crossbow, instantly loading another bolt, and squeezed the trigger. *Clatch-Zip!*

A second bolt whizzed into his belly.

"Augh!" Razor stumbled backward, tripped over a boulder, and fell onto his back. He rolled back up to his side and stood again.

Scar and Shamrok jumped from their gourns and came at him with swords.

Razor drew his last long sword from his back with his good arm. He licked his lips and said, "Here come the cowards. Prepare to die, worms!" He lunged at Scar.

Scar swept the blade aside with a block so hard that it knocked the blade free from Razor's fingers.

He stumbled, clutching his burning gut, and fell. When he looked up, Scar and Shamrok loomed over him with their blades at his neck. "If I didn't have two holes in me, the both of you'd be dead by now." He managed a painful laugh. "Look at your friend over there. His arm and leg are missing."

Scar poised his blade to strike. "We'll have the final word."

"Scar, no!" Drysis said as she dismounted. "I need him alive."

"Heh, heh, heh, a good thing your mother is protecting you, or you'd both be in worse shape than your two-limbed friend," he said.

Scar kicked him in the gut, and Shamrok did the same. Razor groaned loudly.

"Pick him up," Drysis ordered.

The Doom Riders lifted him off the ground and held him before Drysis.

Razor caught his first good look at Drysis the Dreadful. She had an eye as black as coal and pale, almost white skin with blue veins showing. "I bet you were a pretty sight once, but you're nothing but ugly now."

She clamped her hand over his jaw and said, "You are very chatty."

"It's part of my charm."

With her free hand, she twisted the bolt in his shoulder.

"Gaaah!"

"Let us rip the information out of him, Drysis," Scar said. "It would be our pleasure."

"Don't be a fool. This man will die before he betrays his friends." Slowly, she started pulling the bolt in his shoulder free. "He is rich in character. A rare quality I despise. Fortunately, I have means to pry the information that I need out of him before he dies."

"I'm not going anywhere," Razor said.

"Your gut wound is grave." She tossed the bolt aside. "You won't survive but will experience a slow and agonizing death." She flipped the eye patch over her left eye up.

Razor tilted his head to one side. A bright-blue sapphire burned inside her eye socket and locked on him. "How much is that thing worth?" An unseen force invaded the deepest recesses of his mind. His past flashed before his eyes. His strongest memories were being dredged up to the surface, from his earliest childhood and beyond. His entire life was exposed. "No, no, stop it. Stop it, please!"

"Tell me what I want to know," Drysis suggested. "Tell me who you travel with."

Razor's iron will bent like a spoon. The walls of his mind collapsed. In a dreamlike state, he said, "I'll tell you everything you want to know."

44

THE RUINS OF THANNIS

GREY CLOAK LED TALON DOWN THE STREET WITH THE ZOMBIE ARMY ON THEIR TAIL. He waved his arm behind him. "This way! This way!" He turned the corner of the next block and came face-to-face with another zombie army. He skidded to a stop. "That way! That way!"

The company took off at a dead sprint down an alley.

"There's too many of them!" Gorva shouted.

"At least they aren't spiders," Zora added.

Grey Cloak didn't comment. Instead, he picked his way through the alleys, hoping to mislead the zombies and lose them.

"Grey Cloak, where are you taking us?" Zora asked. "We're going in circles."

"I know what I'm doing." He jetted down a narrow alley and raced by another one that was logjammed with zombies. "Don't go that way."

They moved deeper into the bowels of the city. The streets buzzed with the noise of zombie soldiers on the loose. He stopped at an alley exit that led into one of the main streets. Zombie citizens wandered the city in an ordinary fashion, going about their daily business. He heard his comrades panting and looked back at the sweat glistening on their faces.

"I think we have an opening," he said.

"Where did the wizard go?" Gorva asked.

"He doesn't share the same worries we have." Grey Cloak looked down the street both ways, and two blocks down, the zombie soldiers ran with their backs to them. "We're clear. Come on and keep it slow."

"Slow? Why?" Zora asked.

"I don't want to draw the other zombies' attention, since it looks like only the soldiers are after us. And keep it quiet." He ambled into the street at a slow walk with his neck bent and put a hitch in his step.

"This looks ridiculous," Zora said.

Everyone followed suit, except for Gorva, who walked tall and with her head held high.

"Gorva!" he whispered. "To get along, you have to play along."

"I'm not doing that. Zombies are stupid. They don't know what we're doing," Gorva said. "I'm tired of running. I want to kill them."

"You can't kill them if they're dead," he said.

Gorva snorted.

They were halfway across the street when a small group of zombie children wandered into their midst. The children were playing with steel barrel rings, rolling them down the street. Several of the children bumped right into them and fell down, letting out high-pitched screams.

The awful sound caught the other zombies' attention, and they started wandering the company's way. Farther down the street, the zombie army halted its chase and turned.

A zombie child latched onto Gorva's leg and sank his teeth into her thigh.

"Ow! Get this thing off me!"

All of a sudden, zombies burst out of the nearby buildings' doors and windows. They were a mix of men, women, soldiers, and children.

Dyphestive grabbed the child and flung it across the street into a barren water trough. "What are we waiting for, Grey? Go!"

The company fought their way through the undead children scratching and biting at their legs and raced down the open end of the street.

Grey Cloak rounded the next corner and saw the temple in the distance. "There!"

A blockade of zombie soldiers several men deep had set up at the base of the temple's steps.

Behind their ranks was the ghostly form of Dalsay, waving them toward the open doors. The wizard's ghostly voice carried down the street. "Hurry!"

Behind Talon, hordes of the undead closed in. Ahead, an army of zombies blocked the temple with sharp steel and gnashing teeth.

"We'll never make it through there," Gorva said. "There are too many."

Dyphestive stepped to the front with a white-knuckled grip on the handle of his sword. Fire burned in his eyes. The gemstone on his sword's cross guard gleamed like a bright bloodred star. "I'll make a hole."

Grey Cloak put a hand on Dyphestive's shoulder and said, "Brother, no. There must be another way."

"There's only one way." Dyphestive pointed his sword at the temple. His jaw muscles clenched. "That way!" He tore away from Grey Cloak's grip, and with long strides, he raced down the road. "It's thunder time!"

Leena chased Dyphestive with her nunchakus spinning.

Gorva and Jakoby moved to the fore.

"We can't let him die alone," Jakoby said. He let out a shout. "For the Monarchy!"

He and Gorva took off with their legs pumping at full speed. They left Grey Cloak and Zora in the dust.

"Stay close to me," he said to her.

"As long as there aren't any spiders, I'll be fine!" She glanced at the zombies charging down the street behind them then kissed him on the cheek, lifted the scarf over her nose, and vanished. "I'll see you in the temple."

Grey Cloak shook his head as he gazed after the others racing to their doom. "I'm going to be last. Rogues of Rodden! I'm never last, but in this case, I'll make an exception."

Dyphestive formed the tip of the wedge, with Jakoby and Gorva flanking him and Leena behind him. He smashed into the first row of zombies like a crashing wave. The iron sword swung forth in a huge sweeping arc and blasted through three zombie soldiers.

The tide of evil crashed down on the group.

Dyphestive's arms pumped with vigor. Every moving body the iron sword met fell in a streak of red. Dry bones burst. Armor rattled. Ancient bodies were stomped and crushed. A gap appeared on the steps.

"Make a hole, brother! Make a hole!" Grey Cloak shouted.

Zombie soldiers collapsed on them from all directions and buried them.

Grey Cloak couldn't see a soul in the grave of evil. He raced on with the Rod of Weapons burning bright in his hands and shouted, "Nooo!"

45

DYPHESTIVE SHOVED THE END OF HIS SWORD THROUGH TWO HEAVILY ARMORED zombie soldiers and watched their bones collapse. A jolt of energy coursed through the sword, into his veins, and into his heaving shoulders. "Thunderbolts!" he exclaimed.

The horde of zombie soldiers crowded them from all directions. They came at them with sword and spear, but their efforts were slow and clumsy. They usually won by strength of numbers, wearing the mortal body down and finally running over them.

But that day, it was not the case. Talon battled its way up the steps, through the ranks of rotting flesh, led by the tremendous efforts of Dyphestive. The Iron Sword blasted through armor and bone. Torsos were cleaved clean through. Battered skulls exploded.

Dyphestive hollered at the top of his lungs, "Release the thunder!" He fought like a man possessed. He swung the great blade from side to side, bursting the metal shells that covered the zombies' bodies.

The undead fell in heaps. Bones were crushed underneath his boots. Three zombies fell, and five more replaced them.

Striking with precision, Gorva sliced off a zombie soldier's arm with one sword and decapitated another with her other sword. "There are too many! We need to get into the temple now!"

"It will happen!" Dyphestive said as he climbed up two more steps. They'd made it halfway up, with Dalsay waiting for them at the top. "Keep fighting!"

From behind him came a breeze on his ear and the distinctive sound of whistling. Leena fought at his back, with her glowing nunchakus spinning like wheels of fire. *Clok! Clok! Clok! Clok!*

Leena's strikes connected with deadly accuracy, striking brittle bones and turning them to dust. She drummed on a zombie's face, pulverizing its skull like an egg.

The horde kept coming.

Jakoby bellowed another battle cry. "For the Monarchy!" His sharpened steel cut off a zombie's sword arm. A backhand swing took a head from another. His long arms rose and came down with bone-jarring power. "The Monarchy!"

Talon's effort created a pocket that slowly moved up the steps. At the very top, the undead horde surged downward.

Dyphestive plowed toward the top, destroying every zombie that came into his path. "Keep going!"

Metal rang on metal. Bone popped and cracked.

They made it a quarter of the way up the steps.

"Almost there!" Dyphestive said. The door at the top was open and waiting to greet them. "Temple!"

Jakoby and Gorva's battle cries fell silent. Only the striking of metal remained. Finally, Gorva hollered, "I can't feel my arms!"

"Keep swinging!" Jakoby said. "Keep swinging!"

Dyphestive felt their pain. His shoulders felt like anvils weighing him down. Behind him, Leena's panting was loud. "We are close!" He gored another zombie and ripped his sword out. He butchered two more where the last one fell.

Talon's strength started to fade. Their surge slowed.

Gorva screamed. "I'm wounded! My leg."

Zombies zeroed in on her blood.

Grey Cloak barred their path with the burning spear tip of his Rod of Weapons. Several quick punches of the blossoming spear point put the zombies down. "Dyphestive, make a hole to the door. Make a hole now!"

"Everybody get behind me!" Dyphestive shouted. "Here comes the thunder!" He stormed up the stone steps, plowing through a wall of zombies and running his steel through their rotten bellies.

The zombies stabbed, swung, and clawed at his arms and legs. They ripped open the flesh of his arms. But Dyphestive charged through them like a war horse. His boots found the top of the steps. A wall of zombie soldiers met him. He unleashed the iron sword and cut a corridor through them.

"Hurry! Hurry!" Dalsay shouted as he stood in the temple doorway, waving them inside. "Hurry!"

Dyphestive pushed his way into the temple. The rest of Talon stumbled in behind him.

He turned and battled the hordes of undead soldiers back. "Close the doors! Close the doors!"

Jakoby went to one door, and Grey Cloak went to the other. They shoved the long metal doors toward the threshold.

"Dyphestive, get in here!" Grey Cloak shouted. "Get in here now!"

"I'm trying!" He mowed down three more zombies. "Is everyone in?"

"Zora!" Grey Cloak called. "Zora!"

"I'm here," she said.

"We're all here!" Grey Cloak said. "Now quit playing with those zombies and get inside!"

Dyphestive backed toward the door. There was still a crack big enough to slip through. Grey Cloak's and Jakoby's faces appeared from behind the door.

"Move your feet, man!" Jakoby said.

Dyphestive split a zombie's face open, severing it straight through the helm. "Almost finished!"

The doors slammed shut behind him with a resounding *wham*.

"What? Grey Cloak, this is no time to jest!" He stood with his back to the door and kicked it with the heel of his boot. "Let me in!" He shoved his back against it. "Let me in!"

The temple doors were sealed shut, trapping him outside with an army of zombies. They swarmed him. All he could do was swing.

46

AN UNSEEN FORCE SHUT THE DOORS, AS IF THEY'D BEEN PUSHED BY GIANT INVISIBLE hands. The lock bar dropped into place, sealing Talon inside.

Grey Cloak pounded on the doors with his fists. "Nooo! Dyphestive! Dyphestive! Nooo!"

Jakoby tried to pry the bar away, shoulders heaving. "It won't budge!"

Leena whacked at the bar with her nunchakus.

"Ah-hahahaaa," came a ghostly laugh. The haunting voice echoed all over the hard walls of the temple's chamber. "Don't be so upset. Soon, your friend will join with the ranks of the undead, and you'll be with him."

Grey Cloak turned.

Mortis stood on the stage at the end of the aisle. Her rotting robes billowed around her body like a living thing. Her pupils burned in the black depths of her eye sockets like bright stars. "I'm impressed. You survived my trap in the treasure chambers and led me to believe you were dead. But here you are, still alive. How delicious."

Grey Cloak ignited the fire on the Rod of Weapons and said, "We're going to kill you, Mortis. We're going to take that crown off your ugly head and shove it down your throat."

"A delightful idea, but how do you suppose you can kill someone that is already dead? I've had more centuries of living dead than all your group has living." Mortis walked down the steps. "You've caught my attention, however, and I offer all of you a great honor. You will be lieutenants in my army." She made a fist of bone and leathery flesh. "You will help me lead and conquer the surface together!"

"Never! You're going to pay for what you did to my friend!" Grey Cloak charged.

Mortis sent him flying backward with a flick of her wrist. His shoulder blades slammed hard into the temple door, and he collapsed onto the floor. Before he could come to his feet, Zora, Gorva, Leena, and Jakoby went flying back into the wall too. They hit the ground so hard that they were knocked out cold.

The only one left standing was Dalsay. He stood in the center aisle with Mortis walking toward him. He held out his hand and said, "Mortis, stop. I would like to parlay."

Mortis slowed her advance then came to a stop. The towering lich looked down on Dalsay. "A parlay? Is this a jest? There is nothing that you can offer me."

"I offer flesh and blood for your bones. I offer life."

"You are a shade. You have no such power," she said.

Dalsay started speaking in an arcane tongue that Grey Cloak couldn't comprehend. The wizardly words spun and twisted on his tongue. Using the rod like a cane, he slowly started to rise with his back against the wall.

He can't stop her. He must be buying time.

Grey Cloak felt helpless. All of his friends were down. Dyphestive was trapped outside. He reached into his pocket, grabbed the Figurine of Heroes, and rubbed it. *Please work. Please work.* He uttered the word of power. "*Osid-ayan-umra-shokrah-ha!*"

No smoke spewed. Not a single spark came.

Zooks! He put the figurine away. *I guess it's up to my charm and good looks.*

"Enough chatter!" Mortis said to Dalsay. She walked through the wizard and marched toward Grey Cloak. "Your time has come to join the ranks of Thannis. Give yourself freely, and I'll make the process painless and easy."

Grey Cloak brightened. "*Painless and easy*? Ha! Why didn't you say so?" He crept closer with the rod hidden behind his back. "And you promised I'd be a lieutenant. What an honor."

Mortis tilted her head to one side, and her dry, stringy locks hung over her shoulder. She stretched out her fingers. "You have chosen wisely, elf. Now, come closer and feed me."

As quick as a thought, Grey Cloak charged the rod with fire and rammed the spear point into Mortis's belly.

Without so much as a flinch, Mortis stood her ground and dropped her gaze on the flaming spear. "You are beginning to annoy me." She grabbed Grey Cloak by the neck of his cloak and lifted him off his feet. "The willpower of the living. I have no use for it." She tossed him over the aisle like he was made of feathers.

He made a soft landing by Dalsay.

Mortis pulled the rod free of her gut and tossed it into the pews, then she walked toward the others and set her eyes on Zora.

Grey Cloak stiffened like a board. "My limbs. What happened? I can't move."

"Her power is great," Dalsay said.

"No." He strained against his bonds with all his might. Only his lips and fingers could move. "We have to stop her, Dalsay!"

"You need to trust me."

Mortis spread out her arms. Zora's limp body rose from the floor and floated toward the glowing fingertips of the lich. Mortis cradled Zora in her arms and started to chant over her. Zora spasmed.

Grey Cloak nodded. "I trust you. I trust you. Whatever you must do, do it!"

"I'm going to join your body—entwine my spirit with yours," Dalsay said.

"You're going to what?"

Dalsay stepped into him.

Grey Cloak's eyes popped. "Whoa, I feel you. Not sure I like it."

"You have an ability you've only begun to understand. I'm going to use it."

A pulse of energy burst from Grey Cloak's body and shattered the unseen force that constricted him. His arm lifted, and the Rod of Weapons flew into his hand.

Mortis dropped Zora and spun around to face them. "What betrayal is this?"

Grey Cloak started to speak, but Dalsay's commanding voice spoke for him. "This is the end for you, Mortis!" Blue energy shot from the rod like lightning and blasted into Mortis. The searing force sent her down the aisle, and she crashed hard into the door.

Dalsay turned up the heat, sending streams of energy into Mortis's shaking body.

We're doing it! We're doing it! Grey Cloak thought.

Mortis brought her hands in front of her chest and caught the energy in her palms. Then she pushed back and started to march forward.

Grey Cloak's feet slid over the stone floor toward the stage. A wave of energy from Mortis shoved him into the stairs, and he fell. *We're not doing it.*

47

"Fools! I am the queen of this realm. No living person can defeat me!" Mortis said. She slung flaming balls of energy at Grey Cloak. "I am queen!"

Grey Cloak dashed through the rows of pews, ducked a fireball, and sprang away from another. The balls of energy blew out hunks of the pews, and stone dust filled the air.

"Dalsay, I don't know what you're doing, but you need to do better than this."

When Dalsay talked, he spoke in Grey Cloak's head. *"I'm weaving a spell. Keep running."*

Grey Cloak jumped, dove, and rolled then flattened out between the pews and rolled under a stone bench. "How about I hide?" he whispered.

"You run. You hide. You only delay the inevitable!" Mortis said. Stone pews rose from the ground and were tossed aside like hay bales. Stone crashed against stone. The entire chamber was rocked.

Grey Cloak crawled underneath the pews. "Dalsay, how long is this going to take? She's tearing this place to pieces."

The pew he hid under suddenly rose off the ground and was flung aside. It rolled end over end and exploded into a far wall.

He wiggled his fingers at the lich and said, "Oh, hello, Mortis. I love the renovating you're doing. Though I'm not a fan of the Gothic style. But I think it works well with you."

"I can't wait to dry up that tongue of yours," she said as she took a step forward.

The ground beneath her came alive in the form of stone hands and locked onto her legs.

"Use the rod!" Dalsay said. *"Use it now!"*

Grey Cloak pointed the tip of the Rod of Weapons at Mortis. "What am I doing?"

"Let go of me!" Mortis demanded. She started breaking out of the stony fingers.

The Rod of Weapons came alive and started firing pulses of mystic blue energy. *Puul-puul-puul-puul-puul.*

The bombs exploded inside the lich's chest. With her legs trapped, she started reeling.

"I like this!" Grey Cloak said. He let out another series of bursts. *Puul-puul-puul-puul-puul.*

Wiry tendrils started to wrap around Mortis's body, pinning her arms to her sides.

"She's trapped!" Grey Cloak hollered. "She's trapped!"

"*I can see that. We must act quickly. Sink the rod's spear point into her skull. Hurry!*" Dalsay ordered.

"Fools! You cannot kill me! I'm dead everlasting!" Mortis wiggled in her bonds and set her burning eyes on Grey Cloak. "I cannot die!"

"We'll see about that!" Grey Cloak summoned the spear tip's energy and charged.

Fiery beams blasted out of Mortis's eye sockets.

Grey Cloak ducked. "Yipes! I didn't see that coming." He danced away and began an attack from behind.

Mortis's head twisted around. Wherever Grey Cloak went, her eyes followed.

"Dalsay, blind her or something. I can't get close."

"*Get as close as you can. I have a better idea,*" Dalsay replied.

"I will destroy you! I will destroy you all!" Mortis said as she unleashed another fiery blast.

Grey Cloak ducked under the beams and rammed his shoulder into her. Dalsay departed his body and dove into hers.

Grey Cloak's knees wobbled, and he steadied himself with the rod as he clutched his chest. "I feel like my soul was ripped out."

"Strike now!" Dalsay said from inside Mortis's body.

Mortis's eyes had cooled, but they began to burn anew.

Grey Cloak leaped high in the air, summoned the spear head's energy, and brought the weapon down on the lich's crowned skull. The mystic blast sank down to the black wood.

Mortis's jaw opened wide. "No! You cannot defeat me! You cannot leave this place."

He drove the mystic javelin deeper. "We'll see about that!"

"You will face my wrath!" she screamed. "It will come! I am not the only guard—"

A ring of energy exploded out of Mortis's body and hurled him across the room.

He sat up from a pew with his ears ringing. Dust and debris created a fog in the air. On shaky legs, he walked over to the remains of Mortis. A hole in her skull smoldered. The crown sat cockeyed on her head. A pile of ash and bones and moth-eaten robes lay underneath.

Grey Cloak caught his breath and said, "We did it, Dalsay. Dalsay?"

"What happened?" Zora asked. She was on her feet and rubbing the back of her head. "Who redecorated?"

Jakoby, Leena, and Gorva came to as well. Gorva's leg was deeply cut and bleeding. She walked with a limp. "Where's the wizard?"

"I don't know," Grey Cloak said. His eyes widened. "Dyphestive!" He rushed to the double doors and lifted the locking bar then flung the doors wide open.

Hundreds of zombie soldiers were piled up on the steps and in the streets. They looked like they had all collapsed under the weight of their armor. The city was dead quiet. There was no sign of Dyphestive.

Grey Cloak cupped his hands over his mouth and shouted, "Dyphestive!"

"The wizard said that we would not all make it out," Gorva said.

"Don't say that!" Zora said.

Jakoby walked over the undead bodies. "Look at the wreckage. Limbs and heads of the zombies are everywhere. Follow the wake of the carnage."

Grey Cloak joined the former Monarch Knight on the stairs and followed the path of destruction. It ended in a pile of zombie soldiers stacked up to Jakoby's neck. "In here!"

Jakoby started dragging the bodies out of the pile. Leena eagerly helped. A limb popped off from time to time, and they chucked them aside.

"They're so brittle," Jakoby said.

Grey Cloak clawed through the dead. He was shoulder deep in the carnage when a gleam of red light caught his eye. "Here! Here!"

With everyone pitching in, they cleared the dead away and found Dyphestive lying on the bottom, covered in his own caked-up blood and not moving.

Grey Cloak pumped his fists in the air and screamed, "Dyphestive!"

48

LEENA PUSHED GREY CLOAK ASIDE AND HELD A FINGER TO HIS LIPS. SHE OPENED Dyphestive's vest and placed both hands over his heart.

"What are you doing?" Grey Cloak asked.

She shook her head and squeezed her eyes shut. Her lips moved quickly, but they made no sound. Strings of white light built up in her shoulder and coursed into her hands. She pushed them into his chest. A shock wave of energy blasted out of her hands.

Dyphestive's body jumped a foot off the ground. He sat up with his eyes wide and said, "Die, zombies! Die!" His arm shot out, and he clamped his hand around Grey Cloak's neck.

Grey Cloak grabbed his brother's wrist and tried to pry his hand off. Dyphestive's fingers were as strong as iron. "Let go of me," he pleaded in a raspy voice.

Dyphestive blinked a few times, and his grip loosened, then he released Grey Cloak's neck.

Grey Cloak gasped and let out a few dry coughs.

"Sorry," Dyphestive said, patting him on the back. "What happened?"

"You were dead," Gorva said. "The tongueless woman saved you from the Flaming Fence."

Dyphestive raised an eyebrow and said, "I wasn't dead. And I won't ever be crossing the Flaming Fence. I dreamed I was on a cloud, sailing across the sunny sky. And I had an anvil." He pushed out of the pile of the dead and pried a zombie's bony fingers from his ankles. He surveyed the wreckage. "I killed them all?"

"No, you had some help," Gorva said as her gaze slid toward Grey Cloak. "He killed the lich."

"And that killed the rest?" Dyphestive scanned the heaps of the dead and started counting with his finger. "I was up to one hundred twenty-one, and I don't remember anything after that. I blacked out." He picked up his sword. The bloodred gem twinkled like a small star. "Something possessed me."

"One hundred twenty-one?" Jakoby asked as he eyeballed the carnage. "Well, something tore a hole through this one." He lay his hand on Dyphestive's shoulder. "It looks like it was you."

Dyphestive nodded. With his massive hands, he covered Leena's shoulders, looked into her eyes, and he said, "Thank you, but I was only sleeping. But I liked that jolt you gave me." He grinned. "It felt good. Like lightning coursing through my veins."

"So, we can leave?" Zora asked.

Thannis, the city of the dead, had fallen silent. No zombies scuffled or dragged their feet across the street. The rattling and squeaking of armor was gone. The zombies lay in piles like trash in the streets. Even the creeping and crawling spiders were nowhere to be found.

"I believe so," Grey Cloak said as he studied the temple's doors. "But I fear that we lost Dalsay."

"How?" Dyphestive asked. "He was a ghost."

Grey Cloak shook his head. His heart sank into his stomach. He'd thought he didn't care for Dalsay, but now that the wizard was gone, he found that he actually did. "I don't know. But he said certain death awaited. I hope it wasn't his. I'd be responsible."

"You can't kill a ghost," Gorva said. "It's not possible."

"Well, we killed a thousand zombies and a lich, and they were dead." He shrugged. "I don't know." He eyed the temple. "I'm sorry, Dalsay."

Zora hooked his arm. "I'm sure wherever he is, he's fine. But can we go. Not to be selfish, but I don't want to be anywhere near those spiders if they return. We have what we came for, don't we?"

He nodded.

In the distant hills, which were riddled with caves, the clamor of hammers and shovels biting into dirt and stone renewed.

Small bodies crept in an orderly fashion along the shadows of the narrow ledges.

Jakoby squinted and asked, "Who are they?"

"I don't know, and I don't care to find out. Our path is clear, and if there aren't any objections, I say we move out," Grey Cloak said.

"You don't have to tell me twice," Zora said. "Lead the way."

He glanced at Gorva's leg. Leena had started wrapping it with one of her bandages. "Are you well?"

"I can move well enough," Gorva said. She patted Leena on the head. "She's quiet and helpful. I like it."

"Let me know if I move too fast. How about you, Festive?"

Dyphestive glanced over his assortment of wounds. "No troubles."

Grey Cloak led the way down the broken roadways, navigating through the field of the dead. Mortis had boasted that they wouldn't make it out alive, but there they were, living and breathing, with a field of the dead lying at their feet.

Not only that, but they'd recovered the Cloak of Legends and the Figurine of Heroes.

I don't know how I did it, but I did. He smirked.

"What are you grinning at?" Zora asked.

"We live. Why wouldn't I be happ—"

The ground rumbled. The buildings rattled and swayed. Ancient shingles slid from rooftops and rained down on the ground.

"Dyphestive," Grey Cloak said, "tell me that was your stomach."

"I'm hungry, but I'm not that hungry."

Grey Cloak looked behind him. The hammering in the hills had come to a stop, and the small figures in the hills had vanished. The tremors tickled his bare feet and sent shivers racing up his spine.

Talon exchanged uncertain glances.

"Friends," Grey Cloak said, "I have an idea."

"We're listening," Gorva said.

A building along the road collapsed like a house of cards. Dust and debris swept down the street. From the smoke, a grand dragon with eyes like purple flames emerged and let out a deafening roar.

Grey Cloak shouted above the clamor, "Run!"

49

"Follow me!" Grey Cloak hollered. "Follow me!" He'd led them through the twisting streets of Thannis once, and he would have to do it again. He moved them as far away from the sound of the dragon as he could.

They could hear the sounds of buildings crumbling and the dragon's thunderous roar. It went on for several seconds then fell silent.

Grey Cloak ducked into a garden made of massive stones. Gorva held her bloody leg and winced. Everyone was gasping but him.

"Listen, we need to go around the dragon. Get to the entrance to Thannis where we came in."

Zora had her hands on her sides and said, "Maybe it's not even looking for us."

"I wish, but I doubt it. Before Mortis died, she said something about another guardian. At least I think that's what she was saying. That thing must be it," he said.

"What do you want us to do, Grey?" Dyphestive asked.

"I might have to lead it one way while you go another."

Zora locked her fingers around his wrist and said, "You can't do it all!"

"I agree, brother. We can all get out of here," Dyphestive said. "Whether we kill that thing or die, we stick together."

Grey Cloak nodded. "All right. Everyone, stay close. No one gets separated. We're heading to the field, but if anything happens, be ready to run for your life. We'll only get one chance at this."

The company formed a single-file line and snaked their way deeper into the bowels of the city, heading back toward the fields from where they'd come. Grey Cloak didn't have any trouble picking his way through the wasteland. He could tell where they were by the alignment of the strange lights in the cavern ceiling.

The patterns worked like stars, and he remembered them from the moment he'd seen them.

"We are almost to the city's border. It's only two blocks away," he whispered to Zora, who passed the message back to Dyphestive, who guarded the rear.

Grey Cloak peeked down the street. Thannis was walled by stone structures and broken sections of perimeter wall. A wide road led right into the city. There was no sign of the dragon. "I can only imagine the dragon hiding and waiting for us to blow through the main gate." He rubbed his chin. "We need to find a broken section in the wall." He gave Zora the Rod of Weapons. "Hold this and wait here."

His fingers found purchase, and he scaled the wall three stories up to the top of the building. Then he stole across the flat rooftop to a point where he could see over the border wall. "Drat."

They were in a quadrant of the city surrounded by a drop so deep on the other side that he couldn't see a bottom. Staying low, he moved back across the roof and looked over the main road with a full view of the gate. He scanned the streets and alleys.

Where are you, dragon? I know you're out there.

Even though the grand dragon was a tremendous beast, the massive city still had countless places to hide its girth.

As his gaze swept over the storefronts, his heart skipped a beat.

Head down and twisting spiral horns back, the dragon slunk out of the back streets into full view. It was bigger than most. Hard spiny ridges plated its body. Its scales were thick like steel armor. But patches of the scales were missing, revealing rotting flesh and bones underneath.

What kind of undead abomination is that?

Its claws ripped up the street when it passed, and its tail swept over the ground, knocking out the porch posts.

Grey Cloak hurried back to his friends, dropped the last ten feet from the wall, and said to his wide-eyed onlookers, "Change of plans."

"There isn't another way out?" Zora asked.

"We're cornered. Unless we go back into the city and hide, the only way out is through the gate, and as you can see, it has a guardian." He eased his staff out of Zora's hands. "Hence, we are reverting to my first plan."

"No!" Zora said.

"Dyphestive, see to it that you take them to safety. Don't worry about me. If I can lead it away, it won't catch me." He smirked. "I'm too fast."

"We stand together, brother."

"Not this time. Promise me that you will lead all of them out, brother. It is my final request," he said.

Zora's eyes watered. "You can't do this."

"It's like the wizard said—one of us won't make it out," Gorva said. "You are a brave elf. I hope you make it."

Tears streamed down Zora's cheeks. "You'll die out there."

He kissed her on the forehead. "I'll take my chances." Fire blossomed at the end of the Rod of Weapons. He waltzed out into the street and waved it at the undead dragon like a flagon. "Yoo-hoo!"

The guardian dragon swung its head around and set its fiery vermillion gaze on Grey Cloak. It let out a spine-tingling roar. The sound wave ripped off shingles and shutters and blasted through Grey Cloak's hair and cloak.

He pinched his nose and said, "Next time, I'll remember not to breathe." He glanced at his friends hiding in the alley and smirked. Then he faced the dragon, lowered the Rod of Weapons like a lance, and ran straight at the dragon, shouting at the top of his lungs, "Beware the wrath of Grey Cloak!"

50

"He's gone mad," Zora said.

Dyphestive watched in disbelief as his brother charged the dragon like a berserker and picked up speed. The dragon opened its jaws, revealing a furnace of purple flames.

Grey Cloak planted his feet in the ground, turned, and raced into a narrow alley across the street.

Purple flames carpeted the street a moment after Grey Cloak vanished into the alley. The flames rose high in the air, creating a wall between the buildings.

The heat slapped Dyphestive in the face as if a sweltering blanket had been thrown at him. He pulled Zora back into the alley and shielded her with his body. The heat scorched his back. Everyone in the alley hid their faces and pushed against the wall.

The flames started to die, and Dyphestive looked down the street. The guardian dragon sprinted after Grey Cloak. Its hulking body smashed through the buildings, turning them to rubble. The last of its serpentine tail slipped through the wreckage and vanished.

Stone smashing on stone echoed throughout the once-grand structures of the city. The clamor got farther and farther away.

"Let's go." Dyphestive led the way down the street, where they passed the smoldering flames the dragon had left. A gaping hole made by collapsed buildings twisted through the city.

"Keep moving," Zora said.

Leena shoved the gaping Dyphestive along.

Jakoby followed Gorva, who hurried through the gate with a bad limp.

Dyphestive caught up with them. "Gorva, let us help. We can carry you."

Gorva pulled a dagger and snarled. "If either one of you lays a hand on me, I'll kill you."

Jakoby lifted his hands in surrender. "No problem with me."

"Go, then. Go!" Dyphestive said.

Dragon roars erupted from the street.

He stopped, and Leena shoved him in the back.

"Don't even think about it, Dyphestive," Zora said. "You're staying with us."

Bright flames exploded throughout the city and lit up the tips of the stalactites.

Finally, Dyphestive started moving again.

They raced past the lake, leaped over the fallen undead, and traversed the final hill, where the tunnel to the first inner surface waited. It would be impossible for the guardian dragon to follow them through that tunnel. They had made it to safety.

"We made it," Jakoby said as he hurried Gorva, Zora, and Leena into the tunnel. He eyed Dyphestive. "After you."

Dyphestive shoved Jakoby into the tunnel. "You know I can't leave my brother behind. Get everyone to the surface. We'll meet you there," he said. "I swear it."

GREY CLOAK LOOKED over his shoulder and saw the dragon bursting through a building and closing in. "Zooks, that thing is fast!"

Of course, he'd been around his fair share of dragons, and they weren't slow, cumbersome beasts. They were as quick and agile as little lizards in some cases. But the undead one was bones and scales. He'd hoped it would move more slowly, but it didn't.

He jumped through a tavern window and raced up a flight of steps. The dragon crashed through the door below and unleashed its fiery breath. The flames incinerated the steps and raced down the hall after Grey Cloak. He jumped through the window at the other end and landed as softly as a cat in the street.

Flames consumed the building, and the guardian dragon smashed through the back wall, set its eyes on Grey Cloak, and roared.

"Flaming fences!" He channeled his energy into his feet and took off down the street at full speed. With the Cloak of Legends as his companion, he'd become confident that his plan would work. He would run the dragon ragged, buying time for his friends to escape. Once he thought a reasonable enough amount of time had cleared, he would run after them. There was no way the guardian dragon could follow them into the tunnels. It was far too large to do so.

He hurdled fallen zombies and took every narrow street he could find. The dragon plowed through everything like a juggernaut while spitting balls of flame at him.

I can't shake this thing!

The dragon didn't have to see him. Once it had his scent, it could follow him blind if it wanted.

Grey Cloak ran to the far end of the city and entered Mortis's temple. He slammed the metal doors behind him. His lungs burned—and his lungs *never* burned.

He ran to the stage then turned and ran back toward the doors, stole his way along the front entrance wall, and hid behind the pillars.

The dragon rammed through the heavy metal doors like they were made of glass. It pushed its great girth into the building, squeezing through the opening. Pews were pulverized as it passed, and it crushed the crown and the remains of Mortis under its feet. It approached the stage, letting out loud snorts through its nose, and released a geyser of flame.

Grey Cloak dashed away from his hiding spot and squirted out the front entrance of the building. He hit the steps running at full speed and ran over the undead.

He'd made it several blocks down the road when he heard the temple explode and glanced over his shoulder. The entire temple was an inferno. The guardian dragon crept out and roared.

My plan's working. It won't catch me now!

He ran even faster. The wind whistled by his ears like an arrow.

Zooks, how fast am I going?

It had happened once before, long ago, when the Cloak of Legends spurred him to incredible speeds that defied reason.

Grey Cloak cleared the main city gate like a shot. Far behind him, the dragon steamrolled after him. The only things between him and freedom were the hills and the glassy surface of the lake.

He smirked. *It would be quicker if I didn't have to go around the lake. Can I? Will I? I have to try!*

Grey Cloak went down the grassy bank, and when his toes touched water, he kept going.

I'm doing it! I can't believe I'm doing it!

He had run over the cool surface halfway when he caught someone waving out of the corner of his eye. Dyphestive stood on the side of the lake, flagging him down.

"No, Dyphestive, what are you doing? Go the other way!" He skidded over the water and started to sink.

The guardian dragon charged through the gate of the flaming city.

"Run, Dyphestive! Run!"

The dragon didn't see Grey Cloak and set its sights on Dyphestive.

Grey Cloak swam for the bank. He reached the edge and climbed up.

Dyphestive stood his ground and faced the dragon with the iron sword in hand.

"No!" Grey Cloak ran to his brother's aid, but he wouldn't get there in time.

Dyphestive lunged forward and thrust hard. Brawn and metal collided with dragon skull and scales. The bloodred gem in the cross guard flashed.

The guardian dragon came to a stop. It trembled and roared. The iron sword pierced its skull between the eyes. It twisted the sword free from Dyphestive's grip and bucked like a mule. Dyphestive backed away.

It burned from the inside out. Scale and bone caught fire. The monster exploded, hurling chunks of bone and scale everywhere.

The guardian dragon lay in a smoldering pile. The light in its eyes was gone. The flame inside it had been snuffed out.

Dyphestive pulled his sword free of the mammoth skull.

"You killed it," Grey Cloak said as he shook the water from his cloak. "I'm not sure how you did it, but well done."

Dyphestive's gaze ran along his blade to the gemstone, which had cooled. "I don't know how it happened either." He smiled. "But what's done is done. We did it."

"Let's get out of here," Grey Cloak said. "I've had my fill of dead people."

They navigated through the tunnels without any trouble and passed through the field of glowing dandelions into the last tunnel, which took them to the Inland Sea's waterfall.

"I can't wait to see the sun again," Dyphestive said, "and eat like a Monarch."

Grey Cloak nodded. "I share your sentiments. A feast is in order. Now that I have the figurine and the cloak and you have a fine sword, hopefully, we can get the world back in order."

"Agreed." Dyphestive was the first to stick his head out of the tunnel, and the mist of the river kissed his face. He stood on the ledge with the sun shining on the other side of the water and washed the blood from his skin.

Grey Cloak frowned. His brother was torn up all over from at least a dozen lacerations and wounds. He didn't understand how he'd made it. He gestured to the rope and said, "After you."

"Let's go at the same time and surprise our friends together."

Grey Cloak smiled. "I like surprises. I bet they're sleeping. I know I would be after all that adventure."

Dyphestive climbed the rope.

Grey Cloak used the small handholds in the face of the cliff.

Side by side, brother and brother, they scaled the sheer wall. Before they crested the top, they grinned at one another and counted in silence. "One... two... three..."

They climbed over the lip, jumped up, and shouted, "Surprise!"

Grey Cloak felt the blood run out of him.

Dyphestive's mouth hung open.

They stood face-to-face with Drysis the Dreadful and the Doom Riders.

"Surprise indeed," Drysis said with her crossbow pointed at Grey Cloak's chest. "Welcome back to the land of the living—well, except for me."

WHAT DO the Doom Riders have in store for the blood brothers?

Can Tatiana stop the underlings before they master the Time Mural?

Where is Black Frost in all of this?

Grab the next boxset below, but first ...

Please leave a Review on Dragons Wars Books 6-10!

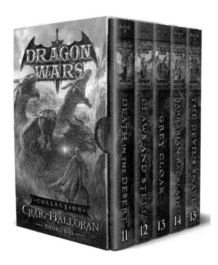

ABOUT THE AUTHOR

Craig Halloran resides with his family outside his hometown of Charleston, West Virginia. When he isn't entertaining mankind, he is seeking adventure, working out, or watching sports. To learn more about him, go to WWW.DRAGONWARSBOOKS.COM.

*Check me out on Bookbub and follow: HalloranOnBookBub
*I'd love it if you would subscribe to my mailing list: www.craighalloran.com
*On Facebook, you can find me at The Darkslayer Report or Craig Halloran.
*Twitter, Twitter, Twitter. I am there, too: www.twitter.com/CraigHalloran
*And of course, you can always email me at craig@thedarkslayer.com
See my book lists below!

CRAIG'S COMPLETE BOOK LIST

OVER 100 TITLES! PURE ADRENALINE!

5 MILLION WORDS IN PUBLICATION!

EPIC FANTASY, SWORD AND SORCERY URBAN FANTASY, SCI-FI, POST-APOC!

FREE BOOKS

The Darkslayer: Brutal Beginnings

Nath Dragon – Quest for the Thunderstone

The Henchmen Chronicles Intro

Dragon Wars Prequel

The Odyssey of Nath Dragon Series (Prequel to Chronicles of Dragon)

Exiled: Book 1 of 5

The Odyssey of Nath Dragon Boxset (Best Deal)

The Chronicles of Dragon Series 1 (10 Books)

The Hero, the Sword and the Dragons (Book 1)

Boxset 1-5

Boxset 6-10

Collector's Edition 1-10 (Best Deal)

Tail of the Dragon, The Chronicles of Dragon, Series 2 (10 book series)

Tail of the Dragon Book #1

Boxset 1-5

Boxset 6-10

Collector's Edition 1-10 (Best Deal)

The Darkslayer Series 1 – 6 books

Wrath of the Royals (Book 1)

Boxset 1-3

Boxset 4-6

Omnibus 1-6 (Best Deal)

The Darkslayer: Bish and Bone, Series 2 (10 Book series)

Bish and Bone (Book 1 of 10)

Boxset 1-5

Boxset 6-10

Bish and Bone Omnibus (Books 1-10) (Best Deal)

Dragon Wars: 20-Book Series

Blood Brothers: Book 1 of 20

Boxset 1-5

Boxset 6-10

Boxset 11-15

Boxset 16-20

CLASH OF HEROES: Nath Dragon meets The Darkslayer

Book 1 of 3

Special Edition - Books 1-3 (Best Deal)

The Supernatural Bounty Hunter Files (10 book series)

Smoke Rising: Book 1 of 10

Boxset 1-5

Boxset 6-10

Collector's Edition 1-10 (Best Deal)

The Henchmen Chronicles 5-Book Series

The King's Henchmen - Book 1 of 5

The Henchmen Chronicles Collection: Books 1-5

Zombie Impact Series

Zombie Day Care: Book 1

Zombie Rehab: Book 2

Zombie Warfare: Book 3

Boxset: Books 1-3 (Best Deal)

The Gamma Earth Cycle

Escape from the Dominion

Flight from the Dominion

Prison of the Dominion

The Sorcerer's Power Series

The Sorcerer's Curse: Book 1 of 5

The Red Citadel and the Sorcerer's Power (All 5 Books)

The Misadventures of Dan - Drama/Comedy

Gorgon Thunder-Bot Incinerator of Worlds (1 book, childrens)

Made in the USA
Middletown, DE
16 October 2023

40883573R00426